# HEART
## OF
# BRONZE

# HEART OF BRONZE

*IRON DAWN*
*JERICHO MOON*

**Matthew Woodring Stover**

SCIENCE
FICTION

# CONTENTS

# IRON
# DAWN

*For Robyn, for giving me Barra*

The author gratefully acknowledges Robyn Fielder,
Paul Kroll, H. Gene McFadden, and Charles L. Wright
for many hours of reading, advice, and role-playing.
Thanks, guys. I couldn't have done it without you.

# Prologue

Dear Chryl and Antiphos,

    This will be the last letter of this packet, I think; if we can make Tyre before winter shuts down the trade, you should be reading this before the Turning of the Sun.

    As you might be able to gather, the last three months have been a bit lean. I've managed to be more-or-less steadily employed as a marine, especially since I hooked up with this Athenian, Leucas. But with the surge in piracy breaking up the trade—particularly here in the East—and stiff competition from Akhaian veterans driving the wages down, we've managed to do little more than support ourselves. These Akhaians, half of them seem to have left their brains in front of the walls of Troy along with the corpses of most of their friends; they hardly seem to care if they get paid or not. If business doesn't improve, I might have to go back to scribing contracts in Knossos next year instead of dealing for myself.

    Don't worry, though; there's rumors of trouble in Tyre, and I'm sure to find profitable employment.

    Leucas' thigh is healing nicely; all the infection seems to have subsided. There's a lesson for you in what happened on Kypros: when hunting boar, especially man-killers who've been hunted before, keep your spear grounded and never try to deflect the boar's charge. It was his own strength that almost killed him, you see. He was trying to shift the beast over toward me for the death blow when the spear shaft snapped. If Kheperu—my newest partner; he's Egyptian, and you know how they are—hadn't

*managed to blind the boar with one of his powders, it would have
certainly savaged Leucas badly, maybe killed him, before I could
get there and sever its spine. Another lesson: when facing a boar
with an axe, come at it from the side and strike for the back of its
neck. It's almost impossible to penetrate a boar's skull—the bone
there is like armor—and if you hit the spine farther down its back,
it can still turn and rip you good using just its front legs.*

*I may be traveling with these two for some time, by the way.
Even though Leucas and I have been together for only a couple of
months, we seem to make a pretty good team, even more so now
that we have Kheperu. I still don't trust him much—he's far too
clever for his own good—but Leucas is steady as a rock (he's not
really bright enough to be treacherous) and he helps me keep
Kheperu in line.*

*King Demetor was very grateful for our help. He gave us
some lovely gifts—I'm sending the bronze sword for Antiphos, and
the silver cup is for Chryl. He also paid us in Athenian coin, sixty
large weights apiece, which will be enough to support us in Tyre
for many weeks, buy a nice gift for your Uncle Peliarchus there,
and have some left over to bank at Knossos.*

*I think I should be able to return to the Isle of the Mighty next
summer, in time for the Midsummer Festival. In the meantime,
tend your lessons—Abdi is a good tutor, and expensive; if the
Phoenikian this letter is written in is too hard for you, he'll read it
for you, I'm sure. You obey Coll, now—I gave her enough trouble
when I was little, she needs no grief from her grandsons; trouble
her too much and your great-grandmother Maeve will turn you
both into goats. Give my respects to Llem, and tell him the tin
trade should be very good next year, and I hope he's having no
more trouble with his underkings. And if your grandda Ouendail
should visit from Eire, tell him to keep his shaggy butt away from
my mother.*

*I love you both very much, and with the favor of the gods I'll
see you in summer.*

*Take care,*

*Mother*

Barra trimmed off the soggy end of her reed brush and returned it to her
pencase made from a bull's thighbone. The whistling, agonized cries of
one of the wounded sailors had faded into silence, and she supposed she

really ought to be up helping to dig his grave. The other wounded sailor only gasped, and occasionally roused himself to ask for water; he'd taken a pirate arrow just below his navel, and Barra figured they might as well dig both graves now. The second sailor'd be filling one soon enough.

The orange glow from the campfire flickered across her face, and the faces of her partners, who drowsed nearby. Trees leaned close around overhead, of the same pine that made the campfire pop and spit. Barra could smell the sea, even through the bitter scent of the burning pine, and hear the low splash of waves on this windless night, but she couldn't see it; the days of making landfall camps on beaches were long gone. She missed it, really, missed sitting on the sand and watching the moon paint silver across the ripples, but these days a campfire on the beach served as a beacon for pirates.

And there was at least one band of pirates, out there maybe even in the darkness tonight, that would be looking for them.

They had come out of the east, a pair of long, low ships rowing hard around a wooded point. She and her partners, trading their skills for passage on this ship, had barely time to arm themselves before the battle was joined. Their captain had tried to run, but their ship was a broad-beamed sea-goer, wide and sturdy to ply the passage from Thrace to Kypros to the Phoenikian coast, and even with every crewman straining at the oars, it had no chance of outracing the sleek pirates. Kheperu's firepots had sent one pirate longship burning toward the bottom of the sea, but by that time the fighting was hand-to-hand. Pirates from the sunken ship swam to the trader and clambered aboard, to join howling pirates from the other ship, that already ranged among the oar-benches, hacking down sailors with short bronze swords. These pirates were Akhaian renegades, probably themselves veterans of the Siege of Troy—skilled fighters, they cut through weary sailors with ease. All that had saved the trader's crew was a desperate counter-board led by Barra and Leucas and Kheperu; with the sailors scrambling behind them, they had abandoned their wallowing trader, captured the pirate's longship with hard fighting, pulled away, and left the trader in the pirates' hands. They'd escaped with little more than their lives and the clothes that they wore.

Barra shook her head as she rolled up the papyrus scroll and returned it to its bone case. In her letters home, she never wrote of how bad things really were, here around the Mediterranean. She rarely mentioned the pirates, the way nearly everybody with thirty friends and a boat seemed to have gone into piracy, these past five years—if they don't have a boat, they become bandits and prey on inland towns. Outside of Egyptian holdings, the only really safe places left were Knossos, Argos, and Mykenai; even the Hittite Empire could no longer summon the strength to put down the Phrygian tribes that pressed on their eastern and northern borders. She certainly wasn't going to tell her young hero-worshiping sons that she was dead-broke—all her silver, all the gifts from Demetor, all the money she'd saved since her last trip to Crete, all had been left behind on the trader; the cup and the sword that she'd written of she'd found under a bench on the longship. She'd only barely managed to save the bundle of letters and the pencase, which now bore a bright scrape where she'd used it to block a pirate's shortsword until she could open his skull with her axe.

She bundled together the scrollcases, tied them with a leather thong, and tucked them into the drawstring bag that held the cup and the smallsword. Fifteen years around the Mediterranean, more than ten of them spent spilling blood for pay, and here she was, burying sailors at a furtive camp on the Hittite coast, barely owning more than the axes that weighed down her belt. She shook her head and got up; she carried the bag over to where Leucas slept, and laid it close by his side— none of the sailors would dare risk disturbing the giant Athenian. If anyone had pointed out to Barra the irony of guarding her few possessions against men that, only hours before, she had very nearly given her life to defend, she would have only shrugged. Sailors are thieves, and that's the whole of it.

Well, she'd only have to deal with this lot for another day or two; Kheperu had done a divination before he'd retired for the evening, and he'd predicted clear weather and hot for the next three days—plenty of time to make Tyre.

She picked her way quietly inland to where the captain sat on a stone outcrop and watched a pair of his men scratch a grave into the stony soil. He acknowledged her approach with a bare nod, and she squatted beside him.

"I'd give him a hero's pyre, if we could risk the light," the captain murmured. "Instead, we must stick him in the ground like a peasant."

Barra said, "Why are you only digging one grave?"

The captain looked at her with raw and bloody eyes. "Paxo is going to *live,* that's why."

"No, he isn't. He may breathe till morning—may—but he'll not see another nightfall. I can smell the bile from the wound." Barra's nose was as keen as a wolf's; there was no chance that she was mistaken.

As if called by her words, the wounded sailor moaned raggedly behind the trees. The captain turned away from Barra's level gaze.

"He'll live," he murmured.

"If wishing could make it so, he will," she said. "But if wishing could make it so . . . well, many things would be different."

They sat in silence for a time, and watched the sailors scratch at the earth with tools meant for shipbuilding.

Finally, Barra said, "What will you do, now?"

The captain shrugged, and let out a long, slow sigh. "Most of the boys, they're hired only as far as Tyre. I'll likely pay them off, and get a new crew . . ."

*And go pirate,* Barra finished for him silently. What else could he do? Unless he had hoarded wealth enough to build a new ship, crew and supply it, and buy a load of trade goods, his only resource was this long, low, sleek pirate ship, useless out of sight of land. It had no room for cargo, barely any for supplies. This man would never captain a trader again, unless he took it by force.

Barra's foster-father was a Tyrian shipmaster; her two foster-brothers were trader-captains, with ships she herself held a part interest in, an investment made after a particularly fat year; she hated pirates more than anything else on land or sea. There should be money waiting for her in Tyre, a return on that investment—unless pirates had hit her ships and killed her brothers.

And yet, she could not bring herself to say anything to this man who would be a pirate in months to come, this man who blinked through fat and rolling tears as he watched two of his men dig a grave for a third. He had sons of his own.

In her mind, she flashed a vivid glimpse of herself, in the spring of her fourteenth year, as she stood at the high-curved prow of a Phoenikian trader and watched the green shores of the Isle of the Mighty recede into the mists. She'd done her duty, fulfilled her obligation to her brother and her gods: she'd given birth to a son, a squalling red-faced baby boy fathered by a traveling prince who'd had a taste for girls at the brink of womanhood. Chryl, she'd named him, Golden, after the color of his father's hair; another heir to her brother's throne in Great Langdale. After that birth her child had seemed hateful to her, as did her life, her family, the very air that carried the oaken scent of the Isle. She'd given her son into the care of her mother, and boarded that ship for Tyre, and she'd stood in the bow and watched the shores of her home fade into moist greyness, and she'd dreamed of coming home someday with a fleet of ships to carry the fabulous wealth of the East, and heroic tales to tell of earning every piece. She'd sworn she'd come home richer than her brother would ever be; she'd come home as a real Eastern princess, with servants and exotic pets— unlike her sisters, who were only chapped-cheek shepherdesses and broodmares.

Now, fifteen years later, here she was: on the Hittite coast without a shekel in her purse, her own cheeks scaly and peeling, nearly as rough as the callused palms of her hands. She scraped her hands together and looked down at the hard muscle of her thighs and thought, *Well at least I've still got my figure.*

And, ignoring the pained, incredulous look from the grieving captain beside her, she laughed out loud.

# PART ONE

# The Job

# 1

# *The Bear*

**T**he sun is the hammer, Barra thought as she swung down to the beach from the high-curving prow of the captured longship, *and I'm the bloody anvil. Kheperu surely called the weather right enough.* She used both hands to wipe sweat from her face back into her tightly tied hair. *Be cold come nightfall, though.* "Leucas! Kheperu! Come on, shag it!"

A rare south wind had brought the smell of Tyre to last night's landfall: cinnamon and pepper in the cedar-laced pine smoke, sharp young wine and close-packed sweating humanity, smoldering hemp and horse piss. She'd been out from Tyre more than a year, broken only by one single-night stopover on her way from Thrace to Pharos six months ago, and those scents brought her blood up like a tired horse in sight of her paddock. Now she was home, or as near to home as anywhere in the bloody burning south could be. No matter that her purse was as flat as a little girl's chest; her foster-father Peliarchus would be holding her share of the profit on the pair of ships she jointly owned with him and her foster-brothers. It wouldn't nearly equal what she'd lost to the pirates, but it'd be better than a sharp stick in the eye.

She'd take the morning to wander the Market, meet people again, take the pulse of the city—remind herself how much she loved this place. And, perhaps, the afternoon as well. Leucas and Kheperu both had a few coins left; surely her partners could stand her a meal or two here, seeing as she'd be putting them up at her foster home tonight.

Tonight, she'd be home, and eating Tayniz's cooking—she'd likely roast ducks with currant sauce, and fry mushrooms in butter, and bake fresh barley bread—and then her own bed in the room that had been hers now for fifteen years, a real feather mattress, not one of these bloody piles of rugs and fleeces that the Akhaians pretended were so comfortable. The thought of so much sheer self-indulgent pleasure brought a sting to her eyes. In between times, she could make a great fuss over Graegduz, the young grey wolf who was her only friend from home, to apologize to him for having left him here in Tyre for so long; and she had a full wagon load of stories to trade with Peliarchus while they sat around the fire, in the courtyard under the Tyrian stars . . .

About half the surviving sailors had debarked, muttering among themselves and giving dark looks to the beachsiders that streamed toward the longship. The *Pelican*—the captain had named her so, for the way she'd scooped them all from the sea—was the first ship in this morning, and the beachsiders pressed curiously around to catch first glimpses of what cargo she might carry, and perhaps to snag a piece or two if no one armed was looking. They appeared more interested than disappointed to find that there was no cargo at all. The captain stood amidships, looking out over the gathering crowd, and Barra read on his face, clear as if the words were burned there, the determination that the *Pelican*'s next landfall in Tyre would be different. He met her eyes, and quickly looked away.

She folded her arms and held herself still in the sunlight to wait for her partners; patience was not in her nature, but she could fake it. The beachsiders took in the look on her sunburned face and her vivid red hair, then the hard muscle of her shoulders and arms left bare by her leather tunic, and finally the wickedly sharp edges of the three stone axes she wore, two small ones of flint tucked behind her wide boar skin belt, and the big basalt broad head that looked like it belonged in a slaughterhouse strapped to her right thigh, its haft in a smallsword scabbard; they wisely gave her a wide berth, muttering among themselves of "damned lunatic foreign women."

Their wariness gave her no satisfaction; on the contrary, it stirred a powerful impulse to raise knots on a skull or two—particularly one big strawheaded guy with a leering smirk on his stupid face. Barra spent a brief, half-smiling moment calculating the profit of the plea- sure she'd get from smacking that smirk off his face with the flat of her axe against the possible loss of offending one of the Great Houses. This fellow was tall enough to have been born into nobility, and his hair was too clean and his clothes, though old and somewhat shabby, fit him too well—he could very well have been a Mursuwallite pur- chasing agent dressed down for bargain-hunting.

On the other hand, he looked more Akhaian than Hittite, and she could always plead ignorance. . . . His smirk grew wider and wider the longer she thought about it, and his stare became ever more insulting: that made up her mind. Among the Picts of Great Langdale, a stare like that is an invitation to bloodshed.

"I can understand why you keep your lips together when you smile," Barra said in conversational Phoenikian. "Eating shit can rot your teeth."

His grin got wider; his teeth were perfect. No beachsider, then. "Don't come all hostile," he said easily, his Phoenikian carrying the rural burr of the Akhaian peninsula. Corinth, maybe. "You make your living with that hardware?"

Barra switched to perfectly accented Athenian Greek. "A girl's got to keep *something* hard with her, these days; I keep meeting men like you, who don't know the meaning of the word."

He shook his head and chuckled, and responded in the same tongue. "Where'd you learn Language? You look like a barbarian— and civilized women don't carry weapons, little girl."

Despite being from a family known for the size and strength of its members—her brother Llem could hoist a full-grown man in each fist—Barra had suffered through a youth and adolescence of japes about her height: she was a full hand shorter than any other woman in her family, and a finger or two below average even down here among the smaller Mediterranean races. It was still a sensitive subject—one among many, as even Barra would admit, including this insulting tendency of folk down here to refer to her people as savages.

Barra's lips drew back from her teeth; she fought to make this reaction look like a smile. "You probably wouldn't know a civilized woman if she knocked you on the head. What do you say we try it and find out?"

His grin began to fade. "A man could get real tired of that mouth on you."

"You think so? Why don't you go find one and ask him?"

"You little whore," he said, reddening. "I ought to break you in half."

Barra made the long-practiced move with her right hand; before the man could blink, the broadaxe was out and cocked back over her shoulder. "Try it. See how you like being able to breathe through your forehead."

A looming shadow blocked the sun from behind her left shoulder. "Barra," Leucas rumbled softly, "why are you about to kill this man?"

Barra kept her eyes on the Corinthian; the Corinthian was speechlessly staring up at Leucas, all nineteen-and-a-half hands and eighteen stone of battle-scarred veteran, dressed in the Cretan style, bare-chested, wearing only a kilt and sandals. Barra said, "I don't like the way he stared at me."

"Mmm-hm."

The Corinthian recovered, and drew himself up. "It's a good thing you got here when you did. Your woman needs to be on a leash. You should muzzle her like a bitch."

Leucas slowly lowered the huge bundle of armor and weapons from his shoulder to the sand. When he straightened, the top of Barra's head came just up to the nipples on a lean, scarred chest layered with deep muscle that looked as hard as a bronze breastplate. In his youth, Leucas had stolen away from his family home in Athens to drive a chariot at Troy. Like so many of the men who'd survived the ten endless years of war, he'd returned to find his home changed beyond recognition; to him, Athens was now just another city, where he'd once lived for a while. Barra had met him only two months before, while they'd both worked as marines on board traders that plied the coast of Sicily, and had already come to rely on him more than she'd have liked to.

Leucas lacked the vicious temperament necessary to make a living as a bandit, or a pirate, as did so many of his former comrades; the profession he practiced when mercenary work was not to be found was proclaimed by his ruined face, a face in which every bone had been broken once or more by fists wrapped in leather and sometimes weighted with bronze in the boxing circles of every Greek-speaking land. Some of the damage was hidden by a short-trimmed black beard shot through with streaks of white, but nothing could conceal the lumps of scar tissue that made up his sharply bent nose and flattened ears. The only feature that had escaped damage was his eyes; eyes that appeared as though they could sparkle with deep amusement, but now fixed on the Corinthian with a look as cold as grey winter ice.

"Barra is not my woman," he said slowly, "and I don't believe I was addressing you, sir."

The Corinthian swallowed. "I only wanted to make a business proposition, that's all."

"He called me a whore," Barra said, her voice flat and hard as the side of her axe.

Leucas winced, then sighed. "Well," he said heavily, "I'm sure you called him worse than that. Didn't you?"

Barra lowered the axe. "Maybe."

"Now, do you want to listen to his business offer, or do you want to kill him?"

"You're asking the woman?" the Corinthian said incredulously. "What kind of a man are you?"

Leucas gave him another considering, long grey look. The Corinthian took an involuntary step backward. Leucas looked back to Barra, and waited.

Barra shrugged; remembering her current poverty shredded her temper like smoke before the wind. She slid the axe haft back into its scabbard. "Why not? It's what we're here for."

The Corinthian coughed his throat clear and patted down his coat, his hands unconsciously reaching toward his shoulders for something that wasn't there. *These aren't his usual clothes,* Barra thought. What was he reaching for? Straps that would hold a breastplate? Shoulder pieces of a corselet?

"How many in your company?"

Barra shook her head. "You'd best start with your name and what you're paying."

"I'm Chrysios," the Corinthian said. "I need about five men who can handle themselves and don't mind a little red work."

"Men?" Barra asked mildly. "Do I count?"

Chrysios shrugged. "That's a nice move you have with the axe, little missy—just for show, or can you swing it, too?"

She was about to show him, but Leucas laid his heavy hand gently on her shoulder. "Wait, Barra, he hasn't yet said how much he's paying."

"It's not enough," Barra growled, irritably shaking free. "A nomarchy in the Delta wouldn't be enough."

"Fifteen silver shekels," Chrysios said. "For one night's—" His eyes glazed over, and he turned his head and coughed harshly: Kheperu was approaching from upwind.

Even in Tyre in late autumn, when fresh water was scarce—the nearest river that runs year-round, the Litani, empties into the sea more than an hour's ride north of the city—and bathing was considered a luxury reserved for those with no better way to use their time, the stench that emanated from Kheperu's person could strike the unprepared like a physical blow. This was more than the goaty reek of the old sweat that caked his robes; the chemicals and aromatic herbs that the stubby Egyptian carried on his person added a sinus-piercing overtone. Barra glanced over her shoulder at him and moved to one side—

standing downwind of Kheperu for a few breaths could numb her nose for hours.

She smiled to herself as he approached; Kheperu was doing his Fat Old Man act, leaning heavily on his stout oak staff, disguising the weapon as a walking stick, the same act he'd done that day he'd introduced himself on the Paphos beach on Kypros. He'd come up and asked their help in the swindle that later became the Kyprian Boar Hunt; the swindle, and the hunt, had worked exceedingly well—it was only bad luck that had brought them afoul of pirates before they could get away with their money. In their brief association, Barra had learned that Kheperu was greedy and treacherous, a whiner and a practitioner of a bewildering variety of perversions; he was also a former seshperankh, a Scribe of the House of Life who had been banned from the priesthood and exiled from Egypt for some unnamed crime, and he claimed to have the entire *Book of the Secrets of the Laboratory* committed to memory. This was almost certainly a lie, as were most things that came out of his mouth, but he did know a great deal of alchemy and a bit of magic and was, on occasion, capable of acts of astonishing bravery.

He wheezed loudly as he labored over the sand, mumbling in a plaintive undertone about the heat. He was only a hand or so taller than Barra, but outweighed her by nearly four stone, his rotund bulk enhanced by the stiff leather armor that he constantly wore beneath his stained, fraying robes. The scalp stubble around his topknot was salted with grey, and only the squirrel-bright glitter in his eyes belied the overall impression of incipient senility.

"Great Mouth," Chrysios gagged. "Doesn't that man ever wash?"

"Best hope he doesn't," Leucas murmured. "It's worse when he's wet."

"You know him?"

Barra said, "He's our third partner."

"Disgusting."

"Tell him so," Barra offered. "He loves compliments from pretty Greek boys."

Chrysios scowled. "How many more?"

"That's all of us."

He looked at Leucas, then at Kheperu incredulously. He said to Barra, "Don't tell me you're *his* woman! How do you stand the smell?"

Barra sighed. It was endless, this automatic assumption that she belonged to a man. In Langdale, the only people who belonged to other people were debt-slaves, and then only until their debt was paid. She tried to be tolerant of the East's barbaric customs, but most of them wore on her, and none more than this one. "I'm tired of you, Chrysios. Go away."

The Corinthian blinked. "My offer still stands—"

"She said," Leucas rumbled, "go away."

The Corinthian looked up into Leucas' cold grey eyes, and decided he'd received valuable advice. He turned with forced dignity and stalked off along the beach.

Kheperu finally trundled up. "Who was that?" he said in bad Greek.

"A job," Leucas said, watching the man's retreating back. "Barra didn't like him."

"Pity. He was lovely."

"Yes, he was," Barra said sadly. "Why are the pretty ones always such jackasses?"

"Your mistake," Kheperu said in a tone of world-weary wisdom, "was in talking to him. Greek men are always more attractive with their mouths tied shut."

Leucas hoisted his bundle back up over his shoulder. "Don't make me hurt you."

"Make you?" Kheperu leered. "I'd *pay* you. Speaking of that, there's an inn in the Greek quarter, run by an old friend of mine— Lidios, his name is—he has the most extraordinary whores—"

"We're broke," Leucas said, frowning down at him. "He'll let you screw on credit?"

"Well, you know," Kheperu patted his robe near his heart, and a muffled jingle of silver was audible. "In Egypt, we have a proverb about eggs and baskets . . ."

"Later," Barra said. "We're going to the Market. We need to drum up some real work."

The Market of Tyre is the centerpiece of the city, an enormous expanse of close-fitted flagstones around which Tyre radiates like a tangled sunburst. Open to the west, toward the sea, the balance of its arc is walled by the golden al-tobe facades of Tyre's oldest buildings, broken only by crowded street-mouths of hard-packed earth. It had been paved more than a hundred years before, by the Hittites, in the days when Great King Suppiluliumas of Hatti had contested with Asshur-ballit of Assyria for the rule of the Phoenikian coast. The days of Hittite rule were long past; Tyre had been an Egyptian holding, part of the Canaan

District, since not long after Ramses the Great had smashed Muwatallis' cavalry at the Battle of Qadesh nearly fifty years ago. Over this century and more, these flagstones had been worn in curving paths by the wheels of wagons and war chariots, by feet of sunbaked Kushites and pale Picts, boots of Bottlers from Iberia and the sandals of Indusians from the Far East, pads of dogs and housecats and the occasional captive lion, hooves of fine-boned Arabian horses, of asses and thick-muscled mules.

From the stone islands around which these pathways weave, rise clusters of tentstalls, ranging from simple pole-and-rope shrouds of linen to semipermanent frames of hard northern cedar, with real doors and framed windows hung with folds of translucent silk. The sites of these stalls, even more than the stalls themselves, have often been in the same family for generations, passed down from father to son as the clan's most precious birthright, and are guarded as jealously as a miser guards his gold. One can judge the success of a Market vendor by the number and equipage of his guards. Even a relative newcomer often has several young men, usually his sons, lounging nearby with knotted sticks in their hands, ready at the instant to drive off with shouts and blows any of the ubiquitous "bedrollers"—transient vendors, usually poor, who carry their wares in blanket-bundles—who might be bold enough to spread their displays too close by.

For Barra, the Market was the heart and soul of Tyre. Tyre was without doubt the most cosmopolitan city of its age; the original inhabitants of this coast, the small, olive-skinned Kena'ani, were outnumbered perhaps four or five to one by the descendants of the Egyptian conquerors and the Hittite conquered, the remnants of the earlier Assyrian occupation, the wealthy Cretan refugees who'd fled Theseus' sack of Knossos, and the steady stream of immigrant fortune seekers from across the known world, for it was well-known that a man could make something of himself, here in the trading hub of the world, that here wit and guts counted for more than did any accident of birth. Of the five Great Houses that controlled most of the trade, not one had existed a hundred years ago.

And so the immigrants came, by ship and by desert caravan, on horseback or afoot along the Coast Road, and they huddled together each in their own loosely bordered ghetto—it was only natural, to prefer to live with those who speak your language, who remember how the air smells and what the sunsets look like back home—but the Market was the leveler, the mixer, the welcoming arms that gathered them all in. The Market was where they all came together.

In the early years of her self-imposed exile from her brother's lands,

Barra had lived for the days she could slip away from the home of her foster-parents and bury herself in the surging, shouting crowds. It was here that she had learned the value of money and the arts of bargaining, here that she sharpened her Phoenikian and Greek, became fluent in Egyptian and the Canaanite spoken by the Amorite princes of Kena'an, studied Akkadian cuneiform and picked up her smatterings of Hatti, Minoan, and the liquid Iberian of the Bottlers. Here she had learned to judge men by action, since words usually lie; here she had learned that a quick punch buys more than a soft word. It was here, in a twilit alley nearby, that she had first fought for her life.

More than the house of Peliarchus, more even than the huge hall of her brother in Langdale or her father's great fortress of Tara, this was home.

The energy of the Market was contagious; after only a few minutes even silent Leucas was animatedly haggling with a vendor over a saw-toothed spear with an intricately carved haft, even though he had no money with which to buy it. Kheperu was already deep in his third shouting match, dark eyes alight as though he'd been sampling his own drugs, shrilling insults and imprecations as he bargained for a pound of cinnamon bark he didn't want.

Barra moved silently through the crowds, keeping within sight of her companions—an easy task: Leucas stood head and shoulders taller than any man in the Market—exchanging greetings with the occasional merchant who remembered her, complimenting this one or that on his wares or the additions to his stall, dodging the occasional knots of the Egyptian garrison troops. Even while enjoying the warm nostalgia of looking over the places where she'd spent her adolescence, she was attentive to the mood of the marketplace, to the slight shift of eye of a sweating vendor, the conversations muttered in urgent undertones. As she had told her companions when they'd reached the Market's western verge: "Now, look, let's stay in sight of each other in there," she'd said, gesturing into the Market. "For now, I only want to shop around, but keep your eyes open. Talk to people. Even you, Leucas; plenty of people around here speak Greek. I've heard rumors of a trade war brewing, and that means people will be looking for guards, at the very least. For the real money, we'll have to hook up with a Great House, and maybe do a little dirty work. And for that, we need to get their attention—you don't just walk up to the gate of a Great House and ask for a job. Maybe we can start with some guarding, and work our way up when people find out we don't mind getting our hands bloody."

Kheperu'd asked, "Well, what about that fellow on the beach, then?"

"He wanted red work—he wants us to kill somebody."

"So?"

"So he was only paying fifteen shekels. Five apiece. I don't blow my nose for five shekels. Come on, let's move. Tyre is a pricey place to visit, and I want to leave with more money than I brought."

"It's always money with you," Kheperu had complained with feigned despair. "What about good food, and straight sweet wine? What about companionship? What about *sex*?"

"In Tyre, they all cost money. A lot. Come on."

Now she was sure the rumors she'd heard in Kypros were correct: some trouble was brewing in Tyre. That Corinthian on the beach had indicated he was looking to hire mercenaries; this had been a good sign, even though he was an asshole-biter. She noted an unusual number of beggars asking alms, many of them doing it poorly enough that they probably weren't professionals—that was another good sign, a sign that business was down all over the city; the Great Houses might be feeling the pinch and getting antsy. The Egyptian regulars she passed here and there uncharacteristically wore their quilted armor in the heat of the day, and they stuck close together in groups of four or five: this was a better sign. She figured that if she and her friends could keep their eyes open, they just might catch sight of some serious profit.

She sensed a shift in the crowd, people starting to drift northwest, toward the central plaza, near the wells. Any disturbance in the Market caused the crowd to flow like sand falling into a sudden sinkhole; when people noticed those nearer to the disturbance moving toward it, they naturally—even unconsciously—followed.

Barra drifted along with them. A simple syllogism: A disturbance indicates an unusual occurrence; Barra and her partners made their living dealing with unusual occurrences; therefore, something might be happening on which they could make a profit. She caught Leucas' eye and nodded him in the direction of the drifting crowds. He returned her nod, shouldered his bundle, and moved off. She stopped along the way to collect Kheperu—she couldn't get his attention, so she marched up behind him and hauled him along by his topknot, ignoring his squealing protests. When she finally released him, she wiped the grease off her hand onto her breeches.

"Thank you," Kheperu said, all seriousness. "That bastard would have taken me for everything I own, plus a year of indentured servitude and my firstborn son."

She shook her head, chuckling. "Didn't I warn you about Tyrian traders?"

"I believed," he said, drawing up with vast Egyptian dignity, "that you were indulging in your usual exaggeration."

"I never exaggerate."

The gathering crowd became more and more noisy as their progress slowed; once the companions gained the central plaza, they were halted by a solid press of human backs. Leucas looked toward the center, over everyone's head.

"It's a bear. A big bear."

"A bear?" Barra frowned. "What's the fuss over a bear? Trappers bring bears through here all the time. Let me see."

Leucas helped her up onto his back. She leaned her elbows on his hard shoulders.

Five armored men held heavy ropes that attached to a specially designed collar around the bear's thick neck. The huge brown beast made muffled grunting sounds through its muzzle of leather and bronze as the men urged it along. It seemed sleepy and docile, and ambled willingly enough through the plaza. To Barra's eye, its skin seemed to hang a bit too tight—the way to keep a bear like this docile is to starve it into submission, and it looked to her like it was a tad too well-fed for safety.

Barra squinted at the designs painted on the handlers' armor. "That's Meneides livery," she mused. "What would Idonosteus want with a bear?"

"Likely to sell it," Kheperu said, one hand on Leucas' arm to steady himself as he balanced on tiptoe. "That's the biggest damned bear I've ever seen."

"Oh, please," Barra scoffed. "It's just a baby! Where I come from—"

"I know," Kheperu interrupted tiredly. "In the Isle of the Mighty the bears graze on the tops of oak trees, right?"

Leucas chuckled. Barra answered innocently, "The top's the tenderest part, you know. Once, when I was a little girl—"

"Don't tell me—you climbed a great brown mountain, and when you got to the summit, it turned out to be the belly of a sleeping bear."

"Well, no, actually, I didn't make it that far—I'm afraid of heights, you know." She grinned at his low-voiced groan of surrender. "That's a northern bear, though, probably from the continent, northeast of the Isle. That means something like two months on shipboard. There's no way he could sell that bear for enough to recoup the cost of just *feeding* the bloody thing."

"Ramses the Living Horus keeps a menagerie," Kheperu offered. "Perhaps this Meneides fellow does as well."

Barra shook her head. ''Idonosteus might fancy himself to be a little pharaoh, but he doesn't like animals—of course, he could be dead, I suppose, he wasn't all that young . . . I don't know who might have succeeded him, I don't remember if he had any sons . . ."

"Bearbaiting."

Barra could feel Leucas' rumble in her own chest, and she craned her neck around to get a glimpse of his face; the huge Athenian's expression was as grim as his tone. An ill weight gathered in the pit of her stomach, and she nodded disgustedly. "You're probably right." She spat on the flagstones, narrowly missing Kheperu. "Sick bastard."

"What is this bearbaiting?" Kheperu asked.

"It's a game," Barra told him. "A vile game. They chain the bear to a post, usually down in a pit, then they send dogs against it, laying bets on how many dogs the bear will kill before it's torn to shreds."

Kheperu stared at her, eyes wide in horror. "That's revolting! I've never heard anything so hideous in all my life!"

"It's the next thing close to murder."

"Murder, nothing! They're just animals! They let that beast kill *dogs?*" Like many Egyptians, Kheperu would cheerfully disembowel a man he caught beating a dog. "Does the Governor know of this?"

Barra shrugged. "Won't make much difference if he does. The Great Houses pay about as much attention to your Governor of the Canaan District as they do their own drooling old king in Byblos."

"Someone should do something." Kheperu's outrage subsided as quickly as it had arisen, falling off to a sullen mutter.

"It's none of our business what House Meneides does for fun," Barra said.

"Funny that it's not in a cage," Leucas said thoughtfully. "That'd be safer."

"In a cage," Kheperu said, "one must drag the entire weight of the animal. This way, the animal carries itself."

"Mm," Barra said, nodding in thought, not in agreement. "And a bear in a cage wouldn't draw this size of a crowd. I wonder what old Idonosteus is really up to?"

Leucas said, in a distant, musing tone, "I've heard tell that Theseus once killed a bear, unarmed—strangled it, the story goes."

Kheperu snorted. "You Greeks and your stories—where did you hear this one?"

Leucas didn't so much as shift his gaze. "From Prince Demophoon—his youngest son, that is. Theseus, you know, he wasn't that much bigger than I am . . ."

"Don't get any ideas," Barra said firmly, slapping him lightly on the top of the head, and Leucas lifted his shoulders in a sighing shrug that ignored her weight on his back.

"Have you seen enough, Barra?"

She squinted at the bear, which was now becoming balky and restive at the noise and smells of the crowd, tossing its head and growling. "Not yet. I don't think these boys know what they've got hold of here. If that bear decides he wants to be free, the five of them won't be enough to stop him."

"Mm, Barra?" Kheperu said dubiously. "If that bear wants to get away, and those men aren't enough to hold him, don't you think it'd be a good idea to be somewhere *else*?"

Barra grinned down at him. "What, you're afraid of a little baby bear?"

"Baby or not, that beast's a long way from little—"

Somebody threw a rock.

It sailed out from the depths of the crowd and hit the bear's shoulder-joint with a muffled thump. The bear reared up, dragging the Meneides handlers offbalance. Barra could see clearly their expressions of sudden panic as they struggled to regain control; they were shouting something that was buried by the wash of laughter from the crowd. Perhaps encouraged by the response, the rock-thrower hurled another, which also landed, this time thumping the bear's thigh, causing it to spin with a muzzled roar, reeling in the handlers to barely beyond the reach of its claws. *Some idiot's messing with them on purpose,* she thought. From her elevated vantage point, she looked for the idiot but couldn't spot him. Now others in the crowd got into the game, pelting the bear and its desperate handlers with everything from stones to apples to mutton bones. The bear howled and twisted and turned, the men clung to the leashes, and then one of them was down and another had lost his grip on the rope, and the bear charged a third with horrifying speed, knocking him flat. One swipe of its claws tore his face off; spouting blood painted scarlet across its muzzle. It pinned its prey beneath one massive paw and looked snarling at the other handlers. Nobody was surprised when their nerve broke.

They dropped the ropes and bolted.

The crowd surged back, away from the plaza. People began to scream. The bear leaned down and nuzzled its feebly struggling victim, trying to bite. Frustrated by the muzzle of leather and bronze, it howled again and charged the crowd.

Barra shouted, "This is our chance! Let's get in there and catch us that bear!"

Leucas had dug in his heels when the human stampede began; the crowd broke around him like surf against a cliff. Barra clung to his back as he now began to breast through the surge, knocking men and women aside with great sweeps of his knotted fists. Kheperu shouted, "Catch it? You're completely insane!" but followed nonetheless in the Athenian's wake.

Over short distances, a big bear like this can outrun a horse; it reached the massed crowd long before the three companions could get clear. It was going the wrong way, northeast into the city, away from them, slashing into the backs of screaming people with its huge hooked claws. By the time Leucas could fight his way into the open plaza, the flagstones were littered with torn and bleeding people, some of them rising to run, a couple only twitching out the last of their lives.

Barra leaped to the ground and shouted, "Kheperu! Turn that bloody thing, get it coming back our way!"

"You're mad!"

*"Do it!"*

Muttering a short prayer under his breath, the Egyptian reached inside his robe and withdrew a small sphere of some black and sticky material; he wound up and threw it past the bear. By great good luck, it hit open flagstones instead of struggling people, and it exploded with a loud *whoosh* into a ball of white fire. The bear reared, howling through its muzzle, and turned to run away from the flames.

Barra smoothly drew one of her twin throwing axes, took half a second to judge the distance, and fired it overhand. The axe sang through the air, a perfect throw, as though it rode a taut line tied from Barra's hand to the bear's head. The flat back of the axe struck the bear between the eyes with a solid thunk. She hummed satisfaction and waited for the bear to fall.

The bear blinked and shook its head, then its beady little black eyes fixed on Barra, and she suddenly thought that this might not have been such a good idea, after all.

The bear dropped to all fours and charged.

Barra drew her broadaxe and crouched, ready to leap out of its path. "Don't kill it!"

"Kill it?" Leucas' voice was thick with crazed Greek battle lust. His face split in a huge feral grin, and his eyes gleamed like fire. "I'm gonna ask it to *dance!*"

The bear shot toward them with terrifying speed. Leucas swung the huge bundle of armor and weapons in a tight arc and hurled it, catching the bear a glancing blow to the head and shoulder, knocking it off stride. The bear reared, howling, clawing at the air; Barra and Kheperu both watched with openmouthed disbelief as Leucas closed with the beast, snapping its head back with a swift jab that was followed by a titanic overhand right hook that crashed into the bear's skull below the ear and rocked it sideways.

Between Barra, Kheperu, and the bear, it was impossible to say who was the most surprised.

The bear recovered first. Still rearing, it towered over Leucas the way the huge Greek towered over ordinary men. It raked at him, a clumsy slash that Leucas easily ducked, but its following slash with the other paw tore open his right shoulder.

Barra snapped out of her daze and screamed at Kheperu to *do something, goddamn you!* She sprang at the bear's back, left hand gripping the collar at its neck, hauling herself up high enough to slam the back of its skull with the flat of the broadaxe in her right. It was a weak blow, with only the strength of her arm to drive it, but it got the bear's attention; it dropped to all fours and shook her off. She hit the ground rolling and came to her feet; Leucas hammered a fist downward into its head.

Kheperu had no faith in the efficacy of his staff against this monster that could shrug aside Barra's axes and Leucas' fists. A panicked glance around the plaza showed him bundles of bronze-headed spears leaning against the wooden counter of a nearby tentstall. As Barra and Leucas frantically danced around the whirling bear, trying to keep it distracted and to prevent it from concentrating on either one of them, Kheperu ran for the stall and reached in, grabbing a bundle of spears, yanking on them, but they wouldn't come clear. He looked down behind the counter, where a sweating Tyrian crouched holding the bundle with both arms.

*"Let go, idiot!"* Kheperu screamed in Egyptian.

"Seven shekels!"

"What?"

The vendor shrilled, *"Apiece!* Seven shekels *apiece!"*

"Fine!" Kheperu yelled. "It's a deal! It's a deal!"

He let go of the bundle, and as the vendor half stood to collect, Kheperu spun his staff end-for-end and cracked the man soundly across the face. The vendor dropped like a poleaxed steer. Kheperu grabbed the spears and ran.

The bear slashed at Barra; she managed to block its claws with the haft of her axe but the force of the blow sent her sprawling. By the time she'd scrambled to her feet, the bear had turned on Leucas, both arms swinging wide. Leucas got his arms up like the boxer he was, blocking with his forearms; for one incredible instant, he matched his strength against the maddened bear's, and held back its claws. Barra blinked, not trusting her eyes: *Nobody's that strong!* she thought—she half expected him next to lift the bloody thing over his head and body slam it like a Greek wrestler, but before he could move, the bear lunged forward and drew him into a hug, clawing at his back. Kheperu had managed to drag one spear out of the bundle, and he launched it from across the plaza.

Barra screamed, *"No!"* as the spear sailed, her mind flooded with an instant's vivid vision of the spear taking Leucas in the small of the back, but the bear twisted and the spear only grazed Leucas, its bronze head stabbing into the bear's side. The bear released Leucas and clawed at the spear shaft.

Bears have one weakness that Barra knew of, one that they share with men; sprawling on the flagstones had given her a fine view of her target. As Leucas staggered back, trying to recover his footing, Barra dove forward into a shoulder roll that brought her to a low, split-legged crouch directly in front of the bear. She swung her broadaxe in a vicious whistling underhand arc that drove its blunt back hard up into the bear's testicles.

The bear said, *"Whuff."*

It stood, swaying, its eyes glazed.

Leucas stepped up and pulled the spear from the bear's side. He gripped the spear just below the blade, touched its end to the bear's face to measure the distance, then swung it with all his might. The spear shaft splintered across the bear's head.

The bear sighed and sat down, rolling slowly onto its side.

Barra and Leucas stood side by side, panting, looking down at the unconscious bear. Leucas touched the torn skin of his shoulder and thoughtfully examined the blood on his hand. "This is our chance?" he said slowly. "Gonna catch us a bear?"

"Don't look at me," Barra said breathlessly. "Nobody told you to *box* the bloody thing . . ."

"You broke my spear!" Kheperu said as he came up, carrying the other four. "I paid sev—*ten* shekels for that spear!"

"I'll owe it to you." He looked down at Barra. "How much is a shekel?"

Barra shook her head impatiently. "We have to get your wounds cleaned and stitched up. And where are the damned handlers?"

"One of them's lying in that pool of blood over there," Kheperu said, pointing.

Barra followed his finger and wrinkled her face. "He won't live. Where are the others?"

Around the plaza the crowd had returned to watch the fight. Barra looked around, searching for the handlers, and saw wounded citizens. Three were down, knots of people clustered around them. Anywhere else she would have ignored them—it wasn't like they were anyone she knew—but here, the thought of walking away from them produced a sharp twinge in her gut. She held out one of her throwing axes and said to Leucas, "Keep an eye on that bloody beast. If it stirs, hit it." The Athenian nodded and took her axe, hefting it thoughtfully.

"All right if I wrap my shoulder first?"

"Ay, whatever. And you"—she jabbed a finger at Kheperu—"come with me."

She led him over to the wounded; his smell was enough to break up the crowd. One was a middle-aged woman torn from ear to shoulder blade, half her neck ripped away, and was clearly dead. The other two were men, one hamstrung and sobbing, the other with a calf wound and a broken ankle; the second was unconscious and had blood on his face—probably struck his head on the flagstone when he fell. "Help me bind them up. And give me some of that salve you use."

"Are you serious?" Kheperu said. "That's expensive stuff. Let their friends tend them."

"I'll pay you," Barra told him evenly.

"What profit is there in this? I simply don't understand why you would—"

"Because I *live* here!" she snapped. "If you need a better answer than that, I'll explain it with my fists."

"No need to be so prickly about it . . ."

It was only the work of moments to stop the bleeding. Barra beckoned to four men in the watching crowd. She told them to carry these two to the Meneides compound and present them there for physicking;

placing her hand on the head of her broadaxe was all the persuasion she needed.

As they carried the wounded away, Kheperu leaned close to murmur in her ear: "How much do you know of this Leucas, our partner? Did you know him well, before we met?"

She shrugged expressively. "Why do you ask?"

He twitched his long beaky nose toward where Leucas stood keeping silent watch over the unconscious bear. The morning sun beat strongly upon his chest and his broad serene brow, brought a golden glow to his bronzed skin and highlit his beard and hair. "Only a madman would charge a bear like that, to engage it bare-handed, if you'll excuse the pun."

"Got away with it, though, didn't he?"

"Mmm, yes. Yes, he did. Just as he 'got away with' fronting the Kyprian Boar after his spear broke. One swipe of the claws tore the face from that handler—killed him outright, or near enough; he won't live an hour—yet Leucas has come away with only bloody scratches, a gash across the back of his shoulder."

"What's your point?"

"I'm not sure I have one," Kheperu said thoughtfully. "I only wonder if perhaps there may be more to our Athenian friend than meets the eyes."

"Guess he's just lucky," Barra said. "You'd have to be, to live through the Siege of Troy. Come on."

She turned her back on him and walked over to the bear, Kheperu trailing close behind.

"No sign of the bloody handlers?" she asked, and Leucas silently shook his head. Barra cupped her hands to her mouth. *"Meneides! Hey, Meneides! Come get your bloody bear!"*

"You're not going to let it go?" Leucas asked, frowning. "You're going to let them keep it?"

"Of course," Barra told him. "Sure, I hate bearbaiting and all, but this is business. When this story gets around, everyone's going to know that we're three bronze-chewing heroes who aren't afraid of anything—even if, maybe, they'll think we're none too bright." She pointedly avoided looking at Leucas. "See? Our price goes up. Meanwhile, the way I see it, Idonosteus owes us a big one. Now we only need those handlers to take us to the House Meneides compound along with the bear, and we can collect."

Leucas and Kheperu exchanged glances. Leucas shrugged, and winced at the pain from his shoulder.

"I have always admired," Kheperu said warmly, "the way your mind works, Barra."

"Have you really?" she said. She looked up into the limitless blue of the Phoenikian sky, followed with her eyes the curving wheel of a gull overhead. "You want to know what my mind's working on right now?"

Kheperu ducked his head, flinching; he recognized her tone. "Well, no, actually . . ."

"I'm thinking," she said mildly, "that if I were to, say, knock you over the head and tie you up, then hang you from one of these balconies, set you swinging back and forth, *blindfold* myself, and start throwing knives and axes and whatever in your general direction, for an afternoon or so, you might learn not to heave spears into a melee where you have a good chance of killing one of your partners. What do you think?"

"I, ah . . ." he coughed, "I don't think that will be necessary . . ."

She bared her teeth. "Are you sure?"

"Now, Barra," Leucas said, "there was no harm done—"

"I'm talking to Kheperu. I have to make sure you're sure, you see, Kheperu, because if you ever do it again, I'll feed you this axe, understand?"

"Quite." Once again fully composed, he shifted his gaze over her shoulder. "The handlers are coming back. We don't want to be bickering in front of the servants, do we? You know how they gossip."

"This bear has become an expensive proposition." Idonosteus mopped wine from his beard with a linen napkin of Tyrian purple, almost the same color as the wine itself. "Lucky that Brachmus had no family, and that he wasn't popular with the men. No compensation, and the funeral can be cheap. You say only one townsman was killed?"

Barra nodded crisply. "Yes, sir. Three or four were injured, but were able to walk away; then there's the two downstairs."

"Lucky again. They'll be presenting themselves for compensation, of course, but if they weren't actually crippled, I may still turn a handsome profit on the beast."

The room was small but lavishly furnished. Barra and Kheperu half reclined on low couches of intricately carved Kushite ebony, piled with silk-covered pillows so soft as to be practically nonexistent. Wide double doors, thrown open to admit the noonday sun, led onto a broad gallery that overlooked the interior courtyard and led to other second-floor rooms. The walls of this room, the informal sitting room of Idonosteus' private apartments, were painted with vivid Cretan motifs of dolphins and octopi, twisting seaweed and playful nymphs. The ceiling was painted with scenes that Barra guessed represented the heroic actions of some ancestor, possibly Meneus himself, during the Sack of Crete.

With the help of Barra and Leucas, the remaining handlers had dragged the bear to the Meneides compound on an improvised travois. Along the way, Kheperu had managed to sell the other four spears for a total of nineteen shekels, despite his continued whining and moaning about the loss he was taking. Under threat of imminent bodily injury, he split these earnings with his partners. When they'd reached the huge bronze door that formed the gate in the compound wall, Barra had an instant's doubled vision: as the door swung wide now, she also saw it as she had a thousand times, passing by here on errands for Peliarchus. As a girl of fifteen and sixteen, she had looked upon these ten-cubit walls, wondering if she would ever see within. House Meneides was second in wealth and power only to House Penthedes; their compound was constructed like a fortress, warehouses full of olives and salt, exotic foods, casks of spices, local wines and Egyptian beer, and—it was rumored—a storehouse of African gold, protected by these walls.

They were received cordially enough, but Idonosteus was "engaged in important negotiations and much too busy to see them," until Barra insisted that the houseboy who'd brought them this message return to Idonosteus and carry the story from the handlers of the bear. The houseboy had bowed minutely, with a skeptical look, and vanished. A few minutes later, a sweating Meneides lieutenant who identified himself as Pharku came scampering out to welcome them. Leucas was ushered off to have his wounds tended by the surgeon, and Barra and Kheperu were led directly to Idonosteus' apartments.

Idonosteus reclined on a broad pile of cushions, and offered the Kushite couches that held similar piles with a lazy wave of his plump, soft, bejeweled hand. The other hand was occupied with a winebowl and a fistful of ripe olives that he somehow held simultaneously. An ankle-height table before him was spread with golden platters of fruit, young cheese, and strips of delicately smoked fish, as well as a pair of golden chalices of wine. The couches were strategically placed so that the table would be within reach of someone sitting on any of them, but only with effort—it'd take a long reach.

The Head of House Meneides was of medium height and round as a dumpling. His sleek black-dyed braids glistened with scented oil; his beard also was braided in the Assyrian style. His teeth gleamed within his wide welcoming smile, but his eyes were calculating and cold as chips of topaz.

"Sit, please, be at home," he said indulgently. "I am curious— Barra? Is that your name?"

Barra lowered herself cautiously onto the bench. "Yes, Lord Idonosteus."

"I am curious, you see, how a trio of scruffy mercenaries—"

"Scruffy?" Kheperu bristled. "I am so far beyond scruffy that—"

Barra kicked him in the calf and said smoothly, "Please excuse my ill-mannered partner, and please continue. I am at your service."

Idonosteus flicked a glance sidelong at Kheperu and the corners of his lips teased upward toward a smile. He went on. "The handlers were five. You, I'm told, are three, and one of you a woman. Yet they ran, while you fought."

Barra lifted her shoulders in an expressive shrug. "How better to get your attention, my lord?"

Idonosteus' eyes glittered, and his smile broadened, and Kheperu stared at Barra as though he could not believe his ears.

"You look vaguely familiar to me," he mused. "Have we met before?"

Barra ducked her head in an obsequious nod. "I scribed a contract for you once, at the Trade Fair on Crete . . ."

"Ah, yes, now I recall—you're the one who's supposed to be the exiled barbarian princess, or somesuch." He nodded and released a wet and bubbling belch. "Odd combination of trades you practice. Well, get on with the tale."

The Head of House Meneides occasionally sipped his wine, or munched olives, while he listened to Barra recount the fight in the plaza, but she could clearly see that he missed not a word. While she spoke, she watched him mentally calculate his losses, toting up the silver he'd have to pay to families of the victims. Once the total had been adjusted to his satisfaction, Barra said, "If you don't mind my asking, my lord—why did your men bring the bear through the Market? It seems to me that an indirect route would have been safer, and less costly."

Idonosteus nodded glumly. "Politics," he said. "Image. Piracy in the Mediterranean has surged in the last five years or so, ever since the end of that business at Troy. It's putting tremendous pressure on me—and the Penthedes, for that matter. We're losing ground to the Mursuwallites, Jephunahi, and Tomitiri, since they used mostly overland routes, north, east, and south. So by bringing in a cargo that could only come from northwestern Europe—"

"You're showing the whole city that your ships can run unmolested all the way from the Pillars of Herakles," Barra finished for him. "Impressive, my lord."

"Exactly; or"—he snorted—"it would have been. You think like a trader."

Barra smiled. "I was raised by one."

Idonosteus waved a dismissive hand; her life was too dull to contemplate. "You told me that you think the same man threw both of the first rocks. Did you get a good look at him? Would you know him if you saw him again?"

Barra shook her head. "The crowd was too thick."

"Someone has been stirring up trouble, and this certainly seems to have been an attempt to embarrass House Meneides. Or perhaps it was simply ill luck; there is a great deal of ill luck going around these days," he said with a heavy sigh. "It's almost as though I've been cursed. Nothing seems to go right anymore; the bloody bear will probably get a fever from that little spear-cut and die, that's the way my luck's been going—I'm tired of it, and it's costing me a great deal, as well."

"On that subject, my lord—"

"Excuse me," Kheperu interrupted, casually leaning far forward to slice off a hunk of cheese with a gold knife. "What do you intend to do with that bear?"

Idonosteus shrugged. "Oh, I suppose I'll bring it to Crete in the spring. If it lives. That's where the big gamblers go to drop their gold."

"*Savages,*" Kheperu muttered under his breath, then continued in a normal tone. "How much, mm, I imagine we saved you a great deal of *money* by our heroic capture of your bear, didn't we?"

Idonosteus' thin-plucked eyebrows lifted minutely, and he glanced at Barra. In the process of shifting her weight on the couch, she managed to tread heavily on Kheperu's foot. His eyes bulged with the effort of restraining a sudden yelp of pain.

"We'll be in Tyre for some weeks yet," Barra said. "You'll be able to contact the three of us at the home of Peliarchus."

"Peliarchus the shipmaster? Penthedes man, isn't he?"

"Yes, sir. And my foster-father. I, however, owe no particular loyalty to Agapenthes, if you follow my meaning, and my two companions are strangers here."

Idonosteus' eyes narrowed, and he gave her one short nod. "I may very well be in touch. Meanwhile, know that you have earned the gratitude of House Meneides, and *that*," he said pointedly to Kheperu, "is no inconsiderable thing."

"The limp-prick bastard stiffed us!"

Leucas frowned down at Kheperu as the three skirted the Market on their way to the home of Peliarchus. His right shoulder had been stitched and neatly rebandaged in fresh white linen by the Meneides surgeon, and more linen wrapped his chest. He claimed that the wounds were shallow, only torn skin; he told them he should heal in two or three weeks, without even much scarring. Barra kept glancing at the bandages as they walked, but the surgeon had apparently done a good job—no blood showed through, yet.

"Not one thin shekel," Kheperu went on. "Like we risk our skins to get some dogfucking olives and cheese!"

Leucas turned to Barra. "What really happened?"

Barra smiled. "Idonosteus will hire us. I'm sure of it. And he'll pay good money, too, because I'm connected in House Penthedes. Something's going on between the Great Houses, maybe another street war warming up. Kheperu damned nearly killed it, though."

"Me?"

"If we had taken a reward for the bear," Barra said flatly, "he would have read us as low on money. Poor."

"Barra, perhaps I'm confused," Leucas said, "but we are poor, aren't we?"

"Idonosteus doesn't know that. By passing off the bear thing as hardly worth mentioning, we come off affluent. Unconcerned. Our price goes up."

Kheperu grunted. "Well, perhaps so and perhaps not. We did not come out empty-handed, though." He reached inside his robe and pulled out a gleaming knife, its broad blunt blade shining gold in the sunlight. "We should be able to sell this for enough to buy an ox or two."

Barra gasped, "Kheperu! Bloody Mother, what were you thinking of? Why would you steal a *gold cheese knife off Idonosteus' table* while he's *sitting* there?"

"Because," Kheperu explained with exaggerated patience, as though speaking to a child, "the chalices were too fucking big to hide under my robes."

# 2

# *Othniel*

**O**thniel bin Jezer pressed himself against the sun-warmed wall at his back, and squinted along the crowded street. There he was, the stone-thrower, a bobbing head of dark hair sun-bleached to the color of dried blood, making the turn in front of Chapli's incense stall. As soon as he was safely out of sight, Othniel broke into a run toward the corner around which the man had disappeared, ignoring the sweat that poured from his brow over his round cheeks. *For a man of forty,* he reassured himself breathlessly, *I can still run—it's only these heavy robes that make me puff so.*

Othniel had walked these flagstones in the Market of Tyre since the day he could first stand upright; he had grown up here, running errands for his father, a prosperous merchant of imported wines. Later, when he'd grown into his strength, he would carry two monstrous jugs dangling from their nets upon his own back, deliver them to the water-front inns, and return unguarded with empties and silver. Often this would take hours longer than it should; he loved to drift through the Market, stroll among the stalls watching people, greeting his many friends and acquaintances, meeting folk he didn't know. This last became less and less common over the years—it seemed that he knew nearly everyone. He knew every twist and turn, every nook and cranny of Tyre; he knew the names of every merchant in the Market and the names and ages of nearly all their children; he knew where this spice seller's mistress spent her afternoons, and where that rug dealer went for pleasures his wife flatly refused to provide. When Othniel was twenty, his father had overextended his credit with the Tomitiri, and the Great House had sent armed men to confiscate his father's inventory. Othniel had returned from his last delivery that day to find his father dangling from a twisted noose made of the carrying nets for the wine jars. He was an only child, and his mother was long dead; alone in the world, he'd drifted back into the Market in search of a living.

In those days, there had been a new trading House in Tyre, the House of Jephunah, Amorites out of the East with strong trade connections to the fading glory of Babylon. They only barely qualified for the appellation House—it was applied mostly by courtesy, out of respect for the enormous sums they had spent trying to establish themselves. Othniel, alone and beggared at twenty, with no resource beyond his strong back and his voluminous knowledge of the city, had boldly reached out to old Jephunah himself and put both at his service.

He rapidly became indispensable. Knowing who could be intimidated, who should be bribed, who must be flattered, and who could be killed without reprisal, he helped build the Jephunahi from fringe-nibbling outsiders to what they were today: a Power of Tyre, a Great House. In the process, he'd made himself into a man who wore rich brocade robes, and gemstones on every finger; a man whose smile could save a merchant's business; a man whose frown could kill.

And he'd done it by simply doing what he loved best, loafing in the Market, killing time, chattering with this vendor and that whore, getting the gossip and sniffing the wind. He could imagine no better life; he served House Jephunah with not only his mind and body, but with his whole heart; and in return, Jephunah had granted him more power than any Jephunahi, saving only the old man's sons—and, Othniel sometimes felt, more respect than he gave even them.

A week ago, a Jephunahi caravan had been ambushed in the Lebanon. The usual inquiries—and offers of ransom—to the Habiru tribes that held the mountains, had produced responses that seemed honestly puzzled; more significantly, none of them had offered to sell back the caravan's cargo. Old Jephunah, always quick to sense a pattern of hostile action, had instantly assumed that one of the other Great Houses was behind it, and had set Othniel the task of determining which. Othniel had returned to his beloved Market and had relentlessly sought information.

House Jephunah was not the only Great House that had suffered recent losses, he learned. The Penthedes had lost three ships, perhaps to pirates; a Meneides wine warehouse had burned; Summilitallas, the aged Head of House Mursuwalli, had died of some mysterious wasting illness, leaving it in the hands of her son, and three of the inns loyal to this House had come under some inexplicable sorcerer's curse that slew all their guests; the Tomitiri had lost a caravan of Kushite oils and a shipful of ivory from Punt. These were only the most blatant manifestations of what Othniel had come to believe was a concerted attempt to foment war between the Great Houses. It was clear that misfortune was more-or-less equally distributed among the five Great Houses.

What he'd been unable to determine was the author of these misfortunes. He became increasingly convinced that old Jephunah was correct, that there was a Great House behind this. The resources of a Great House would be required, to sponsor the sort of powerful magic that was being used to stir things up. Even the lost ships of the Penthedes—there was a rumor that they'd met no pirates, but instead sank due to a sorcerer's curse that had been burned into their bows, a curse at which their captains reportedly had laughed. Another curse of a similar sort was said to have been found, charred and barely legible, in the ruins of the Meneides winehouse. Which of the Great Houses had deliberately inflicted a loss upon themselves, so that they might appear innocent?

Ordinarily, he'd approach such a problem by determining who had the most to gain from the ensuing war; unfortunately, any of them would gain immensely from winning a trade war, and would gain even more by letting two competitors fight one, while waiting to mop up a weakened winner.

Next, he tried to discover which Great House had *not* been recently hiring sorcerers and workers of magic, reasoning that the House behind these various curses would need hire none for defense. Again, he was frustrated. The only Great House that was not aggressively seeking even the lowliest kinds of charm-wrappers was the Penthedes: they controlled the priesthoods of both Ba'al-Berith and Ba'al-Marqod, and thus were defended by the gods themselves. They also, as the greatest of the Great Houses, had the most at risk in a general war.

Days passed, but Othniel never became discouraged; from long experience, he knew that if he kept pecking away, eventually he'd hit the corn among the gravel. Finally, when the Meneides handlers had tried their silly bloody stunt of bringing an uncaged bear through the Market, Othniel himself had been standing not five paces distant from the dark-haired man who'd thrown the first two stones. Interestingly, this man had not thrown anything else, once the crowd picked up his game—that fact alone led Othniel to keep an eye on him, even through the panic of the bear's escape and its foolhardy but lucky capture by those three foreign mercenaries. This stone-throwing individual had drifted slowly out of the crowd immediately after the bear's capture—not as though he had someplace in particular to be, but casually, as though he had all day to loaf and wander. But, if he had all day, why didn't he stick around to watch the aftermath of the fight, to see who lived and who died? Nobody else was leaving; in fact, once the bear was down, the crowd grew ever larger and thicker.

But the stone-thrower sauntered away, and Othniel followed him.

The stone-thrower would stop now and then, turn at some stall or other, and examine their wares. Othniel could clearly see that this was pretense: the man's eyes flicked this way and that, scanning the crowd to see if he was being followed. Othniel was an old hand at this; he stayed barely in sight of the man, keeping himself screened by people between. Once when the stone-thrower turned a corner, Othniel reversed the stole he wore over his robes to show the plain white linen underside; on another occasion he removed the stole altogether and covered his head with a newly purchased burnoose. Of such small details is made success, in following unobserved. Now he was sure he'd made his lucky find; he was positive that this stone-thrower would lead him to the secret enemy. His scalp tingled, and he wore a tight but happy smile—he felt young again, as he followed this man through the Market. This was like the old days, and it warmed his spirit to find that he'd lost none of his skill.

*I can still do this as well as any man in Tyre,* he thought as he followed the stone-thrower into a narrow alleyway. As he peered around a corner within it, he was thinking, *Probably even better; I'm probably the best follower in Tyre* even as the fist-size leather sock half-full of beach sand slapped him precisely on the top of his head. His vision showered sparks, his knees buckled, and he pitched forward toward the dirt.

Even stunned, he understood what was happening—he'd been sapped once before, many years ago. He brought up his hands to protect his head, but the second blow crushed the bones of his fingers against his skull. The third struck him solidly where the base of his skull joined with his neck, and darkness exploded within his mind.

He must have been slowly awakening for some time, because he found himself unsurprised that he was alive. When he'd tumbled toward the hard-packed dirt in the alley off the Market, he'd been quite sure that he'd never open the eyes of this body again. The burning ache in the shattered fingers of his left hand nearly covered the dull throb from his head—the fire that lanced his fingers when he tried to wriggle them pushed a groan past his lips.

It also came as no surprise that he was bound hand and foot; not tied, but shackled to a table that felt rough but not uncomfortable through the layers of the robes he still wore. Shadows danced on a ceiling that had the creases and folds of natural rock, as though he were within a cavern. Although he could smell nothing, not even the smoke from the tripod braziers that cast this reddish light—he must have been shackled here long enough to numb his nose entirely—he could taste, when he licked his lips, some bitter tang, a faintly nauseous taste that reminded him of jugged lamb that had gone over into white webs and decay.

By turning his head, he could see other tables flanking the one upon which he lay. They were empty, though they had shackles at the corners and grooves carved into their surfaces—these looked like drains, not unlike butcher boards, and the dark stains that painted them he found alarming. And on his right hand, past which he looked, glittered the precious stones of the rings he wore on every finger.

This, particularly, was bad. If the rings had been missing, he would have allowed himself to hope that he would merely be robbed and beaten, or held for a fat ransom. But there they were, untouched. A cold, sharp-fingered hand of apprehension clutched his belly; this might be very bad indeed.

"He is awake," said someone softly, behind the head of the table, where he could not see.

Othniel licked his lips again, and cautiously tried his voice. "Come, this is not necessary." It came out a weak, ragged croak. "I'm sure you know who I am, and know that Jephunah will ransom me. Failing that, he will also avenge my death."

A stocky, broad-shouldered man stepped around the table into view. His deep chest was bare, either shaven or naturally hairless, as was his head. He wore a beard in the Egyptian style, bound in a stiff rod from the point of his chin, but his skin was as pale as cave moss, and when he spoke, his Phoenikian had the native accent of the southern ports. "Your throat is dry, mm? Here, drink this."

He offered a cup, from the rim of which hung a curving straw of bronze. Othniel turned his head away; he squeezed shut his eyes and wished with all his heart that this man had worn a mask. He wanted to live through this.

"Don't—*hrakhakh*"—the pale man coughed harshly—"don't imagine that you can refuse. Drink."

"This isn't *necessary*," Othniel insisted, face averted and eyes still shut. "The man I followed is the only one I've seen—and he can't be very important. Truly, I am less trouble alive and free."

His captor said, "Let me explain."

His broken hand was seized, his fingers forced apart. A freezing line drew itself across his thumb, accompanied by a crunching thunk, like a butcher's cleaver hacking through bone into the wood of the block; he felt the shock through the table. Something small and light struck him on the chest; he opened his eyes to see the first two joints of his left thumb, ragged and bloody, caught in a fold of his robe. The polished tourmaline set in its familiar thumb ring of gold gleamed bright and uncaring; he'd worn that ring for nearly ten years.

"Drink," the man told him, again offering the cup.

"Please, you don't *understand*," Othniel pleaded, trembling now uncontrollably. His stomach spasmed and burned the back of his throat with half-digested salt fish. He had to explain, he had to make them understand, this was unnecessary! "Don't you know who I *am*?"

The man with a Phoenikian face and Egyptian beard leaned close and said kindly, "We know who you are, Othniel bin Jezer, faithful servant of Jephunah bin Abieizel, of course we do. We know you have been asking about us. Now, you must drink, or—*hrakhakh*—or I must hurt you again."

Othniel could see now that this man's smooth cheeks were cosmetic; even beyond the kohled eyes that were common among men of rank, his face was painted like a whore's. And within the paint that caulked over the lines of age and slackness, his lips were loose and wet, and his eyes glittered remotely with the disinterested glassy stare of a fish. No appeal could reach through this utter lack of human connection and no appeal would he make: fear paralyzed Othniel's will. He took the straw with trembling lips and drank. It was wine, with a sharp, resinous bite and a sweetish undertone.

"Good, that's very good," his captor muttered distantly, as he turned to the task of binding the spurting stump on Othniel's left hand.

Now spoke another voice, from back behind the table's head; Othniel recognized that this was the voice that had spoken first. Now it spoke in Egyptian, in the aristocratic dialect of the Nile Delta. Did this man, whoever he was, imagine that Othniel, who'd spent his entire life in the Market of Tyre, would not speak the language of this land's rulers? He said, "Really, it's a piece of luck, Sim, this fellow falling into our hands. I think I shall not punish Haral at all for letting himself be observed. After all, had he not seized the opportunity presented by the Meneides' bear, we wouldn't now have our little friend clipped to the table here, would we?"

"No, Remmie," the man who bound Othniel's hand agreed. "It's luck. It must indeed be."

"Luck, perhaps. Perhaps destiny. Perhaps they are the same. The play of chance; the roll of dice, and here I am. I have been searching for a prominent citizen on which to make our next demonstration, and now one is delivered unto my very door who is known and loved by all. A gift of fate, perhaps. Yes, I like that." His rich voice had become a smug purr. "I like that a great deal. But I am curious about these three foreigners who captured the bear. An extraordinary feat, hmm? Haral thinks that they are probably mercenaries; perhaps I can hire them myself—I admire boldness. Ask him if he knows who they are, or anything about them."

While Sim unnecessarily translated the question into Phoenikian, Othniel concentrated on what he was learning: three names, so far, Sim, Remmie, and Haral. He had faces for two of them. If this fellow behind him continued to chatter in Egyptian, he might learn a great deal. He swore to himself that he would survive, that he would escape. He would carry these names to Jephunah, and exact tenfold revenge for his torture.

He answered, "I saw some of the fight. Two men and a woman. One of the men is a boxer—Akhaian, I think—and is crazy; he fought the bear with his fists. The woman throws stone axes, and she's crazy, too. The other man, well, I don't really know, but he looks even crazier than the others. I don't know who they are, or where they are; they're foreign, though. The woman looked faintly familiar, but if the other two were Tyrian, I'd know them—they are both extremely conspicuous. They looked poor, but mercenaries often do." He swiveled his head around, trying to get a glimpse of the man behind. "Do you see that I am trying to cooperate? Do you see that I am not even asking why they interest you?"

The next question he expected—Why did you follow Haral, the stone-thrower?—he had an answer for, and for the next one after that, and after that, a conversation that spun out in his mind and led inevitably to proof that he was innocent, and harmless, and that they'd be much better off if they pleased Jephunah by releasing him. Even the throbbing of his battered skull faded behind this happy expectation; new warmth suffused the room, and brought a glow to his cheeks.

From behind his head, Remmie said in Egyptian, "Of these inns that we are prepared to curse, are any loyal to the Jephunahi?"

Sim, murmuring, "Yes, Remmie, one is," completed tying off the stump of Othniel's thumb with a dirty rag that was crusted with some cracked brownish substance. This Sim must be a fine surgeon; any lingering pain in Othniel's hand was forgotten. He struggled to contain himself, to give no sign that he'd understood Remmie's words. He'd been right all along! A single agent behind the curses! Now, all he needed was to discover which Great House these two worked for—and then to escape, of course, but that was a mere detail; he took it for granted.

Remmie continued, "I wish to make clear that Othniel is no random victim; we must demonstrate to Jephunah that we despise his paltry power. The next inn to fall under the curse shall be this Jephunahi one. Furthermore, we shall escalate these proceedings. Let us . . . mm, have a Jephunahi tax collector killed—and no sneaking about, knife in the back kind of thing. I want as many witnesses as can be gathered; I want it to be spectacular, to be the talk of Tyre for a week. Perhaps we should maim a few of the witnesses, just to give the scene more impact. Yes, I think so."

"A tax collector will have guards," Sim murmured. Now he held Othniel's chin with one hand, while with the other he peeled down Othniel's lower eyelid and peered at it thoughtfully. Othniel tried to form words to ask Sim what he was doing, but his mouth seemed packed with cotton.

Still, the warmth of his impending release kept Othniel happy; until, at least, he began to try to remember if they'd ever asked him that question he'd been expecting . . .

"Of course he'll have guards," Remmie said expansively. "The more the better. I'll put the Greek on it; he likes this sort of thing. He can hire some of the street trash, as many as he needs. And, I think, we should put the word out about those three bear-fighters. I want them."

Sim nodded distractedly, and turned away to fiddle with a tray of winebowls set nearby.

"Sim?" Remmie's voice took on a new tone, a dangerous tone.

Sim's head jerked up from the bowls, and they rang faintly as his hands twitched. "Yes, Remmie?"

"Don't you *yes-Remmie* me, you shit." The words were those of a woman, or a whiny adolescent, but the low, lethal tone in which they were spoken robbed them of all comedy. "When I speak, you *listen.*"

"I was listening! I was, Remmie, I really was."

"All right, then," Remmie purred. "What did I just say?"

"You were, you were going to have the Greek kill a tax collector, and, and something about those three mercenaries with the bear. You, er, you want them." Othniel fought back a smile as he watched Sim try to conceal a sigh of relief. "I'm—*hrakhakh*—I'm sorry, Remmie. I get caught up in my work, you know—he's ready, almost."

*Who is?* Othniel wondered fuzzily. *Is he speaking of me? Ready for what? Are they going to let me go now?* And, belatedly: *What was in that wine?*

"I want them," Remmie went on calmly, as though the previous exchange had never occurred, "because of the way they've entered my life. The play of chance is the hand of destiny. Haral happens to be in the Market; he stumbles across the Meneides' foolishness of bringing a bear through the crowd. He makes a snap decision to interfere. This decision brings Othniel to me, just now, when I have need of him. These three mercenaries also happen to be there, the right place at the right time. They, also, are a gift to me: a gift of fate."

"Then," Sim murmured, "you should take them. You should have them. You will."

"Of course I will. Have I ever been slow to accept the gifts of fate?" He breathed a long, satisfied sigh, like a fat man after a heavy meal. "Is he ready, then?"

"Oh yes, Remmie, I think so."

"Go ahead."

Sim looked down at Othniel and said in Phoenikian, "How are you feeling?"

"Ahll . . ." Othniel found that with great effort, he could make his tongue work. "A lid . . . liddle sstrannge . . ."

"Good, that's very good." Sim turned away from him for a moment, and when he turned back he held a long rod of bronze by its wooden handle; the other end was a molded disk of bronze that glowed yellow with heat. Othniel could smell it, the coppery, bloody smell of hot bronze, and the yellow glow seemed to flow and pulse from side to side, and drip toward the floor, and trail behind it when Sim moved it toward the tray of winebowls. He stuck the hot end into one, which caused a great hiss and a plume of steam—or was it smoke?—that drifted upward in the cavern's still air, twisting into fantastic shapes, a dog-headed man, a crocodile with human arms and legs . . .

Othniel giggled. "Frr . . . for a momen', I thought you were gonna use tha' on me . . ."

"I—*hrakhakh*—I am."

He lifted the branding bronze once again, and now it dripped pale green fire, of whatever substance had been in that bowl. He dipped it in another, and when it came up it flared blue. Sim once again took Othniel's broken left hand and spread its fingers gently, then struck with the hot bronze, searing deep into the flesh of his palm.

Othniel screamed. Sim leaned on the bronze, driving it deeper and deeper into Othniel's charring flesh as his body twisted convulsively. He screamed until his voice failed, until from his throat came only the hiss of escaping air.

It ended slowly, as contact with Othniel's flesh cooled the bronze. Sim dropped the bronze casually on the floor, reached over, and plucked Othniel's severed thumb out of the fold of his robe. "I'll have need of this."

His hand was already growing numb, and the numbness grew along his forearm, crept past his elbow toward his shoulder. "Wha' are you going to do?" he whispered.

"With this?" Sim said, holding up Othniel's bloody thumb. "I'm going to burn it. A bit, *khm*, a bit later on. It's part of the ritual. For now, though, you should be seeing shapes in the air. Tell me what you see."

The numbness reached his shoulder and surged down his chest to his heart. Almost instantly, he could barely feel his body at all. His eyes rolled in terror as absolute as his earlier confidence had been. Things were moving in the shadows, becoming more and more clear. The cavern began to fill with ghostly forms, smoky outlines of obscene shapes that seemed to enter through the stone itself and drift out again. Some of them swirled and stayed near the braziers, as though they lusted for the oil's paltry heat and glow. And their bodies, their forms seemed to have no shape at all, or rather too many shapes, and they flowed from one shape to another, and they twisted and warped, and the only parts of them that seemed to have solidity were teeth, and claws, and eyes, far too many eyes.

Sim said, "Never mind. Your face shows all I need. What you see are the Children of Apep, the divine monsters that tear the souls of the dead. Spirits, you'd call them, or demons. It doesn't matter. You see, they are around us all the time, everywhere—*hrakhakh*—everywhere we go, they are inside us, in our mouths, our nostrils, our bowels. Perhaps they are a bit thicker here, as jackals cluster more thickly around graves of the poor. They take no notice of us, while we live, nor we of them. Well, except for you, Othniel bin Jezer. You have been granted a rare gift; even I have never seen this. You can see them now, faintly, no doubt, their glory dimmed in this faint light. They'll be so much more solid, so much more *potent* tomorrow after dawn, under the gaze of

Ra. You'll see them perfectly. Of course, this means that they also can
see you."

Othniel's chest heaved. "Please. I beg you. I swear I won't tell, I
swear I won't tell anything!"

Remmie's rich baritone came from behind him again, in Egyptian. "Tell whatever you like, to whomever you like. In fact, please
do." Othniel flinched helplessly, and Remmie's voice took on a
chuckling undertone. "Oh yes, I speak your filthy little pidgin, though
I choose not to soil my mouth with it. And I imagine that you speak
Egyptian as well. I certainly hope so. Nothing that happens here, Othniel bin Jezer, is a *secret* at all . . ."

A warm, dry hand stroked Othniel's cheek, almost a caress. "That
is why I shall set you free. Oh, not now—it shall be several hours yet.
Just before dawn, I think. Then you may tell anyone you like."

Remmie laughed, deep and long. "Tell *everyone*!"

# 3

## *Old Friends*

The home of Peliarchus stood to seaward of the Penthedes compound. It was large, by the standards of crowded Tyre, but not ostentatious: the second floor, which had been under construction when Barra was here briefly last spring, was now completed in the same simple, unadorned style as the centuries-old ground floor, smooth straw-colored walls broken by narrow windows shuttered with wood.

Barra fought down the familiar twist in her stomach when she saw the main door. When she'd first seen this house, she was fourteen and bitterly homesick; she spent every waking instant regretting her rash decision to sail to the East. Seeing the house from the outside always brought that back to her, the despairing weight of the knowledge that her home was far beyond the edge of the world.

Before she knocked, she gave Leucas and Kheperu strict instructions to be polite, and to look cheerful and prosperous; nothing burned Barra's spirit more than coming home in need. At least she'd been able to bring some gifts.

After some moderately heated discussion along the way from the Meneides compound (Kheperu: "I stole it; it's mine!" Barra: "But if you'd been caught, we'd all have been in the shit." Leucas came in on Barra's side, which decided the matter) they'd managed to discreetly sell the golden cheese knife for five bolts of brightly dyed silk. One of the bolts bought them an array of lovely faience spice pots; another bought them a thick bundle of exotic incense from Dilmun. It cost two more bolts for the matching bracelet and belt buckle of rope-worked silver from Punt. These things, with the one remaining bolt of silk, Barra judged to be suitably impressive, and she calculated that they'd traded up the value of the cheese knife by at least a third, maybe by half.

The porter who opened the spy gate at her knock had been opening doors and sweeping the hearthyard in the house of Peliarchus for ten years before Barra's first arrival. He recognized her instantly and pulled open the door. "You come on in right now, Barra! 'S improper for a young lady to be standin' on the street alone with men, people'll think you're a whore!"

"I'm not all that young anymore, Milo," she said through a smile as she gripped his wrist. "This is Leucas of Athens, and this is Kheperu, and where are my parents?"

"You just wait here, right? I'll get everybody. Missis is just back from the Market, and Mister's in his chart room, and your bloody dog is upstairs asleep on my bed!"

"He is? Graegduz! Hey, *Graeg!*" She whistled sharply, and Graegduz streaked down the stairs and across the hearthyard like he'd been shot from a bow.

Four years ago, she'd spent a summer at home, on the Isle of the Mighty; she'd made the six-week journey aboard one of the ships she part owned, the *Skye Swift*. She'd spent the summer reacquainting with her family, teasing her brother Llem about the grey that had begun to raddle his black hair, slowly getting to know the happy, golden-haired eleven-year-old that everyone claimed was her son. She'd also crossed the Eirish Sea to make the obligatory visit with her father at his fortress of Tara, bringing gifts and stories of the wide world. One of the gifts her father gave her in return was a wolf cub, only a month old. A wolf pack had been raiding Ouendail's flocks, and he had ridden out with his hounds to hunt them down and kill them himself, as befits an Eirish king. When the slaughter was done, he'd found this cub shivering silently in the hillside cave that had been the den, this cub which he could not kill—to slay the innocent young is blasphemy.

Barra had brought him back to the East and raised him with her own hand. She hadn't trained him, exactly; one doesn't train wolves as one does dogs. She'd come to a certain understanding with him, a sort of mutual respect and affection and cooperation. She treated him as a junior partner; he accepted her as his pack leader. But he didn't like the sea—he became uncomfortable and snappish on shipboard, which could terrify any crew—so she had left him here in Tyre for the past six months while she sailed in search of money, and had missed him terribly.

She staggered under his joyous rush; he was big enough to put his paws on her shoulders and lick her face. She hugged him and kissed his nose and crooned to him in Pictish until Leucas and Kheperu began to look mildly nauseated. She went through the ritual of introducing him to her partners; he was particularly interested in Kheperu, and kept coming back to sniff him again, even though the Egyptian's reek made him sneeze. Leucas was more than a bit bemused by all this.

"I've never seen a tame wolf before," he said thoughtfully.

"You're not seeing one now," Barra said with a grin. "Graeg isn't tame, he's just respectful. Be polite to him, and he'll treat you the same way."

"He's big." Leucas crouched in front of him, gravely bringing his head to the same level as the wolf's.

"So are you."

"I think the word Leucas is looking for," Kheperu said, "is *fat*. That is the fattest wolf I have ever seen."

"He's put on some weight," Barra allowed. She patted his flanks. "How'd you get so bloody fat?"

"Peliarchus spoils him mercilessly." Paused regally at the head of the stairs from the second floor was Tayniz, wife of Peliarchus and Barra's foster-mother. She swept the partners with a gaze that made Barra acutely conscious of the six days it'd been since she'd last had a bath. "I could feed three slaves on what that beast eats."

Her hair was piled and wrapped upon her head like a polished silver helmet, held in place by a number of mother-of-pearl combs; her dress of deep Tyrian purple draped flawlessly across her ample curves. "Barra," she said warmly, descending toward the hearthyard. "What a wonderful surprise! Welcome home." It was a peculiar talent of Tayniz's, to be both sincerely welcoming and regally intimidating at the same time.

When Barra had first met her, all those years ago, Tayniz had terrified her. On first look, Tayniz had frosted her with a glare like a northeast gale—she'd assumed that this slim young redheaded savage had been purchased in the West to warm the bed of her aging husband. Peliarchus had reassured her, of course—over and over again—that Barra had been given into his care by the High King of Langdale, Barra's brother, and that she was to be treated as a daughter. But that initial freezing reaction had colored her relationship with her foster-mother forever. It hadn't helped that for twenty years Tayniz had prided herself on being Peliarchus' first and only wife. As she and her friends aged, her friends' husbands had married again and again, bringing in ever younger girls to swell their households; Tayniz had, deep in her heart, held herself above these other women because she, alone among them, could hold a husband all to herself. After finally becoming convinced of the truth of the situation, she had cared for Barra as though Barra had been one of her own children, even loved her in the cautious, distant sort of way that one loves a half-wild pet that might at any moment disappear back into the forest, but there had always remained a core of reserve between them, an unspoken recognition of a fundamental gap in understanding. Barra could no more imagine herself living her foster-mother's life than Tayniz could picture herself opening someone's guts with an axe.

As a trader's wife, Tayniz had seen far stranger and more disreputable guests than Leucas and Kheperu. She made warm, admiring comments about the spice pots and silk, and accepted Barra's introductions of her partners with perfect grace. Within moments, the household staff had relieved the companions of their gear and led Leucas and Kheperu to a comfortable couch on which to wait for a bath to be drawn; Leucas had accepted Tayniz's offer of a bath with thanks, after Barra's translation—Kheperu, unsurprisingly but unfortunately, had demurred. Tayniz blinked, once, at his refusal, but her expression never altered. "And for you, Barra?"

"Ay, sure, draw a bath, I can use it," she said. "But first I have to talk to Peliarchus. He's in the chart room, Milo said?"

Tayniz nodded. "Doing accounts, and not to be disturbed."

"Good then, I can surprise him." Barra stood on her toes to give her foster-mother a peck on the cheek; from this close, she could now see new lines under Tayniz's daypaint, and puffy flesh under her eyes. "What's wrong?" she asked softly, holding Tayniz's shoulders. "Something's wrong, I can tell."

Tayniz shook her head. "I don't know. You know Peliarchus doesn't discuss business with me—but he's worried. And I think he's frightened. It's the times, I think. The whole city is . . . changing. Everyone is worried, these days."

"He'll tell me," Barra said, giving her shoulders a squeeze. "Then I can tell you. It'll be just like the old days." With one last squeeze in lieu of a hug, Barra slipped back into the inner house, Graegduz padding happily at her heels. At the chart room, she told Graeg to stay outside—the last time he'd been inside the chart room he'd upset Peliarchus' sandtable, destroying several hours' worth of calculations, and had been banned ever since.

When Barra swung open the heavy door of the chart room, Peliarchus nearly knocked over the sandtable himself in his rush to leap to his feet and gather her into a bear hug that left her gasping. "Great bloody Ba'al!" he said, setting her down. "Oh, Barra, I'm glad to see you!"

Peliarchus was a barrel-shaped man a hand shorter than his wife, and his sunburned scalp hadn't seen a scrap of hair since before Barra could remember. One of her earliest memories was of this man, this bright-eyed bald Phoenikian trader bellowing with laughter as he bounced her on his knee—she couldn't have been as much as three years old. Every summer his ships would put in at Langdale's western coast, and he and his men would spend a month in trade and good guesting at her brother's great hall. It was he who'd taught her Phoenikian, who'd first told her tales of Egypt and Assyria, Babylon and Ur; he was one of the bare handful of men in Tyre who could converse with her in her native tongue. As she grew up, she'd marked the years by anticipating Peliarchus' summer arrival; when she'd chosen to leave her home, there was no other man in the wide world her brother would have trusted to care for her. He was a loud and joyous man of sudden passions and swift decisions, but level judgment. Her brother Llem, a deep and silent man, described him as "steady, with a brave heart"—the highest compliment that he would bestow on anyone.

Barra and Peliarchus held each other at arm's length, each enjoying the sight of the other's grin, and traded happy barbs about their weight: from him about her skinny shanks, from her about his round and jiggling belly. She released him and looked at the sandtable, its moist surface grooved with figures of this and that, various additions, subtractions, and multiplications, but mostly dominated by doodlings of some sort of two-masted ship. "I thought you were supposed to be doing accounts," she said with a sideways glance.

He shrugged. "There's not all that much to do."

A faint echo of despair under his offhand tone warned her not to let the silence stretch out too long. "Well," she said quickly, rubbing her hands together, "the *Skye Swift* and *Langdale's Pride* should make port any day now. Then we'll be able to feast and trade tales all week long—and I have a whole bundle of letters for my sons to be sent back with them. Come on out here, I want you to meet my new partners."

Peliarchus looked pained, and he laid a heavy hand on her shoulder. "They won't be making port in Tyre. Not this year."

A high, buzzing sound sang in Barra's ears, and a cold knot of apprehension twisted tight in her stomach. "What do you mean?" she said carefully. "They're all right, aren't they? Nothing's happened . . . has it?"

"No, oh no," he told her, shaking his head. "I sent letters to Knossos for them, told them to sell off on Crete and make their turnaround from there, that's all. They'll winter in Langdale as planned, and come back first thing in the spring."

Breath that she wasn't aware she'd been holding whooshed out from her. "Oh, thank Lugh," she gasped. "I thought you were going to tell me that pirates got them, or a storm, or some other . . . hey, wait. You changed their itinerary?" Her ears suddenly flamed crimson. "You changed the itinerary of *my ships*?"

"Now, calm down, girl. They're only part yours, and their captains are my sons—practically your brothers. Things in Tyre are, well, a little unsteady right now. Agapenthes has lost three ships in the past month; he can afford to. We can't."

"Shit," Barra said. She bit her lower lip and turned away, clenching and unclenching her fists. She'd been counting on her share of the ships' earnings, depending on it. "Shit, shit, bleeding *shit*. I need that money, Peliarchus. I really do."

"What's the matter? Are you in trouble? You have a bad year?"

She shook off his paternal hand and sagged onto the stool; it was still warm with the heat of his body. "No, I'm having a great year. A fucking *glorious* year. Right up to the day when a pair of bloody pirate ships made off with everything I've earned. I am dead fucking broke, Peliarchus. Outside of the stuff I've sent back to Langdale, all I've got left in the world is my share in those two ships, three stone axes and a bronze cuirass that's been mended so many times it looks like a goatherd's cook pot."

"Well, y'know, listen," Peliarchus began cautiously. He knew Barra too well to offer her money; he'd experienced her temper too many times. "I could advance you something, against your share . . ."

"No. Absolutely not," she said. "I won't do that, and you know it."

"It's only a loan—"

"Don't insult me." Her face suddenly blazed to match her ears. "I earn my own living and pay my own way."

"It's no shame to admit you need help—" Peliarchus took in the white line her tight-stretched lips made against the angry red of her face, and shook his head with a sigh. "All right. Have it your way. You always do, anyway."

Barra shrugged and looked at the scrollcases stacked on their shelves on the other side of the room as though they were suddenly interesting; while the color drained back out of her face. She said softly, "Don't tell Tayniz. I don't want her to worry."

"No fear," he said warmly. "Come on, let's go meet these partners of yours."

Introducing her partners took a bit of doing, since Leucas had no Phoenikian, and Peliarchus, though of Argive heritage (three generations back) had only enough broken Greek to trade linen for wine and the like—not to mention the familiar difficulty of introducing Kheperu to anyone; Barra really admired the self-discipline of her foster-father, who was able to shake Kheperu's hand without so much as a blink or the faintest wrinkling of his nose.

Peliarchus made appreciative noises when he was presented with the bracelet and belt buckle; he instantly put them on and found a silver mirror in which to admire them.

Eventually everyone settled onto couches around the hearth, munching on grapes and cheese and strips of smoked pork while Tayniz got the cook working on a more substantial meal. Shortly, Leucas retired to his bath, muttering sourly about keeping his stitches dry.

The first question Peliarchus had for her was how long they would be staying in Tyre. When Barra told him their plans were indefinite, they might even winter here, he looked both relieved and vaguely worried at the same time.

"Good, then, you'll stay with us"—a pained expression crossed his face—"starting maybe next week."

"Next *week*?" Barra's ears flamed, and her eyes went wide. "What do you mean, next week?"

Kheperu noticed the color of her ears, and began to unobtrusively edge away from her.

"Now . . . now, Barra, don't get mad—" Peliarchus began.

She came to her feet. "You don't want me to get mad, y'shouldn't embarrass me in front of my partners! I told them we'd have a place to stay in Tyre! You'd make a liar of me, now?"

"You *do* have a place to stay! You will—as soon as I can clear up this crap with Agapenthes . . ."

"Barra," Tayniz said, "you know that this is your home as much as it is mine and his. It's only that we're committed to these guests—it's a favor for Agapenthes, and you know that when he asks for a favor, we can't refuse."

A favor for the Head of House Penthedes . . . She was right; refusing to do a favor for the Great House that employed you could have terminally serious consequences. Barra took a deep breath, and huffed it out disgustedly. She plumped back down onto the couch. "Well, all right, fine. What's going on that I can't stay?"

Peliarchus sighed. "There's a distant cousin of Agapenthes coming in for a visit. The lord is planning to have his household so full that this idiot and his entourage will have to stay here, with me."

"Why? Who is this guy?"

"Like I said, he's an idiot. Agapenthes hates the guy, can't stand to be around him—I'm told all he does is talk, drink, and fuck, and the only one he's good at is the drinking. A letter came last week—a special ship chartered straight from Kypros—he's on his way here with seven or eight of his nobles. They might even be here later tonight; it depends on the weather."

"From Kypros . . ." Barra said slowly.

Kheperu suddenly snickered. "Do you think it could be possible?"

"Oh, no," she said, starting to laugh, "oh, it couldn't be! Please tell me we're not talking about the king! King Demetor of Kypros?"

"Yeah, his name's Demetor." Peliarchus scowled at their laughter. "Why? What is it?"

"This is a man," Kheperu said with relish, "who has more brains in his eleventh finger than he does in his whole head."

After that, of course, Barra had no choice but to tell the story of their visit to Kypros. They'd arrived the morning after an unsuccessful boar hunt—it was all anyone was talking about at dockside. Two men had been gored, one fatally—Barra and Leucas had been on the beach only a few minutes when they were approached by Kheperu. Kheperu drew laughs from Peliarchus with his re-creation of his Wandering Seer act that had all-too-easily convinced King Demetor that this boar had been sent by the gods to punish his people for their king's impiety.

"What impiety?"

Kheperu leered. "Fucking. Not enough fucking. They worship Astarte, do they not?—even though they call her Aphrodite. I told him Astarte was *verrry* angry with him because he had not been fucking."

Tayniz blinked, and Peliarchus smothered a laugh. "How'd you know?"

"He's *old*," Kheperu said with a careless shrug. "I told him that to appease the goddess, he had to futter seven women a day for seven days. He went white and began to stammer; I had him by his limp old dick. I told him not to worry, Great Poseidon would send him two heroes from the sea, a man and a woman—you see, still harping the Astarte/fucking/lovers angle—and they would be the only ones who could slay the boar. So quite naturally, when Demetor went down to the docks, he found Leucas and Barra swimming, innocently naked, in the surf."

Peliarchus shook his head, chuckling. "And did it play?"

"Hundred and eighty Athenian large," Barra told him. "Pretty good wages for two days' work. That's when Leucas and I took on Kheperu as our third partner; the whole gag was his idea."

Tayniz leaned forward seriously. "But weren't you concerned about your own impiety? Don't you think the gods might take revenge on you for taking their names for a swindle?"

"Not at all," Kheperu said loftily. "Who's to say it really was a swindle? I would never presume to actually know the mind of the gods—it's entirely possible that I was telling the truth without even knowing it. The gods often use us mortals to work out their will without our knowledge; trust me on this—it is a doctrine known by every priest in Egypt. Who's to say that Barra and Leucas *weren't* there by the will of Great Poseidon? I met them by chance on the beach; it is often said that what seems chance to us, is the hand of a god at work."

"Hmpf," Tayniz sniffed. "I still think it seems needlessly risky."

"But it worked on Demetor," Barra said. "And it's probably Kheperu's fault he's coming for this visit."

Kheperu spread his hands. "The day we left I sold him a salve, a private recipe," he said with a broad grin. "I told him that rubbing it on his cock every day would keep him hard come earthquake or hurricane for a week. So he would be able to—*ahem*—to satisfy Astarte, even at his age. I'd wager he is coming here to try it out away from the wife and kids."

Peliarchus, the old trader, answered his grin. "And you thought you'd be far away when he finds out it doesn't work."

"Doesn't *work*?" Kheperu bristled. "Of course it will work. Am I a cheat? Am I a swindler? Shit, I use it myself!"

When twilight had painted purple across the sky and there came no sign of Demetor's arrival, Peliarchus and Tayniz had insisted that Barra and her friends should stay the night. The feast had been eaten—the roast duck in currant sauce was every bit as delicious as Barra'd remembered—and the servants dismissed to their quarters. Now brilliant stars gleamed overhead and the fire in the hearthshrine had been built up with hard oak, to burn long and low, keeping off the night's chill. Pale moths, some as large as Barra's hand, fluttered around the hearthyard, circling the fire, occasionally sizzling in the flames, some falling prey to the sudden jittering swoops of a pair of brown bats.

Barra lay back on her couch, watching the bats, Graegduz's great grey head warm in her lap. She swirled the warm wine in her cup and took another tiny sip. On the couch nearest to hers sat Peliarchus and Tayniz, arms about each other's waist, quietly at ease in the late autumn silence. Kheperu had already excused himself to the room he would share with Leucas, muttering about some poultice or ointment that must be prepared before midnight. The huge Athenian lay sprawled on a couch nearby, snoring softly under the blanket Tayniz had spread over him after he'd drifted off. Leucas was unaccustomed to the straight wine of Tyre; he had drunk it as though it were the three-parts-water mix that was common on the Akhaian peninsula. Combined with the fatigue of his wounds and the heavy meal, the wine had leveled him like a blow to the head; even his snoring was only a pale shadow of its usual grinding roar.

"I've been thinking about those letters of yours," Peliarchus said. "I'll be sorry if we can't get them to the Isle before winter; I'd hate to have your boys think something's happened to you when the *Swift* and the *Pride* arrive without them."

Barra shrugged tiredly. "Tomorrow I can see if any ships are heading north for the winter. Perhaps I can pay for the letters' passage."

"Oh, you can't do that. Most Tyrian sailors'd take your coin and toss the letters into the sea. I was thinking, maybe, I might want to take them myself."

Barra sat up on the couch, drawing a whine of protest from Graeg as she dislodged his head from its comfortable spot. "You're serious? You're going out to sea again?"

"In fact," Peliarchus went on, "Tayniz and I have been talking about going out to sea together. I've been thinking, y'know, I haven't been to the Isle of the Mighty in more than ten years, since that time I had to go and tell your brother you'd run away. And Tayniz's always wanted to see it, y'know, and meet your boys, that are almost like grandchildren. And I was thinking, maybe it's time you went back for a visit yourself. Take the letters in person."

Barra stared into the flickering hearthshrine as though searching for a vision. "Are things really that bad here?"

"Moving in that direction, maybe."

"You would not believe," Tayniz murmured, "what's happened to prices in the Market. Everything's down, way down. Except for weapons and armor."

Barra nodded silently; she'd made most of the cheese knife profit in the initial trade for the silk. Gold was valuable everywhere and easy to hide or transport.

"Mercenaries are coming in from all over the Med. Nearly every ship brings a few more. Way I hear it, most of them don't have much trouble finding work." Peliarchus gave her a sad smile. "And I have a feeling that you and your partners didn't come to Tyre right now just to visit with an old married couple."

"You think it's going to be war."

"Maybe that's the best we can hope for." The shifting light from the hearthshrine painted bloodred shadows across his face. "House Penthedes is still the big dog in Tyre. In all Phoenikia. In an open war, we have the resources and manpower to wipe out any other House, maybe even any two together, and do it before the Governor can get any sizable force of Egyptians in here to stop it. We'd come out of a war with a stronger position than we have right now. Agapenthes has been spoiling for a fight for months."

"So what's stopping him?"

"He can't make the first move. The other Houses would all line up against us—there isn't one of them that wouldn't like a piece of what we've got—and we can't fight them all together." He shifted forward, elbows on his knees, fingers knotting together to pop his knuckles one by one. "I'm thinking this is a good time to take a vacation for six months or so."

"I've noticed that everybody seems tense," Barra said, absently ruffling the fur behind Graegduz's ear. "Has anything actually happened? Has anyone made a move?"

Peliarchus shook his head. "Not openly. But things are going on. Three Penthedes ships are a month overdue. So is a Tomitiri caravan. A Mursuwallite warehouse burned a week ago. You ask me, I say it's the Jephunahi behind it."

"What makes you say that?"

"They're Amorites," Peliarchus said, as though this was a full explanation. "You can't trust 'em. They've only been in Tyre twenty years. Young and hungry, out to carve off a bigger slice . . ."

"And they're sorcerers," Tayniz put in with a whisper.

"Don't start that crap," Peliarchus told her.

"It's true," she said firmly. "Everybody knows that Amorites are sorcerers. The Habiru are Amorite tribes, and look what they did to Jericho! Not to mention Beth-Horon—they have *magical powers*."

Barra smiled. "That's what the New Tribes say about us, back home, and the only real sorcerer I've ever met is my grandma Maeve—and she's New Tribes, a Gael, herself."

"What about your friend Kheperu?" Tayniz asked.

"He's no sorcerer, though he'd like you to think he is. He was once a seshperankh, and he can do a few tricks with powders and potions; it's magic, I guess, but it's not like real magic."

"Well, what about the curse on Nicoras' public house? Everyone who goes in there *dies*! What about that?"

"Probably just his terrible food," Peliarchus grumbled.

"But Nicoras is still alive, and his family, and all his slaves. And I heard that one of his slaves tried to run away, and she got so sick that she would have died if she hadn't come back." Tayniz leaned forward and lowered her voice. "Everyone who was living at the public house when the curse was laid lived—only new guests die. And nobody can leave . . ."

Peliarchus scowled darkly. "Tayniz—"

"And nobody knows how to break the curse. Four underpriests of Ba'al-Berith performed a protection, and an exorcism, and all four of them died right there in Nicoras' common room!"

"Hush up. I'm tired of hearing about this." Peliarchus appealed to Barra. "You see what this situation is doing to people? Everybody's getting crazy, believing any damned rumor that flies into their head. I hear the bloody Governor is already on his way in from Byblos. With the full division. Nobody wants Egypt involved in this; the garrison here is no trouble, most of the officers have been here for years, and they know the tally, but . . . well, no offense to your friend Kheperu, but once those bastards leave Egypt they shed their precious civilization the way a cobra sheds his skin. The Governor himself is a well-meaning old fart, but if he takes it into his head to let the army loose on us, to 'keep the peace,' well . . ." He shook his head. "Once King Demetor is here and gone again, I think we're going to go. And you'd better come with us."

"Peliarchus—" Barra began.

"No, I've decided. We're leaving. Demetor probably won't be here more than a week or ten days, then we're gone and you're coming with us."

"I'm not."

"Barra, dammit, this is no time to turn stubborn."

"If I winter on the Isle," Barra said patiently, "I could miss the Trade Fair at Crete in the spring. One bad storm is all it'd take, then I'm screwed for a year. Maybe more; I could lose everything I've been working toward these last ten years."

"None of that will do you much good if you're dead."

"You worry too much." Barra yawned and stretched. She stood, rubbing her eyes. "It's been a long day. Help me get Leucas up to his room, will you? Between the two of us we should be able to carry him."

Peliarchus pushed himself to his feet. "Well, even if you won't go home, there are a lot of places on the coast that'll be safer than Tyre."

"Relax, will you?" Barra said with her best friendly and innocent smile. "Believe me, I have no intention of getting mixed up in any trade war." This might have fooled Tayniz; the look she got from Peliarchus said he knew exactly what her intentions really were.

By the time the sun peeked over the mountains on a clear and bright morning, the three partners were already headed back through the Market. Tayniz had prepared a huge breakfast from the leftovers of last night's feast, which Barra and Kheperu had dug into with a will. Leucas spent breakfast time leaning his head on his hands and grunting monosyllables. His one burst of language had been a heart-felt prayer of thanks to Polydeukes; Leucas' nose had been broken so many times in boxing matches that he no longer had any sense of smell, for which he was profoundly grateful. The mere sight of so much food painted a greenish tinge under the tan of his cheeks.

Conversation at breakfast was limited; Peliarchus had obviously wanted to pick up the argument from the night before, but was stopped by the knowledge of long experience: once Barra had set her heels, any further pushing would only dig her in that much deeper. She made it easier on him by chattering away on a variety of trivial subjects, but silences tended to grow and deepen whenever she stopped to chew and swallow a mouthful of food.

After some debate, and much insistence from Kheperu, they decided to take up residence at the inn of one Lidios, an expatriate Argive whose substantial establishment (eight private rooms and a staff of twenty) was in the Greek quarter on the southwest side of the city, a short walk from the beach and not too far from the Market. He charged only three shekels a day for full service in a private room; this gave Barra two days' grace before she'd need to start cutting purses for a living.

Before they left the home of Peliarchus, Barra handed over the packet of letters and left strict instructions that anyone looking for her or her friends should be directed to Lidios.

"Especially anyone in Meneides colors," she'd said.

"The Meneides?" Peliarchus grunted. "You're not mixing up with those bastards, are you?"

"Maybe," Barra had told him. "It depends on how much they're willing to pay me."

It was too early yet for the streets to be crowded with traffic, and the golden morning sun gave only a promise of the day's later heat as the three companions walked slowly across the city. Here and there the streets were dotted with half-skirted slaves carting jugs of water back from the communal wells—once Leucas stopped one with a threatening hand, grabbed a jug from his handcart, and drank it nearly dry, pouring the remainder over his head and shoulders. He paid the slave with a shrug and a copper coin, and the slave, muttering sourly, headed back toward the wellhouse. The companions walked on, past scowling merchants tying back the flaps of tentstalls and tired-eyed men who scraped the street smooth before their doors with bronze rakes. In deference to the wounds on Leucas' shoulder and back—not to mention the self-inflicted ache in his head—the bundle of their possessions had been divided three ways, and each carried their share. Graegduz padded sleepily alongside Barra, toenails silent on the hard-packed earth, while she explained in low tones her conclusions drawn from last night's conversation with Peliarchus. The prospect of a trade war seemed to cheer Kheperu considerably; he was nearly dancing as he led them through the streets, laughing and humming snatches of Egyptian songs.

"I don't mind you being happy," Leucas rumbled dangerously, "but do you have to be happy so loudly?"

Kheperu only shrugged and grinned—but he did so silently.

Barra frowned at the buildings around them and squinted up at the sun. "Uh, Kheperu? Are you sure you know where this place is?"

"Of course. I lived there for two months only a few years ago."

"We're going the wrong way."

"No," Kheperu told her with a grin that stopped just short of an outright leer, "we're going the right way."

"You're lost."

"I'm not. I know exactly where we're going. In fact," he paused at the street mouth, where it opened onto a broad avenue, and spread his arms, "we're here!"

A slight shift in the wind brought a light breeze against their faces; now she could smell the place. Barra, who never forgot a scent, would have known it with her eyes closed. Juniper and crushed amber rubbed into human skin to mask the rank smell of fear sweat, that was the distinctive note. Broad walkways circled the building, mirroring the gallery with no railing that ringed the upper floor. Brightly dyed awnings of saffron and scarlet shaded both gallery and walkway, and a third set stretched over the roof. Each wall of the building was set with a wide door of solid bronze, and above each, carved into the stone in Phoenikian, Akkadian, Egyptian demotic, and the Cretan script that served as the written form of Greek, was the simple legend: SLAVES.

Barra said, "I'm not going in there."

"What is this place?" asked Leucas.

"The Mursuwallite Slave House," Kheperu answered cheerfully. "The best slave market in the Canaan District. They have slaves from all over the world! Assyria—Skythia—dwarfs from Punt, Kushite tribals—they have *blondes*, Leucas! Golden-haired women from Europe beyond the Alps! The best part is, they don't speak a word of Language, so you don't have to listen to them *talk*. Think about it."

Leucas frowned. "I can simply walk in that building and *buy* a slave. With money, if I had any. They *sell* them, there."

"Of course. What's the matter?"

"It doesn't seem right."

Kheperu appealed to Barra, "Talk to him. I don't think he appreciates the quality of this opportunity."

Barra shook her head. "Leave me out of this."

"It's wrong to buy slaves," Leucas said slowly. "There's no honor in it, to pay with money for something that should be bought with sword and spear."

"So you're not going with me?"

"Where I come from, a slave is taken in battle. Wives and children of defeated men. You don't buy them. You don't sell them. If you can't support a slave, you marry her off or let him go."

"Fine, you can wait here. Come on, Barra."

"I told you," Barra said, "I'm not going in there."

Kheperu threw up his hands. "What's your problem?"

Barra shifted uncomfortably. "It's none of your business."

"What, did somebody sell you for a slave once? There's nothing wrong with that; could happen to anybody. Even whatsisbugger—Herakles—was slaved once; ask Leucas."

"I told you it's none of your business."

"Oh, come on, we're partners, aren't we?" Kheperu wheedled in a weaselly tone that set Barra's teeth on edge. "We must be honest with each other. No secrets, remember?"

Barra surrendered with a sigh; even after only a few weeks in Kheperu's company she was well aware that the stubby Egyptian was fully prepared to stand here and badger her all day long. She said, "It's because every time I go into a slave market, I end up buying five or six."

"What's wrong with that?"

"You don't understand. I buy the sick ones, the weak ones. Then I end up spending all my money to get them healthy and strong. What do I need with five or six slaves? I've got nothing for them to do—and by that time I'm so attached to them I can't sell them back. I end up letting them go. A few times I've even paid their passage back to the Isle of the Mighty—and with a purse of silver and a letter to my brother asking him to sell them a little land of their own. The last time I—" She stopped herself just in time, just before saying *I adopted one.* She had no reason to tell these men about Antiphos, the broken, brutalized little boy she'd bought four years ago at Crete; she'd told them far too much already. Friends or not, she wasn't in a line of work where one advertises one's soft heart. She'd trust them with her future, but not her past. She shook her head and spat, "It's revolting. And expensive. So I don't go into slave markets anymore."

"But this time you are safe," Kheperu pointed out. "You can't afford any."

"That just makes it worse."

Kheperu eyed her, aghast. "You mean there's something in that heart of yours beyond the clink of silver being stacked in coin? Barra, I'm shocked. Shocked and hurt. Disappointed—"

"Shut up. Go enjoy yourself. I don't know what you're going to be able to afford, either."

He shrugged, a cheerful smile on his face. "Children are cheaper—you have to feed them for a few years before they can do any really useful work, so you can get them for a discount—"

"I don't want to hear about it. Go on; Leucas and I'll sit here in the sun."

Head resting against the wall at his back, Leucas snored like an approaching thunderstorm. Barra left Graegduz at his side to watch as she strolled off into the Market; a growl from the grey wolf should be more than enough to discourage any would-be mischief-maker from bothering the sleeping Athenian or his possessions.

She wandered idly through the swelling crowds, pretending to take an interest in the wares of this stall or that. Nearly every man in the Market was armed, which was not so unusual: most Tyrian freemen carry at least a dagger as part of their normal clothing. What made it unsettling was how many of them supplemented their daggers with shortswords worn ostentatiously outside their overcloaks; there were a number of the small trumpet-faced Egyptian handaxes in evidence as well, not all of them in the belts of the quilt-armored Egyptian regulars from the garrison. Also unsettling was the number of foreigners about, many of them wearing armor of bronze plates as they sat guard near the stalls of wealthier merchants. Tall Northmen, hair shining white-gold in the morning sun, red-faced Kelts and broad-shouldered Picts—Barra avoided the Kelts and Picts; many of those from her lands who traveled the Mediterranean might recognize her—grim, sweating Hittites who likely were deserters from the army King Mutuwalli had raised against the Phrygians, and an astonishing number of Akhaian men with wind-etched faces and the flat cold stares Barra knew from seeing the look on Leucas' face in unguarded moments. These were the empty eyes of men who'd survived the ten years of endless warfare on the plains before Troy.

Barra found herself unconsciously testing the edge of her broadaxe. She gave it a week, two at the outside.

When she returned to where she'd left Leucas, he was awake and sitting up; Kheperu was seated at his side. She could hear the whining tone in his voice before she could make out the words. "What happened?" she said as she walked up.

"What happened is your damn dog almost took my leg off when I tried to wake up Leucas," Kheperu said.

"Did you, Graeg?" Barra chirped in Pictish, ruffling the wolf's fur. "Good boy!" Graegduz responded with a warbling croon.

"You know, Barra," Leucas said with a faint smile, "I'm starting to really enjoy your wolf's company."

Kheperu grunted sourly. Barra told him, "Actually, Kheperu, he likes you. He says you smell like a big pile of fresh shit."

"Does he, now? I suppose you really expect me to believe you can talk to each other."

"All animals speak Pictish," Barra said innocently. "Didn't you know that? And all Picts understand animals."

"Really? Then why didn't you tell that damned bear to roll over and play dead?"

"I did. Bears are contrary by nature, and besides, it's half-deaf. It thought I said come here and eat me. It apologized, later."

Kheperu shook his head, surrendering. Leucas chuckled. Barra said, "So what's doing with the slaves? I expected you to come out of there with at least a little girl or two."

"Ah, they have none," Kheperu said sourly. "Nor boys, either. Some rich Egyptian outside of town comes in once a week and buys up everyone under twenty. You would not believe the going price for a fourteen-year-old."

"Hard luck. Come on, get up. Let's get to Lidios' and stow our gear."

Voices of men shouting in anger and fear suddenly erupted deep within the Market. Barra grinned at her companions. "Sounds like a fight. Want to go watch?"

Leucas shrugged, and Kheperu said, "Why not? If they're not too backed up when we get there, I might get some side bets down."

But as they moved toward the disturbance, the shouting faded away to a single voice: a man's, shrill with terror, screaming barely comprehensible words. Beyond that, all was deathly silent.

Leucas looked down at Barra. "Not a fight. What's he saying?"

Barra frowned. "I'm not sure; he sounds drunk. I think he's saying something about getting something off him. Or someone off him. Other than that, it's about what you'd expect. 'Ba'al-Berith, god of my fathers, help me, save me,' and that sort of thing."

Leucas hissed through his teeth, then said abruptly, "Follow me." He set off crashing through the press of people, battering them aside with the swift ease of a chariot company galloping through a mob of farmers; Barra and Kheperu followed easily in his wake.

They broke free of the press, and stopped. The broad street was empty save for the screaming man; people watched from doorways or pressed back against buildings as he staggered along, lurching and spinning like a scarecrow in a windstorm.

Clear morning sun struck brilliant splinters of light off rings on every finger when he lifted his hands to beg for help or to bat at the air like a man caught in a cloud of stinging flies. A bloody rag was bound around his left hand, and his face was smeared with blood that had splattered a gleaming crimson trail back down the street; patches of blood darkened his striped overcloak and dyed his ankle-length robe.

He screamed until his voice cracked and danced his aimless whirl; the crowd watched in silence.

Kheperu spat on the ground. "Just a damned lunatic. What's wrong with these people? Don't you have lunatics in Tyre?"

"He's no lunatic," Barra muttered grimly. "Look at his clothes. That's a rich man."

Leucas moved cautiously toward the screaming man. "What is it, sir?" he called in Greek. "How can you be helped?"

"Shut up, are you *crazy*?" Barra hissed. "Do you want to catch what he's got?"

Leucas looked back over his shoulder at her, frowning, uncertain. The screaming man had seen him, though, and he rushed at the huge Greek, clawing at him desperately. At Barra's heel, Graegduz crouched, holding his head low and snarling.

"Kill me!" the man croaked, his voice gone. "For the mercy of god, kill me! Don't let them take me!"

Leucas held the man's arms, supporting him like a child. His ruined face twisted into a mask of helplessness. "What's he saying?"

Barra was at his side in an instant. "He's saying he wants you to— *Loving Mother!*"—she whispered in sudden awe.

Even as she spoke, the flesh on the side of the man's neck tore and his blood spurted across her face. She reeled back, arms up to protect her, gagging.

The wound was small and curved: like a bite.

The man convulsed with shocking strength, tearing free of Leucas' grasp. His bowels and bladder voided themselves into a pool at his feet, and he fell back, screaming and writhing in his own waste, wisps of steam rising vividly in the bright sunlight. His back arched, and his feet hammered the hard-packed earth. The three warriors watched in helpless horror as his convulsions quieted; the last of his life fled.

The street was still and quiet, sharp-shadowed as an Akhaian fresco.

Barra said hoarsely, "I know this man. His name is Othniel." Graegduz bent his head to the body, sniffing at the blood. He sneezed abruptly and backed off, whining.

Kheperu knelt beside the body, parting the robes to examine it. "Friend of yours?"

"Not really," Barra said, wiping his blood from her face. "I just knew him from the Market—he's a fetchit for the Jephunahi."

"Look here," Kheperu said, holding the robe aside. "All these wounds, they look like bites of some kind, like man-bites. But the robe isn't torn above them. And do you smell that?"

It was a strange, bitter scent, like that which sometimes rises from hot springs. Barra nodded. "What is it?"

"Burnt sulphur; that is, brimstone."

Leucas shuddered, sharply, only once. "This shouldn't happen by light of day."

Kheperu spread the clenched fingers of Othniel's left hand, and pressed aside the crusted rag. "Someone cut off his thumb, and not long ago, either. And look at this."

On the palm was a fresh brand, the flesh red and angry at its edges:

"You know this sign?"

Barra shook her head. "Egyptian glyph; I don't read it. Contracts are written in demotic or Akkadian cuneiform."

"It means," Kheperu said grimly, *"Behold."*

Barra and Leucas looked at each other, and at the curious Market crowd, now pressing close around. Hundreds of people had watched Othniel die, and hundreds more joined them even now and got the story in a rising buzz of frightened voices. This tale would be all over Tyre before sundown.

"Behold," Barra repeated. "Well, we did. Everybody did." She looked down at her hands, smeared with the blood she'd wiped from her face. She rubbed them together, and the blood scraped off in half-clotted little wormlike threads. "Let's get out of here before some Jephunahi asshole shows up and decides this is our fault."

# 4

# *Murder*

**L**idios wiped his hands on his blood- and grease-stained smock as he stared critically up at the breaking clouds. He nodded sharply, his chins echoing the gesture, and turned away from the doorway, a small smile of satisfaction buried between his massive cheeks. "The skies are clearing," he said to no one in particular, muttering in his native Greek. "We might get enough sun this afternoon to bake off some of the mud."

He waddled back into the common room and grabbed the ear of a passing slave, giving the boy a list of goods to bring from the Market, and a coin purse barely the size of two doubled fingers. After barking at two others to accompany the boy, he dragged a low stool through the nearly empty room and sat heavily at the open end of the triclinium table, where Barra sat with Leucas. Graegduz, who'd been napping, comfortably snuggled against Barra's feet under the table, opened one eye, and sniffed lazily. Recognizing Lidios, he went back to sleep.

"Folk had best come out tonight," Lidios said. "It's the tenday, and I owe two large weights to the bottomless purse of Jephunah. Though what I'm paying for, I can't say. Haven't had a single Jephunahi tough in here since Othniel was killed and you folk came, three days now— they can't get mud on their precious feet—and he can't even protect his own bloody captain!"

Barra nodded sympathetically and sipped the rich Egyptian beer that filled her mug. Leucas grunted, chewing on the last mouthful of his stew, then he lifted the big wooden trencher and tipped the last of the broth into his mouth. He belched and set it down. "One more, Lidios."

"One *more*?" Lidios said incredulously. "That's your third and it's only midday! You'll eat me right out of business!"

Leucas wiped his lips with the back of his hand. "I'll pay double," he offered with a ghost of a smile.

"Oh, very good! Very funny! If it wasn't for Kheperu—may the blessings of Astarte follow him all of his days—I'd make no money from you folk at all. And even he cost me my second-best whore!"

"If you'd prefer," Barra said icily, setting down her mug with a thump that slopped beer onto the scarred tabletop, "we can take our custom elsewhere."

"What's the matter with you people? Can't a man even *gripe*? Please! Eat up! Drink up! Let the bloody storm god destroy my livelihood! I'll breathe not a word of complaint!" He heaved himself to his feet and collected the trencher, heading toward the back door and the cauldron of stew that sat on the hearth built over flagstones behind the inn. "No, let the bloody sorcerer's curse fall upon my house as it did upon Nicoras and Xuros! Will I complain? Not a word!" Without even pausing for breath, he disappeared through the door.

Leucas grinned. "I like him."

"Ay," Barra said glumly, "me, too."

For three days, they had waited here for some offer of employment from Idonosteus. Barra had grown afraid she might have miscalculated. If she had pressed for a reward for the bear, at least they'd have something to show for their efforts, something to pay for Leucas' wounds. The huge Akhaian, stolid as ever, had said nothing on the subject, but the only relief she got from Kheperu's needling came when, as now, he'd paid a shekel or two for a couple of Lidios' whores and was amusing himself with some unnatural acts in a private room.

So far, their only reward for the bear was free food and lodging with Lidios.

Lidios had recognized Kheperu and had greeted him by name when they arrived, in the afternoon shortly after Othniel's death, just ahead of the first thunderstorm. The common room was nearly empty then, only four or five men and three whores; at the sound of Lidios' bellowed "Master Kheperu!" one of the whores had started to her feet, her face suddenly pale and twisted under its paint. "Hello, Belthe," Kheperu had said pleasantly. "It's flattering to be remembered. And this time, I've brought friends." The whore had shaken her head wordlessly, then uttered a piercing screech and bolted for the back door. The only sign of her thereafter came the next morning, when one of the whores, a Kena'ani named Lenka, smilingly claimed that she'd glimpsed Belthe at the edge of town, heading north at a dead run. Everyone played along with the joke; Barra loudly calculated that if her wind were strong, she could reach the outskirts of Sidon sometime this afternoon.

Lidios had seemed confident she'd return eventually, and he'd welcomed the three companions warmly, if somewhat nervously. Rumor of their heroic capture of Idonosteus' bear was by that time all over Tyre, and there was no mistaking the combination of gigantic Akhaian, red-haired axe-woman and reeking Egyptian. He offered them the free hospitality of his public house, asking in return only that they make themselves visible in the common room, so that word of their presence in the inn would get around and perhaps bring in folk who'd be curious to get a look at the subjects of the hottest rumors in months. Then the first of the winter storms had come; three solid days of rain had kept Lidios' common room as empty as a plague house, but Lidios had not recanted on his deal. Even on their first night there, Barra had figured out why.

All businesses in Tyre are affiliated with a Great House; they pay taxes to this House or that, and in exchange they receive the House's protection, and other considerations. A merchant who is in dispute with another can go to his patron for justice; an innkeeper nervous about lodging a rough crew of sailors can go to his patron for armed and armored toughs to help him keep the peace. Transactions between affiliates of the same House take place at reduced prices, and in dealing with foreign traders or affiliates of another House, a merchant has the might of a Great House behind him to ensure that contracts are honored.

Lidios paid his taxes to the Jephunahi. Othniel had been the right hand of old Jephunah himself. Othniel, so the rumor went, had been torn to pieces in broad daylight on a crowded street, with no man's hand raised against him. Barra and her companions had considerately refrained from revealing their personal knowledge of the truth of that rumor.

Any freelance robbers, or thugs from other Houses, might think twice about causing trouble for the inn of Lidios—no matter how weak and threatened the Jephunahi might be rumored to be, now that they seemed the target of some sorcerer's vendetta—while three budding heroes took their ease in the common room.

Lidios kept up a fair pretense of good cheer, but in unguarded moments his face would go slack and sag, revealing the dark purple rings of his tension beneath his bloodshot eyes. Lidios was frightened;

many of the slaves were outright terrified. Barra wondered if perhaps all that kept them going was their talismanic faith in her, Leucas and Kheperu.

That was fine with Barra; she was perfectly comfortable playing scarecrow in exchange for free room and board—her purse still held six shekels—and it bought them time for Leucas' shoulder to heal, which it was doing with the Akhaian's usual swiftness. It also bought time for her to recover from some minor illness. She and Leucas both had been troubled in stomach since they'd come to the public house, sweating and hot of face, and the occasional shafts of sunlight that had showed through the rain clouds had spiked her head like a sword through the eye. Kheperu had seemed immune, happily whoring away whole days, and now she and Leucas seemed to be recovering. The day before she'd felt well enough to drag herself across town in the rain, to share a quiet meal with Peliarchus and Tayniz, and listen to their complaints about the trials and tribulations of hosting King Demetor and company. As for Leucas, even intermittent vomiting hadn't dulled his appetite, and now he was joyously making up for lost food; Barra felt clearheaded for the first time in three days. She only wished that she'd played things differently with Idonosteus.

Lidios returned, the trencher heaped with steaming stew. He set it before Leucas and said, "You'll excuse me if I don't stay and watch you eat me out of house and home. If I don't start sanding the mud outside my door I'll get no trade, sunshine or not."

Leucas nodded, already shoveling stew into his mouth, and gestured for him to be on his way. Barra sipped her beer as she watched him waddle to the sand barrel that stood by the front door and fill a pair of pails.

*Idonosteus, you worthless jiggle-prick bastard,* she thought, *why don't you send for us?*

Kheperu rejoined them as twilight began to close down the day, a whore leaning upon each of his arms, exhaustion counterfeiting affection. As he approached, winding between the posts that supported the ceiling and the now-crowded tables, it became apparent that he was all but carrying them. When he finally released them, the whores—a boy of perhaps seventeen and a woman a few years older—staggered stiffly away to collapse onto the couches with the other whores in the business corner of the common room. Kheperu watched them go, shaking his head sadly, then came to the table and slid onto the bench beside Leucas. "It's a sad commentary on the state of the world," he said. "Even the whores no longer take pride in their trade. No stamina. Lidios should make them run along the beach in the mornings, build up their wind. When I was young, a small silver weight would buy you a woman who could bounce you on her lap two nights and a day together and stop only for a mug of wine and hunk of cheese. Now they start whining about being tired after only a single afternoon. Hardly worth the money. That bloody boy's arm began to wear out after less than thirty lashes—"

"Kheperu." Barra cut him off firmly. "No details. I just ate."

"Oh, relax, it wasn't even a real whip, just a length of cane no thicker than my—"

"I'm warning you."

"—finger," Kheperu finished innocently.

Barra looked at Leucas, who was smiling behind his beer mug. "What's so damned funny?"

"Don't snap at me, Barra," Leucas said mildly. "I'm not the one you're mad at."

"What difference has that ever made?"

Kheperu lifted an eyebrow. "No word yet from our great and lordly bear-master, I take it?"

Barra shook her head disgustedly. Kheperu murmured something in a mincing, effeminate tone, that sounded to Barra very much like "Our price goes up . . ."

"One more word out of you," she hissed, "and I'll slam your face on this table so hard you'll have to pry that beak of yours out with a knife!"

Kheperu made his customary hand-to-heart *Who, me?* gesture of injured innocence, and Barra subsided, scowling. A moment later, she nudged Graegduz with her foot and told him to go to the room; the common room was filling rapidly and the last thing she needed was for the grey wolf to get playful with some unassuming trader. Graegduz gave her one long, reproachful look, then padded toward the dormitory corridor with his head hanging low. He didn't even look at the people he passed—he was accustomed to humans stepping aside to make way for him, and these were no exceptions.

The bright afternoon sun had worked its magic on Lidios' trade; now, with night falling, the common room of the public house was becoming crowded with sailors of all nations and tradesmen with their women, even two youngish women Barra had tagged as freelance whores. Lidios, if he spotted the pair, would toss them bodily into the street, so Barra didn't point them out; she begrudged no one the opportunity to earn an honest living.

A pipe-and-lyre duo performed on stools set up on a table in one corner, earning meat and beer with an evening's entertainment. They weren't very good, the lyrist chanting Phoenikian sailing lays in a rusty bellow; most of the folk ignored them, some even singing songs of their own in a variety of languages. The crowd was well lubricated already; for a single silver shekel—about a tenth the size of an Athenian weight—a man can eat and drink to his heart's content. Another shekel buys him a space on the floor if he can't walk home, as well as breakfast in the morning. As darkness wrapped the inn, Lidios hung oil lamps from pegs on the ceiling posts, their steady yellow light blending with the orange flicker from the hearthshrine, and soon the light attracted the swirling clouds of moths and mosquitoes that were an ever-present part of night in Tyre.

A group of five bearded men in belted chitons occupied a corner table; when they bellowed at the lyrist in Greek for a song of Akhilleus on Skamander's banks, Leucas rose and excused himself. "One of them looks familiar," he explained. "I may have fought beside him at Troy. It's proper for me to greet a brother-in-arms, and to share in a libation to the gods." He moved off with slightly sodden dignity.

"Sentimental mope," Kheperu muttered at his retreating back. "Troy this, Troy that, if the Akhaians were so bloody heroic, why'd it take ten years to sack one city?"

"Shut up," Barra said wearily.

"Ramses the Great sacked Qadesh in three days," Kheperu went on. "Even the Habiru—a pack of thieving savages—took Jericho in a week. But every time you mention Troy, every Akhaian in the damned room gets all misty-eyed over their great heroes who spent ten years playing with themselves on the coast of Thrace."

"Troy was on the coast of Lydia," Barra said, "and if you don't shut up about it, I'll break your jaw."

"Aren't we testy?"

"Shut up."

When Barra had first arrived in Tyre on Peliarchus' ship the Siege of Troy had been already in its second year; no one in Tyre knew of it—or, if they did, thought much about it. But later, as the Akhaian ship raided for supplies and slaves up and down the coast to support their troops, some even reached as far south as Tyre. They came not to raid—the swift response of Phoenikian charioteers ensured that—but to trade their loot for food and wine. Stories the Akhaians told began to filter through the Market, of the epic battles of sons and grandsons of gods on both sides, of the Aiantes, of Diomedes and Odysseus, of Agamemnon and Menelaos the Red King, of Hektor and Aeneas, of Sarpedon and Penthesileia the Amazon Queen. Once, in the half-light of early dawn, Barra had glimpsed an Akhaian captain on board his mighty hundred-sweep warship as it pulled out to sea with the tide. Tall and straight he had stood, his hair the shining, impossible white-gold of spring sunlight on the crest of waves. The armor he wore was curiously worked, of some metal that did not shine with the warm glow of polished bronze, but was a dull, matte grey-black; it was not until years later that Barra would again see arms of iron, the sky-stone metal the secret of whose forging was closely held by the royal house of the Hittite Empire.

Even now, after ten years, she nursed and cherished in her heart the notion that the man she had glimpsed once, briefly in the dawn, was Akhilleus the Godlike. Less than a year later, at the age of seventeen, she ran away from the house of Peliarchus, all her thoughts fixed on reaching Troy.

Events had intervened, painfully; she'd never reached the city. Among the many regrets with which she regarded her past, missing her chance to see the great heroes, Akhaian and Trojan both, fight before the god-built walls of Troy was one of the sharpest.

She strained to her the lyric of the lyrist's song, but it was hopeless through the babble of competing languages. She sighed and sipped her beer. Kheperu surveyed the room with eyes bright and beady as a drunken squirrel's, muttering to himself; she kicked him under the table.

"*Ow!* Hey!" Kheperu said, rubbing his shin. "What was that for?"

"For being an asshole," Barra told him moodily. "Just on principle."

She felt a presence at the triclinium's chest-high wall behind her; even before he spoke she smelled the sour wine on his breath, underlain with juniper and cinnamon and the faint organic decay that comes of too much meat in the diet.

"Hey, little fella," the man said. "What say I dance with your girl?"

An evil grin began to spread across Kheperu's face, until he noticed Barra's expression. He coughed into his hand. "She's not my girl. You'd better ask her yourself."

"Not your girl? Oh, I get it. What's your price, honey?"

Barra carefully set down her beer mug.

"That hair of yours, it's really something," the man went on. "I'll take you, even if you are skinny as a boy."

Barra slid out from the bench, stood and faced him. The man grinned and took her arm. "Come on, then! I'm horny as a goat."

"You like that hand?"

"What?"

"You'd better take it off me before I feed it to you."

"Hey, hey," the man said, looking down at her with an expression puzzled and hurt. "I didn't mean anything by that skinny crack. That's just *negotiation*, you get it? I got money to spend, and plenty of it."

Barra stepped forward, bending her neck to look up into his face, inches from hers. "If you only knew," she began quietly, "how tired I am of every cockeyed Phoenikian son of a bitch I meet assuming I must be a whore because I've got breasts and I'm not married."

"Hey—hey, now . . ."

"You see this axe?" She held her hand level with the broadaxe's head. "I said, *do you see this axe, you worthless goatfucker?*" The shrill power of her shout quieted the common room; even the musicians stopped to watch.

The man nodded and swallowed, taking a step back. Barra took a step forward, staying right in his face.

"How would you like to have this axe planted so far up your ass you'll be shitting flint till Midsummer's? Hey? How would you *like* that? *Answer me!*"

The man's backward pace accelerated. "I, uh, come on now—"

"If your ugly ass is still in this building by the time I count three, I'm going to kill you. You understand? I'm going to fucking *kill you right here and right now! Understand?*"

"Hey, but, I didn't mean anything—"

*"One!"*

The man bolted for the door.

Barra watched him go, smiling with a little sigh. Nothing could cheer her mood faster than shouting down a jackass; she hadn't had to lay a finger on him, hadn't even drawn her axe. The common room rocked with laughter and applause, which she turned and graciously acknowledged with a sweeping bow.

A familiar voice spoke from behind her, in Corinthian-accented Greek. "Hey, it's the axe-girl."

She looked back. "Chrysios?"

He still wore the long-sleeved overrobe of a Phoenikian merchant, although below it he wore only a belted chiton. He flashed those perfect teeth of his and said, "I caught the end of your little scene, Axe-girl. Were you really going to kill him? Over that?"

His legs, Barra noted, were fully as beautiful as the rest of him.

She shrugged. "Maybe. Uh, listen, is that job still open?"

"Something fall through for you?"

"No, no, I was only wondering. My friends and I might have a day or two free."

Chrysios nodded, still showing his arrogant smile. "And I heard about your dance with the bear. We should be able to work something out."

"Why don't you join us at our table," she said, unconsciously smoothing her tunic. It took a conscious effort for her not to check her hair. His, she decided on second look, was closer to golden than to straw-colored. "We can talk it over."

"What, sit with Stinky? Hey, Axe-girl, I came here to eat and relax. I might sit down after supper, if my stomach's up to it."

"All right. And, Chrysios? My name's Barra."

His smile spread. "Yeah, I know." He moved off toward a long table that had a seat open. Barra watched him go, measuring his breadth of shoulder against the loose way the robe moved around his hips. She shook her head and went back to her table.

"Wasn't that the Greek boy you chased off the beach the other day?" Kheperu said as she sat down. "I never forget a pretty face."

"Forget his—you're not his type."

He shrugged. "With Greeks, you can never tell. He *is* pretty, though, isn't he?"

Barra drained her remaining beer and waved the empty mug at Lidios, who nodded at her from across the room. She said, "He's an asshole."

"Is that so? I notice you didn't kick him."

"Shut up."

Lidios arrived at the table with another brimming mug. "Master Kheperu, Miss Barra," he said with a short bow, "there's a tradesman, name of Murso, he'd like to meet you without putting his life and health at risk. You think he could come over here without you chasing him off? Like you did that other paying customer?"

"Sorry about that," Barra offered, not too sincerely.

Lidios shrugged. "Oh, I don't really mind, you know—I'd already collected his coin. Once I get the money, the faster they leave, the less they eat and drink, the better my profit. Just please don't run off any-one who still owes, all right?"

Barra leaned back to be able to see around Lidios' bulk. "Which one is he?"

Lidios was far too old a hand at public-house assignations to turn and point. "Skinny and tall, against the wall to your left of the hearthshrine. Brown cloak with the hood up."

The man Lidios described sat on a crowded bench, spooning stew from a trencher that rested across his knees. He seemed to be watching the musicians between bites, eating with such concentration that he seemed quite alone, despite the shoulders that pressed against his to either side.

"Shy, is he?"

"He said it's the three of you he wanted to speak with. Want I should get rid of him?"

"Loving Mother, no! It might be a job."

Lidios looked pained. "You *have* a job. You have any idea what it costs me just to feed you?"

"Yes, in fact, I do," Barra told him. "Send him over."

Lidios sighed, nodded, and waddled off.

Kheperu eyed the trader lazily. "This won't be much. Look at the way he's dressed—if that's a rich man I'm a camel."

"You smell like one."

"That, dear girl," he said haughtily, "is a disservice to camels everywhere." His face brightened as he caught sight of something behind her. "Now him, *he* looks like a rich man!"

Barra twisted on the bench to look over her shoulder. Through the street door came a tall man who was nearly as fat as Lidios, dark of skin and hair, carrying a lamp of polished brass. He was flanked to either side by surly, competent-looking men in halfcoats of layered bronze; each of the pair had a short broadsword belted to his waist and carried a heavy, wide-bladed spear half again his own height. Gems glittered from rings the tall fat man wore; on the thumb of the hand that held the lamp gleamed a heavy gold seal ring. He strode into the common room with the effortless authority of a man born to power.

"He looks," Barra corrected her companion, "like a Jephunahi tax collector. Poor Lidios—it must burn him like a hot coal up his butt to pay this guy."

Kheperu coughed significantly. Barra turned back around to find the tall trader in the brown cloak standing at the open end of the table. He gave the two a minimally correct bow.

"Kheperu. Barra. May I sit?"

Barra inhaled deeply through her nose, but any scent of the man that might have carried in the thick air of the common room was masked by the heavy perfume of crushed amber. His face was skeletal, cheekbones standing like knife blades, his skin fair—and his eyes were blue. "Murso," Barra mused. "Your name's Phoenikian, and so is your accent, but your face isn't."

The man's thin lips stretched into a humorless smile. "Murso is not my name," he explained softly. "I represent House Meneides."

"You have," Barra said, "my complete attention. What should I call you?"

"Murso will do, for now. May I sit?"

"Please," Kheperu said expansively, "make yourself at home. My table is your table. Lidios! More beer!" He winked broadly at Barra and mouthed: *Finally!*

Murso slid onto the bench next to Kheperu. "Will you summon the Athenian? I have business to discuss."

Barra squinted at Leucas. He was on his feet now, drunkenly pantomiming a jab-jab-hook combination to a chorus of admiring laughter from the Akhaians: she guessed he was telling the bear story. She shook her head. "Make your offer. He'll stand by whatever deal I strike."

She watched him closely as she said this. The man calling himself Murso had a good trade-face, but she could see the slightest widening of his eyes as he took this in. "Really?" he said slowly. He turned to Kheperu. "And you, as well?"

Kheperu shrugged. "Of course."

"It doesn't bother you to have a woman do your speaking?"

Barra smiled thinly. Kheperu edged away from Murso, drawing himself out of the line Barra might swing an axe through.

She said calmly, "In my homeland, men and women are judged more by their abilities than by their genitals. Does this bother you, to deal with a woman?"

Murso lifted an eyebrow consideringly. "I suppose . . . a deal is a deal, isn't it? Regardless of whom it is made by."

Kheperu breathed a sigh and visibly relaxed. "Where's that beer?" He called, "Lidios! Beer!"

"All right, Murso, let's deal. What do you want us to do?"

He leaned toward her and spoke rapidly in a low tone, barely moving his lips. "In Tyre, lately, there have been any number of mysterious . . . difficulties. Unexplained fires, mysterious deaths, caravans delayed or diverted, murders without motive. Idonosteus believes that one of the Great Houses is fomenting war; he believes, specifically, that the House responsible has employed a sorcerer or group of sorcerers to weaken its intended victims and turn them against one another. There are no reliable indications which House is behind it; one act will point to one House, the next to another, the following to a third. The situation is volcanic; open war may erupt at any time. Idonosteus believes that if the sorcerer can be found and his affiliation uncovered, the worst effects of war can be averted. The other Houses will join together to destroy the offender with minimum disruption of trade."

"Do you want him only found? Or do you want him dead?"

"Barra?" Kheperu said, looking off across the room.

"Don't bother me, I'm doing business. Well, Murso?"

The man smiled appreciatively. "You're correct; Idonosteus wishes to hire you to find this sorcerer. But only to find him; his death may alert the Great House at his back, and precipitate the war we're attempting to avoid."

Barra thought of Othniel. "Dangerous work," she said.

"You are mercenaries, aren't you? You'll be well paid."

"Barra," Kheperu said more urgently, "you might want to watch this."

She ignored him. "How well paid?"

"How much do you want?"

"A round hundred."

Murso shrugged. "Shekels," he offered.

Barra snorted, "Egyptian debens. Do I look cheap?"

"Athenian large."

Barra pretended to think it over, then smiled. "Done."

Kheperu put his hand on Barra's arm. "Listen, your boyfriend Chrysios is about to get a new arsehole carved across his belly. Don't you want to watch?"

"What?" She looked up, finally.

The common room had gone very quiet without her taking notice. Chrysios was standing, swaying drunkenly, facing the Jephunahi tax collector. He had one hand on Lidios' chest, holding a handful of the publican's greasy apron, and he seemed to be making a speech, slurring his words and spraying spit. ". . . Just don't think y'should pay this goatfucker, thass all! Whadder y'paying him for? Huh? What work does he do? Howz he earn it? Suck your cock in the alley?"

Lidios was sweating profusely. "Your pardon, Melchazar," he said hastily. "He's drunk, and you know what Akhaians are like with too much wine in their bellies. Please don't hurt him—I haven't had a killing here in weeks."

"Hurt me?" Chrysios wheeled unsteadily on Lidios. "Hurt me? Who's gonna hurt me?"

Men were drifting toward the scene from around the room. Barra thought: *He didn't seem this drunk when he came in* . . . She stood up on her bench. She called, "Hey, Chrysios! Add a little water, huh? Come on over here!"

"Here?" Murso said dubiously.

"Shh," Barra hissed. "I'm trying to save his life."

Chrysios peered around the room until he finally located her. "I'll deal with you later, woman!"

"I strongly suggest," the tax collector said silkily, "that you take the lady's suggestion. Or I may be forced to have my two companions here"—indicating the pair of armed and armored guards—"quiet you down."

"Oh yeah? Oh yeah?" Chrysios held his belly as though he were either about to burst into laughter or be violently ill. "Well, try it, then. Go on, try it! *Now!*"

The onlookers that had been drifting toward the scene suddenly sprang on the guards. One man pinned each guard's arm from behind, while others produced gleaming bronze daggers and, with very professional speed and economy of movement, cut the guards' throats. Chrysios straightened up; when his hands left his belly one of them had a knife in it, and he didn't look drunk at all. He drove the knife into the belly of the tax collector, sawing upward with a sound like the tearing of wet cloth. The tax collector made a high, confused squealing noise as he looked down at his intestines uncoiling onto the floor. The two guards spun in staggering circles, air whistling through the red-lipped lunatic's grins that opened beneath their chins, spraying blood. Chrysios stepped back neatly as the tax collector collapsed slowly to his knees, still trying to gather up his entrails with both hands.

There came a moment of stunned, motionless quiet in the common room while everyone watched the three Jephunahi die. Barra's eyes drifted closed as she shook her head disgustedly. "God damn shit," she said heavily, her words carrying clearly in the silence. She opened her eyes and spoke softly to Murso. "Excuse me."

She stepped up onto the tabletop. She counted six of them, all told, two for each of the guards and another who'd been coming up behind the tax collector. "Chrysios!" she shouted. He turned toward her, his arm drenched crimson to the elbow, the hem of his overrobe dripping blood. She said, "Nice moves, you son of a *whore!*"

With the last word she smoothly drew the throwing axe at her right side and hurled it overhand; he saw it coming and dodged, but he couldn't avoid the second axe, coming sidearm with a left-handed throw, that whirled toward him while the first was still in the air. It struck him just below the breastbone and he folded around it with an agonized outrush of breath.

The common room exploded into action.

Whores and patrons dove for the floor or jumped up, screaming, running for the street door. Lidios clutched at Chrysios, who drove him back with a slash of his knife that opened a long diagonal gash across the publican's chest; Lidios fell back, squealing and holding himself to stem the streaming blood. Murso slid beneath the table as Kheperu struggled to get clear, staff in hand. "Barra, damn your eyes!" Kheperu shouted. "Warn me before you start something!"

Every year, when springtime brought Barra to Knossos for the Cretan Trade Fair, she'd arrive several weeks early to practice and train with the bulldancers, the sacred acrobats who tumbled about the horns of bulls in celebration of the heritage of Minos. She was, compared to them, a bit old and a bit slow—she'd never quite had the courage to perform the bulldance with them—but she kept up her practice, and incorporated some of those skills into her fighting style; by the standards of the wider world, she could do some spectacular things.

Barra leaped from the table and somersaulted over the triclinium wall to the next booth. She landed on the table there, which tipped and dumped her to the floor, but she was ready for that: she landed catlike on her feet and sprang back over the downed table, drawing her broadaxe, leaving the table on its side before her as a wall to hold off the two assassins who now charged toward her.

Unlike Kheperu, Leucas needed no warning. When Barra had thrown her axes, he'd leaped to his feet and picked up the huge oaken table he'd shared with the Akhaians. Now he roared *"Athene!"* and thundered across the common room like an oncoming avalanche, the table held before him as a battering ram, crashing through the struggling mass of patrons to slam into the three assassins between him and Chrysios. Two of them went spinning to the ground on either side; the third, less fortunate, was borne backward into the hearthshrine and fell across it, screaming as the coals set fire to his clothes and seared his flesh. Leucas held him pinned there for a moment, his drunken battle lust making him laugh like a demented god.

Chrysios yanked the throwing axe out of his belly; some blood flowed through the rent in his chiton, but not much: he must have worn light armor beneath his clothing, perhaps a girdle of boiled leather. His gaze fixed on Barra and rage twisted his face beyond recognition. As he charged, screaming like a mandrill, Kheperu skipped toward him, unexpectedly nimble for such a short fat man. His staff whickered down to rap Chrysios sharply on the shin and send him sprawling. The Corinthian turned the sprawl into a clumsy shoulder roll and came up swinging. Kheperu retreated, parrying the slash with the middle of his staff, between his hands; his counterstrike thumped Chrysios on the hip without apparent effect. The Corinthian advanced on him, long knife reversed in his left hand so that the blade lay flat along his fore-arm, held high to defend his head and chest, the axe in his right swirling and slashing. Once Kheperu blocked the axe and committed to a head strike, hoping to drive through Chrysios' guard; the Corinthian ducked the blow and slashed with the knife, slicing through Kheperu's layered robes and deeply scoring the thick leather beneath. Without that armor Kheperu might well have joined the tax collector on the floor—he swore silently that if this bastard killed him, his shade would haunt Barra to an early grave.

Barra had trouble of her own: the two assassins weren't fools enough to clamber over the downed table too close to her—wide two-handed strokes of her broadaxe assured that—but now they split to either side to come at her over the walls of the neighboring booths. If she turned to strike at one of them, the other would be over the wall to stab her from behind in an instant; if she left her improvised fort, the two of them with their knives—lighter weapons, much faster than her axe—could cut her to ribbons on the open floor. She backed toward the wall, trying to watch both of them, and someone on the floor behind her wrapped arms around her knees. She shouted word-lessly as she swayed and almost fell. Instinctively, she glanced down: a trader who had hidden beneath the table she had toppled now crouched low, clutching her knees in supplication. *"Leave off, y'bas-tard!"* she shrilled, her sudden panic returning her to her native tongue. *"Let me go!"* The trader, likely hearing Pictish for the first time, only held her tighter.

Even that swift glance nearly cost her life. Only a flicker of motion in her peripheral vision warned her in time to sway back from the assassin's knife that came stabbing at her throat over the wall. She cut at his arm but only grazed it, not even drawing blood; she caught a glimpse of cross-hatched leather strips that wrapped his forearms. She entertained an instant's notion to simply kill the whoreson who held her, but even that second's work could be fatal. Her desperation left her only one option: she drew her lips back from her teeth and gave a piercing whistle. She wrenched around in the trader's grip to face the assassin nearest to the street door, still whistling sharply. The assassin at her back never saw what hit him.

As he leaned over the wall to stab at her, Graegduz slammed into his back like a grey thunderbolt. The impact of the wolf's leap drove both of them over the wall, tumbling into a scrabbling tangle at Barra's feet. The wolf rolled away, scrambling to get upright; the assassin had time only to look up and see the edge of Barra's broad-axe an instant before it was buried in his skull. A twisting wrench splintered bone and freed the axe; the assassin's mangled brain gleamed wetly through the wound.

The other assassin stared wide-eyed at his companion's shuddering corpse, and made a gagging sound.

Barra hefted her bloodstained axe, a few shards of bone still clinging to the smooth basalt. She tasted blood when she smiled at him. "That's one," she said in Phoenikian. "Now it's just you and me."

He leaped off the bench and broke for the door.

Graegduz started after him. Barra commanded him sharply in Pictish to guard the door; she didn't want the wolf to get sliced up bringing down the fleeing man—better to have him in a position to give warning if the assassin summoned reinforcements.

The merchant who clung to her legs sobbed and shook. Barra clubbed a fist and pounded at the back of his neck until his grip began to loosen. She looked for her companions as she struggled free. Kheperu seemed to be holding his own, his staff blurring in defense against Chrysios' knife-and-axe combination.

Leucas was in trouble.

The table he'd used as a ram lay atop the booth walls on the far side of the room, below a wide splintered dent on the wall; she guessed he'd been trying to swing it as a weapon and had lost his grip. Now, unarmed, he was caught between two assassins, while a third, clothes still smoldering, clambered to his feet. His battle-rage enhanced by the huge amount of wine he'd drunk, he seemed blind to the third man joining his opponents. His left hand, extended for defense, caught at the tunic of one of the assassins; the assassin made the mistake of cutting at the Athenian's forearm instead of raising his guard, and Leucas' huge fist blurred into a right cross that snapped the assassin's head back with an audible *crack!*

*Someday,* Barra thought as she overtopped the downed table with a smooth dive roll, came to her feet and sprinted toward him, *charging into the midst of his enemies is going to get him killed.*

Leucas spun like an athlete throwing the discus, whirling the limp body of the assassin in a wide arc to crash into his companion; they both went down in a skidding heap. But the third assassin, the smoldering one, lunged at the Athenian's unprotected back with both knives. Barra screamed, *"Behind you!"*

Leucas turned: right onto the blades.

She skidded to a stop as he took both knives low in the belly. Leucas roared his berserk joy and seized the assassin by the shoulders, lifting him off the ground and shaking him like a dog killing a rat. Sharp dismay drove the breath from Barra's chest and sudden hot tears started in her eyes: men don't survive deep belly wounds. Leucas might breathe a few more days, but he was already dead.

It didn't seem possible.

She swept the tears from her eyes with a quick hard shake of her head, then turned and ran toward Kheperu. He, at least, might still be saved.

Fat beads of sweat rolled down Kheperu's face as he blocked and parried furiously. Chrysios was no mere barroom thug: he was a highly skilled professional killer who attacked with lightning speed that rivaled Barra's, and greater strength. Chips flew from Kheperu's staff every time he blocked a slash of the axe; the staff itself was weakening, flexing dangerously against every blow. His counter-strikes were limited to occasional raps at Chrysios' knuckles and forearms, trying to disarm him. He'd gotten in a poke or two at Chrysios' ribs, stabbing the staff like a spear, but now he was backed against a wall and had no clearance as Chrysios pressed him. To extend for a swing at the Corinthian's body or head would buy Kheperu a split skull or a span of bronze between his ribs. He glimpsed the vivid red of Barra's hair as she came up behind Chrysios, and his face suddenly split into a broad grin.

"What's so funny, dead man?" Chrysios rasped.

Barra said, "I am."

Chrysios whirled instantly, the axe whistling through a downward cut at the joining of Barra's neck and shoulder. Kheperu poked the end of his staff into the weapon's arc from behind, catching the axe's haft below the flint head, for an instant holding the Corinthian wide open.

More than an instant, Barra would never need.

Her broadaxe whirled up through that same vicious underhand she'd used on the bear and hacked into Chrysios' groin. The boiled leather beneath his chiton slowed it no more than did his pelvic bone; the axe chopped up into his belly and emptied his guts onto the floor. His eyes bulged, and he swung the knife in his other hand in a last desperate attempt to take her with him into the Grey Lands, but behind him Kheperu had reversed his staff and struck the blade away to clatter against a wall.

Barra braced one foot against his chest and yanked her axe free. Chrysios swayed, his face drained of blood.

"To answer your question?" she said. "Ay, I can swing it, too."

Chrysios crumpled, slowly, his face showing uncomprehending disbelief.

She turned, seeking other opponents. Leucas still held the man who had stabbed him: one hand tangled in the man's hair, the Athenian held the assassin's head facedown in the hearthshrine, still laughing that demented roar, oblivious of the blood from his belly that painted his thighs.

He caught her eye. "One of mine got away!"

"I'm on it," she answered. She turned to Kheperu and said more softly, "See if there's anything you can do for Leucas." Then she sprinted out the door, calling for her wolf.

Kheperu spent a moment leaning on his staff—which bowed under his weight, he'd have to cut a new one—breathing heavily in the sudden silence. People began to tentatively move out from their shelter under tables, looking about cautiously to reassure themselves that the killing was over. Lidios sat on the floor, his back against a wall, holding his bleeding chest and cursing steadily in a low monotone. Leucas lifted the assassin he held out of the hearthshrine, grinning; the man's face was half burned away. "You can carve this roast," he said laughingly. "He's done." He dropped the corpse at his feet.

Kheperu made a quick survey of the bodies. Chrysios was unconscious and dying; the man whose skull Barra had split was well dead; another lay on the floor a few feet from the hearthshrine, his neck broken by Leucas' punch.

"Leucas," Kheperu said gently, moving toward him, "you're hurt."

"Nonsense," Leucas said heartily. He lifted the hand with which he'd held the assassin's head in the fire. The skin was reddening, but not charred or even scorched. "See? Just a little broiled, that's all."

Eerie, resonant laughter came from behind him. Kheperu whirled, bringing up his staff, but a moment later he realized that the laughter came from Chrysios, still lying on the floor. The Corinthian writhed in pain, his back arching as he convulsed, blood pouring from his mouth, yet still he laughed; the sound raised prickling hairs on the back of Kheperu's neck.

*"You think you've killed me."* The voice that came from Chrysios then was thick and choked, but still somehow chillingly potent. Kheperu scowled and plodded over to him.

His eyes were open, but they rolled blindly at the ceiling. *"I can never die!"* His neck twisted with more gurgling laughter.

"Really?" Kheperu said tiredly. He reached within his robe and brought out one of the black, tarry balls. He murmured the charm under his breath as his thumbnail scraped away a strip of the tar. The ball began to smoke.

*"Never! Never! Nev—"*

Kheperu crouched and tucked the ball into Chrysios' open mouth. "Shut up," he said. He turned and walked back toward Leucas; a moment later there came a muffled, wet *whumpf* and a burst of flame as the ball exploded, then a scattering of clicks as fragments of Chrysios' jaw and teeth hit the floor around the common room.

Leucas looked slightly green. "Why'd you do that?"

Kheperu shrugged, looking numbly at the sluggish crimson that flowed from Leucas' belly. "I didn't like him. Now, come on, you'd better sit down over here," he said, taking the big man's arm. "I'll see what I can do for your wounds."

"I told you, I'm all right!"

Kheperu looked down. "No. You're not."

Leucas followed his gaze. "Oh," he said softly. "Oh, my. I barely felt it. Oh, damn."

# 5

# *Secrets*

The moon, still three-quarters full, cast an oyster-shell glow on the streets and limned shadows black as holes into nothingness. Barra walked slowly, head down, sick at heart. The splattered wash of blood drying on her face and arms, and across her thighs—none of it hers—itched and flaked away as she rubbed at it. Graegduz kept pace at her side, looking up at her occasionally, crooning low-voiced whimpers of concern. Ahead of her, the assassin she had captured also whimpered, tears rolling down his face as he dragged the corpse of his companion by the heels, the dead man's head bumping along the street.

The two who had run away had gotten only a few heartbeats' head start: they'd had no chance to escape. Barra had loped along the moonlit streets, Graegduz ranging slightly ahead. When she'd caught sight of the trailing assassin, a simple Pictish command to the wolf, "Ankle," had sent Graegduz streaking toward him. The wolf's grip on the assassin's ankle brought the man crashing to the street; Barra killed the man with a single stroke of her axe, hardly breaking stride. She'd spared the second for no reason other than that she didn't want to drag both corpses back to Lidios' inn by herself; she'd kill him once they got there. Why work harder than she absolutely must? It wasn't like she was being paid for this.

*It was my duty,* she told herself. *What else could I have done?* Arawn, Lord of the Grey Lands, required of his children that they suffer no murderer to live to slay again, or so the druids taught. But she could have waited, she could have hunted them as she'd done to others in the past, caught them one at a time.

No matter how she might twist or turn to evade it, the simple truth was that she'd lost her temper, and now Leucas must pay for that with his life.

*Damn you, Chrysios, you bastard! May the Ravens of Arawn tear at your soul for a thousand years!* If only he hadn't been so damned beautiful! She well knew that she'd lost her temper like that because she'd been attracted to him; she didn't often meet men who caused her pulse to quicken, and now when she did, he turned out to be a damned bloody-handed murderer.

Now she could see the lamplight spilling out from the door of Lidios' inn. The stew she'd eaten tried to rise back up her throat; she had to swallow hard before she could speak.

"Take him inside," she told the assassin. "And remember, I'm right behind you."

"Don't kill me," he whimpered. "Don't kill me."

"Move."

Murso stood anxiously by the door, peering out from beneath his hood. His eyes widened when she entered behind the crying assassin. He touched her arm and hissed urgently, "We must leave here. We should go immediately."

She ignored him, saying to the assassin, "That's far enough. Lie on the floor, facedown, hands behind your neck."

The corpse's feet thumped to the floor; the assassin looked at her with tearful eyes. "I didn't hurt anybody . . ."

"Get down and live a few minutes. Stand and die now."

He got down.

Murso's grip on her arm tightened. "Barra, it is essential that—"

"You don't want to touch me right now."

His hand dropped, but he persisted. "If you're going to work for me, you must learn to follow my orders!"

"Teach me later."

She moved away, leaving him standing by the door clenching his fists in frustration.

The common room was littered with corpses, and the air was thick with the slaughterhouse stink of blood and shit. All the patrons had left. A slave dabbed at the blood that still flowed sluggishly down Lidios' chest. Kheperu bent over the body of Chrysios; he'd removed the chiton and light underarmor and was examining the corpse with great attention. Leucas sat on a stool, his back against the wall. His face was grey and drawn, as he bound his own wounds with ragged strips of linen. The pink tip of his tongue showed at the corner of his mouth as he tied off the bandage with drunken concentration. She had to step over two bodies to make her way to Kheperu. Graegduz nosed at one, and dipped his head to lap at the blood. When she told him sharply to get out of that, Kheperu raised his head at the sound of her voice.

"Barra." His voice held crisp excitement, and he beckoned to her. "Here, come here, I have something to show you."

She crouched next to him, looking at Leucas, and said softly, "How bad is he?"

"Leucas? Forget him, he's fine. The knives didn't penetrate his abdominal wall," Kheperu said impatiently. "Look at this." He lifted Chrysios' lifeless left arm, but she ignored it. She rocked back on her heels.

"How do you *know*? How do you know he's all right?"

Kheperu gave her an exasperated look. "Plenty of onions in that stew he's been packing away all day long, aren't there? Sniff the wounds for yourself." He shook his head and muttered something about "ignorant savages."

"Leucas?" she said wonderingly. "You're all right?"

Leucas' bloodshot eyes gradually focused on her. "I'll live."

In an eye blink she was at his side, her arms thrown around his chest. He felt solid, warm, and very alive. "Loving Mother, I thought you were dead for sure! You must be the luckiest bastard who ever lived!"

Leucas blinked slowly and said with sodden dignity, "Weapons often do not bite me as deeply as they do other men." He smiled weakly. "Although I do think I owe a bull to Athene for this one."

Barra laughed, a small chuckle that swelled to a shout of joy. "I can't believe it!" She shook her head sharply, and her gaze fell on two knives that lay on the floor near the hearthshrine, and her laughter trailed off to awed silence.

One of them was *bent*.

She let go of him and walked toward the knives slowly, with great care, as though she expected the floor to give way beneath her at any step.

"Barra?" Leucas asked. "Is something wrong?"

She bent down and brushed her fingers along the bent knife, its blade stained with blood. *Someone stepped on it,* she thought. That's it; that must be it. It bent in the middle—this had to be the result of being stepped on. . . . And the point—the point of the other knife as well—was rounded, and blunted, as though it had been driven into stone. *These probably aren't even the same knives*, she told herself.

These probably belonged to one of the other assassins. But when she looked from the blunted and bent blades to the puzzled expression on Leucas' face, she was powerfully struck by the realization of how little she actually knew of her companions.

Since their meeting and their decision to travel together, two months before, Barra had been constantly aware of keeping her own secrets from Leucas, and later from Kheperu. She had told them little of her family and her life in the Isle of the Mighty; when she had, she'd always carefully made sure they thought she was playing her game of Tall Tale. She'd told them nothing of her sons, or her share in the ships, nor of the merchant fleet she dreamed of building; she'd barely told them three words of her whole life. With so many secrets to keep, it had never occurred to her that her companions might have secrets of their own.

Now they both stared at her as she crouched there by the hearthshrine. She felt a dizzying alteration of perception, as though she'd been hit by one of her grandmother's spells. This new awareness was so potent that it verged on pain; for the first time, regarding them, she became aware of them as people, as human beings with lives and histories of their own, completely separate from hers. Up to now, she realized, Leucas and Kheperu had inhabited her life only as surface figures, as a collection of characteristics like painted heroes in a Cretan fresco. In her mind, this man had been Leucas the Warrior, strong and slow of speech, faithful and none too bright. The other had been Kheperu the Pervert, greedy and clever, an adventurer who fought only to finance his disgusting tastes. She had made of them archetypes, familiar characters from a campfire legend. This sudden shift felt like awakening from a long dream; now she saw, stretching behind them, the vague ghosts of their experiences, the choices and turns of chance that had brought them here, that had made them what they are. This seeing was not visual; their appearance had not changed. The change was somewhere within her, in how she looked at them: she saw them with new eyes.

*Sceon tiof,* she thought. *Loving Mother, it's the sceon tiof!* Barra's heart pounded, and she dug her knuckles fiercely into her eyes. Coll, her mother, was well-known for it, this power to see into the makings of a man, but it was no skill for a warrior. Among the Old Tribes in the Isle of the Mighty, the *sceon tiof* was revered, a gift from the Mother that could mold a blood-mad tyrant into a wise and gentle king; for one who makes her living as a warrior, it could cripple as surely as an axe to the hamstring. She pressed her hands against her head, the hafts of the knives she held digging into her temples. The dizzying spin of perception faded, and her breath began to ease.

She opened her eyes and glared blankly at the floor. An offering . . . she'd best make some offering to the Mother, and soon; the gods take it ill when their gifts are refused.

She shook her head again, as though throwing off a dream, and stood up.

Kheperu asked, "Is something wrong? Are you hurt?"

"No," she said. "I just got a little dizzy for a moment. What was it you wanted to show me?"

He beckoned her over once again; she casually dropped the pair of knives into the hearthshrine. The hearthshrine of a Tyrian household is never extinguished—by the time someone fished those knives out again, this fight would be old news, and there'd be no way to connect those bent and blunted blades to Leucas.

She knew how to keep others' secrets, as well as her own.

Now as she stood over Kheperu she saw the mangled ruin that had been Chrysios' face. She winced and looked away. *So much for being handsome,* she thought. "What did you do to him?"

"I blew his face off," Kheperu said briskly. "It's not important now. Look at this!"

He lifted Chrysios' left arm. On its pale underside near the armpit, half hidden by the silken gold of his underarm hair, was a figure designed in careful tattoo:

"Another Egyptian glyph," Barra said.

"Just like Othniel," Kheperu agreed. He lowered his voice and gestured for Barra to crouch beside him. "Well, not just like: the location, of course, is different, as is the method. Othniel was branded; this is a tattoo, a much more tedious, and ultimately more painful, process. Furthermore, it's not difficult to brand a man against his will, but if you notice how clean and precise the line of this glyph is, you must conclude it was done either while Chrysios was unconscious, or with his willing cooperation."

"And it's a different glyph. What's this one mean?"

"Oh yes, well, there is that. It means: Destroy."

Barra rubbed her face with both hands. "So," she said slowly, "you're thinking that Chrysios is—was—a henchman of whoever it was that did that to Othniel."

"To you, Barra," Kheperu said solemnly, "my mind must be as an open book."

"An Egyptian sorcerer."

Kheperu raised a pedantic finger. "A sorcerer using Egyptian magic. Whether or not he, himself, is of my race, is an open—"

"You know what I'm thinking?" she interrupted.

Her tone warned him. "No . . ." he said warily.

"I'm thinking that we've just been hired to locate a sorcerer who's been stirring up trouble in Tyre. I'm thinking that we could have questioned Chrysios—he would have lived long enough that we'd've probably found out who this guy is and where he lives . . . if some *idiot* hadn't *blown his face off!*" She punctuated her statement with a hard shove that sent Kheperu sprawling across the gore-smeared floor.

He levered himself up onto his elbows. "Perhaps I was a little impulsive. . . . You, on the other hand, have always been the very model of self-restraint."

She stood and looked around the room. "Just count yourself lucky there's nothing within arm's reach that I can throw at you," she muttered. It was difficult to fight down a creeping grin, though; against her will, she found herself in the grip of a cheerful mood. Forget the bloody carnage around them; she and her partners were alive, they'd won, and—most important—they had a job.

Murso came toward her, fastidiously skirting the corpses, robes gathered in his hands to keep their hems above the blood. "I insist that we leave this place," he said urgently.

She raised a hand to acknowledge him, and turned her face toward Leucas. "Are you mobile?"

He nodded solemnly. "I should go to our room," he said, patting the bandage around his midsection. "I'll need to sew these cuts."

"Later. Lidios? Are we square?"

"Square? You're asking me if we're square?" The fat publican's voice was a pale shadow of its usual outraged bellow. He tried to push himself to his feet, there against the wall, but his hands were occupied in pressing his wadded apron against the long slash that divided his chest, and he sagged down once again. "Oh, bloody fuck," he said weakly. "I suppose we are. I'm too bloodyfucking tired to scream at you for tearing up my house and trying to get me killed."

"You better have somebody stitch up that wound," she said.

He shrugged. "Lenka—one of my girls—she was a camp follower with the League of Five Cities; she picked up a bit of surgery."

"All right, good. Listen, we're going to clear out of here. Anyone who comes asking for us, or asking about the fight, you don't know where we've gone. Have a couple of your girls pack up our gear—we'll be back tomorrow or the next day to collect it. And to drop a shekel or two into your hand for your trouble."

"A shekel or two? That's what a mugful of my blood is worth? A *shekel?*"

"Anyone who does ask about us? If you get names and where to find them, that'll be worth a few shekels, too."

She turned her back on his grumbling and helped Kheperu to his feet. He indicated her hand and suggested she should wash it; she rubbed her palm on her chiton. A bit of searching located her throwing axes. She wiped them, and her broadaxe, clean on the tax collector's clothing, then returned them to her belt.

"Well, Murso? We're ready."

"Ready for what?" Leucas asked, using the chair to push himself upright.

Barra waved him off. "I'll explain on the way."

Murso pursed his lips, and twitched half a nod toward the surviving assassin. "What about him?"

The man was still facedown on the floor, fingers laced behind his head. His back trembled with an occasional sob. Barra spat on the floor and moved toward him, drawing her broadaxe. "I'll take care of it."

Leucas said, "Barra, wait."

"What?"

"You can't just kill him. Not while he's helpless."

"Why not?"

"At least give him a chance to defend himself."

"He's a murderer," Barra explained patiently. "Those Jephunahi had no chance—there was no challenge, no warning. They might as well have been poisoned. The Grey Lord demands his life."

At this, the assassin cried out, "But I didn't kill *anyone!* I didn't even draw blood!" To Barra's surprise, he spoke in Greek—he must have understood the whole conversation.

Leucas came toward her, his palms up and faced toward her. He patted the air with a *Be calm, now* gesture. "If you kill him while he's helpless, what does that make you?"

"An executioner."

"I swear I hurt no one!" the assassin said, still in Greek. "May Zeus Skyfather, keeper of men's oaths, strike me dead with his thunderbolt if I so much as bloodied my knife!"

Leucas reached down and took the man's wrist, hauling him easily up to his knees. He peered into the assassin's tear-streaked face. "Are you Akhaian, son?"

He nodded, wiping snot from his upper lip with his sleeve. "My name's Mykos, lord—I was born in Thebes."

Barra said, "He's lying. He would have been, what, three? Thebes was sacked sixteen years ago." Thebes had been put to the torch, its men slaughtered, women and children slaved, by the combined armies of Athens and the Epigoni, the sons of the seven great heroes who had fallen before those walls in a war some five years earlier. The victorious Thebans had dishonored the corpses of their enemies, and for that crime had paid with all they had: their city, their lives, and the lives of their sons.

"I know that, Barra." Some haunting memory hovered behind the Athenian's eyes. "I was there," he said softly. "My mother's brother and his four sons fought for Kreon, against us."

He paused, and Barra wondered if he saw within his mind the leaping flames and greasy, pork-scented smoke of the funeral pyres that must have ringed the city when all its men were put to the sword. Finally he continued, "If he escaped the sack, that would explain why his accent's not Theban, as he grew up in a foreign land, away from all his kin."

Barra scowled. "That doesn't change what he is, or what he's done."

"No, I suppose it doesn't," Leucas said heavily. He turned away. "Do what you must, but I'll not watch."

"Please," Mykos whimpered. "Please . . ."

Barra looked into his face, saw the youth there, saw the terror of death. Now he was no longer simply an assassin; the *sceon tiof* drew aside that veil. Against her will, she looked on him as hardly more than a boy, facing death in a foreign land. And she realized that he'd spoken the truth—he was the man who'd been coming up behind the tax collector when Chrysios stabbed him: he himself had harmed no one.

*It makes no difference*, she snarled mentally, drawing back her broadaxe. Mykos closed his eyes, tears leaking from beneath their lids.

She remembered having seen him in the common room over the last three nights, eating and happily swilling beer; she remembered thinking that he wasn't much older than Chryl, her own son.

She spat a curse and threw the broadaxe to the ground before him. "Pick it up," she said, drawing the pair of smaller axes. "Go on, pick it up. *Fight* me, you bastard!"

He only pressed his eyes more tightly shut and continued to whimper.

"Shit." She placed her fists against her hips, and looked at Kheperu.

He spread his hands. "Your Grey Lord is your god, not mine."

Barra sighed and shook her head. "All right, you little limp-prick bastard, listen. In my land we sometimes allow a killer to pay wergild—to buy off his guilt. If you can tell me who was behind Chrysios, who he was working for and where to find him, I'll let you go."

"I don't know!" Mykos cried. "He hired me and my friends at the beach. I didn't see anyone else!"

Barra nodded disgustedly; she'd suspected that Chrysios had been too smart to trust any secrets to a third-rate street thug. "What am I going to do with you?"

Lidios called from behind her, "You could make him clean up this bloodyfucking mess! Little rat bastard—"

"That's an idea . . ." Barra said. "Ay, all right. Mykos, you're going to clean up all this, and . . . and serve Lidios here as a house slave for a . . . for *one year.* You will perform any task he gives you, no matter what it is, but you will never leave this house. If I ever see you on the street, or if I ever learn you've run off, I'll hunt you. And I'll find you. And when I do, I'll kill you. No begging, no tears—you won't have time for them. You won't even see me coming. One moment you'll be alive, the next you'll be dying. Painfully. You understand?"

"I understand." Mykos pitched forward and clutched her knees, his tearstained face slimy against her legs. "Thank you, mistress! Thank you!"

She kicked him off her, sending him sprawling. "Don't ever touch me, you pile of shit." She put away her axes and turned to Murso. "Let's get out of here before I throw up."

The *sceon tiof* showed her the boy's hurt and humiliation, and she felt their shadows on her spirit; she clutched her determination with both hands and said a silent prayer to the Mother, that she be relieved of this gift.

\* \* \*

The tenement that loomed into the night sky before them might once have been the home of a wealthy landed family, a century or more ago. Successive generations of owners and tenants had built on to it haphazardly, connecting rooms to neighboring buildings; what once had been public thoroughfares around it had become mazy passageways, roofed by rickety floors of rooms above. The passageways were choked with piles of food scraps and the contents of chamber pots, as well as the pallets of men and women: many of the folk who lived here could not afford the price of a room of their own. The light onshore breeze that had followed the storm drew a stench from these passages as it would draw smoke from a chimney, a stench that could bring a retch to anyone's throat, saving only, perhaps, Kheperu; for Barra, it was nearly unendurable.

Murso moved across the street. He said, "Observe. You must do this whenever you return to this place after dark."

"Or?"

"Or the men who guard the place where you will be staying will try to kill you. They've had some trouble with thieves, and bandits; they care little for either."

He lifted his lamp high enough to illuminate his face and held it there for a long breath.

"How do you know they've seen it?"

"They have. Come."

He headed toward the dark mouth of a passage. Barra looked at her companions. Leucas shrugged; Kheperu gestured her onward with a slight, mocking bow.

On their long walk through the night-shrouded streets of Tyre, Barra had stuck closely to Murso, maneuvering herself to stay downwind. Soon she'd been able to get the man's scent, even through the perfume he wore. There was no immediate reason for this, beyond general principle; like the wolf who walked by her side, she could identify many of the people she met by smell alone, and she firmly believed that talents exist to be used. She noted that he favored food heavily spiced with tarragon. To give herself an excuse for walking so close to him, she'd kept up a conversation, pretending to seek information about the job. She found that he knew little he hadn't already revealed.

She changed the subject. "When do we get our front half?"

"I beg your pardon?"

"Half our pay. Up front, before we begin the job. That way, if something should happen—say, you're taken suddenly ill—we haven't done all our work, risked our lives, for nothing."

Murso looked offended. "You have the promise of House Meneides guaranteeing your pay."

"That's why I'm willing to trust you for the other half."

He sighed. "I will personally deliver silver equivalent to fifty Athenian weights into your hand tomorrow morning. Satisfied?"

Barra squinted at the sky as they walked along. "There seems to have been some misunderstanding about our deal. The hundred weights—that's *apiece*."

Murso stopped in his tracks and stared at her. He made a gargling noise, as though something was caught in his throat. "That's three hundred weights!"

Barra nodded. "That's the deal."

"That's *outrageous*!"

Behind him, Leucas and Kheperu looked at each other and grinned. Barra said, "Shh, people are trying to sleep."

"What service could possibly be worth three hundred weights?" Murso hissed.

"Well," Barra said slowly, "you saw our little scuffle at Lidios' house. You can take that as a guarantee that money paid us is a sound investment—we'll definitely survive to complete the job. The job itself, well"—she shrugged and puffed out her cheeks—"that's probably worth only, say, fifty apiece. The other half, you should think of as being the price of our silence. You said you didn't want the other Great Houses to learn of this; the extra fifty apiece assures that we won't be so strapped for cash that we have to sell some information to cover expenses."

"This is extortion."

"This is negotiation."

Murso scowled. "I will convey your . . . offer . . . to Idonosteus."

"You do that."

Now, as he led them along the mazy, evil-smelling passages, climbing stairs and turning corners, lamp held high to illuminate their progress, he said, "The men with whom you'll be staying are mercenaries like yourselves. They are trustworthy, and can be depended upon to conceal your presence here. Nonetheless, they are not to know of your mission."

"What should we tell them, if they ask?" Barra said.

"They will not," Murso said positively. "Only their captain has the Phoenikian tongue, and little enough of that. Have you three a common tongue beyond Phoenikian and Greek?"

Barra glanced at Leucas, and shook her head.

"Then I suggest that you limit your conversation to trivia."

Barra said, "Dozens of people saw you at our table. Someone may see us come and go here. How are we supposed to keep secret our connection?"

Murso smiled thinly. "My face is not generally known, nor is my association with Lord Idonosteus. I serve him in confidential matters only. These mercenaries have contact with him only through me, and they are neither sociable nor talkative. They, also, have been explicitly instructed to conceal their employment. Is that sufficient?" There was just enough extra emphasis there to betray impatience, nothing more.

"That'll do," Barra said.

As they rounded a corner into a short hall, a door ten paces ahead swung slowly open, spilling yellow lamplight that silhouetted a tall, broad-shouldered man, one hand holding a shortsword low and casual by his side. "Lysandros?"

"Yes," Murso said in Greek. "I've brought the guests you were told to expect."

The broad-shouldered man swung his body aside to clear the doorway. "They, and you, are welcome."

"Lysandros?" Barra whispered. "Is that your real name?"

Murso only smiled.

"Barra," Kheperu said softly, "we are being watched from both ends of this hall." Barra looked ahead and behind; ahead, through a crumbled hole in the far wall, she saw a glint that might have been eyes picking up lamplight.

"Do not worry," Murso told him. "They are archers who guard this hall. Now that they've seen you with me, you are in no danger."

Inside, the room was softly lit with a pair of large lamps. A number of straw-stuffed pallets—Barra counted twelve— covered the floor. Makeshift armor stands of rope-lashed pine lined the walls, most of them full. A few bits and pieces of bronze plating lay here and there about the room, near to pouches of fine sand and moistened rags. There was only one small table, set with a pelike and cups of fired clay. Seven men came to their feet when the companions entered; they, and the man who had opened the door, looked enough alike to be close cousins, if not brothers. They were all stocky, broadly built through the chest and shoulders, dark of hair, and wore close-trimmed beards over the heavy bones of their faces. The man who had opened the door was missing one ear, and had a long diagonal scar across his cheek that connected a white streak in his hair to one in his beard. "I am Kamades of Phthia," he said in formal Greek. "I invite you to share our food and wine."

*Phthia?* Barra's heart suddenly pounded, and she found herself short of breath. Was it possible? With great self-control, she introduced herself in equally formal fashion, and accepted.

Leucas said, "I am Leucas Deodakaides, of Athens. I am honored to accept."

Kheperu said nothing for a moment; Barra kicked him none too subtly in the shin. Akhaians hold the guest-host relationship to be nearly as sacred as the bonds of blood; even to hesitate could be taken as a deadly insult. He jumped at her kick, and said in his badly accented Greek, "I am Kheperu of Thebes."

Kamades' eyes widened in astonishment. "Thebes?"

"The *real* Thebes. Er, Thebes of Egypt," Kheperu amended hastily, then offered a small bow. "I am honored to accept."

Kamades gestured to one of the other men, who tore chunks from a loaf of hard bread and poured wine into four cups, handing one to Kamades and the other three to Barra and her friends. Together they poured a libation to the gods, wine splashing into little sawdust clots on the floor, then ate and drank.

Kamades set down his cup. "Lysandros. Is there word from Lord Idonosteus?"

"Only that your service is valued, and to hold yourself in readiness. Now, duty calls me to the side of my lord." Murso's response had the flavor of ritual formula.

Kamades held the door for him when he left.

These Phthian mercenaries were a strange and silent group; they passed their time as do any soldiers who must wait for action, telling stories, drinking, dicing, yet all their activities took place within a shell of hushed tranquillity. No voice was ever raised, in anger or in song, and even their laughter was muted. The only voice ever louder than a murmur was Kheperu's; he'd immediately joined a game of dice with three of them, near the window, and occasionally loudly exclaimed over his "unusual luck." Barra scowled; he was cheating, of course. He had a small pot of incense burning near his ankles—even though nearly all the smoke was drawn out the window, Barra knew its smell, and knew that the three men who were breathing it would see whatever number on the dice that Kheperu told them to see. She hoped he'd have the good sense not to win too much.

Kamades directed one of them, an older man with a grizzled beard and thinning hair, whose left forearm ended in a leather-bound stump, to tend Leucas' wounds. His name was Peroön, and he cleaned and

stitched Leucas' wounds swiftly and neatly, packing them with cobwebs he carried in a pouch at his belt before bandaging them with
fresh linen.

He pulled the last knot tight with his teeth and sat back on his
haunches. "What god is it that stands at your side in battle, Leucas?"
he said with a slim smile.

"God?" Leucas said, frowning.

"Come on, boy. Those were no ladylike little slices; they're stab
wounds from somebody trying to empty your guts. Without a god to
turn the blade, we wouldn't be having this talk, you follow?"

Leucas shrugged and shook his head. "I don't precisely know,
unless it's Athene. I was born in her city."

Kamades spoke musingly from his seat at the table. "Leucas of
Athens . . . I know you, I think. Weren't you charioteer to Pylaimenos?"

"I was, sir. Until Alexandros took his life with his cowardly arrow
from the wall."

Kamades nodded. "I remember you from the funeral games for
Patroklos. You boxed with Diomedes Tydeides." He smiled broadly.
"He beat the snot out of you."

"Yes he did," Leucas said, returning his smile. He touched his nose
and cheekbone. "He gave me my first two fractures. I didn't mind—it
was honor enough even to step into the ring with the lord of Tiryns.
Epeios revenged me, though, and took the prize. But I'm afraid, sir,
that I don't recall you."

Kamades lifted his hands. "No surprise, Leucas. I was in the company of the Prince of Phthia and, well . . . wherever Lord Akhilleus
stood, all eyes fixed on him."

"I well recall."

"You're *Myrmidons!*" Barra breathed. She'd suspected, even
hoped, but still found it difficult to believe.

"Some name us so. We take it as a name of honor."

Kheperu looked up from his dice. "Ants?" he said in Egyptian.
"What do you mean, they're ants?"

"It's just an expression," Barra snapped in the same language.
"Shut up."

His fingers waggled an obscene gesture behind his back as he
returned to his game. Barra once again barely managed to restrain the
urge to throw something at him.

She could have sat all night and listened to them trade stories of
the war. Leucas was in an unusually expansive mood—no doubt he

was still a little drunk—and Kamades and Peroön and two or three of the other Myrmidons vied with each other in their storytelling, as men will do when they find a fresh and attentive audience. Barra wondered if it would always be this way, if Akhaians would define themselves by what they'd done at Troy—Akhaian men of a certain age, from their late twenties to their late fifties, all seemed to know with a simple look at one another, a silent *You were there, weren't you?* As if the Siege of Troy was the center of their lives; as if most of their lives had been spent there fighting on Skamander's banks. No matter that the siege lasted ten years, and most of these Myrmidons were near forty; Leucas had been twenty when he left for Troy, and thirty at the end, but the twenty years before the war were irrelevant, and the five years since were a slow slipping-down anticlimax.

Barra drank in every word of these tales; even ones she'd heard before brought a knife-edged pain to her breast and a glimmer of tears to her eyes. She'd seen her share of wars, and knew the truth of them, the dirty, bloody business, unheroic and terrifying—still, she wished with all her heart she could have seen this one. It was a childish longing, for something she couldn't have, but somehow, deep within her, there lived a hope that she'd never outgrow it.

Strangely, though, the Myrmidons' stories only rarely concerned foes they themselves had faced, or feats they had accomplished; they were always of the great heroes, usually of Akhilleus himself, some of Patroklos, or Aias, Diomedes, Agamemnon, Odysseus—as narrators they were self-effacing to the point of invisibility: ". . . and when Patroklos' spear drove into the joining of the shoulder and neck of Sarpedon the blood sprayed even across my legs, and as he fell the skies were torn with thunder and we all turned our faces up to taste the sudden tears of Zeus' grief for his son . . ."

Leucas, on the other hand, soon drifted into tales of his wanderings since the war, displaying surprising skill and lyricism. When he told the story of the Kyprian Boar Hunt, the Myrmidons began to give Barra curious sidelong glances. By the time he finished his rather embellished version of the fight at Lidios' house, their looks were of open puzzlement.

Finally, Kamades had to ask. "Is Barra your captain, then?"

Leucas blinked. "I never really thought about it," he said slowly. "In a way, I suppose, yes."

"Well," Kamades said, frowning, "is it her orders you follow? You take orders from a woman?"

Barra sighed. She'd really wanted to like this guy . . .

"No, not exactly . . ."

"Then, whose orders do you follow?"

"We don't exactly work that way," Leucas told him. "We never actually decided who's in charge."

The Myrmidons exchanged doubtful looks. "Then, how do you organize?" Kamades asked. "I don't understand."

Leucas turned his head to one side and thought for a moment. Then he said, "We each have our particular talents, you see. I'm very strong, and good with the spear or sword, or without weapon. I'm the best fighter, though we all give potent account of ourselves in battle. Kheperu is very clever, and he is skilled with powders and potions, at figuring things out, and making plans. Barra is, well . . ."—Leucas looked at her and shrugged—"well, she's Barra. She doesn't give us orders, but somehow we end up doing what she wants anyway. I fight. Kheperu calculates. Barra, well, leads."

Kamades scowled. "It's not natural."

Barra sat up, forcing an easy smile. "In what way, Kamades?" Her friendly tone and appearance of nonchalance would have been more convincing if Graegduz hadn't come to his feet, staring at Kamades and growling low in his throat. She put her arm around his shoulders and murmured in Pictish, "Be calm, Graeg, I'm not that angry yet."

"A man needs to know his place," Kamades said firmly. "My men, they take orders from me. I take mine from Lysandros. Lysandros serves Lord Idonosteus. It's the natural order of things."

Barra blinked. This wasn't about her sex? She squinted at him. "You're not really Akhaian, are you?"

"What do you mean? Are you trying to insult me?"

"No, no, Great Mother, no," Barra said hastily. "I'm just surprised, that's all. Tell me something, Kamades—what are you doing in Tyre?"

"Serving House Meneides," he answered simply.

"No, no, I know that. I mean, why did you come to Phoenikia? What made you leave Phthia?"

Kamades' voice went flat. "Lord Akhilleus led us to Troy." He held her eyes for a moment, then deliberately shifted his gaze to Graegduz. "This is a fine dog. What's his name?"

"He's not a dog, he's a wolf," Barra said dismissively. "What I meant was, why didn't you go back to Phthia after the war?"

Kamades nodded. "I have heard of wolves. How do you call him?"

"Look, forget the wolf, all right? I'm wondering—"

"Barra," Leucas interrupted.

"What?"

His answer was a long, significant look, a tilt of the head and lift of the brows.

"Oh, all right," she said disgustedly. She sighed. "His name's Graegduz."

"Grigdoozh," Kamades repeated. He looked politely interested. "Does that have a meaning?"

"Well, sort of. It's two Pictish words, kind of mashed together. *Graeg* means grey, and *greduz* means, like, hunger."

"Does he bite?"

Kamades himself and two of his men gave up their pallets to their guests. Most of the Myrmidons had settled in for the night, including four who came from outside in full armor. Peroön and the three men Kheperu had been dicing with armed themselves and went out. Kamades had extinguished one of the lamps and tucked the other's wick down within it, so that the room was only dimly lit. Barra lay on her stomach, absently ruffling Graegduz's fur. Her axes were carefully arranged under the pallet, so that she wouldn't cut her hand reaching for one in the dark. Leucas snored steadily but more softly than usual, a constant rumble that faded into the background of her consciousness. The sleeping Myrmidons made no noise at all.

Beside her, Kheperu rolled over and she saw that his eyes were open. He grinned at her.

"How much did you win?" she whispered in Egyptian.

He dug out a pouch and opened it, revealing a handful of the small, irregular coins. "Eighteen," he responded softly. "These poor shits are paid only a shekel a day; if I win too much, none of them will game with me."

"Lose it back."

"What?"

"Shh. I know how you were cheating; you've used that incense before. If you don't lose it back, I'll tell them. They won't just beat you bloody and take back the money. These are Myrmidons. They'll kill you."

"That's kind of harsh . . ."

She nodded. "You're a guest. Cheating your host is just as bad as murdering him in his sleep, as far as they're concerned. In fact, I think you'd better lose a few shekels of your own."

"You can be a real bitch sometimes, you know that?"

"You'd best believe it."

Kheperu thought about this in sullen silence for a while, then whispered, "Doesn't it worry you, to sleep in a room with a band of bronze-chewing mercenaries?"

"Not really," Barra said. "They won't try anything. And if one did, Graeg'd have his hand off before he could touch me. How do you think I survived on the road before I met you guys?"

Kheperu levered himself up onto his elbows and looked around at the sleeping Myrmidons, lips pursed musingly. "Still, there are twelve of them . . ."

Barra chuckled softly. "From what I've heard about Phthians—Myrmidons especially—you have more to worry about than I do."

Kheperu sighed, smiling wistfully. "I should be so lucky."

"Get some sleep," she told him, rolling onto her back. "Tomorrow morning, we're going to work."

Barra was up with the dawn. She looked at the Myrmidons, who were awakening about her, and she gingerly squinted and otherwise felt around in her head, searching apprehensively for any sign of the *sceon tiof*; she found none. Perhaps the Mother had retrieved her gift—she breathed a little easier and again resolved to make an offering.

The watch had changed during the night: Kamades wasn't there. Peroön, who seemed to be his lieutenant, insisted on checking the status of Leucas' belly before he'd let them go out. He found no sign of suppuration, and Leucas maintained that he felt just fine, other than a massive headache from Lidios' wine.

Peroön shook his head, smiling. "You're healing well. No fighting though, or even heavy lifting, for at least a week; you'll tear the stitches. Give the flesh time to knit."

Leucas rumbled, "I'll try to avoid it. Sometimes, it's not up to me."

Peroön grinned broadly, and spread his hands. "You can always run away . . ."

There was an instant's shocked silence, then Leucas burst into roaring laughter and slapped Peroön on the back. "And folk say that Myrmidons have no sense of humor!"

The other Myrmidons joined his laughter, in their quietly restrained way, and Peroön said, "Truly, though, be careful. I did a fine job on those stitches, and like any craftsman I hate to see good work go to waste."

Barra told Graegduz to stay here and behave himself, and she promised to bring him some scraps from breakfast. He hunkered down sullenly, head on his front paws, but whined only a little as they left.

One of the Myrmidons led the three companions through a different winding way out from the building. The alleyway they came out in was empty, save only for the morning fog that swirled pearl-grey in the slanting sunlight.

They'd decided to breakfast at Lidios' house, and pick up their gear now, in the early morning, before the mist burned off and the streets became crowded. The mist would help them return with their possessions to the tenement without being seen; Barra didn't want anyone seeking revenge for the fight at Lidios' house to be led to the Myrmidons.

Only a few slaves moved about on the street before Lidios' inn; as the companions approached, they saw a pair of water-carriers pause to look at something over the door, then exchange a glance and hurry away with their heads down, making the horned-god gesture with their hands.

Barra muttered, "Oh, no," and broke into a run.

When Leucas and Kheperu caught up with her, she was standing in the street, looking up at a design that seemed to be burned into the very stone of the huge lintel. Barra recognized the twined-snakes sign of *Forever*, the upraised arms of *Soul*; the whole glyph was boxed within the representation of *House*, and her heart began to boil within her chest.

She didn't look around as Kheperu approached, only continued to stare at the design and said, "Does that shitcake thing mean what I think it means?"

Kheperu translated in a low voice: " 'This door is the threshold of the death eternal.' Oh, it's definitely a curse—that death being not only the death of your body, you understand, but a sort of infinite rotting of the *ka*—"

"Bastard," she interrupted harshly. "Fucking son of a whore."

Now she turned to look at them. Leucas gazed up at the design thoughtfully; Kheperu looked a little sick, sweat standing out on his forehead and cheeks.

She spat in the street. "Well, what are we waiting for? Let's go in."

# 6

# *The Prince*

**H**aral Mesti paused before the gaily painted door to his prince's bedchamber to catch his breath and gather his courage. The bright paint of the door was shaded into silvery grey in the moonlight. The only sounds in the broad moonlit antechamber were his own harsh breathing and the high, thin sobs that came from beyond the door. In a way, those childlike sobs came as a relief; that meant the prince had one of the slave children in his bed this night. When there was no slave child within the prince's chamber, one always ran the risk of encountering Simi-Ascalon—even when a child was there, the risk was only lessened, not eliminated. Haral well knew that Simi-Ascalon was in town this night, supervising the laying of the curse upon that Jephunahi inn, but the nervous tightness in his guts did not abate; who knew what powers that man might have? If any man alive could be in two places at once, it would be Simi-Ascalon. Haral was as brave as most men, he thought, but no man could meet the dead-crocodile eyes of the prince's steward without a coil of fear twisting into his belly— especially if he encountered Simi-Ascalon after dark.

Haral moved on tiptoe to a nearby couch and lowered himself gingerly onto it; his heart froze as one of its joints creaked piercingly in the silence, but the sobbing within the bedchamber continued without pause, and now was joined by the low grunts of a man's voice in passion. Haral looked down at his hands; a shaft of pale moonlight fell across them, and they trembled like the wings of a moth in the wind. He clasped them together and pressed them between his knees.

Only four days ago, Haral had been followed by that Jephunahi fellow. He'd redeemed himself by sapping the man in an alley and delivering him to Simi-Ascalon, but he knew that he'd come close to disaster, that it was only by a whim of the prince that he himself had not ended his life on Simi-Ascalon's table. Now he arrived with more bad news; this is why his hands trembled so. But his faith in the prince's affection drove him to bring the news himself—it was this faith that passed for courage in Haral's character. And the prince's inspiration had turned the Othniel incident to his advantage. Perhaps he could do the same with this.

The grunting crested in a child's shriek of pain, then both faded to silence. Haral stood, taking a deep breath and coughing once to clear his throat. He knocked lightly upon the bedchamber door.

"My prince? It is Haral, with news."

The prince's voice came back thick and languid. "Go away, Haral. No news can be so important that it cannot wait for dawn."

"My prince, it is the Greek, Chrysios. He is dead."

*"Dead?"* The prince's shout came like a thunderclap. An instant later the bedchamber door was yanked open. The prince stood naked, his broad chest heaving, sweat glistening across his heavy muscles. Haral could not meet the lightning of his eyes, and so looked down; the prince's groin and trim flanks were painted black with blood.

"Tell me," he commanded.

Haral coughed. "He is dead; killed at the Jephunahi public house."

"That fool! What, did he attack the tax collector alone?"

Haral shook his head vigorously; when the prince was in a mood like this, Haral knew that he himself might pay a heavy price for Chrysios' mistake. "No, no, lord. He hired men, at least six; some tales say as many as fifteen."

"Some *tales*?" the prince repeated in a low and deadly tone. "You had best explain."

"It's the p-pub-talk tonight all over Tyre," Haral stammered. "Chrysios followed your command, and attacked the tax collector in a crowded public house, so that all could see. The tax collector is dead, and so are his guards, but those three mercenaries—you know, the ones you were interested in . . ." His voice trailed off.

Dark clouds gathered along the prince's brow. "The three foreigners? The ones who caught the bear?"

Haral took a step back; his legs trembled until his kneecaps jumped like a drop of water on a hot skillet. "Y-yes, my prince. The story is told that these three alone—and their dog, the girl is said to have a huge dog—killed Chrysios and all his men."

"So," the prince growled, "you say that instead of spreading a tale of madmen who do not blink at slaughtering Jephunahi tax collectors in a crowded pub, they are speaking of these mercenaries?"

"I, ah . . . well, yes, lord . . ." Haral fought desperately against the urge to flinch and cringe away from him, but the prince did not strike him.

Instead the prince's brow began to clear, and now a smile quirked at the corners of his lips. "Extraordinary. Three against seven—at the very least. Quite extraordinary. Do you know what this is?"

"N-no, lord."

"It is a sign," the prince said. "I see now—it is their fate to be entwined with my own destiny. The gods themselves tell me to reach forth my hand and take them. Summon my captains. I will have these three; they will serve me." The prince turned back into the bedchamber and strode toward his wardrobe. Through the open door Haral could see the bed, and the small body trembling and bleeding upon it; the prince spared it not a glance as he selected a kilt from his rack. Haral backed away until he was out of the prince's presence, then turned to run.

"We meet now, because at dawn I must ride for Sidon," said the prince. He reclined on a couch in his antechamber, while Haral and the other five captains stood in attitudes of respectful attention before him. Watching him, Haral was powerfully reminded of a glimpse he'd gotten once of the Pharaoh's pet lion, a great dusky beast named Akhu, sunning itself near the corpse of a cow it had fed on, there in the Pharaoh's park in Per-Ramses. The prince had that same blend of power and boneless relaxation—but he was much more frightening than any lion.

A pair of lamps supplemented the moonlight, and gave the prince enough illumination to read the scroll in his hands. "The Governor will be there soon, and I must deliver an invitation to guest with me. Persip, it will be your responsibility to have the estate prepared to receive him, since Sim shall be riding to accompany me."

The captain named Persip inclined his head. "It will be done."

Haral thought that it would be a relief to have Simi-Ascalon out of town for a few days; as he looked at the faces of the other captains, he saw expressions that could be read as private agreement.

"Illush and Tekt," the prince went on, brandishing another scroll, "the two of you will begin preparations to curse these inns; also, if you see any opportunities to burn a building here and there, or a ship, you will do so. Very shortly, we should be able to quit with these things, as the Houses turn on each other and do them for us. Bezai, you will take over for Chrysios. I want as many public murders as you can manage; and, I think, you should start with a Tomi-tiri tax collector—we have a Tomitiri public house that is just about ripe. Any high-ranking Great House officers that you can identify, you will abduct and bring to Simi-Ascalon—especially any of Nephrol Tomit's—that would have a certain symmetry that will please me a great deal. And, all of you, think about who would make a suitable replacement for my unfortunate Greek."

He sat up suddenly, and gripped his knees; the captains stood like statues, barely breathing, as they watched color drain from his knuckles and veins stand out along his forearms. "And Silam, this you will do. These mercenaries, the ones that killed Chrysios. I want them. You will find them, and bring them to me."

"But—but my prince, if I cannot find them—? If they will not come?"

"It will be bad," the prince said, in a tone more chilling for its matter-of-fact bluntness, "for you to fail. But you will not. They are fate's gift to me—all three of them. They will come." He clapped his hands together twice, loud enough to make every other man in the room twitch. "That is all for the five of you. Go. Haral, remain."

The five captains exchanged glances, and all five of them gave a look of apprehensive pity to Haral. Haral was acutely aware of the cold sweat that trickled down his spine. The five captains left. Haral didn't move.

The prince slowly rolled the scroll that he'd consulted and returned it to its case. "For you, Haral, I have a special task."

"M-my lord?" Haral fought to control his trembling.

"Yes, yes indeed." The prince suddenly stood, and stretched with a deep yawn. "Take two men—two of our men, not hirelings—and bring Chrysios' body to Sim's cavern."

Haral blanched. "But, but my prince—"

"No excuses, Haral. Oh, you don't have to do it tonight; but he'd best be there by, say, midnight tomorrow. Sim can wait that long, I think, and catch up with me in Sidon in time to meet the Governor—it's only a few hours' ride."

"B-but, but what if I can't . . . or what if, well—"

"There are no what ifs, Haral. Deliver his body to the cavern by midnight tomorrow." The prince sighed, yawned again, and headed back toward his bedchamber. "I made a promise to him, Haral, the same promise I made to you. In exchange for his service, I promised eternal life." The prince disappeared within his bedchamber, but his voice carried hollowly out to Haral. "You would regret making me a liar."

Haral never doubted this; he was still shaking when he left.

# *The Curse*

**B**arra rattled the door; finding it locked, she pounded on it with the heel of her hand. "Lidios! Lidios, open up!"

"Have you lost your senses?" Kheperu said, staring at her.

She shook her head. "The story on the curse is that folk who were living in the cursed inns already don't die. We were living here; we should be safe." She pounded again. "Lidios! Shake your ass!"

Kheperu caught her arm. "*Were* living here," he said. "But we weren't here when the curse was laid. How do you know it will not kill us?"

"How do you know it will?"

"I do not . . . For all I know, we could die from *not* going in—that is what's supposed to happen to people who try to leave, is it not?"

She shook her arm free and faced him, hands on hips. "For a sorcerer, you don't know bloody much about magic, do you?"

Kheperu scowled up at the glyph on the lintel. "Not this kind," he said grimly. "I have never seen anything like it. What about that precious grandmother of yours? Could she do something like this?"

"Probably," Barra said with a shrug. "I don't know."

Leucas reached up, toward the design. Kheperu barked, "Don't touch that!"

Leucas snatched his hand away and looked with mild inquiry at the Egyptian. "Why not?"

"Because I don't know what will happen when you do," Kheperu said. He laced his stubby fingers together and popped his knuckles one by one. "This worries me. Curses on inns and public houses are usually economic, you see. Curdled milk, spoiled beer, mold on the cheese, wine goes to vinegar, that sort of thing. You cost the publican so much money that he is forced to close his doors. About the worst you can do is make the men impotent or cause the occasional miscarriage. But this, this business of wholesale death . . ." He shook his head.

"I've heard stories like this, though," Barra said doubtfully.

"Superstition. Campfire tales to chill the ignorant. Trust that I know more of magic than most, and I can tell you that magic is *orderly*. It operates by rules that are very clear, at least to the initiated. This, though, this is outside the bounds, so far as I know. This is more like some work of a god: a disease or somesuch."

"I was curious," Leucas said, "about the design itself. Looks like it's burned into the stone. Even that must have been done by magic, mustn't it?"

"Hmpf," Kheperu grunted. "That's hardly a mystery. It's easy, I could do it myself. This sandstone, it's very soft, and porous. All that's required is some of this—" His hand dipped within his robes and came out with one of the black, tar-covered balls; he spun it between his fingers, making it disappear and appear again. "Worked into rope, it could be applied directly to the stone—or, better yet, to a thin plank, you could lay out the design beforehand, reversed, and carry the plank with you, then press it against the lintel and fire it. But the glyph itself has no power, you see, except perhaps as a deterrent to the superstitious. You'll find these sorts of designs somewhere on nearly every tomb in Egypt. If the glyphs themselves had any effect, there would be many, many dead tomb robbers, and looting graves would never have become the popular pastime it is today."

"Then why put it there?" Barra said, frowning.

"As I said before, as a deterrent to the superstitious," Kheperu explained. "The vast majority of the populace is uneducated to the point of bestiality—"

"Not on the tombs, idiot!" Barra snapped. "Why here? Why put it on the lintel? Why set a killing trap and then *announce* it?"

"Well," Kheperu said thoughtfully, "if I was laying curses, I'd probably be going around to the publicans—or even to the heads of the Great Houses—pretending to be a white sorcerer, and get paid for lifting it again."

Barra lifted an eyebrow, then shook her head. "No. It's too much trouble for a simple protection racket." She looked at the door and hissed impatiently through her teeth. "Where is that fat bastard?" She drew one of her throwing axes and hammered at the door.

Lidios' voice came faintly from within. "Go away! Can't you see I'm under the curse? Do you want to die? Go away!"

"Open this goddamned door!"

"Barra?"

"If this door isn't open by the time I count five, Leucas will break it down!"

"I will?"

"Shh."

She heard the heavy scrape of the bar being lifted and set aside, and the door creaked open a bare handbreadth. Lidios peered out, squinting and shading his black-ringed bloodshot eyes against the sunlight. "What do you want?"

"Our gear. You've got all our armor and spare clothing."

"Oh, your gear, is it?" He threw open the door and stood aside. "Well, come right bloodyfucking *in*, then! Come on! Come on and die, you worthless bitch! Do you know you've *ruined* me? I've run this house for twenty-three years, and it took you one night to destroy it forever! *One night!* Never mind me, who cares about poor Lidios? *Come in and get your bloodyfucking gear!*"

Foam flecked the corners of his lips; he stared at them, panting, his head twitching to one side, his hands trembling. He seemed to have lost weight overnight—his jowls sagged, and purple-black shadows streaked beneath his eyes. The bandage that wrapped his chest like a ceremonial sash was already brushed brown with dirt, and he smelled strongly of vomit. Behind him in the darkness of the shadowed common room, his slaves and whores sat clustered in frightened groups, some of them crying, some only staring at the door.

"Hey, cheer up," Kheperu said. "If you have any luck, it'll kill us, too." Barra's foot came down on his instep, but he only shrugged at her.

Leucas said, "Do you think you were cursed because we fought those men last night?"

Lidios only stared at him, still twitching; his brown eyes looked almost black.

Barra stepped toward him, to the threshold of the door. Now that she'd come up against it, she couldn't quite bring herself to go in. She said, "Lidios. Lidios, listen."

Slowly, very slowly, he turned his head to look at her.

"Lidios, has anyone died?"

His brows drew together, and again his head jerked to one side. "No. No, not yet. Everyone knows the curse only slays guests—all my guests left. You chased them off with your brawl. None will return, either. None will ever return. I wish that knife had struck deep," he said, slapping the bandage on his chest. "I wish Zeus had loved me enough to strike me dead before I ever saw this day."

"Hush," Leucas said severely. "Do not wish worse luck upon yourself; the gods hear such prayers."

"Worse? Worse than *this*?" As he got excited, working himself up to another explosion, his twitching increased and expanded from hands and head to his whole thick body.

"Lidios," Barra cut him off. "What about that boy, Mykos, your new slave? He became part of your household only last night—does he live, or did the curse kill him?"

Lidios blinked at her like a day-blinded owl. "He's gone."

"But . . ." Her tongue felt suddenly thick and clumsy, and she had to force her words through her tightening throat. "But you said no one had died . . ."

"I didn't say he died, I said he's gone! Ran off in the middle of the night! I hope he's lying dead in the street! I hope he's choking on his own blood!" Once again, his trembling and twitching increased; this time, though, as he stepped through the doorway to shake his fist in her face, he came into full sunlight. His tirade twisted into a cry of pain; he clapped a hand to his eyes and pitched forward to the ground, flopping spastically like a game fish in the bottom of a boat. Barra and Kheperu stepped back instinctively; equally instinctively, Leucas stepped forward and knelt beside him. He took Lidios' head firmly in one tremendous hand, and with the other he drew a knife.

"Help me hold him," he said.

Kheperu flinched. "What, *touch* him? Are you mad?"

"Help me!"

Barra forced herself forward and knelt. "What do you want me to do?"

"Sit on his back and hold his head," Leucas said. "Keep him still for just a moment."

Her flesh crawled at the thought of his twitching body against hers, but she complied. He bucked under her like an unbroken horse. Leucas pried Lidios' jaws apart and inserted the hilt of the knife between his teeth.

"We must get him inside," Leucas said. "He's been seized, and he can die of it; I've seen it happen."

Kheperu went to the doorway and shouted, "Hey! Hey, you lazy shits! Get over here and drag him in!"

A couple of the slaves started tentatively to rise; Barra shouted, "No! Stay where you are!" She snapped at Kheperu: "Stepping out here did this to him. You want to kill them, too?"

"Then what are we supposed to do? Carry him ourselves? In *there*?"

Grimly pinning Lidios' jerking body to the ground, Barra looked at Leucas. He returned her gaze steadily and said, "If he isn't put somewhere warm and soft—like his bed—he'll probably die."

"Better him than us," Kheperu insisted.

"We guested in his home," Leucas replied simply.

Both of them looked at Barra.

Lidios made a choking, gurgling noise around the knife hilt. His breath reeked of vomit, with a bitter, nutlike underlay, like acorn tea.

Barra looked down at him. Why should she risk her life for him? She owed him nothing—the lodging he had given was in return for the business they'd bring in. Her attack on Chrysios had probably saved his life. She wasn't Greek, to be bound by their obsession with guest-friendship. There was no reason why she shouldn't come down on Kheperu's side, and the three of them could turn their backs and walk away, especially after the way this stinking prick-bastard had cursed at her only moments ago.

No reason except one: the *sceon tiof* flared up behind her eyes. She saw how years of hard work had carved his face, the warm and generous heart that supported his slaves in their declining years, the ready laugh, the stout resistance to adversity . . .

*Dammit*, she thought, *why can't I unlearn this trick*?

She gathered in a flailing arm that had escaped her grasp and pressed it tight against his side. She turned her head and spat in the street.

"We're taking him in."

The slaves stared in open astonishment when Barra and Leucas carried Lidios into the inn. Kheperu remained outside on the street, on the dubious premise that if his friends were struck by the curse, he, as a seshperankh, was the only one of them who'd have a chance to save the others' lives. They carried Lidios to his darkened bedchamber and wrapped him in blankets, where his convulsions quickly quieted, and he passed directly into a fitful sleep. Leucas carefully wiped Lidios' mouth foam off his knife hilt onto the bedcovers before returning the knife to its sheath. While Leucas gathered their possessions, Barra questioned the slaves. None of them had seen Mykos make his escape, not even the pair who'd slept on the floor at the thresholds of the two doors, front and back. One of the slaves pointed out the blankets Mykos had used as a bedroll, and Barra, muttering dire curses through clenched teeth, folded one and tucked it under her arm.

When Barra and Leucas returned unharmed to the street, Kheperu looked mildly surprised, then deeply thoughtful. "Very curious indeed."

"So," Barra asked, "what do you make of it?"

Kheperu shook his head, frowning. "Obviously, we haven't been hit with the curse ourselves, or being outside the inn would have the same effect on us that it had on Lidios, don't you think? So, we escaped that part of the curse, the way it affects the resident. But, on the other hand, if we weren't affected by the resident's portion, you and Leucas should have been struck by the guest's portion. But apparently you weren't."

"Perhaps that's because we didn't go in as guests," Leucas mused.

"Nonsense. You think the curse determines your intentions before deciding whether or not to kill you? That's ridiculous!"

Leucas shrugged. "You explain it, then."

"I cannot, yet," he said, fuming. "But I will. There is something shit-rank peculiar about this magic, and I'm going to figure out what it is."

"While you calculate," Barra said dryly, "why don't we work on a question we know we can answer?" She waggled Mykos' blanket significantly. "Come on."

They quickly made their way back to the apartments of the Myrmidons, Barra and Kheperu toting the gear to preserve Leucas' stitches. Murso/Lysandros had come and gone again in their absence; they found, when the Myrmidons escorted them inside, a large leather purse bulging with silver. Barra favored Kheperu with a predatory smile. "Weren't you mocking me, yesterday afternoon?"

The Egyptian hefted the purse, weighing it in his hands. He whistled appreciatively. "Mocking you, Barra?" he said warmly. "Never! I wouldn't do such a thing."

"I seem to recall, over the last couple of days, hearing you saying 'Our price goes up' in that mincing, effeminate tone—"

"Really, Barra, I can't be responsible for how you interpret my tone. I've never had any but the greatest faith in your abilities and judgment. Why, only yesterday, I was telling Leucas how I thought you were being far too hard on yourself; I was telling him that our unemployment wasn't your fault, and that if you only had patience, I was quite sure something would come through. Wasn't I, Leucas?"

Leucas lifted an eyebrow. "When was this?"

"Oh, you were drunk, of course you don't remember—"

"Never mind," Barra sighed. She went over and crouched beside Peroön. The one-armed physician sat cross-legged on the floor, a plate of thick barley gruel balanced on his ankles. He grunted a hello, and said, "Did you breakfast?"

Barra shook her head. "No time. Listen—"

"You should breakfast early, you know," he said, mopping at the gruel with the chewed heel of a loaf of bread. "Wait till too late in the day, it'll make you sleepy; that's a medical fact."

"Ay, thanks. Listen, Peroön, you're Kamades' second, right?"

"By his authority, yes."

"We have to go out again. All our gear and our"—she couldn't say *money*, that would have been too bald—"other possessions will be safe here with you guys, won't it?"

Peroön stopped chewing and fixed her with a long flat stare. He said softly, "You're a foreigner, and likely know no better, so I'll let that pass. We are not thieves."

"Oh, no no no," Barra said hastily. "I'd never even think it."

"See that you don't."

"I only wanted to make sure that you fellows wouldn't, like, all go off to the Market, or something, and leave the place unguarded."

"We won't. Your possessions will be as safe as our own."

"Thanks," she said, with her best friendly smile. "I just wanted to hear you say it."

She whistled up Graegduz out of his corner, tucked the blanket under her arm again, and looked at her companions. "Let's go."

After they hit the streets and the Myrmidon who had led them there returned to his post inside the building, Kheperu murmured, "You think that's wise? There's more silver in that purse than any of these fellows see in a year."

Barra nodded, smiling dryly with half her face. "They're a bit underpaid, don't you think?"

"They are stinking peculiar, is what I think. And I think you are mad to trust them with our money."

"The money is safe," Leucas rumbled.

"How do you know that, though?"

"Peroön said so."

"Oh, fine. Oh, lovely. And you'll simply trust his word."

"Yes, I will," the Athenian replied stolidly. "You, Kheperu, shouldn't judge men's characters by your own."

"Well, I like that!"

"What Leucas means, I think," Barra said, "is that these men are Myrmidons—in Akhaia, their name is a byword for faithful service. Their honor is tied to how well they follow orders, and how well they keep their word; and their honor is everything. It's all they have."

"Too right!" Kheperu murmured. "At a bloody shekel a day, they cannot afford anything else."

"Tell me again why we're doing this."

Barra ruffled Graegduz's heavy fur as she held the blanket for his inspection. The young wolf shook his head and snuffled at the blanket's folds, ears flicking. "There's a good boy," she murmured in Pictish. "This is the fella we need to find." She looked up at Kheperu and switched to Greek. "I think I've made that clear."

"Of course you have," he replied. "And if I did not know you so well, I would likely believe you."

"I'm telling you, something spooked him," she said with flat assurance. "I had that boy so scared he should've been still shaking this time next year. The only reason he'd have bolted is the curse. One, he knew about it in advance. Two, he saw our sorcerer lay it in. Three, he learned of it somehow after the fact. In the first two cases, we need to have a little talk with him. In the third, just finding out if he's still alive will tell us more about the nature of the magic involved. All right?"

"If you say so," Kheperu said with a shrug. "But, for some reason, I suspect that we are tracking him simply because he did not do what you told him to, and you want to kill him for it."

"Really?" Barra's smile stopped well short of her eyes. "In that case, I'm telling you: shut up and follow along. Think you can do that?"

Kheperu sniffed. "Empty threats."

"You think so?" she said, standing up.

"Now, Barra," Leucas said, his hands up in that *be calm now* gesture. "Much as I'd enjoy seeing you knock him down, we ought to get on with this. If he's heading for the beach . . ."

She nodded. "You're right. Graegduz," she said in Pictish, "let's go find this little bastard."

The trail was short: it ended at a dung heap less than two hundred steps away.

Barra stood before it, her nose wrinkled and her hands on her hips, and said grimly, "Or, on the other hand, maybe he wanted to take a nap on a big pile of shit."

The dung heap was nearly as tall as Kheperu, and it occupied the central two thirds of a cul-de-sac formed by the rears of three buildings. Huge glossy flies lumbered in clouds around it, and its lower edges gleamed with busy scarabs. Graegduz nosed all the way around it, but in the end he sat down and eyed the dung heap mournfully. Barra rubbed the loose skin behind his ears. "It's not your fault, Graeg. Good job."

Leucas said, "In there, eh?" He untied his belt and pulled his chiton off over his head. "I suppose this is my job," he said, touching his battered, useless nose.

"I think not," Kheperu told him, rolling back the long sleeves of his overrobe. "Shit—especially human shit—has certain magical properties, carrying away as it does all residues of the failed magical and evil influences to which a man is subjected each day. One must deal with it cautiously, if at all. If, for example, the smallest amount came in contact with your wounds, Leucas, it could put you down with a raging fever. Insidious stuff, shit is. Best to leave it to an expert."

"You don't have to persuade me," Leucas said, stepping aside with a slight bow.

"Humpf," Barra grunted. "This is all only an excuse for you to dig your hands into a dung heap."

"Oh, please," Kheperu said haughtily. "As though I need an excuse . . ."

Barra crouched on her haunches, Graegduz at her side, her back against the chilly al-tobe rear of a building on the upwind side of the cul-de-sac, watching Kheperu probe the dung heap with his staff. He didn't seem to mind that the countless flies found him nearly as appetizing as the heap; he didn't bother to brush them away unless they landed on his face.

Not far from Barra's feet, an industrious scarab toiled along, rolling a ball of dung twice its own size. Two others approached it, as though to help, but shortly they had stolen the ball and were fighting over it between themselves. They shone in the sunlight like burnished brass. Barra scowled at them; they reminded her of her life. You work hard and apply yourself, and just when you're starting to make headway, to get somewhere, somebody steals everything you've worked for, and then somebody steals it from them, until nobody can figure out whose it was in the first place—and through it all, nobody seems to realize that in the end it's just a big ball of shit. Barra suddenly gritted her teeth and brought her foot down on all three scarabs and the shitball, smashing them to crackling paste.

She settled back against the wall, her face frozen with cold anger. She'd tried, she'd really tried to save this little bastard Mykos' worthless life—she'd played fast and loose with her own principle, risked a stinging slap from her gods—and here he was, dead as dead and stuffed into a pile of shit. And he'd been only a few years older than Chryl, her own son.

Leucas crouched beside her and draped her shoulder with his hand. "He might not be here, you know." She looked into his grave grey eyes, and saw there his all-too-clear understanding of what she felt. "He knows you hunt with the wolf; it's how you caught him last night. He could have rolled in the dung heap to confuse his scent. He could be on a boat to Egypt even now."

Barra turned away to squint along her shoulder at the mid-morning sun, now a fist above the building across the alley. It was only the sunlight that brought the quick sting of tears to her eyes. "Thanks, Leucas," she said softly.

"For what?"

"For reminding me that if he wasn't dead, I'd have to hunt him down and kill him. Sweet Mother, sometimes I don't understand myself at all."

A smile tugged gently at Leucas' lips. "Aren't you a little old to be noticing that for the first time?"

"Found him," Kheperu said cheerfully. He pulled his staff free of the dung heap, wiped it with his hands, and set it to one side. He bent at the waist, to reach into the dung heap at about knee height; his face lit with a smile when his probing fingers found an arm, warm as life from the dungheap's internal heat. It was the work of a breath or two to pull the body free—it hadn't been buried deeply, and the outer levels of the heap were still loose. "Well, my my my." Kheperu straightened up and beckoned to his companions. "This is interesting. Look here. And I thought we'd have to wash him off before we'd be able to tell what killed him—to look for a brand, or a tattoo."

Barra nodded, looking down at Mykos' body. There was a deep dent in his forehead, above his left eye, and his throat was cut raggedly, as though the killer had sawed through it with a small knife. "Damn," she said tightly. "God damn."

Leucas sighed. "Well, it probably wasn't a bandit—a robber would have settled for the crushed skull."

"Oh, no, that is, yes," Kheperu agreed. "Oh, absolutely. No, my guess would be that he came out Lidios' window just as our sorcerer and his friends were laying in the curse. He saw them, and they killed him for it."

"Friends?" Barra said.

"Well, friend, at least. There must have been two of them—you do not stop in mid-murder to change weapons, do you?"

Barra shrugged. "All right, two of them." She shook her head, swallowing past the sick constriction in her throat. Graeg leaned against her thigh, crooning consolation. She ruffled his fur absently, fighting to keep her mind on business. "This is too peculiar. It's too strange. I mean, if this boy was killed by a sorcerer, why would they cut his throat? Why didn't the sorcerer blast him, or strike him dead with a glance, or change him into a lizard or something?"

Kheperu cleared his throat importantly. "There are a number of possible explanations—"

"But the most likely one is that he didn't because he couldn't, right? I mean, I've seen you fight—you never use that staff unless you don't have a spell that'll do the job."

"Perhaps he was otherwise engaged." Kheperu began scraping his hands clean on the flagstones. "Perhaps laying a curse of this type is a lengthy process, and his confederates killed our young friend to prevent interruption."

"They could have chased him away," Leucas rumbled.

"Yes they could have, easily enough, if all they cared about was protecting the sorcerer," Barra agreed. "But they killed him, suddenly and without warning. I mean, if I saw somebody burning glyphs into solid stone, I'd head the other direction as fast as my feet could carry me—but the club hit him from in front, and hit him before he could cry out, or he would have been heard by Lidios or the slaves inside. And then they hid the body. That's strange, isn't it? Why not just leave him there in the street, the way bandits do?"

Kheperu picked up his staff and regarded his smeared hands with distaste. "Fascinating, Barra. Now, if you please, I must find a place to wash."

Leucas stared at him in wonder. "Wash? You?"

"Only my hands," Kheperu said stiffly. "Because of its magical properties, shit can interfere with my—"

"Be quiet, both of you," Barra snapped. She spread her hands, slowly, frowning her concentration. She raised a forefinger. "Think about this. Why did they hide the body?"

Kheperu blinked and looked at Leucas, who responded only with a shrug. "Well . . . I suppose . . ." he began, then suddenly grinned. "Well, it would look bad, would it not? A guest of Lidios found on the street with his throat cut. Might make people think the curse is not all that potent—sorcerers can be touchy that way, you know."

"You say that as a joke," Barra said, her eyes gleaming with inspiration, "but you know what? I think you are dead-center right. You understand? You're right as the bloody rain. Plumb line straight on the bloody target."

"Oh, come now, Barra," Kheperu scoffed in his most avuncular, patronizing manner, "a curse works precisely the same way whether people believe in it or not. Why would our sorcerer worry about people thinking it did not work? That would, if anything, only increase the number of deaths. I mean, the only reason he would care is if . . ." His voice trailed away, and his eyes widened in astonishment. "Well, bless my bloody balls."

"Exactly. Oh yes, indeed," Barra said, a grin lighting her face like the sunrise.

Leucas' frown deepened. "Are you saying that—"

"We need to get a look at the other cursed inns," Kheperu murmured.

"Yes we do," Barra said. "Right now."

"What I want to know now," Kheperu said with hushed determination, as though he could drive his words through the hard oak of the door by sheer force of will, "is how many of your slaves have tried to leave—and what happened to them." He pressed his ear against the door to hear the soft, despairing voice of Xuros the innkeeper.

Xuros' establishment was not so grand as Lidios' place, but it was part of an overbuilt block that fronted on a broad right-of-way just south of the Market and only a few steps from the beach. The curse had been on this place the longest—more than a month—and it was only by long and persistent cajoling that they persuaded Xuros to speak with them at all. Money was useless to him, when he couldn't come out to spend it, and threats were equally useless, when his only activity was to sit at his door and wait to die.

On the other side of the right-of-way, Barra leaned against a brick pillar that was warm in the sun and rough against her back, Graegduz drowsing at her side. The pillar was one of a series that supported a broad, gently sloping roof over an open expanse of flagstones; this roof served as a rain shed for the disordered clutter of tradesmen beneath, mostly vendors of roasted pork and spiced mutton, of smoked flatfish and boiled shrimp. At Barra's side, Leucas kept stealing longing glances over his shoulder into the grill court, his sighs reminding Barra that none of them had eaten more than a crust of bread and a mouthful of cheese snatched on the run, with the sun bending now from afternoon toward evening. Though he couldn't smell the food, he didn't need to—the sizzle and crack of fat dripping onto the coals was all the encouragement his appetite required.

The cursed inns had been easy to find; there was always a slave about who'd make the horned-god sign and whisper hasty directions. The inn of Xuros was the last—they'd already spoken with Nicoras, at his large house not far from the Penthedes compound, and they'd dealt through a closed door with the wife of the late Sutuliumas, who had died two weeks ago from a seizure not unlike that of Lidios.

The various inns themselves had little in common save their general design. All were two-story affairs built around a central court—roofed over in the case of Lidios and Xuros, open to the sky for Nicoras and Sutuwallas. In the open-court inns, the kitchens were under rain sheds in the main yard; in the other two, the kitchens were behind, below the rain barrels that squatted on the roofs.

It seemed clear to Barra that their sorcerer was trying to implicate the Tomitiri. Three of the Great Houses deigned to dabble in local inns; Nicoras, Xuros, and Sutuwallas were all Mursuwallites, and Lidios was a Jephunahi; none of the inns loyal to the House headed by the Egyptian Nephrol Tomit had been cursed, and the sorcerer was certainly taking pains to present his curse as Egyptian magic. This, of course, had nothing to do with the sorcerer's actual affiliation. If, for example, it was the Hittite House of Mursuwalli that was trying to spark the war, cursing three of their own inns would be an inexpensive bit of misdirection—inexpensive for the Mursuwallites, less so for Nicoras, Xuros, and Sutuwallas.

Shortly, Kheperu left off his questioning and joined them. "Not much to be learned," he said, leaning heavily upon his staff. "No affray with his tax collector here. He had nine guests the night of the curse; all dead by noon. Two slaves and one of his daughters made it as far as the Market before they went into convulsions and died."

"I told you the business with Chrysios was coincidence," Barra said. "It wouldn't surprise me if the curse was an afterthought—the House behind our sorcerer was trying a new tactic, and when we got in the way they went back to their old one. Or, if the curse had already been planned, the killing of the tax collector was just a new way of stoking the fire, you know? The next step in the plan. Chrysios was Akhaian—if he'd gotten away with it, the murders might have looked like they were ordered by the Penthedes." She shook her head sharply. "Forget why. I'm wondering how. In the food, you think?"

Kheperu nodded, fingernails scratching thoughtfully on the knob of his staff. "The question is, what food? All of it? You'd need to dose everybody, or the illusion collapses. Seems difficult. More likely, some spice or something that would be commonly used . . ." He brightened suddenly. "In the salt!"

Barra shrugged, unconvinced. "I don't know. You'd still have to get into and out of the kitchen—or the storeroom—and I don't know about these other three, but Lidios kept a bloody peeled eye on his stores."

"Do you think we could eat now?" Leucas murmured, still gazing wistfully into the grill court.

"In a moment," Barra told him. "We need to work this out."

Leucas sighed. "What about the water?"

"If you had your mind on any business more urgent than the cry of your belly," Kheperu sneered, "it would be obvious. Water comes from the public wells, fresh every morning or two. There'd be no way to renew the poison, as the inn would be already closed under the curse. Is it *clear* now? Do you *understand?*"

Leucas nodded slow acceptance. "I was confused. You're right, of course. I guess I was thinking that these four inns wouldn't use the public wells till their rain barrels ran dry."

Barra frowned at Kheperu. He grimaced back. They both looked up at the rain barrel on the roof of Xuros' house. Lidios had a similar one, and Barra remembered rain barrels on the roofs of Nicoras' and Sutuwallas' houses, as well.

Kheperu said softly, just above a whisper, "Do you suppose he does this on purpose, to make me feel like a fool?"

Barra glanced over her shoulder at the huge Athenian, who was once again staring at a mutton shank the size of his thigh. There just might have been the tiniest twitch of a smile at the corner of his mouth, but she couldn't be sure.

"I don't know," she said, "but I hope so. Come on, let's take a closer look."

The companions put a corner of the block between them and the crowded food court, and not far along the side of the block found an alleyway narrow enough to force them to walk it single file. The lowest point within it where they could reach the roof was two stories high, slightly more than three times Leucas' height. Barra squinted critically at the wall. "I'm not sure I can climb it," she said. "It's pretty smooth."

Leucas made a basket with his fingers. "If you jump as I toss, I'd imagine you won't need to climb at all."

Kheperu snorted. "You're mad. You're a strong lad, Leucas, but be serious!"

Leucas replied with a shrug. Barra said, "It's worth a try." She looked at the wolf. "Stay here and watch," she said in Pictish. "Howl if anyone comes, and don't bite Kheperu." Graeg whined, but sat obediently.

"Ready?"

Leucas nodded, took a deep breath, and bent his legs. She stepped into his hands, crouched, and sprang upward as he heaved. She was still rising as her hands passed the rim of the roof; she latched on and had enough momentum left to swing smoothly onto it. She lay there for a moment, then shook herself and poked her head back over the rim. "I'm impressed."

Leucas shrugged. "At the Olympian games we tossed a bronze ingot that weighs not much less than you do."

"Oh, sure," she said, "but someday you'll have to come up to the Isle of the Mighty, and try hurling the caber—that's a *real* test. It's a great log the size of a mainmast, not some teeny bit of bronze—"

"I'm sure of it," Kheperu interrupted. "Very interesting, Barra, I'm sure we'd both love to hear all about it. Later."

"Oh, fine," she sighed irritably. Then her eyes went wide. "Leucas—what about your *stitches*?"

Leucas looked momentarily puzzled, then put his hand to his belly and winced. "I forgot." He pulled his chiton out away from his chest and peered down through the neck hole. "Don't seem to be bleeding, though. Peroön is a fine surgeon."

"He'd have to be," Kheperu muttered, "if he's sewing up you scatterbrained Akhaians all the time."

Leucas looked at him consideringly, as though calculating precisely how hard Kheperu could be hit without killing him outright. Barra said, "Don't even start. Either of you."

She rolled to her feet and ran lightly along the rim of the roof toward Xuros' rain barrel, avoiding stepping out onto the probably more fragile—and certainly more noisy—open roof. Leucas and Kheperu followed her from the ground, picking their way around the piles of trash that nearly blocked the passage. Graegduz stayed on guard at the alley's mouth.

The barrel rested at a back corner, slightly overhanging the walls that supported its weight. It was deeper than Barra was tall, and wide enough that she could have lain full length within it and never touched the sides. She leaped upward over the narrow alley that separated the inn from the rest of the block, as the inn's roof was slightly higher, and swung herself to safety. Nearby, a small door was set flat into the roof, and up one side of the barrel were nailed a set of rungs. The hinged lid of the rain barrel was closed for fair weather, to keep out bird droppings. She lifted it briefly, and took a deep sniff. The water's dominant scent was simply the musty smell of being closed up and stale, but underneath that, she detected a familiar bitter, nutlike aroma. A moment's thought told her where she knew it from: she'd smelled the same scent on Lidios' breath. Another moment of searching the roof discovered all the confirmation she required: she brushed her fingers across a roughened scuff mark on the rim of the roof.

She called down, not loudly, "Leucas—you were right. There's a mark here, probably from something like a siege ladder."

"That explains why your little friend was killed," Kheperu said, nodding. He and Leucas stood in Xuros' back-alley kitchen, unused now that no slave dared leave the building. "Our pretend-sorcerer wouldn't want anyone talking about seeing a couple of men running around in the dead of night carrying a ladder. Get a sample of the water."

"Why?"

He leaned casually on the cold brick of the hearth and examined his fingernails. "Because, with the right equipment, I should be able to isolate the poison. That sort of thing is rather my specialty, you know. There are several poisons that might have this effect; they are all expensive, and none come from anywhere close by. All we'll need to do is talk to the alchemists, to find out who's been buying it and . . ." He snapped his fingers insouciantly.

Barra blinked in astonishment. "You're brilliant, do you know that?"

"I've been waiting for you to notice."

# 8

# *Chrysios*

**B**arra sat on the street, her back against the pine door frame of the shop of Tekrop-nekt. The interior of the shop smelled worse than Kheperu, so she had left him and Leucas to deal with the alchemist while she sat out here feeding strips of smoked fish to Graegduz as the lopsided moon rose over the black mass of the mountains.

Before the moon had come up, she'd amused herself by watching the dancing glow of a shop—she was pretty sure it had sold carpets—that had burned merrily in another part of the Market. A few of the rugs themselves had been lifted into the night sky, writhing as they burned within the thunderhead of smoke, salamanders blindly seeking wood or cloth on which to spawn. She'd listened to the distant, desperate shouts of merchants as they'd pursued the salamanders, guessing at the next move of the shifting wind. By the time the brow of the moon had peered over the mountains, the Market was once again dark, and quiet.

Occasionally, she heard Kheperu and Tekrop-nekt speaking in low-voiced Egyptian together, of temperatures of volatility and rates of distillation; the alchemist's shop was one of the merely semipermanent structures in the Market, framed in pine but walled only with heavy striped cloth.

Leucas pulled aside the door curtain over her head. "You'll want to hear this."

"I would've anyway," she sighed, but nonetheless rose, told Graeg to guard the door, and followed Leucas inside.

Within, the shelves and racks that divided the floor were empty, the alchemist's wares already packed away for the evening—the day had been fading from the sky when the three companions had arrived. Another curtain led to an inner chamber; beside that door stood Met, Tekrop-nekt's massively rotund guard, arms like hams folded over his bare chest, one hand close to the hilt of his long, broad-bladed scimitar. Barra noticed Leucas gazing at the sword with something akin to lust; its blade had the dull grey-black sheen of Hittite iron. Tekrop-nekt himself was a thin, languid man who looked at the world through eyes kept half lidded by mandrake root.

"Fascinating stuff," Kheperu told her, in Egyptian. His color was high and his eyes danced with excitement. He waved a small glass bottle at her, within which was some milky, viscous liquid. "This is an extract of the pukenut, which grows far and away on the other side of the Cape of Comorin. It does all kinds of things, really, useful and otherwise, you know."

"Hm-hm," Tekrop-nekt murmured. "In its undistilled form, it is a powerful emetic, used for cattle, and occasionally men. In small doses, the distilled form is a potent stimulant, increasing alertness and strength. In slightly larger doses, it produces convulsions, and death by choking of the lungs."

"You see? You see?" Kheperu said gleefully. "It produces a *tolerance*, you see. A dedicated user can safely take dosages that would kill an inexperienced horse. And, the convulsions can be triggered by excitement, a loud noise, even a bright light—do you get it?"

"So," Barra said, "they would take a few days, even a month, putting tiny doses—"

"Oh yes, yes indeed absolutely," Kheperu interrupted her forcefully. He stepped grandly in front of Barra and swung himself to face Tekrop-nekt. She restrained an impulse to punch him in the kidney; not even Kheperu would be foolish enough to interrupt her without a bloody good reason. "Our only other question regarding this is: who would be importing pukenut extract?"

"Well, the only place one would find pukenuts commercially available would be the isle of Dilmun, through the overland route south of Babylon . . ." Tekrop-nekt said consideringly. "Where, mm, where did you come across this sample?"

"That's our business, I believe."

Tekrop-nekt shrugged. "As is the name of the importer mine."

Kheperu hissed through his teeth and stepped forward. Behind Tekrop-nekt, Met unfolded his arms and smiled. Kheperu stopped, his face contracted into a pout. "Very well, then. Another shekel."

"Five."

"Fine! Five! Who is it, then?"

"In advance."

Muttering vile curses under his breath, Kheperu dug five shekels from his purse of dice winnings. Tekrop-nekt accepted them graciously, and said, "The House of Jephunah holds the sole contract to bring pukenuts to Tyre."

Kheperu's eyes went wide, and he slowly turned toward Barra, until Tekrop-nekt added, "Of course, many alchemists maintain a substantial supply, buying them from the Jephunahi. I do, myself."

Kheperu deflated. "Ah, well," he sighed. "I suppose that would have been too easy."

Barra asked, "Has anyone come around buying up unusual amounts of your pukenuts, or the extract?"

Tekrop-nekt's eyelids drooped as he considered holding out for more money, but apparently he decided to be merciful. "Why, yes, in fact. A man bought every scrap I had, six weeks ago. A tall, fair-skinned fellow with golden hair. Had an Akhaian name, as I recall."

"Chrysios," Barra said.

"Why, yes, I believe that was it."

This time, she did punch Kheperu in the kidney, a short right hook hard enough to buckle his knees.

Barra recounted the conversation for Leucas, who had no Egyptian, while they walked slowly through the moonlit streets toward the apartments of the Myrmidons.

He nodded and sighed when Barra told him who the sorcerer's agent had been in purchasing the poison. He looked over Barra's head at Kheperu, who walked sullenly behind. "Is it too late for me to hit him, too?"

Kheperu made a complicated, two-handed gesture that was unquestionably obscene. Leucas shrugged. "Perhaps we should go to Idonosteus with what we've learned so far."

"Oh, please!" Kheperu sputtered. "Why are you both so eager to cast aside our commercial advantage? I give thanks to the watchful Uraeus that I thought quickly enough to stop Barra's babbling—"

"Which reminds me," Barra cut in through clenched teeth, "I don't like to be interrupted. Don't do it again."

"Piffle. You should bless me. Do you not understand the *opportunity* we have here? We are not being paid to determine the nature of the curse, but rather to discover its author. Once that is done, and we have been paid, *we are the only people in Tyre who know how to lift the curse!*"

"What, all this is about making a few shekels off the poor bastards that run these inns? So you can lift the curse, big deal—they can't afford to pay much, no matter what."

"My dear lady! I would not waste your time with squeezing shekels. Why 'lift the curse' . . . until *after* we have bought the inns?"

Barra stopped in the street and stared at him.

"Do you appreciate how little we would have to pay?" Kheperu continued. "Practically nothing! These men would pay *us* to take these establishments off their hands!"

"Kheperu." Leucas looked down at the little Egyptian with pity. "You are the most thoroughly venal and disgusting man I have ever met."

"Brilliant, though," Barra said thoughtfully. "No one could accuse you of thinking small."

Leucas frowned at her. "Please say you're not considering this!"

Barra squeezed her eyes shut, then shrugged and shook her head sharply. "No, I won't go for it."

"Barra—"

"Think about it, Kheperu. If we bought four inns in Tyre, we'd have to stay here and run them. Do you really want to be an innkeeper? It's a shitty life. And it's boring."

Kheperu pursed his lips, then nodded surrender. "It was a pretty idea, though, wasn't it?"

Barra started walking again, thumbs hooked behind her belt and Graegduz at her heel. Leucas and Kheperu fell in behind them. "On the other hand," she said, "if we were to buy them, lift the curse with some sort of spectacular public ceremony—Kheperu could put something together—and then *sell* them again . . ."

Kheperu's head jerked up when he realized he was alone. He rubbed his eyes, cursing his absentmindedness under his breath. He'd been walking along, thinking hard, watching the creeping tendrils of mist swirl before his feet, and somehow had continued straight at some point where Barra and Leucas had turned. Now as he looked about himself, the mist rose up more thickly from the moist earth of the street and the black-shadowed faces of unfamiliar buildings pressed close around.

"Lost." His voice rasped loudly in his ears, and he tightened his grip on his staff. He repeated, this time only a whisper, "I'm bloody lost."

His friends couldn't be far away—and when they noticed he was gone, they'd search for him. He'd simply retrace his steps and probably find them around the first corner.

But as he turned to go, he found that he was no longer sure from what direction he had come. He'd gotten turned around somehow. North, he told himself. They'd been walking north, so if he turned and put the moon on his left, he'd be heading back south toward the missed corner. But the mist had extended a milk-pale shroud above his head, and hid the moon behind a shifting veil that glowed faintly silver.

He drew breath to shout for them, but held it and listened, instead. He heard only the whisper of a breeze and the unsteady thump of his own heart. Why weren't they calling for him? Had they ditched him on purpose, as a joke?

Had something happened to them?

The sorcerer—could he have sent some otherworldly servant, one of the beast-headed demons of whom the other apprentices had whispered dark tales during the endless nights of Kheperu's childhood? If Kheperu called out, would he draw down upon himself the same hideous death that had taken his friends?

*Nonsense*, he insisted, but silently. He shook the knots out of his shoulders, firmly grasped his staff, and set out toward his best guess of south. The street narrowed as he walked, becoming little more than an alley that he could span with his arms, the buildings leaning together high above his head to shut out the sky. Obviously, this wasn't the way he'd come—he snorted and turned resolutely, then stopped. Footsteps— that sound was clearly footsteps, approaching through the mist. He started toward them—this must be Leucas or Barra, looking for him— but the stride was wrong, neither the sharp staccato of Barra's step nor the measured beat of Leucas; this step shuffled more than it strode, and it was *moist*, scraping through the alley's dirt with a wet sucking sound that lifted the hairs on Kheperu's arms and made his heart stutter.

His nerve broke; he turned and fled, deeper into the alley.

The buildings that made up the walls closed overhead, blotting out the light. Kheperu pressed on, stumbling through trash and slipping on unnameable slime; he couldn't get enough traction to gain ground on his pursuer. The walls squeezed against him in the darkness, the colored eyelights of utter night were all he saw, but he felt the moisture on the walls. They were sweating in the unbearable heat, and he forced himself between them, onward, turned sideways, half trapped, unable to breathe, and still the footsteps came behind, closer.

With panicked strength he burst free of the alley, and found himself in a small cul-de-sac that was thick with mist and bounded by high blind walls. He turned, panting, to face his pursuer, visible now as a vague man-shape. He whirled his staff whistling through the air before him and snapped it into a guard position.

"Come on, then!" he shouted. "Come on, you bastard! I'm ready!"

*"Kheperu . . ."* The voice was as thick and wet as its step, guttural and moaning. *"Kheperu, I want my face . . ."*

The figure shuffled forward, and now Kheperu felt his staff softening under his hands, flowing limply like supple rope that wrapped around his wrists and tied itself into unbreakable knots, pinning his hands helpless before him.

The mist parted around his pursuer and a shaft of silver moonlight lit its face, glossing the dead fish-belly white of its skin, turning the bloody shreds that dangled in place of its lower jaw to gleaming black. The fine corn-silk hair glistened; the shredded lump that had been its tongue pulsed. Slowly and deliberately it came, pushing Kheperu back against the sweating wall, its hands clutching his face, forcing its fingers into his mouth. He tried to scream, but the fingers choked him; he bit down and their flesh burst with squirming foulness that filled his mouth, but their strength was irresistible as they took hold of his tongue, his teeth, his jaw, ripping bone and tendon, tearing it free . . .

*"I want my face!"*

Then, from the back of Kheperu's head, came a burst of white light.

". . . A burst of white light, not unlike one of these," he said, producing one of his tarry flame balls. "And then, of course, I woke up, because the boot whatsisbugger threw hit me in the head. That could have been what produced the burst of light, I suppose."

Barra nodded thoughtfully, keeping her eyes on the sleeping Myrmidons from where she crouched beside Kheperu. It had taken a long time to settle them down again after they were awakened by Kheperu's moaning and his eventual scream, but now they lay dreaming on their pallets, scattered across the apartment's floor, except for those on guard, who were once again outside, and Kamades. She couldn't tell if Kamades was awake, or if he was dozing there in his chair with his chin on his breast. The scar-faced captain might well be cagy enough to pretend to sleep while he listened.

"There's gratitude:" Kheperu went on in his deeply offended whisper, "a boot to the head. One would think he might have been a little solicitous, a little concerned for my welfare, even friendly, after all the *money I lost* to him this evening." Under Barra's watchful glare earlier that evening, with the aid of the persuasive incense he'd used the night before, Kheperu had cheated himself out of twenty-one shekels during the nightly dice game.

Barra shrugged. "If you're trying to make me feel sorry for you, Kheperu, you're shopping at the wrong store."

Leucas sat cross-legged on the bare plank floor, his back to the Myrmidons. He scratched gently at his bandages and said, "What significance do you give this dream?"

"I am not sure that it *is* significant."

Leucas regarded him with lifted brows. "That's why you told us every detail, because you don't think it's—"

"Oh, all right," Kheperu surrendered disgustedly. He leaned forward, glancing past Leucas at Kamades, and lowered his voice even further. "I am wondering if it might be a threat."

Without perceptibly altering his expression, Leucas managed to look deeply skeptical.

"It's not as silly as it sounds, Leucas," Barra whispered. "My grandmother can send dreams, and folk she's mad at might ride the nightmare for weeks at a time."

"And Chrysios was saying something about how he can never die," Kheperu said, licking his lips as though his mouth was suddenly dry. "Right before I killed him."

"When I was a little boy," Leucas said, "my father told me about the dreams sent by the gods, false ones through the gates of ivory, true through the gates of honest horn. He never spoke of dreams being sent by a mortal."

"Yes, yes," Kheperu said impatiently, "I've heard the same story. That doesn't mean it's true."

Leucas regarded him steadily. "My father wouldn't lie."

"Aren't you a little old to still hold that opinion?"

"Aren't you a little small to be calling my father a liar?"

"Stop it, both of you," Barra cut in. She took a deep breath and released it slowly. "The sorcerer couldn't have sent you this dream— he doesn't really have any magic, remember?"

"We have not established that," Kheperu said primly, forefinger lifted to make his point. "We know that he didn't use magic to curse the inns, not that he has no magic at all." He coughed into his hand, and gave a nervous little laugh. "Remember Othniel?"

The shadows cast by the steady flames of the lamp on Kamades' table seemed to lengthen, and to deepen to a darker black. Skin tightened across the back of Barra's neck, and she found herself glancing behind—just to be sure the wall of bare planks at her back was still there, still bare and empty.

"Well," she said heavily, turning back to her friends, "in my homeland, they say that many dreams come from deep within the mind of the dreamer, to remind him of something he's forgotten. The way I see it, whether this dream comes from the gods, from our boy the sorcerer, or out of your own twisted little mind, Kheperu, there's one thing we should do, first thing tomorrow." Barra cracked her knuckles, and took a deep breath; she rubbed her arms to smooth away the gooseflesh, and when she spoke, she had to whisper to keep her voice level. "We need to find out what happened to Chrysios' body."

Barra lay in the semidarkness for a long time, thinking about Chrysios, about Lidios and Nicoras and Xuros, about Peliarchus and Tayniz living in the same city with the man who'd branded Othniel and dropped poison in rain barrels. Thinking about finding a brand like that on her own palm, about drinking that water. Thinking about the seizure of Lidios, about how it would feel to have her muscles betray her and flop her like a landed fish. Thinking about how it would feel to have her flesh torn by demons that only she can see, as people press away from her on a noonday street. Fingers laced behind her head, she stared up at the ragged glow of lamplight on the ceiling, and decided to think about something else.

She lay for a while wondering about Kamades. The solemn Myrmidon captain had sat with her for more than an hour earlier that evening, filling her eager ears with stories of the Siege of Troy. She gathered that he'd been well respected, and had held a very responsible position in the Phthian force that had followed Akhilleus, although—in the self-effacing way that seemed common to him and his men—he never came right out and said so. She was helplessly, irresistibly fascinated by any story that had to do with the Akhaian heroes, especially Akhilleus, and she'd slowly become interested in just how in the names of a thousand gods a man like Kamades had come to be a mercenary captain in Tyre. After all, he wasn't a greedy money-grubber—as Barra occasionally saw herself—nor was he, apparently, ambitious or bloodthirsty. He seemed to see soldiering as a trade, like carpentry; a trade where he would routinely risk his life for a salary a bit smaller than what a decent cooper would make in the Market. But no matter how she tried to steer his stories, he would never refer to why he and his men didn't simply go home; the best she could gather was that there had been some sort of difficulty with Akhilleus' son and heir, Neoptolemos; Kamades' face would gently flush whenever the young man's name was mentioned. On the other hand, Kamades didn't seem to mind her probing. If he hadn't had to take his turn standing watch, they might still be sitting at that table, speaking softly across a lamp flame that wavered with each word.

It was that central mystery of him that drew her; Barra couldn't bear a mystery—the knowledge that someone was keeping a secret from her would buzz in her ears like a persistent mosquito. In fact, if she let herself think about it, she could very well lie awake here all night. Once again, she resolutely determined to think about something else.

She thought about Leucas. The *sceon tiof* was showing her much, letting her see a man who was intelligent and thoughtful, but only when he stopped to think; a man who lost all caution—all *reason*—whenever weapons were drawn and blood began to flow; a man who didn't need caution, because he had luck. Barrels of luck. He'd been a charioteer at Troy; if the songs Barra had heard were true, it was always the charioteers who were killed by the first spear casts between opposing heroes. *Weapons*, he'd said, *do not bite me as deeply as they do other men.* Nor do the tusks of boars, nor the claws of bears . . . It was probably one of his gods, watching over him; the Akhaians had a shipload of gods, starting with a ruling council of twelve, along with all their attendants and servants and children, then they had more minor deities than she had hairs on her head, gods of this mountain and that stream and such-and-such wind and on and on and on till it made her head spin to think about them. It was easy to see how one of them might have taken a liking to him; there was charm in his grave equanimity, in his sly humor so dry that sometimes you couldn't tell whether he was really joking; he was generous, and openhearted, and his rare flashes of anger were always the swelling fires of an open furnace, never constricted into bitterness, never twisted to petty treachery; he was as honorable as a Myrmidon. He could, she thought, have the blood of gods running through his veins—some immortal ancestor would explain much. And really, she mused, squirming down deeper beneath her blanket, if it wasn't for that busted face of his, she'd probably be in love with him. Actually, busted face or not, Leucas was an enormously attractive man . . .

During her years on the road as a mercenary, Barra had developed a mental discipline, a rule that she used to govern her thinking; there were some things that she did not allow herself to do, or even think about. She had a list, in her mind, of topics that she wouldn't address, even in daydreams, topics like "What if Chryl's father hadn't left me?" and "What would my son be like if I'd stayed at home to raise him?" She called this list, privately, the Suicide Table; thinking too much about any entry on it could lead her into doing the kind of foolish things that tend to buy people in her line of work a short trip to a shallow grave. Very high on the Suicide Table was "I'd like to bed one of my partners"; it fell right between "I'd like to bed my employer" and "I'd like to bed my target."

This semiconscious state, drowsing half asleep on her pallet, had always been a dangerous time for her; still awake enough to spin fantasies, she was too close to sleep to keep them tightly reined. But now, as the lean battle-scarred figure of Leucas drifted across the inside of her eyelids, she found that he brought no heat to her loins; she felt affection, but no lust. She wondered, in her vague and aimless state, if he felt the same for her, if he felt this same serene *philios*. She realized that she did love him already: the same way she loved her brother Llem, and, perhaps, trusted Leucas a little more. After twenty-five years as High King, Llem was now an accomplished diplomat; Leucas wouldn't be as smooth a liar if he lived a thousand years.

Kheperu, now, he could drive the flow of words through his mouth as the gods drive water down the Nile, and whether they're true or false had as little effect on whether you'd believe him as the color of your hair has on the path of a thunderstorm. Even knowing that he prided himself on the quality of his lying didn't help; you could catch him in five lies and fall for the sixth. A shift of the shoulders, an inclination of the head, a softening of his tone, all to imply, "All right, I was only joking before, but now, *this* is the truth," and you're swept helplessly along. Drifting, she wondered if even Kheperu knew how *angry* he was, if he still felt the rage that fueled his contempt for the social mores; the *sceon tiof* could not show her what injustice the world had inflicted upon his life, but the lingering scars were all too clear. Perhaps he entertained fantasies of returning one day to his home city, wealthy as a nomarch, to live in luxury and lord it over those who'd scorned him; perhaps he intended to waste his life as some obscure revenge against a half-forgotten parent, or lover. Or perhaps some terrible despair had taught him that he deserved no better than what he sought. In her lands, a man with even half of Kheperu's habits would be regarded as a *silba'itan*, an eater of self, to be pitied and avoided. Here in the decadent south, his behavior must be even more extreme—or else he'd blend right in with the crowds, which is the equivalent of death to a *silba'itan*.

Kheperu, blending into the crowds . . . the very thought was ridiculous. Sorcerers don't blend, it's contrary to their nature; they irrevocably set themselves apart from the balance of humanity when they begin to study magic . . .

This led her to consider sorcerers, and soon she found those thoughts of the brand on Othniel's palm sneaking past her guard. Before she could drive them away once more, the shutter slats on the window began to glow crimson with the first bloody rays of dawn.

The grey-faced, groaning innkeeper still lay twisted among the blankets on the bed where Barra and Leucas had placed him. When the three companions were led in by a pallidly silent slave, Lidios' clouded eyes rolled toward them within an otherwise slack and motionless face. The room was heavily shuttered against the morning sun, gloom so deep that Barra wasn't sure he recognized them. The slave bowed, a pained look on her face, and discreetly stepped back out into the passageway.

Leucas and Kheperu both favored Barra with an expectant stare, as though to say *this was your idea.* . . . She pressed her lips together, sighed through her nose, then stepped forward to crouch beside Lidios' bed.

"Lidios?" She gently touched his shoulder. "Lidios, can you hear me?"

" 'Course I can hear you!" he snapped so loudly it made Barra flinch. "I'm dying, not deaf! What do you want now?"

Barra straightened up. "That Akhaian I killed in the fight the other night—Chrysios. Lenka, out in front, she told us that some men came and took his body away late that night. Do you remember?"

His brows drew slowly together. "Yes . . . yes, surely. Korab and Yeshu—a couple Jephunahi toughs, they came with a few hirelings to clear the bodies."

"Do you know what they were going to do with them?"

"Why, bury them, of course. I mean . . ." He lifted a trembling hand to smooth his hair. "I mean, they would bury them, wouldn't they? They wouldn't . . . wouldn't do anything to the bodies, would they?"

"I don't know."

"I'm, well, I'm not, I suppose, the most pious man who ever lived, but I know what Zeus promises to those who dishonor the dead. I mean, you remember what happened to King Kreon, and his city Thebes . . ."

Leucas rumbled, "I remember." Barra could hear his knuckles pop as he unconsciously knotted his fists.

"I don't want to be mixed up with anybody who'd do anything like that," Lidios murmured, rubbing anxiously at his face. "The vengeance of the God spills over sometimes— you don't want to be standing next to the man who catches a thunderbolt. You don't, you don't suppose that . . . oh, they wouldn't! You don't think they might have left the bodies out to rot into flies and be picked at by buzzards—that could be why I've been cursed! It's the vengeance of Zeus!"

He sank back into the bed, his eyes drifting closed as though this outburst had exhausted him. Barra looked down at him, at this mound of sagging flesh that only two days ago had been a fat and jolly man, and at the large stoneware pitcher that rested on a table at his bedside. The pitcher drew her eyes, and the mug that sat beside it; the scent of the pukenuts was strong in the room, probably strong enough for even Kheperu to smell it. She looked over her shoulder at him. He must have somehow seen her thought, for his eyes widened and he began to gesture frantic negatives. She shrugged a half-rueful apology and turned back to Lidios.

"You're not cursed, Lidios."

His eyes fluttered open. Kheperu said warningly, "Barra . . ."

She leaned down to speak softly and clearly, directly into his face. "Tell no one of this, do you understand? No one. There is no curse. There's poison in your rain barrel. Drink only wine and beer, or take all your water from the public wells, and you'll be fine."

"But . . . but . . ."

"Listen to me. No one must know of this for a few days yet. If word gets out that you've broken the curse, the men who poisoned your water will be back; they will kill you and everyone else in this house. Do you understand?"

"I don't understand why . . . you're telling me this. I cursed you, and you saved my life—now you give me this gift as well. Why?"

Barra shrugged and shifted like there were ants inside her tunic. "You were our host."

"We're a long way from Akhaia, and you're not even Greek."

"Ay, well . . . whatever." She turned and pushed Leucas and Kheperu ahead of her. "Let's get out of here."

Once out on the street, Kheperu wheeled on her. "I'd like to know just what you thought you were doing, telling him that?"

Leucas said with hefty finality, "The right thing."

Barra shook her head, and scratched at her scalp, and said, "No, I don't know. I was afraid he'd die, that's all."

"So? Since when do you care?"

*Since the* sceon tiof *showed me he was a person.* She shut her lips against that thought; the *sceon tiof* was an embarrassing secret that was none of their business. "I don't know. I just do."

"You're changing, Barra," Kheperu said severely, "and I am not sure it's for the better."

She shrugged and whistled to Graegduz, who nosed at a rat hole down the street. "Let's go talk to Jephunah."

The House of Jephunah was of a different style than the walled compound of the Meneides or the sprawling palatial home of the Penthedes. It resembled the mazy block where the Myrmidons kept their apartment: a huge mass of interconnected buildings, three stories and more tall. The original street doors and outer windows of all these buildings had been bricked in over the last twenty years, patches of rich bloodstain-red set sporadically within the sun-bleached walls. The only remaining entrance faced east, a low-ceilinged passageway wide enough for two carts, closed at each end with a heavy bronze gate instead of a door so that the *potameus*—the east wind—could blow freely through it into the courtyard within. That front wall, facing the mountains and the rising sun, was also pegged with bronze hooks the size of Barra's bent arm, all of them crusted and stained black-brown. Below one hook close by the gate, still in shadow as the companions approached, was a blackened patch in the sand from which Barra could smell rotting blood. Kheperu nudged Leucas and nodded toward the hooks. "An unlikely spot to hang meat, don't you think?"

"I was," Leucas rumbled, "thinking just that."

The sleep-ragged voice of a sentry answered their banging on the gate. Barra's demand for a meeting with Jephunah was greeted with blank refusal until she identified herself and her friends as the warriors who had avenged the death of the tax collector.

"Old Melchazar?" the sentry said, a sharper edge coming into his tone. "You're the ones who killed the Greek? Wait there; I'll ask Jephunah if he will see you."

Moments later, a pair of older men came to swing open the gates. They wore only belted robes of striped linen, their faces appeared as weathered and cracked as mountain stone; their invitation to follow them within was grimly polite, but held no hint of deference. *Not slaves,* Barra decided, *likely they're family. Nephews, perhaps even sons.* The low passageway through which they were led had numerous vents in the ceiling. Barra could smell the armed men who watched them from above—she knew they were armed by the pungent scent of the oiled cedar of their spear shafts, distinct from the oiled-bronze smell of the gates. Obviously, the Jephunahi took the events of the last few days very seriously indeed.

Graegduz growled, low in his throat, and pressed close to Barra's leg as they came out of the passage. The courtyard looked deserted; even the balconies that ringed it one atop the other were empty, but it still carried the strong scents of people and dogs. Likely the courtyard had been cleared just now, so that the companions could get no hint of the numbers and capabilities of the inhabitants: here, it seemed, precaution piled upon precaution to the point of absurdity.

Kheperu touched Barra on the shoulder, and murmured, "They certainly know how to welcome guests, do they not?" This earned him a hard look over the shoulder of one of the guides, a look that stopped just short of open hostility.

Leucas barely moved his lips as he whispered, "Be polite."

Barra nodded fervent agreement. She had a feeling that if old Jephunah took a dislike to them, or decided that they were any kind of a threat, they'd be buried here in this very courtyard.

Jephunah himself greeted them in a ground-floor room just off the courtyard. A large chair was this room's only furnishing; he leaned against its back. He was tall, perhaps only a hand shorter than Leucas, and gaunt as a shipwrecked sailor. His close-set eyes held the glossy, inhuman stare of an eagle below brows the color of salt, and his braided beard was dyed ebony-black. His dress was similar to the two guides, a simple shift of striped linen over pants of the same, and his hands, neck, ears, were all bare of jewelry. He took a single step toward them without any hint of a smile of welcome. He said, in fluid Phoenikian that still held a trace of his native Canaanite, "Please excuse my poor hospitality. These are difficult times, and this is an exotic hour to be entertaining mercenaries. What is your desire?"

The chill in his tone gave all the warning Barra needed. She ducked her head and carefully thickened her accent. "Please, sir, I'm sorry t'be botherin' you at this hour in the morning, but I must get a look at that Greek boy, the dead one." It galled her like bee stings to pretend to be stupid and harmless, but she didn't need the *sceon tiof* to show her that Jephunah was the sort to see plots against himself in every heart; the state of siege in his household made that all too clear.

Jephunah's brows drew together. He looked up at Leucas, and snapped, "Why is this woman speaking to me?" Leucas looked back at him, gravely puzzled.

"Your pardon, my lord," Kheperu interjected smoothly. "My friend here has but little of your language, and his woman is from a far foreign land, with strange customs and no knowledge of the proper way of things."

"See that she is instructed."

"I will, oh yes, I certainly will, my lord. Please, though, sir, if it is not too much trouble, we must know what was done with the body of Chrysios, the man who killed, er, Melchazar."

"Why?" he snapped.

"Well, my lord, that's the real question, is it not? I mean, you might well wonder why we should be asking for such a boon . . ." He looked at Barra, and she could see the dawn burst over his brain. He turned easily back to Jephunah and spread his hands, wearing a self-deprecating smile. "It's a religious rite, my lord, to the gods of far-off Albion. She needs a piece of him—a lock of hair, a finger, nothing large or difficult—to be burned in a ritual to honor his shade and to thank her gods for bringing her through the fight."

Jephunah snorted. "I have no interest in barbarian ritual. I meant, why did you not see what you must see and do what you must do without disturbing me? Have the buzzards made him unrecognizable already?"

"I'm sorry?" Kheperu said carefully.

"His is the body that hangs from the hook by the east gate; it is the one that wears the sign 'I Killed a Jephunahi' in three languages."

Barra and Kheperu looked at each other. It was clear that the hook he spoke of was the empty one above the clotted blood that they'd passed on the way in. Barra bared her teeth, and one of her hands curled into a fist at her side. Kheperu sighed and shrugged.

"What is it?" Jephunah barked. "What? Tell me what you know."

"Well, mm, my lord," Kheperu said, "perhaps you—or some others of your household—would like to come outside with us. I wouldn't have you think that we stole the body ourselves."

"The body's gone? Someone *stole* it?"

"I'd assume so, unless you think it got up and walked a—" He suddenly looked acutely uncomfortable. "I apologize, my lord, please forget I said that." He shivered, once, like a man shaking off goose bumps.

"Why would someone steal his corpse?"

"I am quite sure, my lord," Kheperu said, "that I do not want to know."

\* \* \*

"I still believe we should have accepted the job," Kheperu said.

"Be quiet," Barra told him. "I think we're getting close."

Graegduz snuffled among the scrub grass and over the rocks and sand. He trotted a ways farther east, and put his head down again. Leucas squinted against the sun—the near faces of the hills, and the caves that opened within them, were still deep in morning shadow with the sun above, shining full on the companions.

"One of those caves," Leucas said. "Any odds you'd care to make, I'll bet. Isn't that the way you Tyrians bury your dead? Block them into a cave?"

"Some do," Barra allowed. "The poor folk burn their dead, or put them in the ground, in passage-graves rather like the ones we have back in the Isle, only smaller and poorer, with no stonework. The wealthier buy a spot in the caves, here. If you're bloody rich, you can buy a cave all your own, sweep out the old bones and have it blocked up with just you inside, and maybe your family and a few choice slaves. But what makes you think they'd bury Chrysios?"

"Because he's *dead*," Kheperu insisted, too loudly. "That's what you do with dead people. You *bury* them."

"Relax, will you?"

Kheperu huffed a sigh through his nose. "Well, I still cannot see why we could not have taken Jephunah's money. Whom would it hurt, if we tell the Jephunahi where to find his body? We're looking for it already; why shouldn't we be paid for finding it?"

"Because, for the tenth time"—an edge crept into Barra's voice—"finding the body might lead us to the sorcerer. Idonosteus is paying us a hundred and fifty large weights of silver to keep our mouths shut about who this sorcerer is. If we give up the location of the body, we might be giving away the identity of the sorcerer at the same time—and I guarantee that we do not want Idonosteus to think that we're cheating him."

Kheperu sniffed. "What can he do, spank us?"

"He can sic the bloody Myrmidons on us, at the very least."

"Oh, piffle" was his response, but he let the subject drop.

Whoever it was who'd stolen Chrysios' body had done a sloppy job of it. It had still been leaking some various fluids when they carried it off—not enough to leave an obvious trail, but an intermittent splat here and there was enough for Graegduz to follow, even through the city. It had shortly become clear that the corpse and its carriers were headed north and east, into the cave-riddled hills where the dead of Tyre were interred. The swirl of the wind as it twisted between the hills and whistled through the wadis made it impossible for Barra to smell anything beyond sunbaked rock and pine resin, but Graegduz still had the trail, and the companions followed in his wake.

The trail led up through wadi after tangled wadi; these dried watercourses left the hills looking as though they'd been carved by jagged knives. It led through and beyond the funerary ground, ending at a deep cave whose mouth was too wide to be easily sealed. Barra called to Graeg to sit there at the mouth while the companions approached, and he obeyed, shifting his weight impatiently. She stood at the entrance and peered into the deep blackness inside, hands on her hips. "Did anybody think to bring a lamp?"

"Fear not," Kheperu said warmly, digging within his robe to the many pockets inside. "I can do better than a lamp." His hands came out with several small pots of hard-baked white clay. After apparently examining them for markings that neither Barra nor Leucas could discern, he selected four of them, pulled the corks, and began measuring out various portions of their contents with a small wooden spoon no larger than Barra's little finger. He placed these powders in the palm of his left hand, spat into them twice, and rubbed his hands together to work the compound into a paste. The smell that came from this made Graegduz whine and Barra gag: it was a scent rich in decay, a foulness like that which comes from the corpse of a tortoise baking in the sun; but soon the paste on his hands took on a pale, greenish-yellow glow that was faintly visible even in the sunlight. "It's called *tekat-neha*," he said. He smeared a broad stripe of it across his forehead, and then held out his hands. "Come on—a bit of this on your face, and you'll have light enough wherever you happen to look."

Barra said, "A bit of that on my face and I'll vomit every meal I've ever had, back to my mother's milk."

"You're so particular," Kheperu sneered. "Leucas?"

Leucas shrugged and allowed Kheperu to paint his face with the light-paste. "It tingles."

"That's how you know it is working."

"Can't you simply *see* it—?"

"That is a joke, Leucas; you know, humor? I'm sure you've heard of it."

"That's enough," Barra said. "Let's do this."

Kheperu wiped the rest of the *tekat-neha* from his hands onto one end of his staff, and led the way. Once within the darkness, the glow of the paste was vivid, and cast considerable light. Kheperu held his staff high up over his head like a torch. The jagged rock of the roof of the cave was faintly stained a flat matte black. Kheperu smiled and said, "This is it. See that? Lampblack on the ceiling."

Barra drew her broadaxe and held it across her chest, at the ready. Leucas watched thoughtfully as she did this, then nodded silently and drew his sword. As they moved farther into the depths of the hill, the cave began to narrow and close in above, the floor rising from hard-packed earth to bare and jumbled rock. Though the light from his and Leucas' faces stayed bright, the light from his staff would gradually dim; Kheperu would renew it from time to time by rubbing his hands together briskly and using them to warm the paste. After a while, a thought struck Barra and she whispered to Kheperu, "Maybe Graeg and I should go a little ahead. In case someone's still here—they might see our light before we see them."

His reply was also a whisper. "Piffle. No man will stay down here in darkness—it is against nature. Anyone here will have light of their own, which we will see. If they can see ours, we can see theirs. Relax. I think you only want to get away from the smell."

"If I was that worried about getting away from bad smells—"

"All right, all right, *shh*. All this whispering is making me nervous."

A few steps farther on, the cave itself settled the question: it made a gradual bend to the left, and ended in a blank chamber perhaps three paces across.

The walls of the chamber were even more ragged and crumbling than the preceding parts of the cave, and its floor was paved with gravel ranging from the size of sand to the size of Leucas' head. Graegduz nosed around its perimeter, and seemed to find something: he stopped at one point, stared at the wall, and whined.

Kheperu came over and stared at that part of the wall, pointing with his staff to supplement the light from the stripe on his forehead. "Curious. Curious indeed."

Barra and Leucas followed, to peer over his shoulders. "What is?"

"Well," Kheperu sighed, "either they've found a way to pass through solid stone, or we must assume that your mutt here has made a mistake."

"Graeg doesn't make that kind of mistake. And call him a mutt again and I'll let him eat you."

Kheperu sniffed and folded his arms, leaning back against the wall. "Then, perhaps you can explain how the men we are tracking managed to walk through this rock?"

"You're the bloody seshperankh—that's your job, isn't it? We know they came in here—the lampblack, remember?"

"I have been a scholar of the magic arts for more than thirty years. I can state definitely that there is no way. It cannot be done."

"Yes, it can," Leucas said slowly; he'd been staring thoughtfully at the wall.

"Oh? Well then, O Master of Mighty Magics," Kheperu sneered, "perhaps you'd care to enlighten us poor mortals?"

Leucas shrugged. "All right." He too leaned against the wall, near Kheperu, but sideways, his breast against it as though he would press his ear to the stone and listen. He braced his feet, and suddenly cords sprang out in his neck and the long muscles of his thighs bulged in sharp relief; a low scraping grind filled the little chamber. The greenish-yellow light of his face-paint flared bright, he grunted once, and a small jagged section of the wall gave way before him, falling inward with a dull thud that Barra could feel through the soles of her sandals. The opening it left was at about waist-height for Barra, like a window, and just wide enough for one man to pass through comfortably. Leucas picked himself up and dusted off his hands, wearing a small satisfied smile.

Kheperu shook his head disgustedly. "May the gods witness how I despise you."

Leucas' smile widened to a grin. He reached out and patted the stubby Egyptian on the top of the head. "Don't take it hard, Kheperu," he said. "You should just remember that sometimes things are simple." The paste on Kheperu's face brightened considerably, but then he frowned and looked behind into the opening.

"What's that smell?"

The stench that rolled out from the opening was beyond description—worse than a slaughterhouse, worse than a battlefield of unburied dead. Barra backed away, gagging, holding her tunic up over her mouth and nose, Graegduz whimpering and sneezing and pressing against her thigh. Kheperu's eyes filled with tears, he shook his head sharply, coughing, and hurriedly began digging within his pockets. Even Leucas, shattered sinuses notwithstanding, made a face and spat—he could *taste* this foulness. For Barra, with her preternatural sense of smell, it was overwhelming; she staggered away into the darkness of the cave, fell to her knees, and spasmed into throat-racking vomiting.

Then she felt strong hands take her head, and something moist and greasy was smeared across her upper lip; its scent stabbed into her nose at once, sharp and unrecognizable—and then she smelled nothing at all. She opened her eyes to the glowing faces of Leucas and

Kheperu—the Egyptian also had something shiny smeared below his nose, and he was in the act of returning a small corked pot to an interior pocket. She took a deep breath, but the stench did not return. She spat and wiped her mouth on her sleeve.

"Again and again I'm impressed with how useful you can be, Kheperu," she said unsteadily. "I don't suppose you'd have anything to *drink* inside that robe, would you?"

Kheperu smiled and offered his hand to help her up. "Nothing that you'd want to put in your mouth, I'm sure. By the way, don't lick your lips—that nose-killer on your upper lip is a bit poisonous."

"Right," she said, nodding, leaning on him as she regained her strength. "Don't put any on Graeg."

"Oh? Can't you simply *tell* him not to lick his nose? In *Pictish*— all animals speak Pictish, do they not?" Kheperu's voice held no hint of sarcasm, but his slight superior smile made up for it.

"Shut up. Let's see what's in there."

Back at the opening, Kheperu looked over the stone plug. "More and more I believe the Tomitiri must be involved in this. See here? From the looks of it, the opening was natural. This was cut and shaped to fit perfectly—this is Egyptian stonework, or I'm a camel."

Beyond, the opening led to a passage only a span or two long, just tall enough for Barra to slip through in a low crouch; both Leucas and Kheperu came through on their hands and knees. It soon opened out into a wide, roughly circular chamber. There were a number of wooden tables in the chamber, five of them that would be chest-high on Barra in a ring around a sixth, somewhat lower, that was slightly slanted, with channels dug into its top, like the drains on a carving board. The five outer tables were crudely constructed, simply boards hammered together with bronze spikes; the one in the middle appeared, by contrast, very sturdy. The table itself was stained and crusted with some substance that looked black in the light from Kheperu's paste; Barra guessed it was old blood, although without being able to smell it, she couldn't be sure. Graegduz whined from the other side of the passage. He didn't want to come in, and Barra didn't blame him.

Various cutting implements rested haphazardly on the outer ring of tables, curved knives and small saws and hammers with long picks on their backs, as well as long-handled spoons and ladles, a selection of bronze tubes of various lengths and diameters, and a few spatulas, some studded on one side with nails. Mounds of unidentifiable detritus littered the floor around the central table; from their appearance

Barra guessed them to be discarded bits of internal organs blackened by decay and caked with a paste of blood, dirt, and gravel.

Leucas examined the central table with interest, running his fingers through designs crudely carved into the wood. "Does any of this mean anything to you?"

Barra looked at the designs, clear in the light from Leucas' face-paint. Some of them resembled Egyptian glyphs, but most seemed to be writing of some sort, in an alphabet that Barra didn't recognize, all short strokes, vertical and horizontal, sometimes connected, sometimes apparently modified by a dot above or below. "Kheperu. What do you make of this?"

"I don't know," Kheperu said hoarsely. He stood very still near the opening through which they'd entered, both hands clutching his staff as though it were a blanket protecting him from a bitter wind. "I, ah . . ." he coughed to steady his voice, then continued, "I simply cannot be sure . . ."

"You haven't even really looked."

"Barra," he began, and paused, turning his head as though to swallow with some difficulty. He wiped his mouth and continued. "There are some branches of magic with which I am acquainted only by rumor. My alchemical researches necessarily restrict my field of view within the—"

"What're you so afraid of?" Barra snapped. "Come on, out with it."

Leucas looked around, rubbing his hands together to dust off the crusted granules of whatever caked the central table. "This is necromancy, isn't it," he said heavily. "I have heard of such practices."

"Oh, *necromancy*," Kheperu said dismissively. "Well, in a way, I suppose, but you must understand that necromancy is a perfectly honest way to make a living, with a long and honorable tradition; raising the shades of the dead to divine the future or discover hidden treasure, that sort of thing, along with preparing the bodies of the dead properly for their journey after their interment . . ."

Barra cocked her head and squinted at him. He wasn't only afraid—he wasn't even *mostly* afraid; it was anger that drove this babble. Kheperu trembled with anger, veins pulsing at his temples, his breath coming in short choppy gasps; it was as though he spoke to distract himself, as though he feared that if he acknowledged his anger, it would swell beyond control and burst his very chest. "So this is no mere necromancy," Barra said carefully. "Can you tell me what it is?"

"Among the implements on the tables," Kheperu said, his voice thin with effort, "are there any of iron? Or even of silver?"

Leucas shook his head, and Barra answered, "No."

Kheperu seemed to become smaller, to press in upon himself like a boar gathering itself for the charge. "You see, necromancers are scrupulously clean. A necromantic workshop is customarily open to the night sky, well lit, and washed with water every day. A necromancer's implements are polished like mirrors, and made of the most expensive materials available, usually silver, sometimes even Hittite iron if he can afford it. All this is to avoid mixing the tissue—the organs, the blood, fecal matter, even hair—of one client with that of another, and thus confusing the influences and possibly canceling the efficacy of the magic in use. But this . . . this *slaughterhouse*"—his suppressed rage infused the word with acid contempt—"this is no work of any necromancer."

He drew himself up and spoke through clenched teeth. "This man, whoever he may be, traffics with demons."

Leucas' brows drew together. "Half-godling children?"

Barra shook her head. "The same word for different things," she told him. "Demons in Egypt are spirits that thrive on pain and suffering, and rend the souls of the dead for their amusement."

"It is forbidden," Kheperu said, "to even speak the name of a demon, for it may come when called, and thus break through into the world of light. This, this *demonist*, summons them deliberately. That is why there are no tools of silver or of iron; these metals are anathema to the Children of Apep. In Egypt, we would be rewarded for putting such a man to death without mercy."

Leucas appeared skeptical. "How is it that you have so much of this 'forbidden knowledge'?"

Kheperu regarded Leucas steadily and silently, without moving, for a long and measured breath. The paste on his brow grew brighter and brighter. Finally he said, in a low and controlled tone, "I was once accused of being such. I learned much from my questioners during the weeks of their inquisition."

"You—?" Barra breathed.

He nodded with stiff dignity. "It is why I cannot return to Egypt. The order for my execution still stands."

"But how . . . why . . ."

"I do not wish to speak of it. We have other more pressing business." He gestured toward another cleft in the stone walls of the chamber, that seemed to lead to perhaps another passage beyond. "Perhaps they have left a trail that can still be followed by your . . . by Graegduz."

Barra nodded agreement, but said, "Someday, you'll have to tell me the whole story."

"Someday. Perhaps."

The three companions lay flat among the rocks and tufts of grass at the summit of a low, gentle hill, mid-afternoon sun hot on their backs.

"How is it," Leucas muttered, "that we always manage to skip our noon meal?"

"Don't remind me," Kheperu replied. Shortly after they'd left the cave, he'd cast aside that strange and unaccustomed dignity like an ill-fitting tunic and slowly, as though awakening from a dream, he'd become once again his familiar whining, petty self. "Next time we go tracking someone, we should remember to bring a few waterskins, as well."

"Whine, whine, whine," Barra said, her hand on Graegduz's back. "All this city living has made you soft. Now shut up and look—riders."

Perhaps fifteen or twenty horsemen filed into view between rolling hills. They were obviously heading for the wide estate, olive groves and placidly grazing goats and sheep surrounding an enormous, palatial house, that centered on the top of the highest hill in view. Barra could see now a small party of riders—three of them—come from a smaller structure near the main house, that must serve as a stable, and ride out to meet the approaching column.

The cleft on the far side of the chamber had indeed led to another cave that opened on the opposite side of the hill. That cave was littered with horse dung and patches of drying urine; Barra was able to determine that seven horses had ridden out from there. The combination of her ability to read tracks and Graegduz's keen nose had led them into view of this massive estate, an hour's ride to the southeast of Tyre. Leucas had been all for assaulting the place themselves: "We could attack them—we wait until nightfall, then sneak in and grab the son of a whore, just like Odysseus and Diomedes went into Troy to steal the Palladion." Barra reminded him that they didn't know who, among the estate's inhabitants, the demonist was. "And, anyway, we're not being paid to kill him. We're being paid to tell Idonosteus who he is."

Kheperu had looked thoughtful. "Do you remember," he'd said slowly, "what I told you about some rich Egyptian coming in to buy up all the slaves under twenty? It's said that the traffick with demons ages a man unnaturally; it's also said that demons can renew a man's youth—provided they have blood of youths with which to work."

Barra's eyes had drifted closed against this thought. "Maybe we should sneak in there and kill him. Just kill him, forget the money."

"Forget the *money*?" Kheperu had said, appalled. "I think not! We can collect from Idonosteus, and let the Meneides kill this man—much safer, and more profitable."

"I think we should steal him," Leucas insisted stubbornly. "Imagine the kind of ransom such a man could pay."

"Forget it," Barra said firmly. "Kheperu's right."

"I am?"

"Ay. Let's collect from Idonosteus, then, maybe if we're lucky, he'll hire us to kill the guy."

But now, as they lay on the hilltop watching the riders, a banner unfurled from the pole of a standard-bearer who rode at the head of the column; it was bloodred and purple, and a matching banner ran up the pole on the estate house's roof, and when Kheperu saw the design on it, he gasped.

"Oh, Great Ra and the Living-bloody-*Horus*! Do you know who that *is*?"

"You're turning pale," Leucas observed with a smile.

Barra said, "Shut up. Who is it?"

Kheperu wiped his mouth with a trembling hand. "What was that you said about being lucky if we're hired to kill him? Perhaps you should rethink that idea, Barra. Perhaps we should think about collecting our fee and taking a nice long trip to Crete."

"Why?" Barra said, barely resisting an urge to throttle him.

"Because when the Meneides kill him—or someone in his household—there will descend upon this pisswater port a storm of war like none of us have ever seen. That fellow down there—who, I'd guess, owns this place—that's a fellow named Meremptah-Sifti."

"Never heard of him," said Leucas, and Barra shrugged.

"Perhaps not. But you've heard of his grandfather. Meremptah-Sifti is a grandson of Ramses the Great."

Barra felt a shock go through her, and her stomach suddenly clenched like a knotted fist. Leucas still looked blank.

"The Living Horus," Kheperu explained. Leucas shook his head.

Barra said, "Ramses is the *Pharaoh*, Leucas. Ramses the Great, this guy's grandfather, is the god that rules Egypt—and, for that matter, Phoenikia as well."

Leucas said, "Oh. Oh, my."

# 9

# *Meremptah-Sifti*

**M**eremptah-Sifti dismounted with acrobatic smoothness, swinging his off-leg forward, over the horse's head, to pivot in the saddle, and slide gracefully to the ground. His horse took this motionlessly. Lesser creatures never defied Meremptah-Sifti's will; if this horse had had the audacity, the bad judgment to shy at such treatment, Meremptah-Sifti would have killed it on the spot, as he had the last two horses he had ridden. This was a whim he was more than wealthy enough to indulge.

He strode away from the horse, leaving it to wander. Now that the prince had touched the earth, the men-at-arms who accompanied him could also dismount; one of them would catch and tend to Meremptah-Sifti's horse. It was of no concern to the prince who cared for his beasts, so long as they were always at his disposal when he wanted them. If they were not, someone would suffer.

He struck a thoughtful pose as he looked down upon his lands; they spread below this hilltop in all directions, groves of olive and fig and citrus trees, and open meadows where goats placidly grazed. He knew that he cut an impressive figure, the heavy muscles of his bare chest and arms bronzed, setting off the broad arc of black iron and shining gold of the pectoral that covered his shoulders, his unbound hair flowing, streaks within it bleached red by the sun.

Meremptah-Sifti was always keenly aware of how he appeared to others; movement for him consisted of flowing from one pose to another with pantherish grace. He stood there, well satisfied with what he saw, and with what he knew his men saw of him, while the sun sank into the sea. On the hill below him, they fell into twilight first, leaving him shining in the scarlet sunset before the high walls of his manor.

The nervous cough behind him was unmistakably Haral Mesti's. "Welcome home, my prince. How went your business in Sidon?"

Meremptah-Sifti moved only his head to glance at Haral, and he showed his gleaming teeth in a broad and predatory grin. "Perfectly. The Governor was pleased to accept my offer. Thank you for asking, Haral."

"And Simi-Ascalon? Did he not return with you?"

Meremptah-Sifti waved a languid hand in the direction of the funerary caves. "He stopped at his workshop to retrieve some tool or other. He was a bit rushed when he left—dealing with not only the Greek but that Tomitiri fellow, that Bezai managed to lure to the caves . . . what was his name? Peth . . . something. Not important; he's certainly dead by now. Sim should be here shortly."

Alongside the nervous captain was a pair of slaves, one bearing a small stamnos of wine and a cup, the other with a tray of toasted breads and slices of cheese. Meremptah-Sifti accepted the wine, and waved away the slave with the food. He drank deeply, calmly, meditatively, and presented the empty cup to be refilled. When he had sipped again, he said, "And where is Silam? Where are my mercenaries?"

"Silam is within, my prince. He—he asked me to tell you, that the mercenaries are, are not to be found . . ."

Meremptah-Sifti turned fully to face Haral, the scarlet remnants of the sunset gleaming in his eyes. He said only a very soft: "Oh?"

Haral swallowed. "The Jephunahi innkeeper told him that they went off with some trader named Murso. But no one seems to know who this Murso is, or where to find him. The mercenaries were seen, though, yesterday, in several different parts of the city. They seemed, uh, Silam said they seemed to be"—Haral visibly steeled himself—"they might have been asking about the cursed inns."

Meremptah-Sifti looked beyond his sweating captain, far to the west, where storm clouds gathered over the thin grey sliver of the sea. Jagged thunderbolts flickered beneath them, and the prince of Egypt fought to keep his rising excitement out of his voice. "Indeed. And why, Haral, is it that Silam does not make this report himself?"

"He, well, he asked me to tell you."

Meremptah-Sifti only gazed into Haral's watery eyes. He knew full well the reason Silam asked Haral to give this message; it is a burden of leadership, that no one wishes to bring bad news in person. He dismissed this; his blood sang to him a more interesting melody: *There is more than chance in this, perhaps more than simple fate*, he thought. *Now they mix in my affairs not by chance, but by intention. I must meet them. I must have them.*

And he would; there was no doubt of this. Meremptah-Sifti had built a lifetime on getting precisely what he wanted.

Meremptah-Sifti's earliest memories were of his aunties, an ever-changing flux of young women that passed through the cool, curtained bedchambers of Kallela's, an expensive and exclusive brothel on the outskirts of Ascalon. Ascalon was a main way station on the Coast Road from the Nile Delta to the Hittite capital of Hattusas on the bluffs overlooking the river Halys; the whores at Kallela's often chanced to bed nobility of one or the other of the allied empires, when these passing men espied their exceptional beauty and compared them with the now-familiar faces and figures of the women they'd brought along from home.

His aunties came and went with baffling regularity, sometimes leaving to join the wives of a wealthy man, more often being turned out as their looks began to fail; occasionally they died of the fevers that seemed to strike Ascalon so regularly. Meremptah-Sifti was a beautiful child, who swiftly learned how to wheedle a sweetmeat or a sip of wine out of any woman, whether they were already friends or not, with a combination of sly smiles and quivering pouts. He was a great favorite among the whores, and a joy to his mother. With best guess, she raised him to have the courtly manners of the Egyptian nobility, and the whores would often gather around to hear him sing or recite a legend, and pay him with hugs and kisses and strokes on his silky hair.

Kallela's had another side, as well, a duplicate courtyard and chambers, on the other side of a high, unclimbable wall. It was well-stocked with young men and boys, but Meremptah-Sifti never saw it; his mother had in mind a more special occupation for him. Despite her sheltering, he knew all about the other side, of course—his brother Simi, four years older, already worked there. Meremptah-Sifti, aged five, knew bitter envy for the first time, when Simi would sometimes brag of gifts given him by wealthy men, in exchange for the simple use of his young body; sometimes, Simi said, it didn't even hurt. Meremptah-Sifti prayed to the immortal Ra every day to give him gifts that would surpass Simi's, and to give him the size and strength he'd need to beat his brother, to grind his face into the ground and make him eat the dirt, as Simi had sometimes done to him. Meremptah-Sifti had his initial glimmering intimations of his special destiny when the first of these prayers was answered.

In the spring of his sixth year, Meremptah-Sifti met his father for the first time.

He still remembered this clearly, even now. In fact, when some minor reversal of fate would threaten his ambitions, he'd call it deliberately to mind, dwell upon it, ease his worries with the warm and glowing memory of being presented to that fat and sweating man to whom everyone bowed. He remembered the terror of walking alone, away from his mother's side, along a carpet lined with grim, threatening-faced men. He remembered the rotten-barley scent of the beer that leaked out through the fat man's pores and impregnated the rich clothing the man had worn, he remembered being taken in the man's arms, onto his minuscule lap and receiving a sloppy kiss that smelled of bad teeth and old meat. He hadn't flinched, though, had given no sign how repulsive he found this man; his mother had schooled him well—it is an essential skill of a successful whore. And then had come the moment, the single instant that defined his life: the fat man had set him back upon his feet and gently turned him to face the gathered assemblage . . . and everyone had bowed to him!

To Meremptah-Sifti, the little whoreson, all these distant, frightening men had lowered their frowning faces to the floor; they had prostrated themselves to honor him. He'd been shaken with some emotion for which, at six, he had no name. All he knew was that this rapture answered some need within him that he'd never known he had.

The fat man was Namisallu, a younger son of Ramses the Great; he was still, in those days, a vigorous man despite the increasing tolls of age and drink, still believing that little Meremptah-Sifti was only one among what would be great hordes of children. He'd given his little by-blow gifts of gold and robes and spices, and prepared to leave; he was only passing through Ascalon on the Pharaoh's business, after all. Meremptah-Sifti had clung to his kilt, weeping the sort of tears he'd learned were most effective, and had touched his father's beery heart. Namisallu promised to call again, to visit his son whenever his business took him through town.

Meremptah-Sifti's rapture lasted only until his father's departure. His mother took his fine gifts away and sold them, and his brother Simi—half brother only, child of some anonymous sailor, or soldier, or beggar, as he now knew—beat him ever harder each time Meremptah-Sifti mentioned his father's wealth, or position. Namisallu was never to return to Ascalon, although a steady stream of gifts came up the Coast Road—gifts that Meremptah-Sifti rarely had a chance to so much as see, let alone touch or play with, before they were sold by his mother.

It was about this time that Simi became interested in death. He'd talk about it, sometimes at great length, to his little brother. He'd spin theories, and try to show Meremptah-Sifti why they were true by slowly killing beetles and spiders, observing them minutely as he pulled off their limbs. Once, when Meremptah-Sifti was seven, a gull had fallen into the courtyard, and Meremptah-Sifti had swiftly gathered it up inside a blanket and carried it to his brother, a reverential offering. The gull was sick, too ill to fly; its black-opal eyes were filmed and crusted with yellowish scurf, and a pinkish froth leaked from its beak. Simi was delighted. He secreted the gull away in a back corner of the wine cellar and spent three happy days sticking it with bronze needles. When it finally died, he lovingly plucked it and gently cut it to pieces with a small knife he'd stolen from the kitchen, and during this whole three days he'd completely forgotten to torment his little brother. Meremptah-Sifti had finally discovered how to handle him.

After this time, Meremptah-Sifti became Simi's enthusiastic accomplice. Pets began to disappear around Kallela's; first birds, then cats, and even small dogs. It was not unusual for a wealthy client to try to please his favorite whore with a well-bred puppy or kitten, and it was hard for any whore to resist Meremptah-Sifti's tearful pleas to be allowed to play with this one or that one. And when he'd return, without the animal, he'd be crying even harder—the bird had slipped from his hands and flown away, the kitten had scampered over the wall, the puppy had bolted through a door left carelessly ajar—and the whore would take little Meremptah-Sifti onto her lap and rock him and comfort him until he could dry his eyes. It was here that he truly began to comprehend his power over women; at the age of nine, he gave his virginity to an achingly beautiful little whore, only five years older than he, whose favorite puppy he had helped Simi to skin alive less than an hour before.

It was not long after this that he overheard a conversation between his mother and the brothel's scribe. It seemed that Namisallu had written a letter asking that Meremptah-Sifti be sent to him, to Egypt, to be raised properly, as an Egyptian prince of the royal house. It seemed that Namisallu's loins had not been as fertile as he'd wished; the other two sons he'd fathered had both died without issue, and Meremptah-Sifti was his only living heir. Meremptah-Sifti's heart had surged with joy, until he heard his mother's dictated reply. No, she'd said, her health wouldn't stand the journey, and she couldn't allow her son to leave her. Meremptah-Sifti knew that what she really wanted was to simply stay here in Ascalon and continue to receive the sumptuous gifts that his father sent for him; it had been four years since his mother had needed to have sex with a client. She was perfectly comfortable here, lording it over the other whores, and had no desire to ever leave. Her letter in response said that she could never give up her little Meremptah-Sifti, not while she lived; and so it was at this time that Meremptah-Sifti began to plan her death.

He never considered simply running away, and if he had he would have dismissed the idea instantly. Egypt was unimaginably far away, and besides, as he'd told himself thousands of times, he was a prince. Princes do not sneak, nor do they hide, and they certainly do not run away from home.

That summer, swamp fever raged in Ascalon. Half the town was sick with it, a fever that would keep a strong man in bed for eight or nine days, trembling in a pool of his own sweat—many of the weak and sickly did not survive it. Meremptah-Sifti's mother was stricken, but she was strong and not yet old, or so the other whores said, and she had lived through a fever like this one only six years before. Meremptah-Sifti was never slow to seize an opportunity, nor afraid to recognize his own limitations; only ten years old, he didn't yet have the strength to battle his mother, even in her fever-weakened state . . . but Simi, he was fourteen, and already showing signs of the breadth of shoulder he'd acquire with manhood.

Recruiting his older brother was simple. After all, Meremptah-Sifti was leaving Ascalon to be a prince of Egypt, and he could offer his brother a simple choice: Help me, and I will take you with me, and I will be your friend and protector, you will always be by the side of a prince of Egypt, even unto the day of your death. With all my wealth and power, I will support you. Help me not, and stay here, poking little birds with needles and taking grown men up your ass until you are too old or your looks fail, and you are turned out into the street.

Simi had readily agreed; he'd been dreaming of studying the necromantic arts of Egypt for years—and this would be his first opportunity to kill a human being.

The murder was also simple. They came to her room while their mother tossed in the grip of a fever dream. Meremptah-Sifti's talent for getting his own way served him well here, as he soulfully requested that the pair of whores who attended her leave him and his brother alone with their mother for a moment; there are things a boy can say to his mother only while they are alone together, and he was afraid she might die before he could tell her . . . and that was all it took. The whores left the room, and Meremptah-Sifti watched while Simi held a pillow over their mother's face, pressing her down into the bed as she started to struggle. Her legs kicked and twitched, he thought, very much like they used to when a grunting man lay atop her, and she was pretending pleasure. Eventually, she stopped moving, and the boys spent a moment working up their tears before rushing out to cry her death.

Within a week, they were on their way to the Nile Delta, to Namisallu's estate on the outskirts of Per-Ramses, the capital. It was on this journey, on the road, that Simi the whoreson became Simi-Ascalon, the prince's manservant; it was also on this journey that Simi first showed his younger brother some of the tricks of pleasure that he'd learned on the other side of Kallela's, as a way to pass the time on the long trip. Their blood bond was never spoken of again, but once in Egypt Meremptah-Sifti proved to be a man of his word, even at ten. After all, princes are supposed to be men of honor, to keep their word, and Meremptah-Sifti saw to it that his father sponsored Simi-Ascalon into the priesthood of the House of Life.

Through the years that followed, it seemed that nothing could ever be denied to him, and so his ambitions grew with his body. As he grew, he learned—as befits a prince of Egypt—to command more, and wheedle less. He joined the army, as was expected of him, and rose swiftly through the ranks by a combination of his native ability with politicking and the occasional convenient deaths, covertly accomplished by Simi-Ascalon, of men who could not be moved from his path by any other means.

Simi-Ascalon, meanwhile, showed talent of his own. He threw himself into his studies in the House of Life with passionate abandon. In a few short years he was confirmed as a seshperankh; a few short years after that he had surpassed his teachers and followed his own path of study and experiment into ever-darker realms. His health began to fail, and he became more and more withdrawn and isolated, even among the priesthood; the other priests would whisper to each other and sidle away when they saw his hollow-eyed form approach or heard his rasping cough, but Meremptah-Sifti always had time and warmth to spare for him, always attended to his interests, listened to his complaints and his enthusiasms, hugged and held him with more-than-brotherly love.

Meremptah-Sifti might have been in Egypt still, were it not for his Uncle Merneptah, eldest surviving son of Ramses the Great and heir apparent to the throne. Merneptah was a gruff, stolid, unimaginative man who'd made his home in the Pharaoh's army for more than forty years. From their first meeting—when Meremptah-Sifti realized that his late mother had given him the first half of his name in a transparent attempt to flatter the next Pharaoh and, in her ignorance, *hadn't even gotten it right*—this seemed to be a doomed relationship. Merneptah seemed immune to every conceivable combination of flattery, bribery, and comradely backslapping; in fact, it seemed that the harder Meremptah-Sifti tried to gain his confidence, the warier and more distant his uncle became. The man seemed to have no vices or shameful secrets, or anything else Meremptah-Sifti could use against him. Worse, the soldiers he commanded were so loyal as to report Meremptah-Sifti's discreet inquiries back to their commander, and late one night Meremptah-Sifti was hauled shivering from his bed, arrested, and brought before his uncle at the army's camp outside of Thebes.

"I do not like you, boy," Merneptah had said. "I do not like you, I do not trust you, and if you were not my drunken brother's only son, if you did not have my father's blood in your veins, I would have you killed. Stay away from me. Stay away from my men. In fact, get out of Egypt for a few years; I do not want to be worrying about what you're up to back here while I'm off on campaign in Kush. Don't think I will tolerate disobedience; I can hurt you in ways that will spill no sacred blood."

Meremptah-Sifti had gathered his scattered dignity and said, "I bow to your will, Uncle. I do not know with what I am accused, and it does not matter; any claim against my honor can only be a lie. There is no man living who loves and honors you more than I. I pray that you will come to know this, and when you do, send for me."

After that, his only hope of remaining in Egypt was a swift and secret poisoning, but Merneptah remained in camp, preparing for his campaign among his loyal men; there was no opportunity.

His uncle's enmity proved to be a blessing in the end, though, as Meremptah-Sifti moved his household north and east into the District of Canaan, where he was born. Here, away from the prying eyes of crowded Egypt, he could do things he'd never dare attempt at home. In Egypt, it seemed that there were endless ranks of royal grandchildren, most of them having precedence of some sort or another over him, and there were countless high priests, and military generals, and friends of the court of this and that variety, all men that he must treat with respect, and deference. But here, here near the frontier with Hattiland, ah, everything was different. Here the politics of Egypt were meaningless.

Here there was no one who could tell him no.

In taking Egypt from him, his uncle had given him the world.

Meremptah-Sifti was dining when Simi-Ascalon rushed in, breathless and sweating. The prince reclined on a couch-length pillow of vermilion hexamitos; a pair of young slaves, brother and sister, knelt to either side of his head and gently fed him steaming bites of lamb and sips of imported Egyptian beer.

Simi-Ascalon, in his wide-eyed panic, did not await permission to speak. "Remmie!" he gasped, "Remmie, someone's been in my sanctum! *Someone's been to the caves!*" He would have gone on, but a fit of coughing overtook him, doubling him over and driving him red-faced to his knees.

Meremptah-Sifti came off the pillow to his brother's side in an instant; he'd done this many times, and he knew what was required. He laid his powerful arm across Simi-Ascalon's shoulders and hugged him tightly, gathered his head to his breast. "It is all right, Sim. Calm down, it will be all right," he murmured softly, over and over again. Simi-Ascalon's coughing began to quiet, to become little more than a shuddering of his shoulders like a child's sobbing that slowly trails to silence. Meremptah-Sifti glared at the boy-slave. "My napkin," he snapped. The boy flinched, and stared back with wide, uncomprehending eyes.

The prince pantomimed wiping his face, and pointed at the napkin. The boy swiftly gathered it up and brought it to him, and received in return a backhanded blow across the face that sent him sprawling, for not understanding Egyptian.

Meremptah-Sifti held the napkin to his brother's mouth, and pounded Simi-Ascalon's back. Simi-Ascalon coughed again, gagged, and finally spat forth a mouthful of bloody goo. Meremptah-Sifti wadded the napkin around it and tossed it aside. "All right now?"

Simi-Ascalon nodded mutely as he regained his breath, then added, "Yes—yes, Remmie, thank you. But the cave—the *cave*, Remmie—"

"Now, do not excite yourself again. Are you certain that someone has been there?"

"Yes—yes, he found the hidden mouth, he—*hrakhakh*—he threw

up there. And I think there must have been more than one; one man alone cannot shift the slab."

Meremptah-Sifti shrugged dismissively. "How many of the hyaenae did we lose, in destroying that Jephunahi caravan? Three? Four? Take the rest to the cave and put them on the scent; have them kill everyone they find. Better yet: have them kill everyone they meet along the way. This will make another lovely rumor to spread terror through the city."

"Mmn, all right, Remmie." Simi-Ascalon breathed more easily now, and the apoplectic scarlet began to drain from his face. "I'm sorry—I'm sorry I got so . . . . well, you know. I just keep thinking of them in there, walking around in there, touching all my stuff—"

Meremptah-Sifti gave his brother's shoulders a comforting squeeze, and gently stroked his face. "But they'll be dead soon, Sim. All of them will be dead before sunrise." Sim nodded silently, and the prince returned to his pillow and accepted another sip of wine from the flinching girl.

"How do you think they found it?" he said. "How could they possibly have found that cave?"

Simi-Ascalon shook his head; he came over and lowered himself into a sitting position near Meremptah-Sifti's feet. "Perhaps someone saw Bezai's men capture Peth An'khefi, and followed them?"

"No, Bezai is hardly that great a fool. Besides, you had that Peth fellow there for hours; I should think Nephrol Tomit would have mounted a rescue, if he'd had any scrap of information. And Haral, with the Greek's corpse . . . could he have disgraced himself again? Could he be followed through a moonless night?" Meremptah-Sifti swirled the wine within his golden goblet; the reflections on its surface, echoes of the lamp flames above him, were as darkly red as a dead man's blood. "But the girl . . ."

His voice trailed off. Simi-Ascalon waited a properly respectful interval—to make sure he was not interrupting—before prompting: "Yes, Remmie? The girl?"

"My mercenaries," said the prince slowly. "My three mercenaries—*the girl has a dog!*" He jerked himself up straight, his face alive with delight; the motion slopped wine from his cup across Simi-Ascalon's leg, but he didn't notice and Simi-Ascalon wouldn't dare to protest. "My mercenaries killed my Greek . . . what if they tracked his corpse?" He threw back his head in gusty, joyous laughter. "Of course it's them! Who else would it be?" He held up a fist, to display the thick gooseflesh that wrapped his forearm. "Look at my skin!" he said. "It's them! Listen, Sim, I don't want them killed—how can we bring them here alive?"

"Alive? But, but, Remmie, you promised—"

"Oh, don't trouble yourself." Meremptah-Sifti patted him on the knee with a fatherly hand. "I would not force you to forgo your proper revenge for their violations; only think how much greater that revenge can be, if they still live when they are dragged to your sanctum?"

Simi-Ascalon looked considerably mollified.

"Still," the prince said, frowning. "I like the idea of the hyaenae running through the streets of Tyre, killing all they meet . . ." He brightened. "I have it—send the Greek with them! He knows my mercenaries, does he not? When the hyaenae come across my mercenaries, he can point them out to be captured, rather than killed."

Simi-Ascalon now looked doubtful. He said, "But, but he's not ready. He's not ready yet, Remmie."

Meremptah-Sifti turned his palms down upon his knees and leaned forward, and his voice took on a dangerous silkiness. "How long before he can walk and talk?"

"Well, for that, only a few hours, but—"

"Do we have another man who knows my mercenaries by sight?"

"I, I, ah, I don't—*hrakhakh*—I don't know . . ."

"Then make him ready, Simi. Before I get angry."

Simi-Ascalon scrambled to his feet, but remained at the foot of the pillow, wringing his hands. "But, but, but Remmie, my control, my control won't be very good—and Chrysios, you know, he was a little crazy anyway, what if he doesn't want to—"

"Do whatever it takes," Meremptah-Sifti told him. "Bargain with him, if necessary. Promise him whatever you like. Only remember: kill *everyone*. Except my mercenaries—I want at least one or two of the three alive and in shape for interrogation. Everyone else, *everyone*—no mistakes—dies. Do you understand?"

Simi-Ascalon bowed to his younger brother. "It will be done, my prince."

# 10

# The Report

The servants' quarters of the house of Peliarchus were quiet again, now that Leucas had rolled over on his bunk and his snoring had trailed off. On the bunk above, Kheperu smiled and murmured something in his sleep, then he, too, quieted and the only sound was the scritch-scratch of Barra's reed pen. Graegduz snoozed silently against her ankles, warming her feet in the late-evening chill. The tiny fish-oil lamp on the table before her cast a ring of light just bright enough to illuminate the long strip of sun-bleached parchment scroll on which she wrote. The smoky grey-black taste of the burning oil nearly covered the inevitable reek of sharing a room with Kheperu, and buried completely the scent of the ink and the lamb fat that had been rubbed into the parchment to keep it supple.

*Dear Antiphos and Chryl,*

*You must be surprised to get this letter. When I sent the last one, I thought that the* Skye Swift *would be my last chance to send you a packet, but your Uncle Peliarchus is leaving for the Isle of the Mighty in a few days, as soon as he clears away some obligations here in Tyre. This time, he'll be bringing his wife, Tayniz. You'll love her as much as I do, I know; she reared me well here in Tyre—she's practically as much your grandmother as Coll is.*

*The three of us—that's Leucas, Kheperu, and myself, you remember—are staying with Peliarchus again. We had to spend a few days guesting elsewhere, because he's been hosting King Demetor of Kypros, who's a relative of Agapenthes, who is*

*Peliarchus' liege lord (in a sense), and well, it's really rather
complicated. This is the obligation I was writing about earlier.*

*I can't tell you much of what I've been doing here. I've been
paid a great deal of silver to keep it secret, and despite the fact
that your Uncle Peliarchus can't read Greek, I'll be sending this
with him, and you know how nosy he is. He'd probably go to the
Market and hire a scribe to translate it for him.*

*I'm planning to take the* Langdale's Pride *north after the
Knossian Trade Fair in the spring. Business is going very well;
Tyre has proven as profitable as I'd hoped, and we may perhaps
even be able to afford to add a third ship to our tiny fleet this year.*

*There are a few things I can tell you about, though. On our very
first day here, some sailors brought a bear through the Market . . .*

She wrote on for some time, dodging details, pausing occasionally
to trim her pen against the keen edge of her broadaxe; soon one corner
of her mouth was blue-black from chewing the reed tip into a suitable
brush. During one of those pauses, she tapped her teeth with the pen,
thinking of the day's events, then shrugged and continued to write.

*. . . in your education. Tell Abdi—as I will in a separate let-
ter—not to neglect the study of politics, especially the dynastic
politics of Egypt. If you boys plan to travel successfully here in the
East, you'd best be aware of some of the civic realities . . .*

The sun had dipped toward the west and extinguished itself in the
sea by the time the three companions had walked back into Tyre from
the estate of the Pharaoh's grandson. They'd walked in silence, mostly,
each in their own way daunted by what they'd learned. Meremptah-
Sifti was, by Kheperu's account, one of sixty-three legitimate grandchildren of the Living Horus; he was descended through the eldest of
Ramses' three living wives, Isinofre. His father was the younger of Isinofre's two sons; there was a rumor that his mother was an Ascalon-
ian whore, but this was not confirmed. Kheperu guessed his age to be
somewhere within a few years either way of Leucas' thirty-five, and
said that while Meremptah-Sifti had distinguished himself as a very
young man during a campaign in Kush—in the Pharaoh's own Ra
Division—and kept a home in Per-Ramses, the capital, he'd lately
been living in Upper Egypt, in the former capital of Thebes, to ingra-
tiate himself with his powerful grandmother Isinofre, who maintained
her household there. "Lately," in this case, meant a few years before

Kheperu's exile—he had no information more recent than the past decade—but even so, he recalled tales of scandalous libertinage and suggestions of two or three hushed-over deaths.

"And Ramses, as you may know, is an old-fashioned sort—his father, Seti, came up through the military, and raised his son the very same way—and so I'd guess that our young Meremptah is none too popular with the court. It could explain what he's up to here. He can set the Great Houses against each other, embarrass the Governor, perhaps get himself the rule of Phoenikia, which, as the main conduit between the two greatest empires of the world—Egypt and Hattiland—it would serve as an admirable base from which to contend for the throne, should Ramses die without naming a successor. This, of course, is possible, even likely, because after all, Ramses is the oldest man in the world, nearly ninety years of age, and even his deific vitality cannot hold out forever. He could die at any time, and the consequences would be staggering. As a matter of fact, I can recall a time when—"

"So," Leucas had interrupted, to forestall another lengthy disquisition of the labyrinthine politics of Egypt, "if the Pharaoh doesn't like him, why can't we simply kill the man?"

Kheperu sighed. "I despair of ever bringing you to any sort of political awareness. Put simply: it is not only the royal blood of Egypt that flows through his veins, it is the very seed of Horus the Avenger. Any spill of the blood of gods must be revenged a thousandfold. It's traditional. You see? In practical terms, if Ramses does not exact a horrific punishment for this sort of crime, then none of his blood will be safe. He could despise his grandson with a searing hatred beyond your understanding, and it would matter not a whit."

"Only cowards count the cost of doing right," Leucas rumbled.

"A fine philosophy, that led to half a million funeral pyres on the plains of Troy," Kheperu countered.

Barra had been too consumed with her own worries to step in; she let them bicker continuously until they reached the apartments of the Myrmidons. They had no lamp to go through the face-lighting business that Murso had shown them, but Kheperu swiftly mixed together a handful of his light-paste to use instead. Within minutes of their arrival, a Myrmidon runner had departed for the Meneides compound with news that they'd completed their mission and a request for a meeting with Idonosteus so that they might give their report.

*I suppose I should also tell you that I've something of a gentleman admirer. He's a mercenary captain, very brave and*

*very smart—he's a veteran of the Siege of Troy, in the company of
Golden Akhilleus, whom you might remember from stories I've
recounted—he's a fine warrior, taken all for all. It came as a bit of
a surprise, though, I must tell you . . .*

All three of them were glad enough to get off their feet. Leucas
and Kheperu had reclined on their pallets, while Barra sat with her
back against the wall, knees drawn up and wrapped by her arms. Graeg
lay beside her, head on his paws. They'd missed the evening meal, and
so snacked on cheese and hard bread. Barra drank water instead of
wine; she wanted her head to be perfectly clear for the meeting with
the Head of House Meneides.

While the companions waited, Barra watched Kamades pace the
length of the room back and forth; he occasionally flicked a glance
toward her and her friends, a deepening scowl furrowing his brow, or
made a conspicuous show of examining some piece of armor hanging
on a rack. She didn't need the *sceon tiof* to show her that the Myrmidon captain was worried about something. Finally he stopped, huffed
a sharp sigh, and strode toward her. "You'll be leaving soon, then," he
said gruffly.

Barra nodded. "Within the next few days, I'd imagine. We've completed our mission—I'd guess we'll be here for a couple of days just
to see what shakes out when Idonosteus beats the rug."

Kamades nodded stiffly in return. "It's been . . . well, it's an honor
to have hosted you, Barra."

"Thank you." She squinted up at his open, craggy face, at the long
scar that joined the streaks of white in his hair and his beard. He colored and looked away, looked back, looked at his hands, rubbed them
together and hooked his thumbs behind his belt, and finally found
something interesting about the straps of his sandals. Barra grinned at
him. "You're just dying to know what we've been up to, aren't you?"

"I am not," Kamades replied, drawing himself up. "Not at all."

"Oh, come. Tell the truth."

Kamades' gnarled hands pulled his tunic straight. He cleared his
throat. "It would be dishonorable to inquire."

"It would?"

"Yes. You are employed by my lord. If Idonosteus wishes me to
know of your mission, he will tell me."

"No offense, Kamades, but that attitude is going to dunk you in a
barrel of grief someday."

"It serves me well enough."

"It serves to keep any thoughts out of your bloody head except the ones your precious lord puts there."

Blood rose through Kamades' face all the way to his hairline. A vein bulged in his neck as he pressed his lips together against some hot reply. Finally, he said quietly, "There are some thoughts, in my head, that my lord did not put there. Good evening, Barra. Leucas. Kheperu." With that, he turned and stalked out into the corridor, his ear flaming.

Kheperu thoughtfully chewed his upper lip as he watched Kamades go, then turned to Barra. "I think he likes you."

"Of course he does," Barra said, frowning dangerously. "What's not to like?"

"No no no, you misunderstand," Kheperu told her with a naked leer. "I mean he *likes* you."

Barra suddenly felt very tired; she sagged back against the wall, painfully aware of her extremely long day. "But . . ." She looked at Leucas, who managed to suggest a shrug with only a twitch of his eyebrows. "But he's a Myrmidon," she protested wearily.

Leucas said, "So?"

Kheperu smirked. "If they were *all* like that, from where would come little Myrmidons?"

Barra pressed her eyes closed and rubbed her forehead with her fingertips. "Y'know, that's one thing I never expected, to have a Myrmidon lust for me."

Leucas rumbled, "Perhaps you should talk to him."

"Oh, no, I don't think so," she said. "I know better. He'll think I like *him*. He'll think I'm playing hard to get."

"You mean you don't?" Leucas said.

"Why should I? I mean, well, I don't know . . ." she frowned and shook her head. "It's not that I dislike him, really—I guess I hadn't really thought about it."

"*He* has," said Kheperu.

Barra took a deep breath and let it hiss out slowly between her teeth. Now that she thought about it, Kamades was a handsome man, scar or no; he was respected, perhaps even revered, by his men; he was almost certainly competent, reliable, probably a fine warrior—what her brother Llem would call *steady*. "Well, Mother's Blood," she said, now more thoughtful than tired. "A Myrmidon captain. Who'd have guessed it?"

"Anyone would, but you," Leucas murmured, a summer's smile warming his broken face. "You always forget how beautiful you are."

"Oh, stop it, you'll make me blush. Beautiful, my eye." She

shifted her weight and pulled back the hem of her chiton to expose the rippling muscle of her upper thigh. "See? Look how skinny I am."

Kheperu peered clinically at her exposed flesh. "Skinny? I should say instead rather: sleek." He coughed into his hand, and stroked his long beak of a nose to hide a smile. "Hmm, well, and remember that in these lands, most wealthy men keep their wives exclusively to produce children and to run the household—for fun, they prefer teenage boys. Some men might look at you as"—he coughed again, delicately—"an ideal compromise."

"Oh?" She dropped the hem, and her voice took on that dangerous hectoring tone. "Are you trying to tell me I look like a boy? Is that it?"

Leucas hugged his knees and smiled at the ceiling.

Kheperu spread his hands, revealing his grin. "That is, my dear lady, only an expression of my, mmm, admiration for your lovely"—his gaze shifted downward—"physique."

Barra leaned her head back against the wall and closed her eyes. If only she could catch a few minutes' sleep. . . . "I don't want to know about it, all right? I just don't want to know."

Soon the runner returned with word that Idonosteus wished to meet with them immediately. The three companions followed him out of the apartment and away from the building without encountering Kamades, for which Barra breathed a sigh of relief—and also felt a bare twinge of disappointment. She found herself vaguely hoping Kheperu was right about Kamades; the attention was flattering, whether anything came of it or not.

*Tell Coll that I seem to have inherited the* sceon tiof *from her,* she began, and then scratched it out. She hadn't yet given up on the hope that it would be only a passing thing, that the Mother would take back this gift that Barra so fervently did not want. She tapped her teeth with the pen, and went on:

> *I wish I could think of a way to teach you two how to deal with the sorts of powerful men you'll find down here around the Inner Sea. I'm only just now learning how, myself . . . and my business here in Tyre has brought me into arm's reach of several of these powerful men. They're different down here, neither quiet and grim-honest like Llem nor a cheerful braying liar like your grandda. I like ours better, I'd say—these pretend princes can't be trusted out of sight, is what I think. The trouble with these Tyrians is that they have no noble tradition; their nobility is a pack of*

*weaklings that nobody pays any attention to anymore. The real power is with the "princes" of the merchant Houses, who are no more than average Phoenikian traders writ large. Even a bloody New Tribes king—like your grandda Ouendail—has a century or more of tradition to guide his hand, to keep him mindful of his people's needs and his own responsibilities toward them. These merchant princes here do no more than keep both eyes fixed on their profit, one hand holding their own purse and the other reaching toward yours . . .*

The *sceon tiof* hit Barra like a thunderbolt, stopping her voice and widening her eyes.

The companions had been making their report, with Barra as their speaker, here in the same room where they had first met Idonosteus, and all had seemed well, until Barra's voice caught like a blade in her throat.

Her *sceon tiof* vision of Idonosteus shook her like a freezing wind. She saw Idonosteus not as a mercenary sees her employer, nor as an ordinary Tyrian sees the head of a Great House; the *sceon tiof* stripped away any lingering aura of wealth and avuncular dignity—rather than a Power of Tyre, what sat before her was an aging fat man with grease in his beard, sweating even in the evening cool, harboring desires and appetites within that quivering flesh that would make even Kheperu blanch and turn away.

*We are in danger here.*

Her hands clutched the silken pillows beneath her, and her mouth worked open and closed; she faked a convulsive sneeze, to cover her sudden incapacity.

Kheperu, ever vigilant, managed to pick up the thread of the story with hardly a break, as though he'd interrupted her on purpose. "It is painful to recount the contents of that chamber in the hills," he said smoothly, "for one is then forced to recall the smell." He glanced sidelong at Barra, as if daring her to comment. When she didn't, he continued. "Put simply, we believe that the man who cursed these inns and murdered Othniel traffics with Children of Apep. With demons, that is, my lord."

Idonosteus' thin-plucked brows drew together, and his piggy eyes narrowed until they nearly vanished within the rolls of his cheeks. In gloom broken only by the light of a single lamp, flame so still that it might have been carved of glass, his face seemed to float above his robes like the harvest moon. The porpoises and octopi of the room's frescoes seemed quietly asleep, and painted Meneus on the ceiling paused in his heroic labors to watch over the meeting like an indulgent Zeus. Idonosteus pursed his rubbery lips and waved distractedly to Murso for more wine. "Troubling, indeed," he said, while watching Murso refill his goblet from a tall amphora that stood at the head of the couch on which he reclined. "Thank you, Lysandros." He took a long draft, smacked his lips, and wiped them on his brocade sleeve. "Very troubling."

Murso/Lysandros returned to his stiff stance in back of the couch, his hands clasped behind his back, his high and narrow forehead bisected by the upward shadow of his long nose. Kheperu sat beside Barra on a similar couch, his hands waving as he described the demonist's workshop and their tracking of the riders. Leucas stood behind with folded arms, looming over them, his face disappearing into the gloom; he had only a few words of the Phoenikian that was being spoken here, and so he settled for looking grim and threatening.

". . . And so it is, unfortunately, almost certain that the demonist who has been troubling Tyre is a member of the household of Meremptah-Sifti."

Idonosteus sagged like a sun-heated wine bladder that's been moved into the shade. "Not Meremptah-Sifti himself, you don't think?"

Kheperu shook his head. "Quite unlikely, if I may make so bold a statement, lord. Magics of this sort require years of careful study; from what I recall of his early reputation, he showed no indication of developing the level of discipline this would require. Wealth, on the other hand, he would have in abundance—our demonist is almost certainly a hireling."

"Even so . . ." Idonosteus murmured, "even so." He sucked on his lower lip for a brief moment, and took another long swallow of wine. "In a way, this is worse. His protection would extend to every member of his household . . . hmmpf. This would be simpler if Meremptah *were* the magician; if that were proved, Ramses himself would order his execution . . ." He shook his head and sighed, lips stretched in a rueful smile. "An outsider—small wonder we were all helpless to detect him. Our eyes remain locked to each other's, we heads of the Great Houses, by the custom and ritual of our ceaseless dance. It took outsiders like yourselves to even consider that the culprit might not be one of us . . . hmmpf." He heaved himself upright into a sitting position and clasped his hands together. "You have done all I asked of you. The balance of your payments will be delivered to you at the apartment of the Myrmidons by noon tomorrow."

Each individual hair along Barra's arms lifted from its place with a tingling like that which heralds a cloudburst thunderstorm. She took a deep breath, forced a smile, and said with as light a voice as she could manage, "If you don't mind, lord, I think we'd just as soon take our silver with us. I'm not sure we'll be going back to the apartment now." Kheperu gave her another swift sidelong glance, but covered his surprise with a sudden feigned sneeze of his own; he wiped his hand on his robe and frowned at her with the half of his face that was turned away from the Meneides.

Idonosteus cocked his head at her, and she continued hurriedly, "With our mission completed and all, and with everything in your capable hands, I don't think we need a safe bolt-hole to sleep in anymore. I should think the whole affair will be over before anyone seeking revenge for that little business at Lidios' house could find us, and so I think I'd like to go back and stay, mm, with my *family*, you know?"

Murso/Lysandros murmured, "Peliarchus the shipmaster." Idonosteus nodded to indicate he remembered, and Barra felt a cold hand clutch her belly.

"So," she went on, "I think it'd be more convenient for all of us if we could just take the other hundred fifty with us when we leave tonight, if it's all the same to you, lord."

"It's somewhat *in*convenient," Idonosteus began. Kheperu murmured in Egyptian, "What are you doing?"

Barra replied in the same tongue, "Shut up and let me handle this." She switched to Phoenikian and said, "The longer we stay with the Myrmidons, the more chance there is of our connection being discovered. After all, we fought Chrysios' men, questioned Jephunah about his body, were seen all over town at the cursed inns, and were no doubt seen moving out toward the funerary caves. It wouldn't be that hard for someone to figure out what we've been doing, if anyone thinks to ask. And, I've had no contact with my family since the day before you hired us—if they begin inquiries through the Penthedes, well, I thought you wanted our association to remain a secret . . ."

Idonosteus' piggy eyes narrowed until again they almost disappeared, and for a moment the naked calculation she saw there chilled Barra's blood. Then he sighed, and pressed himself to his feet, and his smile was warm, almost fatherly, as he said, "You're good at this, Barra—but then, you were reared by a Tyrian trader, weren't you? And I never heard that Peliarchus the shipmaster was anyone's fool." He waved a hand over his shoulder, and Murso/Lysandros expressionlessly backed into the shadows and slipped from the room.

This seemed to call for no reply, and so Barra bit her lip to hold one back; if it pleased Idonosteus to believe that she'd have grown up stupid and gullible if she'd been reared by her own people, well, that was fine. She was getting what she'd come for—there'd be no profit in cursing him for a bigot.

Before the silence could become awkward, Lysandros returned with a large purse. He stepped around the couch to hand it personally to Barra. She weighed it in her hand, and felt her face slowly growing hot: he couldn't have counted out this much silver in the tiny interval of his absence. The purse must have been waiting in the corridor since before they'd arrived. Idonosteus smiled into his goblet, wiped his lips, and said, "This is a free reminder: sometimes *your* maneuvers can be anticipated, too. You may go now."

Lysandros showed them to the door. On their way out, as on their way in, they encountered no one. Barra retrieved her lamp from the stand by the door, and lit it from the one Lysandros carried. "Pleasure doing business with you," she said.

"It would be as well," Lysandros said softly, "if we do not meet again." He closed the door in her face. Barra shrugged and gestured for her companions to precede her.

As they walked away, Kheperu said, "Now will you please tell me what that was all about?"

"Actually," Leucas murmured thoughtfully, "I'd appreciate it if someone would tell me what any of it was about."

"Just keep walking until we're out of sight." Barra held the lamp high to illuminate their way, even though the three-quarters' moon above was plenty bright for walking.

Kheperu summarized the conversation for Leucas, who listened in his usual gravely attentive manner. He said, "Someday I should learn this language. It's tiresome to watch and listen when I have no idea what's being said."

When they'd turned a corner from the Meneides compound, Barra snuffed the lamp, said, "Come on," and started to jog swiftly through the streets. Kheperu, puffing after only a few steps on his plump stubby legs, gasped, "Why are we running?"

"Because if we hurry, we might beat Lysandros to the Myrmidons. I only hope Idonosteus didn't send his orders back with the runner who led us here tonight. Just in case, one of us will have to stay outside, so they can't make it clean. That'll be you, Kheperu. I'll need Leucas to carry all the gear, and Graeg won't follow anyone but me."

Leucas' long legs carried him smoothly and effortlessly alongside her. "What orders? What are you talking about?"

"Idonosteus wanted to send us our money at the apartment. That's why I reminded him that I have family here who'd be making inquiries if they didn't hear from me. If he thought he could get away with it, he'd have had the Myrmidons kill us all. Better there than in his home, where we'd have made a terrific mess, and might have drawn a cup or two of *his* blood, as well."

"Kill us?" Leucas' voice rose at this suggestion of dishonor. "Why? To save a few bits of silver?"

Barra grinned at him. "More than a few: three hundred Athenian large. That's my guess, anyway. Maybe he'd have a different reason, but the result would be the same. He's a treacherous bastard who'd sell his mother for a fistful of pepper and a blowjob."

Kheperu gasped, "If you've known him . . . all along . . . as a cheat and a murderer . . . why did we . . . ever take his employment . . . in the first place?"

"It's too complicated to explain. Now, shut up. Save your breath for running."

*And here's another thing: never be ashamed to plan for the worst. Sometimes it can seem a bit cowardly, and insultingly distrustful, but as a rule of thumb, I'd tell you to keep one hand on your axe and a sharp ear cocked for the soft step behind. You'll be wrong three times for every time you're right, but don't fear that; just consider that if you're brave and open and trusting, you'll pay for it with your life the first time you're wrong. Though, I must say, when you get older and you know a bit more of what drives some men, you can use a certain pretense of trust to bring out the better side of a man who might otherwise be your enemy . . .*

They loped through the streets under the swelling moon. There was little enough night traffic in Tyre at any time, but tonight they seemed to be entirely alone. Early though it was, the only glimpses of lamplight they got was what little leaked through chinks and gaps in windows tightly shuttered against the night, as though the townsmen believed that these slats of wood could block out the creeping uneasiness, the deepening uncertainty and mouth-drying apprehension of *something about to happen*: even those dull souls who missed all hints of trouble gathering like thunderheads on the horizon, even they couldn't help but register the tension in their neighbor's voice, in the quick shift of the eyes, the tendency to startle at any sudden noise, and they too locked their doors and windows and huddled around the warmth of their hearthshrines.

Three blocks from the apartment, Kheperu made a flame to relight the lamp, and then found himself a comfortable doorway in which to relax. He pointed up at the declining moon. "You have until the moon goes behind that rooftop. Then I go straight to Peliarchus and tell him you've been taken by the Meneides, yes?"

"Yes. Don't even think about trying to come in after us."

"Fear not," Kheperu said, sighing gratefully as he leaned his butt against the wall and slid to the ground. "I have little interest in heroic gestures, and I'm quite comfortable here. It has been a tiring day."

"Don't remind me," Barra said, fighting back a yawn. She gave him the purse and he plumped it into his lap. She looked up at Leucas. "Are you ready for this?"

His cracked face smiled down at her. "Always."

"Ay, I know, stupid question."

They left Kheperu behind; on the street outside the apartment block, they went through the face-lighting business and then went inside. Without a word to the Myrmidons, who lounged about the apartment polishing armor or casually dicing, Leucas set about bundling up their gear, his and Barra's armor, his weapons, their bedrolls, and the like. After she reassured an anxious Graegduz that indeed she did love him by letting him lick her face, Barra made small talk while she collected the purse and tied it over her shoulder.

One of the Myrmidons, on watch in the darkened room adjoining, called, "Rider," and an instant later Barra heard hoofbeats approaching at a canter. "It's Lysandros," the watcher said, appearing at the connecting door, a light of sudden hope illuminating his youthful features. "Perhaps he brings orders to action!" The other Myrmidons sat up straighter, a couple of them rising and flexing their arms and legs to work out the kinks of long inactivity, some grumbling murmurs of support, some expressing cynical disbelief. Leucas looked around the room at them, exchanged a meaningful glance with Barra, then very deliberately finished securing the knots that held his bundle of armor and weapons. He slung it over his shoulder, then drew himself up to his full height—this alone was enough to quiet the room—and he said, in a soft but penetrating voice, "Bring Kamades here to me." When no one moved, storm clouds gathered on his brow and a tone of command that Barra had never heard from him before gave his voice an edge of authority like the clash of bronze blades. "You," he said, pointing to the youthful watchman. "Bring Kamades here. *Now.*"

Suddenly the door was empty, the only sound the clatter of his sandals on the wooden floor.

Barra said softly from the side of her mouth, "I hope you know what you're doing."

He frowned down from high above her, then through his frown cracked an instant's fleeting wink. "Me, too."

Kamades appeared in the doorway and strode into the room. "Leucas Deodakaides. You sent and I have come." He came forward and stopped only an arm's length from Leucas. Barra admired his nerve: the huge glowering Athenian looked as threatening as a mortal can, and Kamades was well aware, from recounting of the flight in Lidios' inn, that Leucas had killed men with a single blow of the fist. The top of the Myrmidon's head came barely to Leucas' lower lip, yet Kamades looked up into those cold grey eyes with perfect calm.

"Let me pose for you this question, Kamades of Phthia," Leucas growled. "Your obedience is legendary. Does your obedience to your lord overwhelm the laws of the God?"

Kamades' brows drew together. "They are the same," he said simply, as though unable to conceive of a conflict between them.

"What if your lord orders you to violate the commands of Zeus? To leave dead foes unburied"—Barra could hear the undertone of loathing left over from the Theban Campaign—"or, worse even yet, to *murder those who are your guests?*"

Movement from the outer doorway caught Barra's eye: Lysandros, lantern in hand, had gained the corridor in time to hear Leucas' question. Now he paused, long face pinched with some unnameable emotion, as Leucas shifted his gaze to look at him over the head of Kamades, and the Myrmidon captain turned to see his proximate superior standing at the door, mouth open as though he wished to speak but was unable to find words that could express his thought.

At once, everyone in the room understood precisely what it was Leucas had asked; there came a pause, a suspension as though everyone collectively held a single breath. Kamades looked at Lysandros for a long time, his mouth grinding shut, muscles bunching at the corners of his jaw. Kamades' eyes slitted, and he released a long, slow breath, and Barra's sight was flooded with the *sceon tiof.*

Kamades stood before her, shining as though cloaked in woven sunlight. The purity of his devotion to the principles by which he lived caught at her heart, and made her ashamed that she'd ever doubted him. No wonder he could stand chest to chest with an angry Leucas: he feared nothing save dishonor.

With serene deliberation, fully aware of the import of what he said, he turned back to Leucas. "My lord would not order such things."

Leucas raised his head to stare directly at Lysandros. "And if he did?"

"He would not," Kamades pronounced with perfect assurance. "Such an order in itself is an offense to God; such an order would be proof that my lord had been forsaken by the gods and taken leave of his senses; thus the order would not have come from my lord, but from the madness which had seized him. I would not obey an order that came from a fit of madness, and I could not remain in service to a madman."

Leucas nodded, once. Kamades allowed himself a slow, grim smile, then turned to Lysandros. "Lysandros," Kamades said with the barest fraction of a bow. "Is there word from Lord Idonosteus?"

Lysandros, nothing if not resilient, stepped briskly into the room and said, "Yes: he wishes that you see to it that your guests get their gear well in order. They are leaving tonight; I had understood that they did not intend to return here, and came to arrange the delivery of their goods."

"It's well, then," Kamades replied gravely, a hint of a sardonic twinkle sneaking into his serious eyes. "We obey—sometimes, before the order is ever given."

Barra smothered a chuckle as a rosy tint crept up Lysandros' neck, and she came to a sudden decision. As she made to follow Leucas out, she stopped beside Kamades and placed her hand on his arm, and the warmth of his skin kicked her heartbeat into a gallop. He looked down at her hand, then his gaze swept upward to meet hers.

"Kamades," she said, just above a whisper, "I may be leaving town in only a few days. Would you like to visit me for dinner before then?" Her face felt hot; she hoped it wasn't too visible.

His eyes widened, and his face kindled an answering blush like a Babylon sunset. He took a deep breath, blinked, and then said in a voice thin with strain, "Yes, Barra, I'd like that very much. Where may I call on you?"

"At the home of Peliarchus the shipmaster—my foster-father. Lysandros knows where it is; I should be there any evening for the next few days, at least."

Kamades bent his head toward hers. "Unless my lord calls me to action, I'll be there. Mm, Barra . . . ?"

"No," she said quickly. "No questions, no talking, no nothing. Just show up, and we'll take everything from there. See you." She was painfully aware of the stares from the Myrmidons and Lysandros as she headed for the door.

Graegduz clicking along at her side, she joined Leucas in the corridor beyond, and together they left the building.

When they arrived back at the doorway where they'd left Kheperu, the stubby Egyptian was happily blowing spit bubbles in his sleep, a line of drool cleaning a path through the dust that caked his face and pooling in a fold of his robe. His hands were folded protectively around the purse on his lap, and he looked supremely comfortable.

Barra and Leucas exchanged another glance, one that spoke volumes, and they together shook their heads and sighed.

Barra shrugged and said, "You know, I'm thinking I could really use a bath myself."

Leucas nodded, lifting one of his hands to smear a cleaner patch through the grime on his chest. He examined his palm thoughtfully. "You think Peliarchus might have enough water left, tonight?"

"Maybe. If he does, though, I get it first."

In the meantime, Graegduz had taken it upon himself to wake Kheperu by licking the Egyptian's face. He smiled and squirmed happily in his sleep—which brought a host of revolting images unbidden into Barra's cringing imagination—and she ordered him sharply in Pictish to back off. Kheperu's eyes popped open and he wiped at his face. "Gyahh—get that beast away from me!"

"He likes you."

"It's disgusting, what you let that dog do."

"Tell me about it," Barra said feelingly. "Just imagine what this'll do to his breath."

Kheperu pushed himself to his feet, grumbling, "Now I must re-grime that whole cheek."

Together the companions walked toward the home of Peliarchus. Leucas filled Kheperu's ear with the scene in the apartment; when he reached their leave-taking, Kheperu's eyes lit up. "An assignation with Kamades?" he burbled delightedly. "Why, Barra! Let me be the very first to taunt you about this! Hmm, let's see, he's over forty, no money, no lands, no education, and no ear—he's perfect for you! When's the wedding?"

By way of answer, Barra wheeled and swung a fist that landed hard enough on the side of Kheperu's head to knock him sprawling. He blinked and rubbed his face, and grinned happily up at her. "Sensitive subject, mm?"

"Don't get ideas. That," she said through her teeth, "was for falling asleep on watch."

Kheperu said to Leucas, as the Athenian helped him to his feet, "Do you know, that's the first time she's ever hit me? I'm relieved—I'd begun to worry that this vaunted temper of hers was all an act. Do you think if I make another joke about Kamades, she'll kick me in the crotch?"

Leucas said, "I hope so."

A pair of lanterns that hung from bronze hooks cast pools of light to either side of Peliarchus' door, even though the time neared midnight. A sleepy Milo, the porter, opened a spy gate at Barra's knock, recognized them, and let them in, then went to wake Peliarchus. The old trader came stumbling out, rubbing sleep from his eyes, and spent the obligatory few minutes grumbling at Barra for dropping out of sight. Barra, for her part, spun an outrageous story about being kidnapped by pirates and waiting and pining for three days for the sight of her foster-father's ships rowing out to rescue her—she said that after three days had passed, she'd figured that Peliarchus had forgotten all about her, so she went ahead and escaped on her own, no thanks to him!

"Oh, sure," Peliarchus grumped. "More likely you got so pissy that they threw you overboard to shut you up. What've you really been doing?"

"Can't tell you," she said with a careless shrug. "You know how it is."

"No, I don't. And I heard about your brawl over to beachside."

"Keep your voice down, you'll wake Tayniz. I gave my word, Peliarchus. I really can't tell you. Listen, I need a favor. We can't go back to the place where we've been sleeping, and it's too late to find an inn. Can you put us up for a night?"

Peliarchus squinted at her and rubbed his palms across his scalp. "Who's after you?"

"No one, honest. We just need a place to sleep tonight—and to stash our gear and some silver."

"Ahh, shit. All right," he said, scowling. "Bloody Demetor and his whiners have the whole ground floor—each of the whiners had to have his own room—but the servants can sleep out here, I guess. It's a nice night, doesn't look like rain."

"Aw, don't push them out, Peliarchus. Just double them up—I don't need a room to myself."

His eyebrows arched, and he looked from her to Leucas, then at Kheperu, and back at her with an unspoken question.

"Oh, no, sir," Kheperu said, with just a hint of his usual leer. "Nothing like that—in fact, she's courting a Myrmidon!" He smoothly shifted his foot out from under Barra's stomp.

Peliarchus grinned at him. "From that fresh knot on your head, I'd guess you've been teasing Barra about something already tonight. Don't push your luck."

He led them up the rail-less inner stairs to the new second floor, still fresh enough to smell of the polished cedar of which it was built. A couple minutes of rousting servants got the arrangements made, and the three companions settled into the room for the night. Peliarchus stood at the door, leaning wearily against the frame. "You maybe don't want to go to sleep right away," he said, yawning. "King Demetor and the whiners are still out on the town; if they decide to come home tonight, they'll raise enough noise to wake Ba'al-Marqod. G'night."

As Peliarchus moved off toward his own temporary room, Leucas turned to Barra. "Did you ask him about the bath?"

Barra shook her head and nodded toward the large pitcher of water and the towels that were folded on the table beside it. "You can wipe down now, I guess. We'll get our baths tomorrow." She began to untie the knots on the bundle of their gear and dig through it.

Kheperu had already flopped, fully dressed, onto the lower bunk. "What are you doing?"

Barra held up the pencase and the roll of parchment. "I'm not sleepy right now. I'm going to write a letter."

"Oh, really?" He levered himself up onto one elbow. "To whom, might I ask?"

"You might. I won't tell you."

"All right," he said easily, and lay back down again.

Barra shook her head and chuckled. "And I'm writing it in Pictish," she lied. There was no need to tell Kheperu that Pictish had no written form.

"Barra!" he said, sounding shocked and deeply offended. "That's not fair!"

"Go to sleep."

Leucas slowly wiped himself off and climbed into the upper bunk. He closed his eyes and within seconds began to snore. Kheperu sighed, rolled over, and began his own wheezing counterpoint. Barra made herself comfortable on the stool, Graegduz settling in around her feet. She rested her elbows on the table, dreaming of home, of the late autumn storms cracking branches from the sky-topping oaks, of the frost that rimes the heather and the pale northern sun that can barely melt it by midday. She yawned deeply, stretched, and then slowly bent her head over the parchment and began to write.

# PART TWO

# Eirish Stand Down

# 11

# *The Favor*

*And, while I'm thinking about it, I want to tell you one more time to not be afraid to do favors for people, because you never know when you'll need a favor in return. You have to not be too shy about pressing for a return, too; don't be afraid to push hard. And don't leave a favor uncollected for too long—you'll get the reputation of being softhearted, which is dangerous, especially so if it's a bit true. Also, a favor becomes more meaningful—a bit more special to the person you're doing it for—if you present yourself as the sort of person who doesn't ordinarily d—*

The thunder of fists against a door and the clamor of shouting men made Barra jump and drop her pen. These were no playful hammerings and prankish shouts: they had the tempo of panic and an edge of desperation. She found herself on her feet reaching for her axes before she really registered what was going on—that the pounding and the shouting all came from outside, on the street, that her axe belt was draped over the chair across from her, that she was barely half-dressed. Graegduz scrambled to his feet shaking off sleep, his ruff fully expanded and a low snarl in his throat. On the bunks across the room, Kheperu tossed himself into bleary-eyed semi-alertness. "What . . . ? Mmm, what?" Leucas snored on, undisturbed.

"Get your butt out of bed and kick Leucas," Barra snapped as she tied off her breechclout and reached for her belt. "Something's wrong."

" 'S just King Dinky and the, the whiners—"

"*Listen*, shit-in-the-head! Does that sound like some happy drunks back from a night on the town?"

Kheperu frowned and cocked his head; his face cleared as recognition triggered his pulse and sleep washed away. He rolled out of the bunk, popped energetically to his feet, and began to shake the snoring Athenian.

"*No time for that shit!*" Barra barked. She sprang over to the bunk and smacked a stinging slap across Leucas' face.

His eyes popped open. "Hey—"

"On your feet and arm yourself!"

Though he slept like a stone, Leucas had the ability to come fully awake in a single surge. In the space of two breaths, he had his round shield of layered bronze and ox-hide on his arm and his man-length spear in hand. Barra spun away from him and kicked open the door to the balcony. In the courtyard below, Milo was unbolting the door. Quicker than thought, she drew a throwing axe and whipped it singing through the air to thud deeply into the door a foot away from his face. The porter jumped back with a cry, the bolt dropped back into place, and Barra shouted, "Touch that door and the next one goes into your skull!"

"Shit, Barra," Leucas murmured behind her. "Isn't that a bit harsh?"

She wheeled and jabbed him in the solar plexus with her stiffened fingers. "We have no *fucking clue* who's out there, and this is my *family*! Any more *stupid fucking questions*?" She punctuated this with a shove sharp enough to make the boxer grunt and step back. She turned away without waiting for a response, snapped, "Now get your butts down there!" and threw herself over the rail. She dropped into a roll on the flagstones and was at the door peering through the spy gate in the blink of an eye.

Kheperu said, "She seems a bit tense."

Leucas nodded tightly. "I'm a bit tense, myself."

Peliarchus and Tayniz both appeared at the door to their room, making inquiring noises and rubbing their eyes; Leucas and Kheperu brushed past them without a word. By the time her two partners made it to Barra's side, the whole house was in an uproar, the seven servants streaming down the stairs jabbering to each other, Peliarchus in the middle of them shouting about the damage Barra's axe had done to his cedar door. Tayniz stopped two steps above the yard, drew her shawl tighter around her shoulders, white-knuckled hand holding her robe closed over her ample breasts, and shouted, "Everyone, *be quiet!*"

Years of haggling in the din of the Market of Tyre had given Tayniz a voice that could pierce a bronze cuirass front and back. Her tone made it clear that she was mistress of this house and by God every single soul who lived here would do as she says or suffer for it. The babble abated as everyone turned to look at her, except for Graegduz, who stood expectantly at Barra's side, and Barra herself, who was already fumbling with the bolt. Outside the clamor had turned to recognizable words, begging for entrance.

Tayniz said, her voice overcontrolled and leaning toward shrill, "Barra. What is happening? Tell me what's happening!" Tough and loud as she might be, an explosion of shouts and hammering in the middle of the night takes some getting used to; even Peliarchus, more accustomed to sudden awakenings due to his travels on the trade routes, was clearly unnerved.

Barra began to swing the doors back. "Leucas—Kheperu. Stand ready." She spoke in Greek—she had always been the lone member of the household who could get away with ignoring her foster-mother. "It's Demetor and his men, and he looks sick. Just be ready until we know for sure there's nobody else out there."

Two of his men carried in the Kypriot king, supporting him by holding his strengthless arms about their shoulders. Demetor was only semiconscious, and Barra knew instantly what had happened to him, even before the light of a lamp held too close to his face made him begin to thrash against the grip of his friends. His flowing white beard dripped vomit, and the rich embroidery of his overrobe and stole were both soaking, and the roast-acorn smell of the pukenut extract was, to her nose, unmistakable even through the overpowering reeks of beer, wine, half-digested meat, and stomach juice. Three of his eight companions were similarly affected, and Barra waited for no explanations and would allow no one to question them until all four men were gently laid on fresh linens in the master bedroom and the windows were safely shuttered against even the light of the waxing moon.

She shooed everyone out, and stood a moment alone in the middle of the room, to look at the stricken men around her and think. They'd have to be cleaned up, have the vomit swabbed off their skin and combed out of their beards, but gently; any sudden movement, noise, or bright light could seize them and kill them. She thought that they just might live—the vomiting must have ejected a substantial amount of the poison, and they wouldn't be drinking any more of it. On the other hand, these were none of them young men, and Demetor himself had seen more than sixty winters, possibly nearly seventy. She looked down at him, at his flowing spray of surf-white hair across the pillow, his eyes rolling behind closed lids, and thought of the cheerful, befuddled old king she'd seen in his hall at Paphos, eyes wide as he'd hemmed and hawed at Kheperu's Wandering Seer act, willing to try or pay almost anything to protect his people from the manslaughtering boar. She'd despised him then, for his pompous foolishness, and laughed at him in memory many times since, but now as he lay before her, that scorn and laughter lay bitter in her throat. How many years would it be before her own father Ouendail would lie as helpless as this? How long before Peliarchus would? In some depth of her spirit, chains of kinship were being forged, how or where she neither knew nor cared; wherever the connection she felt with this fallen king came from, it was undeniably real. She felt the slow, rising surge of her temper coiling upward to aim at Meremptah-Sifti and his demonist, and clamped mental hands around it to hold it in check. The Meneides, she told herself, would handle that problem for her. Her efforts would be better spent right here.

The Kypriots clustered like nervous sheep around the courtyard door. Barra had to force her way between them as she strode out from the bedroom, back into the crisp night air of the courtyard, and took a deep breath to clear her nose. She ignored the questions they pressed on her and grabbed the arm of one of the Kypriots. "You, and maybe one other guy, can stay in there with them. Clean them up, gently, and keep them quiet—nothing loud, keep your voices down, no lamps, no nothing. If any of them get seized, try and hold them so they can't hurt themselves. Understand?"

The Kypriot, a tall man with a bloated face behind his beard, glared blearily down at her. "Who th'fuck are you?"

Barra was a past master at handling drunks; she grabbed a handful of his beard and hauled his face down even with hers, ignoring the watering of his eyes and his yelp of pain. "I'm the woman who'll split your thick bloody skull if you don't do as I say. If you don't, and King Demetor dies tonight, so do you. You understand?"

He nodded mutely, and she released him. The other Kypriots wisely refrained from questioning her orders. She left them behind; she went to where Kheperu and Leucas stood at the street gate, side by side, peering out into the darkness beyond. "There's no one else outside," Kheperu said. "King Dimwit and the whiners—it's the curse, isn't it?" A pair of servants, inching close to eavesdrop, gasped and skittered away to pass along this tidbit.

Barra sighed tiredly. "Oh, well done. Very nice. You're a fine one to be calling someone else a dimwit. Now they'll all be in a panic."

In seconds Barra was at the center of a crowd. All the Kypriots unaffected by the curse yammered questions at her, since she seemed to know things they didn't; the servants clutched at her and begged to be told if the king had brought the curse down upon this house as well. Barra howled at them to shut up, but even Graegduz's snarled support was lost in the noise. Peliarchus gave no help—the shipmaster sat on one of the yard couches, his head in his hands. Finally, Barra raised her head and caught Tayniz's eye; the pleading expression on her face spoke clearly. Tayniz took a deep breath and blared, *"Quiet!"*

Once again, it worked.

With Tayniz's support to lend authority to her orders, Barra swiftly got the courtyard under control: the Kypriots calmly seated, with mugs of wine at hand, and the servants—except for the porter—packed off to their room. It took a bit of work to get the near-incoherent story.

Demetor's party had split into two groups, when the king had wanted to move on from the brothel where five of his men—these five in the courtyard now—had cheerfully passed out. They'd heard a story earlier about a Tomitiri tax collector and his bodyguards being murdered on the street, and in their alcohol-dazed state, they'd decided it would be fun to see where the killings had taken place. Massacres and brutal murders, after all, are subjects of the most enduring interest—especially when they're so recent. They'd ended up at a nearby inn, one nearly deserted, where they more or less took over the place and drank themselves stupid. This place had been, Barra surmised with some assurance, a Tomitiri inn; the pattern seemed identical to what had happened to Lidios. Meanwhile the men they'd left behind had regained consciousness, though not sobriety, and these had decided to venture forth into the night in search of their friends. It was the bowl of water that Demetor and his friends had downed to clear their heads for the walk home that had struck them with the curse, Barra knew, though she said nothing; the curse and all knowledge surrounding it was covered by the contract with House Meneides. She had given her word, and been paid, and even Idonosteus' presumed treachery didn't release her from the obligation to keep her mouth shut.

Peliarchus was near shock; the devastating image of Demetor dying while under his hospitality drew haunted shadows under his eyes. Though Agapenthes himself was as Tyrian as any sharp-eyed trader in the Market, the House Penthedes traditions traced proudly back to Mykenai. By the sacred laws of hospitality as practiced in Akhaia, Peliarchus—as host—was personally responsible for any untoward fate that befalls his guest, even one hosted unwillingly. Add to that bonds of blood—Agapenthes may despise his cousin, but blood is blood, after all—and the future Peliarchus saw before him was bleak indeed.

Barra crouched before him and gripped both his shoulders. "Hey, cheer up, Peliarchus," she said softly. "I think we can save him. Save them all."

Leucas and Kheperu frowned at each other. Peliarchus said, "You think so?"

"Kheperu can . . . lift this curse. Can't you, Kheperu?"

The Egyptian looked doubtful. Barra said leadingly, "If we can find the right components . . . if we go out for a little while . . . and talk to a friend of his . . ." She nodded and smiled at him, but the knot of muscle at the corner of her jaw and the tight-clenched teeth said, *Back me up or I'll smack you one.*

The realization that Barra was, for once, *asking* him to lie brought a bright manic gleam to Kheperu's beady squirrel's eyes. He rubbed his hands together briskly. "Oh yes, well, actually, she's being a bit overly delicate. Yes, in fact . . . I must go out into the darkness and summon a spirit, yes, well really a sort of minor god, if you must know—yes, that's indeed what must be done. The only question is, *when* will it come?" He stretched his thick neck to ostentatiously scan the sky. "All portents appear to be good, and, of course, I can make it clear in my summoning how urgent the matter is; this is done by the melody of the chant which accompanies—"

"Save the details," Barra interrupted firmly, "there may not be time. Leucas and I will go with you—to . . . er, guard against dangerous influences." She looked up, and chanced to meet the eyes of Tayniz. Her foster-mother stood behind Peliarchus, arms folded and her lips pressed together. Tayniz had a way of looking at you that reminded Barra of Coll, her real mother. They both had a manner of silently gazing into your heart, like they know you better than you know yourself, and they're mildly disappointed in you but love you in spite of it, like there's something that you would know you should be doing right now, if you were any kind of proper daughter. It always gave Barra a mild case of the creeps. Tayniz lifted her eyebrows by a hairsbreadth, and suggestively swung her gaze down to where the porter stood sulking by the foot of the stairs. "All right, all right!" Barra muttered through her teeth. She grabbed Kheperu's sleeve and slapped Leucas on the shoulder. "Come on, get a couple lanterns, we're going out."

Leucas said, "Out?"

"I'll explain later." With an exasperated glance back over her shoulder at Tayniz, she marched over to the porter. Milo pretended to be examining his folded hands, while flicking fearful glances toward Barra from beneath his lowered brows. "Look," she said, "I'm sorry I frightened you."

At this, the porter's head came up, while Barra cast around in her mind for something else she could say, to make the poor man feel as though she valued him and his service. "My friends and I are going to go out now, for a while. While we're gone, don't let anybody in, all right? It's very important, and we're all counting on you for this. Don't let in anybody at all, not even me, unless Peliarchus or Tayniz personally tells you to. All right?"

"I weren't frightened," Milo mumbled. "You was always excitable. I knew it weren't personal. I'll take care of it, Miss Barra, you know I will."

"You're a good man," she said. Tayniz, above and behind the porter's shoulder, gave Barra an infinitesimal nod. Barra sighed—that was her foster-mother all over, to be worried about proper handling of the servants while the world burned down around her.

Milo held the door for her while she retrieved her throwing axe, and the companions went out.

Once the door was closed behind them and they were moving away in Barra's wake, Kheperu said, "Let me see if I have this wrapped and tied. We're going to the Market to see Tekrop-nekt, are we not? We shall haul his ass out of bed and pay his exorbitant price for whatever useless herb he claims will cure pukenut poisoning, and for what? For King Demetor, whom you despise?"

Leucas said softly, "It is our obligation. He was our host on Kypros; we are guest-friends."

Barra nodded. "That's right. You're both right. We're guest-friends and I despise him. So what?" She smiled thinly to herself as she thought of the words she had just written in her letter to her sons. "First, though, we're going to go down to that Tomitiri inn and knock a hole in their rain barrel."

"But why?" Kheperu insisted.

Leucas looked down at him. "Because we might be able to save several lives."

"So? What good does that do for us? It will stir up Meremptah-Sifti—he'll know someone is on to his pukenut curse."

"He already knows somebody's on to him," Barra said grimly. "I yarked my breakfast at the demonist's chamber this morning, remember? The next time he shows up to do a little magic, he'll bloody well know someone's been there. As for the inn, I don't expect you to understand." How could she explain? She didn't know what the *sceon tiof* might show her on a corpse, especially one whose death she could have prevented; she didn't know what it would feel like to see deeply into the life of someone she'd chosen not to save. She never wanted to find out.

"What about our *rest*?" Kheperu went on. "Have you lived through the same day I have? Do you remember what *sleep* is?"

Barra nodded and fought back a yawn. The last thing in the world she needed right now was to be reminded how tired she was. "Let's say only that I feel a little responsible. I live here—these are my people, I guess. Nobody chooses where they're born, but you can choose where to live your life, and—ah, forget it. I don't need a reason. We're going to do it because I want to, that's all."

"Oh?" Kheperu replied haughtily. "And what if I do not?"

Barra grinned at him. "Nobody asked you."

Even the moon was slanting toward the sea as the companions threaded through the silent maze of the Market toward the shop of Tekrop-nekt. They moved cautiously, carrying no lamp, through strips of silver moonlight separated by shadows so deep that to step into one was to wink out of existence. When Kheperu stumbled against some carelessly left rake, with a sharp clatter and a sharper curse, Graegduz whirled snarling to face him, and Barra found her axe had come to her hand and her heart seemed to choke her throat. Even stolid Leucas jumped, and after that, walked with his shield in place on one fist and his naked sword in the other.

Ever since they'd left the Tomitiri inn, its rain barrel draining through the hole chopped by three swift strokes of Barra's axe, Graegduz had walked pressed against Barra's thigh, and she'd felt his long, low growl rumbling warmly through his deep chest. It was then that she'd had Leucas and Kheperu douse their lamps, and follow a path that wound through alleys and along rights-of-way between houses with barred doors and locked shutters; the prickling at the nape of her neck persisted, though, and had grown to a skin-crawling conviction that they were no longer alone on the starlit streets of Tyre. A shifting breeze hushed in her ears, and the occasional scrape of stone or wood might have been as much a natural sound of settling buildings as a sign of pursuit; twice, though, her nose had caught a whiff of animal musk, underlain with meat rich in black decay and the faint greenish reek of an egg left for days in the sun. On the first of these, the wind had been from the west, and the second had come from the south. Dark masses of clouds roiled there, in the south, flickering tongues of thunderbolts between them, and the scent of rain was also in the air. Barra nursed a prayer in her heart that whatever was out here had nothing to do with them, and that they wouldn't attract its attention.

All three of the companions were exhausted; a day of relentless activity from before dawn to well after midnight had left Barra's legs heavy and stiff as stone. Even Leucas walked with his head down, his shield and bared sword swinging limply beside his thighs, and Kheperu was so tired he'd barely said a word since they'd left the inn.

From ahead, now, came definite sounds of activity, low voices snapping irritably just below the threshold of comprehensibility, the clap and clatter of boards being stacked and the fresh rip of tearing cloth, and one voice raised in a fulminating Egyptian curse.

"That sounds like Tekrop-nekt himself," Kheperu murmured. "Perhaps we should hurry."

Leucas frowned. "It might not be a good idea to rush up on them."

"Oh, ay," Barra said. "On these streets in the middle of the night? They're likely as nervous as I am."

"True enough, I suppose," Kheperu said with a sniff. "There's no honest business that would take a man to the Market at this hour."

When they came in sight of Tekrop-nekt's shop house, Tekrop-nekt and his huge bodyguard Met were busily stacking the pine slats that had formed the frame of Tekrop-nekt's shop onto the back of a mule cart. There was no mule in sight; Barra suspected that those empty traces would end up going around Met's meaty shoulders. Nor were there lamps; like the companions, these two Egyptians relied on the moon's intermittent illumination. Barra cautiously hallooed from well down the street. They both startled like spooky horses: Tekrop-nekt clutched his chest, gasping, and Met leaped wild-eyed in front of him, that grey-black scimitar finding his hand with impressive speed.

"An odd hour to be out of bed, Tekrop-nekt," Kheperu called softly. "It is I, Kheperu, with the northern girl and the Greek."

Met shifted his weight forward into a more assured fighting stance, both hands on his sword. Tekrop-nekt came up behind his shoulder, squinting suspiciously through the moonlight. "I know you, Kheperu. What do you want?"

"Only a few moments of your time," Kheperu said soothingly. He spread his hands, showing his empty palms, and began walking toward the nervous pair. Barra beckoned to Leucas, and followed. "I take it that you have suddenly discovered urgent business in some less troubled city?"

Tekrop-nekt's answering laugh was thin to the verge of being shrill. "Urgent business? Oh yes, it *became* urgent when Peth An'khefi was slaughtered by invisible demons in bright Ra's afternoon glory this day in Nephrol Tomit's very courtyard!" His mouth twisted, and his hand speared out over Met's shoulder. "And that is *close enough!*"

Kheperu slowed, but kept approaching, speaking in his best wheedling undertone. "You won't turn us away, will you? On a night like this, I suppose our next destination must be that very home of Nephrol Tomit, to carry the tale of his oath-bound alchemist taking his powders elsewhere in the middle of this dark night . . ."

This brought a clear tic to Tekrop-nekt's thin and lipless mouth. "No, no please—what do you want, I can help you . . ."

Without taking her eyes off Met's glowering face, Barra put her hand on Leucas' arm, and said softly in Greek, "He's leaving because one of the Tomitiri men was killed the same way as Othniel."

"Hmm, I don't blame him," Leucas said, nodding with a thoughtful frown. "Ask the fat one if he wants to sell that sword." Barra rolled her eyes at him, and he said defensively, "I haven't seen an iron blade since the Sack of Troy—a sword like that should be in the hands of a man who can use it."

In the meantime, Kheperu had explained what they were after. Tekrop-nekt scratched at his topknot and chewed his lower lip; like many men who love their work, Tekrop-nekt could be put almost entirely at ease by calling upon his expertise. "Well, there is no cure for pukenut poisoning; that is, no antidote," he said slowly. "The best one can do is offer an infusion of poppy oil and nightshade in straight wine—it's commonly the convulsions that kill, not the pukenut itself. Of course, the cure can be deadly, as well, if too much is taken."

"Yes, yes, of course," Kheperu said irritably. "Am I a bloody novice? I'll take the poppy oil and nightshade straight—I can prepare the infusion myself."

"Oh, no, no," Tekrop-nekt said, his eyes going wide once again. "I was not proposing to *sell* these things to you. All of my wares are packed away; I cannot spare the time to unpack them." Met, who still held his scimitar before him, emphasized his agreement with a twitch of the blade.

Kheperu's hand dipped within his robe and came out with a fist-sized leather purse that jingled suggestively. "How much is your time worth?"

Tekrop-nekt's feathery brows drew together as he considered the question, and the wind shifted, blowing now full on Barra's back. The fine hairs on the nape of her neck lifted, and Graegduz began to growl: that musky reek of decay and rotting eggs forced its way into her head, strong enough now to wrinkle the noses of the Egyptians, even Kheperu. Barra said in Greek, "This negotiation? Kheperu, I tell you, make it fast. I want to get out of here."

Kheperu nodded and turned back to the other Egyptians, but before he could speak, Met lifted his head to peer beyond Leucas' shoulder and said in a high, fluting eunuch's voice, "We are not alone, here."

A thick bank of cloud blotted out the moon; suddenly the Market vanished into darkness so complete they might as well have been struck blind. Barra cursed under her breath and reached out to touch Leucas. When her hand found his massive oak-hard arm, she drew one of her small axes and slid around to put her back against his; his back was as reassuringly solid as a wall of stone, but through it Barra could feel the pounding of his heart. The smell was thick enough to taste on her tongue.

As she moved into place, she murmured in Greek, "Kheperu—ready some light."

His reply was low but crisp. "Two steps ahead of you, my dear."

The voice that grumbled in the darkness spoke Greek, but nothing else about it suggested that it came from a human throat. Lisping, with a halting stammer that chopped at its vowels, it spiraled between a moan and a shriek and back again without any recognizable inflection, or aspect of reason, as though it were a first attempt at speech by a creature who had read of the concept, but had never had anyone with which to converse.

It said, *"My Master . . . has instructed . . . me to extend his hospitality . . . in this invitation . . . to you, Leucas, Barra, and Khe . . . and Khe . . . Khe . . . Kheperu! Khehhperrruu!"* This drawn-out shriek became a scream of inhuman rage, a bubbling roar of berserk fury that battered Barra's ears and leeched strength from her knees—she could feel even Leucas flinch. The scream cut off cleanly, as though chopped through with an axe, and in the ringing silence she heard Kheperu's wordless moan of terror and a sudden patter of fluids on the street— from the sound, his bladder had let go.

The scream returned, louder than before: *"Kheperuu! Kheperu! I want my faaace! I want my face Kheperrrrruuuu!"* It was joined by Kheperu's rising howl of mortal fear, and then by other voices, yipping laughter from a dozen throats, from lunatic giggles to high-pitched screaming guffaws, staccato bursts of mindless hilarity from every direction.

She felt, rather than heard, the rumble of Leucas' low chuckle against her spine. "What's so funny?" she snapped, and in his reply the warm beginnings of his berserk battle joy heated up each word.

"After all this time in this godsforsaken hole," he said with a laugh, "how pleasant it is to finally meet someone who speaks Greek!"

An instant later, all voices were blasted away by the explosion of a brilliant thunderbolt directly overhead. The vivid flash stilled forms already in motion, capturing a single instant of the arc of the leaps that brought the creatures forward to attack. Only one man hung screaming in the blaze of afterimage that filled Barra's eyes—an unarmed man, who wore only a girdle and Egyptian kilt—but at his side bounded nightmare dogs, powerful forequarters leading to long, flexible necks thicker than their fox-like heads, foam trailing from their jagged needle teeth, tails that seemed to hang loose and limp between their short and spindly hind legs.

It was the *dogs* that laughed.

Another thunderbolt opened the sky, and rain drove down upon them. Barra reached down and grabbed a handful of Graeg's ruff, with a sharp command in Pictish to stay at her side. She felt Leucas tense at her back, and knew that these nightmare dogs must be racing in from his direction as well. She couldn't tell what had happened to Met and Tekrop-nekt, though she could hear Kheperu's shriek still rising. The rush of the rain covered the footsteps of the dogs, and they'd stopped their insane laughing, so she waited, blind and deaf, trying to breathe past her hammering heart. The moment stretched out agonizingly, endlessly, an eternity passed between each heartbeat; when they hit her it was almost a relief.

They hit her low, going for her legs—needle teeth sank into her calf, and she swept her axe downward. It struck something that gave a hollow thump, not like flesh at all, but the teeth released her. She heard Leucas shout, and the sure support of his back left her, and scrabbling claws were all around her, and the dogs crashed into her and took her facedown to the street that was rapidly turning to mud. She tried to scream past a mouthful of water and earth as strong jaws gripped her wrists. She felt power in these jaws that could bite through her bones like dry pastry, but she also felt the restraint that stopped them; they pulled at her arms so she couldn't turn over, trying to hold, not to maim. And then one stepped onto her back, and its jaws took her neck.

In her mind, the words spun crazily: *My Master has instructed me to extend his hospitality in this invitation to you.* Maybe in some insane way, he'd meant it. Maybe if she didn't struggle, they wouldn't hurt her. Maybe resisting would only make it worse. Maybe—

Then light came, some kind of flickering orange glow like torch-light. And something from behind her hit the one whose teeth gripped her neck—the teeth raked free, and the dog rolled into the mud before her, locked in a snarling maelstrom of fur and fangs with Graegduz. Barra yelled and twisted desperately, swinging her legs up to kick at one of the dogs holding her arms. They giggled high in their throats, and stared at her with malevolent yellow eyes, and held on.

It was the limberness of her bulldancing training that finally freed her. She managed to get her left foot locked against the jaw of the one that held her left wrist—she shoved with her foot and yanked her arm, her flesh ripped through its teeth and her arm came free. Its drool burned like fire in the wounds, and it scrabbled to regain its hold, but Barra had already freed her broadaxe. She struck it a glancing blow that set it back on its haunches, then swung the axe in a whistling arc at the forelegs of the one that held her right wrist. It connected with a thud, and the dog barely seemed to notice. She twisted and got her legs under her, came to her feet to get a real swing, and this time the axe bit into the dog-thing's spine just behind its skull, a decapitating blow that didn't decapitate. No blood spurted; the axe didn't penetrate more than a finger's length. The dog-thing released her, though, and Barra watched it for an instant of frozen disbelief.

It stood, unsteadily, its head dangling from the thick muscles at the front of its neck, nose twisting an inch above the mud, the ends of its severed spine clearly visible in the dry, bloodless wound, then it turned uncertainly and trotted off into the darkness, moving half-crabwise so that one eye of its dangling head could be kept pointed in the direction in which it moved.

The thought, when it came, made her hair lift and her hands tingle like a near miss by a thunderbolt: *Graeg is fighting one of these monsters.*

She sprang up and over the snapping jaws of another one, an aerial somersault that brought the blade of her broadaxe into its skull with crushing force—again, the sound it made through the shouts and hideous laughter of the battle was a hollow, bloodless thump, as though she'd struck a leather-wrapped barrel—and when she landed skidding in the mud, the dog-thing jumped at her belly as though it had felt nothing, as though the gaping wound showing splinters of bone was no more than a scratch. She batted its slashing jaws aside with the haft of her axe, and on the backswing she buckled her knees and swept the axe in a flat arc only a span off the ground: it still wouldn't cut deeply, but the dog-thing's foreleg snapped with a satisfying crack. She turned away from it instantly, in search of the young wolf.

Graeg still struggled, held down in the mud by a pair of them: one's jaws chewed a hind leg and another's teeth sank deep into his shoulder. Barra shrieked and leaped among them, straddling Graeg's body and swinging wildly before and behind. Her axe struck them again and again, doing no very serious damage but driving them snarling back long enough for Graeg to gain his feet. Barra risked a quick look around, hoping to find some help on the way or an inviting piece of wall that she could get her back to.

The light by which she saw came from flame that sprang out of the mud, as though it was the street itself that burned, the rush of rain hissing into steam above it. It flamed in a broad ring around the place where Kheperu struggled with the dogs' master. The man's clothing was on fire as well, and his smoking hair was blackened and sparked here and there with glowing coals. As she watched, Kheperu tripped the man up with a very neat sweep of the staff, sending him falling back into the flames once again.

Understanding came to her in a single instant flash: that piddling sound, when Kheperu had first moaned in terror—that hadn't been Kheperu's bladder emptying onto the street, it had been one of his potions, some distillation he must have carried within his robe. Clever man—no matter how frightened he got, it never stopped him thinking of ways to shave the odds in his favor. And he needed it: the dog-master—even now, Barra couldn't think of him as Chrysios—climbed back to his feet, out of the flames.

Kheperu struck him a wicked blow across the temple that split skin back from bone, and the dog-master didn't seem to notice. Kheperu followed with a whistling overhand, and the dog-master caught his staff with one hand, twisted, yanked it away, and threw it aside. His howl, "*I want my face!*" was matched by Kheperu's scream, and Barra could hear the difference now, the raw ragged edge of true terror. The dog-master clubbed a fist and, almost casually, battered Kheperu to the ground with a single blow. Kheperu's shrieks never stopped; he covered his face with his arms and tried to roll away, but the dog-things closed in laughing upon him.

Barra drew her remaining throwing axe and hurled it through the flames; it struck the dog-master in the back, and bounced off his bare flesh. He did not trouble to so much as turn and look.

"All right, I admit it," she muttered. "We're in trouble." As always, when in desperate circumstances, there was one thing she could do. She shouted, "Leucas!"

The giant Athenian danced among a giggling, snapping mass of the dog-things, weaving a whickering net of bronze with his short-sword. The small shield he used also became a weapon, hammering left and right with crushing force. The dog-things kept a respectful distance around him, not willing to press too closely, always trying to dart in to snap at his heels. Any that came close enough to bite paid for it with a dry cut or a broken skull. He matched their lunatic laughter with some of his own, and his eyes danced with manic joy. At his feet lay the massive mound of Met, scimitar lying carelessly alongside—two dog-things still tore at his unmoving body, their heads disappearing within the yawning wound, lipped with yellow globs of fat, that opened across his belly. Barra thought, *I guess he wasn't invited.*

"*Leucas!* Quit fucking around, Kheperu's in trouble!"

Leucas lifted his head at her shout like a chariot horse hearing distant battle horns. She had no chance to see what he did about it because she had to turn and cut at another one of the dog-things that tried to take advantage of Graeg's unsteadiness. Graeg limped badly, struggling on three legs—his left rear leg, the one the dog-thing had latched on to, could bear no weight. He still snarled and half-lunged at the snapping dog-thing, but Barra could tell his heart wasn't in it, it was only a show, a pretense. He was seriously hurt.

The pelting rain had pulled Barra's hair free of the pins that held it, and now she had to slap it out of her eyes as she searched desperately for some place of safety. Leucas waded slashing through the pack of dog-things that harried him, heading toward the fire and Kheperu. Most of the dog-things now circled the ring of flames, panting and chuckling as they drooled at the sight of their braver companions tearing at Kheperu, while the dog-master judiciously applied an occasional vicious kick to the ribs or crotch—but they *circled*, they didn't cross the flames, and that made up Barra's mind. It was the only place where the dog-things wouldn't come at Graeg.

"Graegduz!" she said in Pictish as she slid the haft of her broad-axe back into its scabbard. "Gimme a hug!"

The young wolf reared unsteadily on his one hind leg, and Barra wrapped her arms around his chest. She grunted as she lifted him up off the ground—it'd been a year since she'd picked him up, and now he was better than two thirds her weight. "You eat too bloody much!" she wheezed as she turned and ran as hard as she could toward the flames, screaming a Pict war howl that startled the dog-things into scattering momentarily, clearing a path. She put her head down and held her breath as she burst through the wall of flame. The heat blazed for only an instant, and then she was through.

Within, the ring was more confined than it had looked from outside; the heat was intense and now the center, the coolest place, was crowded with the dog-things that chewed at Kheperu, and the dog-master, who grappled with Leucas. Leucas' shield lay in the mud nearby, not far from the hilt of his sword—the blade had snapped off a handbreadth above the guard. Barra released Graeg and drew her broadaxe. She leaped over the whimpering wolf to attack.

The dog-master had Leucas in a bear hug around the short ribs, lifting the Athenian off the ground. Leucas' knotted fists, manslaughtering weapons, hammered at the dog-master's head and shoulders without effect. Barra skidded across the mud behind it, took a solid stance, and swung from her heels. Her broadaxe bit deep into the small of the dog-master's back: the razor-sharp flint sheared through the base of its spine, and the blade sank in to the very haft. She braced one foot against its butt to yank the axe free—but even as the axe tore loose, the dog-master tossed Leucas carelessly aside. Leucas tumbled bonelessly through the flames like a broken doll, and the dog-master turned to Barra and smiled.

*"Hey, it's the axe-girl."* The words were familiar, but its voice shrieked and howled like a damned thing. *"Remember meeeee?"*

Firelight gleamed in its eyes, but there was no other suggestion of life there. The blackened flesh of its face still smoldered—smoke drifted from the glowing charcoal of its upper lip, and its jaw—its jaw didn't look human, some kind of piece of some animal's mouth, jagged tusks on bone that had been sewn to its face with leather thongs. Some milky fluid oozed like cold oil from the holes where the thongs entered the bone. Similar thongs strapped across a huge cut from its crotch to its breastbone, exposed now that its clothing had burned away, and when it stepped toward her, its walk was liquid and ungainly at the same time, a swaying, dipping unhuman stagger—for a numbing, nauseous instant, Barra thought she could hear the ragged ends of his pelvis scrape together with each step, grinding where her axe had split them days before.

When it said: *"Let's tryyyy that one again, shall weeeee?"* she knew exactly what it meant.

Her throwing axe had bounced off its back—its skin must be like leather boiled in brine. She hoped that, like the dog-things, its bones would be as fragile as a mortal man's. The bite wounds on her wrists bled along her hands to slicken the haft of her broadaxe with her blood. She stepped back as it lurched at her, axe up in both hands before her; it came with arms spread wide like a favorite uncle. She'd picked her target to attack—maybe she could break its knee, get it off its feet— but somehow she couldn't step up to swing. The heat at her back increased painfully, and the scent of scorching linen and hair told her she'd run out of room. Her axe became suddenly heavy in her hands, weighing on her arms like bronze shackles. The simple *unfairness* of this stung the most bitterly: she and her friends could beat any *human* foe—and they wouldn't even be *out* here if she hadn't come to the aid of a man she despised.

She summoned up her will and whipped her broadaxe into a singing arc around her head. Remembering how bloody fast he'd been when he was alive, she eye-faked to its neck and continued the arc of the axe into a circling slice at the side of its left knee.

It was faster now; and stronger.

One hand met the arc of her swing, *one hand* to take the haft of her axe and stop a flint blade weighing more than half a stone that moved with every ounce of force Barra could muster. It disarmed her with a casual flick of the wrist and caught her elbow with its free hand. It lifted her into the air; she kicked like a thief in a hangman's noose. Its eyes blazed, and its blackened tongue snaked out to lick at the milky fluid that leaked like tears down its face.

*"I'll bring your corrrrpse to my Masterrr. You'll live as I do. And He'll giiiivve you to meeee!"*

Its skin was like armor of boiled leather; its muscles were like plates of bronze. But neither leather nor bronze can stop a heavy, curved blade of cold-forged iron swung by an enraged Athenian giant; no more so did the arm that held Barra.

She found herself staggering to her feet, Chrysios' severed arm dangling from the grip it still held upon her elbow. The thing that had been Chrysios roared an ear-ripping shriek and wheeled on its attacker.

Leucas towered over it like a god from the songs of Troy, outlined in rain and fire, his down-plastered hair and beard trailing smoke, glowing cinders climbing the hems of his chiton. The thing reached for him, the scimitar flashed, and its other arm tumbled away from its shoulder and splashed to the mud. Its legs buckled, pitching it forward as though to clutch at Leucas' knees to beg for mercy, but it had no arms with which to grab, and the scimitar's merciless downstroke clove its skull and split its mutilated face like a length of firewood, one eye to either side of a gaping slash that drove down to open its whistling throat and notch its collarbone.

It swayed there on its knees while Leucas regarded it with a breathless snarl. He gasped in air, his shoulders heaving, then wrenched the scimitar with a sideways twist that freed the blade and flopped the halves of the thing's head apart from each other like petals of some flower of flesh and bone.

Leucas thoughtfully wiped the blade on the thing's blackened chest, and said, "I like this sword."

Barra caught at the severed arm above the elbow with both hands; then she had to pry the fingers loose one at a time to break its bruising grip on her arm. Two dog-things still tore at Kheperu, whose struggles seemed weaker. There was nothing Barra could do for him, unarmed as she was with her weapons beyond the wall of flames, out with the circling pack. "Leucas! Help Kheperu!"

"All right."

"Oh, don't bother!" Kheperu snapped. Suddenly, one of the dog-things reared back gibbering away from him, its entire body engulfed in flames. An instant later, the head of the second exploded with a muffled *whump!* and Kheperu sat up.

"Do you think you could have taken a bit *longer* to deal with him?" the Egyptian groused.

Barra threw the severed arm disgustedly down into the mud. Leucas merely stared.

Kheperu turned up his palms. "These creatures couldn't do much harm to me through the armor under my robes. It was simply a matter of keeping them off my face and hands until the two of you could handle Chrysios. He was certainly too much for me." He offered a winning smile. "I knew I could count on you."

The rain had ended, and the ring of fire around them was dying away. The hyaenae—the name Kheperu had for the dog-things—had slunk away into the night; even the one with no head had dragged itself blindly off. Obviously, they had come of the same sort of magic that continued to animate Chrysios. Its body still twitched aimlessly; even the severed arms flexed, clenching and unclenching their fists. Leucas kept one foot on its chest, holding it pinned to the ground.

Met, the guard, was thoroughly dead, his massive form sprawled near the mulecart of his master's goods, his guts spilled in the mud around him. Tekrop-nekt had fared no better; the lanky alchemist's body lay in an alley nearby. Apparently, he'd either tried to run, or a couple of the hyaenae had dragged him there to chew on undisturbed; he was barely recognizable.

"What I don't understand," Leucas murmured, surveying the scene, "is why no one came to *help* us. We must have woken every soul in the Market."

"Think about it," Kheperu advised sarcastically. "You're awakened in the middle of a thunderstorm by bloodcurdling screams and lunatic laughter, and when you peek out you see, well, this." His gesture took in the whole scene. "Who in their right mind would get out of their warm, comfortable, safe bed to fight for someone they don't even know?"

Leucas frowned. "I would."

"Well, all right," Kheperu conceded. "But, remember, I said 'in their right mind.' "

Neither Leucas nor Kheperu was badly injured. Kheperu had another swelling knot on his face to match the one Barra'd given him earlier; Leucas was mildly scorched—both he and Barra would need to trim their hair—and his ribs were tender, but that was all. Both of Barra's wrists were torn, and she had a nasty-looking bite wound on her calf, but she wouldn't let her friends bandage her until she'd seen to Graegduz.

The wounds in his shoulder still oozed blood, thinned by the rainwater held in his fur; all she could do there was wrap some wet cloth around it—nothing more could be done until she had the time and a dry spot to shave the fur away. Nor was there much to be done for his hind leg: it was broken.

Barra's eyes filled with tears when Graeg licked her hand, tears that dropped one by one across the jagged ends of bone that showed within the wound. Kheperu rested a surprisingly gentle hand upon her shoulder. "We can set that bone, once we get him somewhere out of the rain," he said softly. "We'll hold him; Leucas can set and splint it. It'll be all right, Barra. Really it will."

Barra angrily knuckled away her tears and stood up. Without a word she went to where Chrysios lay writhing. The scorched linen of her chiton tore easily; when she had three long strips, she took them in her teeth. She reached down and took the halves of Chrysios' head in her hands, the charred muscles crusty and jumping against her skin.

She pressed them together, the two halves roughly aligned, and the eyes rolled and focused on her. She looked up at Leucas and said through her teeth, muffled by the strip of linen, "Hold him like this."

Leucas looked extremely dubious, but complied nonetheless.

Barra swiftly tied Chrysios' head in place with the linen strips. One went around his throat to stifle the whistling of his breath, another across his mouth, and the third just above his eyes. All three were instantly soaked through with the viscous, milky fluid that leaked from every wound. Barra said grimly, "I know you can still hear. Blink twice if you understand me."

The fierce blaze in his scalded eyes never wavered, but he did blink slowly: once, twice.

She said, "You go back and tell your master that we know who he is. Understand? We *know*. And you tell him that, as far as his invitation goes, we have a previous engagement for the rest of our lives."

Kheperu snorted. Barra shot him a *shut up or I'll pound you* look.

"Tell him we're leaving town tomorrow," she went on. "If he wants us, he'd better move fast. On the other hand, if he's smart, he'll just let us go. His business is none of ours, you understand? We don't care what he does in this shitcake town. We're already gone, you understand?"

Chrysios blinked, twice.

"All right. Leucas, let him up."

Leucas frowned. "Are you sure?"

She shrugged. "What's he gonna do, bleed on me? Let him go."

The Chrysios-thing slowly climbed to its feet. It looked at the three of them as though its gaze could kill them where they stood, then it wove off into the night, its dipping stagger fading beyond sight.

The three companions watched it go, and then Kheperu turned to Barra. "What now?"

She could barely hold up her head. "Now we're going home. It'll take him at least till dawn to make it out to the caves or the estate, whichever. We'll take care of Graeg and then catch a few hours' sleep."

"No, I mean, what is your plan? What shall we do about"—he gestured around them—"this?"

"Exactly what I said. We're leaving."

Leucas looked stunned. "You're joking!"

"I'm not."

"I was sure," Leucas said, "that this was strategy, that you didn't really mean to . . . run *away*."

She stepped up to face him, and sudden anger shrilled strength into her limbs. "Look around you, you shit-eating idiot! Those . . . things . . . could have found us at home! Go over to that shitcake alley and take a long look at what's left of Tekrop-nekt. That could just as well have been my *family!*" She paused, gasping in her rage. "That asshole-biter Idonosteus wants us out of the way—not even the gods know why—and the goddamned demonist knows who we are, and there is no one in this town that will lift one shitcake finger to save our lives. You had best believe that we are leaving. Tomorrow."

Kheperu nodded silent, grim agreement, but Leucas still looked hurt. "I never thought you'd let someone run you out of town, Barra."

She looked over to where Graegduz lay in the mud, panting out his pain, then looked down at the earth at her feet. "That's the thing about me," she said grimly. "I'm just full of fucking surprises."

# 12

# *Scent*

**T**he Governor was coming.

It was all the buzz under the harsh morning glare in the Market of Tyre. Forward outriders had arrived at dusk last night, and the contingent of the Canaan Division that accompanied the Governor's Household would reach Tyre by noon. Opinions were mixed as to the significance of this occurrence. For some, the storm that had blown through the night before represented the current unrest and troubles in the city, and the Governor himself was the sky-cleansing wind. Others spent the morning locking up their best wares along with their daughters, and hunkered down to wait out this visit with the same stolid patience with which they'd greet a cloud of locusts or a long drought. Still, overall, the mood among the smaller merchants and innkeepers seemed to be one of cautious optimism. There was a certain sense of being rescued, just in the nick of time—the mangled corpses of Tekrop-nekt and his bodyguard Met had been found in the Market this morning, and the rumor went that they were only two of more than ten corpses strewn in streets and alleyways across Tyre. Someone had seen a pack of ghostly dogs jittering with unearthly laughter as they pursued a screaming man in the Egyptian quarter, and it was generally assumed that the rogue magician was responsible for these murders, as well; everyone hoped that the Governor could bring it all back under control, and in the meantime, here was an opportunity that was literally golden. The streets were packed today, filled with slaves and shoppers streaming into the Market, stockpiling food and horse feed and spice and beer, in anticipation of a local economic surge as 5,000 Egyptian regulars poured into the city.

Barra listened to an Assyrian horse dealer chatter about this in Egyptian, to Kheperu, while she examined the spavined joints of the pair of mules he was trying to sell them. Apparently, the Assyrian owned a part interest in a medium-size brothel, and was most excited by the army's arrival. She palpated the poor mule's swollen hock one last time, then stood, shaking her head disgustedly and crossing her arms to scratch at the bandages wrapping both of her wrists: they'd already begun to itch. "They'll do," she said in Greek, "but don't pay more than ten shekels for the pair." Kheperu nodded his understanding, and she left him to handle the haggling. She went over by Leucas, who sat on the al-tobe wall that surrounded the horse yard and thoughtfully watched the passing crowds.

"I see lots of folks going around dressed like that," he murmured, nodding toward three boys wearing very clean, new-looking kilts and stoles of bloodred and purple: the colors of Meremptah-Sifti's banner. One held the leads of a pair of oxen, and the other two walked behind, occasionally encouraging the oxen with slender switches. "You think those belong to our buddy outside of town?"

Barra said, "I'd imagine so."

"Why so many, you think? Why today?"

Barra shrugged. "I'd guess Meremptah-Sifti is throwing a party. The Governor's supposed to be an old friend of the Pharaoh; he was a standard-bearer or drummer or something in the Ra Division when Ramses took Qadesh—like, fifty years ago. Maybe sixty. Anyway, I'd make a bet that Meremptah-Sifti is having some kind of feast to welcome him. To show respect, get in on his good side. It's what I'd do. And the Governor can't turn him down—when the Pharaoh's grandson invites you, you come. Period. He might even invite the Governor to stay at the estate while he's dealing with Tyre. I'd do that, too. Easier to keep an eye on him, make sure he doesn't get any wrong ideas."

Leucas' eyebrows pulled together, and a low grumbling grunt resonated through his chest. "That'll cause a problem for Idonosteus, getting at the demonist, won't it?" he said softly.

"Doesn't matter," Barra told him. She touched the gold ring on her first finger, twisting and turning it—not yet comfortable with it, nor with what it represented. "It's not our problem anymore. We're leaving."

Barra had been literally staggering with fatigue by the time the companions had made their way back home the night before. They'd found an overhanging roof with a dry spot beneath where they could set Graegduz's leg with a piece cut from one of the pine slats off

Tekrop-nekt's dismantled shop. He took it like a champion, panting mostly, only one little yelp when Leucas pulled the leg straight and the bones ground together. She'd carried the young wolf in her arms, all the way home.

Once there, she'd passed off their wounds and Kheperu's shredded robes as coming from the "deadly influences and supernatural creatures" attendant to "Kheperu's summoning"—explaining the truth to the cluster of anxious, red-eyed Kypriots would have taken too much time and effort. One of Demetor's men had convulsed and died in his bed while the companions were away; his body, wrapped in a winding sheet, lay on one of the couches where the servants eyed it fearfully. The Kypriots were grieving for their friend and terrified for their king; Barra wisely kept her explanation brief and reassuring. Explaining the large bronze-bound wooden chest they brought back with them was less easy.

The chest had been Tekrop-nekt's, and it contained all of his alchemical wares, hundreds—perhaps thousands—of shekels' worth of rare powders and poisons, bits of this bark and that shell, everything from old toenail parings to gold-filigreed shark's teeth. In the words Kheperu had used, his beady squirrel's eyes gleaming with avarice: "Little point in leaving it here—I'd venture Tekrop-nekt has no use for it any longer." To Peliarchus, he'd airily described it as a "gift of Thoth, God of All Knowledge—for I am his most faithful servant," as Leucas carried it up the stairs on his back. At her foster-father's sidelong glance, Barra wearily promised to explain everything in the morning. Leucas, returning, appeared acutely uncomfortable at the flow of Phoenikian around him; Barra translated the conversations, and Leucas shook his head sadly and murmured in her ear, "I suppose this means I won't be able to brag about the fight."

"No, you won't. Not for a while yet, anyway."

He laid himself sprawling along the length of one of the courtyard couches and laced his fingers together behind his head. "Hardly seems worth winning in the first place, if you can't brag about it."

Kheperu had vanished into the second-floor bedroom and swiftly prepared the infusion. Barra administered the potion; she half feared the effect Kheperu's smell might have on men in their sensitive condition, and by the time the potion was ready, Leucas was sound asleep, snoring thunderously on the couch.

Demetor and his two surviving friends lay wide-eyed, staring and terrified in the dark. Barra shooed out the Kypriot that sat with them, gave them each one of the three winebowls Kheperu had prepared, and sat with them while they drifted off into a drugged sleep. In the darkness Demetor did not know her, but he clutched her hand and swore his gratitude in words increasingly slurred as the potion took effect, and held her hand in his strengthless fingers until he fell asleep.

After that, it was all Barra could do to drag herself up the stairs to their room. Even Graegduz's occasional whimpering—he shared her bed this night—couldn't keep her awake. All of them overslept; the sun was well up, streaming through the window while Barra freshly re-bandaged her wrists and Leucas' belly and shoulder, and then tied a patch around her calf. Kheperu spent the time sewing shut the bite tears that riddled his overrobe. She chipped a new edge on one of her throwing axes, and used it to gently shave the fur around Graeg's wounds. Leucas held him still while she cleaned them with fresh water and re-bandaged those, as well. She'd shaken her head grimly at the array of wounds and observed that Tyre was chipping away at them, little by little, and it was a good thing they were leaving.

There was much consternation in the household when their imminent departure was revealed. Especially among the Kypriots—Demetor seemed to have passed the crisis during the night and was well enough to sit up and take broth for his breakfast. The old king was dazzled that it was the three boar-slayers who had saved his life; in the full light of day, he recalled them from their meeting in Paphos—where he claimed they'd saved his kingdom just as even now they'd saved his life—and he pressed three gold rings into Barra's hands; not as payment, for it would be impious to offer a fee to ones who were so obviously servants of the gods, but as tokens of the gratitude he owed to them for saving him. He invited them to guest with him whenever they passed Kypros, and asked them to join him at the funeral feast and games for his slain friend, and then passed into a long and windy exposition of how well Kheperu's ointment had served him at the brothels here in Tyre until Barra began to feel a guilty regret for saving his life and thus inflicting him upon her family once again. Whatever chains of kinship had been forged the night before may only have been the result of exhaustion and the warm letdown that comes after one has escaped danger; by morning's light she found him absurd and more than a bit repellent.

Tayniz had saved a breakfast of barley toast and lamb gravy for them, and she and Peliarchus sat with them while they ate. Tayniz was not the sort to give sighing, sidelong glances or make oblique comments; she leaned toward Barra and said, clearly enough that the servants had no need to inch closer to eavesdrop, "It's *shocking* that you'd leave again so soon. We've barely had a chance to say hello, and now you tell us you're off again. And look at you. You're a mass of bandages, your clothes are barely more than filthy rags, and I'll bet you can't even remember the last time you washed your hair."

Rather than rise hotly to the challenge—she bloody well *could* remember, it was at Lidios' house, only four or five days ago—she had held on to her temper and beckoned Tayniz close, gesturing for Peliarchus to lean in as well. "Please don't be angry with me," she'd said, low. "We did a little job this past week, and it's turned out to be—well, we're in a certain amount of danger. It's not too serious, really, but I don't want to bring down any more trouble here than you already have, with Demetor and all. There are a few people who are a little upset with us; we're going to head overland to Sidon and stay there until they calm down a bit here—shouldn't be more than four or five days, maybe a week, then we can come back."

"I've never liked the whole idea of you traveling like this," Tayniz said. "I don't understand it, I don't like it, I don't know why you refuse to simply settle on some good Tyrian boy. I know you're getting a bit old for a first marriage, but you still look like a girl, he wouldn't have to know . . ."

Barra examined her hands, callused and powerful for all their small size, spent half a moment picking at the bandages on her wrists. Every time this particular conversation had begun in the past, it had ended in shouting or tears, commonly both. She resolved to make it different, this time, so she clamped her teeth against the reminder that if she were a simple Tyrian housewife, Demetor and his friends would be dead right now and this whole household would be swimming in Agapenthes' shit-pot. All she would say was, "Maybe I'm just stubborn."

The companions swiftly packed up their belongings, under the watchful eye of Tayniz. Barra had to explain twice that no, she didn't need any money for new clothes or food or lodging or pack animals or anything else, thanks anyway, she'd made plenty off this job. She gave careful instructions as to the care of Graegduz, and recommended that the Kypriots handle it; "He got hurt saving their bloody king, let *them* look after him." She spent a few minutes alone with the young wolf, feeding him hunks of gravy-soaked bread and fresh cheese, trying to make him understand that she would only be away for a few days. He licked her hands, and her heart hurt in her chest as she left.

Kamades wasn't home when the partners arrived at the apartment block with their new mules in tow. Barra had decided—reluctantly—to tell Kamades that she was leaving town. She didn't want him to think she was ducking him; he was the best man in years who'd shown a spark of interest in her. She didn't want to think about how many years it'd been, and she didn't want to slam the door against any future chance.

The lone Myrmidon present was Peroön, the one-handed physician, who wouldn't tell them anything about the others until he'd had a chance to re-bandage Leucas and tsk-tsk Barra for the sloppy way she tied bandages. He also insisted on rubbing some salve into her bite wounds—"What in the name of the Moonbitch did these? That hairy beast of yours finally go feral?" Barra assured him that it was none of his business, and pressed him about Kamades.

"Oh, they're out," he said, scratching his stump absently. "Shopping. Probably be in the Market till mid-afternoon. Lysandros came by with a stack of new clothes, to dress 'em up like servants, and a list of stuff they're supposed to buy and cart out to the Egyptian's place."

Barra winced. "The Egyptian's?"

"Oh yeah. Throwin' a big do for the Governor, all the Great House folks're invited. I'd suppose," he said with a wise squint, "that Lord Idonosteus is having them dress up to keep an eye on things, like he doesn't exactly trust this Egyptian fella. That's why they left me here; with the arm gone and all it's pretty clear I'm either a veteran or a thief, and somebody has to watch the armor. Don't know why all the fuss, but then, we never do."

"Yeah," Barra said heavily. "Listen, can you give him a message— ah, forget it. I'll find him and tell him myself." She left, muttering darkly, "This whole having-a-suitor business is complicating my bloody life before I even have a suitor."

Amber and tarragon.

Barra's head came up like a hound's, and she scanned the upwind crush of the Market. The gentlest of breezes came off the sea, and on its salt wings rode a thousand scents. There—there it was again, tarragon and crushed amber, over the clean-sweat smell of a freshly bathed man, and beneath that a rich, corrupt trace of a diet heavy in veal and lamb. Barra's nose was not as sensitive as her wolf's, but it was nearly as accurate, and she recognized that scent as one might recognize a familiar voice within a crowd's babble.

Murso. Lysandros. Whatever his name might be today.

She stopped, still looking for him, some unexplainable apprehension trickling into her belly. He couldn't be far away, if his scent was readable in the midst of this press. Leucas and Kheperu, walking alongside with the leads of their pack-laden mules, also halted and scanned the crowd, an instinctive reaction to Barra's peering.

"Uhm, Barra?" Leucas said after a moment. "What are we looking for?"

For an instant a corridor opened within the moving crowds, a channel straight toward the sea, and there he was, his back to her, skeletal shoulders obvious beneath a gaily dyed robe and a square cap in the Hittite style, not even a stone's throw away. He moved with deliberate speed toward a large oxcart that was being loaded with barrels and sacks by sweating slaves, and the two men who sat on the driver's bench wore livery of bloodred and purple.

A cold hand clutched her guts. Without any knowledge of *how* she knew, she murmured in Pictish, "This is a problem," and knew the words were true.

The channel within the human sea surged closed once again, but now she saw the men on the oxcart conversing, and one of them pointed toward a nearby warehouse.

Murso's words came back to her: *I serve him in confidential matters only.*

"Barra?" Leucas repeated. "Are you all right?"

She turned back to them, and her expression was as bleak as her flattened voice. "You two stay here. Better yet, stay over there." She pointed to a narrow walkway between a farrier's and a shop that sold wine. "You're too damned conspicuous, both of you," she said, tying her hair up in a twist. She pulled a robe from one of the mulepacks and slipped it on over her clothes and weapons, then plucked out the long strip of cloth that had been bought as a new breechclout, and wound it around her head, tying it off like a Tyrian sun bonnet. "I'll be back soon."

Kheperu and Leucas had watched this whole process with identical bemused frowns. Kheperu said, "Are you going to tell us what this is all about?"

"I'll know more when I get back," she told them over her shoulder as she vanished into the crowd.

The man that Murso met coming out of the warehouse was clearly not himself the Pharaoh's grandson: he looked more Phoenikian than Egyptian, for all his sumptuous southern attire. The bloodred and purple colors of his dress were blazingly vivid and his torc gleamed with gold and lapis lazuli, matching the bracelets that clasped his upper arms. He was of medium height and stocky build, perhaps could have been very strong if he'd gone for a laborer or a warrior, but now gone mostly to fat. His beard was bound into a stiff rod down to the middle of his smooth chest, and though his head was shaven like a priest's—

and his skin was fair—his head was pale, showing no sign of exposure to the sun.

The man began issuing orders before he'd even cleared the doorway. White-kilted slaves and liveried servants scampered around him, heading inside. In the midst of this flow, Murso stepped up to him, head bent respectfully. The man jumped visibly at Murso's words and looked around nervously, and Barra—watching from the corner of her eye while pretending to consider the wares of a fabric merchant at whose stall she stood—carefully lifted the cloth she held as though to examine its weave in the sun. The two men conversed briefly, then the man took Murso's arm and led him around the corner of the warehouse. Barra dropped the cloth to the ground and walked through a wide arc to get a view around the corner, ignoring the curses of the merchant that faded into the crowd's babble behind her.

*Idonosteus, you cocksucker,* she thought, blood freezing in her veins. *You worthless jiggleprick bastard.*

Alongside the warehouse stood a line of wagons, all draped in Meremptah-Sifti's colors. One of them, actually painted thus, was also hung with roof and curtains of heavy brocade. The man respectfully held the curtains aside and allowed Murso to precede him into the wagon, and Barra—as if from a distance—felt her knees buckle and breath drive out from her lungs as the *sceon tiof* took her.

This came not as it had before, a deep sense of the forces that drove the man she looked at; this came like a sudden storm wind that pushed her toward a precipice.

The sun faded in her eyes. The breath that left her was pulled out, torn from her by the whirling winds that were sucked down into the maelstrom of darkness within this man's spirit. She put out a hand to steady herself, and found nothing there to clutch. A dizzying vertigo, like that which may come of leaning out too far over an abyss bottomed only with mist, nearly overcame her.

*It's him,* she thought. *No person inside, only a gulf, an emptiness—that's the bloody demonist. An ordinary little man standing in broad daylight—Oh, Loving Mother!*

And he paused there, hand on the curtain and one foot lifted to climb into the wagon, and now his head cocked to one side as though he'd heard a familiar voice behind him or some unseen hand had politely tapped his shoulder, and he turned—

And from far across the Market, a swirling crowd of hundreds between them, he looked directly into her eyes.

\* \* \*

"I don't know what might have happened if I hadn't pulled away and run like a bloody deer," she said grimly. "I don't know if he could've done something to me out in the open, in broad daylight and all, or not. I don't know if he's got some sense of me, like I've got a sense of him, or if it might be worse than that. But I do know what I've got to do now."

Kheperu stared morosely into his mug. Leucas drained his and set it down. He rested his forearms on the table before him and said, "You know I'm with you, no matter what. I never liked this idea of letting them run us out of town."

Barra looked around the smallish common room of this smallish public house, at the benches that were beginning to fill with hungry shoppers as noon approached. The big bowl of straight wine she'd drained had stopped her shaking by the time she'd gotten halfway through her story, but her arms and legs were still pimpled with gooseflesh.

"There's a chance," Kheperu said slowly, fingers pressed against his eyes as though he tried to massage away a headache, "that you misjudge the situation. It's possible that this is some maneuver preliminary to destroying them."

"A chance," Barra allowed. "That's all. Believe me when I tell you that I know things about Idonosteus"—she had *seen* them—"that make this all too convincing. That's why we were isolated from the beginning, why no one was to know of our job. That's why Idonosteus tried to get the Myrmidons to kill us—it had nothing to do with the money, it was because we're the only people in Tyre that know he knows who's behind all this. Mother's Blood—that's probably why he hired us in the first place! We're foreigners, all of us. If we're killed, he'd only have to pay a blood price to Peliarchus, maybe, and a blood price doesn't come to much for a twenty-nine-year-old spinster. For you two, nobody cares. A couple of anonymous bodies in an alley somewhere. And if he misses, so what? Who can we tell? Who'd believe three foreign mercenaries against the word of a Head of a Great House?"

"So. Where does this leave us?" Kheperu said, examining his fingernails. "On our way out of town, purses heavy with silver, as I recall."

She shook her head stubbornly. "We're the only ones left who know what's going on. House Meneides has joined the bad guys. If we leave now, we're handing Tyre to them on a platter."

"So?"

"Bloody Idonosteus is selling us out!"

"I say again"—Kheperu shrugged—"so?"

Barra gripped the edge of the table and lowered her head like a bull, struggling to keep her voice down regardless of her temper. She understood Kheperu's point all too well. They were foreigners here, even she—how much of her life was really invested in this city, after all? Three years? Four? She'd arrived on Peliarchus' ship at fourteen, and at eighteen she'd run away to see the Siege of Troy. In the years between then and now—more than ten, now, incredible as that was— Tyre had been only a stopping place in her mercenary travels around the Inner Sea, a place to come and rest, sometimes to heal. Tyre was small, and the world was large.

She hardened herself against a certain twinge at her own ruthlessness; she knew how much what she was about to say would hurt. She growled slowly, grinding the words out between her teeth, "This man—this demonist—practices the very art that you were accused of. You were taken, and tortured, and exiled on threat of death. You were innocent. He is guilty. He lives in comfort and honor, and his art will bring him wealth beyond your dreams."

Kheperu had gone ashen when she began; now his fingers whitened around the fired-clay mug and his voice rasped with real pain. "That's low, Barra. You shouldn't say that to me. That's not fair."

She didn't press him further, for she knew she didn't have to; the insight about him that the *sceon tiof* had given her told her well that his own mind would push the idea harder than she could.

She laid her palms flat on the table and looked around the common room, filling now more and more with townsfolk patiently waiting to be served the noon stew, chattering at each other in five different languages, talking of the army, of the weather, the prospects for trade; in her mind, each of them became a staggering, lurching Chrysios leaking milky ooze from its eye sockets. She said, "I never expected us to get this deep into something this dangerous. If I'd known, really known, what we were getting into, I'd never have taken this job—"

Leucas interrupted her with a gentle smile. "I don't think that's true, Barra. I saw it in your eyes when you looked at that fellow who died in the Market, that Othniel."

Barra shrugged irritably. "It doesn't matter. The point is that the Great Houses could have banded together against an outsider like Meremptah-Sifti, and probably beaten him, Pharaoh's grandson or not. But Idonosteus got a bright idea. He said to himself, 'Let's hire me some mercs who're smart—but not too smart. Let them find me that sorcerer so I can go to him and form a new partnership. Between the two of us, inside and outside, we can take over Tyre in no time, and leave me in the chair beside the new tyrant, whispering in his ear.' And, you know what? I think he's right." Muscles bunched at the corners of her jaw, and pulsed at her temples. "Don't you see? If it hadn't been for us—for me—Tyre might have had a chance. This is *my fault*, and I've got to fix it."

Her hands unconsciously sought the hafts of her axes and stroked them lovingly. "And Idonosteus used me in a way I don't like to be used. You'd best believe I'm not going to let him get away with it."

"Even . . . assuming," Kheperu said, his voice still harshly rasping, "that you are not completely full of shit, what can you do? What could we do? You said it yourself: we're outsiders here, we have no status that puts our words on a plane with those of the Head of a Great House or an Egyptian prince. Who would even listen to you, let alone believe you?"

Barra tried to drive the butterflies from her belly with a deep breath. She heard the distant thunder of her heart's blood in her ears. "Well, see, I've an idea about that. I don't need all of them to believe me, just one or two who can convince the others. Or maybe just one man: Tal Akhu-shabb—the Governor."

"What makes you think the Governor of the Canaan District would spare one minute for a bedraggled Pictish mercenary?"

"Well . . ." Her stomach knotted around the wine she'd drunk. "He wouldn't. However, he might be willing to spend a few precious moments with a nice-looking redhead who approaches him at a party . . ."

Kheperu looked thunderstruck. "You cannot!"

"I think I can," Barra said. "I'm sure Peliarchus was invited, or will be, as the Penthedes shipmaster. He can get me in."

"But, but," Kheperu sputtered, "the party's on his estate, on the bloodyfucking *home ground* of Meremptah-Sifti!"

"That," Barra said, "is what makes it, well, challenging."

Leucas leaned forward, his brows drawing together. "I don't like it. You'd have to be alone. I'd be recognized instantly, and Kheperu—"

Barra shrugged. "I'm not helpless. And if things go bad, there wouldn't be much you could do except die at my side."

"That is not such a little thing," Leucas said.

"Well, forget it," she told him. "I'll be perfectly safe; that feast is the last place on earth Idonosteus would expect me to be—and, believe me, I won't be looking like I do right now. Meremptah-Sifti has never seen me. I can do this. I'm going to do this. This is my home, my problem. My job."

"But you're working for free, Barra," Kheperu said, shaking his head grimly, "and that is a dangerous way of doing business."

# 13

# *Idonosteus*

**"S**o, my prince," Idonosteus said, smacking his lips wetly as he inhaled, "though I know your plans as I know my own name, and could certainly interfere if I chose, I do not intend to. Quite the opposite, in fact." He shifted in his sedan chair; the noonday sun had snuck around the edge of his embroidered linen shade. The day was, in fact, growing uncomfortably warm, out here near the reflecting pool behind Meremptah-Sifti's manor house; sweat began to prickle on the backs of his hands. "Do you think you could invite me inside, my prince?"

Meremptah-Sifti stood staring down at the Head of House Meneides with undisguised loathing, as his steward translated this request. Idonosteus could well imagine what this extremely fit, extraordinarily handsome and youthful prince of Egypt thought of him; Idonosteus had dealt with several of Egypt's military-raised minor royals in the past. He knew how he appeared, with his pale flesh smooth over its rolling hills of fat, with the perfumed oil in his braided beard and the kohl shaded beneath his brows to make his piggish eyes look larger. Meremptah-Sifti would be thinking, more likely than not, that he resembled some plump, bejeweled maggot feeding on the corpse of an honest man. *Well, fair enough,* Idonosteus thought. *So long as he thinks I have the intellect of a maggot as well—it's always useful to be underestimated.*

The prince said something in Egyptian, in that tone both languid and peremptory which Idonosteus admired so much—one must be an aristocrat born to command with such a tone. The steward, Simi-Ascalon—a strange, pale man who never seemed to blink—didn't bother to translate this, as he had their earlier conversation, but then a

translation was not required. The action of the two Egyptian men-at-
arms, as they strode forward and pulled their axes from their belts,
made the prince's meaning perfectly clear.

The Myrmidons, standing around Idonosteus' sedan chair in their
servants' guise, made no move to intercept; they played their parts very
well. They only watched Kamades, and Kamades watched Idonosteus,
waiting for his signal. Idonosteus, instead of giving this signal, only
examined his polished fingernails.

Kamades and his men could certainly handle the approaching soldiers, as well as the other two armed and armored men who stood
stiffly nearby, even though the Myrmidons wore no armor, only their
white servant's chitons, and carried as weapons only daggers concealed in sheaths strapped to their thighs. Handling the prince's men
was not the issue; Indonosteus wanted the Myrmidons to still be available, still be regarded as mere servants, in case the time came when
they'd have to handle the prince himself. Idonosteus turned back to
face Meremptah-Sifti, and offered him an oily smile. "If those men
touch me, you'll lose Tyre, and most likely return to Egypt in shackles."

He'd already seen that Meremptah-Sifti understood Phoeni-kian,
by watching the play of expressions across the prince's face while
Idonosteus had spoken earlier; he didn't know why the prince refused
to speak it in return, and he cared not a whit. Meremptah-Sifti held up
a hand to halt the approaching men-at-arms, and murmured a few
words in Egyptian, to his steward.

Simi-Ascalon cleared his throat explosively, and said, "My prince
instructs me to inform you that he is not susceptible to extortion. I,
ah,—*hrakhakh*—assume that you have committed your knowledge to
paper, or confided in someone who will go to the Governor or the other
Great Houses in the event of your untimely . . . whatever." He shook
his head irritably, and wiped his mouth with a linen handkerchief.
"Now you want my prince to cease and desist, or to pay you not to
interfere. He will do neither, and now your life is forfeit for the insult
of making such a presumptuous demand."

*So much for the packets of letters I left with Lysandros.* Idonosteus
spread his plump, moist hands. "Not at all. You mistake me, entirely. I
come, not to demand, but to offer. My services, and those of House
Meneides."

At this, the prince's eyebrows lifted, and he fixed Idonosteus
with a penetrating stare. "Have your warriors withdraw," Meremptah-Sifti said distinctly, in perfectly accentless Phoenikian.

"My warriors?" Idonosteus struggled to conceal a sudden surge of panic. "I don't know what you mean." *How had he known?*

"You are a fool, Idonosteus Meneides, to think that I could mistake the discipline of warriors for the obedience of servants. To persist in your failed deception would be a deliberate insult; you might as well call me a fool to my face. If you do so, I will have you killed." Meremptah-Sifti folded his arms. "Have them withdraw."

Idonosteus' hand fluttered a slightly shaky gesture, and Kamades looked silently at the prince of Egypt while he waved his men toward the reflecting pool. Meremptah-Sifti returned this impassive look with a smile and a mocking lift of the brow. Kamades dropped his eyes in a minimally correct bow, and he too stepped back to join the others near the fountain.

Meremptah-Sifti watched him go, then swung his contemptuous gaze deliberately back to Idonosteus. "So, Idonosteus. What can you do for me, that I should let you live?"

Idonosteus licked his lips. The steward, standing at the prince's side, stared at him with a lizard's unblinking fixity. Rolling sweat the size of teardrops painted Idonosteus' cheeks. "I, well, I . . ." Idonosteus coughed and leaned out around his sedan chair's canopy to squint up at the blazing sun. "Do you think we could get out of this heat?"

Meremptah-Sifti's lips stretched into a broad, mocking smile. "Ra blesses our meeting with the passion of his kiss," he drawled. "We shall stay here."

And he and his steward stood with folded arms and watched him sweat, waiting for him to continue.

"Hm, well," Idonosteus said, mostly to fill the uncomfortable silence. "As a guest of House Meneides, the prince would have access to each of the Great Houses; I could arrange an invitation for the prince with any Head—"

"My grandfather is the Living Horus. I have no need for such as you to be my pimp. No Great House would dare refuse me."

Again silence extended like the sudden yawning drop of an unexpected cliff. The rings on his fingers clicked loudly as Idonosteus rubbed his hands together. "I have extensive resources on the streets of Tyre, men whose only job is to bring me news of the city—"

"So do I."

It seemed now to Idonosteus that the blankness in the steward's eyes had taken on a new expression: no longer a lizard's bored stare, it was now more the gaze of a cobra coiled at the mouth of a rat hole.

It went against Idonosteus' nature to come right out and say what he wanted. There was a cherished dream, an idle fantasy in which he had indulged on the ride out from Tyre, a dream that he'd intended to work his way toward gently, and subtly, making his services indispensable, slowly gathering power until his fantasy became truth. He'd look at this building, and that shop, and this stable and that inn and imagined what he would do there, with them and to them. He'd looked at young men on the street, and little girls playing in the sun, and he imagined what he would do there, too. Now he realized that he had little else to offer . . .

"Perhaps," he said, "my services can be of only little value in the taking of Tyre. I would not presume to imagine that I can do anything for the prince that he cannot do for himself. I would, however, venture that once the prince has taken Tyre, after the conquest, as it were, perhaps it would be the prince's desire to rest and enjoy the fruits of his labors, rather than taking on the onerous duties of actually administrating the city's business. This is where I can be of service. I have a thousand loyal men to do my bidding, men whose whole lives have been spent in learning the intricacies of the Tyrian trade. With House Meneides administrating Tyre, as a, well, satrap, as it were, Tyre would become an ever-increasing source of revenue, pouring gold in endless streams directly into the prince's coffers . . ."

"Money?" Meremptah-Sifti barked a laugh. "You think this is about *greed*? You poor, shortsighted, bumbling fool. I *have* money! When I am done with Tyre, you can turn the city into your own personal bordello, for all I care."

Idonosteus' heart leaped within his chest. "Your word on it?"

The prince waved a hand dismissively. "I have said so."

"I am, ah, only curious," Idonosteus said, "about how you plan to take Tyre. My agents didn't seem to know—"

"I am not planning to take Tyre," Meremptah-Sifti said smugly. "I am planning to accept it, when it is given to me."

"Your agents?" Simi-Ascalon the steward seemed to suddenly come to life again, as though he were a statue that had been animated by a passing god. His voice became disagreeably sharp, and he stepped forward and grasped the chair's canopy-poles in white-knuckled fists. "Did you have someone following me in the Market this morning, someone other than the Lysandros that I spoke to?"

Idonosteus flinched back from the fine spray of spittle that flew from his lips. "I, ah, well—" Really, this man had appalling manners, for the steward of a prince!

Meremptah-Sifti said warningly, "Sim, don't become excited—"

The steward whirled upon his master so quickly that for a terrifying instant Idonosteus thought he would strike him. "I told you—about that boy in the Market today, the one who . . . did that, who looked and, and *did that to me*! It felt like, like . . . I didn't like it! I told you! Someone was, was, I don't know what!" He spun back to Idonosteus, and the Head of House Meneides looked into eyes that were utterly deranged. "A boy, fifteen perhaps, no beard yet. Hair red as sunset. Is he your agent? I want him. I want him here, where I can *hurt* him."

Idonosteus' mouth went dry as desert sand. He shook his head hastily and spoke in a rapid stammer. "No, no, no, my agents were, they were foreign mercenaries, two men, Greek and Egyptian, and a woman from the north, she claims to be some sort of Barbarian princess—"

Now Meremptah-Sifti suddenly appeared at his steward's shoulder, looming over him with blazing eyes. "They were your agents? My mercenaries?"

Idonosteus cringed helplessly. What sort of madmen had he involved himself with? "Y-yes, my prince, those three were—did you say, *your* mercenaries?"

The prince brought his hands together in an explosive clap loud enough to make Idonosteus jump. "*I knew it!*" His eyes burned, not with anger but with some sort of mysterious exhilaration. "The woman, her hair is red, isn't it?"

"Y-yes, my prince . . ."

The prince pounded his steward on the back, and grabbed his shoulders, their eyes locked together. "You see? What have I been telling you, all these days! Now they have brought me another gift—a viceroy for my city!"

Simi-Ascalon said, "The boy, it could have been a woman . . . a slender one, in man's clothing. I want her. Remmie, I want her here where I can hurt her."

"Hush, Sim, it's all right. You'll have her." Idonosteus watched in disbelief as the prince kissed his steward gently on the cheek. He slid his arm about the steward's shoulders, and turned back to Idonosteus.

"Now, Idonosteus," Meremptah-Sifti said, his face alight with anticipation, "you will tell me all you know about these three foreign mercenaries."

# 14

# *The Feast*

The sweep of hill below and around the manor house of Meremptah-Sifti's estate blazed with countless constellations of torchlamps, as though the rippling Phoenikian countryside were in fact the sea, and the hill a cresting wave reflecting the glory of a midnight sky. Ba'al-Marqod looked kindly on the gathering this night, and sent his servant Karbas, the dry desert wind, to sweep the sky clean of storm clouds. Even Karbas trod gently here, as he was out of his accustomed season, and flames of the torchlamps flickered only pleasingly. Sweating slaves in livery surrounded the fire pits, faces red-lit from below by pulsing coals that hissed with fat dripping from the slaughtered lambs which turned slowly on spits above them.

The manorial house itself was three majestic stories, surmounted by a flat roof that was itself torch-lit and scattered with guests, surrounded by a sprawling complex of wine vats and olive presses, stables and storehouses and barracks, pools and even one cunningly constructed fountain, all connected by roofed colonnades that shone with whitewash. Around and through and over it all wove the party, hundreds upon hundreds of guests and dozens of servants hustling throughout carrying huge two-handed trays of winebowls, or baskets piled with fruit from as far away as Kush or Doria, loaves of bread still steaming from the ovens, or golden plates piled with spiced lamb and roasted apples, smoked oysters and broiled shrimp. Strolling musicians offered songs sweet and tuneful or cheerful and openly bawdy, per the request of those nearest, or played accompaniment for the dancers, jugglers, acrobats, and minor conjurers that entertained here and there throughout the grounds.

The feast had begun at noon, and now, long after dusk, it showed no sign of abating. All the most important men of Tyre were there, even the hapless, somewhat nervous commander of the Egyptian garrison, who stood around licking his lips and looking like he very much hoped that his garrison troops wouldn't start something foolish with the Governor's Canaan Division personal guard. The heads of the Great Houses had arrived in early afternoon, accompanied by their retinues of servants and hangers-on.

Regal, silver-haired Agapenthes, tall and still trim with a hunter's athleticism, walked in a cloud of Penthedes retainers, his gait having acquired a stately weave. He was rarely found these days without a winebowl in his hands, and today had been no exception. Nephrol Tomit held court not far from one of the fire pits, his vast bulk comfortably ensconced within an even vaster mound of cushions, his booming laugh ringing out infectiously, bringing chuckles out of men and women even on the far side of the feast. Five maidens reclined on the lower slopes of his silken mountain, sampling bites of this and that before offering them to their master; he'd eat nothing unless it came from the supple brown fingers of his slaves.

Xuxusimilli, grandson of Mursuwalli, who had founded his House, was the single Great House Head who had arrived openly armed, a straight broad-bladed sword thrust behind his wide leather girdle, and five of his thirty-odd companions were armed and armored with a king's ransom of grey Hittite iron. He took no chances anymore, not since his mother—the former Head—was poisoned a few weeks ago. But no one at the party so much as looked twice at these weapons, and soon Xuxusimilli had begun to look a bit shamefaced and defensive at the implied melodrama of bringing armed guards to a feast of welcome. Even grim Jephunah seemed to unbend a bit, fleeting ghosts of smiles skittering across his skeletal face, but he kept his sons close around him—eighteen sons total, from his five wives—and his glinting eyes never paused in their suspicious scan.

It was Idonosteus, of course, that Barra watched most closely. Now in the evening, the sweating Head of House Meneides still worked the crowd tirelessly, shaking hands, introducing himself to anyone he didn't already know, doing quite the opposite of the other lords, who held themselves apart and relied on their companions to sift out any unwelcome petitioners, or even the merely boring. Barra herself had been put off by several; she'd given up on the lords of the Great Houses. The Myrmidons came and went around him, in their servant's guise, playing their parts convincingly enough; it was actually only Kamades among them who looked acutely uncomfortable. Close observation enabled Barra to spot the weapons they carried strapped to their thighs, by their occasional brief outlines through their chitons. She had been looking for them, reminded by the continuing friendly discomfort of the two bronze daggers she wore beneath her skirts.

She wondered how many servants of the other Great Houses here tonight were actually disguised warriors—there were undisguised ones enough, here and there, Egyptian regulars and men of various races in armor painted with the colors of the prince of Egypt, eyeing each other with friendly mutual contempt. The Myrmidons scrupulously stayed entirely away from the masculine chest-bumping that the other guards indulged in.

None of them had seen her; or if they had, they didn't recognize her.

Tayniz's lead clay had paled Barra's sunburned face and throat to a fashionable white, kohl enlarged her eyes, and crimson wax had been gently spread to emphasize the delicate bow of her lips. Her hair, freshly washed and lightly brushed with scented oil, piled up above her head in a gleaming mass of sorrel curls, set off by the ribbons of Tyrian purple that held them in place. A flowing dress of the same color, heavily draped in the Athenian style, softened the hard lines of her muscular figure; Tayniz, frowning, had added an extra drape across the shoulders that such a dress normally leaves bare. She had forgone jewelry—she didn't have the resources to compete with wealthy Tyrian wives and courtesans, and so had decided on a daring simplicity. Tayniz had swiftly sewn together elbow-length gloves, more in the Cretan style, out of fabric to match the dress. These hid not only the wounds on her wrists, but also her callused, grimy, nail-bitten warrior's hands. As they left their home in the late afternoon, Tayniz had declared herself satisfied, and had promised that if Barra didn't receive at least five proposals of marriage tonight, she'd eat that dress.

For her part, Barra felt clumsy and ridiculous, and vaguely helpless. She'd become convinced that the custom of wearing long dresses was invented by men, and intended precisely to make women helpless—you can barely fight, and you sure as bloody death can't run. If something went wrong, the daggers strapped to her thighs would be of little use beyond making sure she was not captured alive. She was completely out of her element; her skills as a warrior and as a sharp-eyed trader were useless here. To catch the eye of the Governor, and convince him of her truth, required the sorts of skills Tayniz had developed in her youth, or Barra's sisters, back home in Langdale, or Barra's mother Coll, who even now in her fifties could catch a man with a sly look and a tilt of the hips. She'd never had time nor interest to devote to such things; now she swore silently that she would study this, and practice it, as she would some new weapon.

She'd arrived with Peliarchus and Tayniz just at twilight—she had no intention of letting Idonosteus or the demonist get a look at her in broad daylight. She'd played for time all day, with changes to dress and hairstyle and such, to make sure that the feast would be in full swing and the day fading, so that no one would take too much notice of their arrival. This worked quite well—rather too well for Tayniz's taste—except for the seven or eight young men who always seemed to be drifting close to wherever Barra would stand, trying to draw her into conversation; not even her most pointed sarcasms seemed to dampen their enthusiasm at all. Finally, she let one of them lure her into a small yard behind the barracks, screened from the torchlight by a well-kept hedgerow. As he tried to pull her close, she delivered an efficient knee to the groin that lifted him off his feet and dropped him crumpled and gasping against a wall. Before he could so much as open his eyes again, he felt the edge of a dagger against his throat. "If you and your boys don't lose interest in me right now," he heard, "I'll make bloody sure you'll never be interested in a woman again, y'hear?"

The barracks itself had interested her somewhat; the strong scents of oiled bronze and leather clung heavily to it, worked into the wood itself. While the estate clearly required a small army of gardeners and other laborers to maintain, gardeners don't sleep with their tools—they would put their tools in the locked sheds that dotted the grounds. There's only one kind of professional workman who routinely sleeps with his tools: a soldier.

She worked her way back to a line of sight on the Governor. He'd been perambulating throughout the crowd, congenially accepting greetings and courteously laughing at stories. His topknot and braided beard were the color of a wave crest whipped by the wind, and the creases in his weathered face were visible even by torchlight from a bowshot away. She'd dared not approach him, for wherever he went, Meremptah-Sifti and his demonist were not far away.

The Pharaoh's grandson was tall and very fit; he wore the embroidered kilt and wide pectoral of the royal house, and his bare chest was broad and heavy with muscle. Looking at him, she doubted Kheperu's stories of drunkenness and dissipation; nothing about him bespoke anything other than strength and capability. His features were sharp, not blurred with drink, and when he laughed, his teeth shone very white. Barra had considered the idea that he might be duped, or even a helpless pawn under the demonist's control—but now, seeing him, it was hard to believe he wasn't in complete command.

She didn't even want to *look* at them too long; should the *sceon tiof* take her, she felt sure the demonist—whose name, she'd learned, was Simi-Ascalon; he posed as the estate's steward—would feel it and point her out, which could be very bad indeed. She needed some sort of distraction, something to draw the pair away. She wished desperately that she hadn't had to leave Leucas and Kheperu behind.

Kheperu had begged off: "I am sorry, Barra, but as you may recall these are Egyptian lands and I'm still under sentence of death. One of the many advantages of my particular personal hygiene is that no one looks too closely at me; if I'm clean and well dressed enough to mingle at this feast, I may be recognized. Meremptah-Sifti and his household are from Thebes, you know—it's not impossible that one or more of them may know me. One word to the Governor and *snick-snack*, there goes my head." Barra could hardly argue with that, and she'd been forced to agree with what Leucas had said; he was just too conspicuous, with his great height and broken face; little could be done to conceal either.

After circling back by the home of her foster-parents to inform them of the change in plans the day before, the companions had indeed headed out—conspicuously—into the desert. This required nothing in the way of further planning—after all, the mules were already loaded with supplies for a journey. They'd spent the night in rotating watches against the chance of being found by those hyaenae or other creatures of the demonist, sleeping in shifts, wearing full armor, tucked into a highly defensible crack in a hillside not far beyond the funerary caves. It was an utterly miserable night of rainsqualls and biting flies, made only worse by its uneventfulness. By morning Barra found herself wishing for an attack; it would have made the torturous semi-sleep that she'd suffered through seem almost worthwhile.

Now—presuming nothing had changed since she'd left them—Leucas and Kheperu lay patiently on or near the hill from which they'd originally observed the estate, taking turns watching the feast. They would have retied the packs onto the mules sometime around sundown. Barra had told them to pick an inn in town, but Leucas insisted, "We'll watch from the hills. So we might know if something has gone wrong."

Both Barra and Kheperu pointed out that there would be little to be done, and less yet that *could* be done by a lone warrior and an Egyptian alchemist from half-an-hour's march away, but their pair of cranky mules had nothing on Leucas for stubbornness. "You don't know," he stated calmly, again and again. "I might be able to help. You don't know." In the end, he got his way through sheer persistence.

Now Simi-Ascalon the steward/demonist had vanished somewhere among the guests and servants. Meremptah-Sifti still hung near the Governor's elbow, but Barra had no better ideas and had run out of patience. She threaded among the knots of guests, keeping a weather eye out for Simi-Ascalon.

Watching the Governor as she closed on him, Barra caught herself wishing for the *sceon tiof*. For once, it would be useful, perhaps even essential, to get a glimpse inside a man. He looked genial enough, with laugh lines deep as knife wounds across his temples, and he had a reputation for being both kindly and tough, if perhaps less than ideally smart. Barra was acutely aware of how far reputation could diverge from reality. Could he be swayed by argument, or would tears work better? If he didn't believe the story, was he cautious enough to quietly investigate it anyway? If he did believe her, was he strong enough to stand up to a prince of Egypt? How close was he to Ramses? Had the Pharaoh sent him here as a reward for past service, or as a politically safe exile to the Hittite frontier? Was Akhu-shabb really a capable administrator whose strength was needed, or was he an annoying weaselly back-stabber that Ramses had shoveled off here where he could do little damage? Once she opened her story, there would be no going back—and she just didn't know. This bitter twist did not escape her, how this gift that she'd earnestly wished the gods would take back would serve her perfectly now, when it wasn't working, but she was too worried to fully appreciate the irony.

Then she was among his personal guard; they lounged at their ease not far from the Governor, and several eyed her appreciatively. None made any comment, however, lewd or otherwise—not even a whisper—and they smelled clean and healthy, even the greying ones who were obviously longtime veterans. This made Barra feel a bit better; you can judge a commander by his men, and these were clearly disciplined, respectful, high-morale troops. But anyone with half a brain will choose his best men for his personal guard, she reminded herself. Still, it was a good sign.

Then she was before them, the wrinkled old warrior and the prince of Egypt. They broke off their conversation and turned to look at her.

Her breath caught in her throat as her eyes were helplessly drawn to those of Meremptah-Sifti.

*Oh, Loving Mother!* she thought desperately, her heart pounding. *That's the most beautiful man I've ever seen.*

Nut-brown skin, smooth and creamy as butter; high, broad forehead above liquid brown eyes; straight blade of a nose and a full, sensual mouth above a sculpted jaw; skin stretched rippling over smooth muscles, powerful shoulders beneath the arc of the pectoral tapering to a trim waist; just a trace of fine black hair climbing the furrow of his belly above his girdle. Then he smiled, his eyes lit from within by a flame of aristocratic assurance, and she wondered how she'd ever get enough breath to actually speak. *Tale of my life,* she thought.

He said, "Why, greetings, child. How is it that the sun has come back from his bed to light your face?"

"I, ah, well . . ." *Can he really see me blush even through this bloody paint?* Even as she stammered, she had the presence of mind to accent her Egyptian with Greek vowels. Meremptah-Sifti only smiled tolerantly; he was clearly accustomed to stopping the speech of women with his grin and a word or two. He reached out and gently laid his hand upon her arm. His touch burned.

"Tell me your name, that the pleasure of introducing you to our Governor may be mine."

"I am Briseis of Argos, Most High—of House Penthedes now," she said, dipping her knees in her best imitation of a courtesan's courtesy; her face heated up even more. *I hope that didn't look as clumsy as it felt.*

Meremptah-Sifti turned indulgently to the smiling man beside him. "Tal Akhu-shabb, it is very much my honor to present to you Briseis of House Penthedes."

The Governor looked her up and down, a frown both critical and avuncular furrowing his brow. He cleared his throat wetly, and held his winebowl out to one side, where it was instantly refilled by a slave bearing a large pelike. His eyes glistened, and his critical frown was replaced by the first twinge of a smile. "You're a lovely young thing, my dear. Are you a slave?"

Barra dipped her head, casting her gaze down at his sandals, trying to look demure. *Everybody likes demure, don't they?* "Yes, lord. Taken at Troy, gifted to Leokalkes, nephew of Agapenthes." This particular nephew she'd lately seen snoring behind a hedgerow. "I am offered again, for this night, as a gift to my lord."

Meremptah-Sifti's eyes danced, and he clapped the old man on the shoulder. "A princely token! I've half a mind to take her myself." He stepped close to her and took her shoulders, looking down into her face. He smelled of fresh bread and open space, of olive groves and wild figs. "How would that be, child? Would you like to grace the bed of a prince?" Barra met his gaze again, melting helplessly at his staggering beauty. She hoped she wouldn't have to kill him.

"I am only a slave, Most High," she mumbled. "I can only go where I am sent."

"Well, then, let us find your master and let him change his direction." He squeezed her shoulders, a frown stealing over his perfect features. "Why, you must be near as strong as a man! What sort of work did those Argive beasts force you to do?"

Barra thought quickly. This wasn't going at all well. "I, I'm a dancer, Most High, and a tumbler and acrobat."

"Hmm. Indeed. Well, then, you shall dance for me, eh? In my chamber. You don't mind, do you, Tal?"

The Governor gestured expansively. "It seems some small repayment for your glorious hospitality. I'm an old man, you know, age and drink have taken their tolls. A gem like this should be polished by a man who yet has some zest for the task, eh?" Meremptah-Sifti agreed with an appreciative chuckle.

"But, my lord Governor—" Barra began, alarmed.

"Yes, child?"

She needed a lie, quick and good. What would Kheperu say? "I, ah, well, lord, I have some small experience in kindling fires from the faintest of smoldering embers. . . . Do you not think . . . ?"

The Governor's spray of snowy eyebrows lifted, and a broader smile twitched at his lips, but then he shook his head sadly. "No, I think not, sorry to say. What trick could you play that I've not seen or done?"

"Well, I, mmm . . ." Barra clasped her hands behind her back and looked shyly at her feet. "I don't like to say."

The two men exchanged a look that burst into shared laughter. "A bashful whore!" the Governor chortled. "This may be an evening's entertainment better than any I've had for many a year."

Barra said, still with her head down, "Perhaps I could whisper in my lord's ear?"

"Oh, well," he replied, "I suppose I can go that far, with no strain on my poor old heart." He spread his arms. "Come here, child."

She folded herself into his arms and pressed her lips to his ear, cupping her hand around to hide them. She whispered, "I am neither slave nor whore. Your life and your command are in deadly danger. There is enemy magic in the air, and the gods do not protect us. If you would learn more, come with me to some place where we may speak in private." The Governor clutched her more tightly while these unexpected words registered in his mind. Around them, Meremptah-Sifti and the Governor's personal guard watched this charade with open amusement.

"By Ishtar and Astarte!" the Pharaoh's grandson said. "I think she's raised the Governor's banner!"

The Governor held her a moment longer, and Barra could feel the quickening of his heart against her chest. Then he released her, stepped back, and offered his arm gravely. "This endeavor may be worth the trying," he said gamely, but Barra's heart sank to see the concern clearly written on his face. Perhaps it wasn't as clear to the others, or perhaps they mistook its source. She had no better hope. As they walked away, she felt the gaze of Meremptah-Sifti blazing against her back.

They strolled arm in arm toward the house, and when they got to the doorway Barra cast a last glance over her shoulder. Across the party, far from his master, stood Simi-Ascalon, apparently deep in conversation with Idonosteus, but:

*He was looking at her.*

Barra leaned out the broad window, pressing back the shutters of polished cedar. The colonnade that led to the stable was empty, as was the small stretch of open yard between. She turned back to the Governor. "I think we can get to the stable without being seen. Come on."

He folded his arms across what once must have been a most impressive chest. "I think I have come far enough, on only your word."

"We may be interrupted here, lord." In fact, if that chilly bastard had recognized her, she could guarantee it. "I only want a bit more privacy." *And to have a horse at hand in case I need to bolt.*

"Not even Remmie would dare to disturb me. Speak on," the Governor said sternly, with a strength in his voice that lifted Barra's spirits.

But: "Remmie?"

The Governor grunted. "Meremptah-Sifti. I've known him since he was a boy. Ramses is like a brother to me."

*Oh, Loving Mother.* Still, he was her best hope. She looked at the dozens of figures painted on the walls that surrounded this expanse of floor; not scenes of battle, or of the daily life of an estate such as this one, but endless erotic variations of men and boys and women and animals and above it all the smiling Osiris, a gaping hole between his legs, giving his loving approval. The room was big enough to double as a dance ring, and was spread with cushions after the Tyrian fashion. She said, "Can we at least move to a smaller room?"

The Governor shook his snowy topknot stubbornly. "I have trusted you thus far, but no further. Begin your tale."

She gripped her nerves with both hands and clenched down on them. After a deep breath, she began. "I know you're here to keep a lid on the trouble in Tyre. I'd guess you already know that someone's been stirring this pot with dark magic."

His brows drew together. "I do know, yes. And I have taken steps to protect myself and my men against it."

"Good, good," Barra said, nodding. "I know who the sorcerer is, and I know why he's doing it."

The Governor's eyes lit up, and a certain thickening of his voice betrayed a rising excitement. "Oh, really? Sit with me here, and tell me this story. I would very much like to get my hands on this black magician, and my sword at his belly."

They lowered themselves onto a pile of cushions. Barra said, "You won't like this story, all right? Just hear it out, no matter how much it surprises or hurts you. All right?"

The old gentleman nodded gravely. "Speak on."

Barra told her story rapidly, leaving out only incidentals. She told of Chrysios, and the fight at Lidios' inn, of Mykos and the curse, of Tekrop-nekt, of Lysandros and Idonosteus, and the theft of Chrysios' corpse. The Governor's face showed his excitement mingling with mounting horror as she approached the end of her tale.

". . . And his banner unfurled, bloodred and purple, and it was this very estate," she finished breathlessly.

The Governor looked stunned. After a moment of dazed silence, he jerked himself to his feet. "Remmie's steward, Simi-Ascalon, was once of the priesthood; he has considerable knowledge of magic. . . . I've, I've already consulted with him on this matter . . . I always wondered how it was that a skilled priest would leave to take service under a minor member of the royal house—but this is madness! Am I to accuse Remmie of leaguing with a demonist on the word of this . . ." He caught himself, and shrugged at her apologetically. "I cannot believe this would be so."

Barra rose beside him. "You don't have to take my word for it. Investigate for yourself, look into it, have Meremptah-Sifti and Simi-

Ascalon questioned, do whatever you think needs to be done to be sure, but for the Love of the bloody Mother don't do it here. *You're not safe here,* do you understand? I don't know what the limits are of Simi-Ascalon's power, but I wouldn't put it past either of them to drop a vial of pukenut extract into your soup, or simply slip a knife into you."

"But, but I don't understand," the Governor said, shaking his head as if to clear it after a blow. "Remmie is a grandson of Ramses himself! The blood of God flows through his veins! He has wealth, women, anything a man can want—why in the name of the Living Horus would he want Tyre? Why would he do this?"

Barra stopped, and thought about it. Why, indeed? "I don't know," she said after a moment. "I can't even guess what drives him."

The Governor met her gaze, but then his eyes flicked over her shoulder and widened in surprise.

"Perhaps it is because," came the rich and resonant voice with undertones of mocking laughter, "I simply cannot bear the thought of having anyone around me that doesn't have to do exactly what I tell them to."

Leaning against the post of the door behind her was Meremptah-Sifti, and at his side stood the cold void of Simi-Ascalon.

Barra thought, *Oh, bloody fuck.*

"Barra. Coll. Eigg. Rhum." Meremptah-Sifti pronounced each syllable with distinct pleasure, as though savoring some unusual sweet. "Do I have that right? Idonosteus is a bit drunk." He flowed into the room, a loose-skinned predatory stalking like the cheetahs in his grandfather's menagerie. "You are very bold, Barra Coll Eigg Rhum, princess of Great Langdale—though Idonosteus tells me that this means only that your family has the largest mud hut—ship owner, tin trader, sometime scribe, mercenary. Whore. I admire you. Why did you not simply introduce yourself? We have a friend in common, after all. He sends his regards, as he is regrettably indisposed."

"Well, I . . ." The pounding of blood in Barra's ears made it difficult to think. She said, "If you don't even have the courtesy to learn how to properly pronounce my name, I'm leaving."

As she whirled toward the open window, Meremptah-Sifti said, "I think not."

It wasn't open anymore.

An instant's vivid image of crashing through the splintering shutters crossed Barra's mind, but now, for the first time, she became aware of their construction: diagonal slats of springy cedar on the inside—and she'd bet the slats on the outside crossed them at the opposite diagonal. No one crashes through shutters like those, and she had a sneaking suspicion that they were being held shut by men outside.

She turned back. "You're a shitty host, you know that?"

The Governor drew himself up to his full height. "Remmie, what is all this? What are you doing?"

An odd, secret smile flitted across Meremptah-Sifti's beauty. "Do not concern yourself, Tal. This is between the princess and myself."

"I, I mean, I suppose—"

"Drop the *princess* crap, all right?" Barra said, taking refuge in her cynical mercenary act. She wished desperately that her daggers weren't buried beneath yards of purple linen. While she kept talking, she clasped her hands behind her and began hiking up the back of her dress little by little, bunching it up above her wrists, hoping that the Egyptians wouldn't realize what she was up to before she could get those weapons in hand. "We don't exactly have kings the way you do down here—it's more like my brother knows some guys who'll stand up for him in a fight, if he asks them nicely. Now, on the other hand, if he finds out his favorite little sister's been hurt down here in Phoenikia, you'll have about a million and a half screaming Picts running around down here burning towns and killing Egyptians and doing all kinds of—"

"Shut up." Meremptah-Sifti strolled toward her, the very image of nonchalance. "Simi, close the door and join us."

The demonist spoke for the first time, his voice surprisingly thin and querulous for such a robust-looking man. "All . . . *hrahkhakh*"—a racking cough—"all right." The door that he swung shut was constructed very much like the shutters, of crossing diagonal boards. Barra realized with sinking heart that this manor house was built like a fortress.

"I do apologize, by the way, for the unfortunate result of my invitation the other night. Who would have known he was so vain? And so determined, in holding a grudge." He smiled, and Barra's mouth went dry as sand.

The Governor said, "I should return to the feast, and let you two handle your business here."

"Well, thanks a bloody lot!"

"Don't blame him, Barra." Meremptah-Sifti turned to the Governor. He spoke as a parent does to an unruly child. "I think not, Tal. I think you'll be staying here."

"I don't much like your tone," the old man replied stiffly.

"It doesn't matter. Sit down."

The Governor sat down.

Barra said incredulously, "What are you *doing*? You're the bleeding Governor of the Canaan District! You don't have to do what he tells you!"

"Yes, he does."

"What, just because you're Ramses' bloody grandson? He was appointed by the Pharaoh himself—and I hear Ramses doesn't even *like* you! I hear he thinks you're a lazy, perverted pile of shit!"

"My, my, what a mouth you have." Meremptah-Sifti shook his head, smiling. "You know, you're so lovely in your gown and face-paint, I had almost decided to keep you for myself. But I could never bear your tongue, so"—he sighed deeply—"I suppose I'll give you to Chrysios after all. You wouldn't happen to recall where you left his arms, would you?"

Barra's whole body seemed to freeze solid, waves of chill radiating downward from the back of her neck; she couldn't move, could barely breathe.

"Chrysios?" the Governor sputtered. "That's the name of the man whose body was—"

"Yes, yes, be quiet," Meremptah-Sifti snapped. "I'm in the midst of explaining something to the princess. Now," he said, drawing himself up and crossing his arms, "it would be traditional, at this point, to simply murder old Tal Akhu-shabb and tell the guests outside that you'd done it. We caught you in the act, you see, still holding the weapon and wearing the blood-smeared gown."

The Governor began to rise. "Murder? Me? But, but Remmie—"

Meremptah-Sifti forestalled his protest with an uplifted palm. "Don't speak until I give you leave." He turned back to Barra. "But that would be wasteful. Waste not, want not. I'm going to let you live, Tal, and you'll never mention what happened here today. I'll even let *you* live, princess, at least for a while."

Barra had the dress almost high enough to get at the daggers. She said, "Why?"

In answer, Meremptah-Sifti showed her teeth that glistened in the lamplight and said, "Tal: dance. Do the chicken dance."

And the Governor, without a word, climbed to his feet, crouched, doubled his arms, and began to flap them like wings. He shuffled grotesquely around the room, capering like an arthritic madman, his face gone purple and veins standing out in his neck.

Barra could only stare, tight pain growing in her chest. The folds of her dress dropped from her nerveless fingers. She said, "Stop." Against her will, her voice took on a pleading tone. "Stop him, you have to stop him!"

"No, I don't," Meremptah-Sifti said warmly. "I never have to stop. That's exactly the point. Tal: strip. Take off your clothes."

The Governor only slowed his dance so that he could pull at his clothing, never stopping, tears running down his face, pulling away his painted shift, exposing the scruff of grey hairs on his chest, his sagging old-man's belly and withered arms. Swelling showed high on his shoulder, where even if he were publicly bare-chested the mark would be covered by his formal pectoral, a dark blue-black mark on flesh still an angry red: a tattoo? He undid his breechclout and dropped it, still dancing. His pubic hair was grey as granite, and his genitals flopped limply, and Barra's vision began to blur with tears of her own.

Meremptah-Sifti, watching, had begun to massage himself through the embroidered kilt that he wore. Simi-Ascalon looked on, an expression of detached appreciation on his face, smiling a private smile and rubbing his fingers together.

Meremptah-Sifti said, "Tal: stop dancing and come here. Kneel before me." The Governor complied, and Barra's breath stopped in her throat.

The Pharaoh's grandson pulled aside the folds of his kilt to expose his erect penis, long and bulbous and the color of spoiled sausage. He looked not at the Governor, but at Barra, directly into her eyes, as he said, "Tal: suck on my penis."

In Barra's homeland, the Isle of the Mighty, they played a game that the Kelts had brought with them in their migration a century before Barra's birth. This game came to be known as Eirish Stand-Down, and its rules are fairly simple. It's played by two men at a time, who stand toe-to-toe. You punch your opponent as hard as you can. If he doesn't fall down, he wins. If he does fall, and then after he falls down he can't get up again, you win. You and your opponent trade blows until one of the two conditions prevail. A good match of Eirish Stand-Down can last for hours, especially since it's traditional to down a mug of beer after each pair of blows. Barra, who as a child couldn't bear to be left out of any activity the boys were up to, grew up playing this game. She wasn't very good at it; small as she was, it was almost impossible to remain competitive against boys half again her height and twice her weight. On the other hand, it led her to develop a truly impressive two-handed haymaker.

Now, as the Governor bent his head toward Meremptah-Sifti's groin, her numb paralysis finally shattered into fury. She shrieked a bone-chilling Pict war howl as she sprang at the prince of Egypt and whirled herself recklessly around: her doubled fists exploded against his face. The blow lifted Meremptah-Sifti off his feet and dumped him on the cushions, shaking his head dazedly and struggling to rise.

A hard shoulder slammed into her back, driving out her breath and bearing her to the floor beside him—Simi-Ascalon had tackled her from behind. She squirmed around within his grasp and got a hand on his face, thumb digging for his eye while her other hand blindly sought the hilt of a dagger within the folds of her gown.

She got a glimpse of the Governor, still pursuing Meremptah-Sifti on his knees, and then the prince was above her, standing, veins bulging in his face, blood pouring from his mouth. Her hand found the dagger's hilt, Simi-Ascalon clutched her tight and tried to bite her fingers, and Meremptah-Sifti snarled, *"You worthless cunt,"* and kicked her in the head.

Stars shot through her vision as the blow unstrung her limbs. He kicked her again, and again, she tasted blood and vaguely felt her nose break as the room darkened around her. Meremptah-Sifti pushed Simi-Ascalon off of her and straddled her, his hard thighs crushing away her air, his fingers tangled within her hair as he slammed her head into the floor again and again and again and as the darkness closed in around her she thought disjointedly, *I thought he said he was going to let me live.*

# 15

# The Sorcerer's Mark

The first vague stirrings of light within the darkness brought pain: face hurt, nose—no breathing here, only throbbing, mouth, taste of blood, ribs grabbing painfully—ah, that's a breath, she remembered what breathing felt like. Someone, something held her, leg and arms, head, everything constricted, no movement, only blind limbless writhing.

*I think she's waking up. You shouldn't have beaten her so hard, you could have killed—*

*Shut up. Hold her. Watch out for her teeth.*

Rape? Was that what was going on? She remembered rape. She remembered—

The road to Troy: eight days up the coast in a Penthedes freighter, off at Rhodes, a ferry to the mainland. Eighteen years of innocent blood-thirstiness and a pair of stone axes on foot through Thrace and into Lydia, spinning dreams of god-sired heroes, her breasts bound and her crotch stuffed. A mistake: the three deserters—Akhaian, she later learned: Mykenaians—were disappointed that she *wasn't* a boy. This was after they'd flung themselves upon her as she slept by the embers of her campfire. By this time, though, they'd already torn her clothes to shreds, and they shrugged and decided to go on ahead anyway. After all, there wasn't much a boy could have done for them that they couldn't get from her.

*Princess, you must speak to me. You must tell me who else knows your pretty tale.*

*Give her to me, I can make her answer. It will take only a moment.*

This was a voice she half knew, simpering and thick as though speaking through a mouthful of drool.

*I think not.*

*I demand that you give her to me!*

*Idonosteus, we are not partners. You should never consider yourself in any way to be my equal. Do not demand. If I choose, you shall have her while she yet lives.*

While she yet lives . . . she remembered—

No question but she was lucky they were so brutal. They used her for two days, there among the jutting rocks, while they ate and drank all the supplies she'd carried for her journey. She was unconscious for much of it, and when they decided it was time to move on, she couldn't walk, both eyes swelled shut, coughing blood with every breath. They gave her a few parting kicks that broke another rib and left her for dead. It could have been worse: they could have taken her along.

*Princess . . .* The voice was chiding now, and half-wheedling. *Tell me. You must tell me who else knows the story.*

She swam up out of the darkness enough to mumble, "Sleep. Just lemme sleep. Ask me later."

*Gibberish.*

*Perhaps. Perhaps it is her native tongue. None among my household will speak this—perhaps your servants?*

*No. Just slap her a few times, wake her up more.*

*Mmm. All right. You do it; this will be a little treat for you.*

Stinging hands sent her back into dreams.

It took her a year, all told, even though they made it easier for her by staying together. A year to heal, a year to replace her paired flint axes. A year to find a basalt blank that she liked, of the proper size, to trim it down with her hammerstone, chipping, chipping, a constant *chik chik chik* that she came to hear in her dreams. In Great Langdale, an experienced weaponsmith could produce a serviceable flint axe in a few hours, one of basalt or granite in a day. She worked hers for two weeks, refining the edge, smoothing the cheeks, rubbing them with a hunk of raw copper until they gleamed a rich killing green. And then practice, learning the broadaxe, learning the sinuous dance that let her slip shieldless aside from spears and swords, and always, always practicing her move, her own move, the one no one else used, the one which no defensive reflex that a veteran learns will counter: that whistling underhand arc, a speed move, useless to the big slow men who depend on strength and weight to batter through an opponent's guard, no power behind it beyond the sheer momentum of the stone blade. Later in life, she'd use it to quiet a bear that stood on flagstones within a ring of buildings pressing back against a mob, she'd use it to gut a handsome Corinthian who'd offended the gods, but now she practiced, and hunted, and practiced, and traveled, and practiced, and prayed, and practiced.

It took her a year, all told, to find them.

Pain from someone's nose brought her swimming up through dark water. Something pressed on it, hard and twisting. Broken, it was broken, she half remembered—Loving Mother, what if she couldn't *smell* anymore, what if she was like—

She mumbled, "Leucas . . ."

*What? What was that? Was that a name?*

*Hm. That's the Athenian, the big boxer. There's a question for you— where are the Athenian and the grubby Egyptian?*

*Grubby Egyptian?*

*No offense, Most High, but he is. He is. He must be seen—smelled— to be believed. He and the Greek are her partners. Where are they?* More twisting, fire bursts showering behind her eyes. *Where are Leucas and Kheperu?*

"Where are Leucas and Kheperu?" she repeated numbly. Well, where *are* they, really? Weren't they supposed to be rescuing her right now, or something? Or was she on her own?

*Tell me! I know you hear, I know you understand! Tell me!*

She'd told the story only once, in eleven years. She never told her parents—either set of them—she never told her sons, neither the adopted nor the one she'd given screaming bloody birth to at the age of fourteen. She'd told the story only to Khemshi, a huge and gentle Nubian, a spearman in the Ptah Division, one long golden-drifting afternoon in the haymow of a stable in Pharos. They lay with limbs entangled, and his face had taken on an uncommon gravity as the tale had leaked from her, not in a steady stream but drop by drop, the way a pinholed wineskin gives up its contents.

". . . And, you know, I only killed the first one. I wasn't quite as mad at him, if you must know. The other two are still alive, I'd guess. Right now they're likely skipping hand in hand through the forest and braiding flowers into each other's hair—if you receive my meaning."

The Ptah Division had marched less than a week later, to reinforce a beleaguered frontier garrison. Khemshi was killed on campaign above the Second Cataract in Kush. She'd heard, later, that the spear he took in the belly had not killed him outright, and in his three days of dying fever he'd asked for her. She'd picked him up to ease an interval when her loneliness had become unbearable; she had barely known him.

Her life was full of regrets and missed chances.

But never for lack of trying.

This time she struggled up into the light by her own will. Her consciousness once again inhabited her eyes, and she decided, finally, very deliberately, to open them.

Meremptah-Sifti's smiling face greeted her, blurred and twisting into twins and back again. Floating near his side was the bulbous jowly mass of Idonosteus.

She was tied, with what she couldn't tell, and someone who knelt behind her held her head—Simi-Ascalon, probably. She lay on cushions that would have been comfortable if not for the bound position of her arms and legs. This was still the room where she'd spoken with the Governor; as this realization came to her she also became aware of muffled sobbing that came from somewhere out of her line of sight. That, more than anything, told her that she hadn't been unconscious more than a few minutes: Tal Akhu-shabb was too tough an old bird to cry for long, even from the shattering humiliation he'd suffered. Soon he should recover at least a facade of dignity.

She squinted blearily at Meremptah-Sifti, whose mouth was swelling nicely, already showing traces of blue-black bruising. "I repeat," she said thickly, "you're a shitty host. And your face is a mess," *though I'm sure it's a sight prettier than mine right now.* "Who's a girl have to maim to get a drink around here?"

"Hmm." His aristocratic self-possession had entirely returned, and with it his superior smile. "We have no very great time to spend, Princess. Tell me now who knows your tale."

Barra sighed. With great effort she could force her swollen tongue to form clear words. "Well, let's see, mm, well, there's the Governor, Idonosteus, you—"

He cut her off by taking her broken nose between the first knuckles of two fingers and grinding it through a short arc. Her eyes glazed and blurred with tears, and she clenched her jaw against a yelp. Through the blur she could see Idonosteus licking his mouth. Fresh blood trickled across her lips.

Meremptah-Sifti sighed, "Let's try that again, shall we?"

When she could trust her voice again, she said, "You're not all that bright."

His eyebrows went up. "Oh?"

"If you'd been thinking, you'd have realized that I wouldn't tell anyone except the heads of the Great Houses or the Governor. Nobody else can do anything about you. And you'll kill anyone who knows."

He straightened up, nodding. "And where are your partners?"

She gave her best approximation of a shrug. "Hiding in the desert."

Idonosteus said, "What about your family?"

A frozen hand clenched in her belly.

"Family?" The word, in Meremptah-Sifti's mouth, dripped with malicious joy.

"Oh yes." Idonosteus' chins jiggled with the nodding of his head. "She lived with the Penthedes shipmaster and his wife. In fact, they are here tonight, at your invitation. . . . This is no doubt how she got past the guards."

"Mmm, well. So." Meremptah-Sifti reached down and gently stroked her chin, the line of her neck. His flesh felt warm and dry, and she couldn't shrink away and she didn't dare to bite him. "I imagine that we'll have your cooperation, then, won't we?"

"I . . ." Barra's voice rasped in her throat; she coughed to clear it. "It won't do you any good to hurt them. They're pledged to Agapenthes, and he'll revenge them if they come to any harm."

"Of course he will." Meremptah-Sifti's gaze drifted over her head as though he was deep in thought. "I suppose it really doesn't matter, much. Slight change, minor adjustment. Hmm. We'll do it right now, I think. Everyone's here, everyone I need for a successful beginning. Sim, are you ready?"

The nervous, phlegm-roughened voice came from close behind her. "I, well, I can be, I suppose. In half of an hour, less perhaps . . ."

"Very well. Idonosteus, you can be of service here again. Gather the Heads and such of their lieutenants as are most trusted and influential. Tell them that an attempt has been made on the Governor's life, and I must speak with them all immediately. Bring that fool of a garrison commander in here as well. Oh, and—get that shipmaster and his wife."

Idonosteus licked his lips, nodded, and scurried out.

"Sim: get your equipment and summon six guards, mm, just tell Haral to bring his five best men—he's over by the fountain."

"All—*hrakhakh*—all right." The gripping hands left her head and Simi-Ascalon stumbled out.

"Tal: stop crying."

The sobbing ceased abruptly. Barra could turn her head now; the Governor sat in a crumpled ball not far to her right.

Meremptah-Sifti pursed his lips. "Tal: from now on, you will believe that you take my suggestions of your own will. You love and adore me and want nothing in the world so much as to please me in every way."

The Governor did not respond, only looked up at the prince with bruised eyes.

"If, after I leave this room, this woman makes any attempt to escape, or even speaks, kick her in the head until she stops moving. And fix your clothing. Make yourself presentable."

The Governor busied himself with his clothing. Meremptah-Sifti once again smiled down upon Barra. "I'll return shortly. Please don't do anything that would make Tal hurt you. I think the old gentleman's actually fond of you, and he'd regret it later."

"What . . . what are you going to do with me? Fix me up with a tattoo like his?"

He gave her a mock frown. "Not at all. Am I not a man of my word? You will be given to Chrysios—although what he expects to be able to do with you, considering the shape in which you left him, I cannot say. No, the tattoo, that's a curious thing, that bit of magic. It only works if you ask for it. If you take it willingly."

He crouched on his haunches beside her. "The human will is extraordinary, isn't it? Perhaps more than anything else, the will is what makes us human; the ability to intend, to see a future and direct our thoughts and actions toward it. A powerful force, a potent force that can bend the course of history, and yet it is so easily surrendered. Sometimes with hardly even a thought. Sim's little tattoo, why, that's just another way of surrendering; it's like a slave's collar that won't close unless one fastens it around one's own neck."

"What future?" Barra asked softly, picking something from his rambling to keep him talking. "What future is it you're going after?"

"That can hardly matter to you," he said, standing again and striding toward the door. He finished the thought without looking back, ". . . since you won't be there to see it."

Helplessness clawed at her; she had to do something more than only lie here and wait to die; she had to fight, to hit back, somehow, no matter how petty or ineffectual it might be. She called after his retreating back, "Y'know what, you bastard? Everyone says your mother's a *whore!*" He kept walking, without so much as a twitch to indicate he'd heard her. "And I hear that you've sucked more than your share of—"

But he was gone from the room now, and the soft step behind her was the only warning she got before the Governor's kick exploded stars across her eyes and sent her spiraling back down into nothingness.

She had never been prone to nightmares, not even as a child, and so she had no recognition of this fog of shrieking apparitions that swam in and out of her vision, doubling and redoubling. Bruising claws dug into her arms and yanked her upright, and torchlight speared her eyes. Light pulsed within her head, flashing at the corners of her eyes in time with her heartbeat. Her head weighed tons, she struggled to bring it upright, and suddenly her throat ripped with vomiting as though a giant had leaped upon her belly. The spasm finally passed, and she hung strengthless in their grip.

Faces crowded in around her, and words wavered into comprehensibility and out again.

gabble *under the charm of the sorcerer, of course* . . . *Here, look here, at* gabble gabble . . . Hands ripped at her dress, the beautiful gown that her mother had made; tears leaked from her eyes as the cloth gave way, and clearly through the haze in her brain she heard the horrified gasps.

. . . *armed, you see? She nearly killed him* . . . gabble *daggers* gabble gabble *barely caught her in time* gabble gabble gabble . . .

Some of the faces she recognized, vaguely, in a sort of distant blurry way—a fat man that she was sure she knew from somewhere, repulsive and quivering; a handsome Egyptian who was doing most of the talking: he frightened her, somehow, though she couldn't remember why. And there—there was Peliarchus, she knew him, she was almost sure that this grey-faced, stricken old man was named Peliarchus, and she loved him very much, but who was the woman he held in his arms, her face buried against the joining of his neck and shoulder? That was, was, was Tayniz, she foggily guessed.

*I'm hurt,* was her first clear thought, and she was obscurely pleased that it rang so true. *People've been kicking my head.*

Now the Egyptian was talking again; she guessed that what he was saying might be important, and so she gritted her teeth and forced herself to understand him.

". . . consulted with the Governor, and he agrees. My steward, Simi-Ascalon, was once a priest of Osiris, and is an expert in these matters.

The Governor and the highest officers of the Canaan Division have been protected from this sorcerer's power—it is a simple charm, merely a moment's work, a tattoo that renders one completely immune. Now that this sorcerer has struck at the very heart of Egypt, in the use of this poor girl to attempt a bloody assassination, I feel that it is my duty to make this protection available to all of you. I am only sorry that my steward could not have done so earlier, in time to save your friend Othniel, Jephunah; or yours, Nephrol; or any of the dozens of unfortunates who have died at the inns, innocent victims of a wizard's vendetta against this city. But at least there is this comfort: all of you here tonight, along with such of your nearest and dearest that so desire, can be completely, almost painlessly, perfectly protected."

They clamored for it—at first, they still tried to hold their dignity, but even through her hazy eyes she could see the wide-eyed lust on their faces, the twisting elemental need like a baby's cry for the tit. They stretched out their hands, asking to be taken ahead of their fellows, ahead of their wives and children, as though in this last moment of vulnerability the sorcerer could come and slay all who delayed. So much fear, so much helplessness, weeks and months of creeping tension as the curses and the fires and the demons struck here and there at random throughout the city—how could anyone resist such an offer? A little mark on the skin: an end to fear.

Barra croaked, *"No . . ."*

None of the clamoring press could have heard her, but Meremptah-Sifti's head came around as she spoke.

She tried again, gathering strength and pushing for volume to cut through the surf of voices. "It's a trick! No! Don't—"

Meremptah-Sifti came to her, stood close before her until his smiling face filled her eyes. He cupped her chin with his strong dry hand, pressing closed her mouth against the unbearable weight of her head. "You never give up, do you?" he said softly, almost lovingly. "Do you not understand that you've lost? Now you must turn your attention to salvaging what can be saved from the wreckage." His smile spread like oil, curving maliciously. "Think of Peliarchus, think of his wife. Think of what could happen if they are not *protected* from the *sorcerer . . .*"

She inhaled a pale spark of anger and spat blood across his face. His eyes suddenly blazed, and a vein pulsed out from his hairline to his brow; his fist clenched and only tendon-popping self-control stopped its flight toward her face.

"Most High . . . Most High, please, lord, may I ask . . . ?"

Meremptah-Sifti turned, and behind him was Peliarchus, ashen and trembling, Tayniz leaning with stricken dignity upon his shoulder. Barra's heart plunged within her breast; she could not risk endangering them further.

Peliarchus said in halting Egyptian, "Please, lord, this girl is like my own daughter. If she is the, the helpless . . . tool of the sorcerer, then she herself is blameless, isn't she? What will you do with her? You won't . . . please say she won't be—"

Meremptah-Sifti smoothly swallowed his rage and lifted his hand to wipe his cheek and mouth. "This is not within my control. The Governor shall make the disposition; it is he who bears responsibility for the administration of justice. For my part, I can do no more than see to it that she"—he half turned back toward her, and smiled with the half of his face that his audience couldn't see—"receives that same special protection from the sorcerer. Beyond that, we must await the Governor's decision."

"Can I speak with her?"

"Of course. I do not know, however, if she will understand you."

Peliarchus stepped close. Barra could taste the fear on him. "Listen, Barra, Barra honey, they're going to help you. I, we, know that none of this was your fault, and I'll go to Agapenthes, he'll understand, and he'll talk to the Governor, and everything will be all right. All right? Everything will come right in the end, you'll see. I promise." He was trying, trying so hard to sound confident, but he was so scared. . . .

Barra's eyes filled with stinging tears, and the story swelled behind her lips, the story of what had been done, was being done to the whole city, but over Peliarchus' shoulder she could see the calm, close-lipped smile and one slightly lifted eyebrow of Meremptah-Sifti. She dropped her head and released her effort, and the world drifted away into fog once again.

*. . . Take her . . . workshop . . . until I arrive . . . may require . . . hours . . .*

Those bruising hands dragged her toward darkness, and she barely felt them.

"Stand aside."

Barra swam up toward the light once again. She'd been occasionally aware of what was happening to her—she knew that she was being dragged somewhere, but she had no idea how long they'd been dragging her, or where they were going, or even if they were still on the estate. Like some great sea creature, she'd surface only long enough for a breath, and then slip back down into the darkening depths.

"Stand aside." The first command had been in mellow, almost indulgent Egyptian. This one now came more forcefully in Phoenikian, as did its reply.

"I don't think so."

When Barra's eyes opened, she at first saw only what her captors saw: a loose semicircle of men in servants' dress of light belted chitons. Something familiar in their faces tickled her mind.

They seemed to be in some sort of cellar—at least, there were no windows. Barrels and sacks were stacked neatly around them, floor to ceiling, labeled flour, salt pork, apples, wine, beer, and on and on in Egyptian demotic. Two armored men half held, half carried her. Two others carried lamps. And the final two carried swords.

"You shouldn't be here. This is the prince's private stores."

One of the men in servant's dress shrugged unusually broad shoulders. "We're leaving, soon enough. And we're taking the woman with us."

The man who spoke was missing one ear, and a white streak in his hair was connected to a similar one in his beard by a long thin scar.

Barra's heart sang.

The leader of the guards looked over the men that faced him. They were ten to his six, but they were unarmed, while he and his men wore bronze cuirasses and helmets, greaves and bracers, and carried broadbladed swords. The leader said, "You're mad. Get out of here before you get killed. The prince won't like it, us killing servants at his feast."

Kamades replied, "I said we're taking the woman, and I'm a man of my word."

"Look," the guard said patiently, "I don't want to hurt you. I don't even know you. But I've got my orders, and if you don't get out of our way, I'll cut you down where you stand and take my chances with the prince."

Kamades spread his hands, smiling, seemingly calm, but there was a certain gleam in his eye. "I'll wrestle you for her. One fall, winner gets the girl." The other Myrmidons also began to crack smiles and nudge each other.

The guard sighed heavily and looked exasperatedly at his fellows, as though to say *can you believe how stupid this guy is?* In the bare second that his eyes were averted, Kamades stepped up and grasped the wrist of the guard's sword arm with his left and unloaded a thundering right cross on the guard's cheekbone. The other Myrmidons were already in motion, no need for a signal of any kind, leaping upon the other guards.

Barra barely had time to gasp a single breath. The lamps crashed to the floor, one extinguishing and one wick still flickering in a spreading pool of oil. Kamades used his grip on the guard's wrist to swing the half-stunned man to the floor, dropped his knee on the man's chest, and in a single smooth motion drew his dagger and sank it into the guard's throat. By the time he could rise again, his men had finished the fight—the other, with sword in hand, had a cut throat that gurgled as the last of his life poured across the floor; the other four had never had a chance to draw. They were all facedown on the floor, being efficiently hog-tied by the Myrmidons.

Barra sagged against a wine cask, barely able to stand. "Loving Mother!" she breathed. "You guys are good."

Kamades flashed her a grim look; all traces of his earlier smile had vanished. "Who's hurt?" he said.

Only one voice responded—the Myrmidon who'd dealt with the other swordsman had taken a shallow cut under his arm. Two others retrieved the unbroken lamp and lit it from the guttering wick of the other before stamping out the spreading flames.

"How . . ." Barra gasped, "how did you find me? How did you—"

"Not now," Kamades told her curtly, then turned away from her and began snapping orders while he gathered up the sword and belt of the man he'd killed and wrapped them in cloth. In seconds one of the Myrmidons had stripped, to offer his chiton to Barra, who only now was becoming coherent enough to remember that she was naked except for the pair of empty knife scabbards still strapped to her thighs. Another took blood from the floor and smeared it across his face, while a third tore his chiton into a strip to bind up Barra's hair in the guise of a bandage.

"What—?"

"You look bad," Kamades explained. "If anyone questions us, you and him got drunk and started fighting. He—the one with the cut—got hurt trying to break it up. I'm taking the pair of you to the stable to sleep it off until the party's over. Got that?"

Barra nodded dizzily. "Ay, surely. But what about your naked friend, there?"

"He'll stay here to watch the guards, make sure they don't get loose, and raise the alarm before you're well away."

She frowned. "You're going to let them live?"

His face kept swimming in and out of focus; she couldn't read his expression at all. "I can do my duty without killing them," he said. "So, yes, I'm going to let them live."

"But, but they'll *tell*! They'll tell it was you that helped me!"

"Barra, you are my guest-friend. I am doing what is right. I'm not going to hide from the consequences."

"Kamades—"

"Hush. Your form can pass for a boy's, but your voice can't. Let's go before we're missed."

Barra tried to fix in her memory the route they took up out of the manor's bowels, but her mind wouldn't hold the facts. While they went, Kamades explained in a low voice that he hadn't even known she was at the feast until the rumor went around that some redheaded woman had tried to kill the Governor. "But I didn't!" Barra protested weakly. Kamades shook his head. "It doesn't matter." He felt his obligation was clear: the only way to save her from execution, or so he'd thought, was to wait for her to be led to wherever they would lock her up and take her away from her guards. He and the Myrmidons had spread themselves through the chambers surrounding the shut-up room where the Heads had gone, and had followed the guards when they dragged her out.

Twice on their way through the feast they were stopped by armed men and questioned about the blood that painted their faces and clothes. Twice Kamades told his story, twice the guards examined Barra's bloodied, swollen face with incurious eyes, and each time the guards waved them along. Everyone seemed much more concerned with the swirling rumors of strange things going on in the room in which the Heads were cloistered. There was much debate about it— even the entertainers had stopped their pointless acts, and stood in little knots, conjurers with acrobats, singers with jugglers, talking mostly in whispers. Word was out that an attempt had been made on the Governor's life, but no one seemed to know what could be happening now within the house.

Barra knew, and the sick twisting in her stomach might have come as much from that knowledge as from the nauseous spinning of her head.

After what seemed endless stumbling progress, they reached the warm darkness of the nearest stable. Hand gestures from Kamades told four of the Myrmidons to search out the stalls, to make sure that there were no surreptitious lovers nestled within the straw. Seconds later, they told him that they were alone, and he turned to Barra. "We have a horse for you—I have a horse for you; she's mine. Take her—

Glandys will saddle her for you. Take this." He thrust forward the cloth-wrapped sword and belt of the lead guardsman. "We can't help you beyond getting you off the estate; Lord Idonosteus has ordered us to stay with him tonight. After that, my duty is discharged and you're on your own."

"Kamades," Barra said, shaking her head, trying to rattle some clear thought back into it, "Kamades, you have to come with me. You all must come with me. You have to leave here now."

"No, we don't." Kamades' voice was cold as mid-winter in the northern fjords. "And we won't. We've been ordered to stay near the side of our lord. We obey. What I've done already tonight is dishonor enough."

"What is the *matter* with you? Why are you acting this way?"

"I believe that Lord Idonosteus regards you as an enemy, but you are my guest-friend. The danger you're in puts me in a place where I must choose between my duty to my lord and my duty to the God. I have . . . dishonored myself . . . to preserve the sacred bond of guest-friendship, but now my duty there is done. If I am ordered to hunt you down, I'll . . ." For the first time, his metallic tone faltered; his voice faded and he looked away. ". . . I will do it, Barra. I beg you to go, and may Zeus spare me that task."

"Listen to me!" she insisted, clutching at his chiton to hold herself upright. "You don't know what kind of man that fat bastard is! He doesn't deserve your service. Cutting his throat would do you more honor than taking his orders."

Kamades' face froze over once again. "You must go, now."

How could she explain? What words could tell all the truth in the little time they had? She ground her teeth in frustration. "You don't know what he'll do to you for letting me go. You have no idea what he's capable of."

"I have sworn my service to him. Whatever punishment he chooses, I'll accept."

"Loving bloody *Mother*! You and your bloody honor, your talk about guest-friendship and duty to the God and duty to your lord and I don't know *what* bloody all! If Idonosteus were here, right now, he'd be ordering you to cut off my head so he can fuck my corpse in the neck! And he'd make you watch him do it."

Kamades' eyes went wide and hot, gleaming in the lamplight. "Then you'd better be gone before he gets here," he snarled.

Barra's temper flared inside her head, sending sparks shooting across her vision. "You thickheaded son of a goat's asshole! Why won't you listen? I'm trying to save your *worthless bloodyfucking life*!" Her battered mouth cracked with her shout, and she tasted fresh blood.

Before Kamades could snarl his reply, distant yelling came from the direction of the manor house. Kamades cast a desperate glance over his shoulder. "I think we've been found out. Can you ride?" His voice held a note of sudden care that tore at her chest.

Barra nodded. "I think so."

He led her to his horse's side and helped her up into the high-built saddle. "Her name's Andromakhe. Steer with your knees. Now go!"

Barra found looking down from this new height to be more than a little dizzying. She gathered the woven-rope reins in one hand, and with the other reached down to touch Kamades' face. "I'll see you again."

His eyes met hers, and they were far warmer than his tone. "I hope not—unless it is by my will, not my lord's order." He spun away from her. "Glandys! Othoön! Cut the girths of every saddle! Lalcamas, open that door and bar it behind her when she goes. Come on, snap!"

The broad doors swung back. Barra leaned forward to wrap her arms about Andromakhe's neck, and kicked her hard in the ribs. The mare sprang forward, scattering a crowd of approaching guardsmen, and galloped off into the night. They'd be on her trail in minutes, saddles or no. She thought she could hear, among the startled shouts and cries that accompanied her passage, faintly behind her the deep growl of Kamades still snapping orders. She told herself that the sharp sting in her eyes came only from the wind.

The ride was a bouncing, jouncing nightmare; every beat of Andromakhe's hooves pounded another spike into Barra's brain. She hung on grimly, arms locked around the mare's neck. Bare moments after she'd burst from the stable, two broad spears of torch-bearing riders had curved out after her, swinging wide to cut off any escape. The wind had shifted, now bringing high clouds in from over the sea, and the declining moon cast huge hill-shadows across her path.

In the dark, every hill looked alike, and shouts might carry to her pursuers. Finally, Barra had to coax Andromakhe to a halt; the mare stood, flanks heaving. Barra put both hands to her face, one on either side of her swollen nose, and suddenly pressed hard while pulling down. The pain made her vision swim, and completed the process that the ride had begun: she vomited convulsively. But after she wiped the last strings away from her lips, she was able to blow, painfully, a huge glob of half-clotted blood from her nose and then she could breathe through it again, just a little. Just enough.

After that, it took only a few minutes of judging the wind and riding back and forth. She knew she was in the right general area, and Kheperu's scent would stand out in a slaughterhouse.

She found it and rode upwind, following, she crested a small rise, and there they were; she dizzily prayed that the Mother might shower blessings on them like rain. She tried to greet them, but her throat constricted and she could barely croak a hail. They both came to their feet, uncertain; Leucas had his spear in hand and his shield in place, and Kheperu reached within his robe, but then the last wisp of cloud was swept away from the moon.

"Great Thundering God!" Leucas said. His shield and spear dropped by his side, and he sprang to her. "What did they do to you?"

She let herself collapse into his arms. He cradled her gently, while Kheperu took Andromakhe's reins. Leucas lowered her to the pile of blankets he'd been using as a cot. She said thickly, "The next time . . . the next time I tell you I want to go in somewhere by myself? You should just beat the shit out of me right then, save the other guys the trouble."

Kheperu knelt beside her, reins still in hand. "I take it things did not go as well as they might?" he said, but the mockery in his tone was only reflexive, almost loving.

"I'll hit you for that later, when I can move again. I am," Barra rasped, "really, really, *really* glad to see you guys." She clutched Leucas' arm with both hands, pulled on it as she tried to sit up.

"No, no," he said, gently pressing her back down onto the blankets, "you just lie there for a bit."

"I wish I could," she said, "but pretty soon the whole shitcake Egyptian army is going to be hunting us. If we want to live through the night, we'd better find a place to hide."

# 16

# *Hostages*

The pair of lamps sprouted flames that rose tall and still in the dead air of the cellar, twisting pillars of lampblack falling upward to the ceiling. The smell here was unmistakable: the blood that had poured from the curling cut across Haral Mesti's throat mingled with the shit that his dying convulsions had squirted into his armor. The unconscious men had been untied and revived; only the two corpses now lay here. Meremptah-Sifti stood with his sandals half an inch from the edge of the pooled blood, and looked down upon his dead captain. The prince held a handkerchief of white linen to his mouth, and every so often pulled it free and examined it to see if his swollen and split lips had stopped bleeding.

Idonosteus hovered nervously near the prince's shoulder, rubbing his sweaty hands together. Meremptah-Sifti ignored him, interested instead in the scar-faced man in servant's dress who stood holding the lamps. He appeared perfectly calm, perfectly relaxed, entirely oblivious of the pair of men-at-arms who held the stabbing points of their blades against his ribs, one to either side of him.

"You did this? *You?*" Meremptah-Sifti said in slow Phoenikian, mindless of the bad taste his milk tongue left on his lips.

The scar-faced man's eyes shifted, looking behind the prince to Idonosteus. The fat merchant must have given some sign, because now the man nodded in response.

"With men—the men I lead," he said, his words halting and thickly accented. "Yes."

"How many?"

The scar-faced man frowned. "Ten—one, there, watching," he

pointed toward the stairs that led upward into the house. "Nine, and me."

Meremptah-Sifti murmured, "Extraordinary." He glanced over his shoulder. "These are the pretend servants you brought with you yesterday, to my patio, are they not?"

Idonosteus' chins jiggled with his nervous cough. Meremptah-Sifti smiled secretly to himself at how much that preparatory throat clearing resembled Haral's; Haral, who lay at his feet here with his throat cleared for good and all.

"Y-yes, my prince, but, you see, I don't think—"

"Six men," Meremptah-Sifti mused, ignoring Idonosteus' panicked sputtering. "In full armor, with swords. Ten men in servant's chitons, armed with, what? Knives?" He shook his head. "Extraordinary. Haral was a good man, and his men are veterans. By all rights, they should have slaughtered you."

The scar-faced man shrugged blandly. "He feared to disrupt your feast, by killing servants."

"Yes . . ." Meremptah-Sifti nodded, chuckling. "Yes he would, wouldn't he? Poor Haral. If I had known of your skill, yesterday, perhaps I would have been more cautious in my dealings with your master. I had no idea how much danger I was in."

His chuckle expanded into a throaty laugh, and he turned back to Idonosteus; the blood painting his teeth and drying on his chin made his grin so gruesome that Idonosteus flinched back as though he feared the prince would bite him. "I hope you have a good explanation for why your bodyguards killed two of my men and let that little whore get away."

"I, well, no." Idonosteus shook his head hastily, having come to a swift decision to tell the truth. "I cannot say—they're Phthians, you know, and all Greek speakers are lunatic."

"Mm. I have heard this said before."

"She and I are guest-friends," the scar-faced man said calmly. "Guest-friendship is a bond that is sacred to Zeus. I could not stand by and allow her to come to harm."

"Zeus?" Meremptah-Sifti said disbelievingly. "What is Zeus, some Akhaian god? Some little hedge-god from halfway across the world? You fear this little unknown god so much that you throw away your life?"

The scar-faced man's gaze had a curiously occulted look to it, as though he didn't really see the prince at all. "I do not fear the God. I respect his law."

"But this is Phoenikia, do you see? Your little god has no power here."

The scar-faced man did not respond.

Meremptah-Sifti turned his face to Idonosteus and murmured, "Yes, he is mad; but mad perhaps in a very useful way."

Idonosteus licked his lips. "Un-until this moment, my prince, I, I would have said that he was completely reliable."

Meremptah-Sifti shrugged. "Perhaps he is." He directed his words once again to the scar-faced man. "You must have known you would be punished."

He shrugged minutely.

"Why did you not run away? Escape with her?"

"I am sworn to my lord Idonosteus' service."

Meremptah-Sifti shook his head in wonder, and then his face broke out into a broad smile, oblivious of the cracking of his lips and the fresh blood that flowed because of it. "I respect your devotion to duty," he said, with only a hint of mockery, "and, I think, your punishment should be . . . mm, deferred to some later date. Your name is, what, Kamades?" He glanced at Idonosteus for confirmation; the fat man nodded. "Meanwhile," the prince went on, "you and your men should be protected from the sorcerer, even as are my own men. Go now, gather your men, and take them to Simi-Ascalon."

Again, the scar-faced man's eyes flicked to Idonosteus, who nodded. The scar-faced man handed his lamps to the men-at-arms, and walked stiffly up the stairs.

"And I hope you won't mind waiting," Meremptah-Sifti called after him with a laugh. "I understand there's quite a line!"

Idonosteus chuckled at his shoulder. Meremptah-Sifti's smile vanished behind the bloodstained handkerchief as he took a step away, half turned, and laid a whistling slap across Idonosteus' face.

Idonosteus staggered back a step or two, hands up to his reddening cheek and tears filling his eyes. "Wha—?"

"This is your fault," Meremptah-Sifti said, his voice low and deadly. "Those are your men, you should have known what they would do. Idiot. I should open your guts right here beside my men."

"B-but, but my prince, how could I *possibly*—"

"Be silent, you contemptible toad. The sound of your voice brings vomit to my throat." He regarded his hand with distaste; his palm was moist with the sweat that had coated the fat man's cheek. With a shudder of disgust, he wiped it on his kilt. "You boasted to me of your thousand men, who know all of Tyre. I have the army to seal the city; she cannot get away overland. If she is not taken tonight, she will go to ground in the city. Find her."

He stepped close to Idonosteus, and leaned into his face until he could feel the man's breath upon his own lips. "You lost her. You'll find her. You would regret disappointing me in this."

"I, ah . . . I, ah . . ." Idonosteus, now that he was recovering from the sting of the slap, looked at Meremptah-Sifti with a certain glow to his eyes. Far from standing up for himself like a man, he was licking his lips in anticipation.

Meremptah-Sifti grunted and turned away; he should have known Idonosteus was that type, he'd seen enough of them in his childhood.

Idonosteus said, "If she is not taken tonight, my men will comb the city—although, my prince, I have an idea that she'll find a way of avoiding such crude methods. She's shown herself to be exceptionally resourceful, and skilled in changing her appearance."

"Is this some childish attempt to excuse failure in advance?"

"N-no, my prince, not at all. I was only thinking that, well, per-haps it might be more effective to have a plan to, well, to draw her out."

"Mm?"

"This can certainly wait for morning—no need to alarm your other guests. But it seems to me that she lived in Tyre for a few years with that Penthedes shipmaster . . ."

"Hostages?" Meremptah-Sifti's mouth quirked upward. "The dif-ficulty with a hostage is that if you don't kill him, you are not taken seriously; if you do, his value is lost."

"Not, not *necessarily*," Idonosteus said. "I have an idea."

Once Idonosteus explained his idea in detail, Meremptah-Sifti shook his head in open admiration. He slid an arm around Idonosteus' soft and flabby shoulders and said, "You have made me become grate-ful that I let you live."

# 17

# *Stand Down*

**B**arra woke to a dully painful pulling sensation, as though a none-too-gentle hand had taken hold of the end of her nose, and a strange unpleasantly tangy taste soured the back of her mouth. She opened her eyes to find Kheperu's greasy beard far too close to her face, and he was rubbing something onto her bruises that stung and made her eyes water.

She didn't have the strength to punch him or push him away, so she settled for saying, "If I could breathe through my nose, I'd probably have to kill you." Her voice sounded thin and weak, alarmingly so, even to her own ears.

Kheperu only smiled distantly and encouraged her to roll over. The bed beneath her was too comfortable; considerable encouragement was required before she was willing to move. On the floor next to the head of the bed was a steaming pot of some kind of watery greenish preparation, with what might have been bits of leaves and flowers floating on its thick and greasy-looking surface. Kheperu held out his hand. "Blow."

Barra grimaced. "It hurts."

"I don't care. Blow."

Barra shut her eyes and blew a burst of bloody goo from her nose. Kheperu caught it deftly and examined it with interest. "Good, good," he murmured. "You are coming along fine. Here, drink this."

He offered her a mug about a third full of some thick milky fluid. She drank it; the taste was vile enough that she was grateful for her impaired nose. She wiped her mouth on the blanket beneath her. "I've been asleep for a while, mm?"

Kheperu shrugged. "You'll be stronger when you wake up. By the way, you did a fine job setting that nose of yours—I think it'll be only a bit crooked, perhaps not at all. We'll know more when the swelling goes down."

"I wasn't trying to set it at all," she mumbled. "Where's Leucas?"

"Out. Keeping an eye on things."

"You've been taking care of me . . ." Clouds began drifting into her mind, gently lifting her and rocking her toward sleep. "I'd've thought you'd be long gone . . ."

Kheperu shrugged again, and his smile became distant and his eyes a little sad. "I should be," he said gently. "I should have left days ago, as soon as we were paid. But—well, where would I find another pair of fighters like you two? I must have *someone* to protect me; might as well be you. And I've become used to you."

"You . . ." Whatever had been in that drink thickened her tongue and made it hard to gather words at all. "You liar . . . y' lying prick, I know better. You . . . jus' wanna get *at* me . . . while I sleep . . ."

He chuckled softly. "That's right. Sleep now."

As hiding places go, this was a beauty. It was Leucas' idea; he had sat on the hillside with his chin on his fist, and watched Barra and Kheperu discuss what to do next. Clearly, Barra was in no shape to be racing around the hills dodging patrols—she was too dizzy and weak to walk very far, and could barely stay on the horse. She'd need at least two or three days before she could do the kind of strenuous traveling that might be required to get away from Tyre, and a week would be better. Kheperu was all for splitting up and losing themselves in some sleazy waterfront inns; Barra held out for staying together at the funerary caves. They'd argued it back and forth for a while, until Leucas had grunted and sat up straight.

"Let me see," he'd said slowly. "The problem with an inn is that someone might recognize us and sell us out, but the advantage is that we're in town, we can keep up with what's going on, and we'll know when is a good time to make a break. The problem with the caves is that we're low on supplies and we're out of touch, but the advantage is that it's unlikely we'll be seen there, and we'll all be together. Do I have this right?"

The other two had nodded impatiently, and he went on. "Then, why don't we go to an inn, in town, where we can stay together, but no one will come and go, so there's no way we'll be seen, and there's no one who'll sell us out?"

"Oh, right," Kheperu said with bone-deep exasperation. "And

where will we *find* this magical place, hmm? Perhaps if we start now, we can *build* it, hey?"

Leucas had only shrugged apologetically. "Sorry—I was thinking of Lidios' inn, that's all. Doesn't he owe us a favor?"

With the curse openly displayed, no one would dare to so much as look through his doors—and Lidios did, after all, owe them his life twice over. Kheperu turned a purple that was visible even by moonlight. Barra grinned at him, though it made her lip split again. He snapped, "How come he never does that to *you*?"

"Because I've learned that when Leucas gets that 'Let me get this straight' tone in his voice, I should just shut up and let him talk."

They carefully helped Barra up onto Andromakhe's back, and slowly picked their way toward town.

Leucas walked along beside the horse, his arm around Barra's waist to hold her in the saddle against her occasional attacks of dizziness. The search seemed concentrated on the routes out of Tyre; careful movement, relying on the intermittent moon rather than torches or lamps, got them safely within the city. They unloaded the mules and tied the packs across Leucas' shoulders—it wouldn't be wise to leave animals tied outside what was supposed to be a deserted inn—and Barra dismounted, leaning heavily on Leucas' strong arm, and slapped the horse on the rear. "Go home, Andromakhe! Go on, go home!"

Leucas watched the horse gallop off with grim bemusement. "Kamades named his horse Andromakhe . . ." he murmured, shaking his head. Barra had told them the whole story on their way into town. "That man really knows how to hold a grudge."

Barra felt herself unaccountably bristling. "What do you mean by that?"

Leucas looked down at her with his gentle smile. "Andromakhe was married to the greatest hero of Troy. Every time he mounts up, Kamades is riding Hektor's wife . . . if you see what I mean."

Kheperu laughed; Barra scowled. She said, "I don't know if I like that, or not."

The streets were quiet tonight, and they encountered no one between the edge of town and the silent, darkened and sealed inn of Lidios.

Lidios had answered his door himself, and when the companions identified themselves he let them in instantly. He was horrified at the wreckage of Barra's face, and he insisted on getting her cleaned up and in a bed before he would let them so much as tell him what had happened.

Barra'd told him, after she'd been safely put to bed: "I won't lie to you, Lidios. We're in a whole shit pile of trouble. A sizable chunk of the Egyptian army is hunting us, and if they find us here, I don't doubt they'll kill you for hiding us."

The fat publican's face went utterly expressionless. "So?"

"I'm just trying to say I'll understand if you can't do this. If it's too much, tell me now and we'll find someplace else."

"Barra," he said seriously, "any other mercenary I've ever known would hold a blade to my throat and lock the slaves in the cellar. From you, though, that offer I take with deep offense."

"Huh?"

"How could you possibly even think that I'd count the danger?" He touched his chest; the soiled bandage that still wrapped it was faintly visible through his bed shirt. "I owe you my life—because my skill is with stew and beer, not with weapons and fighting, that doesn't make me a coward."

He stood up and smoothed his bed shirt over his massive belly. "You just lie there and get better, I'll take care of everything. 'S been too long since I've belted on my apron, anyway."

He went out, and as sleep closed in around her, she'd pulled Leucas close. "Keep an eye on him, huh?"

He frowned. "I'm sure he wouldn't—"

"Just watch him, all right? Can't trust, trust anyone . . . Now"— her eyes drooped and she yawned enormously—"now I gotta sleep . . ."

Over the next three days, Barra woke only long enough to take food and water and relieve herself. Then Kheperu would arrive at her bedside with another of his sleeping powders, which took away the pain in her head and pushed the world off behind thick clouds. Whenever she woke, there would be someone sitting by her side, sometimes Lenka, Lidios' loyal house slave who had some minor medical experience, more often Kheperu or Leucas; and sometimes Lidios himself, often smelling of the thick lamb stews he cooked, always smelling of beer or wine—he claimed that water was at a premium, since the only water that was safe to drink had to come from clandestine visits to the public wells after dark; Barra suspected that the lack of water was going a long way toward sustaining his courage.

It was in the first hour of daylight when the thunder of fists against a door tore Barra from sleep and shoved her upright in bed. *Just Demetor and the whiners,* she thought fuzzily, then: *No, that happened already . . . the poisoning, the fight. What in the name of the Loving bloody Mother—?*

Lenka stood near her bed, looking off toward the public house's street door, her face blank with sudden terror. Abruptly Barra remembered where she was and why she was here, and she fought with her tangled, sweat-damp quilts until she could struggle up out of the bed. She swept up her weapons and lurched toward the door; her fingers wouldn't seem to work very well, as she tried and failed and tried again to tie the belt over her bed shirt.

"Where are Leucas and Kheperu?" she snapped, leaning against the door frame and gritting her teeth against a blinding swirl of dizziness. *Curse that shit-eating Kheperu and his shitcake potions!* Lenka only shook her head.

Now the shouting from outside resolved itself into a voice, demanding entrance in bad, Egyptian-accented Phoenikian. Lidios was already there; she could hear his reply: "I'm under the curse! Go away! Do you want to die?"

"Open door or door will broken!"

Barra pushed open her door, and Lenka clutched her from behind. "Don't! You must go out the rear! You must go!"

Barra irritably slapped at her hands. "Like it would do any good." She gave the woman a good shove that sent her backward toward the bed. "Sit down and shut up." Barra pulled her broadaxe out of its scabbard, and huffed a little as she hefted it; it felt heavy as a barrel of beer.

From the outer room she heard Lidios again. "I beg you to go away! If I open this door, you will all die!" He sounded very certain of that, and when Barra peered out around the doorpost—through the deep gloom that filled the shuttered common room, its only light a dull orange pulsing from the hearthshrine—she could see why. Lidios crouched among the tables, well away from the door, and in the shadows to either side of it stood darker shadows, the barely visible forms of Kheperu and Leucas, and the boxer's hand was on the bar.

"No death fears us more than anger of prince. If red-hair girl not is here, we go. Open!"

The huge silhouette to the door's right lifted a shoulder in an eloquent shrug, and flipped the bar off its hooks. The soldier outside kicked the door open, tearing it out of Leucas' grasp and slamming it around into the waiting Kheperu, who let out a muffled grunt. The soldier jumped in through the doorway and threw his weight against the door, pinning Kheperu in place. He wore Meremptah-Sifti's red and purple painted on his armor and a supercilious grin on his face. He said in Egyptian, "Oh, hiding, are we?" In his hand he carried the small trumpet-faced bronze axe of the Egyptian army, and his day-blind eyes, in the gloom, didn't see Leucas at all until the Athenian stepped into the doorway.

The soldier yelped and sprang deeper into the room, to get fighting space; Leucas ignored him, reaching instead out through the door to grab the soldier's partner by the clavicle of his corselet and drag him inside. With a sound like rock hitting bone, a huge fist fell once; the man's head snapped violently back, and Leucas opened his hand to let him fall.

The first soldier, deep within the inn, Leucas silhouetted between him and the light and freedom outside, between him and the rest of his life, said in awed Egyptian, "Oh, my god . . ."

With a slight push from behind, the door swung shut, cutting off the daylight with the finality of an axe.

Kheperu said, "Yes, in fact, I *was* hiding. How impolite of you to notice."

The soldier whirled to run toward the back, but his day-blindness betrayed him and he stumbled into a table. Kheperu needed no more than this; he skipped nimbly toward him and struck his knee with a sharp blow of the staff. The soldier's leg buckled, and he dropped to the floor, wailing, until the hard oak smashed his lips and scattered his teeth about the room. A third stroke quieted him, and Kheperu said in Greek, "There's likely one more, watching the rear; perhaps there may be two."

Leucas nodded grimly. "I'll take care of it." He reached into the shadows along the wall and brought out his man-length spear, its haft as thick as his wrist and its blade as long as his forearm. "You handle these two." He slipped out through the front door, and in the momentary light Barra could see that he carried the iron scimitar behind his belt as well. She shuddered in a brief instant of empathy for the soldiers in the alley behind.

Lidios cautiously straightened from his crouch among the tables. "It's over?"

"Nearly," Kheperu said cheerfully. His hand came out of his robe holding a long, narrow knife. "All that's left to do is kill these two and hide their bodies."

"*Kill* them? Don't—I mean, do you, I wish you really—"

"Lidios, please. You can't keep them here—what will you do when the next group comes to search? If we keep them somewhere else, they'll get loose eventually, or be found, or starve to death. If we let them go, they'll tell, and you and all your slaves will be tortured to death. Besides, you told them if they opened the door they'd all die." Kheperu spread his stubby hands, and his teeth seemed to shine yellow in the gloom. "Do you want me to make you a liar?"

The fat innkeeper's mouth opened, then closed again; he wiped his hands on his apron and looked around at the floor. "Always cleaning up someone's teeth when you're around," he muttered distractedly. And he wandered off, barking at his slaves to quit cowering in the storeroom and bring him a broom.

At this moment Kheperu noticed Barra leaning on the door frame. He smiled. "I was just now coming to wake you up. I think we should be leaving."

Barra looked down at the huddled shapes of the two unconscious soldiers. She wondered where they'd come from, if one of them had a girlfriend he really loved, if the other might have a favorite horse, or a dog. She wondered who'd be crying for them when they didn't come home tonight. *That's the bloody trouble with this whole stinking* sceon tiof *business,* she thought. *Even when it's not working, you're wondering what you'd be seeing if it was.*

Kheperu said, "What's wrong?"

Barra began to speak, a rasping sleep-clogged croak. She coughed hard to clear her throat and spat on the floor. Kheperu's logic was unassailable, even though it turned in her stomach like a blade. "I'm tired of this business," she said softly. "I'm ready for another line of work."

"What?"

"Nothing," she said, stronger. "They were warned. Kill them."

Behind her, Lenka gasped. Barra ignored her.

Kheperu picked up the ankle of the soldier Leucas had felled, and started dragging him toward the back door. The soldier stirred and groaned, lifting a hand to let it fall back limply. "You want to help?"

Barra shook her head. "I . . . better get started packing up."

"Since when are you squeamish?"

Faintly, through the back door, came a hoarse cry of alarm that was cut off by the vivid *sluutch* of a blade tearing through a man's belly so that his bowels spilled to the ground. Someone sobbed in Egyptian, "Oh, shit, shit I'm really hurt, I'm hurt . . ." and the heavy barley-sack thump of a falling body was followed by a crunch of metal on something hard, like a skull.

Barra flinched—she couldn't help it, and she knew Kheperu had seen it. She shook her head. "Just kill them, all right? Then come help me pack. We've got to get out of here."

Kheperu and Leucas washed the blood off themselves using the last of the previous night's water. The dead soldiers were safely stashed in a refuse heap three doors away. ". . . That's why it was Meremptah-Sifti's men, rather than regulars, who came here," Kheperu was saying, as he strapped on the tight-fitting armor of the portliest of the three. He had already shaved the stubble from his cheeks and chin, and tied his beard into military braids. "They'd already have the tattoo to 'protect' them. What I don't understand is why they'd still be searching for us. What harm can we do him now? He owns this city already—why, from what you've been telling me about things out there, Leucas, I'd have to say that he controls this city more completely than any tyrant has ever held a city before. What good does he get from all this time and effort of searching? What makes us so special to be worth this? What does he get?"

Barra had quietly bound her breasts tight—to pass as a boy yet again—and tied off bundles of clothing and weapons while listening to Kheperu's nervous post-fight chattering. Now she said, "He gets me."

Kheperu snorted. "No offense, my dear, but I hardly think you are worth—"

"You weren't there," she said flatly. "You didn't see him, or hear him talk. He won't stop until he gets me. Just take my word for it. That's why I'm leaving. Like I should have done a week ago. Let the cocksucking bastard spend his life searching for me."

"Hmm," Leucas said. "This may be hard."

"Why?" Barra said. "With a hood up to cover my face—and as long as you remember to keep your knees a little bent and your back hunched—no one should question us. We just need to stay away from anyone else in red and purple."

Kheperu twirled for them, like a girl showing off a new skirt. "How do I look? Like one of the new masters of Tyre?"

"You'll see," was all Leucas would say. "You'll see."

Soon all three were ready to leave. Barra paused at the alley door to clasp forearms with Lidios. The publican licked his lips, and released one of Barra's arms so that he could mop pale sweat from his jowls. "You be careful," he said hoarsely. "And if you're ever back in Tyre—"

"I know," Barra said with a smile that bent her swollen face painfully. "Stay the bloody fuck away from here."

Lidios chuckled wanly and hugged her. "I owe you more than silver can repay. You have the freedom of this house forever." He pressed
her close. "I hope you make it."

"We will. Remember—anyone who comes asking after those three
men? They were here, you let them in so they wouldn't break down the
door, they looked around, then left. That's all you know, right?"

"Right." He released her and stepped back. "May Zeus guard your
path."

Barra took a deep breath. "May the Mother stand behind you and
smile on every pot."

Lidios held the door for them as they shouldered their bundles and
slipped out into the blazing Tyrian day.

*You'll see,* Leucas had said. Barra saw. On the streets of her
adopted city, everything that came before her eyes tied another coil
around the knot in her guts.

She saw the pinched faces and fearful eyes of Tyrian freemen
when they looked upon Kheperu in his livery.

She saw the instant outward respect he got from Egyptian regulars, and their expressions of relief when he had passed.

She saw the slamming of doors and latching of windows that preceded them down every side street.

She saw little children watch him with wide, numbed eyes. Some
of them screamed and ran. Their mothers stayed silent, their faces
filled with hopeless, empty defiance.

At the beach, ships were drawn up gunwale to gunwale, barely
space for a skinny man to slip between them; a man could walk the
length of the beach deck to deck, without ever touching the sand. Carelessly unshipped oars made untidy, bristly stacks between the deck
benches. The sand inshore was piled here and there with mounds of
cloth and spices and goods from across the known world, some still
guarded by sweaty, nervous crewmen, most standing abandoned and
forlorn, left to the beachsiders, the gulls, and the flies.

Also on the ships this day were people. Hundreds upon hundreds
of Tyrians, some with bundles of possessions, some clutching children
close by their legs, stood anxiously among sailors and marines from
every foreign port. They crowded onto the decks, shading their eyes to
look out to sea, many standing up on the benches for a better view. Far
out on the sea, a small spot on the endless expanse of shimmering
greenish blue, the crew of a merchant ship pulled desperately at their

oars. There was no wind; the hammering of the oarmaster's drum came frantic over the calm waters. For a while it seemed that they might escape, but no one on the dockside cheered. A murmur would ripple through the crowd, from time to time, that was always accompanied by flickering glances at the scattered pairs and trios of soldiers and men in bloodred and purple, skating glances, long enough to read an expression but too short to truly meet the eyes. No one was willing to meet their eyes.

Out on the water, a pair of slender dark warships fairly skipped over the sea, closing rapidly on the slower merchantman. Soon fire arrows trailed their sooty smoke in arcs over the water; shortly after that the warships overtook her, and the long spiked boarding planks swung down to lodge in the merchantman's deck. The planks swarmed with soldiers, and the cries and screams came clearly to the shore. In minutes the warships were curving away, pulling back for the city, leaving the merchantman burning, a pyre for its fallen crew.

Leucas looked down at Barra. "Any ship can enter. None have managed to get away."

Barra nodded grimly. "Then we'll have to go overland."

On a bright, wide side street not far from the Market, another silent crowd was gathered. Barra turned aside from their path through the city toward the northern road to Sidon; she insisted on knowing what was going on.

Leucas shook his head. "You don't want to go in there."

"What's happening?"

The Athenian's rumble was barely audible. "It's a rape."

Barra's eyes widened. "How do you know?"

"I have been about the city, these three days. I've seen this before."

Now sobbing, high and thin, a child's voice, the sobbing that remains after screams have failed, could be heard among the rough grunting and low, coarse laughter. Barra looked at the backs of the people, down the street.

"Why are they just standing there? Why doesn't someone do something?"

"Because a man who wears Meremptah-Sifti's colors—or the armor of an Egyptian regular—can do anything, in this city."

Barra turned toward the crowd, her battered face set as stone, her hand beneath her cloak on the head of her broadaxe. Leucas caught her shoulder. "Don't go there."

Barra shook him off. "I have to see for myself."

"No, you don't. What'll happen, you'll go there, you'll see some man pounding his hips into some boy, or girl. Maybe the child's mother lying dead in the dirt nearby. In broad daylight, in the middle of the street. You'll try to kill him; you'll likely succeed. Then the ten or fifteen Egyptian soldiers that are holding the crowd back will kill you."

"Maybe," she answered grimly. "Or maybe that crowd will stand with me."

"Barra, no. Watch them," he said, taking her shoulders and gently turning her, holding her so that she faced them.

Even as he turned her, a sound like a gentle breeze came to her ears, though the air was still. Then the sound came again, and this time she saw it, the sigh that moved the crowd gently as though it were some softly creeping beast. Barra's stomach suddenly spasmed, and she had to turn away. Even Kheperu looked pale.

Leucas' voice was as bleak as she'd ever heard it. "Why do you think they're *watching*? Why do you think they're not running away to lock themselves indoors and hide? Those soldiers, they don't hold the crowd back to protect the *rapist* . . ."

"That's sick," Barra said, swallowing a thin burning trace of vomit. "That's sick."

Kheperu murmured, "You'd perhaps be surprised how many men share my tastes—or worse—within their hearts, lacking only the courage to give themselves permission to indulge them. They may have to pretend outrage, later, to salve their conscience, but they won't have to hold themselves responsible—they can say, within their hearts, 'There was nothing I could do to stop him.' "

Barra stared at the crowd; another sigh, stronger now, rippled through it. "And not all of them are men," she said thickly. "Let's get out of here before I throw up."

A full company of Egyptian infantry sealed the north road out of Tyre, politely but firmly turning back all who tried to leave. Any who tried to duck around them and strike out despite their orders were easily taken by the cavalry that backed them up, ten two-horse chariots. No attempt was made to capture these fugitives; their flight would be stopped, each and every one, by a spear in the back or a hatchet blow to the head. By the time the three companions had made their way there, the gently rolling coastal plain to the north was dotted with corpses left lying in the sun, most surrounded by squabbling rings of vultures, arguing over which gets the eyes and which the tongue. Farther out, dim in the distance, two encampments were visible, one straight north near the coast and one far to the northeast, nothing between them but open, rolling hills. Even if it were possible to organize something like a mass rush for the hills, Barra could see no chance of escape. They didn't even bother coming up to the soldiers themselves; they just faded back and let the current of the crowd carry them into the city once more.

"How could he have done this?" she asked. "In just two or three days . . ."

"Simple, really," Kheperu told her. "He controls everyone who has the power to resist him."

The companions worked their way in a wide arc through the outskirts of Tyre, even though Barra foreknew it would be useless; the city was clearly sealed. She wondered, as they walked, how long Meremptah-Sifti could get away with this. A long time, certainly; it would take months, perhaps a year or more, for the rumors to get around to other ports, as traders failed to appear on their usual routes, and traders who didn't call at Tyre began to expand their territories. Barring some unusual event to the north—say, a disastrous loss in battle by Hattiland, who then would call upon its ally Egypt for reinforcements—that would bring a large army marching through, Ramses might never learn what his grandson was doing, up here on the Phoenikian coast. The Governor was the author of all official reports regarding events in the Canaan District, and Egypt had troubles of her own.

Meanwhile, the population would continue to grow. Tyre was already crowded, straining its wells to support the people who lived here now—this was why so many inns and private homes had their own rain barrels. Every caravan that came to Tyre would add to its numbers, as would every trade ship. Even thinking about this made Barra's breath run short; the crowds becoming thicker, spreading to fill every street, every house . . . The gods take it ill for men to live too closely pressed together; they strike the densest cities with sicknesses that kill and kill and kill until the gods judge that the crowd has thinned enough; and they send madness, too, that bends the minds of even honest, sober men toward bloodshed.

Leucas walked beside her, his back bent and head jutting forward, scanning any crowd for faces that might be even vaguely familiar, so that the companions might be able to turn away before they were recognized. Kheperu made himself strut a bit, playing up his Lord of the City act, but his face showed pale strain and he rarely spoke; whenever another man in the prince's colors came into sudden view, he'd clench his jaw and his fists, and breathe deep, trying to hold on to his courage.

Barra tried to distract herself as they walked, tried to think of other things, of spring flowers in Great Langdale, of the sun sparking fire off the white limestone that faced the tomb of Khufu, of the sunrise sacrifice on the Horns of the Bull in the midst of the thousand-chambered hall of Knossos; but somehow each attempt spun into some wild fantasy of revenge, of retribution on Meremptah-Sifti. In one she led an army of howling Picts against his estate; in the second she stood before Ramses the Great and denounced his grandson to his face; in the third, the prince himself was tied between the Horns and it was Barra who stood before him, saluting the sun with the double-faced golden axe.

The platform rose in the eastern quadrant, on a field not far from the edge of the city, along the road crudely known as The Tongue, since it led from the city toward the funerary caves. The field was ringed with bored soldiers, drinking and dicing and joking among themselves, but making very sure that the mass of people there remained orderly, and within the field's confines. Many persons in that crowd wore the clothes and head wraps of white linen, rubbed with ash until it is a mottled grey, that are the marks of mourning. There was some small traffic from the city into the field and even less returning.

Three liveried soldiers of the prince stood on that platform. Two of them had scribe's tablets and pens; the third held in his hands whatever item they were offering for auction: sometimes weapons, or jewelry, or cups of precious metals, more often rugs, or large squares of brocade, sometimes only the painted cerements, the funeral wrappings cut from a corpse.

As each item was lifted to the sun, wailing keens rose to meet it, high shrilling voices of men and women who saw again items they'd buried with their own hands, in the graves of their loved ones. And there were curses, too, low-voiced so that the soldiers could not hear, invocations to Ba'al-Berith to avenge the disturbance of mortal remains; the less pious whispered pleas to Great Mouth. Sometimes two different families would each believe they recognized the same piece; the bidding became tragic, as well as shameful.

Not all the bidders on these items were bereaved; many, here and there, were clearly well dressed, cynical merchants and agents of merchants who saw an opportunity for easy profit—the same sort of men that will cut purses on a sinking ship.

The companions watched in silence from the rear of the crowd, until a woman in ashen linen spotted Kheperu, took in the colors of his livery, and clawed through the crowd toward him. "Lord, oh, lord!" she screeched, her hands extended in supplication. Kheperu stepped back, but she threw herself at his feet and caught the hem of his purple kilt. "Please, lord, please, in the name of whatever god pleases you," she sobbed, her voice half muffled from pressing the kilt's hem to her lips. "Great Mouth swallowed my husband only five days ago, lord! I have . . . I have no . . . I have nothing to pay for his cerements! They were sold, lord, and my husband . . . My children, I had to . . . *Please*, lord, can you . . . ?"

Kheperu swallowed, and looked a plea to Leucas, and to Barra. Barra, mindful that maintaining Kheperu's disguise was their only hope of evading capture, slowly shook her head; that tiny motion cut her like knives. She and Leucas began fading back toward the city's edge—others were taking notice, heads turning toward them. Kheperu nodded his resignation. He looked down at the sobbing woman and harshened his voice. "Leave off, woman!" he rasped. "Soil my kilt and I'll have you whipped!"

"*Pleeease!* I beg you, don't let my Thomi wander freezing forever!" Broad streaks of tears washed away the ash that clung to her face, and her eyes were raw. "I'll do anything! *Anything!* I'm still young, men desire me, please, please lord I'll do anything . . ." She tore open the front of her mourningshift, exposing small breasts that quivered red and helpless. *"Anything!"*

Kheperu recoiled, horror twisting his face. She clutched at him again, and he kicked free. "Leave off! Let me go!" He got loose and hustled to rejoin his companions. Behind him the woman writhed in the dirt, wailing, "Please! Please!"

They hurried back into the city; the woman's screams faded behind them.

Barra shivered uncontrollably, though the late-year sun was warm. "I can't take this anymore," she said. She found the cool brick wall of a nearby building to lean against and put a hand over her eyes. "We can't run, and we can't hide, and I can't stand it. I have to do something. We have to do something about this." Leucas stood beside her and silently laid his huge warm hand upon her shoulder.

He squeezed once, and said, "We'll find a way."

Kheperu paced circles before them, clasping and unclasping his hands, wiping his brow, tugging at his beard. "Find a way, yes, oh, certainly. Neither of you is thinking. You're just *feeling*. Think! Don't you see what's going on?"

Barra said grimly, "This whole city is being raped."

Kheperu snapped his fingers. "Pah! That's nothing, an amusement. Why do you think they're selling those grave goods over there? It's not the money, that's not why they're opening the caves—that's peripheral, you understand?"

"You've always been the clever one," Leucas said heavily. "Just explain."

The Egyptian took a deep breath, and rubbed his jowls; he frowned, as though saying this would hurt, as though putting it into words would make it irrevocably real. "The few shekels they can earn from selling grave goods are hardly worth the effort of digging them up. This is a *sideline*, do you understand? They're opening the caves anyway, may as well make a bit of silver here and there, selling off what's left after their real treasure has been taken away."

Barra and Leucas both frowned at him, uncomprehending.

"You do not see, only because you close your eyes," he sighed. "What they're after is the *cadavers*—why do you think your bloody-fucking Simi-Ascalon has his bloodyfucking workshop right there among the caves?"

"Chrysios . . ." Barra breathed. Leucas had turned decidedly pale.

Kheperu still talked as he paced nervously before them, but Barra was lost in tales of her childhood. In the Isle of the Mighty the bards still sing of Bran the Blessed, who with his brothers led the men of the Isle against Matholuch the Red at Tara; Matholuch, who held the Cauldron of Rebirth. In the hour of his defeat, he filled the Cauldron with the corpses of his men and they rose to fight again, soulless, shambling, and unkillable. Of the great host Bran had led, only seven men came home. That endless army of corpse warriors had haunted Barra's nightmares as a child—now they filled her daylight mind. The shivering, that had subsided while listening to Kheperu, came back with a vengeance, full-fledged trembling. She hugged herself tightly, leaning against the cool-shadowed wall, and wished there were some way for her to get warm.

"... And remember," Kheperu was saying, "Chrysios had been dead only a day or two; any Tyrian of reasonable means would be able to afford full Egyptian necromantic rites ..."

Leucas and Barra only watched and waited for him to finish; from experience they knew that Kheperu, once going, needed no further encouragement.

"Do you see? You felt the strength of Chrysios, and the toughness of his skin. Imagine if his corpse had been properly prepared—it is the difference between skin, and leather; between cutting fresh meat and meat that has been smoked and dried. . . . These corpse-fighters like Chrysios—chryseids, if you will—they will be very tough, indeed. Tough beyond tough."

"But who would he attack with these fighters?" Leucas said, frowning. "Why create an army of corpses? What would he do with them?"

Barra said grimly, "Whatever he wants to."

"That's not a very good answer."

"It's the exact truth," she said. "Believe me. When he loses interest in Tyre, he'll be able to go anywhere, do anything, take any city. He can do what he's done here to—to anywhere."

"And," said Kheperu, "I do not believe there is any way to change it."

"We have to find a way out of town," Barra said. She thrust her hands under her arms to stop their shaking. "We have to get a message to the Pharaoh. It'll take an army to stop him now."

"Yes, well, and . . ." Kheperu said slowly, uncomfortably. He turned away and looked at the street near his sandals, and dug beneath his armor to scratch. "I think you may have to do that without me."

Leucas said, "Of course we'd never ask you to go into Egypt again—"

"It's not that." He tugged on his beard, and his expression was one of actual pain. "I've been thinking I might give myself up."

"What?" Barra barked, taking a sudden step forward.

Kheperu matched her with a step of retreat. "I do not see any profit in fighting the wind," he said, and spread his hands. His face reddened in a way Barra had never thought she'd see: a blush of shame. "One might as well strike at the tide, or attack a mountain. I think I should get on the winning side while I still have the chance."

"And what about us? What about *me*?" Barra snapped.

"Please, Barra, if I planned to betray you, I'd hardly be telling you this now. Perhaps if I can establish my usefulness to Meremptah-Sifti, I can persuade him to give over his search for you. Or, at least, misdirect the search in such a way that you'd have a better chance to escape."

"I have used many low names for you, Kheperu," Leucas growled, "but coward was never among them."

Kheperu wrung his hands until the knuckles popped. "Listen— please try to understand. This is not my city, these are not my people.

I am a mercenary—as are we all. You two seem to have forgotten that, but I haven't. I want to *live*. Meremptah-Sifti has outplayed the sharpest traders on the Middle Sea; he holds every stick, and I don't think his grip can be broken."

Barra examined him, the smooth round chubbiness of his cheeks, glistening now with sweat, the oiled braid of his beard, a look of defeat she'd never seen before in his beady dark eyes. She said, "I understand. You should understand, too, that if I do get away, if I get to Egypt and get to Ramses, this will have been the worst decision you've ever made. You follow?"

Kheperu nodded miserably. "But, you see . . . I really do not think you have a chance."

"I understand something else, too," Barra went on. "I understand that you didn't have to tell us. You could have simply made up some excuse to slip away, and never come back—that would have been the smartest thing, the most practical thing. You could have gone three days ago."

Kheperu looked away. "If, well . . . you're hurt, you see. I had to know you are all right. Blows to the head . . . they can be very dangerous." He turned back with a forced smile. "Look what it did to Leucas . . ."

No one laughed.

Barra reached out to him, took his arm. "I told you, I understand. Now, listen, I want to ask one thing of you. One favor."

"Ask?" Leucas growled. "We should ask? I think we should kill him. Now, while we have the chance."

Barra never took her eyes from Kheperu's face, though her words were directed at the giant Athenian. "Can you? Look at him. This man we've come to know so well—better even, maybe, than we wanted to. That we've fought with, and drank with, and laughed with. You think you can look him in the face and take his life?"

"Well—"

She knew better than to wait for an answer. "This is the favor I want, Kheperu," she said. "I want you to come and eat with us—we'll go to that grill court in the Market near Xuros' inn. We can talk about what to do next. Maybe we can come up with something that'll change your mind. All right?"

Kheperu swallowed, and nodded.

Barra looked over her shoulder. "Leucas?"

The boxer scowled, and huffed, and finally shrugged. He shook his head, surrendering. "Whatever you say, Barra."

\* \* \*

Most of the Market was deserted, or nearly so, eerily empty stretches of dirty flagstones between the very few tentstalls that remained open for business. Footsteps scraped loudly over the whisper of the sea breeze; the only voices to be heard were held to mutters, from knots of men looking sidelong; and even these mutters trickled away to silence when the companions approached. Signs of activity began to appear only when they came near the central plaza, where they'd fought the bear—Barra counted days blurrily in her head. Was that twelve days ago, or thirteen? She couldn't remember; it seemed a lifetime.

Perhaps three quarters of the businesses were open, around the plaza; the merchants here seemed to feel safer, where they were in plain view of so many people, than did those in the narrow and twisty byways deeper within the Market. And, perhaps for the same reason, there were more citizens as well—even in a state of siege, or occupation, or whatever this was that Meremptah-Sifti was doing to this city, people must eat and drink. Some even continued their normal routines, as though by pretending that nothing had changed in Tyre, they could make it so. The plaza couldn't be said to be full, exactly, but there were enough people there to obscure the exhibit, on display in its center.

Leucas' great height allowed him to see it first; even hunched over as he was, he stood a head taller than either of the other two. He said, "Something new in the agora."

Barra and Kheperu had been walking along in silence, both staring at Leucas' stiffly uncommunicative back; now they both stopped and strained to see around it. Barra said, her voice weary, "Well, what is it?" She wasn't at all sure she could stand any more ugly sights today—and, now that she was paying attention, it seemed that an uncomfortably large number of people simply stood and stared thoughtfully into the middle of the plaza. After what she'd seen this day already, it took only this to kindle a sickly twisting dread within her chest.

"Looks like some kind of a cage," he replied slowly. "Set up on a little platform with guards around it. Meneides guards." He straightened, lifted himself up onto his toes and stretched his neck; then as he took in the view he seemed to shrink, to fall in upon himself, and when he looked back down and met Barra's eyes, his face was pale as the sand on the beach, save for the scars that crossed his shattered nose and bridged his cheekbones and brows: these flamed red. "There are two people in it."

A weight settled upon Barra's shoulders, the bodiless hand of some god crushing her into the earth. She struggled to hold herself straight, to make herself move forward over the flagstones that paved the plaza. Kheperu touched her arm, said something; Barra shook him off and kept walking.

As she passed a pair of men, she overheard one say to the other: "Well, it looks like rain's coming. Huh, if the weather's bad enough, they might live for a tenday."

"No—too old, I think they—" The second man never had a chance to finish this thought, for Barra wheeled on them and grabbed the nearest by the front of his robe.

"What's that mean?" she snapped, pulling his face close to hers. "What's that mean, if the weather's *bad*?"

"Hey, I, uh, listen . . ." he sputtered, waving his hands as though he wanted to push her away but was afraid to touch her.

Barra's eyes blazed, and she whispered a snarl: "Talk to me, you shit-eating prick! What's that mean?"

"There's a, a, an old couple, an old man and his wife, they got them in that cage there," he stammered. "They say they're keeping them there with no food nor water until some girl—some girl they're hunting for—gives herself up. So I figured, I figured, if it rains a lot, they might be able to get enough water to live for a while, that's all, catch it in their mouths or something. That's all, I swear!"

Her hands opened; his robe fell from her fingers. She rocked back on her heels. "A cage. Open. Open so everyone can watch . . ."

Leucas and Kheperu had caught up with her by now. She looked up at Leucas and said, "Everyone can watch them die." The Athenian and the Egyptian both could only stare; Leucas' hands twisted into fists, then relaxed, helpless. He said, "Don't do it."

He reached for her, but she spun and dodged away into the crowd. "Wait!" Leucas called, and Kheperu, too, surging after her, but she was too agile and far too quick.

And then she came in sight of the cage, and it was open-worked, with head-size spaces between cedar poles bound together with ropes, and within it were Peliarchus and Tayniz.

She stopped, panting harshly, wordless growls rasping under her breath. Townsfolk nearby edged away from her, slowly, so as not to attract her attention. The guards around the cage all faced outward, toward the plaza, eight of them in quilted armor painted with the sigil of House Meneides, spears grounded and shields in place upon their arms. They scanned the crowd, their faces full of serious self-importance, each deeply aware of the gravity of his task.

They were looking for her; she knew this, but she couldn't stop herself drifting closer.

Tayniz lay huddled in Peliarchus' arms; he knelt, grimly holding his head up. The cage floor was littered with garbage, dark and slimy bits of what might have been fruit, much of the cedar of the cage was stained with it; some of the townsfolk had been amusing themselves by throwing stuff at her parents as they sat caged there. Probably the guards had put a stop to it—it wouldn't do to have the townsfolk's cruel amusement provide food for these two who were intended to starve to death. Both wore only torn and dirty bed shirts, showing plainly the filth and bruises on their skin.

The afternoon sun struck hard upon everyone there, but hardest of all upon Peliarchus; he sat so as to give his wife what shade he could, and beaded sweat glistened upon his bare scalp.

And there was something else, there on the floor of the cage, something grey and furry and still, not a body, too flat for that: a pelt.

A pelt. The skin of a wolf.

Barra's mouth stretched wide, and her vision blurred and a trembling took her hard, shaking, shaking so she couldn't move, except her eyes, she looked up to Peliarchus' face, to her father's eyes, meeting her gaze, he saw her, he recognized her, he pushed aside his wife, and he came to his feet and pointed at her and shouted:

*"There she is!"*

His bed shirt fell away from his shoulder, and she saw the angry mark there beside his throat, the swollen redness that surrounded the tattoo, and from somewhere beyond the world a howl began that came ripping from her throat, pinning her there on the plaza, motionless, screaming, howling, mindlessly wailing out her unconquerable pain. She saw the guard come toward her, felt him grab her arm, but she couldn't pull away, couldn't move, couldn't think, until from behind her she heard the bark of Kheperu, "Barra! *Catch!*"

The simple order struck through her paralysis, and she turned . . . the small bronze axe looped gently through the air toward her . . . the guard's grip held hard her right arm, she couldn't pull it free, but Barra was that rare warrior for whom both hands are right and she deftly snatched the axe from the air with her left hand and buried it between the startled eyes of the young man who held her . . . it stuck in the bone as he fell twitching away and she let it go, reaching behind for her own axes of honest stone, she remembered now that she still wore them pushed behind so that they were covered by her cloak and the scream of rage and pain twisted into a war howl as she threw herself toward the other guards.

Arms caught her from behind, arms irresistibly strong, lifting her up, pinning her axes against her legs, and she struggled and fought and screamed and kicked, but the arms carried her away, charging through the crowd like a maddened bull as she screamed, *"I'll kill you! I'll kill you! I'll kill you!"* in her native Pictish; only Peliarchus, of all the folk in that Market, could understand her, and he was unable to care.

They paced slowly along an anonymous alleyway, side by side, as night drifted into the sky. Kheperu now wore most of Barra's cloak, to cover his livery; Barra kept only the hood, cut away and tied under her chin to conceal the telltale red of her hair. Leucas walked straight now—his back ached from being held hunched all day. Since that mad, headlong rush to escape the guards in the plaza, none of them had spoken.

They came to a small dung yard, a heap piled within it not much smaller than the one in which they'd found Mykos. As they passed by, a small door in one of the surrounding buildings scraped open; an old woman shoved it wide with her hip and stepped out to slop a couple of piss pots onto the heap. Flies lifted off in a buzzing, iridescent cloud, and its fringes gleamed with scarabs. The old woman caught sight of the companions, pushed a straggle of grey hair off her face with the back of her wrist and gave them a gap-toothed grin. "Not much here to eat, boys—and girl," she said, "but whatever you find, it's yours. You can pay me later." Chuckling, she slipped back in through the door, and Barra heard the heavy thunk of a bar settling into place.

"Hmpf," Kheperu mused, eyeing the dung heap thoughtfully. "How is it we always manage to skip our day meal?"

Leucas shrugged. "Maybe your prince will feed you," he muttered in a bitter undertone.

Barra moved away from them, silently sliding into the dung yard; beyond the heap, she'd spotted a spray of green in the fading light. She skirted the heap, and on the other side, pushing its twisted, stunted way up between the flagstones, was a young tree. It couldn't have been more than a few months old—it barely reached her chest—and its leaves were pale and sickly, but someone, in one of these buildings, must be caring for it, or it would have been uprooted long ago. The flags were scraped in a small ring around it, not clean, but cleaner than the rest of the dung yard. Barra crouched before it and ran her fingers over the roughening texture of its maturing bark. How long had it been since she'd touched a living, growing tree? She couldn't guess, not now, not here. She gently touched the leaves, pale and almost translucent, their shape that eldritch blend, midway between a human hand and the paw of a wolf.

A wind howled in her mind, roared like an angry sea; a wind from long ago and beyond the edge of the world.

She looked up to find Leucas and Kheperu standing over her. "You see this? You know what this is?" Her voice came out rough and thick; these were her first words since the scream in the plaza.

Leucas frowned, puzzled. "It's an oak," he said slowly. "Isn't it?"

Barra nodded. "It's an omen."

Kheperu snorted. "Oh, really, Barra, please—"

"It's an omen," she said stolidly. "Don't argue with me. How did she know I'm not a boy?"

"I, well, the shape of your face—"

"Shut up. She said, she told me that whatever I find, is mine." Her fists knotted until the knuckles popped. She straightened, and her expression of grim determination reached only to her eyes: her eyes burned like offering pyres to the god of war. "I tell you this. I'm not running, not anymore. I am not going to Ramses to tell on his grandson like a whining child. I'm going to beat him."

"Barra, really, I think you are a bit—"

"Shut up." She grasped the top of the little oak in her right hand, and took her axe in her left, and her voice rang like an iron bell. "I swear, by the life of the Mother that runs through this sacred oak, and by the power of her wedded Grey Lord that drives this weapon, I will whip Meremptah-Sifti cringing from this city. He is a dog, and as a dog will I whip him."

Kheperu and Leucas looked at her, then at each other, at the dung heap and the little oak. Finally, Kheperu took a deep breath and broke the silence.

"One should be cautious with oaths, I mean, really—"

"And you," she said, her voice level and calm, her axe pointing directly at Kheperu's long nose, "Kheperu, you will either help me do this or I will kill you right now. I will cut you down where you stand. Will you help?"

The Egyptian looked affronted. "How in the name of every living god do you expect to do this?"

"That's not your problem. Are you with me, or are you dead?"

"Barra, I've been thinking over my position . . ." he began uncomfortably.

"Yes?"

"Well, you see, much as it pains me to admit it like this, I . . . hmpf. Well. I do not care about this city. I do not care, really, about nearly any of the people in it. Meremptah-Sifti can, so far as I'm concerned, do what he likes with them. It's what he's done to *you*, Barra. That cage, in the Market—and to kill poor Graeg—!" Words failed him for a moment; he could only shake his head. "I'm with you."

"Leucas?"

"How can you ask?" the Athenian rumbled. "You know that I am always beside you. No matter what."

"All right." Barra tucked her axe back behind her belt. "Let's go."

"But—" Kheperu said, "what are we going to do?"

Barra smiled. The clouds that had hung within her mind all day had begun to break even as she'd made her promise to the gods. Ideas began to hum and shimmer behind her eyes. "I said it'd take an army. I've got an idea where we might be able to find one." Her smile widened, and it was not a happy smile; in the fading day her teeth gleamed and the light in her eyes became feral. She reached out and clasped the shoulders of her two companions. "That cage, there in the Market, Peliarchus and Tayniz, that tattoo, and, and Graeg—that was Meremptah-Sifti's best shot. He can't hit me any harder than that. He hit me with everything he's got, and I'm getting up again. I'm awake, and winding up."

She let go of her friends, and her fists tightened. "We'll see who's standing, at the end."

# 18

# *Barra's Army*

**D**own in the courtyard, Leucas measured his scimitar against the throat of the bull. The huge animal, drugged on honeyed wine, lowed contentedly. The flames of bonfires leaped up around it, painting its white flanks golden, and the two men holding its horns patted it and made comforting noises, and Leucas, with a solemn invocation to Athene, slit its throat.

The pouring blood was caught in a golden bowl, and the bull slowly knelt, going down on its front knees, and its rear legs buckled, and its front legs gave way, its chin coming to the flagstones, and finally, ponderously, it toppled to the right.

Up on the roof, among the green and growing plants of an incongruous garden, Barra knelt. Before her, on the roof, lay a small wooden trencher filled with hunks of dried clay. She spat on them, again and again, and ground the hunks together, mixing her fluids into the flesh of the Mother until they softened and combined into a paste. The keen edge of her throwing axe against the heel of her right hand drew blood, nine drops into the clay.

She gathered a handful and lifted it to the gleaming, grinning moon.

"Mother, my blood, Your Flesh. We are One. I am Your Mountain, it is my strength; I am Your Earth, and I endure."

As she spoke, it became true; this is Joining the Earth, the First Link of the ritual by which a Pict prepares herself for war.

In the deepening twilight after Barra's oath in the alley, the companions had gone straight to the home of Peliarchus. When they got in sight of the house, Kheperu had instantly observed, "This looks like a trap."

Barra and Leucas agreed; the house stood dark and unguarded, no sign of activity of any sort, and certainly no appearance of watchers. Barra's response: "So what? Follow me."

She led them around the corner of the house, into the narrow right-of-way beside it, found the window she wanted and knocked on its closed shutter.

Kheperu was horrified. "What are you *doing?*" he whispered urgently.

"Relax."

"But you don't know who's in there!"

"That's my room. It's the one where Demetor is staying."

"What if they're with him?"

Barra snorted. "Given the choice, how much time would you spend in a room with Demetor?"

The shutters swung outward, and a man leaned out—the startled, horrified look on his face when he saw the companions let Barra recognize him: it was the Kypriot she'd bullied in the courtyard on the night of the poisoning. He turned instantly red and put his hand to his mouth. "Shhh! Oh, great Ba'al! *Shh!*"

Barra whispered, "How is King Demetor? Did he make a full recovery?"

"Yes, well, yes, he's fine, but the courtyard is full of men—they're *waiting for you!* They took Peliarchus and Tayniz—your wolf . . ."

Barra silenced him with a firm gesture; she couldn't bear to hear about this right now. "Let me talk to him."

The Kypriot stepped away from the window, and within the room there was much whispering, and then came a familiar whining moan that struck tears into Barra's eyes—and then, blindingly, she realized that she had not imagined it.

She never knew how she got into the room; her next cogent memory was of lying on a pile of rugs beside Graegduz, and he was happily nuzzling her under her chin. The blankets, the whole room, reeked of him—if not for her damaged nose she would have smelled him instantly. The bandages on his shoulder and leg were clean, and clearly new, and now the tears did flow from her eyes and she clutched him to her chest, and he was warm, and breathing, and stinking in terrible need of a bath, and she told him so in her Pictish baby talk.

She lifted her tear-streaked face, and the smile that brightened it brought answers from Leucas and Kheperu, peering in through the window, and from the Kypriot, and from King Demetor, who stood over her grinning into his snowy beard.

Demetor said, "When your father left, those men, why, they wanted to kill this wolf. I told them you'd placed him under my care, and I found myself a sword and ordered my men to fight to the death to protect him, and they decided they could do without. I told them this wolf had been hurt saving my life, and while I had life they weren't to touch him."

That pelt—why, they must have simply bought it, or stolen it from some shop in the Market. Just a jab, a stinging slap for her—they probably hadn't even guessed how deep a wound it would inflict.

Barra rose, and clasped forearms with him, and when she could trust her voice, she said, "May the Mother of All shower blessings upon you like the rain in spring."

"It was only my duty," mumbled the old king, a bit shamefaced but obviously enjoying himself. "I only wish I could have done the same for your parents, and I would have, y'know, I really surely and certainly would have, except that Peliarchus himself told me that everything was all right and I shouldn't worry, that they weren't going to be hurt or really even very inconvenienced—"

That had been the tattoo's magic talking, Barra knew; but there was neither time nor reason to explain that to King Demetor and his man. "You know what this is?" she asked, talking to her friends outside, her eyes alight.

"Let me guess," murmured Kheperu. "Another omen?"

"Best believe it," Barra told him. "I thought he was dead, lost forever, and here he is alive, and soon to be well. Saved by blades and boldness. It's an omen of victory."

"Victory?" Demetor said, obviously puzzled. "Over what? Against whom? I'm sorry, I've been a bit out of touch, recovering and all—that's thanks to you, y'know, and I can't tell you the depths of my gratitude—but it does keep one out of circulation. By the way, how was the Governor's feast? Sorry I missed it, I wasn't quite well yet. And, you know, you look like someone's given you a bit of a beating . . ."

"My lord." Barra once again firmly dammed the river of words. "I must ask you for a favor. You have done me so great a service in saving my friend that I don't want to demand this as a right, as guest-friend and all, but instead I only ask."

"Anything, Barra," he said firmly. "Anything at all. I owe you my kingdom, and my life."

"What I'd like," she said slowly, "is a private interview with your cousin Agapenthes."

His brows drew together. "Agapenthes? Why, certainly. I've been keeping out of his way while I'm here in Tyre—just between you and me and this wall, I don't think he likes me very much—but I should think he'd see me if I presented myself at his gate."

"Good," Barra said, nodding. "Great. Now, just one more thing before we go—"

"Now? You want to go *now*?"

"Oh yes, we have to. Tomorrow might be too late." She took a deep breath and rubbed her hands together, gave Kheperu an encouraging smile.

Kheperu coughed, and reached within the small purse that hung at his belt. "Yes, well. Up in the servant's quarters, on the second floor, there's a large box. This key will open it. There are just a few items that I'd like you to bring for me—carefully, casually, so as not to shake them up too much, or alert those men who are waiting out there . . ."

Down in the courtyard, Leucas busily gutted the bull, while the two handlers stripped back the skin, starting with the head and front legs. There was none of the laughter and cross-talk that normally characterizes such a task; a sacrifice such as this is a solemn occasion.

Up on the roof, Barra shook a powder out into the palm of her hand, a powder that comes from boiling the crushed leaves of a small shrub that grows in the Isle of the Mighty. Her pouch, containing this powder, she'd carried with her for years, since her last visit home; this powder's blue showed clear and vivid even under the pale light of the moon. When she judged she held exactly the right amount, she shook it gently over the moist clay, and kneaded it in, until the clay took on the color of a threatening sky. Slowly—a bit awkwardly—she unbound her long gleaming red hair, silver-black under the moon. It fell free around her shoulders, and she began to work handfuls of the clay into it, in long, sweeping ritual gestures. She built it up with the clay into a fan above her head, with straight spikes descending like rain scattered in the wind. A few dabs of powder on her clay-moistened fingers drew spirals around her eyes and slashes below her cheekbones.

"On my brow, Your Thunder, that is my voice. In my eyes, Your Lightning, that is my fist."

As she spoke, it became true; this is Joining the Sky, the Second Link of the ritual by which a Pict prepares herself for war.

King Demetor had easily persuaded his men to lend the companions their clothing, and after a bit of low comedy in getting the old king safely out the window, the four of them snuck off, looking for all the world like four Kypriots creeping drunkenly toward the nearest brothel. Kheperu made his preparations on the way; by the time the four of them presented themselves at the gate of the Penthedes compound, the closed censer in his left hand leaked a minuscule amount of sweet-smelling smoke, and he had concealed in his right a folded paper packet that contained some brownish-grey powder.

Demetor had a fine time, pretending to be a bit drunk ("In my youth I performed the occasional dithyramb, here and there, rather well, I might add—") and bullying his way in past the Penthedes guardsmen. Whenever he was refused, whether by a guard or a servant or the house steward himself, he simply raised his voice, louder and louder, demanding to see his cousin Agapenthes, until finally the four were allowed in solely to shut him up. Barra's face was swathed in bandages, and Demetor merrily pretended that she was one of his men, who had come out on the losing side of a brawl with some imaginary Penthedes tough, and now he'd come to see his cousin to demand restitution.

Agapenthes finally greeted them in an inner room, broad and low-ceilinged, richly carpeted, layer upon layer of rugs overlapping across the floor in a garishly contrived arrangement, and other rugs from Dilmun and Punt were hung about the walls. He looked considerably less regal than he had at the feast; his silver hair was tied back in a hasty horsetail, as though he'd just awakened, although the strong scent of wine that came even to Barra's damaged nose suggested that if he had been sleeping, it hadn't been for long.

He offered warm, if somewhat wary, greetings to his cousin from Kypros, while Kheperu paced slowly around the room, watching the smoke from his censer to judge the air currents. A slow smile crept over his face when he saw that by standing just *here*, he could twist open the censer's ports and get both Agapenthes and Demetor in the path of the smoke. Barra and Leucas leaned away, in their chairs, not so much that Demetor or Agapenthes would notice, only enough that they wouldn't breathe it: the incense in the censer was the same compound that Kheperu had used to beat the Myrmidons at dice.

"What is this?" Agapenthes demanded, and when Demetor went into his story about Barra's supposed fight, Agapenthes shook his head. "No, I mean this—this smelly incense. You—what are you doing?"

"I'm cleansing the room, my lord, of spirits and adverse influences," Kheperu said smoothly. "With all the rumors of magic and sorcery, I thought it best our little gathering be protected."

"I am *already* protected," Agapenthes huffed. "The prince's steward drew the mark of protection on my shoulder with his own hand."

Kheperu glanced at Barra; she gave him a tight-lipped smile and a tiny nod.

"And, here, see now, Demetor," Agapenthes went on, "this man's Egyptian—he's not from Kypros at all. Since when do you keep company with Egyptians?"

Demetor looked utterly blank. "Since, why, er . . ."

Barra closed her eyes and sent a swift prayer toward the Grey Lands.

"Well, since, you see, I'd been hearing about all this, all this, this magic and all, so I . . . hired this man to look after me, you know . . . protection from this sorcerer everyone's always talking about . . . and, well, that's it, you see."

Agapenthes nodded, and the cloud of suspicion cleared from his brow. Barra thanked her gods that he was drunk, and already a little woozy from Kheperu's smoke. He said, "Well, perhaps we can take some refreshment, and you can tell me of your trouble with my man."

Kheperu watched the pair of cousins while servants streamed in, bringing wine and bread and fresh goat's milk cheese. By the time the servants had left, Kheperu was satisfied; he nodded to Barra, and she gave him a tiny gesture of *get on with it.*

As Demetor began to once again trot out his invented story, Kheperu interrupted. "You may be too tired for this, Demetor. You're very tired. Agapenthes—he looks tired, doesn't he?"

Demetor yawned. Agapenthes leaned toward him, concern painted clearly across his face. "Why, you look absolutely exhausted, cousin."

Kheperu said, "You'd best offer him a bed for the night."

"Demetor, we can deal with this difficulty in the morning. Won't you be my guest, sleep here this evening?"

"Why . . . why, Agapenthes, awfully kind—" he stretched, and yawned again.

"In fact," Kheperu said, "Demetor, you're about to fall asleep. You *are* asleep." Demetor's head dropped to his chest, and his eyes closed, and he made comfortable burbling noises into his beard. Kheperu grinned at Barra. "Told you I could do it."

"Then quit fooling around," Barra growled.

Agapenthes peered at the two of them drunkenly. "Do what? What have you done?"

"Nothing," Kheperu told him firmly. "Agapenthes, do you recognize me?"

"Erm, well . . ."

"I am Meremptah-Sifti."

The Head of House Penthedes squinted, frowning. "Most High? You seem different."

"I'm in disguise," Kheperu said irritably. "Agapenthes, stand up." He stood.

"Spin around."

Slowly, with a certain graceful stateliness, the Head of House Penthedes spun himself in a circle. Again, Kheperu grinned at Barra, and this time, he spoke in Greek, so as to include Leucas in the conversation. "Want to see him dance like a chicken?"

"No!" Barra snapped. "That's not funny."

Leucas leaned forward, resting elbows on knees. "Does it bother you," he asked softly, "to use the same methods Meremptah-Sifti does?"

"Where I come from," Barra told him evenly, "that's called cutting a man with his own knife—and it's counted as quite a coup." Leucas shrugged, looking unconvinced. She turned her attention back to Kheperu. "What about his tattoo? Is that going to cause a problem? When, say, we come across, well, someone in particular that I'm not going to mention?"

"Perhaps; perhaps not. If my hold is good I can tell him day is night and he'll see what I tell him to. On the other hand, this spell fades over time . . ." He opened the paper packet he'd carried in his right hand and swirled its contents into a half-full winebowl. He gave this to Agapenthes to drink, and the old man did so with pathetic eagerness to please. "This potion is a more concentrated, potent form—its effects should certainly last until sunrise; perhaps until midmorning."

"I'm still worried about that tattoo. Is there anything you can do to nullify the mark itself?"

"I don't know. There's no way to be sure without extensive experiment. Probably the surest way is to kill Simi-Ascalon; magics often die with their creators."

"Fine," Barra said. "I'm going to do that anyway. What about the meantime?"

Leucas, ever practical, said, "What if we simply slice it out of his flesh?"

Kheperu nodded dubiously. "That would probably work—but it might not; I'm unsure about the actual mechanism behind this spell. However, doing so will certainly break *my* spell. Any sudden physical pain will wake him right up, and then we will all be in a bit of trouble."

Barra nodded. She waved a hand at Agapenthes, who still turned himself in slow circles. "Ask him how many men he has under arms."

"Agapenthes, you can stop now."

"Thank you, Most High," he gasped. "I confess I was getting a bit dizzy."

Kheperu smirked. "Yes, well, whatever. Now. You will answer all questions and follow all orders that come from this person as though they come from me," Kheperu said, indicating Barra. He turned back to her. "Ask him yourself."

Barra switched languages, back to Phoenikian. "How many men do you have that can be gathered, ready to fight, within the hour? I'm not talking about houseboys, here; I mean veterans, blooded, with their own armor and weapons."

"Now? In the middle of the night?" He frowned, calculating. "Three hundred, perhaps. Or a bit more."

Barra's heart thundered. That was *three times* what she'd been expecting! She said to herself, *This could work.* "How many chariots?"

"Only forty—the garrison keeps the rest locked up for emergencies."

"Forty is plenty. All right. Get your messengers going. I want all three hundred men and forty chariots assembled in that big courtyard out there within the hour, with all their gear, and weapons, and horses. Oh, and wait," she said as he turned to follow her orders. "Is there a garden around here somewhere? Some place with a few plants and maybe a tree or two?"

"On my roof," he told her. "It's the best view in Tyre. I like to sit up there and have a bowl of wine or two at sunset—"

"That's good enough."

"And a bull," Leucas said.

"What?"

"I want a bull. His best bull."

"Leucas, in the name of the Loving bloody Mother—"

He set his jaw stubbornly. "Remember those cuts I took at Lidios' house? I still owe a bull to Athene for protecting me, and I'd be a fool to go into battle without paying up."

Barra sighed and said to Agapenthes in Phoenikian, "And your best bull. Have him brought to the courtyard, too."

"Of course. May I go now?"

Agapenthes' eagerness to please gave her a greasy, slightly sickly feeling in the pit of her stomach, but she told herself that this was no time to get squeamish. Plenty of time for that after the battle, while they bury and burn the dead.

As the companions watched Agapenthes scurry off, Leucas nodded toward Demetor, who now snored softly. "What about him?"

"Let him sleep," Barra said. "By the time he wakes up tomorrow, this'll all be over."

Down in the courtyard, Leucas wrapped the entrails of the bull in its skin, along with the fat from its thighs and belly; he tossed the bundle onto the central bonfire of sweet-scented cedar. The offering bundle crackled and popped in the flames, and the dark, rich-roasting meat smoke rose gently into the sky, drifting on a breeze westward, out to sea. Leucas' song followed it, his powerful bass voice surprisingly pure and sweet, in his hymn to Athene.

Up on the roof, Barra stripped off her Kypriot tunic and leggings and set them aside. Her nipples hardened instantly in the chill night air. Clad only in her breechclout, sandals, and weapon belt, she began to paint herself with the clay, spirals out from her nipples and waves across her belly, long curving stripes from her bandaged ankles to the curve of her hips.

"My breast is Your Waters, struck but never injured; my legs are Your Wind, swift and inescapable."

This is the Joining of the Sea, the Third and final Link in the ritual by which a Pict prepares herself for war.

"The Earth does not tire, the Sky does not clear, the Sea does not rest, until war is done."

Barra stood, and took the hilt of her broadaxe in her teeth; she must carry a weapon naked, never set it down or tuck it away, until the battle is done. She took the trencher, which was stained blue and still contained a handful of blue-grey clay, over to the largest of the pots that housed the green and growing plants around her. With her hands, she scooped aside the moist earth, and laid the trencher within it, covering it over once again in reverent burial.

"That's quite a spell," Kheperu said from behind her.

She hadn't known he was there, she didn't know how long he'd been watching, but she didn't startle at all. She took her axe in her right hand and turned to face him.

Any lingering doubts she might have had about Kheperu's loyalty or determination to see this through were instantly washed away: she was in the grip of the *sceon tiof*, and she saw that his commitment,

once made, was unbreakable. She looked over her shoulder, down at
the men gathered in the courtyard, at Leucas as he donned his armor,
and she saw into the hearts of each and every one. The fear and dismay that had always accompanied the *sceon tiof* were absent, though;
Barra was calm, and sure—and when any of these men fell, she would
grieve for them as though they were her blood kin.

This she accepted; it was the inevitable price of fighting her war.

And the *sceon tiof* did not pass; it was no momentary, flickering
thing, but it rested within her spirit and looked out through her eyes.

Kheperu wore his old robes once again, faded, stained, and
patched, with many, many pockets, and beneath them his familiar
armor of boiled leather. Those myriad pockets bulged with every bit of
magic he thought could possibly be of use—he walked carefully, as he
stepped toward her.

He said, "You know, I'd really feel better—more comfortable—if
you'd put on some armor."

"Armor?" Barra said. The serene consciousness of the Mother's
Love drew her lips into a thin smile. "I'm not even going to put on my
shirt."

Kheperu had concocted a fantastic story about an impostor taking
over Meremptah-Sifti's name and lands, with the connivance of
Idonosteus and Simi-Ascalon, and they were now holding Tal Akhu-
shabb, the Governor, hostage; the impostor must be brought down, and
the Meneides punished, and the Governor rescued, and no matter how
ridiculous the story sounded, Kheperu had no difficulty at all in selling it to Agapenthes, so thoroughly was he magicked.

He'd had a bit more trouble with Agapenthes' wives. All three of
them had come screeching after their husband, swearing and moaning
about the noise and confusion and snapping questions about what the
drunken old fool thought he was going to do now, until finally Kheperu took pity on the stammering old man and offered the women bowls
of wine that contained double doses of one of his sleeping powders,
and breathed a heavy sigh of relief when they nodded off.

Agapenthes also had some difficulty in persuading his men. He
stood on the back of a chariot and exhorted them in a penetrating—if
somewhat slurred—voice of command. Kheperu stood beside him,
just behind his shoulder, and whispered occasionally into his ear. More
than three hundred men had answered the call; they clustered about the
courtyard in ragged, undisciplined knots. They wore armor and carried
weapons, but they seemed more interested in keeping close to the

warmth of the bonfires than in chasing about and fighting a pitched battle in the dark; especially with all these Egyptians around—nobody wanted to get on the wrong side of an Egyptian axe company. Not one of them was unaware of what had been happening in Tyre over the past few days, they just didn't think that they should be the ones to risk their lives trying to fix it. The appearance of Barra at the edge of the rooftop, looking like some wandering spirit from a children's tale, didn't help matters any. Barra, watching from above while Kheperu fed Agapenthes his lines, shook her head. She would have traded the whole three hundred of them, chariots and all, for twenty-five Myrmidons who knew when to shut up and follow orders.

Finally, Kheperu hit upon the magic phrase to turn the tide of opinion in the proper direction: "Equal shares."

*Equal shares.* The phrase whispered through the untidy ranks; it was as though they'd learned that some god would stand at each man's side, an almost superstitious shivering of awed semi-belief. Would Agapenthes really let every fighter share equally in all the loot? It was unheard of!

Kheperu shrugged, and made Agapenthes seal the promise with an oath by the witness of Ba'al-Berith.

The shout that went up from the courtyard warmed Barra's heart.

She went in, and made her way downstairs to where Leucas was dressing in his armor. He took a long, long look at her, frowning, squinting, then finally he nodded. His only comment was, "You be careful. Whatever magic that is, it won't work as well as bronze plate." He shrugged. "On the other hand, it won't itch and make you sweat."

The greaves were already strapped about his shins, and the interleaved bronze plates of the corselet about his chest. He strapped on the girdle, to protect his loins, and then tied back his long grey-salted hair into a pile on the top of his head, to serve as additional padding under the helmet. He lifted the great helm and regarded it solemnly, shaking his head at the ratty, bug-eaten look of its crest of horsehair. "I don't think I've been in full armor since Troy," he mused. "Should keep better care of it." He snugged the helmet over his head, sighed, and tapped the nasal, the long bar that extended from the helmet's brow down to the tip of his nose. "Makes me go cross-eyed. Blasted thing always gives me a headache." He slung his scabbarded sword across his back, stuck the iron scimitar through his belt, then got his massive shield, five layers of alternating ox-hide and bronze. He lifted his man-length spear of heavy ash, and said, "How do I look?"

The *sceon tiof* glowed behind her eyes, and made his every gesture shine with joy. Leucas was a huge man, already; with the helm's crest adding to his height and the corselet deepening his chest, he looked more than human. "Happy," she said. "You could be the very son of manslaughtering Ares."

One of his rare grins split his ruined face. "I admit, I'm looking forward to this."

Barra nodded. "Let's get started."

The fires began at midnight.

All over Tyre, buildings burned, lighting the clouds with an orange glow. Fifty men, ten teams of five, raced through the city torching skins of lamp oil and throwing them onto roofs, or through windows.

Roofs of Meneides warehouses. Windows of Meneides inns.

In some of these, there were guards, or watchmen, or guests sleeping off heavy meals and too much wine. The teams knew their lines; at each, shouts were heard: *"Barra Coll Eigg Rhum makes war! Let Egypt beware! Death to Meremptah-Sifti!"*

At approximately the same time, the Egyptian garrison commander was startled out of a sound sleep by trumpets of alarm and cries that the city was under attack from the sea. At the camps north of the city, breathless riders reported that sea pirates had landed south of the city; at the southern camps, the word was that Joshua ben Nun and his Habiru horde were attacking from the Lebanon, to the northeast, and forward elements were already within the city.

Every camp of the Canaan Division suddenly burst into the furious activity of a kicked-over anthill.

Barra watched it all from the roof garden, Leucas, Kheperu, and Agapenthes at her back. Down in the courtyard below the remaining two hundred–odd men were formed in ranks, surrounding the forty chariots.

Barra said softly, so that only Leucas could hear, "You know, the first time I went to war I was only eight years old. My brother—that's Llem, the High King—he said I couldn't go out hunting with the boys, that I wasn't old enough. My father was visiting from Eire and I told him about it, asked him what he'd do. He said, 'Fuck it. Go to war!' So I did. Painted myself up and marched into my brother's hall, where he was holding a big meeting feast with a bunch of northern chieftains, and proudly informed him that I was at war with him." She sighed, shrugging into the warm regard of Leucas' grey eyes. "Wasn't much of a war. There were exactly two casualties; I still sit on both of them."

"This one's a little different," Leucas murmured.

"Don't I know it."

They stood in silence for a moment, watching the growing flames that sprang up in the night like toadstools. "If Zeus sends no rain," Leucas said, "we might end up burning down the whole city."

Barra shook her head. "No. We won't. Tyre won't burn."

"How do you know?"

She looked calmly, deeply into his eyes. "I know."

Perhaps he saw something of the *sceon tiof* certainty within her gaze; perhaps he only wanted to believe her; at any rate, he nodded. "I understand the fires," he said. "We need to stir up the Egyptians and get a lot of people out on the streets so that we can move around without being interfered with. But why the announcement? Why give warning?"

Barra leaned on the parapet and looked out over the city. "Because we don't know for sure where Meremptah-Sifti is. He could be out at his estate, or here in town at the Meneides compound, or staying in the garrison, or practically anywhere. It won't take more than a couple of hours for the Egyptians to get things back under control; we don't have time to pick a place, and be wrong."

"I still don't understand."

"That's because you don't know Idonosteus." The *sceon tiof* insight she'd gained of the Head of House Meneides had given her this tactic, and there was no doubt within her that it would work. "He panics. He's smart, but he's weak; his nerve'll break. I have ten horsemen surrounding his compound, watching from all sides. I'm just waiting for him to get word of the fires. For him to get word that I'm the one doing it. Because the first thing he'll do is send a message to his master and beg for protection. Then we'll know where Meremptah-Sifti is."

"But they'll be warned."

Barra showed her teeth. "So?"

A clatter of hooves interrupted them. A strong voice shouted hoarsely from the street below. "My lord Agapenthes! Twelve riders and a light coach left House Meneides and galloped out of the city. Toward Karbas' home!"

"Southeast," Barra interpreted grimly. "He's heading for the estate."

"No messenger, then," Leucas said. "He's going himself."

"I suppose he's thinking he'll be safer out there. I told you he's weak."

"Twelve riders, though." His voice was freighted with grim meaning. "Twelve."

Barra knew what that meant: her worst fear had come to pass. "The Myrmidons are with him," she said flatly. "Kamades is with him. They saved my life."

More than that: she thought of the pure joy she'd felt, seeing Kamades in that cellar, and the stunning efficiency with which the Myrmidons had dispatched her guards. She thought of the throat-tightening purity of courage with which he'd faced an angry Leucas. It was possible that he'd fall in this war she'd begun; it was possible she'd find herself matched against him, to kill him or be killed herself.

Leucas, never one to waste words, snaked an arm around her shoulders and gave her a gentle, solemn hug. The smooth bronze of his corselet struck a chill into her bare flesh.

After a moment, she shook him off. "Kheperu—get Agapenthes into a chariot and move 'em out. Let's go do this."

# 19

# *Fun*

**M**eremptah-Sifti listened with interest to Idonosteus' breathless tale, nodding and encouraging him with thoughtful questions. He reclined on a high couch, his hair unbound, his mouth still swollen and ugly with a purple-yellow bruise from Barra's fists. He winced, just a bit, with each sip of wine; this wine was resinous enough to sting his lips.

Idonosteus, by the time he finished his tale, was practically hopping with panic. "Well? So? Well? What will you do about this?"

Meremptah-Sifti shrugged languidly. "What do you suggest I do?"

"Well, you'd better, er, we . . ." he sputtered, then finally controlled himself. "My prince, I think you should send riders to the army immediately, tell them that we're going to be attacked."

Meremptah-Sifti shook his head dismissively. "Not at all. We have the Governor's personal guard here, as well as my personal retainers: over a hundred men."

"But, but she has *more*! Ba'al alone knows how many! They're burning Tyre even as we speak! Where could they have come from? She could have *thousands*!"

"It does not matter."

"What do you mean? How can you say this?"

Meremptah-Sifti twisted his battered mouth into a knowing smile. "I have been hoping for this." He pushed himself upright and swung his legs down off the couch. "Sim has moved his operations downstairs, since his workshop at the caves was discovered. I am well prepared for this occurrence."

"But, b-but still, my prince, shouldn't we have the army—?"

"No."

"B-but—"

Meremptah-Sifti suddenly stood, towering over Idonosteus; Idonosteus cringed like a whipped slave. Meremptah-Sifti smiled, and decided not to hit him.

"No, if the army were here, it might frighten her off," he murmured with deep amusement. "Then I would have to go into Tyre after her. This will be much more convenient." He touched his mouth thoughtfully, running his fingertips over the swollen curve of his underlip.

"This will be much more fun."

# 20

# *Barra's War*

The clouds had not yet stretched east to the mountains, and the rising moon still gave light for the march, illuminating the rolling ground enough for the horses to step confidently. The orange glow of burning buildings in Tyre faded behind them.

Barra stood beside Leucas in the chariot, wearing only her breech-clout, her axes, and a long coil of rope that looped diagonally over her shoulder. The huge Athenian enjoyed himself immensely, driving again for the first time in more than five years. He handled the reins expertly, and chuckled with pleasure when the horses took his direction smoothly and eagerly. "Fine animals," he rumbled. "Greek-trained; they know all the right signals." Barra thought privately that it was more likely that the Greek style was derived from the Phoenikian, but saw fit to keep her mouth shut on the subject—Leucas was the expert, not she.

Alongside them drove Agapenthes, leading his men; Kheperu stood beside him, holding on to the chariot's rim with both hands.

There had been a good deal of laughter and back talk among the men when they'd left Tyre; it had now faded into expectant silence and harsh breathing. Barra pushed their pace as fast as she dared. "Remember," Leucas had said, "these are townsfolk, really—they're warriors only by a sort of accident. You can't expect them to run for an hour in full armor and be able to fight at the end of it." Barra's solution was to keep the pace at a steady jog, and rotate the men through the chariots—at their most crowded, each could hold four men. With this reduced force—numbering now, subtracting the men who still raced around and burned buildings, and the others spreading lies and confusions among the Egyptian camps, perhaps two hundred and twenty or thirty—well over half could ride at any one time. The battlefield she'd chosen would be small; better the horses should be tired and the men strong.

The fires and diversions had their desired effect. On the march toward the estate, they were challenged only once. A large group of horsemen had galloped toward them out of the south—an Egyptian patrol-in-force, investigating rumors of the Habiru invasion—and Barra had crouched low behind the chariot's wall while Kheperu explained to the officer in charge that this ragtag group was a force of Penthedes irregulars, heading out to reinforce the troops protecting the prince at his estate. Kheperu's reply had captured perfectly the nasal arrogance of the Egyptian aristocracy, and the moonlight bleached the stains from his robe; the officer waved them on and the patrol galloped away.

Barra's army marched on, footfalls and hoofbeats muffled by the grass. Conversation was muted, if any took place at all; to Barra's ears came only the hush of the west wind and the creaking of the chariots, the occasional snuffle of a horse and slap of reins.

In the Isle of the Mighty, when the men—and sometimes women—march to war, it is a great and festive occasion, with dancing and singing of songs, with much drinking and more fucking, a celebration of fragile life for the many warriors who will not return. Here in Phoenikia, war was a quiet, grave thing, and the men had no song to keep the dread from their hearts.

Barra didn't like it; to her, it smelled of disaster.

Barra squinted up at the manor house, where it squatted on top of the hill. At this distance, little could be seen of it save the tiny pinpricks of light from its windows. The moon, still fairly low over the mountains, let her see clearly the terrain and the waiting men. "He wants us," she said softly, near Kheperu's ear. "He hasn't even closed the shutters—he's trying to draw us in pretending we can surprise him."

Kheperu gave her a sickly smile. "It's going to work, too, I'm afraid."

"That's right."

She looked at Leucas. He nodded, and extended both fists clenched before him, then slid his shield into place in the grooves of the left side chariot wall and reached back to check that his spear stood firmly in its holder. He was ready.

She looked at the men around her. Their shuffling and snuffling had faded into expectant stillness as they'd caught their breath from the hour's hard march out here.

"I've told you," she said softly, so that only Kheperu and Leucas could hear, even though she spoke in Greek, "that the house up there is built like a fortress. I don't know how many men he has—there is at least one barracks that could hold, say, fifty men or even more. Remember that we don't have to beat them. We just have to get inside, get our hands on Meremptah-Sifti. And, for the Love of the bloody Mother, *don't kill him*. I don't intend to save Tyre only to have it destroyed by Egypt. Simi-Ascalon, Indonosteus—they're fair game. The sooner they're dead, the happier I'll be."

She took a deep breath and gestured toward the manor. "Now, I figure that his best defense is to hold his men inside the house, fight with arrows from the second floor and third, maybe sortie once or twice to keep us back from the walls. For our part, we have to get in close. We need to be fighting right up against those walls, which should produce enough confusion that we can get inside. I'm thinking the roof—you see that colonnade, there?" She pointed it out, ghostly in the moonlight. "If we can get up there, Leucas, you can toss me up onto the roof, just like you did at Xuros' inn. I lower this rope"—she patted the coil over her shoulder—"and all three of us are up there. We should be able to get in from the top—nobody should be expecting that."

"Why the roof?" Leucas asked, frowning. "The house may be built like a fortress, but it's not a fortress. If we get to the walls, we can force those doors, or the shutters on the windows. Why go to all the trouble of going to the roof?"

"Because," Barra said tightly, "that's where he'll be. If we go in from the ground, we'll have to fight our way up. He might be on the third floor, but probably he's on the roof."

"How do you know?"

She shrugged. "That's where I'd be."

Agapenthes was given his final instructions in an undertone by Kheperu, leaning with both hands on the old man's armor. "You must lead your men in close, and do not fall back. Keep them with you, shame them if need be, but bring them to the house and surround it, and break the windows and doors, and take the house. Those inside who do not resist, take prisoner. Take only the ground floor, do not go up into the house nor down into the cellar." Barra had decided this was safest; she didn't want Meremptah-Sifti killed by some Penthedes bully who got his blood up. This wouldn't stop the Penthedes men from running up and down those stairs looking for things to steal and people to kill—no leader has that much control over his men, except perhaps the late Akhilleus—but it should slow them down.

Kheperu ended his instructions with, "And, once the attack begins, follow no other order, from me or anyone else, until the battle is done." This risky command was given in hopes that it would prevent Agapenthes being turned by a shout from the real Meremptah-Sifti; Kheperu didn't know for sure whether it would work, but it seemed to be the wisest precaution.

"Oh, and"—Kheperu winced, and made a superstitious warding gesture against bad luck—"when the arrows come at you, keep your shield up."

The orders were given. No trumpet sounded, no shouts or songs rose toward the sky. The chariots were deployed in wings, to the right and left of the body of footmen, where they could respond swiftly to any sortie, except for the chariot of Agapenthes and his driver, and the chariot that Leucas drove, carrying Barra and Kheperu: these were in the center.

The army advanced, up the hill, toward the house, at a walk.

Blood thundered in Barra's ears, and she gripped the chariot's low wall with her free hand, more to keep herself still than to maintain her balance. She kept telling herself that Meremptah-Sifti couldn't have more than fifty or sixty men here, and if he'd sent riders in search of reinforcements from the Egyptians, they'd have a hard time finding the necessary officers, who were spread out all over Tyre looking for raiders or fighting fires in the city, and even if they did find the officers, they wouldn't be able to get any substantial force here in time to alter the outcome, and that Meremptah-Sifti had some extremely fast-looking horses in his stable and so if things went badly she could steal one that just possibly might be able to outrun the Egyptian chariots.

She turned, into the trailing wind, and now they'd risen up the hill far enough that she could see the distant fires, and she scanned the rolling ground for any sign of troops marching toward them—she had no illusions about how her little army would fare against Egyptian regulars. The orange-tinted clouds were reaching inland now, and the moon rose to meet them, and she had another thing to worry about: if the moon went behind the clouds, the only light they'd have to fight by would be whatever fires Kheperu could quickly set, which would be a stunning advantage to the archers within the house.

And she kept looking at the ornamental groves of olive and fig trees that they passed, these stands of trees that were scattered artistically about the grounds. The blackness within them was impenetrable, and any one of them could hold enemies lying in wait.

She looked around her at the apprehension, the stomach-knotting dread, that showed so clearly on the faces of the men who walked alongside the chariot. Which of them would live to tell this story? Who would take an arrow through the lung? Who would return home to his wife with a gangrenous stump where his arm had been? Who would scream for his mother as he lay on the ground and tried to stuff his bowels back inside his slashed belly? The *sceon tiof* couldn't show her that; it did show that they feared humiliating themselves in front of their comrades more than they feared death or injury; it showed the resolve, deep within each man, that if he was wounded he'd bear his injury bravely, silently, that if need be he'd die without a sound, so that he could be remembered as a warrior. It showed that not courage, but shame, would keep these men fighting in the strong encounter.

Leucas, glancing back, caught her expression. "I've seen that look before," he said.

"What look?" Barra shook herself free of the gaze that had held her, and shifted her grip on her axe.

"Your face, just then, could have been Agamemnon's, at Aulis. I saw him there, when he put his daughter to the knife for a fair wind to Troy," he rumbled thoughtfully. "I saw Diomedes gaze on his young companions, in front of the seven-gated walls of Thebes, and he too wore this look that you wear now."

She shook her head. "I've never led men into battle before."

"Well, actually," Kheperu said, "*you* are not really leading them, you know, if anyone could be said—"

"It doesn't matter," Barra said, interrupting him with a slice of her hand. "This is my fight, but it's going to be their blood that pays for it."

"It's hard, your first time," Leucas said. "Or so the poets say. Maybe there'll be a song about us, someday."

"About this?" Barra said skeptically. "This dirty little fight? I don't think so."

"You never know," Leucas told her. Then: "Look up there. They're coming out."

Above them, at the crest of the hill, the lights in the windows winked out, one by one, like fireflies dying in the cold. Out from the main front door issued a long file of men. In the moonlit distance, it

was hard to tell if they were armed, or not. They came out onto the
front lawn, and formed a ragged line, and stood, waiting.

"What's he doing?" Barra muttered. The army continued to
advance while she counted them silently. Twenty-five men, perhaps
thirty, that was all. What could Meremptah-Sifti be thinking of, to put
thirty men outside the safety of the walls, to face two hundred? Some
still trailed out the door, and none of them seemed in any great hurry
to get into position. For a moment, she nursed a wild hope at her breast
that Meremptah-Sifti, arrogant as he was, might actually come out to
parley, to find out why one of his tattooed slaves had turned against
him.

Then the breeze shifted, only for a moment, whispering from the
east, and a chill understanding made Barra shiver. Bad eggs and rotting meat . . . "Smell that?" she said. "Those are—what did you call
them?—corpse-warriors."

"Chryseids," Kheperu murmured, then suddenly his gaze sharpened. "You can *smell* them?"

"I'll explain some other time." She shut her eyes, briefly searching for some of the serenity the Rite of War had given her, but she
found it nowhere within her. *Well,* she thought, *better they should be
out here, against the army, than waiting for me inside . . .*

She opened her eyes. "Cry the charge," she said softly. "Kheperu,
tell Agapenthes to cry the charge."

Leucas answered her with a laugh that thundered like a happy
Zeus. "We don't need words to cry the charge!" He snapped the reins
against the horses' rumps. *"Hyah!"*

The horses surged ahead, leading the way, leaving the men behind,
and as they saw this, the men of the army roared with a single voice
and broke into a run.

The footmen overtook the chariots, tired as the horses were, and
once again the army surged up the hill as a single mass. Agapenthes
shouted something wildly about the impostors sending servants and
slaves against them, because the chryseids wore no armor, only carried
spears and knives, and then the battle was joined.

During the initial shock and crush, Barra was most concerned with
keeping her feet in the bouncing chariot. Kheperu crouched below the
chariot's walls, preparing some spell, and Leucas stood like a ship's
captain holding the tiller in a storm. Hands clutched the chariot's rim,
and Barra cut at them, feeling again the leathery shock as her axe
failed to slice through the skin.

The army's war cries turned to shouts of alarm and dismay, when they found their weapons often failed to bite the skins of their opponents. The chryseids fought silently, delivering blows of tremendous power, driving spear points through the very bronze of the Penthedes corselets, ripping through the livers and unstringing the knees of many a man. Against enemies of such strength, the footmen's armor served little use, providing scant protection and slowing them to make them easier prey.

The chariot lurched, knocking Barra sprawling against Leucas' legs, as a lunging chryseid slashed his spear blade through the neck of the left-hand horse. It reared, screaming horribly, spraying blood that drenched Leucas and made the clay paint begin to smear on Barra's skin. Leucas gathered the reins in one hand, cursing, and then with a single smooth motion drew the bronze sword from his back and cut away the traces holding that horse to the chariot in one swift stroke. "Learned that trick from Nestor himself!" he roared with a laugh that spread his mouth within his blood-drenched face like an open wound.

He fought the reins as the other horse reared away from its injured partner, still driving for the house. A chryseid clung to the rim, and Barra got her feet beneath her and chopped a two-handed gape into its skull. The viscous milky fluid that served it for blood splashed across her face, and the chryseid stabbed clumsily at her with its knife, and she shouted, *"Kheperu! Help me kill this bastard!"*

"I'm right beside you," he snapped. "Don't shout." He reached toward the chryseid, his hand full of some black-tar substance that he slapped across the thing's snarling lipless face. "Stand back."

The tarry substance burst into brilliant white flame, and the chryseid lost its grip on the chariot as its flesh melted and its brain boiled within its skull. Kheperu held up his hand and examined both sides. "Must be sure none of it clings—that would smart quite a bit!"

Something *spangged* off Leucas' armor and dropped into the chariot's bed: an arm's-length shaft tipped with bronze and fletched with gull pinions. *"Arrows!"* Barra shouted, and soon the cry rose across the battle. Men cried out in pain as another flight struck among them. She looked around, searching for the archers—that arrow had hit Leucas in the *back*. There—pale grey in the moonlight, she saw a flight of gull-fletched arrows arching toward them from one of the ornamental groves; and another flight rose from a different grove, and she clenched her jaw. Meremptah-Sifti meant to crush them against his house, and let none escape.

Arrows showered thick as rain around them, the archers uncaring whom they hit. If a chryseid was struck, most arrows would bounce from its leathery skin; any that pierced it were yanked out or had their shafts broken off, and forgotten. A Penthedes man only steps from Barra threw his arms up, his spear tumbling away, as he clutched vainly at the arrowhead that stuck out through his eye; he crumpled to his knees and slowly pitched forward onto his face.

Then Leucas cursed and before Barra could see at what he swore, she found herself tumbling helplessly forward, over the front of the chariot to the ground, where she scrambled away from the screaming, struggling horse. The horse lashed out convulsively, and one hoof caught Barra a glancing blow across the hip that sent her spinning again to the ground. She got a glimpse of its sheared-through front leg and then Leucas rose to his feet and drove his spear through the guts of the chryseid that'd savaged the horse. The chryseid flopped on the spear point like a fish; Leucas roared and lifted it into the air. It clutched at the shaft, howling wordlessly, and Leucas whipped the spear like a staff sling and threw the chryseid tumbling high over a nearby melee—it landed among the struggling men and instantly came to its feet and attacked the nearest. Leucas' eye found Barra.

"Are you all right?" he bellowed. "Where's Kheperu?"

"I'll find him," Barra yelled, coming to her feet at once. "Don't let that horse suffer!"

Leucas stuck his spear headfirst into the ground and drew the iron scimitar, and Barra turned away. Kheperu she found almost instantly; he'd been crouching in the chariot when the horse went down, and had hit his head against the wall. "I'm all right," he insisted dazedly. He staggered a bit as he came to his feet, and he had to lean on Barra in order to stand. "I'm all right," he said again, his voice getting stronger. "We'd best get to the house and settle this business."

She plucked an arrow out of the folds of his robe; spent of its force, it hadn't penetrated the armor he wore beneath. She shook it in his face. "Stick close to Leucas! Try and cover behind his shield!"

Leucas had struck off the wounded horse's head with a single blow. Now he returned the scimitar to his belt and recovered his spear, and pointed off behind Barra. "I think we better run!"

She followed his finger with her eyes. From around the corner of the manor house pelted men wearing the quilted armor of the Egyptian Army, and the colors of the Governor's personal guard. Barra groaned; small wonder the arrows had flown so thickly! The bloody Mother alone knew how many men there were still inside the house. Chryseids, the prince's men, now the elite of the Canaan Division . . .

She whirled back to her partners, whom she had led here to die.

"Guess we'd best go that way," she yelled, pointing to the opposite corner of the house. She took the coil of rope in one hand and her axe in the other, and took off running hard for the colonnade.

Leucas thundered along behind her, his much longer legs nearly capable of pacing her, even carrying Kheperu; he'd said to Kheperu, "Hold these," and handed the Egyptian his spear and his shield. Kheperu, too startled to refuse, took them, and Leucas gathered him up in a bear hug and carried him in Barra's wake.

She rounded the corner of the house and pressed close to the wall, hoping that none within could see her. No one appeared to be up on the colonnade's roof, and when Leucas and Kheperu joined her, the Athenian was able to lift her high enough that she could get a grip on the edge of the roof and scramble up. So far their luck was holding; no one within the house seemed to know they were there.

The battle raged around them as she helped Kheperu up onto the roof beside her, and then they both held the rope for the armored Leucas. She paused a moment, to catch her breath once Leucas was safely up, and looked across the unbelievable carnage that spread throughout these grounds. The flagstones ran with black blood, and the grass was painted with it, and corpses lay strewn here and there like the dolls of a careless child. It seemed incredible that only a few days before she'd been here, on these very grounds, for the Governor's feast of welcome. She'd sat on the rim of that fountain, over there, where now a Penthedes man lay facedown and darkened the water with his life's blood. Agapenthes and his men struggled with the chryseids and the Egyptians close to the wall—and, even as she watched, an arrow struck Agapenthes in the thigh, below his girdle. Blood began to flow, and the old man shook himself like he was awakening from a dream.

*Any sudden physical pain,* Kheperu had said, *will wake him right up, and then we will all be in a bit of trouble.*

If Kheperu ever decided to get out of the mercenary trade, Barra decided, he could make a fine living as a prophet.

She bleakly pointed this out to him and Leucas. Kheperu looked stricken; even now Agapenthes began to yell at his men to fall back, or surrender. Leucas only shrugged and said, "I suppose this means we'll have to hurry."

Barra put her hand on his arm, and gave his stone-hard bicep a grateful squeeze. "All right."

She shook out the coil of rope. "I'll hold it in the middle," she said. "You keep both ends down here, so once I'm up there I won't have to waste time tying it off. There's a low wall around the roof up there, and there are torch stands sticking out of it—I can just throw the loop over one of those."

"Mmm, wait," Kheperu said, digging within his robe.

"You have something to say, or are you just scratching?"

"Here." He brought out two small pouches, teased them open; within each was a glass pot about the size of her fist, wound in linen that Kheperu carefully unwrapped. "This one, when broken, makes light—quite a blinding flash, actually—and this one makes thick smoke. Just in case you were right, and he's on the roof."

She snatched them out of his hands. "Great, that's great—" He flinched back from her.

"Be careful! They're fragile! You must protect them with your body—hold the rope in your teeth when Leucas throws you."

"What are you, crazy? I'm not going to *carry* these things up there!"

"Barra—"

She looked up at the roof and whistled piercingly through her teeth. "Hey!" she yelled in Egyptian to get their attention, "Meremptah-Sifti takes it up the ass!" and followed this with the two glass pots, one only a second after the other. They burst with a crash of glass and a hissing sound like a nest of cobras, and the flash of light flared across the sky. Voices cried out from above. "They're up there," she said. "Let's go!"

She stepped up into Leucas' finger-laced hands, gripped the rope, and nodded. He returned her nod, and bent his knees. So did she.

With an enormous surge he threw her into the air; she leaped with the throw and arrowed up over the lip of the wall. She tumbled onto the roof, and into a stinging cloud of smoke that hung near the deck; she popped to her feet and instantly looped the rope around one of the torch stands, before even looking to see where her enemies were. *"Come on come on!"* she yelled, and Leucas sprang to the wall and began to swarm up the doubled rope, Kheperu right behind him.

The smoke drifted in the breeze, beginning to clear already, and the flashpot still burned brightly, lighting the smoke from within, and she could hear Meremptah-Sifti's voice, that chilling Egyptian drawl, calmly ordering someone to "take the bitch." So he knew; he knew it was her on the roof. She hefted her axe and grinned into the smoke. Her nose was useless here, but she could follow the sound of his voice. It wasn't a conscious decision that sent her loping around the rim of the roof; she didn't *decide* that she couldn't wait for Leucas and Kheperu; she heard his voice and she went for him in the instinctive blood lust that sends a wolf pack against a stag. She stuck close to the upwind wall so that she could see her footing, and was startled to hear voices shouting from below: *"The Wild Woman! It's the Wild Woman, on the roof!"*

Penthedes men, weapons down in the act of surrendering, stared up at her uncertainly. She realized that with the flash and the smoke, those below must have thought she'd transported herself up here by sorcery. Silhouetted against the white-lit smoke, she shook her axe at them and howled, "Fight! Fight, you sons of shit-eating dogs! *Fight or I'll come for you next!"*

They swept up their weapons and threw themselves against the Governor's personal guard below, and Barra turned once again to go after Meremptah-Sifti. The smoke had now cleared so that she could see shapes within it, moving uncertainly toward the sound of her voice.

Then the wind gusted, and whipped the last of the smoke away, and the men who crept toward her were Myrmidons.

Back beyond them, Barra saw Meremptah-Sifti, and beside him the round form of Idonosteus. She howled again; faster than thought she drew a throwing axe from her belt and hurled it spinning for Idonosteus' head. And she screamed, *"No!"* as the Myrmidon beside him threw himself into the path of her axe.

It was the young one who'd been excited by the prospect of action, the same one that Leucas had terrified into summoning Kamades, all those days ago. He covered Idonosteus, and the axe struck him full on the breast and stuck into his armor; he staggered back, blood welling around the pitiless flint.

Meremptah-Sifti said, "I want them alive. Damage them as much as you like, so long as they are still breathing."

Kamades, his face expressionless, nodded. "Take the Akhaian first, then the Egyptian. Lalcamas: you and I have the girl."

They closed on Leucas. He'd left his spear behind, since he couldn't climb and carry it, and he'd lost his short straight bronze sword somewhere out in the battle. He whipped the scimitar around his head menacingly enough, but uncertainty showed on his face—these were guest-friends, and an injury to them would be avenged by Zeus. This momentary uncertainty was all the Myrmidons needed; six of them leaped upon him together. He roared and cut one at the joining of the shoulder and neck, the keen iron slicing through bronze, but the other five bore him to the ground. Kheperu waded in behind them; he killed the wounded Myrmidon with a staff blow at the base of the neck, below his helmet, then he had three Myrmidons of his own to face. They forced him back, and he gave ground, blocking desperately with his staff against their stabbing spears.

Kamades and Lalcamas, the man who'd held the stable door for her to escape from this place, advanced on her, shields up to their eyes; Lalcamas held a spear low, by his thigh; Kamades held a sword.

"Kamades," Barra said, "call off your men. Remember what you said? You wouldn't obey the order to harm guest-friends, because those could only come from a madman! Remember?"

Kamades' expression never changed, and the *sceon tiof*, that lived now within her eyes, looked at him and saw nothing at all. No will, no choice, none of those things that make a man what he is, in himself.

Across the roof, still clear in the fading light from Kheperu's flashpot, Idonosteus smirked at her. "We decided he should be . . . decorated. Seems now like that was a wise choice."

From beneath the struggling pile of men, Leucas arose with a roar, a Myrmidon hanging upon each arm. The huge Athenian whirled and bellowed and slung one of those two men over the rim of the roof; the Myrmidon screamed as he fell, and hit the paving below with a thunderous crash that cut off his voice.

Kamades turned his head at the scream, only for an instant, and Barra broke past him, streaking for Idonosteus, her broadaxe up and a wild howl erupting from her throat. She was fast; no man could catch her at a run, but they didn't need to catch her. Even as Leucas' knees were unstrung by a spear shaft clubbed into his jaw, even as Kheperu went down beneath his attackers' pounding, Lalcamas cast his spear and struck her deep through the front of her thigh, the spear slicing through and tangling her legs, and she tumbled to the roof. He was to her in a blink of an eye, but that was too slow—she popped to her feet with the bulldancer's kip, feinted at his bare thigh to draw down his shield, and swung full force at his head.

She was no Akhaian, to be god-bound in the oaths of hospitality, and iron is not the only thing that will cut bronze. Her broadaxe sheared through the helm that he wore and opened Lalcamas' brain to the night sky.

She did not pause to watch his shuddering fall, but turned again to make for Idonosteus and something struck her shoulder with staggering force; her right arm went numb and limp, and her broadaxe dropped clattering to the roof.

She spun, and clapped her left hand to her shoulder and howled when she felt the lips of an open wound and the jagged ends of bone within. Kamades stood there, blood on his sword and no expression on his face. She drew her remaining throwing axe with her left hand—and remembered losing her breath at his courage as he faced Leucas and Lysandros in the apartment; and remembered his gruff commitment to save her life, no matter the cost to himself—and in that instant of hesitation, Kamades slapped the axe out of her hand with the flat of his blade and battered her off her feet with his shield.

Stunned, she could only lie there as he put his foot upon her throat and held his sword pointed at her eye.

Some few shouts and screams, not too many, still sounded from the grounds below; on the roof all was quiet.

Meremptah-Sifti strolled casually up beside Kamades, and looked down at her with mock concern. "Your little war is over, Barra Coll Eigg Rhum."

A glorious smile spread across his face like the dawn.

"I win," he said warmly. "You lose."

# 21

# *War's End*

**K**amades' foot pinned her to the roof. She didn't struggle.

Meremptah-Sifti said, "Let me once again extend the hospitality of my home. You won't refuse me, this time, will you?" He turned to Kamades. "Take them down to the workshop. Tell Sim not to start on them until I finish up with this." His gesture took in the struggling men on the grounds around. "Do no more than restrain them until I get there; I want to watch."

Idonosteus sidled up to him and licked his lips. "*I* could go—"

"Stay with me. There will be nothing to see until I get there."

It took three Myrmidons to carry the unconscious Leucas in his armor, one holding his legs while two more took one arm apiece; another two had Kheperu gagged and his hands bound, and they kicked him stumbling along before them. Kamades took his foot from Barra's chest and knelt beside her. "I'm sorry I hurt you, Barra. I didn't want to, but you shouldn't have killed Lalcamas."

Barra's throat rasped from the screaming she'd done. "It's all right, Kamades, I know you couldn't help it."

The ends of her broken collarbone ground together as he lifted her in his arms, but the wound was still numb—it only made her dizzy, instead of faint with agony. He carried her gently, as a father carries an injured child. "I'm told this Simi-Ascalon is a fine surgeon," he murmured as he carried her down through the open stairwell. "I'm sure he can save your arm."

Her last view of the sky also held the silhouettes of Meremptah-Sifti, standing with legs apart, hands clasped behind him, looking proudly out over his handiwork, and Idonosteus, standing identically, imitating mastery as he had imitated manhood.

Barra looked up into Kamades' face, searching it for any understanding of the reality of what was happening. She wondered idly which shoulder his tattoo was on. "He's not going to heal me, Kamades; he's going to kill me. Simi-Ascalon will torture me to death."

"Now, Barra, that's just not so," he said, sounding so much like Leucas that it hurt her chest.

The last two Myrmidons walked close behind him. Barra's mind whirled, racing through fantasies of escape—but Leucas showed no signs of awakening, he might be dead, Kheperu could do nothing, gagged and tied, and she was weakening rapidly, going fuzzy with blood loss and defeat. Kamades carried her across the third floor, archers turning curiously away from the windows to watch the procession, and down more stairs, deeper into the manor.

"Your hair looks funny, Barra," he said. "What did you do to it? I liked the other color so much better. And it looked soft."

"Kamades, I know you can't help yourself," she whispered, "but I hope you'll remember. Someday, when this power wears off, remember that I don't hold you responsible for this."

"For what?" he said, frowning. "No one will hurt you, Barra."

She understood now what was happening within him; he was spinning fantasies, to justify following these orders. He was making himself believe that since he was doing this, it must not be wrong—the only way he could justify hurting her as he had, was to believe that he was now carrying her to someone who would help her. Under the power of the tattoo, he was forced to do things which were against everything he believed in, and his mind was searching for ways to convince himself that these things were right.

He would go right on convincing himself while he watched Simi-Ascalon slice her and shred her into bloody death.

She looked at the others, the ones carrying Leucas, the two shoving along Kheperu. They had the same bland certainty that painted away all thought from Kamades' face. And again, she understood: getting Kamades to accept the tattoo would have been easy. Idonosteus would have just told him to. Then, he would pass the order along to his men; they would obey unthinkingly.

Ironic, that the magic only enforced behavior they already practiced.

Barra turned her head painfully to look at the two who brought up
the rear. "You understand what's going on, don't you?" she rasped.
"You know the dishonor you bring upon yourselves."

One of them—the young one who'd saved Idonosteus by leaping
in front of her axe, he had a rag stuffed into the gap in his armor to
stem the bleeding—said hesitantly, "The only dishonor I fear is disobedience."

"What are you, *dogs?*" she snapped in sudden anger, and would
have gone on at length had Kamades not gathered her head to his
corselet and clamped a warm, dry hand over her mouth.

"Don't abuse my men, Barra," Kamades said reproachfully. "If
you don't promise to leave them alone, I won't let you talk at all."

They passed through several rooms on the first floor; in one of
them, Barra's rolling eyes caught a glimpse of the Governor, sitting
morosely on the floor, alone in a corner. In nearly all the others were
any number of soldiers and servants of Meremptah-Sifti; of course he
had sent the Governor's personal guard into the battle and held his own
men back.

Finally, Kamades looked down at her and said, "Do you promise
not to say anything against my men?" When she nodded agreement
with her eyes he released her mouth.

"All I want," she gasped, gritting her teeth against the grinding of
broken bones that she could hear inside her head, "all I want,
Kamades, is a favor from you. We're guest-friends, and I'm going to
die—"

"You're not going to die," he insisted, but as they descended into
the cellar, where he'd risked his life and the lives of his men to save
her, he sounded a little less sure of himself, and a slightly puzzled
frown came over his face. The other two, who'd been bringing up the
rear, now carried lamps they'd lit from the ones on an upper floor.
They looked at each other, also frowning.

"Listen, Kamades, whatever happens, you and I both know I'll
never see my home again. But, at the house of Peliarchus, my foster-
father, there's a bundle, a . . . a packet. I want you to go there, please,
get it, make sure it's sent on a ship to Albion."

"Well, why . . . I don't know—"

"Please, Kamades." She clutched at his armor with her working
hand, and tears welled in her eyes. "I'm begging you. I have two sons,
one of my own and one a little Akhaian boy that I adopted—and that
packet, that's my letters to them, and if you could just write something,
to let them know how I died . . ."

She heard the sounds of shifting stones, a heavy scraping with hollow, echoing undertones; some sort of underground door was being opened, here in the cellar, and a wash of air, a breeze warm as human breath, spread a stench around her that she instantly recognized—that mingled black decay and chemical reek could only have come from the demonist's workshop. There was an overlay of burning cedar that hid the worst of it; she clenched her teeth grimly against the gagging rebellion of her stomach, and kept her eyes on Kamades' face. She was getting through to him, not much perhaps, but she thought she saw answering tears in his eyes.

"Please," she whispered, "I don't want to die alone and unknown in a foreign land. Don't leave my sons to forever wonder what happened to me, to look for me at Midsummer's and when I don't come, think it's because I've forgotten them. They'll think it's because I don't love them . . ."

"I . . . Barra," his voice was husky with emotion, "Barra, I swear, I wouldn't bring you here if, if I thought you'd come to any harm. Please—"

Now they descended along steps cut into living rock, and the stone that bounded these stairs to either side showed faint reliefs carved beneath the layers of lampblack. Barra clutched at him again. "Promise! Promise me!"

A single tear rolled down Kamades' cheek, a jewel more precious to Barra than any stone, slowly moistening the creased scar down to his beard. Somewhere, deep within him, she was getting through, some understanding was coming clear. He said solemnly, "You have my word."

The shackles were of bronze, strongly bolted to the rough, unpolished wood of the table. Their edges were sharp, cutting into her ankles and scraping her wrists alongside the bandages that still covered the hyaenae-bites. Against her back she felt the grooves carved into the table, channels that led to three different drains drilled through the table's surface. She hadn't struggled when they bolted her down to this table, even after she'd seen the rich brown stains and blackened flecks of decayed flesh that covered it; with a broken collarbone and a stiffening gash through her leg, she could hardly hope even to hurt someone before they brought her down, let alone escape. Lying flat and still on this table was the only way she could keep the growing pain tolerable, although the blood that trickled from her thigh and her shoulder and into the channels of the table made her flesh crawl, like it was a trail of ants marching down her back.

Simi-Ascalon's workshop was a natural cavern, like the one at the funerary caves, that had been subtly enlarged with skillful stonework. Small tripod copper braziers stood about the cavern, holding pyres of cedar to both light the room and combat the horrible stench. Shadows shifted across the rough stone folds of the walls. This place was larger and better furnished than the one at the caves, lacking also its hasty, improvised look. Simi-Ascalon's workbench was much bigger here, a long well-carved table that bent in the middle to follow a natural corner of the rock, and shelves rose above it, so high that the uppermost would be out of reach of even a very tall man; it was crowded with boxes and scrolls and bottles and implements of every description. A ladder rested against one end of them.

Four worktables held the center of the room; one of them was empty. Next to Barra, Leucas was bolted facedown on his table, and Kheperu, on the other side of him, had given Barra a look that pulsed with some sort of undetermined significance as they shackled him facedown as well. They hadn't bothered to remove Kheperu's robes— none of the Myrmidons had wanted to touch them, and Simi-Ascalon assured them that he'd cut off the clothing himself. The Myrmidons had stripped Leucas of his armor, and now beside her, Barra could see his naked, scarred back slowly rise and fall.

He was alive, then. Another tear leaked from her eyes. *Thank you, Zeus, Athene, whoever it is that watches over him. If we are not to escape this, though, I beg you not to let him wake up.*

Leucas moaned and shifted a little bit, and his eyelids fluttered, then he relaxed back into unconsciousness.

On the other side of the cavern, where Barra tried not to look, were bodies—cadavers, corpses. They were stacked in untidy heaps like shipbuilder's planks, some in roughly pyramidal piles, some leaning up against the walls, five, seven bodies deep; men, women, even boys and girls. Hundreds upon hundreds of them, stacked on the walls in a cleft in the cave that receded into darkness: the dead of Tyre, brought here piled in wagons, no doubt. Now that there was no longer any need for secrecy, the less-comfortable workshop at the caves had probably been abandoned. Barra tried to keep her face turned from there because that was where Simi-Ascalon worked, but the sucking void that was his spirit drew her through the *sceon tiof*; whenever she glanced toward him that blackness grew once again within her mind, drawing her down like a ship caught in Kharybdis.

He was working on one of the corpses, where it stood against the wall, incising designs in its leathery flesh with some kind of gouging tool like a chisel. She glanced at him, unable to stop herself, and his hand twitched and he cursed in fluent, accentless Phoenikian. He stood, and threw down the chisel in disgust. "More warriors, he says. Always more warriors. How am I supposed to work under these conditions? Does he think this is *easy*? You there—Kamades, is that your name?—stack this one with the others, that pile, over there."

Kamades rose; unlike the other Myrmidons, who were clustered nervously near the stairs, he'd been squatting beside Barra's table. Silently he complied, and as she watched him, Barra's eye caught something that she'd missed before: leaning against the wall, half concealed by the stack to which Kamades carried the stiff corpse, was one that stood without arms, and with its split head bound together by soiled linen. She let her eyes drift closed and sent a prayer to the Mother that Meremptah-Sifti had forgotten his promise to give her to Chrysios.

Simi-Ascalon said, "And you! You stop that, stop that *looking* at me. I don't like it."

Barra opened her eyes and glanced toward him. "You mean like this?" Darkness sucked at her, but she ground her teeth and pulled with her right arm against the shackle. The hideous pain of the ends of her collarbone grinding together anchored her against the pull of his void, and she held her gaze on him, and he stepped toward her, his face twisting.

*"Stop it!"* His voice took on a querulous whine; as he came close, Barra could see the thick makeup on his face, the paint he used to cover the decay of his flesh, and he smelled—even through the stenches of this room, that were fading now as she became accustomed to them, she could smell the acid sweat on this man, the animal musk: fear.

It made her smile.

"I'm tired of it," he said. "I don't like it. I told Remmie he should have killed you before. It feels like, like I don't know what. Like something's *crawling*, inside my skin. Like you're *doing* something to me."

Within her mind, winds tore at her, driving her spirit toward him, but she wrenched her shoulder and clung to the pain. "All I'm doing," she ground out through her clenched teeth, "is *seeing* you. I'm seeing you, for what you really are. If you don't like it, you should have been something else."

His fist flashed out and cracked her across the cheekbone, she tasted blood—and Kamades came at him from behind. "That's *enough!*" he shouted.

Simi-Ascalon whirled in surprise, and Kamades grabbed him by the shoulders and shook him like a rag. "You're supposed to be *help-ing* her! You're supposed to be healing her!" He lifted the demonist off the ground; Kamades' face was red as an open wound, and his eyes bulged in fury. "Hit her again and I'll kill you!"

"No, you won't," Simi-Ascalon said hastily. "Put me down, and don't touch me again. You others"—he snapped toward the other Myrmidons, who had started toward their captain—"don't move. None of you move."

Kamades' face went blank; he released Simi-Ascalon, and the demonist dusted himself off and recovered his composure. The other Myrmidons stood like statues.

"Now, you will stand where you are, all of you," Simi-Ascalon said, his lower lip jutting out like a pugnacious little boy's. "Don't move until I say. Don't speak. You and I, Kamades, we'll have some fun later. I'll pay you out for putting your hands on me. I think I'll flay you and wear your skin as my new robe. Or something."

Kamades stopped moving; he stood like a statue beside Barra's table, but she could see the veins twist beneath the reddened skin of his neck—and, just peeking out of the collar piece of his armor, the black-ink rim of the tattoo that held him.

"And now for you, you, you *cunt*!" Simi-Ascalon spat. "You want to see what's going to happen to you? Is that what you're looking for?" Down, far down deep within his swirling blackness, Barra saw a little boy, faceless, nameless, playing alone, always alone, hurting things, pulling legs off frogs, putting hot coals into a cat's rear, hurting himself, cutting his hands, scraping his face with broken glass. This wasn't his past she was seeing—it was his nature. He felt it, he felt it again as she watched him; his face contorted into a snarl and he writhed convulsively, like a man covered by fleabites that he can't scratch. "Stop it! I didn't like it in the Market, and *I can't stand it now!*"

He sprang to the workbench and started throwing things off the shelves, digging for something, finally coming up with an octagonal bronze rod as big around as his wrist and as long as his arm. It was studded with bits and pieces of metal, castings of hieroglyphs bolted to it. He waved it at her, his eyes shining with anticipation, his mouth slick with saliva.

"First, I *fuck* you with this, you see it? You understand what it's going to *do* to you? Then, after you're good and torn up inside, I leave it in there, you see, and I heat this end in a brazier, until the whole thing gets red-hot. See? That's why your boyfriends are face*down*, see? You take it in the cunt, they get it up the ass! And that's only the beginning! You want to see it all? Keep looking!"

A sound came from Kamades' throat, a horrible low growling moan, and tears streamed down his face, but he could not move, could not even blink. Barra wrenched her shoulder, again and again, grinding bones, holding on to the pain, glaring at him, her eyes locked upon his void. He snarled, "Or maybe I'll dig your eyes out, first!"

"It doesn't matter," she whispered. "It doesn't matter at all. I have seen you, Simi-Ascalon. I know what you are. You felt me at the feast; I can feel you now, whether I look at you or not. You can take my eyes, but you'll have to kill me to take the sights I already have."

"I, I would, I would, but Remmie wants me to wait—"

"You're such a frightened little man." Barra managed a forced sneer, contemptuous through her pain.

*"What?"* He lifted the phallus like a club, like he would beat her with it; his eyes bulged and his face colored with blood.

"You just about crapped in your robe when Kamades grabbed you," she said. "I bet you didn't think he could do that, under your tattoo. You're finding out that your power isn't good for much after all, and it's scaring the shit out of you. You're afraid of Meremptah-Sifti, you're afraid of Kamades—shit, you're afraid of *me*. All your power, and you can't even make one sad-ass wounded Pict girl shut up."

"I can—I can shut those eyes. Don't you doubt it."

"Yeah? What'll Kamades do while you try?"

"Nothing! My power—"

"Is shit. You can't make him do *anything*, really. He just does what you tell him because he's used to following orders."

Simi-Ascalon's eyes bulged as though they would pop from his head, the skin around them turning black with apoplectic rage. "All right," he said, no longer talking to her. "So I will. I can apologize to Remmie later. Things got a little out of hand, that's all. He always forgives me. So—" He chuckled under his breath, and the flesh of his face began to sag as he relaxed. "Kamades, you like her so much, you kill her."

That shivering moan grew louder within Kamades' throat, but he still didn't move.

"You can move," Simi-Ascalon said irritably. "Oh, hurt her a little first—stick your hand into that wound, there, or something."

Kamades' eyes bulged almost like his master's, but he couldn't stop himself: his dirty hand, covered with salt sweat, found the sword-cut and the ragged bone within it. Agony burst white fire into Barra's brain, but she didn't cry out in pain, not quite—this was what she'd been waiting for. She screamed, "Kamades, I love you! Kiss me!"

Simi-Ascalon said, "What?"

Kamades looked down at her, puzzlement suddenly written across his face.

Barra pleaded with her eyes. "Kiss me once before I die!"

He leaned down, tears streaming, to kiss her, and Simi-Ascalon shouted, *"No!"* and Barra lunged up convulsively, ignoring the shattering agony that blazed from her shoulder, and sank her teeth into Kamades' shoulder where it joins the neck.

Right into the tattoo.

Kamades howled from the sudden pain, and blood spurted salty and metallic into Barra's mouth, but she hung on, biting down, shaking her head from side to side like Graegduz worrying a piece of meat off a stag.

Simi-Ascalon sprang to the table, beating at Kamades with the huge jagged bronze phallus, screaming, "No! Get away from her! Get away!" and Kamades shoved himself back from the table with a mighty heave—but he left a chunk of skin behind, in Barra's mouth. He staggered back, hand clutching his shoulder to stem the blood, and his face cleared.

He bent to a fighting crouch, and veins stood rippling out on his forehead and around his eyes, and he moved toward Simi-Ascalon with the slow, lethal grace of a hunting cat.

He said, "Now, Simi-Ascalon, give me another order."

The demonist looked from him to Barra, horror plain as paint on his face. She spat the bloody hunk of skin out onto the floor and grinned fiercely through the gore on her lips. "Go ahead," she said. "See what it gets you."

Kamades sprang at him, but Simi-Ascalon ducked aside and darted around Kheperu's table, still holding the phallus like a weapon. Kamades drew his sword. "You won't leave this room alive," he said.

*"Myrmidons!"* Simi-Ascalon shrilled. "You can move! *Kill Kamades!"*

They moved slowly out of their statue-like freeze, hands grasping blindly at their sword hilts, tentatively lifting their short spears and sliding their shields into place, and a number of things happened very nearly at once.

Kamades, still unconvinced that Simi-Ascalon's power would prevail over Myrmidon honor, pointed his sword at the demonist. "Take him!" But even as he spoke, Simi-Ascalon snapped, "Ignore all orders but mine, and *kill him now!*" The Myrmidons advanced on Kamades, weapons coming hungrily free; they fanned out into a shallow arc, still the consummate professionals. Simi-Ascalon drew breath to order them again, but yelped in surprise instead, as blinding white fire rose hissing from the shackle that bound Kheperu's left wrist to the table. Simi-Ascalon stared across the table at it with openmouthed incomprehension and while his eyes were held there, on the other side of the table, a small round ball of black tar flicked from Kheperu's right hand and bounced to the floor, unseen by all but Barra, coming to rest between Simi-Ascalon's feet.

The splintering, moaning crackle of wood being ripped apart drew Barra's eyes away from the smoking tar ball, and she shouted for sudden joy: the scars on Leucas' naked back had turned crimson as every muscle bulged out in knife-like definition. The table beneath him creaked and shuddered and moaned in protest, and one of the shackles around his ankles squealed and shrieked as it tore free of the wood. Barra shouted, *"Now, you bastard! Now you're deep in the shit!"* and her shout was nearly buried beneath the rolling thunder of Leucas' basso laugh.

In the next moment:

Kamades slid under the stab of a spear and drove the man stumbling back with a sharp kick in the guts; he ducked behind Barra's table, where only two of his men could come at him, one to either side. Even as he did so, Simi-Ascalon looked down, horror growing on his face as he realized what was smoking between his feet. He said, "Ah-ahh . . ." and the rest of his speech was obliterated by Leucas' roar of berserk battle joy as his other ankle tore free of its shackle; with a titanic splintering sound the table beneath him broke into pieces and Leucas rose from the wreckage, shackles still on his arms, head-size hunks of wood to which they were bolted still attached.

The sight of naked Leucas, upright and angry, gave the Myrmidons pause. He looked more god than man, and no one was eager to engage him. Leucas didn't wait for them; he roared, "Come on, then! Cowards!" and waded into them, battering to right and left with the huge hunks of wood shackled to his wrists. The Myrmidons scattered; they hadn't been ordered to fight Leucas, and they couldn't get past him to come at Kamades. Simi-Ascalon could have easily amended his orders, but he had problems of his own.

The tar ball at his feet smoked and sizzled; in one rush of recognition, he had realized what it was and now he tried to leap away from the coming explosion, but his single second of frozen realization had been one second too much: with a breath-stealing *whoosh* the tar ball detonated into a huge globe of eye-burning white fire. His robes burst into flames; he staggered back, beating at the flames that licked up his clothing, the jagged bronze phallus clanging on the stone as it fell from his hands.

Kamades, the perfect soldier, had never lost sight of his real objective, of the key to victory; freed by Leucas of the need to defend himself, he sprang like a lion onto and over the tables and launched himself through space to slam his powerful body into Simi-Ascalon and drive the demonist stunned and bleeding to the floor.

The Myrmidons, occupied with Leucas, couldn't find their target, and couldn't get themselves together to handle the whirling, roaring, pounding boxer. A couple of them saw Kamades now, though, struggling to hold Simi-Ascalon down, and turned away from Leucas to come at him from behind. Barra stretched up agonizingly from her table and shouted, *"Kamades! Kill him if he doesn't call them off!"*

Kamades' fist thundered down onto Simi-Ascalon's face once, and again, and the demonist ceased to struggle; he knelt on Simi-Ascalon's chest with his sword at the demonist's throat. "Call them off or die right now."

Simi-Ascalon shouted desperately, *"Stop! Don't move!"*

Barra shouted, "Leucas! Hold it!"

The Athenian stopped and looked around; he still held a semiconscious Myrmidon struggling weakly in midair with one hand, and his other was drawn back to punch. When he saw that the best of the Myrmidons were no longer moving, he let the man go. The Myrmidon collapsed bonelessly to the floor. Leucas said, "Oh. Sorry."

Everyone looked at each other for a long moment.

Kheperu said into the sudden silence, "Could someone get this damned shackle? I can't reach it, and I seem to have burned the shit out of my hand."

And it was over.

Soon Simi-Ascalon was tied up and gagged, and Kheperu was free, and Leucas worked on freeing Barra. The Myrmidons still stood where they had been at the instant Simi-Ascalon had given them their last order.

"How long have you been awake?" Barra asked, as Leucas pulled the bolts out of her shackles.

He shrugged. "A while. Since before you and him started talking."

Another one of his rare smiles lit his wintry eyes, although this was a weary one. "I was waiting for what seemed like a good moment."

"Well, you picked it. Any earlier, the Myrmidons would have killed you; any later, they would have killed Kamades."

He shrugged again. "Luck."

"And you," Barra said, looking over at Kheperu, who now sat up on his table and thoughtfully rubbed salve onto his burned hand. "When did you palm the fireball? And you did the shackle with that same gunk you burned the chryseid with, right?"

Kheperu nodded. "I palmed both back up on the roof, while I was pretending to be unconscious. I must say, though, you did a fine job yourself. I really didn't expect to get a chance to use it effectively."

Leucas drew the last bolt, and Barra sat up, wincing and holding her arm very still. "Nothing much," Barra said. "I just never gave up, that's all. Neither did you, either of you."

"Need I remind you?" Kheperu said. "We're an awfully long way from being home safely."

Kamades still stood over Simi-Ascalon. Even though the demonist was now bound and gagged, Kamades kept his sword near the man's throat. Kamades' armor was painted with his blood, that still leaked from the bite wound on his neck.

He said, "What shall we do with this garbage? Will he make a hostage?"

"We don't do anything with him until we get a bandage on your neck," Barra said.

Kamades flashed her a grin. "You could use some bandages yourself, Barra."

Leucas pulled things off the shelves over Simi-Ascalon's workbench until he found some relatively clean cloth. Kheperu bandaged Kamades while Leucas packed Barra's shoulder with folded linen and tied her arm tightly to her chest, shaking his head all the while. "What did I tell you about magic?" he murmured. "Your Pictish battle-magic is all real nice and all, but you should have been wearing armor."

Barra winced at the pressure on her arm, and thought privately that her battle-magic had served her very bloody well, thank you. "Next time," she said hoarsely. "Next time maybe I will."

"Speaking of magic," Kheperu said, standing close by and pretending to be thoroughly interested with wrapping his burned hand with a long strip of cloth, "what was it you were doing to Simi-Ascalon there that got him so upset?"

"Looking at him," Barra said innocently. Truthfully. "That's all.

Who knows why it bothers him so much—" She glanced down at
Simi-Ascalon; he writhed within his bonds and moaned into the gag,
and she had to lean hard on Leucas' shoulder to maintain her balance.
"He's probably just crazy."

"Mm-hmm." Kheperu nodded; it was clear from his expression he
didn't believe a word of it. "First you can smell the chryseids from far,
far away. Now you can drive men mad with a glance."

"I told you before," she said, sliding down off the table and turning this way and that, to check the range of motion she could use without causing her shoulder to scream with pain, "I'm just full of
surprises. Now let's kill this piece of shit and get moving. We've got
some unfinished business on the roof."

Kheperu stared at her, dumbfounded. "Are you mad? There is still
a *battle* going on up there! Or, worse yet, it might be over, and the soldiers returning to the house. You can barely walk, let alone fight. We
are unarmed."

Barra said, "But we have the Myrmidons. They have weapons, and
we can get some of our own."

"We have a hostage," Kheperu countered, and he gestured toward
the darkened cleft in the wall. "And I'd wager that we have a way out
of here, as well."

"We're not going to use him as a hostage. We're going to kill
him."

"Barra—"

She blazed with sudden anger, and she thumped Kheperu's chest
armor with her good hand, even though it hurt her shoulder enough to
shoot stars through her vision. "If I thought you'd let him live, after
what he was going to do to you, I'd kill you *myself!*"

Leucas rumbled, "I don't much like this idea of killing a helpless
prisoner."

Barra wheeled on him. "Maybe if you go over there and look at
that, that *thing* he was going to jam up your ass, you might change
your mind. Kamades?"

The Myrmidon captain's face was as grim as his voice. "I don't
have a problem with this."

"Do it, then."

"All right."

Simi-Ascalon screamed, but his voice was tied within his mouth;
and struggled, but his limbs were bound with belts; and begged with
his eyes, but found no mercy on any face around him.

Kamades, in his very matter-of-fact, businesslike way, stuck his short straight sword into Simi-Ascalon's belly, slicing upward with a back-and-forth sawing motion as though he were carving a roast, until the blade found the demonist's heart and cut it into a furious crimson fountain.

Barra watched it all, watched the abyssal darkness of his spirit dwindle, recede, and finally fade to nothingness, leaving only the stocky corpse of a Phoenikian-looking man dressed as an Egyptian seshperankh. She nodded to herself; she had a strong feeling that this simple cut of a sword had left the world a much better place. "Take his head," she told Kamades shortly.

It took two strokes of the sword. Simi-Ascalon's head, mouth still tied with the gag, bounced on the floor like a child's rag ball.

The Myrmidons, who had stood and watched this without volition, unmoving, living statues, suddenly staggered and gasped and looked as shattered and stunned as a sleepwalker awakening in the noonday sun of an unfamiliar town. Even the one that Leucas had dropped to the floor pulled himself unsteadily to his feet. Not a face among them looked less than stricken as they comprehended what they had almost done under the demonist's spell.

Several of them extended their hands to their captain; one even threw himself down to clutch Kamades' knees and beg forgiveness. He shook the man off and gruffly brought them to order, and then the screaming began.

Wild, howling eldritch screams echoed in the chamber around them, scaling up from a deep-throated roar to a shrill ear-piercing falsetto and back again. Everyone cringed and covered their ears—in that small, stone-bounded room the screams were deafening. After the first instant of shock, Barra found the source of the screaming.

It was Chrysios.

The armless thing that had been Chrysios writhed on the chill stone of the cavern's floor, screaming beyond breath, halting, sobbing shrieks of unendurable agony. And now a few within the stack of cadavers began to move as well, scattering the stiff corpses around them like branches before a wind, staggering and falling and rising again, tearing at their own flesh with their fingernails, ripping back hunks of it over the bone and arching their necks to scream and scream and scream.

Barra didn't stop to count them—in the condition she and her allies were in, one or two could be too many. She had to shout at the top of her lungs to be heard over the deafening shrieks. *"Let's get out of here!"*

She found no argument among her companions; they all scrambled for the stairs. She caught up the demonist's head by its long braided beard and ran with the rest. Her wounded leg betrayed her as she tried to race upward, buckling suddenly, but strong hands were there to bear her up: on one side, Leucas, and on the other, Kamades.

They boiled out of the stairwell into the pitchy cellar, lit now only by the faint reddish glow from the braziers in the cavern below. The Myrmidons shifted the heavy block of stone that closed it, and blocked away the screams, and suddenly there was no light in the cellar at all. Barra said, "Er, does anyone have a lamp?"

No one did, and certainly no one was interested in going back down to the workshop to get one. Kheperu said, "One moment—this is surprisingly difficult to do in the dark."

A few long, dark breaths later that familiar horrid smell permeated the cellar's air, and Kheperu's *tekat-neha* began to glow, providing enough illumination for them all to find their way up to the house above, and to find and light lamps of their own.

They went in close order, the Myrmidons clustered around them with weapons drawn as though Barra, Leucas, and Kheperu were prisoners; but the deception proved unnecessary: no one paid any attention to them at all. A chorus of screaming chryseids surrounded the manor house, hammering blindly at the walls with their bare fists. More screaming wails sounded out from around the grounds, and within the house all was confusion, panicked soldiers and servants rushing from door to door and window to window, trying to understand what was going on or to find a place to hide. In some rooms the soldiers struggled with Simi-Ascalon's hyaenae, the nightmare dog-things, cutting again and again at their unliving flesh. These rooms the companions passed hastily.

Kheperu nodded, mostly to himself. "His magic is dying with him," he murmured distractedly, as though he spoke while taking notes, "but the life in his chryseids comes from the gods, or from demons—it is his *control* of them that has died."

They came to a doorway that Barra remembered, and instead of passing by to the stairs, Barra said, "Wait here for a minute." She held out Simi-Ascalon's head to Kheperu. "Hold this."

He took it, and she slipped into the room. There, collapsed into a corner and sobbing upon his arms like a brokenhearted boy, lay Tal Akhu-shabb. He didn't look up at Barra's approach; even as she crouched beside him, he only moaned, over and over again, "What have I done? How could I be so weak?"

She touched his arm. "Governor . . ."

He lifted his head and startled back from her with a gasp, pressing himself against the wall. "What are you?"

"I'm Barra, Governor, ah, Briseis—the girl from the feast. Do you remember?"

He squinted at her, trying to see that lovely young girl beneath the clay-spiked hair, and the painted face that was now streaked with sweat and blood, blood that caked her mouth and chin. "There was a girl," he said uncertainly. "She tried to warn me . . . but it was too late . . ."

"I know what he did to you, Governor. It wasn't your fault. You couldn't help yourself."

Fresh tears streamed from his eyes. "I, I did things . . . I allowed things, even ordered them . . ."

The *sceon tiof* was still with her, and it lent unanswerable conviction to her words. She saw within him and knew that everything she said was true. "Your only fault is that you trusted a man who is unworthy of you. You understand? You were *magicked*; you could not have done any other thing than what you were told. You are a good man, who has been betrayed."

Hope blossomed within his wounded eyes; he almost dared to believe her. "Who . . . who are you, really?"

"I'm the girl . . ." she began, then bared her teeth. "I'm the girl that's going to give Meremptah-bloodyfucking-Sifti a bloody good spanking. If you want, you can come and watch."

The view from the roof was a fever nightmare of carnage. Bodies lay everywhere about the grounds, and chryseids staggered drunkenly around them, ripping limbs off corpses, biting into bellies, attacking each other or simply writhing on the ground and screaming at the moon. The survivors of the Penthedes army had run away when the corpse-warriors had gone mad, as had most of the surviving Canaan Division contingent; the chryseids no longer made any distinctions between friend and foe. Some of the hyaenae had escaped from the house and ranged about the battlefield, tearing randomly at living and unliving alike. Every now and then a human-throated scream would join the chorus, as the body of a chryseid savaged turned out not to be quite so dead after all.

The companions had been able to hear Meremptah-Sifti's curses from the floor below. Kamades and Tal Akhu-shabb led the way up the stairs.

The prince of Egypt stood at the retaining wall, shouting, "No! Stop it, do you hear me! *I command you to stop it!*"

Idonosteus stood beside him, his hand out as though to reassure the prince, and he saw them coming up the stairs. "Most High—"

"Something's gone wrong," Meremptah-Sifti said. "This is *wrong*, this isn't *happening.*"

"Most High—" Idonosteus said more insistently, now tugging on the prince's elbow.

"I told you never to touch me," he snapped. "What is it?"

Idonosteus pointed a fat finger.

Meremptah-Sifti turned and snorted, seeing at first only the Myrmidons and the Governor. He looked annoyed. "Tal, I told you to stay downstairs. Go back down and wait until I send for you. Kamades— as long as you're here, go and tell Simi-Ascalon that something's gone wrong with the warriors . . ." His voice trailed off as it registered on him that the Governor hadn't yet moved to comply with his order.

"Did you not hear me? I ordered you to go back downstairs."

Tal Akhu-shabb slowly shook his old grey head. "No, Remmie. I came up here to watch, and I'm staying."

Meremptah-Sifti looked thunderstruck. "Are you defying me? What is *wrong* here? Has the whole world gone mad? Kamades, take him with you when you go. If he resists, kill him."

Kamades took a deep breath, and sighed it out. "You're not really so much, after all. I think I'm enjoying this."

*"What?"*

Kamades barked, "Step to the outside," and the Myrmidons parted.

Barra stood there, Kheperu behind one shoulder and Leucas behind the other.

Meremptah-Sifti staggered as though his knees had lost their strength. *"What are you doing here?"*

Barra showed him her bloody teeth. "I came to get my axe."

It still lay on the roof, not far away. She stooped and picked it up with her good left hand, flipped it end for end and caught it again. She held it up at arm's length and sighted along its top, measuring Idonosteus' face. The Head of House Meneides let out a low moan.

Meremptah-Sifti still thought he was caught in a dream. "This is *impossible*! Sim has done this a hundred times! He wouldn't *dare* fail! You can't be here! You can't be doing this!"

Barra said, "Kheperu?"

Kheperu gently tossed the demonist's head so that it bounced across the roof and rolled brokenly to stop at Meremptah-Sifti's feet. The prince looked down, and his hands clutched convulsively at the air, and he gasped *uh—uh—uh*, as though he'd forgotten how to breathe. He fell to his knees and cradled Simi-Ascalon's head in his arms, bundling it to his chest like a baby, and he screamed, "*Noooo! Ahhh, gods, no!*"

Barra looked on him with the *sceon tiof*, as tears streamed from his eyes and he lifted a sobbing face to the sky. There had been some deep connection between them, that went far beyond master and servant; she couldn't see what it was, but seeing Simi-Ascalon dead, holding his remains like this, wounded Meremptah-Sifti in some way so fundamental that it left a sickly taste in Barra's mouth. She turned away from him and fixed her gaze upon Idonosteus.

He backed away from her. "You don't dare harm us," he said hastily. "Shed one drop of the prince's blood and the whole might of Egypt will fall upon this city like an avalanche."

Barra paced toward him. "That protects *him*; what's it do for you?"

"Kamades," he said desperately, "stop her. I order you to stop her!"

Kamades shrugged. "I quit."

"You can't!"

"I have. We'll find a worthy lord to serve, somewhere else."

*"But she'll kill me!"*

"That's right."

Idonosteus turned his sweat-slicked face back to Barra and licked his lips, still retreating before her. "I'll pay you. A mountain of silver, gold, anything! I'll give you anything!"

"All right," Barra said. "I'll take your life."

He fell to his knees and clasped his hands before his face, squeezing fat tears from his eyes. "Please! I'm begging you! Please, please don't kill me!"

Barra stood over him. Fury filled her, but the cold determination that battled it was what found its way into her voice. "You're worse than Meremptah-Sifti. You're a disgusting little toad—that's an insult to toads. Even a toad will stand and fight to defend its nest. You sold out your own, Idonosteus. You sold us all, and you put my parents in a cage in the Market, and now you're going to die."

"But, but they're not *hurt*, they're all right, it's not like I *killed* them . . ."

"Look around you," Barra said. "Look out there. A hundred men died tonight, and more. How many more were burned on their ships, or were cut down as they tried to fell the city? Every one of those lives is a debt you owe, and this is the only way you can pay up. And you know? It's not even all that, so much, in the end. It's not so much for what you've done, as for what you *are*. Kind of like Simi-Ascalon over there. The world will be a better place without you in it."

She drew back the axe.

He screamed, *"Pleaaaaaa—"*

She buried the axe in his skull, and wrenched it out again with a sound of splintering bone. She stood over his corpse panting, and sweating, and in tremendous pain.

Eventually, Meremptah-Sifti recovered his composure, kneeling there on the roof, with the head of Simi-Ascalon upon his lap. Kamades and the Myrmidons had accompanied the Governor down-stairs, to try to organize the surviving soldiers and servants. Leucas and Kheperu remained up on the roof with Barra, and the corpse of Idonosteus.

Barra leaned on the wall, in nearly the same place where Meremp-tah-Sifti had stood to watch the battle. He said from behind her, "What now, for me? What am I to do?"

Barra turned to face him. "Whatever I decide. Understand? You'll do exactly what I tell you to."

He still knelt on the roof with the head in his hands, but his fea-tures had returned to their aristocratic mask. "And if I don't?"

Barra shook her axe at him; she hadn't cleaned it, and splinters of Idonosteus' skull and bloody fragments of his brain spattered across the prince's face. He flinched helplessly, and lowered his head in shame.

"If you don't, I'll probably just kill you and take my chances with Ramses."

He said, his face still lowered, "You know, in the end, we're not so different, you and I."

Hearing this, Kheperu snorted, and he translated for Leucas, who shook his head.

Barra, though, nodded thoughtfully. She said, "You know the dif-ference between us? Why you lost? It's this: all you had was slaves." She looked straight at Kheperu, and at Leucas. "I, on the other hand, I have *friends*."

Kheperu gave her a tight little smile, and there was a faint gleam in his eye that might have been a hint of a tear; then he turned away to translate this for Leucas as well.

"So you beat me," Meremptah-Sifti said. "You won, in the end. How does it feel?"

Barra looked out across the bloody battlefield, and listened to the screams of the chryseids.

"This isn't winning," she said softly, painfully. "I beat you, but didn't win."

Then she brightened, and looked back at him, and said in a stronger voice that held a touch of a grin, "You sure as bloody death *lost*, though, didn't you?"

# 22

# *Barra's Peace*

**L**ater, during the weeks of her convalescence, Barra would often wake screaming from nightmares of being shackled once again in the reeking cavern beneath the manor house, and having her mouth tied shut, or having no teeth, or Kamades not being there: having no escape while Simi-Ascalon approached with the bronze phallus. She'd sit up gasping in the darkness, clutching the warm down of the quilts on her own feather bed, in her room in her foster-parents' house, and wipe the freezing sweat from her face, and slump there to wait for Kheperu to bring new cups of cold willow-bark tea to lower her fever.

Sometimes in the cool evenings, when her fever would recede, she engraved a new entry on the mental stone of her Suicide Table: *Take a job in your home town.* She calculated that she'd likely not survive another one.

Sometimes, when the infection in her shoulder made the fever worse, she dreamed of being dead, her blood replaced by milky oil, walking again beside the battered armless corpse of Chrysios.

Sometimes, too, as the fever finally broke, and her collarbone began to knit, the Mother answered her prayers and sent her dreams of the fires, instead.

Grey dawn over the battlefield.

The crows began to flutter down among the dead, and vultures wheeled on the wind high above. Flat clouds the color of slate roofed the world.

Barra sat on the ground, and watched the corpses burn.

Agapenthes had been found, wounded but alive, and he had sent back to Tyre for priests of Ba'al-Berith to perform the funeral rites for his fallen men. Initially, the arriving priests had been horrified at the idea of putting the corpses on pyres and burning them—this was a custom of the barbaric West. The survivors' stories had quickly changed their minds; Barra guessed that cremation would be very fashionable in Tyre for some years to come. The hundreds of corpses from the workshop below had been sent piled in wagons back toward the funerary caves; word would be sent out, and any that were claimed by friends or relatives could be returned to their crypts.

The rest would be burned, even as these fallen soldiers, Penthedes and Egyptian alike, were being burned.

The priests still resisted, until Agapenthes made his offer of one shekel per man. At this, they huddled together and conferred among themselves, and soon a delegate returned to inform the exhausted old man that such rites could be devised—for three shekels per corpse. Eventually, a price of two was settled upon, and the priests went efficiently to work with their improvised rites, counting silver in their heads; this was Tyre, after all.

Each man had his own small pyre. Meremptah-Sifti's olive groves had been cut down to make them, and they burned quickly, scattered across his grounds like the cook fires of a mighty army. The oily, resinous wood snapped and crackled and poured thick black smoke into the sky. Sometimes the wind whipped blinding plumes of it across Barra's eyes.

She sat on the ground and breathed it in, never blinking, as tears ran down her face.

The big bonfire in front of her, the one she looked at more than the others, was by now very nearly burned out. At one point it had towered high, licking the starry night sky with its crackling flames. Now it only smoldered here and there, and blackened bones showed everywhere among the ashes, and skulls answered her stares with lipless grins.

Barra had sat in this very spot, Kheperu on the ground beside her, and Leucas standing with folded arms behind, while she'd watched the chryseids, led by Chrysios himself, form themselves into a wailing line and march toward the huge bonfire, and one by one throw themselves screaming into it, and writhe shrieking among the flames as the blaze consumed their very flesh.

Chrysios had found her, after he'd staggered from the cavern by way of the underground cleft. Barra was still on the roof, and Chrysios fell to his knees on the flagstones below. He'd had some perfunctory repairs made to his face—he could speak, barely, with much drooling and slobbering and repeated attempts to find words that his shattered mouth could form—and he explained that Simi-Ascalon had had no time to do a better job; Meremptah-Sifti had been pushing him mercilessly to create new corpse-warriors. With a line of milky tears leaking down his torn cheeks, he had begged a boon of his victorious enemy.

*"You mus' des'roy uz,"* he begged, with difficulty. *"You canno' know the agony . . ."*

"It's a tough life," Barra had said, her mouth twisting with revulsion.

*"Pleazz,"* he said. *"I did no' choose thiz . . . Thiz was done do me againz my will . . . Ih hurzz, hurzz un'il you can' belee . . . belee . . . you can' unnerssann how ih hurzz. I can 'eel each wound . . ."*

He writhed on the ground before her, the straps that held his head together coming loose.

Barra said, "You can feel each wound? That's what you're telling me? Every one?"

*"Where you cu' me, be'ween my legs—I can s'ill feel ih . . . hurzz. Hurrzz. Others . . . they feel their organs ripping ou' from their bodies, feel uh s'raw tha's in their gutz . . ."*

"The other ones can feel the straw they were stuffed with? Inside? And they still feel their . . . and the rest?" Barra looked away, imagining against her will how it would feel to walk in agony like that, and know that you are immortal, and that your pain will only increase.

*"Pleaz . . . Fire . . . need. Burnnnn . . . pleaz burnnnn . . ."*

Barra could only nod.

Chrysios had struggled to his knees, and his improvised mouth worked agonizingly to make one last sentence intelligible. *"Burnnn mee, and I forgi', forgive you, forrrgivvve you for killinnng me . . ."*

Barra looked down into his parboiled eyes, and remembered that she'd once found him handsome. Her gorge rose, and she hurried away from the edge of the roof, so that he wouldn't see her vomit.

And so he got his fire, he and those like him. There were rumors, in the days that followed, that not all of the chryseids burned themselves, that some still roamed the streets of Tyre in the night, when they would not be seen for what they were, and stood near to the homes where they once lived and called in soft, despairing voices for their loved ones. But these were only rumors.

Many of the unliving hyaenae had escaped into the night; they would be hunted by packs of nervous men for weeks to come.

Barra had watched the burning of the dead, and felt cleansed in her spirit.

All the dead were burned, even Simi-Ascalon and Idonosteus; vile though they had been, they received cleansing pyres that would send their spirits with some honor into whatever lands they might tread.

The gods pass judgment only on the acts of the living, and dishonoring the dead never goes unpunished.

After some consultation with Barra and the Governor, Agapenthes (as the sort-of general, willy-nilly, of the winning side) decided to accept, on behalf of the citizens of Tyre, compensation from Meremptah-Sifti. This was arranged to take place some days later, after Barra was able to be up and about again. She wasn't well; sickness had settled into her lungs, she coughed a great deal and tired swiftly. But her fever had broken, and she insisted on being present nonetheless. Long experienced in scribing contracts, and thus having detailed knowledge of the proper forms of Egyptian official communication, Barra herself dictated the letter that Meremptah-Sifti wrote to his grandfather.

In that letter, the prince described how he had been duped and magicked by his steward Simi-Ascalon, who would certainly have raped Tyre and would perhaps have made of himself a power that even Egypt might fear, with his army of animated corpses. This letter described how Simi-Ascalon had taken Tyre and how only the heroic actions of Leucas Deodakaides of Athens, Kheperu of Thebes, and Barra Coll Eigg Rhum of Great Langdale had stood between Tyre and utter ruin.

In "gratitude for my timely rescue" he wrote that he was donating all his Tyrian holdings to the people of the city, to be administered by Agapenthes of House Penthedes. The letter also asked for an immediate loan of one hundred thousand silver debens—each deben contained silver equivalent to about three Athenian weights—to "compensate the good citizens of Tyre for the horrible suffering my treacherous steward inflicted upon them," which he would repay from his personal holdings as soon as he could return to Egypt to sell them off.

"One hundred thousand!" Meremptah-Sifti had said. His fist clenched, and the reed pen snapped. "This will *pauper* me!"

Barra had shrugged, and looked across him to the Governor, who also stood behind him, reading the letter over his shoulder. She said, "I think the prince here could have been hurt in the battle against his treacherous steward, maybe even *badly* hurt."

The Governor put on a mock frown and touched a finger to his pursed lips. "You mean the unfortunate incident that cost him, oh, let's see, perhaps his left hand? Ramses will be most upset—but, of course, still grateful that the life of his grandson had been saved. Don't you think?"

Meremptah-Sifti looked from one to the other, and decided that despite their bantering tone, they were both deadly serious. He drew another reed pen from the case, dipped it, and continued to write.

"This is not over, between us," he muttered. "This will never be over, not while you live."

Barra draped her left arm across his shoulders—though the infection in her shoulder had begun to subside, her right arm was still bound immobile to her chest—and she leaned down so that she could speak directly into his lovely face. "You've got that backward, Remmie. This won't be over while *you* live. And the only place in the world that's safe for you is right here in Tyre. Of course, here in Tyre, everybody either thinks, one, you're a dummy who got taken by his steward or, two, you're a rotten prick who got his ass whipped by three rag-tailed mercenaries. You're a joke. I don't imagine you'll be staying."

He shook her arm off as though her very touch were loathsome. "Don't think that I fear you. Don't think I can't find you."

"I don't want you to fear me, Remmie," Barra said. She summoned all her energy, to force a tone of solid conviction into her voice. "I want you to forget all about me. That way, when I catch you someday outside this city—someplace in Egypt, maybe—it'll come as a nice surprise. If you can find me, I can find you. And I will. My gods have a law concerning murderers."

The prince gazed up into her eyes; the swelling her fists had left on his chin was gone, and the bruise nearly faded; he was again heartbreakingly beautiful. "When I first heard of you—when I heard the tale of your capture of Idonosteus' bear—I knew that our destinies would tangle. I thought of you as a gift of fate. I thought that you would be mine."

"Not bloodyfucking likely," she said tiredly.

"If we had met—"

"Don't even try," she told him. She shook her head. "If I'm a gift to anybody, maybe it's to some of these poor bastards in Tyre, don't you think?"

After a moment, Meremptah-Sifti once again bent his head to the page, to write at her command.

The Governor frowned, and stroked his snowy braided beard. "I wish there was something else, something more we could do to you, Remmie. I don't suppose there is any way to punish you as you deserve, but I wish . . ." His voice trailed off wistfully.

Barra shrugged and drew her broadaxe. Though to her weakened arm it felt heavy as an anchor, she flipped it into the air, caught it again. "Want to see him dance like a chicken?"

The Governor frowned at her and began to shake his head, but as he watched the image in his mind, his eyes lit up.

Lysandros—Murso, or whatever name he chose—must have slipped away on the night of the battle. He, Barra figured, was as guilty as Idonosteus; she added his name onto her mental list, right behind Meremptah-Sifti's. *Someday*, she promised him in her heart. *Someday, you murdering bastard.*

Agapenthes threw a grand feast of celebration, for the victory that freed Tyre, and put on games in honor of his fallen men. He could well afford to; in addition to all of Meremptah-Sifti's holdings, Agapenthes had now merged House Meneides and all its possessions into House Penthedes. Idonosteus' sexual tastes had, unsurprisingly, left him without heirs. Agapenthes had been, even before this, the wealthiest man in Phoenikia; now his wealth rivaled the great fortunes of Babylon and Knossos.

Barra attended in a place of honor, along with Peliarchus and Tayniz, Kheperu and Leucas, Demetor and the Kypriots. It was an all-day affair within the Penthedes compound, and at intervals it spilled out into the streets, with drunken dancing and singing and scattering of gifts. The occasional fight was let run its own course, without interference. The Governor had wisely pulled the entire Canaan Division out of Tyre, and ordered the garrison commander to keep his troops indoors; the uniform of the Egyptian army would be unpopular here in Tyre for some time to come. As for the soldiers of Meremptah-Sifti, none could be found. Here and there burned pieces of bloodred and purple livery were discovered, but no one would ever admit to having worn it.

The days of Meremptah-Sifti's domination of Tyre faded into the past, a half-remembered nightmare for most; for some—some battered children, some widows, some cripples—it would fade more slowly, if at all.

At the feast, Agapenthes and Demetor both got staggering drunk, and ended up in each other's arms, swearing eternal friendship above

and beyond the blood ties that bound them. Kheperu vanished period-
ically, for an hour or two at a time, to return with a gentle smile on his
lips and, often, the arm of a prominent Tyrian about his shoulders.
Leucas took part in the games, winning both the boxing and the
weight-throw, taking runner-up in wrestling, and placing third in the
spear-throw. Barra watched the games enviously, especially the runners; she was sure, that if she hadn't been injured—and trying, even
now, to cough up her lungs—she could have placed high, even against
the men, perhaps even beaten them all. She'd been nursing a secret
dream to compete in the Trade Games at Knossos in the spring, and
run against the fastest men in the world. She tucked away choice bits
of meats and cheeses to take home to Graeg, whose leg was healing
nicely.

She looked around the feast for Kamades, and the Myrmidons, but
they weren't there. Kamades had been to see her a few times during
her fever, but he had seemed uncomfortable: he hadn't said much, nor
had he stayed long.

Peliarchus and Tayniz sat quietly at the feast, and ate little. A
cloud seemed to hang over them, darkening their faces, and once Barra
noticed, she pestered them until Peliarchus told her what he was upset
about.

"I can't seem to get over it," he told her, running his finger over
the now-powerless tattoo beneath his shirt. "Sitting in that cage, waiting for you to appear. I *wanted* them to catch you, Barra; I can't
believe—I don't care what magic it might be, I can't believe it would
make me want to hurt you. Great bleeding Mouth. If you listen to
Agapenthes over there, he broke the spell over him by a heroic effort
of will and led his men to glorious victory."

"Mm, well," Barra said, "not that I'd accuse the lord Agapenthes
of being less than truthful, but he's a bloody liar. He came out of it at
the same time you did, the same time everyone else did—when
Kamades killed Simi-Ascalon. And as soon as he did, he dug down
under a pile of dead men and hid."

Peliarchus only grunted.

"And seeing you at the feast, when they held you like that and
showed you to everyone," Tayniz said. "Your poor face—I've never
been so frightened in my life. I have nightmares about it."

Barra turned her head, looking away to where Kheperu chatted up
a blushing Penthedes cupbearer. "I have nightmares of my own, now
and then. They'll stop, in time."

"And this is the sort of thing you do all the time?" Tayniz asked. "How can you bear it?"

"It's not usually this bad," Barra told her. "Sometimes, it's kind of fun."

"I remember when I first met you," Peliarchus said. "I think you were about eight or nine years old, your whole body covered with freckles 'cause you weren't old enough to rate summer clothes, and the whole month I was in Langdale you followed me around and pestered me to teach you Phoenikian. Looking back on it, I guess I have to say it's a good thing I'm such a soft touch."

Barra didn't need the *sceon tiof* to tell her what her foster-parents needed to hear. She reached toward them, and took a hand of each. "I really love you, you know. You are the parents I always wanted, when I was little. I dreamed about having a mother who'd take care of me, and a father who didn't live across the Eirish Sea and I . . ." She blinked back sudden tears. "I'm just really lucky, that's all."

"We're the lucky ones, Barra," Peliarchus said. "And every person in Tyre today would agree with me."

Tayniz snuffled, and wiped her eyes, and said, "And what about this Kamades? He came to see you three times. Is he married?"

Days passed, and Barra's lungs gradually began to clear, and her strength began to return.

Word had trickled through the House Penthedes backstairs gossip that Agapenthes had sold the apartment block where the Myrmidons kept their household to the Jephunahi, who were evicting all the tenants and converting the apartment block into a fortified warehouse for spices, oils, and wines. Hearing this rumor, Barra had sighed, "I'd better go talk to Kamades." Leucas and Kheperu had insisted on accompanying her; in Kheperu's words, "Anyone who takes orders that well cannot be trusted."

On the walk to the apartment, Kheperu had badgered her until she reluctantly began to talk about Kamades. "It's not that I want him as a lover," she said. "Not really at all. I mean, he's very attractive, in a weathered kind of way, but—"

"Kamades, I love you! Kiss me!" Kheperu snickered.

Her shoulder itched fiercely beneath its bandages, reminding her that punching him would likely hurt her more than it would him. "That was *tactics*," she said severely. "Don't laugh—that kiss saved your life, too."

Kheperu acknowledged this with an acquiescing bow.

"He's just so serious," Barra went on. "If I wanted to get married,

I'd give him some real consideration. But I don't think he'd be a lot of fun at parties."

"So why," Leucas rumbled, "are we going to see him?"

Barra grimaced. "I feel bad for him. I feel responsible, you know? I'd bet it was rescuing me at the feast that made Idonosteus have him tattooed—tattooed because he's too useful to kill. That feast was when he found out that Kamades couldn't be trusted." She shook her head. "He found out that Kamades couldn't be trusted to do something rotten and dishonorable just because he was told to."

"And you killed one of his men."

"That's got nothing to do with it!" Barra flared. "That son of a dog just about *gutted* me!"

Leucas only shrugged. The Myrmidon he'd thrown from the roof had broken a leg; he'd broken the heads of a couple more down in the workshop. The other Myrmidon, the one Leucas himself had killed, had been named Glandys; and Leucas' face would fill with blank pain whenever he thought of him.

Nothing more was said on the subject. Barra made Leucas and Kheperu wait in the street while she went up alone.

The Myrmidons had little gear beyond bedrolls, armor, and weapons; everything was well packed away when Barra was admitted to the apartment. Kamades was silently policing the rooms, to make sure his men had left no trace of their passing. When Barra entered, he acknowledged her uncomfortably, and went back to his inspection.

"Kamades," Barra said, coming close to him, but his cold reserve stopped her from taking his arm. She let her hand fall, defeated. "Where will you go now? Back to Phthia?"

He glanced at her, then went back to examining the dust at the base of a wall, and shook his head. "We can never return. We will find some new lord to serve, one with some honor of his own, perhaps."

"You know," Barra said slowly, "you never told me why you left Phthia in the first place."

Now he regarded her, his mouth a grim line. He spoke softly, so that his men would not hear. "I suppose it doesn't matter. You have seen me disobey, and abandon my lord in danger, even to allowing his death—no further dishonor could lessen your opinion of me."

"Lessen? Kamades—"

"Neoptolemos, the son of Lord Akhilleus—after Troy, when we returned to Phthia, he had the rule, and our service. But"—his face twisted—"but he wanted us to return to the farms our fathers worked, we whose trade was war, we who had known no other life for ten years, but war. His father had made of us warriors; we had no skill with land. We met among ourselves, and elected one man to go to the lord Neoptolemos, and ask him if we mightn't find some other employment. Neoptolemos, he has a temper, and when . . . this man . . . presented our suit, he was angered. He shouted that we were disloyal, for questioning his orders, and that if we wouldn't be farmers, then we should be gone. This is why we cannot go back to Phthia."

"He sounds like a jackass to me," Barra said.

Kamades frowned severely. "He was my lord. I should never have questioned him."

"It was you?" Barra said. "You were the one who went to him?"

Kamades looked away. "That was the seed of rot; that is when I started down this path of dishonor."

"Loving bloody Mother!" Barra exclaimed. "Kamades, you are more in need of a drink than any man I've ever met! I know a place—"

"Barra," he began, misery showing plainly on his face, "I must apologize to you. I think I have led you on."

"Hah?"

"I know that I approached you . . . ah, as a man does a woman, and I do find you desirable, really I do, but . . ."

"But. . . ?" Barra led, hoping that her rush of relief didn't show on her face.

"But, Lalcamas—I know you couldn't help it, it was in battle, but every time I look at you, I see his poor dead face, and, and well, he and I, we were friends, we were boys together. And my men are my responsibility, and I lost Glandys as well; it is my fault they are dead, my fault for having taken service with an unworthy lord . . ."

"Don't think about it," Barra said. "So, what you're saying is, that you just don't think you can get involved with me, is that it?"

"Barra, I'm sorry—"

"No, no," she said, acting like she was putting up a brave front, while underneath she was so relieved that her knees had gone weak. "Can we still be friends, do you think?"

Kamades looked dubious.

Barra said, "There is this publican, who owes me his life, you see? His name is Lidios, and he told me the other day that I have the freedom of his house for as long as I live. That means, I can take you and all your men there and get you so drunk you can't see, and it won't cost me a copper shekel."

"You would do that? Even though . . . you and I don't . . ."

"On one condition," Barra said. She scratched at her bandages thoughtfully. "You have to promise that we won't talk about Tyre at all. All I want to hear about, all night long, is Akhilleus and Patroklos, Diomedes and Odysseus, Agamemnon, Menelaos—nothing but the Siege of Troy."

Kamades thought it over, and slowly he sighed, and allowed himself a gentle smile. "All right."

As she took his arm to lead him out, she murmured, "And, I've heard that the silver mines at Laurium, just down the coast from Athens, have been raided pretty hard over the past two years or so. The Twin Princes might be looking for some good men to keep order down there . . ."

"Oh, really?"

As her shoulder healed and her cough faded, Barra took to a habit of long walks in the hills around Tyre; now that winter had come, the days were shorter and cooler, and if one doesn't mind getting wet in the occasional thunderstorm, the walking was very pleasant. Graegduz went with her on these walks, limping at first but soon running with all his old speed after hares and snipe, and she was always armed—she wasn't fool enough to believe that Tyre was any safer than it had ever been.

Sometimes she walked for hours; sometimes she'd just find a comfortable hillside and sit, or throw rocks, or strengthen her arm with some halfhearted axe practice. But always, always looking out over the dark, straggling greens of the bushes that clung to a precarious existence among the sand and rocks, always looking into the desert and dreaming of home, of the lush grassy hills and dense, impenetrable forests of the Isle of the Mighty.

Leucas and Kheperu found her there, sitting on a stone outcropping and chucking rocks down the hill. Graegduz ranged the dry watercourse beneath her, nosing for hedgehogs among the rocks.

Leucas crouched beside her; on the other side, Kheperu plumped down and dangled his feet down the rock face, kicking his heels against it like a child.

Kheperu said, "He's healing well," indicating Graegduz, who seemed to have discovered something in a sheltered cleft; he happily skipped back away from it, and darted in again. "I'm glad of that. And I was curious about your shoulder."

Barra shrugged. Six weeks had passed since the battle; the season had advanced nearly to the Turning of the Sun. The wound was still covered with the remnants of a ragged scab, that Barra picked at when no one was looking, and her shoulder was still sore, and weak, but soon she'd be fully recovered.

"We've been thinking," Leucas said, "of moving on. Tyre is expensive."

She nodded, still not looking directly at either of them. They'd elected not to wait for the caravan from Egypt that was even now on its way with the hundred thousand silver debens; by arrangement with Agapenthes, they'd taken their shares out of Meremptah-Sifti's household goods. In addition to some fine clothing, and household implements of silver and gold, the companions had received five of Meremptah-Sifti's beautiful mares, three geldings and a dazzling white stallion. Barra had spent most of her share buying the spare horses from her friends; they'd make a princely gift for Idomeneus, king of Crete, when Barra went there for the Trade Fair in the spring. A gift like that should get her bumped up from the merchant quarters of the palace at Knossos to the royal chambers—then she could *really* do some business. Kheperu and Leucas, on the other hand, finding themselves cash rich, had been living high for this whole past month of Thirisin: throwing parties, buying expensive gifts for their expensive whores, gambling almost endlessly. Barra had known for days that the two would be ready to go pretty soon: they were running out of money.

Leucas said, "We wanted to know if you'd be coming with us."

Barra looked down at her fingernails. Under the forced inactivity of her wound, they'd grown out, and Tayniz had tended them, and her calluses had begun to fade. Her hands were slowly beginning to look almost ladylike. She said, "I lied to you, Kheperu."

"Really?" The Egyptian seemed more interested than surprised. "When?"

"That night. In Simi-Ascalon's workshop, when I said I didn't know what it was that was driving him so crazy."

"Oh?" he encouraged her.

She sighed. "I have a power, I guess. It only began to develop recently. It's a Pictish thing, called the *sceon tiof*. It comes and goes; I never really know if it's going to work, or not. But when it does work, well, I can look at someone and know them, like I've known them all my life."

"Hmpf," Kheperu murmured. "You have so many little secrets, Barra."

She could hear the frown in Leucas' voice. "You mean you can know their past, like a diviner? Or know their thoughts like a god?"

She shook her head. "Neither one. It's like, I don't know anything about them, except what kind of person they are. It's like when you look at a brother, or a friend you've known for twenty years, you don't think about things that have happened to them, but you just have a sense of what it is that makes him who he is, what makes him unique, I guess. You *know* him. I never wanted to be able to do this. In fact, I've been worried sick about it."

"An interesting ability," Kheperu said, squinting at her narrowly. "Why do you fear it?"

Barra grimaced. "Just imagine—imagine that every time you go into battle, you're fighting your best friend. Every time I see a man with this power, I see him like, like a beautiful sculpture—I see that there is no one else like him in the world, and if I kill him, I'm taking something away from the world that can never be replaced." She shook her head again, exasperated. "It's not even that. I don't even have words for it, really. I still, even now, feel bad about Idonosteus."

"It didn't seem to bother you at the time."

She turned and looked into his eyes. "I've been thinking about retiring. I probably would have quit before this, but Meremptah-bloody-Sifti would have . . ." Her voice trailed away.

"Let me see if I have this straight," Leucas said. "You're wanting to retire because it, kind of, *hurts* you when you fight. But you didn't quit before this, because . . . it would have hurt you *more* to watch what was happening to Tyre, and to your parents, and everything else. Have I got this right?"

Barra nodded. "But now it's over."

Kheperu smiled knowingly. "It's never over, Barra. Why, even now, a pair of Kena'ani kings are in Tyre, hiring mercenaries to defend Jebusi. It seems the Habiru are gathering their tribes together for another round of conquest, and you know what they're like. You've heard, no doubt, what they did to Jericho?"

"Yes," Barra said slowly. The massacre of every living creature in the fortified town of Jericho had been a campfire tale for at least ten years. "Yes, I have."

"It seems to me," Leucas said, "that you don't have to quit. Maybe you only need to be more careful who you work for. The way I see it, the only thing that's really changed is that you've found out that there are some things more important to you than money."

"Bite your tongue!" Kheperu snapped.

"Let's say, *as* important," Barra said. She got up, and whistled for Graegduz. "I said I'd been thinking about retiring. I didn't say I was going to. Jebusi is a good destination— overland, so we don't have to worry about storms at sea, and it takes us to the fringe of Egyptian control."

"And you'd be helping people defend their homes," Leucas said with a wise smile. "Maybe you're less of a mercenary than you've always thought, and more of a hero."

"I don't think so," Barra said. "You'd best believe I wouldn't do this work for free."

"So wait," Kheperu said, rising beside her. "If it's not an excuse to quit, why'd you finally tell us about this seeing thing of yours?"

Barra smiled. "We're friends, aren't we? Maybe I'm getting tired of keeping so many bloody secrets." She clapped Leucas on the shoulder, and almost did the same to Kheperu—she stopped herself barely in time, remembering that out here there was no water with which to wash her hands. "Besides, I can't quit now. I have just enough money for a down payment on another ship."

Leucas said, "*Another* ship?"

"You have a *ship*?" Kheperu screeched.

Barra looked down to where Graeg scrambled up the rocky sides of the watercourse toward them, and she bit her lower lip. "Well, one," she lied. "I'm a part owner. Just a little one, for short coastal trips . . ."

The beach at Tyre was no longer packed with ships, but a fair number came and went, sticking close to the coast to ply their routes, risking winter storms for the greater profits of the winter trade. The storyteller squatted on the beach, bent back resting against a sun-warmed hull, cloak wrapped tight around and hood up to keep old bones warm, perhaps, or to shade a pale face from the sun.

This was the fourth straight day the storyteller had been here, on the beach, telling again and again *The Rescue of Tyre*. Children and beachsiders knew the story, some almost by heart; often children would imitate the storyteller, sitting cross-legged on the sand and chanting along with the lines of the tale. Sailors from the calling ships often clustered around, listening intently; they'd heard confusing rumors about what had happened in this city, but this storyteller seemed to have the whole truth, and was able to tell it in a bewildering variety of languages.

". . . And with the mighty crash of the thunderbolt, Barra appeared on the roof, for the barbarian gods that love her set her down there to win the war. She cut her way through the prince's bodyguard with swift ease, her axe whirling as though it held life of its own and danced for its joy in the battle. And then Kheperu the Cunning cast a mighty enchantment that broke the spell of the treacherous steward," was the point the storyteller had reached on this particular day, when Leucas and Kheperu appeared on the beach, walking thoughtfully to the back of the crowd that listened so intently to the story.

The storyteller looked up and caught Leucas' eye, and went on with a wink: "And then Leucas, a man like the god-sired heroes of old, whose like has never been seen since Herakles the Mighty was set upon Olympus, crushed the great stones of the wall to powder with a blow of his fist . . ."

Leucas turned to Kheperu and murmured in a low voice that no one around them could hear, "Every time she tells this story, it gets bigger and bigger."

Kheperu shrugged, smiling. "She's right, though; if we want to command the top rates, it'll help if people have heard of us."

"I only wish she wouldn't exaggerate so. It's embarrassing."

On the beach, surrounded by her rapt audience, Barra went on, ". . . when warlike Odysseus and Diomedes the spear-famed scaled the god-built walls of Troy in the pitchy night to steal the Palladion from the very Temple of Athene, it was but a poor foreshadow of the valor and skill of the three heroes of Tyre . . ."

*I'd call this success,* she thought, smiling to herself as she spun out her tale. *I'd call this being happy.*

# Epilogue

*Dear Antiphos and Chryl,*

*I hardly know where to begin. It's certainly been an eventful few weeks. There was a little bit of difficulty with my last job, here in Tyre, but everything has turned out well, in the end. My shoulder is healing nicely. Here's a good rule for you: never turn your back on a man with a sword, even if you're pretty sure he won't hurt you. If you're wrong, it's a nasty surprise.*

*That mercenary captain I told you about—my admirer—has left with his men for Laurium. I'm not going with him. His name, again, is Kamades. When you two boys travel down here, if you're ever in need of help in the vicinity of Athens, go to Kamades. He is one of the finest men I have ever known, and you can trust him with your lives.*

*I wish I could give you similar advice about Tyre, but if I were you, I'd trust no one here but your Uncle Peliarchus. I've had about enough of this city, and I'm glad to be leaving.*

*King Demetor—he's the one from Kypros, you should remember from the last packet—he visited here in Tyre, and he had a little trouble again, and we saved him again, and actually, he's a pretty good old man. He's another one you could always come to, if he's still alive. If you tell him you are my sons, he'll give you the palace and all its furniture.*

*It looks like I'll be traveling with Kheperu and Leucas for some time to come. We had some testing times, here, and I've learned that these two are as brave and trustworthy—and as skillful—as any men alive. Leucas turned out to be a lot smarter than I originally thought, and Kheperu is a lot more honest—*

*down deep, anyway. I think someday I'll even bring them back to Great Langdale, so you can meet them.*

*I suppose what it is I want you most to know is this: wherever you go, find the best men and women there are, and do your best to be their friends. You can never have too much money nor too many friends, that's what I say. It can save your life.*

*I can't make this a longer letter; I have a caravan to catch. Give my love to everyone, and mind Coll, and do your lessons. I still think I should be able to be home for Midsummer's. Tell Llem that I should be in a prime position for negotiating new tin contracts at Knossos in the spring; I've found a bribe that I know King Idomeneus will love. If your grandda Ouendail should visit, tell him I hit a fella with the haymaker he taught me, maybe twenty years ago, and got my face busted for my trouble. And Coll. Tell Coll that she and I will have a lot to talk about, when I get home. A lot.*

*I love you both very much.*

*Take care,*
*Mother*

*P.S. I'm sorry there's no gifts with this letter; I'm a bit short of money right now. However, I've got a job, coming up: there's this people called the Habiru, and they're getting together to attack a big city called Jebusi, under their old general Joshua ben Nun. They're kind of a queer people, from what I hear. The story is, they carry their god around with them in a box, can you imagine? I don't know that this is true, but I do know they have decided that their god has given them Jebusi to be their own city. Adonizedek, the Jebusite king, is hiring lots and lots of mercenaries, so I'm going to go and help him defend his city. These bloody Habiru don't even know the real name of the place; they call it Jerusalem.*

*Sounds like easy money to me.*

# JERICHO MOON

*For Robyn, again—and for the same reason.*

The author wishes to acknowledge Robyn Fielder,
Paul Kroll, H. Gene McFadden, and Charles L. Wright
for their invaluable time and support in developing
this story and its background: thanks again, guys.
Neither of these books would have happened without you.

The author would also like to thank Dr. Nick Wyatt of
New College, Edinburgh, and Mr. Eliot Braun of
the Israel Antiquities Authority, Tel Aviv,
for the selfless gifts of their time and expertise in compiling
the research bibliography for this novel. Any errors of fact
or interpretation are wholly the responsibility of the author.

# Prologue

The storyteller sat cross-legged on a thin cloth pallet stuffed with straw; a shallow bowl holding a scattering of silver coins lay on the sandy flagstones near the storyteller's bony knees. An enormous wolf drowsed alongside, his head resting on massive paws. Only the clink of silver coin would prick open the wolf's eye, and his low growl was more than enough to discourage those who might think to take a coin, rather than leave one.

The storyteller's pallet rested on the fringe where the Market of Tyre, the centerpiece of the Phoenikian mercantile empire that stretched from the Indus Valley to the Pillars of Herakles and beyond, bordered upon the protected beach where the Phoenikian sailors—the greatest sailors the world had ever known—drew their longships up onto the land to unload their exotic cargo.

This same storyteller had squatted here for months, now, through a long and bitter winter, and had told endless variations of a single tale: how the Three Heroes of Tyre—Leucas of Athens, Kheperu of Thebes, and the barbarian princess Barra of far-off Albion—had saved the city from a mighty sorcerer of ill intent. Passing sailors would stop to listen, and sometimes drop a coin in the bowl, and they had carried the tale with them on their journeys across the sea; caravan guards did the same on the overland routes. It was a good story; it told well, and better yet, it was mostly true.

But even the best story goes stale in time, and now few children ever gathered around to hear it, and of men fewer still. On one chill spring morning with the waning moon still high in the sky, in a mist that billowed in from the sea, there was only a single listener, an older, hard-looking man wearing the hooded burnoose of an inland Canaanite. He squatted before the storyteller and listened with squinting attention, nodding to himself as familiar parts of the tale came around; the parts where the magician Kheperu burned a thousand men with the flame from his fingertips, where Leucas broke stone walls with a blow of his fist, where Barra disappeared and appeared again with the flash of a thunderbolt, and fought with a magic axe that danced in her hands like a living thing.

A coin rang faintly in the bowl, and the man asked the storyteller, "And if a man wanted to find these Three Heroes of your tale, how would he do that?"

The storyteller looked down at the bowl in amazement: the coin this man had dropped was no silver shekel, but a disc of solid gold. She looked back at the man with a mercenary gleam in eyes the unsettling blue-green color of a stormy sea.

"Shit," Barra said, "for that kind of money, I'll introduce you myself."

*Dear Chryl and Antiphos,*

*Well, it looks like we'll be heading out to Jebusi after all. This ought to shut up Kheperu's eternal bitching about how poor he is; he is absolutely the whiniest man I have ever met. Leucas, of course, never complains about anything, but he was getting pretty antsy, too.*

*Neither of them trusts me, is what it is. I mean, the king of Jebusi is paying five shekels a day—which is a bloody good wage around these parts, what with all the Trojan veterans driving the price down, not to mention the deserters from the Hittite army now that the Phrygians are carving them up in every battle—but it's a flat rate, no shares of loot involved. Sure, it's easy work (I don't think even the bloody fool Kelts would attack a city jammed full of mercenaries), but there's no future in it. At five shekels a day, it'd take me years to build a new ship; when you figure in living expenses, I'd never make it.*

*I kept telling them that if we held out for better, something better would turn up. As usual, I was right, and they were wrong. It seems the prince of Jebusi was out riding where he shouldn't be, and he got captured by one of these bandit tribes, the Manassites, up in the hill country south of Beth Shean. The king down in Jebusi is offering a reward—a* hefty *reward—to anyone who brings him back. Now, this is the kind of job I like: we grab the prince, take him home, and stroll back to Tyre with saddlebags full of silver.*

*I know it sounds a little tricky, but don't worry. These Habiru—that's what the locals call the bandit tribes up in the mountains—can be dangerous when they all get together, but otherwise they're nothing much. Kheperu, bless his clever little heart, knows all about them. Apparently these same tribes caused some trouble in Egypt a few years before Kheperu was born, until Ramses kicked them out of the country. There was a rumor, last fall, that they were getting together to start another war, but that turned out to just be the usual donkey gas.*

*So, tomorrow we head out along the caravan road toward Beth Shean with some extra horses and a few scraps of this prince's clothing—the fella who told us about it had a whole bundle of them. I figure Graegduz and I can sniff him out once we find the right camp. Finding him is the hard part. After that, I don't figure we'll have much trouble at all.*

*Give my love to your grandma, as always, and tell your Uncle Llem that once we save this prince, I'm putting together a terrific scheme to cut the Phoenikians out of the tin trade. Why should they make all the money? It's our bloody tin. Keep doing your lessons—I guess I don't need to remind you how expensive it is to support an Egyptian tutor—and while you're at it, get after Llem to come and sit down for a lesson or two. After twenty-five bloody years as High King, don't you think it's time he learns to read? Then I could write straight to him. And if your grandda should visit from Eire, tell him I miss him, and I'm planning to stop by Tara on my way if I should make it home this summer. I'll have a few stories that even you haven't heard, I think.*

*Take care, and behave yourselves, and with the favor of the Goddess I'll see you in summer.*

*With all my love,
Mother.*

BOOK ONE

# *The Jericho Road*

# 1

# *In the House of Joseph*

**T**he bloody sun sank toward the western hills, and the hope of Agaz of Jebusi sank with it.

He stood with one hand upon the flap of the black goat-hair tent that the Manassites had given him, and watched the sun's crimson smear spread across high strings of cloud, the sort that fly before an approaching storm. The light caught the deep creases in the weathered skin of his face, and pinked the scatter of grey in his tied-back hair.

The camp of Manasseh was spread across dozens of meadows like this one, a shallow bowl ringed by Galilean hills; hills that were covered with thousands of the squat tents of goat hair, shading from black as tarnished brass to red as rust on iron, pegged in random scatterings and clusters, the gaps between filled with communal cookfires, with stalls of impromptu markets and pens for goats and asses, reeking sheep and precious horses. Agaz was lost within an ocean of Habiru raiders: his very foreignness trapped him here more tightly than any chain.

Every man of them knew his face; he had a thousand jailers.

For a month he had been held here. The moon that would rise tonight from the mountains at his back would be the barest sliver short of half-full, the same as it had been the night his men were slaughtered like cattle.

He glared at the two Manassite warriors who squatted nearby, keeping one eye on him as they picked dripping hunks of roasted goat meat from the bowl that held Agaz's dinner. He'd been good today, docile and even friendly, and so he hoped they might leave a chunk or two of meat for him.

One of them grunted in thickly accented Canaanite, "What? You got a problem?"

"I was only thinking," Agaz replied evenly, "how much I'm enjoying your hospitality."

The tribesman nudged his companion, and they both chuckled. "Enjoying our hospitality. Huh. Enjoy it more if you could eat my heart, huh? That's what you Jebusites like, isn't it? Man meat?"

The other snorted. "I got some man meat for him here, if he's hungry. How about it, Jebusite? You want a taste of my man meat?"

Agaz's smile was cold as the winter dusk. "Sure," he said. "Bring it here." His smile spread to show his teeth.

The tribesmen nudged each other again and laughed some more. "Kind of like you, prince. I do. Be sorry to kill you, later."

"Kill me when you want," Agaz told him, "so long as you feed me now."

They looked at each other from under the hoods they wore tied about their brows, and traded a shrug. "Here," one said carelessly, offering the bowl. "Eat up. It's getting toward that time again." *That time* was the hour when his keepers would pound hot bronze rivets through the shackles on his wrists and ankles, to bind him for the night.

Agaz ate standing, fishing in the bowl with his fingers. For a moment, he wished it was true, the persistent fantasy that his people ate the flesh of men; he stared over the rim of the bowl at his guards as he chewed a mouthful of goat.

*You I would eat, whoreson,* he thought. *You I would stew like a kid in the milk of your mother's teats.*

This had been his life for a month, while he waited every day for the ransom from Jebusi. Every day since the day that even now rose within him, and turned the food in his mouth to ashes and bitter gall.

The sky was grey that day, thick clouds bringing dusk to the noon, and a bitter wind from the north had stung their cheeks. In the cold light of afternoon, a quarter of Agaz's men had surprised a patrol of Manassite foragers. The Jebusites fell upon the luckless foragers like a landslide, and had killed every one before Agaz could arrive to stop them.

He'd come north six weeks ago with a hundred picked men, blooded veterans, some of them companions from his distant boyhood. Armed with bow and spear, with remounts for each man, more than two hundred horses in all, they had come to scout the rumored gather-

ing of Manasseh and Ephraim, the twin tribes of Habiru raiders that
held the hill country surrounding Beth Shean.

They'd learned the stories that had come to Jebusi were true: the
Habiru were massing, gathering their men in camps strategically
placed to threaten the low-lying towns of the surrounding Canaanites.
No longer content to steal sheep and raid the occasional caravan, they
stood poised for a new round of conquest.

There in that little valley, standing over the bodies of the Manassites, Agaz had feared there might have been stragglers, away from the
main group of foragers; stragglers who might have watched the
slaughter from hiding, and then made their escape.

Despite his grim command to bury the bodies—he would brook
no dishonor to the dead—his men rode from the battleground in high
spirits, joking among themselves of the scant loot they'd collected: a
few knives and a bare two spears, most of the Manassites having been
armed only with round smooth stones for their slings.

His men—even his friends, his companions from boyhood—had
smirked as he'd ordered them to turn and ride for the south. He had felt
the doom hanging over them like the fist of winter, but he was alone in
his premonition.

The smirks from his men had turned to grumbles when he'd ordered
a cold camp for the night: a cold camp has no fires which might alert a
watchful enemy. At the tail end of winter, a cold camp meant his men
went to their bedrolls wet and chilled and miserable. Looking back on
this decision, he regretted it. He should have let them have their fires and
hot food, for all the difference it made.

At least they would have died warm.

The strangled gasp of a man choking on the blade of a bronze
knife had drawn Agaz from his fitful dreams that night. He'd yelled his
alarm, but by then it was far too late: the Habiru were among them in
the dark, slaughtering with knife and spear. Some twenty of his companions gathered about him, and together they fought their way free of
the killing ground—but only because the Habiru had let them go.
These Habiru were seasoned raiders, who knew better than to corner a
man beyond hope of escape.

Faced with certain death, a man fights with desperation beyond his
strength.

Instead the Habiru had pursued them through the dark, herding
them like cattle. Agaz remembered that bitter night as a tortured fever
dream of running on broken ground, stumbling over ankle-turning

rock, pursued by the screams of dying friends, listening for the burred hiss of death from the shadows.

When dawn finally came, only Agaz and three of his companions still lived, shattered and staggering, as the Habiru closed in around them.

Agaz had neither closed his eyes nor turned away as his friends were cut down, speared through the guts like wild pigs. He'd been their leader; the guilt of their blood was his as much as the Habiru's.

They'd seen by his gear and the quality of his clothing that Agaz was set apart from the men he led; questioned at spearpoint, he'd admitted his name, and the Habiru had needed no more than this. Jebusi was a great city, and he was known as its prince.

One month he was held, waiting for the ransom to arrive. He had no fear of his father's will—he knew that his father would ransom him.

But the money should have arrived a week ago, and more. That it hadn't boded ill. These were troubled times in the lands between the walled cities of Canaan—the tribe of Manasseh wasn't the only band of Habiru bandits roaming these hills. If the ransom party had been taken by another—say Ephraim, or Benjamin, or even Naphthali—he wouldn't live long enough for a second ransom to be raised.

One month had been set as the limit of his life, and that month expired tonight. His only hope lay in the long experience of the tribesmen of Manasseh with ransoming captives and caravans: he could hope they'd want the money more than they would his blood.

The smith set his anvil between Agaz's ankles while the guards stood watchfully nearby, their hands upon their knives; Agaz had attempted escape before, and they'd take no further chance.

Once the shackles upon Agaz's ankles were properly aligned on the anvil, the smith pulled a dully glowing peg of bronze out of the coals in his firepot with short tongs; he threaded it through the leaves of the shackles and gave it three sharp taps with his hammer to spread the ends. The process was repeated with the manacles around Agaz's wrists, but only after his arms encircled the thick center pole of the tent.

The smith stood up, clipping down the cover of his firepot. "That's done," he said with a sigh. "Same time in the morning, then?"

"No need," said one of his guards with a smirk—and got in reply a sharp look of warning from his partner, and an expression blankly puzzled from the smith.

Agaz understood before the smith did: there'd be no need for the smith to return in the morning to cut the rivets and set him free, for only one reason: once Agaz was dead, it'd be simpler to cut through his wrists.

His death was decided, then; decided for this very night.

He said nothing, only stared into an invisible distance, far beyond the black-woven walls of this tent, as the smith packed his gear and left. He saw nothing of his guards as they settled themselves to watch over him in comfort.

His sight was taken by his father's face, and the slow tears that would roll into the white beard of the king; he saw the towering white walls of the Citadel of Jebusi, upon which he'd played as a boy in the company of boys, and stood armed watch as a man in the company of men. He saw the fair curve of his wife's hip in their bed, and felt for an instant the softness of her skin beneath his hand; his wife, taken by the same fever that had taken his sons so many years ago; his wife, whom he would rejoin tonight.

Agaz was, above all things, a practical man. He raised no fantasies of escape to ease his heart with false cheer; he only prayed the Habiru would neither play with his hopes nor torture his flesh, but make an end with one swift stroke.

He had been wounded once, in battle, a Philistine arrow he took while leading the pursuit of a raiding party back toward the coast. In the high blood of battle, he had not known he was injured; he'd felt no pain until his best friend cut the barbed arrow from his flesh with a bronze knife that wasn't as sharp as it could have been.

He had borne that pain without shaming himself; he prayed now that he could face his death the same way, as a prince and a warrior, no shaking or pleading, no tears to burn his cheeks. He prayed that he would leave these Habiru bastards no scornful stories to pursue his shade with mocking laughter.

As the night wore on, he brooded helplessly on this, picturing himself going through every possible variation of courage or cowardice. He told himself that he could do it, that he could bear his fate well—but his insides were growing loose, and his stomach turned toward knots, and the long-stretching silence became more than he could bear.

"When will it be, then?" he demanded suddenly of his guards, his voice overloud and overharsh. "Tell me. Don't make me sit and wonder."

"When will what be?" one guard said disingenuously, but the other laid a hand upon his partner's arm and regarded Agaz with something like sympathy.

"Don't know, for sure," this second tribesman told him. "Someone will come for you. It's, ah—well, y'know, it's not something *I* wanted to do. I'd just as soon not watch it, either. I mean, if you'd tried to escape again, sure, I'da cut you down, but this . . . I don't know, it's different, somehow." He shifted uncomfortably and looked away. "This'll be no treat for me, either, y'know."

Agaz nodded and gave a cold smile. "You'll forgive me for not offering my sympathies."

The unsteady nerves his guard showed helped to ease him, some-how; that this hardened desert raider could be so shaky put his own squirming fear into a less humiliating perspective—and perhaps his fear would get no worse than this; perhaps this fear was the most he could feel.

This much fear he could bear like a prince, and go with honor into the darkness.

Then the door-curtain was drawn aside, and a youth stuck his head in, peering about the tent with arresting sea-green eyes. "Where's the prince?" he said, with a certain edge of puzzled suspicion in his voice.

*Someone will come for you.* And Agaz had been wrong, of course, about the fear; what he'd felt a moment ago was but a pale shadow of the terror that seized him now. He tried to respond as a warrior should, he tried to say *I am the prince*, but this terror closed his throat with an iron grip, and he could only stare as his guard nodded reluctantly toward him.

"This is him."

"You?" said the youth, disbelieving. "You don't look like a prince. You guys wouldn't be ribbing me, would you?"

With a great exercise of will, Agaz found his voice. "I am Agaz, prince of Jebusi."

"Hah. How about that," the youth said. "I guess I was expecting, I don't know, a littler tear-stained goatling that smells of powder and perfume—you look like you can handle yourself."

Before Agaz could summon a reply the youth turned away, and muttered something incomprehensible to someone outside; the words had the almost-understood quality that comes of overhearing a foreign language.

And there was something strange about this boy, about his eyes, about his accent . . . and then Agaz's own eyes widened and he stifled a gasp; now through ice around his heart shot a lance of wild hope.

Those murmured words hadn't been uttered in Canaanite, true, but he *recognized the tongue*: it had the liquid music he'd heard in the speech of some of the mercenaries his father had been gathering to Jebusi—this odd boy with the Philistine eyes had spoken in *Greek* . . .

Now the boy came fully inside, and behind him a man ducked through the tent flap, a man with black hair and beard both shot with grey; when he straightened and stood, the tent seemed to shrink until its roof brushed the top of his head.

"You've come for the prince?" the guard said.

"That's right," the youth replied. "Don't bother to get up."

The other guard squinted at this pair as he heaved himself upright. "You don't look like sons of Manasseh . . ." he began slowly.

"Listen, don't make a fuss. Everything's under control," the youth told him; the words and the tone that carried them were both reasonable, but beneath them there was a curious air of command, as though this boy, inexplicably, was accustomed to being obeyed without question. "Sit there and keep quiet, and we'll all stay friends, all right?"

Without waiting for a response from the guards, he once again said something in Greek, and the huge man nodded and stepped over beside the center tent pole; he knelt there to take a closer look at the manacles that fixed Agaz's arms around it. From this close vantage, the huge man's face had an extraordinary *broken* look to it, like a stone statue that had been shattered and then mortared together again by an inexpert craftsman, and his eyes were as grey as storm clouds in front of the sun. He noticed Agaz's regard; a corner of his mouth twitched wryly, and one eyelid drooped in a solemn wink.

"Here, what are you doing there?" the guard said, rising with his hand upon his spear, stepping close to see what the huge man did. "I'm not sure you two should be in here at all."

The boy said, as though in answer, "Leucas."

The huge man glanced over his shoulder and then spun with astonishing speed, still on his knees. His massive fist blurred through a short overhand arc to strike the guard in the middle of the chest. With a sound like the crush of bone beneath the blow of a club, the guard flipped into the air to fall gasping to the ground, collapsed around his broken ribs.

The other guard leaped to his feet as well, lifting his spear and drawing breath to shout an alarm, but the youth skipped forward and kicked him full in the crotch: the guard's shout died in its birth, trailing to a strangled whine. The boy had produced from somewhere an enormous broadaxe of what looked like worn-smooth copper, and he held it like an expert.

"Now," the boy said, "are you gonna be quiet and behave yourself, or am I gonna open your skull?"

"You'll never escape," the guard wheezed. He moaned once, curling around his injured groin, and then went on, "Why d'you think there's no guards outside? This whole camp guards—"

"Shut up," the boy told him, hefting his axe significantly. "Didn't I say I have everything under control?"

The huge man had already turned back to Agaz's manacles, and now he spoke for the first time, a basso rumble that seemed to come from the earth beneath their feet. The boy's response was definitely snappish, and the huge man shrugged expressively.

He looked into Agaz's eyes and lifted one finger as though to say *Wait a moment*; then he took hold of the manacles, one in each hand. Muscle rolled like boulders beneath the thin overrobe he wore, and Agaz could only stare in awe as the manacles gave forth a thin squeal of bronze *stretching* under intolerable strain, then a pop like a finger snap, and his arms were free, the manacles now hanging like bracelets upon his wrists. The broken pieces of the rivet that had held them dropped onto his leg—it was hot, so hot it scorched him through his kilt.

He finally found his voice. "Who *are* you people?"

"Mercenaries." The boy flashed a grin at him that showed teeth white and even, and an array of crow-foot creases around his eyes, inexplicable in one so young as to have no trace of beard. "Your father's put up a reward for your safe return. A big reward," the young-old boy said. "We're going to get you out of here."

"You're not like any mercenaries I've ever seen," he said blankly.

"I'll take that as a compliment. This time. Mind your manners."

Kheperu's long, hooked nose twitched in disdain. Goat, everything in this bloody place smelled of goat, and worse: *sheep*, which have the most appalling odor of any creature on earth, excepting possibly Kheperu himself.

He dipped a hand in the lambskin purse within his robe and palmed the next to last of his contributions to this rescue: a lime-sized ball compounded of a number of esoteric ingredients, including white phosphorous and naphtha, covered with a thin layer of tar and two wrappings of water-soaked kidskin. In the pouch he had one more identical to this one, save that it had only a single layer of watered skin.

"Come along, you great dirty beast," he muttered to the enormous grey wolf that padded patiently along at his side. "We're almost done."

Graegduz, the great dirty beast in question, made no response.

Kheperu wove with studied uncertainty through the forest of goat-hair tents, looking this way and that, occasionally muttering to himself in senile fashion. He leaned heavily on his walking staff of stout oak. For purposes of this rescue he had brushed a heavier white into his already-greying topknot, and had unbound his stringy beard to lie loose and wild upon his chest. As he passed, he'd collar various random Habiru and whine something half-comprehensible, usually beginning with, "Do you speak a civilized tongue, you vile savage?"

Even if they did, they were rarely able to take offense; Kheperu had not bathed in more years than he cared to remember, and he'd rub the leather armor that he wore beneath his robes with lamb fat from time to time to keep it from cracking; many of the alchemical substances with which he worked were volatile and noxious in the extreme, with an array of nauseating stenches that soaked into his skin and oozed out again through his pores; now in his late forties, his teeth were going, making his breath resemble the exhalation of a slaughterhouse; and it was not uncommon to find within a pocket of his robes something roughly resembling a dead rat in an advanced stage of decay.

Therefore, it was a rare tribesman—who, through an astonishing contortion of his nimble mind, Kheperu managed to think of as "the filthy Habiru"—that could do more than gasp and try to rub the sting from his watering eyes, and choke out some impromptu excuse about urgent business elsewhere, usually upwind.

In this fashion, he moved with deceptive speed toward a large fire pit over which hung numerous large strips of what might have been lamb, smoking slowly on a greenwood rack. Several large bronze cook pots sat upon the coals, and the scents of mutton and stewed barley brought a surge to his mouth and a snarl to his belly, reminding him that he hadn't eaten since the morning.

He made his way to a knot of men that squatted near the lip of the pit, warming themselves at its coals, and said in a whiny, querulous simper, "I seem to have lost my way. Can any of you revolting peasants direct me to the tents of Elihu?"

They exchanged glances among themselves, and one of them piously muttered something in this tongue of theirs, which sounded to Kheperu's ears like a nasty hawk-and-spit gabble compounded of corrupt Egyptian and the lowest gutter slang of the Phoenikian Coast. Kheperu caught the words *mitsree*, Egyptian, and *geyr*, strangers, and he knew this man quoted a familiar saying from their seemingly endless store of laws; this one had something to do with being nice to Egyptians because this whole tribe of filthy Habiru were once strangers in Egypt. Kheperu had heard this phrase repeated over and over again till he was bloody sick of it, in this past week of searching the Manassite camps for the prince of Jebusi.

One of the men rose uncertainly, eyeing sidelong the wolf at Kheperu's side, and gestured vaguely westward. Kheperu stepped close to the man, to give him a good whiff of his breath, wheezing, "Where? There? Are you certain?"

The tribesman's eyes glazed over and he involuntarily flinched back from the stench. His companions giggled into their hands; Kheperu favored them with a frosty glance, and they instantly looked away, swallowing their chuckles and pretending perfect innocence.

During this brief moment while all eyes were averted, he dropped the hide-wrapped ball that he had palmed; it fell unobtrusively to the earth, and a tiny twitch of his foot flicked it into the fire pit.

*Almost too easy,* he thought. *Where's the challenge in baffling these ignorant* shasu?

He thanked them effusively and began threading his way back toward the surrounding darkness, Graegduz beside him. He had one more of these little beauties to deliver, and then he'd have perhaps a hundred breaths to join up with Barra and Leucas before the first one—of the dozen or so he'd planted—would detonate.

He shook his head in private derision. Barra had been so worried, so careful to plan this rescue down to the most minute detail. Really, this wasn't going to be difficult at all.

Kheperu had known tales of these tribesmen of old—he'd grown up in Thebes, on the fringes of the court of Isinofre, the eldest surviving queen of Ramses the Great. Ever since Ramses had established her there and then wisely escaped to his capital in the Delta, the bitter old bat had loved to tell the story; she'd trotted it out whenever she'd had a few cups of wine and the subject turned to her husband.

It was, perhaps, the single most embarrassing failure of the God-king, when this pack of savages had stolen their neighbors blind and then beat it into the desert on foot. On foot!—in Egypt, they were still known by the derisive nickname *shasu*: the Pedestrians. Kheperu hadn't understood how the *shasu* had ever believed they could get away with it, but when Ramses himself had led the cavalry of the Ra Division in pursuit, he'd lost most of his horses and nearly all his chariots to a freak thunderstorm and flooding in the Sea of Reeds.

By the time he'd assembled another column, these *shasu* Habiru had already scattered and buried themselves among the people of Canaan so thoroughly that they could not be rooted out. In the sixty-odd years since then, they'd been hardly more than a nuisance, a pest like the biting flies on the Coast Road; *really,* Kheperu thought, *I cannot comprehend from whence comes their fearsome reputation. They're virtually a nation of simpletons.*

It was one of these simpletons who now said from behind him in heavily accented but fluent Phoenikian, "Excuse me, friend, but did you say you're lost?"

"Why, yes—yes I did," Kheperu replied in the same tongue, turning. "I'd taken my dog, here, outside the camp to relieve himself, and I must have gotten turned around . . ."

Seven men stood arrayed in a tight arc behind him, their faces shadowed by the firelight from the cookpit; three leaned casually on man-length spears, and the rest had bronze knives prominently displayed at their belts. One stepped forward, and when he spoke there was a glint in his eyes that appeared neither simple nor friendly.

"Then how come the directions you got at the *last* two cookpits didn't serve? Why'd you have to come here and ask *again?*"

"I'm sorry?" Kheperu said with careful blankness. He swallowed through a suddenly dry throat. *They've been following me.*

A single droplet of sweat slid like ice down the entire length of his spine.

The Manassite stepped closer, and placed a hard and competent-looking hand on the hilt of his knife. "You're the Egyptian, aren't you? The one with the Greek pack bearer and the red-haired eunuch. Elihu was chosen to host you."

"That's correct, sir," Kheperu affirmed with a wetly obsequious snigger. *Although if you call Barra a eunuch to her face, she'll knock you on the head.* "In some fashion, I cannot seem to find my way about these tents—everything looks so much alike here, you know . . . I thank you for your concern, but I think this kind gentleman has set me upon the proper course . . . so, with your permission, I'll be going . . ."

And soon, too; the layers of wet hide that wrapped the pyrotechnic balls were inexact fusing devices; the bloody things could start exploding any second.

The lines of suspicion graven around the Manassite's eyes hardened further. "I think I know why you can't find your way."

"Oh?"

"Yeah," he said, with a certain grim mockery. "You must find us *deficient* in our *hospitality*, don't you, a sophisticated city-fellow like you? I think maybe we should have given you a guide, and an *escort*, from the beginning."

"Oh, yes, well," Kheperu said, "you did, I mean they did, he did— you know, Elihu himself, but somehow we became separated . . ." *at about the time I poisoned his entire household,* he finished silently. "I'm sure he's somewhere about, looking for me . . ." *Listen closely and you can likely hear him snore, you ignorant oaf.*

"You just come along with us, friend," the Manassite said flatly; for all his pretence of civility, he clearly intended to keep Kheperu within arm's reach. "We'll make sure you get to his pavilion safely— and right away."

"You're very kind," Kheperu told him.

They would be somewhat *less* kind, on arriving at the pavilions of Elihu, and finding Kheperu's host, his wives and children, even his slaves, in a heavily drugged slumber.

These fellows obviously partook of a nastily suspicious nature; Kheperu reluctantly decided that he'd passed the point where he could talk his way out of this.

He glanced down at Graegduz, who stared at the Manassite with unblinking yellow concentration. If the tribesman moved to draw the blade from his belt, Graeg would bite the fellow's hand off, right through the wrist. Then one of those spearmen would stab the cursed beast, so that even if Kheperu managed to get clean away, Barra would open his skull with that bloody great axe of hers for getting her bloody dog killed.

He half snorted a sigh through his enormous nose, hard enough to ruffle his unbound beard. "I thank you deeply, a thousand times," he wheezed absently, making a show of patting his robes as though searching for something, then his hand dipped within. "Let me give you something for your trouble."

He brought out a small folded paper packet of a silvery grey powder that he emptied into his palm; on the thumb and middle finger of that hand, he now fixed a pair of small metal thimbles.

"Here," he said brightly, offering the powder to the Manassite. "This is *Barra sokjan.*"

Graegduz's great yellow eyes swung up toward Kheperu, and he blinked in what might have been expressionless puzzlement.

The Manassite peered suspiciously at the powder. "What is it?"

"It's *Barra sokjan!*" Kheperu said forcefully. Was he mispronouncing it? "*Barra sokjan,* you idiot!"

*Barra sokjan* was not the name of the powder; the powder was called *sh'asbiu*, fire-sand. *Barra sokjan* was one of the very few phrases that Kheperu knew in Pictish, a tongue which Barra was fond of insisting that all wolves understand. It meant simply: *Go find Barra*, and now Graegduz heaved himself reluctantly upright and trotted off into the darkness, with a single reproachful glance back over his shoulder.

Kheperu hissed silent relief through his teeth—now he had only his own life to worry about—and saw his relief echoed on the faces of the Manassites, who all relaxed somewhat now that the great wolf was leaving.

Kheperu made a show of confusion, calling, "Thesem!" after the departing wolf as though it were his name. "Thesem, come back here! Where are you going?" and then turned back to find the hard eyes of the Manassite staring into his.

"You shouldn't call people idiots, you stinking fool," the Manassite said through his teeth. "They might get angry. Now what is this *Barra sokjan*?"

"Oh, that," Kheperu said. "Here, I'll show you."

A snap of his wrist tossed the powder into the air, a snap of the fingers that wore the thimbles struck a spark within the cloud of powder. Kheperu prudently closed his eyes just as the entire cloud ignited with a loud *whoosh* into a ball of flame bigger than a man and brighter than the noonday sun: it struck like a dagger into the eyes of every man that beheld it.

The tribesmen staggered back, shouting in startled fright, stumbling into each other and rubbing at their faces. Kheperu wasted one single second to shift his grip upon his staff, transforming it from a walking stick into a deadly weapon: he spun it hissing through the air and cracked the skull of the hard-eyed man. Blood spurted from the Manassite's scalp as he collapsed to his knees and pitched forward onto his face.

"That's for calling me 'friend,' you *shasu* scum," Kheperu snarled, and then he turned and ran.

He ran hard, surprisingly fleet and nimble for such a short fat man, dodging around tents and skipping over guy ropes. The *sh'asbiu* trick bought him a head start, but as soon as he got away from the glow of the fire pits, the uncertain moonlight forced him to slow his pace on the uneven ground, and now the camp rang with the shouts of his pursuers. Voice joined to voice—in a moment, the entire bloody camp would be up in arms.

He made to slip within a nearby tent, to hide for just a moment to collect his wits and form a plan, but just as his hand reached for the curtain, it was drawn aside and he found himself faced with a spear-armed Manassite who gabbled something at him in that revolting tongue of theirs, some question to which Kheperu's answer was a quick punch in the mouth with the end of his staff. The Manassite's knees buckled, and Kheperu didn't waste the time to finish him. He sprinted away into the darkness, his breath now going short.

He stopped some distance away, huffing and gasping for air, and looked about. Around him was a forest of goat-hair tents, one looking much like the other, their colorful dyes bleached by the moonlight. With irony that stung like a slap, he realized that he was now lost in truth, irretrievably lost.

"This," he said aloud, "isn't turning out quite as well as it could have."

A voice cried *"Hane!"* and its triumphant note provided all necessary translation: Kheperu had been spotted.

He spun and saw a large group of armed men pelting toward him. A fist-size slingstone hissed past his head so closely he could feel the wind it brought with it, and as he turned to run again, a tent peg caught his ankle and he fell, saving his life: a hail of stone sizzled through the space where he'd been standing.

He struggled to rise, gulping air; by the time he'd found his feet, the pursuers were well within spearcast. He ran again, but spears rained around him.

One heavy blade, expertly cast, struck him squarely in the back, shearing through his robes and the armor beneath them to slice into his flesh. Its impact drove him sprawling across the earth; he twitched once, then again, and then lay still.

"Something's wrong."

Leucas squatted beside the prince, but his stare was a thousand miles away. The two guards snored peacefully, stretched out by his ankles.

"Nothing's wrong," Barra snapped. She continued to pace, snarling under her breath, one hand within her galabiyeh to scratch beneath the cloth that bound flat her breasts. "He'll be here. He's good at this shit. Give him a little credit."

"It's you that doesn't give him credit, Barra," Leucas rumbled. "Kheperu's a professional. He'd be here by now, if he could."

"I'm telling you, everything's all *right*," she snarled, still seeking the itch. *Mother rot this stinking wrap, rot this tiny reeking tent, rot this whole fucking culture.* She stamped back and forth, swinging the enormous basalt head of her broadaxe dangerously in the confined space.

Agaz, the fortyish prince of Jebusi—who was really a lot more handsome than any backwoods hedgegoat had any right to be, kind of leathery and serious-looking—looked up at her and asked in Canaanite, "What's wrong?"

"*Nothing,* dammit!" Barra snapped back in the same tongue.

"Then what are we waiting for?"

Barra took a deep breath and sighed out her temper. "We're waiting for our other partners. They should have been here by now."

"Greek, are they?"

Barra gave him a sharp look. "You speak Greek?"

Agaz shook his head. "My father's been hiring mercenaries—it seems as though half of them are veterans of the Siege of Troy. I recognize the sound, that's all. How many men do you have?"

"One," Barra said through her teeth. "One childish, perverted, whining, stinking son of a whore, who's so *late* that when he gets here, I'm gonna give him a knock he'll never forget."

"That's *it*?" Agaz said, blinking. "The three of you?"

Barra showed him her teeth. "More men only means more shares in the reward. If we three can't do it, more wouldn't help anyway."

The prince seemed to fall in upon himself, and his head sank toward his breast. He murmured, "And for a moment, I allowed myself to hope . . ."

"Hey," Barra said, "none of that shit. We got *in* here, didn't we? We'll get out again."

He looked up again, and his eyes were empty as the face of a corpse.

"Do you think you're the first to have come for me?" At Barra's blank look, he laughed bitterly. "You're not even the first to have made it this far."

Barra swallowed, and something cold thumped down into her guts. "Oh?"

"It's easy to get in," he said. "You'll never get out. Now I'll have the dubious privilege of watching you and your partners hauled to the edge of camp and stoned to death. Ever see a stoning, boy? It's ugly. And it takes a long time."

"Shit, you're just a regular sunbeam, aren't you?" Barra forced a laugh that sounded more or less confident. "Betcha a thousand shekels we get you out alive."

The leather of the prince's face cracked briefly; Barra thought it might have been an attempt at a smile.

"All right," he said slowly. "It's a bet."

Leucas said, "Listen."

With no grasp of the Canaanite tongue, the giant Athenian had nothing to do but wait and worry while Barra and Agaz conversed; now, outside, the wind had shifted, and it carried distant voices raised in shouts, like the cries of hunters who have flushed their prey.

Barra knuckled her forehead, as though in pain. "Something's gone wrong."

Leucas made no reply, only stared at her patiently with calm grey eyes. She shook her head angrily and hissed through her teeth; she had to make the call, and the wrong move here would cost lives.

She tightened her grip on her axe, taking comfort from its reassuring weight. "We go for the horses," she said. "If they're chasing Kheperu, he'll he heading that direction. Let's move."

Leucas rose, and so did Agaz, when she repeated herself in Canaanite. The two guards snored thinly on the ground, unconscious with one of Kheperu's sleeping draughts apiece—given the choice between drinking the draughts or eating the edge of Barra's broadaxe, both guards had sensibly decided to sleep on it.

The hooded burnoose taken from one of them already disguised Agaz; now Leucas lifted their spears. "I think we'd best go armed."

Barra nodded, and looked at Agaz. "Can you handle a spear?"

"I can fight," Agaz said, taking a spear from Leucas' hand. He smiled grimly at the bronze manacle that still hung like a bracelet upon his wrist, as though he saw there the faces of his jailers. "Just watch me. They decreed my death for this night; I thank you that I may take some few of them with me into the Muck."

"Ay, muck is right," she muttered. "Come on."

She held aside the curtain, and they slipped into the night.

They moved at a swift walk; to run would draw undue attention from the men and women who now stuck their heads out from their tents to see what the shouting was about. Barra held her broadaxe low by her leg, keeping it as unobtrusive as possible, and squinted up at the sky. Thickening clouds swung before the moon, darkening the ground toward invisibility.

"Where's this bastard storm coming from?" Barra snarled under her breath. "We need that bastard moon . . ."

"Fire," Agaz said quietly beside her. "We should fire some of the tents."

Barra shook her head crisply. "No need."

"It'd keep them busy—with Manassites poking their heads out like this, it's only a matter of time before we're stopped. We need some kind of diversion, and fire works best. Fire has a power over people, a power—"

A boom like overhead thunder echoed through the camp; Agaz jumped like he'd been stung. Barra gestured toward the sound: there, far across the camp, a cascade of glowing coals and cinders showered like falling stars onto the tents that had surrounded a large fire pit.

"I told you: no need," she said. "Didn't I say we have everything under control?"

Flames licked up from the tents there, and men rushed out around them from all sides, some only half-dressed, some fully dressed and already armed with shield and spear. Another of Kheperu's incendiary bombs detonated in a different part of the camp, and now there was so much confusion of running and shouting and flames that the three fugitives could move at speed.

*That's kicked over the anthill for good and sure,* Barra thought. *Now all we have to do is get out of here.*

The growing firelight from the burning tents pushed back the night and made the going easier; it also brought clear their foreign features to the Manassites around them. They stayed off the main avenues, dodging along the backs of the clustered tents, but still they had gone only a hundred paces when a man stepped out not far from them and shouted, "Where you going? Fire's that way!"

He pointed, but then his arm fell and his brows drew together and he said, "Hey—hey, it's the *Jebusite! The Jebusite's loose!*"

He turned and ran, shouting his alarm, and Barra snapped in Greek, "Take him."

Leucas' reply was a spearcast, a whipping overhand that drove the spear singing along a flat arc toward its target thirty yards away. It took the fleeing man full in the spine and drove straight through, bursting from his chest in a fountain of gore. His hands flew up in a gesture of strengthless surrender, and the force of the throw lifted him from his feet and pitched him face first into the dirt. He lay pinned to the ground, squirming spastically, choking out his life.

Leucas jogged toward him, muttering, "Gonna need that spear."

"Through the ribs front and back," Agaz murmured in wide-eyed awe. "He's *strong.*"

Barra grinned at him. "He was holding back: a full throw would have sent the spear right through him and lost it in the darkness."

Agaz turned his wide-eyed gaze on her, and then she saw his eyes shift to over her shoulder—this was all the warning she needed. Even as he drew breath to shout *"Behind you!"* she was already moving, slipping to one side, away from the spear blade that stabbed at her back.

That cursed itching breast-binding wrap nearly cost her life: her acrobatic bulldancer flexibility was so restricted that the spear grazed her, and tangled in her galabiyeh. She spun, her broadaxe cocked back over her shoulder to strike, but as the Manassite behind her yanked back on his spear haft to free the blade, it pulled the loose robe into a twist and she stepped on its lower hem, stumbled, and fell flat on the ground at the Manassite's feet.

She tried to roll away as he lifted his spear to spit her like a lamb, but he stood on her clothes and held her in place. She had time to think, *Shit, this is a stupid way to die,* and then she looked up, and met his eyes, and knew him.

All in an instant, she saw him as though she'd known him all his life. She saw his fear, his fury at the sudden murder of his friend, she saw his courage in battle and raid; she saw a dutiful son, a loving father, a loyal friend—maybe a little earnest, a little humorless, the butt of the occasional practical joke, but good-natured and forgiving, able to laugh at himself in the end; not quite stingy or miserly, but perhaps somewhat reluctant to share a cup of wine or shank of lamb with a neighbor who had none; a rock-hard believer in square dealing and honest work. He must have been awakened by the shouting and the explosions, grabbed his spear and run bravely outside, just in time to see the life torn from a man he'd known since boyhood. In fear and fury he'd struck at the nearest killer, and now he was about to take her life.

It was a Gift of the Mother, called by her people the *sceon tiof*; those who have this gift of looking into the hearts of men are thought blessed among the Picts of Great Langdale. Barra called it her mother's curse: Coll, her mother, was famous for it, and it was great talent for a judge, or a queen.

Barra had only a touch of it, a trace in the blood, and it had nearly crippled her: for a mercenary, empathy can be lethal. It came and went unpredictably, often taking her at the most inconvenient moments imaginable, sometimes showing her nothing of value, and at other times, such as this one, bringing great pain.

As the Manassite stabbed downward, Agaz struck the blade aside with his own spear, following the parry with a buttstroke across the Manassite's teeth that loosened his limbs, then with ruthless efficiency he reversed his spear again and raked the edge of the blade across the Manassite's throat.

Blood sprayed in a black shower from the Manassite's jugular; he staggered backward, dropping his spear to clutch at his throat, trying to scream his shock and despair, but making only a gargling croak from the wound that tore his windpipe.

Agaz extended a hand to help Barra up. "Told you I can fight."

Barra struck it aside. "I don't need your help."

Agaz dropped his hand and his face frosted over. "Perhaps I should have let him kill you."

Barra, on her knees, looked over to where the Manassite lay dying; this man she knew like a brother, like a son—better, in fact, than she knew her own sons, growing up without her on the Isle of the Mighty.

Like a painting, like a sculpture, a living work of art, there was only one of him; there could never be another, and the world was a darker place for his passing; a single irretrievable action had lessened the world, and the loss weighed like a stone on Barra's spirit.

How many men had she watched die this way? Hundreds? *Add one to the list.*

Now Leucas was beside her, a hand on her arm to help her up. "Be nice to the prince," he rumbled in Greek. "I know you're embarrassed, but you shouldn't refuse a helping hand."

"Embarrassed? Leucas, I'm not . . ." Her voice trailed away, and her eyes went distant; the wind had shifted.

Through the scorched-hair stench of the burning tents, through the chemical reek of the incendiaries, the scents of goat and sheep, pigshit and horseshit and manshit, through the ionic crackle of the approaching thunderstorm, she could smell him. Barra's nose was as keen as a wolf's; she could ken a scent the way another might recognize a familiar voice.

She said, "Kheperu's in trouble."

Leucas brought her to her feet with a heave of one arm. "How do you know?"

"The horses are that way," she said, pointing, then swung her arm to point upwind. "Kheperu's over there."

"All right," Leucas said. "Let's go, then."

A high shrilling scream came out of the nearby darkness, a woman's scream: the wife or daughter of one of these dead men had put her head outside and seen them. Another voice joined the scream, and another, and now the shouts of men approached.

She should be used to it by now, she'd seen it happen so many times before, but even so she registered an instant's fleeting wonder that so many things had gone wrong so fast. It was always this way: once the smallest leak breached the dike of their luck, troubles cascaded upon each other like the widening rush of a flash flood.

Desperate times, desperate measures.

Barra snapped in Canaanite, "Follow me," and ran upwind as fast as she could without tripping on her robe. Leucas' long strides kept him easily by her side, and Agaz was at her heels.

"Where are we going?" the prince asked. "They know we're out here, now—shouldn't we be making for the horses?"

"Our partner's in trouble," Barra said shortly.

Agaz snorted. "So? Isn't that just one less share in the reward?"

Barra stopped short and wheeled on him; her eyes blazed, and a vein pulsed in her forehead. She gathered Agaz's robe in her free fist and snarled right into his face, "I'd trade your life for his right *now*, you sack of shit. Now come on—or stay here and die."

She released him and whirled away to run without waiting for an answer. "What's the matter with you Jebusite mama's boys anyway? Can't you fucking *run*?"

Agaz ran behind her, huffing his breath in grim determination to keep up. "That thousand shekels," he gasped, "is starting to look like a good bet."

He was at her side when she and Leucas stopped short. A little distance away, nine spear-armed men surrounded a dark figure stretched full length upon the ground; a couple of them prodded at the figure, tentatively, as though they couldn't quite decide whether or not to actually stick it through. Fire leaped from tents around them, carving the night into dancing shadows. Thunder rumbled from the clouds that covered the moon.

"That's him," Barra said in Greek. "Help me get this shit off."

Leucas began dubiously, "Barra—"

"Don't argue with me, dammit!" she snapped, pulling the galabiyeh off over her head. "I can't *fight* like this!"

Under the robe she wore the traditional Canaanite spiral-wound wrap from knees to shoulders; Leucas drew the bronze knife from his belt and cut it off her with a single stroke. Agaz watched in wide-eyed astonishment as Leucas sliced away her breast wrap as well; Barra stood revealed wearing only her heavy cloth breechclout and the wide boarskin belt that held her twin throwing axes of flint, and the smallsword scabbard that would carry her broadaxe.

Her long hair, the color of the flames around them, fell below shoulders as lean and hard as a leather saddle; cords of solid muscle stood out along her thighs, but his astonished gaze was taken mostly by her small, firm breasts and the way her nipples hardened in the chill night air.

She said dangerously, "What?"

Agaz blinked. "You're a *woman* . . ."

"Brilliant, sunbeam. You're a fucking genius. Now come on, we don't have time to be clever."

With no more warning than this, she threw herself into a sprint toward the knot of armed men. Not even Leucas could match her at a full sprint; she outstripped him with ease, and as she ran she drew the left-hand throwing axe from her belt. Barra's left had strength and skill equal to her right, and she threw the axe in perfect stride.

Lightning flared from the clouds above, and a third incendiary detonated nearby with an earsplitting roar and fountain of cinders reaching for the sky; when her axe took one of the men in the back of the shoulder and drove him to the ground, it was as though he'd been felled by a thunderbolt.

She sprang high over the downed man, an aerial somersault like a Cretan bulldancer diving over the slashing horns of the sacred bull; she landed bestride Kheperu's body and howled like a rising wind among rocks.

The Manassites drew back in surprise and she threw herself toward the nearest, whirling like a sand devil, a stroke of her broadaxe knocking aside his spear. She let the weight of her stroke pull her into a spin that ended with the edge of her broadaxe taking the Manassite full in his open mouth.

Nine pounds of basalt, honed sharp enough to shave with, moving with all the speed that eleven years' fighting experience can give it, is unstoppable by any mortal flesh or bone.

His teeth shattered, and his cheeks parted around the upward slice that sheared through his skull into his brain. Barra wrenched the axe free, with a twist that splintered bone and teeth, before his falling body could pull it from her hand. His jittering corpse fell to the ground, and Barra shook her bloody axe at the others, spraying them with bone splinters and bits of their friend's brain, all the while screaming wordlessly at the top of her considerable voice.

"It's Anat Herself!" someone shouted in tones of panic. "Anat Headsmasher—*the Slaughterer fights against us!*"

The eight remaining Manassites froze for one instant of superstitious terror, staring in awe at her; for that instant, the issue could have gone either way—they were eight to her one, after all, and she didn't *look* like a goddess—but in that moment of indecision, a great grey wolf paced out of the red-shadowed darkness to stand by her side, its head held low and dangerous, its legs coiled to spring.

The Manassites, as one man, took a step back.

An instant later, a flick of Kheperu's wrist made a brilliant flash burst from the ground to sear their eyes, and Leucas arose behind them, nineteen and a half hands of blood-mad Athenian, roaring like a wounded bear. He seized one Manassite in each massive hand and slammed them together like an angry child smashing pots. He released them and they fell, then they dazedly scrambled back to their feet and ran away, and that decided the matter: the Manassites scattered into the darkness, yelling for help.

Barra watched them go, breathing harshly. Graegduz sidled up to her and laid his head against her leg.

"Hey, Graeg," Barra murmured, ruffling the fur behind the wolf's ears. "You're a good boy, aren't you?"

She stepped over to where Kheperu was slowly coming to his hands and knees and squatted beside him. "You know what? You're late."

Kheperu's round face seemed drawn under its layer of grime. "Barra, I'm hurt."

"Ay, sure, whining about your feelings when I've just saved your life—"

"No. I mean I'm *hurt*," he said thinly, with none of the edge of mockery she'd expected. He sounded tired, and a little frightened. "In the back. I don't know how badly. One of these filthy *shasu* got me with a spear."

Barra quickly wiped her broadaxe clean on the ground and stuck its haft into the smallsword scabbard tied to her leg. She got a hand under Kheperu's arm and helped him up. "Can you walk?"

"I don't know. I've been playing dead. I can feel both my legs," he offered hopefully.

"We'll take no chances. Leucas?" she called softly, and the Athenian came over, with Agaz sticking close by his side.

"What's wrong?"

"Kheperu's hurt. You'll have to carry him."

Leucas nodded. "Your axe is gone," he said as he lifted Kheperu's bulky form as easily as a child's. "The fellow ran away with it still in his shoulder."

Barra shrugged. She had three spare blanks of good flint in her pack, back with the horses. "Agaz," she said, "this is Kheperu, our third partner."

Agaz nodded politely to him, but eyed the grey wolf with open apprehension.

Barra said, "*His* name's Graegduz, and he's our fourth partner. He's the one that found you in the first place; he sniffed out your tent when Elihu gave us a little tour of the camp this morning. Graegduz," she said with a certain formality, "this is Agaz, prince of Jebusi. Be nice to him." The wolf gravely sniffed the prince's hand.

"We must keep moving," Agaz said. "These Habiru are very tough, and very brave; it will take only a moment for them to recover their nerve and return with more men."

Barra nodded, and squinted at him appraisingly. "That was you, that shout about Anat the Slaughterer, wasn't it?"

"It seemed appropriate," he replied with a cold smile.

"Pretty clever, sunbeam. Damned clever. I could learn to like you."

Lightning flared above them, with thunder close upon it, and raindrops of the size that herald a big storm began to spatter the dust.

Barra scanned the sky and shook her head. "Let's go. The storm'll give us some cover, but we need the fires for light until we get outside the camp; we'd best be gone before the rain gets heavy. We can make the horses by midnight, and cover some miles by dawn."

"That's your *plan*?" Agaz said disbelievingly. "Do you have any idea how many Manassites there are? You think they won't be out there after us? They've held these hills for *fifteen years*—they know each rock of them, and there's enough fighting men among them to cover every pass between here and Jebusi."

"Ay, I know," Barra said. "Don't make me out for a fool, prince."

She led them off through the camp at a steady jog. Leucas kept pace with her easily, even carrying Kheperu; the Egyptian grunted each time a sharp step jolted his wounded back. The rain thickened around them, and Agaz continued to protest in a hissing half whisper at her side. "How can you possibly expect to escape to Jebusi—"

"Because we're not *going* to Jebusi, all right?" Barra hissed in response. "We're going the other way—north, to Beth Shean. Now shut up and run."

"Beth Shean? The garrison city? What's in Beth Shean?"

"Don't take orders worth a shit, do you?" she said dryly. "The Governor's in Beth Shean, that's what. Along with a few thousand regulars of the Canaan Division."

"Tal Akhu-shabb? What could an important man like the Governor possibly have to do with *you*?"

"He owes me a favor," Barra said. "More than one."

"I hardly think—"

"Hey," Barra said sharply. She pulled up short, and Agaz nearly fell over her. She straightened her back and stuck her face close to his; the stiffened fingers of her right hand poked the prince of Jebusi hard in the chest. "Didn't I tell you to mind your manners?"

Agaz looked into the eyes of a woman that he had only moments ago compared to the battle-god of Canaan, and from her up into the winter-sky grey of the eyes of Leucas; then to Kheperu's, beady like a squirrel's, and finally at the great yellow orbs of the wolf.

He coughed, and swallowed, and blinked, and said, "I, ah, I suppose I'm sorry. No insult intended, ah . . . ah—I don't believe I know your name."

Barra grinned at him. "Barra Coll Eigg Rhum. Pleased to meet you. No more talking. Run."

They ran.

Thunder cracked and rain roared down past the mouth of the small cave, high among the rocks. The small meadow outside, a patch of straggled scrub grass barely the size of a house, was invisible; the wall of rain reflected the light of the small campfire like a curtain.

Six horses snorted and stamped at the rear of the cave, nervous in the storm, and not liking much the scent of wet wolf; Graegduz wisely stayed well away from them, resting his head upon his paws up near the cave's mouth. Kheperu sat on the ground with his back to the fire, while Barra examined his wound.

She spread the lips of the wound with her fingers, and swabbed away the welling blood with a piece of dirty rag. The layer of fat that covered the Egyptian's body was thick here along his spine, yellow-white globules streaked with scarlet that greased Barra's exploring fingers. Kheperu shuddered and chewed the base of his thumb as her hand went in nearly to the knuckle.

She could feel the jump of muscle within, but no grating ends of bone, and there were no bubbles in the blood, which meant the blade had stopped short of his lung.

"I think you're all right," she told him. "If you don't come up with fever, this'll heal clean."

Kheperu's face was moist; whether this was sweat or rain was impossible to tell. "The salve's in my case—you know which pot," he said thinly. "Pack the wound with it before Leucas sews it up."

Barra nodded at Agaz, who squatted nearby, watching. "That wooden box over there with the packs—get me the red-and-gold faience pot that's in the top tray."

Agaz frowned darkly. "Excuse me?"

"Just do it, all right? I have to help him get his clothes and armor off."

With the look of a man biting back a cutting reply, Agaz pushed himself to his feet and went over the neatly ordered mound of their gear. Kheperu glanced over his shoulder, and a trace of his usual mockery leaked back into his voice. "Pretty," he murmured appreciatively. "You like him, don't you?"

"Don't start with me," she hissed sharply. "Get this stuff off."

"Oh come," he said. "I know you do. You're never this rude to men who don't warm your breechclout a bit."

"You think that's funny?" Barra muttered. She flicked the wound with her finger as though snapping at a fly; Kheperu flinched and smothered a squeal. "I can just as easily pack this wound with *salt*, you little bastard."

She glanced over at the prince, who thoughtfully scanned the topmost trays in Kheperu's voluminous trunk. "You want to know what I see, when I look at him? A ship."

"I thought you already *have* a ship."

"Ay, sort of. I've a quarter share of two, but that's goin' nowhere. They're not big enough for the kind of trade I'm seeing. With my share of the reward, I can build my own. A three-master—a hundred oars, go into the tin trade. And no more hauling raw ore from the Isle of the Mighty. That's for suckers. I can pick up refined copper in Cyprus and carry it up to the Isle—we can smelt our own tin, and I can make the run back down with finished bronze ingots. A single season's run'll pull enough profit to build another ship, and have some left over to play with. I'm gonna have a *fleet*, Kheperu. Not only merchantmen, but battleships. Let some fucking pirate come after my bronze—I'll slaughter his whole fucking crew and take *his* ship, too."

Kheperu chuckled wetly. "You have an impressive imagination,

Barra. I've always said so. In Egypt, we have a proverb about counting chickens when all you have is eggs."

"You'll see," she said solidly. "You'll see."

She breathed an inward sigh of relief that Kheperu seemed to be
buying her tale. She glanced at Agaz, where he crouched over Kheperu's trunk, sorting through the faience pots with the grim concentration that he seemed to bring to everything he did. He had a serious
mind, did Agaz, serious like her brother Llem, the High King; serious
like Kamades, the Myrmidon captain with whom she'd almost had a
fling back in Tyre. Her *sceon tiof* was conspicuously absent, when she
looked at him, and she thought it was just as well: she didn't *want* to
know him that way. She didn't want to see him as anything but a job.

He was a prince, after all, and she was nothing but a grubby mercenary with skinny legs and arms like a man's.

And that, too, was a thought unexpectedly bitter, more bitter than
she really wanted to think about; to discover why it stung so much
would take her down some road that she didn't want to walk right now.

She stood up and switched her language to Greek. "Leucas, come
on. You'd best sew him up now."

Despite his enormous hands, Leucas had a deft and gentle touch,
and wide experience with surgery; ten years of war on the plains below
the walls of Troy had taught him the rudiments, and he'd had plenty of
chances to develop his skill in the years since. Barra herself carried a
few scars that had been stitched by Leucas, including a knotted sword
cut that crossed the arc of her right shoulder, front to back. It showed
red-pale against her skin and now ached in the rain: this scar was still
young, taken only at the beginning of this now-ending winter, back in
Tyre.

"Leucas?"

He stood at the cave's mouth, staring thoughtfully out into the
storm; his hands curled into fists, tight enough that his knuckles
popped, then relaxed again.

He turned away from the rain, his face set in a thoughtful scowl,
but instead of coming over to Kheperu, he went to his gear and lifted
out the broad leather belt from which dangled a scimitar in a homemade leather scabbard. This sword was his most prized possession: it
had a blade of Hittite iron, and could cut through bronze armor like
hard cheese. He buckled on this belt, and said, "I don't think we have
time, Barra."

Agaz watched him do this, the pot of salve forgotten in his hand.
"What's the matter with him?"

"That's what I'm trying to find out, if you don't mind," Barra snapped in Canaanite, then switched to Greek again. "What's the matter with you?"

"It's this storm," he rumbled in a voice like an echo of the thunder outside. "I don't like it. It feels wrong."

"I've felt better myself," Kheperu began; Barra shut him up with a light slap on the top of his head.

"Wrong how?" Barra asked.

"I can't rightly say. I don't think we should take time to stitch you up, Kheperu. I think we should load the horses and go."

"In *this*?" Kheperu squawked, flapping his fingers at the sheet of rain that closed the cave's mouth. "You're mad!"

Leucas lifted his heavy shoulders and dropped them again in a silent shrug. It was not in his nature to argue; he merely stared at Barra, and waited.

Barra compressed her lips and squinted through Leucas, through the rain and the rock. She put one hand on the basalt head of the broadaxe that rode her hip, letting its cold solidity seep into her fingers.

This was often how she made decisions, standing still and holding her axe as though it were some sort of touchstone, a talisman that could bend her toward the right path. She didn't exactly think it over; there was no comparing of options and logical chains of probability. Instead, she spun within her mind visions of struggling over the rocks on foot through the rain, leading the horses, hearing their half-spooked neighs and Kheperu's continual undertone of whining complaints, feeling the inevitable scrapes and bruises and twisted ankles; then she set beside that vision an image of being discovered, and trapped here in this meadow, in this cave, by the pursuing Manassites.

She looked at Agaz. "These Habiru of yours—you think they could find us, up here?"

Agaz frowned. "I can't say; they tracked my men three leagues—at night—and found us in a cold camp. It's possible. I don't know how they found us then; they may be able to do the same again."

"All right," she said in Greek. "Pack them up. We're moving out."

Leucas nodded and set to work, loading the packs onto the nervous horses; Kheperu muttered in a bitter undertone of lunatic Akhaians and gullible Picts, and said through his tight-set teeth: "If my back goes septic from this, I swear that my shade will hound you all to early graves."

Barra snatched the pot of salve from Agaz's hand and smeared some of the evil-smelling paste into Kheperu's wound. She folded the dirty rag, the one she'd been using to wipe away the blood, and tucked it in through the rent in Kheperu's robes and armor, tying it into place with a piece of rope that she cinched tightly around his midsection.

"Get to work on the *tekat-neha*," she told him. "We'll need it. Leucas, go start pulling the rocks, I'll finish loading the horses."

Agaz watched all this with an expression of puzzlement that verged on awe. "You can't mean to go *out* in this . . . ! Have you any vaguest clue how *dangerous* these mountains are when Ba'al opens the sky?"

"Don't lecture me on storms, sunbeam. These aren't the only mountains in the world," Barra said as she tied down a saddlepack. She winced at a sudden overwhelming stench: the *tekat-neha*, the light-producing paste that Kheperu now compounded out of several ingredients and moistened with his spit, smelled of the gases that come from the stomach of a corpse decaying in a swamp in high summer. Warmed by the heat of his body, the *tekat-neha* threw a cold yellow-green glow like a paste made of fireflies, but many times brighter; it lit the cave like a blazing torch.

Kheperu smeared the paste on his own brow and cheeks, then did the same for Leucas, who took it unflinchingly; his nose had been broken so many times, by so many fists wrapped in leather or weighted with bronze, that it was packed with scar tissue; he had lost forever his sense of smell. Once fully painted, Leucas went out into the rain to unblock the narrow defile that was the only way out of the tiny meadow.

"Even with this foul stuff to light our way, the going will be near to impossible," Agaz said.

"On my *good* days," Barra told him, "I am not a patient woman. Help or shut up."

"I'm not going out in that," he insisted.

"You are. Leading a horse or tied to one: your choice."

"You," Agaz said in low and icy voice, "have an odd notion of gratitude, and a crass manner of addressing a man who's saved your life twice already tonight."

"*Crass?*" Barra snarled. She turned toward him, a dangerous vein beginning to bulge at her temple, and her hand was on the head of her broadaxe, and Kheperu suddenly appeared from somewhere and stepped smoothly between them, his face and hands shining like lamps with the *tekat-neha*.

"Excuse me," he said unctuously, in Phoenikian, "but I have none of your tongue. Most of you inland aristocrats have some Phoenikian, yes?"

"Some," Agaz admitted, his cold stare never shifting from Barra's hot one.

"Fine, then. Lovely. Let this be our common tongue, then; even that great dullard outside has a word or two. Well." He smiled, showing a ragged array of teeth that shaded toward light umber. "Since no one has been thoughtful enough to provide a proper introduction— barking names at each other hardly counts, does it?—I must present myself. Kheperu, late of Thebes, honored to place myself at your service, your highness. Forgive me for not offering the proper bow—my back, you understand. Now: I do not know what you two have been arguing about, but I can inform you of at least one general principle apiece. First, prince, you should know that no matter how irrational Barra may seem, she almost always knows what she's doing, and to insult her, defy her, or cross her in any way risks a swift and rather hideous death. She would regret it later, you understand—especially since we do not get paid unless we deliver you alive. She might even shed a tear . . . but right now, she is extremely cranky, and no one to be trifled with."

He turned to Barra, and held up a hand to forestall her angry snarl. "And you, madam, should realize that you cannot order him about as though he is a stableboy. He is a crown prince, and must be treated with a semblance of the respect to which he is accustomed. Furthermore," and here he switched to Greek, "if you don't behave yourself, I'll tell him you're only rude because he makes you wet."

"Say what you want, you son of a whore," Barra responded through her teeth in the same language. "I know where you sleep."

"Fine, then. Good," Kheperu said brightly. "We can all be friends."

Barra glared through Kheperu at the prince of Jebusi, and he returned her stare fiercely. They measured each other with their eyes until Barra forced herself to look away; she turned her gaze inward instead, onto an image of a hundred oarsmen sweeping in cadences, and the smell of salt on the west wind.

*He's a job,* she told herself. *He's just a job.*

Outside, the storm howled and screamed, and Leucas toiled grimly within it. The *tekat-neha*, chilled by the icy rain, cast barely enough light to illumine the rocks upon which he put his hands. A defile so narrow that the horses had to be led nose-to-tail was the only exit from the meadow; to keep the horses within while he and his partners had infiltrated the Manassite camp, Leucas had piled boulders more than head high to block it. They'd scrambled over these boulders on foot a few moments ago, but now several tons of rock must be shifted to clear the path for the horses.

When he'd built this barrier, Leucas had thought to have some few hours to clear it away; he'd planned to arise early, in the darkness of the next morning, and have it cleared in time to move out at dawn. Not one of these rocks he now took in his hands and tossed to one side weighed less than he did himself, and most weighed considerably more, yet his pace never slowed and his grim-set expression never altered, not even when his flesh tore and the blood from his hands washed thin upon the stones as he threw them. The flung stones cracked together like a tiny echo of the anticipatory snap of the lightning that battered nearby peaks.

Leucas had always loved storms, loved the slashing rain and the head-bursting roar of thunder. As a boy in Athens, he would slip away from his mother's side when she and his sisters would head for shelter against the storms that swept in across the Corinthian Peninsula; he'd race the storm to the outskirts of the city, to play and dance in open fields and tempt the thunderbolt of Zeus.

He'd never understood the fear that drove his family indoors—his mother tried to teach him that these storms spoke of Zeus' anger, but he could never believe this. He felt no anger in those storms, only an exuberance of power, a wild joy of release, not unlike what dancers and poets spoke of, when they performed at their very best; not unlike what he himself felt when he faced another man in battle, or in the ring.

If storms weren't dangerous, they wouldn't be any fun.

But this storm felt somehow different, darker, uglier; the play of a sullen boy when he's angry at his parents, a surly rack of stone upon stone, like pebbles tossed into an anthill; a petulant snit forgotten in a day or two—but not by the ants.

And there seemed to be something unexplainably *specific* about this storm, as though it were not only angry, but angry at *them*.

Now within the swirl of rain and shout of thunder, Leucas felt the hairs upon his head straighten and tingle; those upon his arms, visible in the light from the paste on his brows, stood straight out. He threw himself flat to the ground in the same instant that a thunderbolt speared between the peaks and struck the very stone toward which he'd reached.

The rock burst from within with a crack like the lightning that struck it, splinters of stone rattling around him like arrows, and an instant later he was on his feet again, shouting, *"Barra! Kheperu! Time to go! NOW!"* for on the slope above the cave's mouth danced a twisting, curling trail of lightning, a searing blue-white bolt brighter than the sun, forking and recombining as it skittered across the slope from rock to rock as though searching for a point upon which to anchor, and destruction followed everywhere it passed; each stone it touched detonated like one of Kheperu's bombs.

The hillside above the cave sagged like spun sugar in the noonday sun.

The lightning danced and spat through the thunder's roar.

The mountain itself twitched, and trembled, and began to collapse.

Within the cave, Barra squinted against the glare that lit the tiny meadow and heard the growing rattle of falling rocks. She could smell the harsh throat-rasping reek of the lightning, and she understood Leucas' urgency without further explanation. She exchanged only a glance with Kheperu; words were superfluous. He took the lead rope of the horse that bore his chest of magic and slapped the beast hard on its flank to get it going.

She screamed to be heard over the lightning's roar. "No more talking, Agaz! Grab a horse and get the fuck out!"

"You're mad!"

Barra snarled to herself and clasped her hands together as though to pray, then whirled and brought her doubled fists up against the point of the prince's chin with all the force she could muster. Barra was a small woman, and not overly strong, but she had grown up playing Eirish Stand Down with boys twice her size; her haymaker was a force to be reckoned with.

Agaz's eyes rolled up, and his knees buckled.

She caught him as he fell and threw him staggering out into the rain; half-stunned, he sprawled across the rock and struggled dazedly to rise.

Barra dashed back in, got behind the horses, and began screaming and slapping at them to drive them out of the cave.

One horse balked, and she shot a desperate glance outside—the rock now came down thick as the rain that brought it, and she turned to save herself . . . but this last horse was the one on which Leucas' armor rode, the fine-worked bronze he'd carried away from the Sack of Troy . . .

Kheperu and Leucas now both shouted for her to *leave the cursed horse and get out of there*, but she clenched her jaw and dragged at the horse's lead, snarling in Pictish, "Come along, y'filthy beast, move it, *move it . . .*"

Now a deeper rumble underscored the thunder, and the cave itself trembled and shook beneath her feet. She swung up onto the horse's back and kicked its flanks as hard as she could, screaming close behind its ear, and the horse leaped forward into the rushing landslide.

Huge stones now crashed around them: one bigger than Barra herself struck the horse on its hindquarters and snapped its leg and the horse went down, screaming a high keening wail of panic and pain. Barra sprang from its back as it fell, but another stone struck her a glancing blow to the back of the head that shot explosions of light across her vision and drained all the strength from her knees.

She staggered and would have fallen, but a grip that was itself like stone caught her arm and dragged her away from the rocks, toward the defile as the mountain shook around them and a million tons of stone and earth poured over the entrance to the cave, sealing it forever.

Her rescuer hauled her stumbling through the defile, away from the meadow.

"Leucas?" Barra said dizzily; she couldn't quite make her eyes focus, and she couldn't quite remember where they were or what they were doing here, but the face of the man who'd saved her came clear in the lightning that flashed anew, rain-plastered hair half-covering the eyes of the prince of Jebusi.

"That's three you owe me, Barra Coll Eigg Rhum," he said loudly, over the storm.

He looked back along the defile, to the meadow now buried under stone. "Although I think this last one, we can call even."

"Y'know, you were right," Barra said unsteadily. "Fucking storm *is* more dangerous than the damned Manassites . . ."

For a moment, she sagged in his arms, and when she looked up, his face was only inches from hers.

She touched his chin gently, her fingers brushing the swelling that had already started. "Sorry about your face, Agaz . . . you're going to have to learn not to argue with me."

His expression was unreadable. "Apparently so."

For Barra, the rest of that night was a staggering nightmare of half-panicked horses and swearing men; she was barely conscious for most of it, dragging herself along, clambering over slickened rocks and down sluicing slopes by sheer force of will. The effects of the blow to her head lessened even as the storm did; her head cleared when the last of the thunder blew itself out in the blackest hours of morning.

Dawn found the companions upon a ridge from which the peak above their cave could be seen. Leucas paused there for a long moment, staring back over the route they'd traveled, the rising sun painting half his face like blood.

Barra looked up at him from a hundred yards below, shaking her head: he was skylined like a beacon fire.

"I'll go after him," she said.

Kheperu shot a glance at Agaz, further downslope out of earshot; the prince had found a hunk of dried beef in one of the packs, and was gravely offering it to Graegduz from his hand.

Kheperu leaned close to Barra to say softly, "I do believe we're going to make it."

Barra scratched dried and flaking blood out of her hair at the back of her head; some of it might have been hers. "Did you ever doubt it?"

"Me? Don't be silly. I have perfect faith in you, madam. I was only thinking: to have a little success here, like this, might ease your nightmares a bit, hmm?"

She turned to look him full in the face, and danger flickered within her eyes. "What nightmares?"

"Oh come," he scoffed. "You wake every morning with a gasp, if not an actual scream; and that is if you haven't done so several times already during the night. This has been going on for weeks. You might remember that I'm not a fool."

"I don't know what you're talking about," she lied grimly, "and you should mind your own fucking business."

She had no intention of discussing these dreams that had slashed at her sleep for weeks, dreams filled with the scorch of roasting human flesh and the shrill despairing cries of murdered children. She fought these dreams in the only way she knew how: she bent her entire attention, the full force of her concentrated will, upon accomplishing the task she'd undertaken.

Once she had Agaz safely back in his home city, and the reward safely banked in Tyre, the hemp cords laid out on the yard-floor in the plan of her ship, *then* she'd worry about the fucking dreams.

"But it *is* my business," Kheperu said with a smug sniff. "I was a Scribe of the House of Life; like every seshperankh, I am fully trained in oneiromancy."

He glanced pointedly down at the young scars upon her wrists, scars left by the teeth of demon hounds in the back streets of Tyre.

"Are they still about Tyre? About Chrysios, and Simi-Ascalon's work-shop?"

She looked at the ground and clenched her teeth, and reminded her-self that nothing would be gained by breaking her partner's jaw.

"I'm gonna ask you one last time to mind your own business," she said flatly. "Don't make me persuade you with my fists."

"Hmpf. Well, let it be known: when you choose to talk of this, I will be a willing ear. All right?"

She looked into his eyes, and saw there honest concern that disarmed her anger. "Ay, all right. Ah . . . thanks, Kheperu." She turned swiftly and jogged up the ridge toward Leucas.

The Athenian boxer stood like an image graven in stone, his gaze fixed miles away, upon the peak that had shadowed their cave. Barra joined him there, and put her hand on his arm. "You'd best come down," she said. "They can see us from there."

Far-off black ants crawled the peaks around the meadow: Barra had no idea how the Habiru could have tracked them, but there they were.

Even if there had been no landslide, the Manassites would have found them there with the dawn.

She suppressed a shiver of apprehension. These Habiru tribesmen were vastly more dangerous than she'd expected, and she had a feel-ing she'd come to regret having crossed them.

"Come on, Leucas. Take no chances. Let's go."

"My armor," Leucas rumbled distantly. Barra needed no further explanation; the horse that bore Leucas' gear had been irretrievably buried.

"Pylaimenos gifted me with that armor in the third year of the war."

The war was the Siege of Troy; Pylaimenos was the Greek hero that Leucas had served as charioteer, had looked upon as a father. Leu-cas had borne that armor, burnished it, mended the rents of battle in it, cared for it as though it was itself his home, for thirteen years; it had been the one constant in his ever-changing life.

"I only want to remember this place," he murmured. "Someday I may return, and dig for it."

Barra felt his pain as though it were a knife in her own chest. A loss like this . . . it went beyond words. If the same had happened to her axe, it would have broken her heart.

"If we both live that long, Leucas," she said slowly, "I'll be here to help you. I swear it."

He turned to her, and some of the clouds cleared from his wintry eyes. "If it had to be you or the armor," he said, sliding his massive arm around her shoulders, "I prefer things this way. You know that, don't you?"

Her eyes grew hot. "Ay, sure." She struck his hand away. "Don't get sentimental, you'll make me blush. Now come on; if they could find that spot, they can sure as death track us here. It's gonna be a straight race to Beth Shean, and we'll need all the start we can get."

She picked her way downslope through the scrub trees and grass. After a moment, she heard Leucas' heavy tread behind her.

A few hundred yards further down, Kheperu and Agaz waited with the four remaining horses—they'd lost one more in the night to a broken ankle among the crags.

"Let's go," she told them, clapping her hands sharply. "Come on, what are you waiting for?"

Kheperu said something snide in a voice just too low for her to catch, but she ignored him. She looked at Agaz; he squinted back at her, the sun in his eyes. The knot on his chin was purpling nicely—and the image of her new ship began to fade in her mind, to submerge below the memory of his arms around her and the scent of his skin.

*He's just a job,* she told herself.

"You," she said, "owe me a thousand shekels."

# 2

# *Soldier of God*

**J**oshua ben Nun reclined in the morning sunshine upon the verandah of his modest home at the center of Timnath Serah, an amphora of strong wine beneath his hand and the sun warm upon his swollen joints. Toward him, down the long and dusty main street that ended at his door, rode a procession of men in priestly garb, most of them on horseback, but one man standing majestically in a chariot that shone like gold; from the sparkling fire that the sun struck on the gem-crusted breastpiece of their leader, he supposed that he was being favored with a visit from Eleazar himself.

He took a long pull straight from the amphora, and shifted his weight on the couch; the chill last night had settled into his bones, and he couldn't get comfortable.

The morning traffic in Timnath Serah ground to a halt to watch the procession; Hivite slaves set their water jugs on the ground, women tilling their gardens in preparation for spring planting set aside their hoes and looked up, men came to the edges of their rooftops and spoke together in low-voiced wonder.

Some years had passed since Eleazar ben Aaron, High Priest to Yahweh Sabaoth, El Shaddai, had last ridden through these streets; this was a sight to remember. From the plate of solid gold that rode his turban's brow, with its legend *Holy to the LORD*, to the glittering array of gems graven with the names of the Twelve Tribes fixed in rows to his breastpiece, every detail of his dress gave glory to the wealth and power of God.

An ill weight gathered in Joshua's belly as he watched them approach. There was something solemn, almost ceremonial, about their stately pace, and Eleazar wore his full-dress regalia: this was official business.

Eleazar wore the trappings of his office only when on an errand from God.

Joshua took another long draught from the amphora and swallowed hard.

He was still a big man, bullnecked, with a chest like a wine cask, short bowed legs beneath the torso of an ox. Now well beyond eighty, his face had gone to folds of sun-blackened leather, sagging low from his cheeks behind a thinnish slate grey beard. Age and drink had swollen the joints of his hands, and brought purple veins out across his painful knees, and brushed his eyes with a pantherine trace of yellow; his face had a rounded look, a lack of flat planes and sharp corners like an ancient statue in a desert, eroded but also refined, reduced to its essential core.

Any who looked upon him would have said that here was a man used hard in the service of his god; used up, even. Used beyond measure.

The god, however, would not agree. Did not agree.

Joshua knew that this was what brought Eleazar and his party to Timnath Serah. To be the Voice of God, that Joshua might once again hear the call.

A knot of children played the Jericho Game in the dust of the street nearby: five or six in the middle would link arms, while the rest ran around them, shouting. When they'd gone seven times around, they'd rush in and try to knock over the defenders, squealing and laughing and shoving each other's faces into the dirt. It was more of an excuse for wrestling and horseplay than an actual game, but now Joshua saw that some enterprising youngster had added a new element: each of the felled defenders was forced to stand up in a line, while one or more of the successful attackers got to punch him, once, in the stomach.

Even this was not so different from other rough games of young boys; each of the defenders, though, on taking the punch, took great relish in doubling over and falling to the ground, and kicking his heels while uttering a sort of bloodcurdling gurgle, a childish imitation of a death rattle.

Joshua felt as though he'd taken a blow himself, and for a moment his throat closed upon a memory of choking dust and the taste of blood on his lips, the stench of human hair burned on corpse pyres, and prisoners, row on row, kneeling in ranks while he and his men ranged among them with bloody swords in hand.

There were gut punches in plenty that day, and all that night, gut punches from fists that held three spans of razor-edged bronze.

He found himself on his feet, trembling, shaking a fist he did not remember raising. "Stop it! Stop that filthy game!" he roared.

Even now, past eighty, the voice that thundered from his bull neck could turn a charging horse, or weaken the knees of an infantry division; the boys in the street froze like startled rabbits.

As he felt their eyes upon him, wide and fearful, some of them starting to well with tears, his sudden fury was overwhelmed by bitter shame, shame that burned within his chest and brought tears to his own aged eyes.

"Go home," he told them. "All of you. Go home and pray."

They scattered like quail from a bush, and he watched them run. Where were the fathers of these boys? Where they should be, at home, in the fields? How many were in the camps in the hills, foolishly waiting, drinking with their friends and dreaming of loot from the rich cities of the coast?

Fools. Fools with fools to lead them.

"Merash! Gibel!" he barked. Merash, a timorous Hivite slave, peered through one of the small windows, and Joshua snapped instructions for him and Gibel his wife to make ready more wine, with bread and cheese and olives for the refreshment of their visitors.

When he turned back toward the street, the priests were reining in the horses. Joshua waited for no greeting, but stumped down from his verandah, the street's dust kicking up at his bare heels.

"What is it?" he said roughly. "It's Jerusalem, isn't it; He wants Jerusalem."

The lead priest, a broad-shouldered man of noble brow and flashing eye, slivers of grey brushed through his thick black beard that curled beautifully with glistening oil, urged his horse forward, and said proudly, "We bear the word of the Lord to his Anointed. Greetings from Eleazar ben Aaron, High Priest to Yahweh Sabaoth, El—"

"Phinehas?" Joshua said, squinting against the glare. "Is that you, boy? Has it been that long? How old are you, now?"

"I . . . Uncle, it's hardly proper—" he stammered, blushing— many years had passed since anyone had last dared speak to him like a child; it took a strong effort to recover his dignity. "The Cloud has lifted up from upon the Tabernacle, and this means—"

"Don't tell *me* what it means!" Joshua snapped. "You forget yourself, boy. I have stood in the Presence, and heard His Voice with my own ears. Can you say the same?"

His fierce glare seemed to demand an answer, and Phinehas' blush deepened toward scarlet.

"I, ah . . ."

"Did you not stand dry-shod between the banks of Jordan, while the Lord piled up its waters like a mountain, that I might lead Israel on to Jericho? What sign has the Lord given *you*, that you should lecture me?"

This bald old man standing barefoot in the street locked gazes with the richly dressed priest high above him on horseback. He held the eyes of the younger man as though he'd sunk his teeth into them; Phinehas dared not look away.

The moment stretched through embarrassment toward actual pain; and might have gone further had not Eleazar himself stepped down from his chariot and come to Joshua's side.

"Joshua, old friend, please excuse him. If he sins, it is only from youth and excess of zeal."

His voice spread like oil upon the old man's anger; Joshua shrugged, and looked away, and Phinehas ben Eleazar found himself once again able to breathe.

"Youth?" Joshua grumbled. "He's what, forty? I was barely half his age when I went out against the Amalekites . . ."

"It has been too many years since last we met," Eleazar said smoothly. "Are you well?"

Joshua snorted. "You mean, am I drunk?"

Every priest stiffened, scandalized; Phinehas actually gasped. Eleazar looked at them all with an expression of patient distaste. "Phinehas, take the horses to water." He waved a hand that sparkled with gems. "All of you. Go. I'll call for you when you're needed."

Eleazar ben Aaron was a small man, trim and graceful even in his sixties; his beautiful shining hair, still black, spilled from beneath his turban toward his shoulders. He had his father's gift of smooth speech, and an elegance of manner unexpected in a desert-born Israelite. Joshua had often thought, looking upon him, that Eleazar would have been better suited to Pharaoh's court at Per-Ramses than he was to his own palatial compound in Hebron.

*But we all,* Joshua thought, *come in and go out at His Word; Eleazar has never had any more choice than I have.*

They stood together for a moment and watched the younger men lead the horses down the street toward the wells.

"He's grown into a fine-looking man," Joshua offered gruffly, meaning Phinehas, Eleazar's eldest son.

"Mm," Eleazar murmured in distant agreement. "I often think that this was how Abraham must have looked, in the pride of his strength. Would have made a fine warrior; as a priest, however . . ."

"Surely he's as fine a priest as he could be."

Eleazar shrugged, and his white teeth flashed within a sudden smile. "He's become something of a fanatic. Astonishing, isn't it, that out of a craven weakling like my father and a spineless flatterer like myself, should come a pillar of righteousness like the patriarchs of old?"

"You say these things too easily," Joshua began, and Eleazar stopped him with a hand upon his arm.

"Only in jest," he said through his smile. "Only in jest. Can we go in? The sun becomes harsh upon all this finery."

Droplets of sweat had appeared across his brow; Joshua glanced at them, frowned, then nodded and led him inside.

The front sitting room of his house was cool and dark, and his slaves had already set up an array of fruits and cheeses on the low tables. Eleazar made himself comfortable on one of the couches, but Joshua paced, unmindful of the pains from his swollen knees.

"This isn't some trick of yours, is it?"

Eleazar shook his head. "No; the fires still burn, but the cloud lifted up. It ranges not to south or north, nor east or west, but hovers above the Tabernacle. It's God, unquestionably, and He waits for you."

"I was afraid of this. I've feared it for years."

"Come now, Joshua." His tone was lazy, almost mocking. "What is there to fear?"

"This is about Jerusalem," he said. "I've smelled it on the wind; He wants Jerusalem, and the blood of every Jebusite that lives there."

Eleazar shrugged and took a long sip of springwater. "You did promise it to the Benjamites . . ."

"If they want it, let them take it," he snapped. "They *have* the city; they have the land all around it, nothing can come in or go out without their leave. What more do they want?"

"It's not what *they* want that concerns us," Eleazar pointed out, rolling a significant glance toward the ceiling. "I'd be just as happy to go on taking the Jebusite tribute. Even divided among the tribes, it's a considerable amount . . ."

"This has something to do with Manasseh, and their captive prince," Joshua growled. "You have heard of this, I would guess?"

Eleazer nodded primly. "Oh, yes, little goes on among the Tribes that does not reach my ear eventually. Mm, perhaps the Benjamites do not hold the land so firmly, if this prince of Jerusalem could reach so far into the country of Manasseh. But it is of no matter; I am told that no ransom is forthcoming, and I seem to recall that this prince was to be executed—why, early this morning, if I'm not mistaken. You think there might be a connection?"

"I do not presume to know what may stir the anger of the Lord." Joshua shook his head, and turned his empty palms upward. "We've taken tribute from Jerusalem for *fifteen years*, ever since the Five Armies met us at Beth Horon. Why can't we go on as we have? Why can't He wait?"

"These are questions that are not for us to ask," Eleazar said. "I gave up asking why when He burned my brothers to death for using the wrong kind of incense."

Joshua responded only with a grim look; he had been there, had stood at the side of Moses when the charred bodies of Nadab and Abihu had been carried from the Tabernacle; he had heard the lamentation keens of Aaron their father and Elisheba who'd borne them.

But he couldn't let this go; it chewed at him sharply, and the words had to be said.

"Jerusalem is built on an *escarpment,*" Joshua said, an insistent note, almost a whine, stealing into his voice. "There's only one side you can come against in force, and even then you're attacking uphill. Have you ever seen those walls? Why does He think we didn't sack the city after Beth Horon? We could lose a hundred men for every one we kill . . ."

He lowered himself painfully onto a tiny wooden stool that creaked loudly in protest at his weight. "I've been a soldier for seventy years. I learned siegecraft in the service of Ramses the Great. If that city is held by determined defenders . . ."

"What? We can't take it?" Eleazar said with a lazily cynical smile. "Is the Lord's arm so short?"

All of the petulance that had gathered within Joshua's breast left him in a long sigh. He bowed his head in surrender.

"We can take it. But in the taking, thousands will die. *Tens* of thousands. I'm an old man, now; can't He wait only a few years? Let me be gathered to my ancestors without . . ."

His voice trailed away, but what he'd left unsaid was clear: *without these thousands of dead men, of widows and numberless orphans upon my head.*

Eleazar shrugged. "Perhaps it's not war He wants. Perhaps He has some other task for you."

Joshua shook his head without lifting it. "No. It is war. The smell of war has been upon the tribes for months; half the warriors of Ephraim are even now encamped in the hills, awaiting the command, and more men slip away to join them every day. And for what else does He use me? War, always war, as though I have nothing else to give Him."

"Well then, perhaps it's some other town. Perhaps it's Tyre, this time, or Gezer."

"Perhaps," he said slowly. "For that, at least, we can hope."

The road out from Timnath Serah led up at a steep angle. Joshua walked along it alone, staff in hand and traveling cloak whipping in a hot east wind, no sandals to protect his feet; he could walk barefoot on the business of the Lord, and no stone would dare to bruise him.

He'd left Merash and Gibel behind to gather his other slaves together and prepare them for a journey, to load his donkeys with provisions and shake the naphtha from his pavilion of desert brown. He'd sent the priests ahead on their horses—he insisted he could make the journey on foot. "I made the night march from Gilgal to Beth Horon. I can walk a good road in the broad day."

He needed the solitude. The thoughts he entertained on his walk might show somehow upon his face, and they were so private he barely dared to think them at all.

The Lord would be angry with him, and well he knew it.

He should have taken Jerusalem fifteen years ago, when he'd destroyed its army along with those of Hebron, Jarmuth, Lachish, and Eglon at the battle of Beth Horon Valley. The other cities he'd taken and put to the sword, as instructed by God, but when they'd come to Jerusalem . . .

*We were tired,* he told himself, *and weary of slaughter.* The walls were so high, and the men who stood upon them, few though they were, had no hope of life after a surrender; they would have fought to their last drop of blood. When the old king had offered tribute instead, he'd taken it gratefully; the Jebusite king of Jerusalem had given sovereignty to the Israelites in exchange for the lives of his people. Joshua had respected this exchange, and so matters had stood ever since.

Until today.

Joshua had taken up warcraft at the age of fourteen, when he was drafted into a conscript infantry battalion under Ramses the Great; he'd fought hand-to-hand against the Hittites at Qadesh. He was twenty, a blooded veteran and officer, when Yahweh raised up Moses to be a beacon for His people, and he had led his entire battalion in revolt to join with the Flight from Egypt.

He had stood at Moses' side when the Lord called the storm upon Pharaoh and his army at the Sea of Reeds; at twenty-two he had smashed the lines of the Amalekites when they'd threatened the nomad nation, and so scattered and destroyed them that it was later said the Lord Himself had blotted that warlike people utterly from the memory of men.

At Moses' side, he had stood in the Presence of the god, and heard His Voice; he was the great prophet's aide, and chief military advisor, and later, his most trusted general. It was said that when Joshua went forth before the Nation of Israel, no people could stand against them.

As the Lord had promised, "Ten of you shall chase a thousand."

So it came to pass, again and again; he smote the Amalekites and the Rephaites, the Midianites and the Perizites, killed men without number, sacked towns so thoroughly that no man could say where they once stood. In the service of Yahweh, he was invincible, and he asked nothing more of his life than that he be allowed to serve the god always in this way.

And always at his shoulder, like a proud father, had stood Moses. Joshua could still see the great man in his mind as clearly as though the twenty-odd years intervening had never passed; could still hear the prophet's voice. His whole life had been spent in Moses' shadow, at his elbow when Moses ate, by his side when Moses slept.

He had stood behind the great man, shaking and sweating his fear, when Moses had *argued with God.*

Moses had chastised even Him for His anger, and caused the Lord to turn aside His wrath. Moses, through incredible courage and sheer stubbornness, had saved the generations of Israel on that day, as he had countless times before, and Joshua, even now, felt humbled by this memory.

Tears that came from more than the desert wind filled Joshua's eyes as he walked in memory at the great man's side. No years intervening could dull the ache of this loss; Moses had been everything to him, the greatest man who'd ever lived, the only prophet to speak with Yahweh face-to-face, in plain language, as a friend.

The awe Joshua felt toward him had never lessened, had only grown as his understanding of what Moses had accomplished deepened.

But the awe mixed with bitterness; for he also remembered how the Lord had rewarded Moses' achievements: with a lonely death on Mount Nebo, and an unmarked grave in Moab. An unmarked grave far from the people who loved him.

Far from Joshua.

It was always thus, had always been, would always be. With one hand, the Lord gave gifts beyond measure, revealed His Glory like the sapphire floor He'd stood upon at Sinai, when the Elders of Israel dined in His Presence; with the other He ripped away gifts and life itself with the dispassionate fury of a farmer poisoning rats in his grain bin. The beneficence of Yahweh, and His vindictiveness, had only the limits He Himself set for them.

He remembered the bursting dawn of pride, when the Lord had named him as Moses' successor, the trembling joy, the humbling awe that had shaken his knees when Moses had brought him before the Elders of Israel and laid his hands upon him, to name him so in their presence.

He remembered the breath-catching reverence he'd felt when Moses had drawn him aside, had taken him within the prophet's pavilion, to impart to him the secret of his great wisdom, the wisdom that had kept him at the head of the nation for forty years.

This revelation had shaken him to the depths of his heart; it shook him still.

"Joshua, I love you as though you are my own son," Moses had said, "and I would have given any treasure, made any sacrifice, if this burden had not come upon you."

"Burden?" Joshua had said, puzzled. "Moses, I'm not the man you are, but with the Lord's help, I'm sure I can lead—"

"The Lord will *not* help you lead," Moses said heavily. "You will not lead. Yahweh Sabaoth leads this nation, and it is presumptuous of you to even suggest otherwise. He does not need you to *lead*."

"But—but, what then shall I do? What is it you have done, all these years?"

"I have fought, every day, to get these stubborn mules of Israelites to *obey the Law*." The bleak and desolate emptiness of his voice gave his words unanswerable authority. "It is their only hope of life, do you understand that?"

"But, but, but Moses—"

"You have seen, again and again you have seen, but you have never understood. It is *not your job* to lead the Children of Israel into the Promised Land, nor to defend them from their enemies. The Lord can do these things without your help."

Moses had paused, then, to take a deep breath and steady his nerves; even his illimitable courage was barely sufficient to bring the unspeakable to his lips.

"Your task is exactly this: *you must protect the people from God.*"

"Protect . . . ? From *God*? From the God of Abraham and Isaac? Moses, I don't understand!"

"Have you forgotten Paran? The plague in Moab? The rebellion of Korah? *Yahweh Sabaoth punishes transgression with death.* You must argue with Israel, and wheedle, beg, and command. Sometimes even slay. You must do *whatever is required* to keep the people upon the path that Yahweh sets for them. His Love for us is real, but so is His Vengeance. He is not patient, nor is He merciful; His Sword is ever poised above our heads. Don't think that you can argue with Him, as I have, and turn aside His Wrath—that effrontery has been reserved for me alone, and I shall suffer its reward soon enough. Every hope that Israel has, will ever have, rests upon you, Joshua ben Nun, and your ability to command obedience. Why else does God choose a soldier to put above his people?"

*And also,* Joshua now thought as he walked up the steep road, in an answer to a man more than twenty years dead, *because after a lifetime of soldiering, I should know how to take orders.*

He'd take the guilt upon himself, when he came before the Lord. It was the only way to protect the people. The transgression was his alone.

He knew well the command that God had given Moses, and had passed on to him: "Of the cities I have given you, you shall save alive nothing that breathes, but you shall utterly destroy them: the Hittites, and the Amorites, the Canaanites, and the Perizites, the Hivites, and the Jebusites."

And he had done so, followed the Lord's command, killed every living creature of Jericho, and Ai, and Beth-El, and Eglon, Lachish, Hebron, and Jarmuth, smaller cities, villages, and farmsteads until only the Children of Israel walked the high country of the Promised Land. The Hivites still existed, but as slaves, condemned by their own treachery to be hewers of wood and drawers of water until the end of time.

Of all the peoples that God had commanded him to destroy, only the Jebusites remained, cowering behind the walls of their fortress-city.

Joshua had foolishly taken the Lord's silence, these past fifteen years, as a sign that He had relented, that He would not waste His People in a bloody assault upon that impregnable town.

He should have known better.

He should have ordered the destruction of Jerusalem all those years ago, should have spent his exhausted army like the flies that die with the first frost, but he was weak, too frightened for the lives of the men he led, and now the Lord called, and he had no choice but to answer.

Let the punishment fall upon him, he prayed, and let the people be spared this war.

If only Moses were here with him now . . .

Moses would have found a way.

Even now, when Yahweh thundered in his ears, it was Moses' voice he heard.


He crested a hill and, waiting beside the road, stood Phinehas, one hand upon the halter of his horse.

"What . . ." Joshua panted, half-winded by the climb, "what are you doing here, boy?"

Phinehas held himself straight as a spear. "Waiting for you, Uncle."

Phinehas had called him uncle ever since he was able to speak. Eleazar his father had once called Joshua uncle as well; Joshua had stood guard outside the midwife's tent on the day Eleazar had issued from Elisheba's loins. For Eleazar the respectful habit had fallen by the wayside some time after he'd become High Priest. Phinehas, on the other hand . . . disrespect of any kind would stick in this one's throat and choke him.

"The Lord protects me," Joshua rasped roughly. "I have no need of you."

"I wouldn't presume to defend you, Uncle," he said stiffly. "I was only, I was hoping, I thought you might do me the honor of riding my horse, and let me walk at your side."

Joshua shook his head, leaning heavily on his staff . . . but the day was growing hot, after all, and the Tabernacle was yet some miles away . . .

Phinehas took Joshua's silence for disapproval, and stood even straighter. "And I'm sorry, sorry for the rudeness I showed this morning . . . I wasn't thinking . . ."

Joshua stumped over to him and studied his face; he certainly was a handsome man—Eleazar might be right, this could be how Abraham had looked—and he was tall and straight, nearly as tall as Joshua himself, and he was so earnest . . .

"It's I that should apologize," Joshua said slowly. "The rains weigh heavy on my old bones, and it makes me irritable." He sighed a slow breath out. "And if you'll give me a hand up, I'd be glad of the chance to ride a while."

Phinehas bent his back and laced his fingers together to help Joshua into the saddle.

"I could only hope to be at your side always, Uncle," he said. "You have seen the Lord. I could live a happy life merely in your shadow."

Joshua looked down on him, an unaccountable sting in his eyes. "Be careful what you ask for," he said.

The front of the Tabernacle stood in black shadow upon the hill-top. The cloud had descended upon it with Joshua's entering; with the sun lowering toward the western hills behind it, flames like tongues of lightning flickered through the cloud until it was hard to look at.

The cloud might have been a hole to another world: the eye could not hold it steady, nor fix on any one thing within it; instead it blurred and sharpened and blurred again so as to make the head ache and the stomach twist. Of all the priests that stood below, in their traditional camp to the east, only Eleazar and Phinehas dared look up to watch.

All around the hilltop, the camp of the Levites was spread by clans, the Gershonites, the Kohathites, and the Merarites. Twenty thousand men came and went here every day, a camp larger than most cities.

Now, no business was done, no wood was hewn nor water drawn. Every man sat in the door of his tent, or with his women, or held a child in his arms. Even the slaves were silent, waiting.

Waiting for Joshua to emerge, and give them the Word of God.

"Let it be war," Phinehas murmured. "Let it be proud Jerusalem. Let the Jebusite women scream and weep; let the Jebusite princes drown in blood."

Eleazar looked sidelong upon his son's enraptured face. "Why so bloodthirsty, Phinehas? You're not a warlike man."

Phinehas turned to his father, and his eyes shone. "I was twenty at Jericho, when the walls fell; twenty-five at Beth Horon, when the sun stood still and slaughtering stones fell from the sky—but more than fifteen years have passed, a whole new generation has come to man-hood, that has never seen the power of Yahweh with their own eyes. How may they fear the Lord, when they've never felt His lash? How may they love Him, when He has yet to smite the enemies that defy them, enemies that openly laugh their derision behind walls of stone?"

Eleazar only nodded; years of practice before the Mercy Seat had trained him to hide all emotion behind a mask of complacent faith.

"I have trained you well," he said, with deliberate ambiguity. He gestured toward the Tabernacle. "It seems your prayer is answered."

Even as he spoke, the cloud lifted up from the Tabernacle, high into the sky while lightning shimmered within it. As the cloud drifted southward, the door-curtain of the Tent of Meeting drew aside, and Joshua stepped forth upon the hilltop.

His age and the fatigue of his journey could be read upon his face, in the sag of his sun-blackened skin, but nowhere else: he stood erect, his back age-curved no longer, but straight and strong as a youth's, and a golden light seemed to shine from his face, and when he spoke his voice thundered across the camp with a sound of trumpets of brass.

Of the twenty thousand, not one had to strain to listen; those a spearcast away from the foot of the hill had to cover their ears with their hands, against the pain.

*"Hear me, Israel! The King of Jerusalem has refused to redeem his son from the Manassites! Instead, he has stolen his prince by night!"*

He paused to gather breath, and roared out with redoubled thunder:

*"ADONIZEDEK HAS SET HIS WILL AGAINST THE WILL OF GOD! LET EACH TRIBE SEND FORTH HIS WARRIORS, AND LET THE LEVITES CARRY THE TABERNACLE. YAHWEH SABAOTH, EL SHADDAI, GOD OF ABRAHAM AND ISAAC, MARCHES FORTH TO WAR!"*

*So*, Eleazar thought, unsurprised. He gave his son a smile that would have seemed shockingly cynical on the face of anyone other than the High Priest himself. "So," he murmured. "Happy now?"

Whatever answer Phinehas might have made was lost in the gathering storm of shouts and cries and howls of battle which seemed to arise from the very earth around them.

# 3

# *The Caravan*

**B**eth Shean was a dirty place, even as garrison cities go; loud and crude, filled with inns selling watered beer, public houses selling rotten food, and dilapidated brothels selling the dubious charms of whores too old and ugly for the pricier trade of the Coast Road. The entire town was devoted to serving the Egyptian troops that garrisoned here, and to entertaining the caravans that slid through like worms following a slime trail; it was the intersection of three major caravan routes.

Garrison cities are always despised by the troops forced to live there. Their diversions and amusements swiftly become stale, and the troops inevitably occupy their time with the kind of casual property destruction and general hooliganism that seem to be the common pastimes of garrison soldiers everywhere.

It becomes worse when the garrison city is also a caravan town. A caravan town has a kind of impermanence: though the city itself might be unimaginably old, very few people actually live out their lives there. Since everyone is moving on, sooner or later, no one can really be bothered to muck out the streets, or scrape the graffiti from the walls, or drag their chamber pots further than the nearest window. Even the innkeepers are a surly and hostile lot. They can afford to be; like everything else when the caravans come through, sleeping space is a seller's market.

The air was thick here, thick with brown haze that shrouded every building like winter fog. This haze was fine-ground sand and ashes compounded with the shit of men and donkeys, of the garbage of generations of travelers and inhabitants alike, desiccated by the harsh desert wind and pounded to powder by centuries of passing sandals, and hooves, and bronze-bound cart wheels. To Barra it had an Egyptian smell, of men dead a thousand years, and it packed her nose until the subtler scents of cooking and the perfumes of the whores, the sweat of the horses and the oil of men's weapons all stopped short— she knew they were there, but she couldn't scent them clearly; they were like half-heard voices within the general roar of a crowd.

The companions were all on foot, leading their exhausted horses; even Graegduz limped along with his nose nearly dragging. Barra kept a sharp eye out—bloodshot, sand-dry and purple-smeared as that eye might be. Everywhere she looked on these crowded streets, she saw knots of men sticking close to each other, and these knots stayed together.

The other traffic of hustling pedestrians and lazy cavalry passing at a walk, the carriages pulled by donkeys and the warhorse-drawn chariots, all broke around these little groups like a river breaks around rocks that are anchored to its bed. And the men that made up these knots always had elements of appearance or dress in common, like the blonde hair of Philistines, or the short-trimmed beards of Akhaians; and every man of them kept one hand free, and close upon the haft of a knife or hilt of a sword, or carried a spear openly at his side.

"Well, my, my, my," she muttered to herself, then caught Kheperu's eye. "Interesting, huh? You see it?"

"I see all of them," Kheperu said musingly, wiping feverish sweat away from his lips, "and yes, interesting is what I'd call it."

"What? See what?" Agaz said loudly.

"Shut up," Barra told him, "and keep your head down and your hood up." Before entering Beth Shean, Barra had pulled the hood of Agaz's burnoose up to shield his face, but she couldn't seem to convince him to keep it that way.

"I don't understand why we cannot go straight to the garrison. I am the prince of Jebusi, and we are loyal vassals to Egypt; they will protect us."

"If you say that too loud out here, you'll never *make* it to the bloody garrison," she said. She nodded toward a knot of blonde men, clean-shaven with hair hacked short. "See those guys? Philistine mercenaries. Those over there? Probably Hittite deserters—some of those whose spear blades are iron, and Hittites favor that curve to the blade. That little group with the kilts on would be Greek. This whole city is lousy with mercenaries; I don't think I've ever seen so many in one place before. And if any of those bastards gets a hint of who you are, they'll cut our throats, throw a bag over your head, and sell your royal butt back to the Manassites, *all right?*"

Agaz glared at her, but he didn't snap back, and he did pull his hood further up over his face. Barra turned away, shaking her head with disgust—at him, or at herself, she couldn't be sure.

This wasn't her usual style of job, and somehow she couldn't seem to find her balance. A straight kidnapping was simpler: when you're transporting a hostile prisoner, you just keep the bastard hog-tied and blindfolded, and only take his gag off when you feed him. She'd have been happier if Agaz had been the powder-and-perfume adolescent she'd been somehow expecting—an ambiguously male maiden-in-distress, she could have dismissed with tolerant contempt; this coldly courageous Jebusite warrior disturbed her in uncomfortable ways.

Their trek to Beth Shean had been a grueling two-day hump through the foothills with the shadow of Manasseh growing at their backs. These Habiru were no ordinary bandit tribesmen: they pursued, not with furious raging speed that would soon tire and leave them exhausted and empty, but with an inhuman dogged persistence, a disciplined implacability that had frightened Barra more than she cared to admit, even to herself. Whenever they topped a rise, she had looked back to find black knots of their pursuers always a little closer than they had been before.

No camps were made, no rest taken—the Habiru came on behind them like the steady march of the seasons. Constant motion held the companions' only hope of escape. Sleep was out of the question, and hot food was only a fond dream. They ate salt beef and hard biscuits from their packs as they rode, and later—when the horses began to give out—as they marched.

Kheperu had been swaying with fever before the first day went down to dusk, barely able to keep his saddle; through that night and all the next day, he had only kept riding with the support of his companions. They had rotated him through the exhausted horses, taking turns walking alongside to hold him in his seat—even Agaz, who set a seal upon his lips and never mentioned the smell.

She'd found herself staring at the prince, trying to summon the *sceon tiof*, trying to see inside him, to penetrate his icily handsome mystery despite her earlier determination not to do so. But the *sceon tiof* would not come, and she'd made herself give it up: he'd caught her staring one too many times, and now she couldn't meet his eyes without feeling a hot flush rise up her neck toward her cheeks.

Barra had read on his face his bleak conviction that he would never see his home again; she'd had no need of the *sceon tiof* for that. Every time he'd looked back to see the pursuing Manassites gaining ground, she had seen in his eyes a curious sort of grim satisfaction, as though he took a certain pleasure in contemplating the inevitability of his recapture and death. Yet he never faltered, never complained, never even suggested giving up.

And all through the dizzy infinity of that second night, when the headaches from the stone that had clipped her skull became blinding, he was at her side with unfailing support, to catch her whenever she stumbled.

Staggering with exhaustion, they had crept into Beth Shean bare minutes ahead of the warriors of Manasseh; the Habiru had been close enough that Barra could read the expressions on their faces.

The Manassites wouldn't come after them in force, she was sure of that—they still had that much respect for the Egyptian army that garrisoned this city. But scouts would follow, to search for them on these crowded filthy streets, and to buy news of them from whatever garrison officers they'd managed to corrupt. The rest of them would be outside the city, lying low in the surrounding hills, waiting for Agaz to come out.

She looked at him now, tucked within his hooded burnoose, and tried to see her ship of a hundred sweeps, tried to smell the salt air and feel the ocean spray, tried to hear the cries of gulls picking over the floating slops cast behind them. *That's all he is to me,* she told herself, but even inside her own head she could hear the overemphasis, the insistence so forced that it belied itself.

He was turning human to her, despite her best efforts to keep him safely tucked away as a job; against her will, she saw him as a man— and worse: a frighteningly attractive man.

"We, ah . . . we were talking about the mercenaries," she said in an offhand tone, a sort of half apology for her earlier snarl. "I get a little nervous around mercenaries. You can't trust 'em."

His eyebrows lifted, and that chilly smile of his quirked at the corners of his lips. "Oh?"

"Don't say it—it's a cheap irony, and I've heard it before," she told him. "Let's just say that most men get into this trade because they're too stupid and lazy to make a living as bandits and thieves." She looked around at the press of these stupid-and-lazy men; they were everywhere. "There's a damn bagful in this town, and no mistaking."

"Little mystery there," he said sourly. "They'll be on their way to Jebusi."

"Really?" Barra frowned. "Many of them?"

"All of them. My father is open-hiring all comers."

She whistled softly through her teeth. "We'd heard that, even back in Tyre, but I didn't really believe it. That's an expensive party he's throwing down there. He's planning to sack a couple neighbors?"

"No." Agaz pulled his lips back in a humorless grin. "None of our neighbors have any loot worth taking. The mercenaries are for defense."

"You can't defend a city with mercenaries; they won't stand a siege," Barra said, in a tone of explaining the obvious to a child. "When they turn, you have enemies on both sides of your walls. Your father's spending a lot of money to buy nothing but trouble."

His eyes went distant and hard. "My father . . . is taking bad advice, from bad advisors."

"I'll say."

They rounded a crook in the street and the high walls of the Egyptian garrison citadel came into view; a scarlet pennon painted with glyphs in yellow rode the position of honor on the flagpole, directly below the flag bearing the Uraeus symbol of the Pharaoh.

Barra nodded toward it. "That's the Governor's flag—we made it in time, he's still here. This shouldn't take more than an hour, but it's getting on toward sunset. Hey, wait for me in there." She pointed toward a shadowed doorway; the sharp stink of human urine from the wet sand in front of it proclaimed that a tavern lay within.

"Why can't we go on into the garrison?" Agaz said.

"Why do you have to question every goddamned thing I *say*?" This got her a sharp look from Leucas and a not-so-subtle kick in the shins from Kheperu; and the anger in her voice brought Graegduz up and bristling, his eyes on Agaz's face, a low rumbling growl starting in the back of his throat.

While Barra still struggled with her temper, Agaz said, "I'm sorry, Barra."

"What?"

"I'm sorry," he said openly. "I'm asking because, well, because you seem to know things that I don't. I'm only trying to understand."

"I, ah . . ." His apology disarmed her so completely that for a moment she had no words, and she felt that familiar hot flush creeping up the back of her neck. "No, *I'm* sorry. I'm, ah, a little short of sleep—and riding straight through from the camp hasn't helped any. Forgive my frayed temper."

Behind Agaz, Leucas gave her an approving nod, and Kheperu mouthed, *Much better,* and the flush spread over her entire face so that she had to turn away.

"Look, with the garrison it's like this. Beth Shean is still Manassite country—they hold this land for a day or two in every direction—and the only difference between the garrison troops and those mercenaries is that the troopers already *have* Manassite contacts; they'd know right where to deliver you, and they'd be able to get a better price. They have no reason to protect you, and every reason to give you up."

"Then—no, never mind, I don't want you to get angry again."

"No, no, no, it's all right, go ahead," she insisted tiredly.

"Then why did we come here at all?"

"I told you: I want to talk to the Governor."

"And he'll see you?" Agaz said, not skeptical so much as mildly astonished. "Tal Akhu-shabb will really have time for you?"

She became acutely aware of the burning scrape of her eyes when she blinked, and the fatigue-born headache that pounded at her temples. With great effort, she forced a smile.

"Just wait for me in that pub, all right? And for the love of the Mother, get a cask of beer and have somebody heat some food. I don't care what it is, so long as it's hot and there's a lot of it."

Lazy curls of soot trailed up from the untrimmed wicks of the pair of lamps on the table, spiraling up to stain the ceiling. The shutters were thrown wide, admitting the noise and dust of the street, but little light in the fading of the afternoon. On a couch across the table from Barra's, reclined Tal Akhu-shabb, the Governor of the Canaan District.

He was a grave and competent old warrior, though his fighting days were far behind him; the thin topknot that coiled on the back of his shaven head was white as frost, and his chest-length beard, bound stiffly with golden wire, was grey as old snow on a mountaintop; the creases of seventy smiling years of life scored his temples like the wounds of a knife.

Barra had been ushered instantly into his presence on the strength of her name alone. His first questions, even before his orderlies had finished setting the table with wine and dried winter fruit, had been of her adventures in rescuing Prince Agaz. He insisted on hearing every detail, and from time to time he would exclaim his regret that his age and responsibilities prevented him from joining her and Leucas and Kheperu on the road.

This was something of a private joke between them. They both knew that if boyhood were somehow miraculously restored to him, he'd spend the second youth as he had the first: serving the Pharaoh as a soldier.

They never spoke of how they had met, at a feast on the Tyrian estate of Meremptah-Sifti, the disgraced grandson of Ramses the Great. They never mentioned any of what had passed between them, in those days at Tyre. In those days, as autumn had waned toward the Turning of the Sun, Barra had saved the Governor's life, and his honor, and more than either of these: his command.

She would never remind Tal Akhu-shabb of the debt he owed her; she had seen into his heart with the *sceon tiof*, and she knew the old soldier, with his rock-hard code of honor, could spend the rest of his life repaying and never call it even.

She set the winebowl down on the table before her with a certain firm finality.

"So, I'm thinking," she said, "that we might hitch a ride with the Canaan Division, since you're swinging through Jebusi on your way back to Gezer."

The Governor had become thoughtful toward the end of her tale, and now looked actively troubled. "I'm not sure that we are," he said slowly. He swung his legs down to the floor and sat up, resting his elbows upon his knees. "You've said the Manassites are preparing for war. Do you have any idea what their target might be?"

She shrugged, and he went on grimly, "We have a policy of non-engagement with the Habiru. If they're as stirred up as you say, I might have to take the Canaan Division up the east trail, come to the Coast Road through Megiddo—"

"Policy of nonengagement?" Barra said. "What's that mean? They shake a spear at you, and you pack up your tents and run away?"

"Roughly, yes." He spread his hands. "You know what things are like up here. The Canaan Division itself is barely above half strength, and even with a full complement there's not much I can do against Habiru."

"Excuse me for a stupid question, but aren't these still Egyptian lands?"

He snorted an unfriendly laugh. "Yes, they are. But only as long as the Habiru let us keep them."

He rose and paced to the window, his hands folded behind him, and stared out into the darkening street. "I can't get replacements from home this year. There's no recruiting anymore, and you can't put conscripts on open frontier unless you have a war on. All our strength is spent holding down the Kushite insurgency into Nubia—the rebellion is bleeding us like a pig for dinner. Ramses believes we can count on the Hittites to hold the north."

"The *Hittites*?" Barra said incredulously. "They can't hold their own lands, let alone Egypt's! Doesn't the Pharaoh know that the Phrygian tribes are cutting them to shit?"

"He knows," the Governor murmured, "but he doesn't believe how bad it is. He thinks my letters exaggerate; he calls me an old woman who jumps at shadows. Ramses is an old man, blood of gods in his veins or not. In his mind, the world is still the bright and happy place it was when he was young; Hattiland is the Northern Power, and he is the Southern, and they divide the world between them."

He lowered his head and shook it sadly. "All I can do, here, is try to keep the roads open for the caravans, and the only way I can do that is by nonengagement."

"I don't get it."

He turned back to her, and smiled, but the smile was sad and pained. "We never go out against any of the bandit tribes in battle. They are still afraid of us; so far, they think that the only reason their raids succeed is that their bands are small, and fast-moving, and we can't catch them. They try to keep their raids inexpensive enough that we won't bother with them. The fact is, we don't dare. It would take only one pitched battle for them to learn that Egyptian regulars die just as easily as any other men—and they can outnumber us ten to one at any point on the map. Once the tribes learn how weak we really are, even the ghost of our control is gone. They'll take everything. It'll be a hundred years before another caravan goes safely through this land."

"So you just give it up? You surrender the entire countryside to whoever can put together thirty men with spears?"

"Barra, you don't understand. They already *have* the land. Egypt takes the long view: in another century, *they'll* be the kings and princes, and Egypt will deal with them as such. As bandit chiefs, they're already beyond our control."

Barra lifted her winebowl and drained it. She wiped her mouth on the back of her hand and said, "Well, shit."

"That about sums it up," the Governor agreed.

"What can you do for me?"

He frowned a moment in thought. "There's a caravan heading

south along the high road that left this morning, medium-sized or a bit less—a thousand asses, five or six hundred men, but most of them are mercenaries heading for Jebusi like yourself, and heavily armed; no one will be bothering this particular train, I believe. I could send you an escort—say, a cavalry company—as far as its tail end. Put you all in new galabiyehs, so no scouts can recognize you from a distance, you should be safe enough. Start early tomorrow, and you might catch them in their night camp by sundown."

"What'll we tell your officer? I'm really not comfortable with anyone knowing who Agaz is."

Tal Akhu-shabb smiled. "We'll tell him you're carrying a message—and it will be the truth. The Jebusi garrison commander might not understand the realities of his situation. Here, take this—" He went to a drawer and withdrew a cylinder seal carved in onyx, strung on a leather thong. "Present this, and he'll know you come from me. Tell him at the first sign of hostile action, he's to pull out and march straight to Gezer."

"Very brave," Barra muttered.

The Governor shrugged expressively. "Who rules Jebusi is no concern of Egypt's, so long as the caravans get through. The most important thing is to avoid an incident that would require a response from us."

Barra held the seal up before her eyes, examined the figures—soldiers, bearing shields and the trumpet-faced Egyptian war-axes of Ramses' infantry. She clenched it within her fist. "You old fox. Here I come asking for a favor, and you get one from me."

"Now, Barra—" the Governor began.

"Humiliating, is what it is, to be used to run an errand." She let her temper flow a little, warming up into a fine tirade. "I can't believe you'd even ask me to do such a menial task; it's *insulting* me, you are, and after I've sat at your table and y'got me half-drunk on your wine, which is too bloodyfucking strong, by the way, and you only fed it to me so you could take advantage of my good nature—"

"There's a hundred debens in it for you," the Governor said, with a broad smile.

Barra blinked. "Well, all right, then." With a wistful sigh, she let her temper subside again. "Oh, and listen, before I go . . ."

She reached into her pack and pulled out a black-rubbed pencase made from a bull's thighbone, smooth and shiny from much use, except for one bright gouge on it where it had once blocked a pirate's sword and saved Barra's life.

She untied the thong that held it shut, and pulled out some rolled sheets of expensive, high-quality Egyptian papyrus. She unrolled one flat on the table, moistened her ink with a drop of wine, and chewed the end of a reed brush into shape before scribbling a few words in Phoenikian at the bottom of the sheet. She rolled the sheets up together again and gave them to the Governor.

"You'll see to it that those get to Tyre, to Peliarchus the shipmaster, won't you?"

"Yes, of course," the Governor said warmly. "To your sons, back in far-off Albion, yes?"

"Ay . . ." Barra frowned. "How'd you know about my sons?"

"Peliarchus let it slip one night over a bit too much of my bloody-fucking strong wine," he said with a smile. "I see you're not the only one here being used to deliver mail."

She responded only with her most charming smile, which was fairly charming indeed. He chuckled. "What was that last little note?"

"Oh," she said carelessly, "I haven't yet had the time to write out the tale for them. I just wanted to let them know that I survived rescuing the prince of Jebusi. It might be a while before I can send my next pack of letters, and I don't want them to worry."

The attack came without warning, in the late afternoon with a hot gritty wind blowing in from the Syrian Desert, only two days' march south of Beth Shean.

The caravan stretched a dusty half mile along the broad watershed road, two hundred wagons with their drovers and private guards, a thousand asses to draw the wagons, four-hundred-odd mercenaries ranging from well-drilled Hittite veterans to ragged knots of barrel-chested, axe-armed Picts from Barra's homeland, the Isle of the Mighty, on the far edge of the world. Kheperu had nudged her while one of these, a hulking black-bearded man with brooding eyes, walked up the line toward a water wagon.

"He looked like you," Kheperu said with a smile, "except for his hair."

"Ay," Barra said shortly, watching the Pict's departing back from the corner of her eye. "He's one of my people—he could be one of my brothers."

Kheperu's brow went up. "Really?"

"My da, he's got bastards all over the Isle. I don't know them all. This guy probably isn't—most of my brothers have the hair, like my father's. And mine." She nodded toward a group of men even bigger than the Picts, enormous ginger-haired men gone to freckles in the desert sun. "Those fellas over there, they're from the New Tribes—a couple of them might be brothers of mine, too. They've got the size— the only man in the Isles stronger than my da is my brother Llem."

Kheperu favored her with one of those indulgent smiles that made her want to slap him. "This is the brother who's supposed to be the emperor, or something?"

"High King," Barra corrected him automatically. She knew he was baiting her—he'd never believed a word of anything she'd told him of her past and her family—but she couldn't stop herself. "Technically, I'm a princess of the Old Tribes *and* of the New—what you'd call the Picts and the Kelts; my da's a Gael."

"You're a half-breed?"

"I'm half everything," she muttered. "Half-Pict, half-Gael, half-crazy and a half-wit to be telling you this. All I've got is half brothers and half sisters—I'm the only child of my ma that was gotten by my da, although he keeps on trying every time he visits, or so I hear."

"Why is it you never go among them?" Kheperu asked. There was a curiously wistful and serious note in his voice, now, that made Barra look at him sharply. He gazed at the group of Picts, but seemed to be watching something within his own head. "I've seen you when they pass. You turn your face away, and never speak."

She shook her head. How could she explain? Though she knew none of these men, any number of them might know her, at least by reputation. She'd returned to her home four times since leaving there fifteen years before, the last two times as supercargo on one of the two ships she part-owned with her Tyrian foster-family, the *Skye Swift* and *Langdale's Pride*.

She'd come when she was flush with coin and jewels, fresh from negotiating tin contracts at the Knossian Trade Fair. She'd bought houses for her boys, and land, and horses and armor and weapons, gifts for her brothers and sisters, casks of Egyptian beer for her father; she had played at being a conquering hero of limitless wealth. How could she face these men who carried in their skulls the memories of her extravagance, and her boasting tales of her exploits, when she walked along in this caravan owning barely more than the clothes she walked in?

She couldn't face the knowing looks that would sneak into their eyes, couldn't face the squirming imaginings that would haunt her, as her traitor thoughts whispered the jokes that they would be telling about her behind her back.

She couldn't keep a spasm of painful self-hatred off her face, but Kheperu's thoughts were elsewhere, and he didn't seem to notice.

Finally she could only shrug, and say, "It's none of your business. You wouldn't understand."

"Oh, but perhaps I would," Kheperu murmured, his fever-sweat streaking trails through the dust on his brow. "Perhaps I can understand how homesickness can become overwhelming."

Suddenly she understood that his question wasn't about her, at all. She clapped him on the back—well above his wound—and said, "Cheer up. At least you've got money."

He looked at her, and the clouds broke from his eyes. He jingled the purse of shekels at his waist, and grinned. "Oh, yes," he said. "Silver is a cure for many ills, is it not?" He turned away, to once again happily chaff one of the drovers.

Barra watched the Pict return from the water wagon, still keeping her face half-averted. Her heart ached to speak with him, for just a moment, just to hear one unfamiliar voice speak her native tongue, but she couldn't; the sharp sting of imagined humiliation stopped her cold.

She supposed it was childish—but she'd been a child when she'd sailed from home on Peliarchus' ship, only fourteen, brokenhearted and weeping for her lost innocence, calling upon the gods to witness her vow of exile. She had sworn then that she would only return as a hero returns, and that no one would ever know her pain.

Something in Kheperu's voice, in his distant eyes, had opened a wound of homesickness within her that would not heal. Perhaps it was because most of her memories of the green hills of home were memories that belonged to a girl who no longer lived, except somewhere in the murky depths of her memory. *Maybe,* she thought, *what I really want is to be that happy little girl.*

She walked beside Agaz, keeping an eye on him. The prince elected to spend the day goading a crazed Assyrian who led a string of pack-laden camels.

The Assyrian—who apparently didn't share the common wisdom that camels can't be domesticated, or was too crazy to care—ran back and forth and up and down his line of camels, thwacking them into order with a knout of braided leather, dodging their sinuous attempts to latch into his shoulder with their evil-looking ragged yellow teeth, all the while insisting in a high-pitched voice that "camels are the ass of the future! Can't you fools *see* it? If anyone would actually give them a try . . . !"

Barra watched him with the pity she reserved for madmen, but Agaz seemed truly interested, questioning the fellow about his train-

ing methods, their habits, and their diets, patiently enduring the Assyrian's endless screeching diatribes.

"Is he actually *encouraging* that man?" Leucas said, massaging
his throbbing forehead and trying to uncross his eyes. "That *voice* . . .
Barra, tell him to stop. Make him stop. If you don't make him stop,
I'm going to kill him."

Last night, after they'd come up to the camp and signed on with
the caravan master, Leucas had managed to find a handful of Argive
veterans of Troy huddled around their own campfire, and he'd spent
the evening with them, downing gallons of half-watered wine and bellowing uproarious songs of fighting and wenching and sailing upon
the open sea—these seeming to be the three main occupations of
Greeks everywhere. Today, he walked along leaning heavily upon the
shoulder of his horse for support, and occasionally groaning in pain
when the sun peered out around the clouds. On arising, and feeling the
depth of fur that had grown upon his tongue, he had begged Kheperu
for a cup of willow-bark tea, but the Egyptian had stoutly refused.
"You brought it upon yourself," he'd said piously. "My medicines
must be reserved for emergencies."

"It'll *be* an emergency if I don't get that willow bark," Leucas
said. "I'll *make* it an emergency."

"Pish. In your state, you can't run fast enough to catch me, and if
you did, you can't see straight enough to hit me."

Eventually Kheperu took pity on him, but even the strongest infusion he could prepare had little effect; Leucas was doomed to suffer.

Barra had no comfort to offer him, either. "I can't make Agaz stop,
Leucas. Nobody can make him stop. Killing him might be our only
chance—and then we don't get paid."

Leucas only sank his head onto his horse's shoulder and covered
his eyes with his hands.

Agaz and his questions . . .

All the previous night, she and Graegduz had stuck close to Agaz's
side, shadowing him on his restless wandering through the various
groups that made up the caravan's camp; he was, after all, roughly the
sum total of her fortune. He would pause at the campfire of any random group that had some little thing he hadn't seen before: a different
hitch on the wagon, or an unusual ass harness, an oddly plated piece
of armor, or any thing at all. If the possessor of this curio had any
Canaanite or Phoenikian, Agaz would interrogate him at length on the
item's construction and use; if, as sometimes happened, they had no
common speech, he'd turn to Barra with respectful requests to trans-

late. Barra spoke five languages well and could get along in three or four more; when mercenary work was not to be found, she'd supported herself as a translator and scribe.

Watching all this, she had gradually realized that his questions to her had never reflected disrespect. Instead, Agaz was possessed of an omnivorous curiosity, a constantly pricking lust to learn. Getting the answers to his endless questions never really seemed to please him, though; he would only nod gravely, and ask another.

This curiosity of his seemed to bite at him like sand flies in the spring, driving him from one man to the next without any satisfaction, or rest. Finally she dragged him bodily away; his Jebusite accent was too pronounced, and here and there a mercenary gave him a sort of considering look that meant he'd been listening to the rumors.

The hottest rumor around the campfires was of the miraculous escape of the prince of Jebusi out of the fist of Manasseh; the tribal leaders had, apparently, not only made no secret of it, but put an enormous price on his head. The amount they had supposedly offered varied wildly in these rumors, from a mere thousand silver shekels to the prince's own weight in solid gold.

She would take no further chances: she installed Agaz on a bedroll with herself to one side and Graegduz to the other, and told him to go to sleep.

And later, in the dark hours of dawn, when she had lurched awake from evil dreams, with the stench of burning corpse-flesh in her nostrils, gasping and biting back a scream, she found him lying awake on his bedroll at her side, staring up at the brilliant desert stars.

"Nightmare?" he'd said softly.

She leaned forward and breathed deeply until she could speak. "Ahh, something I ate."

"What was it about?"

For a moment, she considered telling him—but no, she couldn't, she couldn't talk about her nightmares like a frightened child crawling into bed with her mother. She only shrugged, laced her fingers behind her head, and stared at the stars.

"What is it with you?" she'd asked at length. "Questions, questions, questions, about nothing in particular. You never stop."

His smile was cold, and a little sad. "About *everything* in particular. I'm interested in everything."

"Why?" she said. "What good does it do you?"

He shrugged. "None at all, I suppose. It reminds me that the world is very large, and I am very small."

"That's a cheerful thought."

"I get many such cheerful thoughts. In the end, Barra, we all go to the Muck. Phht. Nothing left. All we know, all we see, all we feel, our loves, our hates . . . phht. It seems a cruel fate that there is so much of the world I can never know, so many things I can never feel or see; but El has decreed it so. Even Ba'al Stormgod bowed before the Mouth."

Barra shook her head and clapped him on the shoulder, chuckling. "And here I am, thinkin' that I've seen too *much*. Y'know what your problem is? A lot of bloody time on your hands and nothing to do with it; you're a brooder, is what you are. Come travel with me for a year or two. Hang your life out on a thin cord once in a while: it cheers you right up."

"I wish I could, Barra. I truly wish I could," he said with surprising wistfulness. "I'd give anything to go with you . . ."

She gave him a sharp stare, her throat thickening suddenly, swelling with the sudden thump of her heart. Had she heard him correctly? She could see him only in profile, now, as he gazed at the heavens above; had he glanced at her as he said that? Had there been a shy truth surfacing within his starlit eyes?

For one stretching moment she didn't trust herself to speak.

Then, she said carefully, "You mean that?"

"It's . . . only a dream, I suppose," he murmured with a sigh. "Run away. Live free . . ."

And that wild midnight hope had turned to ashes in her mouth. He hadn't been thinking about *her* at all, and she should be old enough to be past this kind of foolishness. Thank the Blessed Mother that the night was too dark for him to see her blush.

She said, more bitterly than she'd intended, "Nothing's *free*, sunbeam. You want to run away, do it after we get the money, all right?"

After that, she rolled over and refused to speak further, but it was a long time before she fell back to sleep, and as they neared the end of this day's march, she felt that restless night dragging at her feet.

Kheperu, on the other hand, was practically dancing along the trail. His earlier fit of melancholy seemed to have burned away in the sun like morning dew. He laughed and joked with one of the drovers; this drover, less cheerful, continued to exclaim loudly over Kheperu's exceptional luck with the dice. Leucas had stitched his spear cut back in Beth Shean, and had pronounced that it was healing cleanly; Kheperu had celebrated his presumed recovery by spending a night dicing with ten or fifteen of the drovers.

For refreshments during the game, he'd purchased several bulging wineskins and passed them liberally among his opponents, who never quite noticed that although he pressed the skin to his lips and gulped as lustily as any of them, the skin was always just as full when he passed it on as it had been when he accepted it. Several did remark on an unusual aftertaste, a not-unpleasant woody tang that none of them could identify; by the time the game had broken up, those poor sods had seen whatever number on the dice that Kheperu told them they saw. He could have told one of them he was the fellow's wife, and gotten a kiss and a pinch on the rear for it—and, for that matter, pleasures of a more intimate nature, if he chose.

In fact, pleasures of a more intimate nature had been exactly his intention—one of the drovers was a pretty young man of perhaps only seventeen—when Barra'd interrupted. She didn't mind so much him cheating at dice, but at this she drew the line; she had a son nearly that age. If he wanted to share that boy's charms, he'd have to try again when the boy was sober.

Still, this afternoon Kheperu walked in the train carrying a purse newly bulging with silver shekels, and despite the almost-but-not-quite accusations of this ill-natured drover, seemed very happy indeed.

As the sun dipped toward the western hills, the Argive mercenaries—who had been dropping back slowly all day, most of them in a condition similar to that of Leucas—saw him behind them and stopped to wait for him, a dozen half-drunk men with spears resting on their shoulders, armor bundled and hung across their backs with leather straps, swaying a bit unsteadily beside the train. They hailed him loudly as he met them, and there was much friendly chaffing in intentionally piercing tones to split their assorted hangover-swollen skulls.

Between the Argives, the screeching Assyrian, and the complaining drover, for a single sunlit moment the babble of conflicting voices was overwhelming.

"For the love of the bloody Mother," Barra said wonderingly, "I can't hear myself fucking think! I wish *just one* of you assholes would *shut up!*"

As though in answer, she heard a dull crack like a punch landing on someone's chin, and when she looked back, blood spurted from the scarlet porridge that had been the complaining drover's face; the teeth that had sprayed from his shattered mouth still bounced across the road like a handful of pebbles tossed by a child.

For a single astonished instant, Barra couldn't comprehend what had happened to the man, but then the donkeys screamed as more slingstones hissed against their flanks with bone-breaking force, and men up and down the line were slapped to the ground as though hit with hammers; one of the Argive mercenaries flipped into the air, the back of his skull pulped and spraying blood in a wide arc, and Barra screamed "Get down!" as she sprang at Agaz, tackling him around the waist and driving him into the rocks of the road.

It wasn't a battle; it was a swift and brutal slaughter that churned the road into a muck of blood and shit.

Barra stayed down, doing her best to cover Agaz with her body. The screams of horses and dying men tore raggedly at her ears; horses reared and kicked and bolted, some of them fell, crushing cowering men beneath them; donkeys brayed in panic and tore their yokes and dragged bronze-bound cart wheels over arms and legs and necks, breaking bones and smashing skulls.

The air sizzled with flying stone, and some arrows as well. She couldn't see Leucas or Kheperu anywhere. A man fell across her legs and she spun like a cat, pulling his jittering body over to cover both her and Agaz like a shield. Not far away Kheperu's horse was down, kicking out the last of its life with an arrow through the skull, and that was the best cover she could see: the wagons were being reduced to kindling, as the slamming impact of the slingstones broke their sidewalls to splinters.

"This way!" she hissed, and rolled the dead man onto Agaz. "And bring that corpse with you!"

She snaked across the road into the shadow of the dying horse's back; Agaz came after her, dragging the dead man with one hand, and between these two shields they hid, feeling dull thumps through the bodies that protected them as more and still more stones flew, and arrows thrummed into the twitching corpse-flesh.

*Three days,* Barra thought bitterly, now that she had a chance to think. *Three more fucking days, we would have been in Jebusi, counting our money.* That was her first thought; her next was *Where's Graeg?*

At the first lull in the staccato drumbeats of the attack, she risked a glance above the horse's back, peering out around the ironbound trunk still lashed to its side. The grey wolf was nowhere to be seen; she could only hope he'd sprinted for cover when he saw her go down.

On both sides of the road, men in hooded cloaks of desert brown and stone grey boiled up, seemingly from out of the earth itself, as they scrambled up from dried watercourses and out of low scrub, ululating a high, piercing wail that chilled her blood. Every man of them was armed, but few with real sword or spear; most brandished scythes and hoes, some carried threshing flails, some had battle-axes that seemed to be improvised by sharpening the edges of a horse barn's mucking shovel.

"*Shit,*" she hissed. "Shit shit shitshitshit. All right, *fuck.*" She lay back down beside Agaz and dipped her hands in the pool of blood that was still spreading beneath them, from the horse. She slopped handfuls of it across Agaz's face and smeared in into his hair.

"What—? Cut it out!"

"Shut up," she snapped in a harsh whisper. "You're *dead,* understand? Dead until I say otherwise. Don't move, and I might be able to get you out of this."

"But—"

"*Lie down!* And if any gods favor you, pray for a miracle."

She forced his face down into the bloody muck and pulled the corpse half-over him, in hopes it might conceal the fact that this particular dead man still breathed. With only a second or two left, she slipped her broadaxe out of its scabbard and jammed it as far under Kheperu's dead horse as it would go.

Then a shadow fell across her; she squinted past the hands that she held up, empty in surrender, at the sun-shadowed Habiru raider that towered over her.

"Don't hurt me," she said thickly, a sob in her voice. "Everybody's dead, you killed everyone . . . don't hurt me . . ."

The raider took her wrist and hauled her roughly to her feet. "Lookit what I got here. Hey, Adab, you ever see one like this?"

All around her, prisoners were being kicked to their feet and disarmed by knots of Habiru. The Assyrian sobbed on his knees, his hands buried in the fur of the lead camel in his string. It was down, and the others honked and brayed nervously, nudging the body.

Some of the mercenaries tried to fight, even now: Barra could only watch grimly as one of the Argives swung a wild blade at a raider, only to be seized from behind by another. The first raider hacked into him with a hand scythe, its blade hooking into his chest; then a couple more joined in, one taking the sword from his opening fist, chopping at his arms and his legs until he fell into the mud, groaning thinly, steam rising like breath from his gaping wounds.

Barra turned away. It'd take the Argive a few minutes to bleed to death, and there was nothing to be done.

She was not in the habit of prayer. When in trouble, she'd depend on her wits and her axe and leave the gods to take care of themselves, but now she took the advice she'd given to Agaz.

*Mother, we could really use a hand here, if you have one to spare.*

Two more raiders joined the one that held her. The first pulled the flint throwing axe from behind her belt and turned it over in his hands, staring. "Stone? A stone axe? You're kidding me, right?"

She ducked her head, sniveling and trying to look helpless. " 'S just a camp hatchet—holds an edge better than bronze . . ."

"Lookit the arms on her—bet she can swing it, too. Shit, she looks like a man."

"Empty," one of them said, touching the smallsword scabbard that had held the haft of her broadaxe. "Where's the sword for this?"

"Maybe she ain't got one," the first raider said with a laugh. "I mean, look at her—I betcha she's never had a sword in her scabbard."

"I gotta sword for her—"

"Ahh, she'd snap you off at the root . . ."

While their speculations went on, Barra surreptitiously looked around. Graegduz was still nowhere in sight, but not far away Kheperu sat uncomfortably on his hands—he still wore his robes, and no doubt the armor beneath them; none of the Habiru would be very interested in frisking him, and she didn't blame them.

He caught her eye and mouthed, *Agaz?*

She flicked a glance toward her feet, to point out where he lay motionless under the corpse, then dropped an eyelid in a slow half wink.

Kheperu mouthed in reply, *Whenever you're ready.*

She gave her head a tiny shake. She saw not even the faintest chance of escape.

Now, on her feet, she could see up and down the caravan train, where Kheperu, from the ground, could not. There were *thousands* of Habiru: everywhere she turned they crowded the road like flies on a corpse. They outnumbered the mercenaries fifteen, perhaps twenty to one, and the deadly accuracy of their slings made fleeing on foot an impossibility. And these were their lands, their home territory.

It couldn't be done.

She flicked a glance down at Agaz. She should have stayed down there, played dead right beside him. Maybe she still could have lived to collect that reward. But instead, she'd stood up, and she couldn't deny the truth: she'd done it to protect him.

Somehow his life had become more important than her money.

Within her mind, her hundred-sweep merchantman seemed to pull out into the fog-shrouded sea, leaving her bereft and empty, standing lonely on a deserted shore.

She thought, *I need a new line of work.*

Now Leucas arose from within the splintered wreckage of a wagon; he was ringed by six of the Habiru, all of whom now had spears they'd lifted from dead mercenaries. Blood trailed down his face from a cut above his hairline, and he looked shaky on his feet; he must have taken a glancing blow from a slingstone.

In his hand was the iron scimitar, and Barra's heart froze within her.

He'd die, he'd go down fighting, he'd never surrender, no matter what the odds. He swayed unsteadily, blinking, trying to focus his eyes on the men around him, and the blade twitched in his hand, and Barra couldn't take it anymore.

"Leucas! Give it up!" she shrilled in Greek. "Surrender and live!"          .

"Stop that jabber." One of the Habiru cuffed her on the back of the head hard enough to send her stumbling over Agaz and the corpse— Agaz let out a thin involuntary grunt as her knee came down on his kidney.

Leucas' head had snapped up at her voice, and the man behind him reversed his spear and slammed the butt of it into the joining of Leucas' head and neck. The Athenian dropped to his knees, his sword falling from limp fingers. His eyes glazed and crossed, but he clung to consciousness, slowly and uncertainly putting his empty hands on the top of his head.

Barra gradually picked herself back up, suddenly aware of goose-flesh on her exposed arms and legs so thick it was almost painful, as though a blast of astonishing cold had descended from some ice-capped mountaintop.

Her first thought was that she'd been wounded, and hadn't noticed; it had happened before that she'd come through a battle and only felt her wounds when the bitter chill of shock set in to shake her limbs like marsh reeds in a gale.

But around her, the Habiru now drew their cloaks of desert camouflage tighter around their shoulders, and spoke to each other in low tones of the sudden unseasonal freeze that seemed to be setting in with the sunset, and the thickening mist that the chill pulled up from the ground.

All but one of them, that is, one smart-looking fellow who peered suspiciously down at Agaz, frowning. He must have heard that grunt . . .

"Hey," Barra said softly to him—she had to distract the bastard, or Agaz would be as dead as he pretended. "How about lending me that cloak of yours? It's freezing out here."

As she asked, she arched her back, just a little, to show him what the sudden cold had done to the nipples behind her soft leather tunic. Now, still holding her back arched just that much, she lowered her chin and looked at him through her lashes. "I'd be really, really grateful . . ."

He forgot all about Agaz for a moment as his eyes raked her from head to foot and back again, then he licked his lips, apparently deciding that not all of her looked like a man.

He showed her teeth worse than Kheperu's when he smiled, a mouth full of greyish stumps. "Room enough in this cloak for two, if you're that cold," he said.

"Piss off," said another. "I saw her first."

"You can have afters," said the first. "But I think we got a live one, down here."

"Yeah?" said the second. He nudged Agaz with his toe. "You alive?"

The freezing mist swirled more thickly around them, and Barra dug under the horse's back with her toe; she found the broadaxe and hooked her foot in the joining of head and haft.

The raider kicked Agaz harder. "Hey! You faking, or are you out?"

Mist rose up like smoke from the earth; now the distant ends of the train had vanished behind its thickening shroud, which swirled ever whiter by the second.

She glanced at Kheperu, her eyebrows up.

Half-hidden by the fog, he gave her a nod.

Another glance at Leucas—he was watching her, clear-eyed now, while the grinning spearmen examined his iron scimitar and exclaimed over its edge and heft. An iron sword of that quality was worth more than its weight in gold.

Deep grey billows of fog rolled across the road.

*Just give me one chance,* Barra prayed. *Just one.*

"Oh, stick the bastard and shut up about it, will you?" the Habiru with bad teeth said. "They'll all be dead soon enough anyway. No prisoners till we settle Jerusalem, remember?"

The second Habiru adjusted his grip on a stolen spear—then a yell and string of curses stole his attention. One of the Habiru had strayed too close to an angry camel, and the beast had latched its teeth into the man's shoulder.

As he wrenched free, he swung a captured sword at the camel's bowed neck, and with a wild scream the Assyrian launched himself at the man who wanted to harm one of his precious pets, clutched him and carried him to the ground. They rolled over and over in the muck, kicking and clawing at each other.

For one instant, all eyes turned that way.

Barra thought, *Fair enough.*

With a graceful swing of her leg, she flipped her broadaxe spinning into the air.

The motion caught the eye of the Habiru who stood over Agaz, and his mouth opened for a surprised shout as the axe reached the top of its arc and began to fall again. Barra snatched it from the air two-handed and let its momentum carry it around in a vicious whistling underhand swing that drove its edge into the Habiru's crotch, chopping him wide open and turning his shout of alarm into a breathless grunt. His guts spilled down his thighs as he dropped gasping to his knees.

The raider with bad teeth sucked air for a shout of his own, and tried to scramble back for spear room, but Agaz's hand snaked out and grabbed his ankle, and he went down hard. Barra sprang over Agaz and split the raider's skull like firewood.

"Get that spear and cover my back," she snapped, and he scrambled to his feet at her side.

Spear in hand, Agaz looked around dimly, peering into the mist that shrouded the road, now so thick that men a spearcast away were barely even shapes in the fog. "Where'd this fog come from?"

Barra didn't have a chance to explain, because the Habiru were everywhere. All around them, men struggled with each other, locked together by their mortal need to pull free the weapons that they each had their hands on.

The mist was growing so thick that now she couldn't tell which were Habiru and which were mercenary until she was close enough to be in danger; she and Agaz took to charging them indiscriminately, short sharp howling attacks that broke off instantly when the nerve of the indistinct men gave way and they turned back to vanish into the mist.

Even as Barra had first moved to kick her axe, Leucas had come to his feet. Between him and her and Kheperu, there was no need for signals.

Gathered around to admire the sword, the raiders didn't see Leucas rise behind them, didn't know he was there until he seized one of them with his left hand and struck the man with a right cross that shattered his cheekbone and snapped his neck. Now they shouted their alarm and backpedaled away from the towering boxer, except for the man who held the scimitar. With a terrified shriek he launched himself at Leucas, swinging the sword at his head.

Leucas, a patiently contemptuous expression on his face, blocked the swing almost casually by lifting the corpse one-handed into its path. The blade hacked down through the corpse's shoulder and caught in its ribs, and when Leucas dropped the body, the sword was wrenched from the raider's hand.

Leucas grinned at him and beckoned. "Come on, little man. Come and die."

The Habiru didn't know the words, but the meaning was unmistakable. He bolted like a frightened rabbit.

The other raiders nearby, armed with spears, exchanged nervous glances as Leucas reached down and pulled the scimitar free with an effortless twist.

He lifted the blade and looked at them. "Well?"

One of them said something in their own tongue, and another said something else, and he didn't need the language to understand, because he knew the tone. Facing an armed man in hand-to-hand is an entirely different proposition from firing rocks at him from a bowshot away—they were nerving each other up to attack, assuring each other that they would all charge together, because none of them wanted to be the one caught with his butt hanging out, alone within the reach of Leucas' sword.

He saved them the trouble: he sprang at them with a howl and chopped through the spear haft of one of the flinching raiders. Another thrust at him and he stepped inside the spear's reach; he was behind the man's guard and a swift pivot sent his blade around a flat quarter circle that hacked through the raider's arm and into his chest.

The hand on the severed arm clutched the spear shaft spasmodically, dangling free. The raider, wide-eyed, made disbelieving huffing sounds before collapsing at Leucas' feet.

Kheperu had been anticipating this chance from the moment the mist had begun to rise. Now he suddenly clutched at the hem of the nearest raider's burnoose, shrieking, "Please, oh, *please* don't kill me, my wife, I have five children . . ."

The Habiru snarled at him and struck at his head with a spear butt . . . and the two substances that Kheperu had smeared upon his burnoose—one from each hand—were now brought into contact when Kheperu bunched the hem together, and flame burst from the man's clothing, snarling upward to claw at the oil in his beard and hair.

The raider's scream was deeply satisfying as he danced and spun away, slapping at himself, and he made a vastly superior distraction to the crazy Assyrian and his wrestling opponent.

Other nearby Habiru rushed at him to help him as the flames consumed his clothes, and Kheperu casually hooked the ankle of one of them with his own. The man went down hard, stunned on the ground, and before he could rise Kheperu snatched the dagger from the man's belt and buried it in the nape of his neck.

He took the spear that lay beside him and yanked off the raider's burnoose, scrambling away on hands and knees through the confusion—and looked up to find himself face-to-knees with Barra and Agaz.

"So far, so good," he said cheerily. "Where's Leucas?"

The fog was now so thick that the companions had to peer through the white-shrouded gloom to see each other, even though they were close enough to touch. Shouts and screams and gurgles of dying men told them that they weren't the only captives who'd seized the chance to fight; the clash of weapons sounded from every side, but grew more distant now, as though the fog itself isolated them, held them apart from the battle that raged around them.

"Leucas!" Barra shouted sharply, and only seconds later his massive shape materialized out of the fog, bloody scimitar in hand.

"These Habiru don't much care for close combat," he said gravely. "I only killed two."

"No armor," Barra pointed out. "With no armor, I'm not so in love with close combat myself."

Agaz swung his spear slowly, watching intently how the mist swirled around it like smoke from a fire of damp wood. "I've never seen anything like this fog," he said. "Not here."

"Me has," Leucas said slowly, struggling with the Phoenikian. "At Troy; Menelaos and Aeneas man to man fought . . ." He gave up and switched to Greek. "Barra, tell him. Aphrodite wrapped Aeneas in a mist like this one, to save him from the Red King, and carried him away to safety."

"Don't start that with me," Barra told him hotly. She didn't want to have anything to do with the idea that the hand of a god had raised this fog; she had a sudden stinging fear that she'd somehow placed herself in someone's debt. "This is just the shitcake *weather*."

"Barra, I was there."

"Shut up. Has anyone seen Graeg?"

Kheperu said, "He ran for the hills when the horses started to scream."

"Great," Barra said, staring into the impenetrable fog. "Which way are the fucking hills?" She drew a deep breath and shouted at the very top of her lungs, in Pictish, *"Sing out!"*

Far away, high up and barely audible over the continuing battle, she heard the howl of a wolf. She turned her face toward it, and looked up, for the fog must have been very shallow upon the earth; the waxing moon had risen from the eastern hills, and it seemed to hover over the spot from which the howl must have come.

*All right,* she thought. *I can take a hint.*

A wounded raider staggered close, mistaking them for friends; Leucas dispatched him with a dispassionate blow that opened his skull, and stared solemnly down at the dying man. "Fog or no fog, we have to go. Now."

"My *case*," Kheperu said with a gasp more like panic than Barra'd ever heard from him. "We can't leave my case!"

"You're in luck," she told him. "Your horse is dead right over here. Leucas, you'll carry his trunk for him, won't you?"

He shrugged. "Of course."

For a moment Barra thought of her own horse with a keen pain, her horse that right now could be anywhere. Bundled on that horse had been her armor of bronze, patched and mended so many times it had looked like a goatherd's cook pot; her blanks of good Langdale flint, from which she'd planned to replace the throwing axes she had lost; and the hundred debens the Governor had advanced her to deliver his message.

But there was another, sharper sting: the loss of her pencase.

She'd carried that pencase for more than ten years; once it had saved her life. More than that, that pencase had represented her link with her sons, back on the Isle of the Mighty. Every pen she'd ever used to write them a letter had ridden in that case. She could hold that case in her hands and almost feel her boys beside her.

Gone, all gone. Not only could she not retrieve them, she didn't even have the time to properly mourn their loss.

"This has turned into a fucking expensive little expedition," she muttered, but in her native Pictish: this was a thought for herself and for the Mother, not for her companions.

"All right," she said in Phoenikian, raising her voice to be heard over the shouts and confusion that still rang out around them. "We're heading for the mountains to the east. If anyone gets separated, just hide; I'll find you." She knew their scents as well as she knew Graeg's; there'd be no trouble finding them in a wilderness.

"Take the burnooses," Kheperu added. "Perfect camouflage in this blasted desert."

"One question," Agaz said, then added with exaggerated courtesy, "if I may . . ."

"What?"

He lifted his hands, and fog swirled across them. "How do we know which way to go?"

"That's easy," she said, pointing at the sky. "Follow the moon."

# 4

# *Prophecy*

**T**hrough the marching Tribes of Israel, the eremite danced.

His sun-blistered scalp showed angry red under wisps of hair white as fair-weather clouds. One eye reflected a milky blindness as though it were a tarn iced over in winter, and the blood that seeped from his toothless gums mixed with spit and trailed down his chin, underlining in scarlet a smile as happily serene as that of a mother who holds her newborn child to her breast.

The tatters that he wore had once been noble robes, now stained with urine and the bloody saliva that dripped from the point of his chin, the cloth painted grey-brown with rot and desert sand wherever they were not black with moisture. His feet were bare and battered; the graceless cavorting of his dance had brought them down hard on stones that had cut them and sticks that had twisted them. Both ankles swelled and darkened as though with sprain, but he danced on, heedless, leaving behind him footprints of blood and murmuring knots of bemused Israelites.

This was his song:

> *I am the fire of the western sea*
> *I am the child of the earth*
> *I sing to the sun but the moon sings to me*
> *my mother was born at my birth*

This he sang in endless, obsessive repetition, with no melody or rhythm, sometimes whispered, sometimes screamed, fast or slow, sweetly or harshly.

The only time he said anything else was when someone among the marching Tribes was unwise enough to touch him, to try to get his attention long enough to speak to him directly. Then he'd fly into a rage, shrieking obscenities in a piercing screech, and strike out suddenly with bony fists. There was no strength in his deadstick arms, but the blaze in his one good eye could be alarming, and his screech could be outright painful.

"I sing to *God*, motherfucker! You reeking dogshit bastard pigslop sack of *fucking guts*! Bring me to God! *I'll sing! I'll sing to Him,* you cock-swallowing turdhole!"

Word of him spread through the Tribes that were assembled, through Manasseh and Naphthali, through Ephraim and Asher, and soon it reached the ear of Joshua himself.

Joshua marched in his accustomed place, at the head of the vanguard of the army of God. At his back were the Levites, the three clans each bearing their appointed share of the Tabernacle and its furnishings. Behind the Tabernacle came the vast Host of Israel, innumerably huge, and it grew every day as warriors and their supporters streamed in from the surrounding countryside to join with it. It had always been thus: before the Host goes the Tabernacle.

Before the Tabernacle goes Joshua ben Nun.

The part of Joshua that was still the Egypt-trained soldier snorted sometimes in contempt at what he saw when he viewed his forces. This was less an army than a migration, a vast mass of humanity a mile across and many miles long, organized only roughly according to tribe and clan. For every fighting man behind him, there marched also a handful of slaves and women to serve each man, horses and donkeys to bear the gear of war and the tents that would shelter the warriors, sheep for mutton and goats for milk, and camp followers of every description. Perhaps only a quarter, or even less, of those that marched with the army would ever touch a weapon—but even that quarter would be formidable. The Host of Israel numbered over a hundred thousand already.

By the time they encamped at the walls of Jerusalem, the Host would be several times larger.

They'd been on the road for some days now, moving slowly to allow the Host time to gather. Already some of the high spirits that had accompanied Joshua's declaration of war were beginning to grind away; instead, much of the talk around the campfires at night was of the height and thickness of Jerusalem's walls.

It was Phinehas who brought news of the eremite. He told Joshua of the madman's song, and that the men among whom he passed had begun to whisper that this was prophecy, and that the eremite had come from God to warn them of doom.

"Uncle, you should have this man put out of the Host," Phinehas was heard to say. "At the very least, you should forbid him to prophesy."

It was reported by the priests who overheard, that Joshua seemed to take the news with an impossible mix of fury and wild hope, as though he could not decide whether to strike Phinehas or embrace him. After a long struggle within himself, they say, he murmured only this reply: "I once used the same words to Moses, many, many years ago, before you were born, Phinehas. At the door of his tent, while we camped at Kibroth-hattaavah, before the plague. Do you know what he told me? He said, 'I wish all Israel were prophets, and that the Lord would put His Spirit upon them.' I think Moses was tired that day, Phinehas, tired all the way into his bones; for today, I am tired and I have the same wish. This man will be allowed to speak—but I will go to him, and listen for myself."

So it came to pass in the waning of the day, that the eremite danced his way into the presence of Joshua ben Nun.

The Elders of Israel stood around the perimeter of a broad circle like a dancing ring, and watched the eremite caper within.

The entire army had ground to a halt, and now men crowded around to see what Joshua would do, those in the rear using the whispers of men before them as their eyes.

Joshua stood with arms folded across his barrel chest, and tried to ignore the grinding pain from his swollen knees. Every day, he'd marched in the vanguard, refusing sedan chair, horse, or chariot. He meant to subdue the grumbling he knew would come from his people on this long march by sheer force of will: if a man who approached ninety years of life can make this march, no younger man has cause to complain.

But the days had been unseasonably warm, and the earth hard as stone; now all that kept him on his feet was a stark refusal of weakness. He would not allow himself to falter, supporting himself with determination and wine, the wine that he drank to bleed pain from his joints and leach evil dreams from his sleep.

Before coming to this gathering, Eleazar had pressed upon him an infusion of one of his many powders, one that he said would give Joshua the strength and alertness of a young man again, if only for the afternoon. Joshua had no doubt that this infusion would work as Eleazar had described, but he refused nonetheless. He had used such powders in the past, years and years ago, and knew too well the transformation they could work upon the very spirit that God had placed within his breast, making him aggressive, and irritable, and rashly inclined to sudden violence.

Now, though, as the wine he'd drunk grew upon him, pulled at his limbs and dragged his eyelids closed, he regretted that steadfast refusal. Now, in the hot, slanting sunlight of late afternoon, he struggled grimly with himself, to fix his mind on the eremite and his words. If there was any chance this man might be a prophet, Joshua would not allow himself to miss it; his determination to uphold the Will of God, no matter what the cost or where it might lead him, snapped at his ears like a drover's whip.

If Yahweh chose this man to speak through, it would behoove all Israel to listen.

But the eremite seemed to have no words beyond his senseless song. He wailed and screeched and danced his aimless whirl, arms unfolding like blighted flowers and waving spastically in caricature of a dancer's grace.

Joshua struggled with mounting revulsion as he watched, a revulsion that piled upon his fatigue and bent his shoulders like a stone upon his back.

*Is that me?* he thought. *I look upon him, and the Elders watch me, and do we see the same thing?*

It was known to all that prophets lose concern for their dress and their body when first they hear the thunder of the Voice; that the Voice in their ears drives them away from home and family and all the affairs that occupy men who are not so blessed. Their duty to God overtakes all other concerns.

*And some men say I am a prophet. Am I? Yahweh does not speak to me in visions, but in commands. The Voice never offers me a riddle—that playful gift He reserves for men like this eremite. Yahweh cloaks the future from me as he does from any other man, and yet—*

And yet his service to God had purged from his existence every semblance of the things that made the lives of other men worth living. No wife had ever come in to him; no child had ever called him father. Even now, in the weakness of his age, when he had finally been given a house and a town to call home, his household consisted only of Hivite slaves.

Every man in Israel held him in too much reverence ever to sit upon his porch in Timnath Serah and share a bowl of wine in the evening to watch the stars come out. Of what would they speak?

The men of Israel feared too much the judgment of a man who'd stood in the Presence of God, ever to truly call him friend.

He might as well *be* a prophet; he had been given nothing in this life to love except Moses, long dead, and nothing to fear except God.

"He's mad," Eleazar muttered at Joshua's side. "The sun has boiled his brain, Joshua. There is no prophecy here."

"I am not so sure."

The High Priest drew the cuff of his robe across the pale sweat upon his brow, and examined the darkening patch on his sleeve with an expression of mild distaste. "It is no great feat to babble a rhyme," he said reasonably. "Surely you don't believe such gibberish needs God for a poet . . ."

"Prophecy," Joshua replied, the weight of years in God's service on every word, "is in the ears that hear. This song troubles me."

Eleazar's fine-drawn eyebrows lifted mock-quizzically. "Tell me one thing which does *not* trouble you, old friend. I know what is in your mind: you are searching for an excuse to call off this war and send these men home."

"Excuse?" Joshua rumbled dangerously. Storm clouds gathered within his eyes as he looked down upon the smaller man. "No. I pray only that God will relent—and that He makes His Will known clearly to us, that we may walk His True Path."

Eleazar pursed his lips together as though he could barely restrain a snort.

"I am told that this man claims to sing to God; not of God, nor for Him, but *to* Him. Yet this song clearly does not glorify the Lord . . ." Joshua's voice trailed away. "I wonder . . ."

Eleazar laid a warm hand upon Joshua's arm. "We can't stand here muttering to each other," he said softly. "Look at them; everyone watches us."

This was true; as minutes passed, more and more eyes of the Elders and the host behind them turned from the eremite onto their leaders. Joshua ignored them, holding his gaze fixedly upon this man who might be a prophet.

Eleazar went on, "The longer we do nothing, the weaker we appear. Joshua, it was you who taught me that the greatest sin of a general is *uncertainty*. We must do something . . . to stand here dithering drains morale from the host like beer through a bunghole. You have to make them think you know what you're doing."

"The Law says, when a man prophesies, and his words come to pass, then those words are from God. If they do not come to pass, he is to be stoned for a false prophet."

Eleazar shrugged eloquently. "And if no one can say *what it is* the prophet claims will happen—?"

"Then he must be made to declare himself," Joshua rasped, and strode into the ring.

His implacable presence silenced the entire assembly. Even the eremite, finding his voice suddenly alone, bit his lips between his toothless gums, his eyes rolling; his song was reduced to a faint humming through his nose. The only other sounds were the shush of the breeze and the chirp of a far-off quail.

"Joshua, *don't*—" Eleazar exclaimed behind him. "This madman might be dangerous—!"

"Joshua?" said the eremite, flecks of foam trailing down from the corners of his mouth. *"Joshua?"* His voice became a scream of rage. *"JOSHUAAAAA!"* The name became a howl that seemed to tear his throat, and the eremite sprang at him, slavering, fist upraised with a dull flash of knife within it.

Joshua stood like a stone, his arms folded as the eremite struck him full upon the breast.

In an instant, Phinehas was beside him with a shout of rage and a knotted fist. He struck the eremite only once, clubbing him on the back of his neck, and the eremite sprawled upon the earth, staining it with his bloody spit. Phinehas raised his foot to stomp upon the eremite's throat, but he was restrained by Joshua's hand upon his arm.

Joshua said, "I told you before, Phinehas. The Lord defends me. I have no need of you for that."

Phinehas' jaw dropped and his mouth opened within his glistening beard. Joshua was unhurt, unmarked except for a smear of dirt on his dust-streaked robe. For a moment, Phinehas could only blink in astonishment as he looked from Joshua's breast to the eremite who squirmed wetly on the earth.

Beside the eremite lay what he'd taken for a knife: the husk of a marsh reed, dried to a light brown and brittle as a crust of stale bread.

He bent his knee and lifted the broken husk with both hands, reverently as though offering it to God, his face alight with sudden awe.

"A miracle," he whispered, then repeated himself in a clarion shout. *"A miracle!"*

He lifted up the husk for all the assembly to see. "You have *seen*!

Your eyes bear witness to the power of God! The knife that would have slain the Lord's Anointed becomes only a broken reed! So shall every weapon raised against Irsael! Cry out your praise, a joyful noise to the Ear of the Lord!"

For a moment, Joshua's breath was stolen by the mighty shout that arose from the assembly. He squeezed shut his eyes against a bitter pang that stabbed far more deeply than the eremite's husk.

*If only it could be so. Please, my God, let it be so,* he prayed within himself, knowing full well that Yahweh would never grant this prayer.

"And this false prophet," Phinehas went on when the shouting receded, "has condemned himself by this cowardly attack! Let him be taken outside the Host and stoned!"

Men rushed forward from all sides; they seized the eremite and dragged him to his feet. His eyes spun madly, and his head lolled upon his shoulders, and his arms and legs twitched like a half-crushed spider, but the voice that now came from his ragged mouth stung their ears like a slap of wine does the eyes; it pierced the assembly's shouts like a javelin.

"Prophet?" he shrilled. "*Prophet,* you crack-sniffers? Is that what I am called, in this gathering of cock-swallowers? Then prophecy is what I bring. I give you my shit for your bread! Here is my prophecy! *Hear the truth!"*

His head lifted as though his spine were held straight by invisible hands, and his one good eye flashed as though lit from within. He spat, "Yahweh Skygod is lord of heaven—but it is not through heaven that you *march,* fuckers of pigs! You are not creatures of the air! You're men! You're men made of the mud that drags at you, and the stone that cuts your feet. From muck you come between your mother's thighs, to the Muck you return! The road to Jebusi is the Tongue to the Mouth that will swallow you! The flame of the moon from the western waters stabs you to the heart!

> *The earth shall be iron*
> *and the sky shall be brass!*

When the sky falls, it is not the earth that breaks! It falls, it falls, Yahweh tumbles from His shitter—"

"Silence!" Pushed beyond endurance, Phinehas punched the eremite hard in the mouth; the eremite's head flopped back, and the power seemed to go out of him.

In the shining westerly sun, Phinehas seemed to burn with right-eousness. *"Destroy this blasphemer!"*

Joshua could only stand and watch as they mobbed the eremite and began to drag him off the road. He was stunned, and saddened. A terrible sense of loss gnawed at his belly. Only now did he realize how much he had hoped this man might *be* a new prophet, after all, might bring a new vision from God of some happy future, some future that had no dead men piled below Jerusalem's walls.

The Elders and the other watching men broke around him like surf as they rushed to follow in the wake of the men who dragged the eremite away; no one wanted to miss the stoning.

Joshua blinked back sudden moisture from his eyes; he was getting old, he thought, old and foolish and weak, to pin so much hope on an empty dream. With a heavy sigh, he roused himself to follow the others, then he felt a hand upon his shoulder and heard Eleazar's soft voice speaking in a private tone.

"Stop them, Joshua. You cannot let them do this."

He turned and looked down at Eleazar, surprised to find the priest's eyes lacking their usual cynicism, and full of honest alarm. "I must," Joshua said. "It is the Law."

Eleazar gave his head a quick double shake. "Don't you see? Few men heard this man's voice, but by tonight some version of his words will be spread throughout the Host. If you hadn't seen his madness for yourself, how would you know he was mad? If you were one of the men who'll hear the tale tonight, what you would hear is that we ordered a man stoned to death, purely for predicting disaster at Jerusalem."

"And the miracle," Joshua said with a bitter heaviness that was almost sullen. "Let us not forget the miracle. The miracle that this madman could find nothing more deadly than a reed with which to strike."

"As to *that*," Eleazar said, a suggestion of his accustomed half smile tugging at his lips, "don't judge too quickly. Did you see the reed in his belt? Did you see it clearly as he struck?"

Joshua shook his head.

"Nor did I. Nor did anyone else, I'd wager. How do you know it *wasn't* a dagger, up until the very instant that it touched your chest?"

Joshua said with solid finality, "Because the Lord does not exert Himself for trifles."

"You're hardly a trifle, my friend. Hardly. At any rate, don't quash the tale of this sudden miracle—a miracle here or there does wonders for morale. And, in fact, if you'll allow me, there might be another miracle in store. Yahweh has done one already today; who's to say he won't do another, and solve our little prophecy problem?"

The old man frowned unhappily. "Do not test the Lord—"

"I don't propose to," Eleazar said easily. "I propose to let the Lord test our prophet."

He thrust his hands within his robe, and on his face was a smile of odd self-satisfaction, the opposite pole of his earlier alarm. "It's one thing if we stone him for predicting that our campaign will fail; that will inspire fear, and quiet some grumbling voices, but nothing more. In the long run, we might even be seen to have feared that prediction ourselves—to have stoned him only to silence him—and thus damage the spirit of the entire army. *But*"—here he raised a finger significantly, and his eyes lit up—"it is another beast entirely if the Elders of Israel see the Lord Himself strike this fellow down for blasphemy. It would be nothing less than a promise of success."

There was no arguing with this; Eleazar was a born politician, and he knew his business intimately. "But will He?" Joshua rumbled in his chest, seeing suddenly within his mind a happy chance—a chance that, at least, this campaign against Jerusalem was not a punishment, that the Lord was not using the Jebusites as another in his long list of plagues, and fires, and military disasters like the first battle of Ai, by which He punished His people for disobedience.

The Lord had only commanded that this war be fought; He had not promised victory.

Even this chance, that the Lord might do this thing in his sight, brightened his spirits like the earth under the kiss of the storm-chasing sun.

"How do we know He will do such a thing?" he asked, not quite daring to hope.

"For that," Eleazar said, his smile broadening until his teeth gleamed like the gems that adorned his fingers, "we must have *faith*."

Bonfires made a circle of light before the Sanctuary.

Alone within that circle swayed the eremite, bruised and battered, barely retaining his feet; Joshua's order that spared his life had arrived barely in time. Blood still trickled from wounds on the eremite's naked scalp, down brown-crusted furrows in his face and neck, like streams with banks of clot.

Stars glittered above, and the waxing moon hung in the sky like a shield upon a wall. The Nation of Israel gathered around, to witness the Judgment of God.

Now Eleazar stepped into the circle of light; upon his head was the priestly turban, with its plate of shining gold; across his shoulders hung the tasseled ephod, and gleaming upon his golden breastpiece were the Seals of the Twelve Tribes, and the shimmering Urim and Thummim. From a chain in his fist swung a censer that trailed sweet-smelling smoke, and behind him walked his eldest son.

He stood beside the swaying, oblivious eremite and addressed Israel.

"Sons and daughters of Jacob, given the title Israel by the gift of Yahweh Sabaoth, El Shaddai, you have heard of the prophecies of this man who stands beside me. You have heard that he predicts a disaster for the Host of the Lord."

His voice, when he spoke full-throated, had a resonant hypnotic power that reminded Joshua of Aaron himself.

"We could answer his blasphemy by stoning, as the Law requires of us, but we have heard the murmurs of the Chosen People." Eleazar's eyes flashed like the flames around him. "We have heard your grumbling, your whispers of distrust. Yahweh Sabaoth is the God of Justice, as He is of all things above and here below, and He knows what has been in your hearts. The answer this man's blasphemies require shall come not from other men, as fallible as yourselves, uncertain and doubting, but from God Himself!"

He handed the censer's chain to Phinehas at his side. He tucked his hands within his robe as though suddenly chilled, and his voice lost its ringing power, became warm and human again.

"It is a simple test the Lord requires. I shall stand beside this blasphemer, and proclaim the coming victory. I shall call upon the Lord to judge between us, and to strike down the man who lies."

There were murmurs from the assembly at this, and Eleazar shook his head sadly, but also somehow humorously. "I know how shocking this must be, to the fighting men around us here. I have heard the mutters, that the priests send you forth to battle and stay safely behind. Here I am, to show you now that we share your risk. We, too, gamble our lives on victory." He took a deep breath, as though steeling his courage, and the assembled Elders and warriors all breathed with him.

"It remains only to be certain that this blasphemer has nothing unclean upon him, to offend the Lord and prejudice the test. I myself will search him, that all may know: when judgment comes it shall be judgment of prophecy, and naught else."

Eleazar stepped close to the eremite, and thrust his hands within the ragged and filth-stained clothing that covered him. He went over every inch that could possibly conceal an offense to God, and then he turned away again, and his voice once more rang like a brass bell.

"Israel prevails at Jerusalem! Israel prevails! Yahweh Sabaoth El Shaddai, strike me dead if I lie!"

Joshua found himself holding his breath, as though it were the only way he could keep his hammering heart inside his chest. If only he could know that he had not already failed in the task Moses had set him; if only the Lord would say to him *I will give Jerusalem into your hands, as I did Jericho.*

Nightmare images of a hundred thousand men lying slaughtered below the walls of Jerusalem had haunted his sleep for days, and had driven him to empty skin after skin of bitter young wine. Every one of those deaths would be an accusing finger, pointed ineluctably at his sin.

If he had kept faith with Moses, if he had truly done his utmost to keep Israel upon the path of the Law of God, the Lord could deliver Jerusalem without the loss of even one life.

Every single death would be a testament to Joshua's inadequacy.

Each death would speak with the Voice of Yahweh: *Joshua, you have failed in My Sight.*

"Now," Eleazar said, turning to the eremite, and extending his hand to point as though he could strike death with a touch, "prophesy, blasphemer. Prophesy, if you dare."

At the word, light returned to the eremite's misted eyes. He raised his head and screeched, *"The lance of the moon strikes the breast of God! Shit, shit, dung-hole god falls into—"*

And he burst into flame.

The Nation of Israel gasped as one man.

Fire roared up the eremite's cloak, and he screamed like a goat in the jaws of Moloch; flames spat from him in all directions; he seemed to become a pillar of fire rooted to the very earth, shrieking his hideous death as the fat beneath his skin melted in the heat and his flesh began to flow like mud, even as it charred and caught fire itself. His eyeballs burst from the boil of pressure within, and he fell writhing to the ground.

No man moved or spoke until the unnatural flame hissed away, and the eremite was only a smoldering heap of coals before the curtain of the Tent of Meeting.

The crackle of cooling flesh was all that could be heard for a long breathless moment, until Phinehas raised his fist and cried, "Behold the Power of the Lord! Like the followers of Korah at Paran, he is consumed! Victory at Jerusalem! *Victory at Jerusalem!*"

His cry was taken up by the assembly, and the shouts rose and swelled until it seemed that the earth beneath them rocked with jubilation. Eleazar stood over the charred remains of the eremite, grinning fiercely and his eyes alight, as he saw the joy of Israel that ringed him on all sides, excepting only one man.

Joshua stood staring hotly, as though struck dumb with fury.

When Eleazar's gaze lit upon Joshua, the fierceness of his grin faded, for Joshua's face had purpled, and cords stood out in the old man's neck.

Eleazar came to his side and raised his voice to be heard above the general din. "Two miracles in one day? Is this not a time for joy? For what else have you prayed, Joshua?"

Joshua ground out his words as though each was a boulder being crushed upon a millstone. "I will see you in my tent. Alone."

The old man spun on his heel and strode away, leaving Eleazar speechless.

Joshua had one more word for him.

*"Now."*

When Eleazar ducked around the curtain of Joshua's tent, the old man stood within, his back to the priest, hands knotted behind him so tightly they trembled, and his knuckles showed white.

"Joshua? Are you ill? What's wrong?" Eleazar went to the old man's side solicitously, but Joshua struck his hand away.

"I know what you did." His voice was a bitter rasp of suppressed fury, and his eyes bulged as though they'd been boiled.

"What I did?" Eleazar asked, his stomach dropping, for he already knew the answer.

"You forget. *I was there* when Korah was swallowed by the earth. I was there when the Lord sent fire to destroy his followers. Their clothes caught fire *from their flesh*, not the other way around. You put something on the man's clothing, something that made it burn. You *murdered* him."

"Ah," Eleazar murmured, then sighed. "I suppose I should have known that you, among all Israel, would be the one I could not fool."

"I am not the only one who sees through you, Eleazar. *God* watches your deceit; He knows your crime."

"I'm sure He does."

"How could you do this? I could have you stoned for a murderer!" Joshua's face suddenly deepened from purple toward black, and he seized Eleazar by his priestly robes with astonishing strength. He lifted the smaller man off the ground and snarled in his face. ''How could you dishonor God in this way?"

Eleazar barely blinked. Icily, he met Joshua's outraged glare while he wiped Joshua's spittle from his face. "You should be asking yourself that question."

Slowly the clench faded from Joshua's jaw, and he lowered Eleazar back to the tent floor. "What do you mean?"

"Isn't it obvious?" Eleazar said carelessly. "I am the High Priest. How can I do anything that is not God's Will? If Yahweh did not want me to kill that man, why didn't He stop me? In fact"—and here he drew himself up and met Joshua's eyes fearlessly—"isn't it a bit presumptuous of you to be so angry? Who are you to dictate to the Lord what tool He will use to show His Will?"

Joshua snarled, "I am not persuaded."

"What will you do?" Eleazar brushed himself off as though Joshua's touch had soiled him somehow, and he straightened his clothing. "To accuse me would be to proclaim before all the Host that the Lord did not decide the matter after all—that, in fact, you believe the eremite's prophecy. The war will crumble in fear. How will that serve Yahweh's will?"

Joshua could not answer the priest's logic, but he looked in no way defeated. There was a power in his voice Eleazar had not heard there since the fall of Jericho.

"Hear me, Eleazar ben Aaron. Such a thing, be it God's Will or no, shall never happen again. *Never.* Do you understand me? Never again will you presume to set your judgment before the Lord's. *Never.* Understand? Say it."

Eleazar flushed angrily. "I am no child, to be spoken to thus—"

Joshua drew himself to his full height, and looked down upon the priest with the full authority of the Lord's Anointed. "Say it."

In the end, Eleazar could not match his anger, nor his commanding authority. "I understand," he said thinly. "Never again."

"From this day forward," Joshua said, "I—*only I*—am the judge of Israel. And you—" His face compressed as though he crushed something with the clench of his jaw. "Get out of my sight."

# 5

# *Jericho*

**F**ilthy with dust, sweat, and the mud of six days' travel, Barra topped the rise. Her face was streaked with tears pricked by dry winds; they followed the purple swipes of fatigue below her eyes and trailed through the hollows of her cheeks. These new hollows had been pulled from hard marching on short rations, and her flesh had drawn tight over her skull. Her hair was no longer the color of a spectacular sunset; it had gone dirty brown and greasy with sweat and dust. Exhausted enough to ache in every bone, she nonetheless broke into an honestly happy grin at what she saw.

On the highest hilltop before her, a black silhouette between her and the setting sun, the ruins of Jericho rose like the rigored hand of a dead man, reaching into the cold and empty night.

"Well, there it is," she muttered to Graegduz, who limped along at her side—he'd cut a paw on a sharp-edged stone three days ago, and she couldn't get him to stop chewing off the dressings Kheperu had put on it.

She sighed and stretched her back, trying to ease some of the knots that hard marching had tied there; her scarred shoulder popped like a giant's knuckle. She rubbed at her eyes, the sweat-salt scraping her face like sand, and when she looked again, blessedly, Jericho was still there.

It was a signpost, one that she'd begged the gods to let her see.

It was a promise.

She saw within its shadow the ghost of her hundred-sweep merchantman, the foundation of her fleet.

That ghost ship had floated before her eyes for days now, beckoning her onward through the rugged hills, leading her deeper and deeper into the net that she knew the Habiru were even now drawing close around Jebusi. Her ship of dreams burned like fire every night, demanding that she march on another mile before she could rest; by day, it shaped itself of cloud, and the wind whispered with the cries of black-legged gulls.

*One more day,* she thought. *Camp in the ruins tonight, and one day's march puts us in Jebusi. One more day till I can sleep in a bed and have a meal that doesn't taste of camel.*

Then up the Coast Road, to Tyre and home—and the finest shipyard in Phoenikia.

On the hilltop, the blackened tumble of stone seemed to whisper something she couldn't quite hear, as though the wind that rustled among the fallen towers carried voices, not talking to her, but among themselves—as though the shattered walls were looking down the slope of the road and discussing her, the way hungry hunters discuss a doe that's creeping toward their blind.

She shivered. "Bloody Mother," she muttered. "Fucking place *does* look haunted."

She turned back along the road and waved broadly at the rest of the tiny column that she led, now in a crease a half hour behind her. She'd been on scout, as usual; throughout this arduous hump through the hills of what Kheperu called the *mâtat Urusalim*—Land of the House of Peace—she had saved herself and all these men again and again from Habiru patrols, detecting them in time for her column to hide or detour. Some of the other mercenaries in her train from time to time had shaken their heads in wonder, and muttered, "It's like she can smell them coming." It became a kind of catchphrase among them, an ironic testament to her extraordinary success as a scout. Only Leucas and Kheperu, among them all, knew how right they were.

It was her keen nose, in fact, that had made this journey possible at all. Late in the night after their flight from the doomed caravan, while they picked their way through the hills by the light of a growing moon, Barra had caught a scent on the wind of muskrat and cat piss, human sweat and almost-but-not-quite horseshit, and she'd recognized it instantly. Bounding off through the scrub juniper and pine, over moon-bleached rocks and up washes still muddy from winter rain, she had found her target.

When the others had finally caught up with her, she stood on the lip of a ravine, her arms folded across her breasts and a triumphant grin on her face.

"What . . ." Kheperu had gasped, nearly retching with his need for breath, "what was this . . . all about?"

Barra gestured grandly into the ravine below; they joined her on its lip and looked down.

Tramping single file along the ravine in the stark moonlight, to the sound of the thick pads on their feet and the ceaseless muttered curses of a madman, was a string of six pack-laden camels, with a crazed and bloodstained Assyrian at their side.

"Those packs are mostly full of food and beer, as I recall," Barra said. "Is anyone ready for supper?"

Leucas frowned and spoke in Greek to Kheperu. "I can't seem to get the hang of Phoenikian. Did she say—"

"Yes, she did. Food, praise all gods. Supper."

"—beer?"

The Assyrian—whose name, they later learned, was Pahshannur—had at first not been at all interested in sharing his provisions. Barra had explained her proposition to him in plain terms: in exchange for shares of the food and drink he carried, she and her companions would undertake to deliver him safely to Jebusi. Pahshannur had protested that he had no real interest in going to Jebusi; in fact, he intended to ford the Jordan River and strike out into the desert. He continued to protest until Barra took him aside and explained to him that whatever he did was fine with her . . . but Leucas, on the other hand, was determined to go to Jebusi, and he had already been speculating how camel might taste, and whether it would be better roasted or boiled. Pahshannur was apparently not crazy enough to ignore the fact that there was only one of him, and that the four of them were armed, hungry and—being mercenaries—presumably ruthless.

He, and his six surviving camels, walked along in the center of the train that now marched up the Jericho Road.

At the head of the train, well off by himself where he wouldn't be forced to converse with any of the others, walked Agaz. Even from this distance Barra could see the anxiety that gnawed at him, just by the way he walked: head down, staring at the ground a few feet in front of him, hands alternately clasped behind him or clenched into fists at his sides.

She wished she could do something to reassure him.

She also wished that she didn't care whether he was anxious or not.

She'd seen her troubles with Agaz coming the very first time she'd laid eyes on him: she'd always had a weakness for a pretty face. Over this march, things had only gotten worse.

It had started only minutes after they'd bolted for the hills under the cover of the mist. Once they were well away from the slaughter on the road, she and Agaz had climbed up above the fog to get a look at what the Habiru were doing—mostly to find out if the Habiru were coming after them.

She should have never let herself be alone with him. That was her first mistake, but not her last.

The mist had vanished, and the long shadow of the western hills stretched over the road. Lying flat on a chilly crag more than a mile away, with most of a mountain below her, Barra watched the Habiru as they ranged up and down the shattered caravan train, collecting bits and pieces of loot from the hundreds of corpses that lay clumped here and there, a random scatter.

The Habiru had left them wherever they'd happened to fall.

Overhead vultures wheeled, waiting for the Habiru to finish their business and move on, so that the vultures could undertake business of their own. Kites soared in, and below them all were squabbling black clouds of crows.

*No prisoners till after we settle Jerusalem.* Jerusalem: the Habiru name for Jebusi, a corruption of the Egyptian *Urusalim*. She muttered, "Shit, those Manassites sure can carry a grudge . . ."

"I suppose they can," Agaz said from where he lay beside her, on his stomach, resting his chin on the backs of his hands as he stared down at the road. Now and again a scythe rose and fell, as a few men still living were discovered among the corpses. "But these aren't Manassites. This had nothing to do with us."

"No?"

His mouth hardened into a grim line. "Nothing to do with you. Everything to do with me. Those are Benjamites. Benjamin holds the land around Jebusi. This is bad. This is as bad as it gets."

"I don't follow."

He rolled his head to one side so he could meet her gaze. "Benjamin is a small tribe, just about the weakest of the Habiru, but they're experienced caravan raiders. When Habiru attack a caravan, they never come from both sides of the road. They're after the donkeys and wagons, and the goods, you see? They're not interested in fighting a pitched battle. All they want is to drive the guards away so they can pick and choose what they want to steal. You can't drive guards away if you don't give them somewhere to run to."

Barra nodded; she'd been around, and she knew a little bit about pirates. These Habiru were pirates of the land, but pirates are pirates nonetheless.

"You think they were after the weapons and the armor."

"I know they were. And I heard them talk about Jebusi. This isn't going to be something my father can settle with Manasseh. It's war. You remember how many warriors Manasseh had? That's only one tribe, half a tribe, really. There are *twelve* tribes."

He turned his bitter gaze back toward the road. "I should have let them kill me. That would have been the best thing I could do for my people. Stay there and die."

Silence stretched between them, and finally, just to have something to say, Barra said, "I'm sorry."

"It's not your fault. It's what the reward is for. How could you have known?"

"I'm not apologizing," she said. "I don't apologize for being good at what I do. I just feel sorry for you. I feel sorry for any idiot who thinks he's better off dead."

He took the jab without reaction; his mind was far away. "Maybe I could . . . Maybe . . ."

"Hey," she said sharply. "Don't even think about it."

He kept his face turned away from her. "I'm not thinking about anything."

"Yes, you are. You listen to me, sunbeam. I haven't come this far to go home with a flat purse. You're going to Jebusi if I have to tie you up and have Leucas drag you the whole way."

"You can still get paid," he said. When he turned back to her, the desperation in his eyes was as stark and undeniable as the stone on which they lay.

She said warningly, "Drop it. You don't want to walk this road with me, Agaz." Using his name in that tone would have been warning enough for any other man, but he ignored it.

"You're a mercenary, aren't you? What do you care, whether your money comes from my father or from Manasseh? Money is money, isn't it?"

She reached over and grabbed his hair roughly, yanking his face close to hers. She snarled from a range close enough to bite him, "For a fella who asks so many fucking questions, you're damned ignorant, y'know that?"

He didn't resist at all; maybe he didn't feel like he had a right to. It was all she could do not to knock his pretty face against the stone— and then she looked into his eyes, full in his eyes as dark as onyx, and the pain there caught at her; not physical pain—what she saw had nothing to do with the tangle of her fingers in his hair. This was a pain of need.

It burned in him sharper than lust, a need to protect, to defend, to put himself between his people and their danger, as a father will stand between his son and a stalking lion.

She released him. Nothing she could do to him would hurt as much as what he was doing to himself.

After a moment, she lowered her face to the stone and let its chill drain the heat from her forehead.

"I'm sorry," he said hoarsely. "I'm sorry, Barra . . . I didn't mean to insult you, I swear . . ."

He wasn't even angry, only sad; his remorse pricked her like a needle.

"Agaz, Agaz," she said, her face turned away against the stone. "When we're not trading apologies we're trading punches. What's the matter with you, anyway? Half the time you don't even fight back."

He'd never meant insult, she knew that. She'd known it even as her temper was flaring out of control. His offer was noble; it was the very *definition* of noble, to give his life to protect his people. Her brother Llem, High King of Great Langdale, did the same whenever he rode out to battle. Her anger might have come because he seemed to make it so cut-and-dried; she might have been angry because of the arrogance of his assumption that the first thing he'd thought of was the only answer. And maybe she was so quick to fury because his instinctive nobility had made him even more attractive.

Unseen behind her, but close enough that she could feel his breath on the fine hair at the nape of her neck, he said, "Perhaps I don't want to take the chance of hurting you."

"Don't say that to me, you bastard . . ." she began, but her command lacked any real force. She stayed frozen where she was, afraid to move, afraid to remain still, hoping for one second of awful weakness to feel his lips there, where she had felt his breath.

After one thin-stretching moment, she did.

Her heart shouted within her chest as his lips barely brushed her spine, and she rolled over, raising her mouth to his for one deep and searching kiss, a sweet caress that tasted of sweat and other men's blood. The kiss drove the breath from her lungs and gathered stars around her head, and the beat of his heart against her chest felt like music.

But it lasted only for a moment; an instant later, even as her pulse pounded louder and louder in her ears, all of her years of self-denial and hard experience rose up and strangled her passion like an Indusian executioner.

Gently but with undeniable firmness, she pushed him away. "This," she said, "is a very bad idea."

"Barra," he said softly, gazing at her as though entranced, "what do you call the color of your eyes?"

"Agaz—"

"I've never seen the sea, but they tell me it has a color of spring leaves and sky together, and that's what I see here. And your hair, it's like fire, like the clouds at sunset—"

"Cut it out." She shoved him away and sat up on the rock. "Look, I know what's going on here. You're feeling all frisky because you almost got killed. You're just looking for a handy hole. It happens to everybody." She looked away. "Even to me."

"That's not true," he said softly. "I'm not a boy, Barra. I've been through battles before this one, and I know that feeling. This is something else. You are something else. I've seen enough to know when I look on something extraordinary."

"Oh, ay, I've heard this before, too. Y'know what I am, Agaz? Ask any slave trader, he'll tell you. I'm what they call an *exotic*."

She slid down the rock, out of sight of the road, then stood up and folded her arms. She couldn't look at him, but she did manage to keep the bitterness out of her voice. She sounded like this didn't bother her at all.

"Look at me, Pict girl—well, not a girl anymore—with red hair, arms like a man, and a stone axe at my belt. *Nobody* around here has seen anything like me before. Every son of a whore I meet wants to fuck me. Even the pederasts—they tell me I've still got the butt of a teenage boy. They *all* want to fuck me." She looked up at him. "Once."

"That's not what is happening here."

"Once his cock goes soft again, every boy wants a girl like his mother. I'm not like anybody's mother."

He slid down beside her, scrambling to her side. "Barra, I swear—"

"Don't swear. Just shut up. I didn't come down here to get laid, Agaz. I can do that anywhere. Now get off your whiny ass and get back down there with the others before I get angry."

She gave him a sharp shove to get him on his way, then turned away and pretended to watch the Habiru while she listened to him crawl back down the crag to where Leucas and Kheperu waited with Graegduz. She stayed up for a while longer, knowing herself well enough to stay away from the others until her temper subsided.

*So much for that romance,* she thought.

Now she stood by the road and watched him walk slowly toward her at the head of the train of camels and men, and she wished things could be different.

Barra had a list that she kept inside her head, a list graven on tablets of mental stone. It carried the lessons she'd learned in eleven years on the road, living by her wits and the edge of her axe. She called it the Suicide Table, because every entry on that list represented a short trip to a shallow grave. *Romance the client* was high upon that list, a mistake she'd only made once, many years ago. It was a mistake she'd barely survived making, and she didn't need to learn that lesson again.

Of course, Agaz wasn't exactly her client . . .

And what she really wanted wasn't romance, so much as it was the scratch of an itch she'd had for more than a year . . . but *Have sex with the client* was on the list right below romance.

Most of the entries on the Suicide Table had dealt with getting too involved, with giving herself too much to risk in a job, with letting the stakes rise too high. At the beginning of this now-ending winter, she'd added a new entry that read: *Take a job in my hometown.* She'd set herself against a renegade Egyptian prince who'd wanted to rule Tyre, and it had nearly cost not only her life, but the lives of her friends, her foster-parents, nearly everyone she cared about in this whole half of the world.

She swore she wouldn't make that kind of mistake again. No matter how much she liked Agaz. No matter how much sympathy she felt for him, with a storm of war lowering upon his city. She'd never been to Jebusi, and she had no reason on earth to give one scrawny rat's ass about what happened to anyone there, and she intended to keep it that way.

Even Graeg liked him . . .

Agaz had made a subtle point of cultivating the grey wolf's affections, keeping back a scrap of sausage or a piece of cheese from every meal on the long journey, and feeding it to Graeg from his fingertips when he thought Barra wasn't watching. Graegduz's fickle heart followed his belly too easily, Barra knew. Whenever he wasn't with her on scout, she'd find him curled next to Agaz, pretending to be asleep while he waited for another morsel. The spoiled beast was the only one of them who didn't lose weight on the march.

Barra thought that making friends with Graeg was kind of a game with him, probably the same sort of game that tickling her breechclout had been. A distraction, something to take his mind off his visions of the coming war.

His desperate fear for his city and his people had only grown on the hard march; she could see it in his face in every unguarded moment. They couldn't walk the road, with the Benjamites holding it closed, and they couldn't risk coming down to the Jordan on the far side of the hills. They'd marched through the mountains, as straight and as fast as they could, hoping to make Jebusi before the Habiru descended upon it and invested the city.

They came this way, to the Jericho Road, because, as Agaz had said grimly:

"It's haunted."

"Really?" Kheperu had purred happily. "Demons? Goblins, that sort of thing? It's really *haunted*?"

"The Habiru think so," he'd replied with a shrug. "Or maybe it's the Habiru that are haunted, by what they did there. They killed everything."

"Everyone," Kheperu had corrected automatically, but Agaz shook his head.

"Every*thing*. The cattle. The cats and the dogs. They burned the city and salted the fields around it."

Kheperu's bristly eyebrows lifted. "They must have been angry."

"Who knows?" Agaz's face was colored from within by imaginings of his own city facing such a fate. "Who knows why Habiru do anything? Anyway, they don't go there."

And so Jericho had become, in a sense, their destination, the milepost they'd been looking for on their grueling journey. Once they'd made the road, they were less than a day from the ruins. The ruins were less than a day from Jebusi.

And Agaz walked as though every step was a prayer that he'd make it in time.

Barra felt for him, she really did, but cities get sacked all the time. It's not the end of the world.

Besides, there was nothing she could do.

Nothing beyond delivering him to his father the king, collecting her money, and running like a fucking gazelle for the Coast Road to get back under the protection of the Egyptian army. Into the city and out again; she'd be damned if she was going to get dunked in the shit-pot that Jebusi would become once the Habiru arrived.

She'd be long gone.

That's exactly what she was going to do. No more, no less.

Long gone.

She looked toward the Jordan River many miles away, where the moon would soon rise out of desert sand, and said, "Please. Please let it be so."

She asked the moon for it, and the earth, because both reflected the Mother. Perhaps the Mother would defend her from those endless, hideous dreams.

She'd find it a shitload easier to deal with Agaz if she could get just one decent night's sleep.

They had grown worse, her dreams of blood and flames and the screams of children, every night along her journey. They were becoming thicker—more immediate, more real, with a gooey tangibility that clung to her like honey drying on her skin, even after she awoke. She woke less often in these nights, but that was not because the dreams were less hideous; it was because she was finding them harder and harder to escape.

It wasn't only recurring nightmares that were costing her sleep. She, Kheperu, and Leucas had stood rotating watches every damned night of this trek, and not merely, or even mostly, for defense from predators and Habiru; much of their watchfulness was spent guarding their belongings and themselves from their companions.

Eleven other mercenaries had marched through these mountains in their train, eleven survivors of the caravan raid. Over the first day or two of their southward trek, they had come across several single survivors—mostly Philistines, and the sea-nomads Kheperu called Sherdanu, all of whom spoke passable Egyptian—and a group of three Hittites, as well as five survivors of the company of Argives, thirteen in all.

One, a Hittite wounded in the belly, had died four days ago, screaming into a piece of dirty rag his two brothers had forced into his mouth, so that his death agony wouldn't alert a Habiru patrol that Barra had scented nearby. The other two Hittites, great hulking brutes with bristling black hair, still marched alongside the camels, though they had been eating little and saying less since they'd buried their brother.

Another mercenary, one of the Argives, was dragged behind a complaining camel, tied onto an improvised travois with ropes made of strips of his own clothing. The travois itself was a pair of saplings Barra had felled and stripped with swift strokes of her axe, and its bed was sturdily sewn—by Leucas—from the chitons of two of his companions. A panicked horse had stepped on his ankle during the attack on the caravan, shattering it beyond any healing. When his friends had made their escape into the fog, he had begged them not to leave him— Greeks, even mercenaries, are softhearted that way, and two of them had shared his weight between them on their dash for the hills. He had helped them all he could, even managing to half run upon his shattered ankle, which forced splinters of bone through the skin.

By the time Barra came across them, the ankle was deeply septic, so septic that it was what had revealed them. She smelled the sweet, throat-cloying scent of dying flesh while she was still hundreds of yards away from their hiding place. Creeping silently close to the cave where they hid, she'd overheard men speaking Greek, and recognized the voices and the scents that went with them as the Argives; she knew that the smart thing to do would be to simply creep away again—but Leucas would never forgive her, and she didn't trust herself to lie to him.

So it happened that by that night, the Argives had joined them in their camp, in a tiny rock-lined fold in the hills, where they could build a fire and keep it well concealed. Barra had wrinkled her nose guardedly at the piney scent, but the mercenaries had chosen their firewood well: there was no smoke, and only enough light to bring a fleshy living glow to the rock walls around them.

Leucas had taken only one quick look at the injured man's leg, and had turned away, expressionless. He pulled Barra off away from the campfire, and spoke with his face in shadow.

"Those red marks," he said in an undertone, "see them? Like stripes left by a lash?"

She nodded. Bloody rags were tied around his foot, and the Argive seemed oblivious to any pain; he laughed along with his friends at Kheperu's mocking flirtation with the youngest of them, a blushing young man of perhaps twenty-five. The stripes did look like whip marks, rising out of the rag bandage, visible even in the shifting light from the tiny fire.

"Those are streaks of fever," Leucas said grimly. "Once they pass his knee, he's a dead man. That foot has to come off."

Barra shook her head. "Seems like a lot of trouble. He'll likely die anyway."

"But maybe not."

"Maybe not," she said with a shrug. "But so what? If he's lucky enough to live, he'll end up a beggar by somebody's city gate. That's no life for a warrior. Would have been kinder to leave him to the Benjamites, and make a quick end."

"Too late for that now," Leucas said. "I want Kheperu to dose him with something, so he'll sleep through it."

"Ay, whatever. You can do what you like, Leucas. Why are you coming to me with this?"

"Because I want you to do it."

"Me?"

"I'll hold him steady. You take off the foot. Your axe—it's the best we've got."

Barra reached down and put her hand on the head of her broadaxe, while she stared past Leucas at the laughing Argive. He was right; even the iron axe that one of the Hittite brothers carried didn't have an edge like hers. Lovingly maintained over more years than she liked to remember, the copper-green basalt edge of her axe was sharp enough to shave with, and the head had plenty of heft—nearly three-fourths of a stone.

*Poor bastard,* she thought. Nothing but bad luck, that's what it was. *Didn't even fall in battle . . . stepped on by a fucking horse.* She could do it, one blow, as swift and as painless as any surgery could ever be. The stone seemed to grow warm as it took heat from her hand, as though the axe itself said to her: *I'm willing.*

She shrugged again. "Ay, sure. Break out one of Pahshannur's casks of beer. I'll get Kheperu to dose him up for you."

It wasn't until the wounded man was safely asleep that Leucas explained to the Argives what they intended to do. All of them were veterans, even the young blushing one; they understood the need. But one of them, the largest, with shoulders wider than those of Leucas and a neck thick as a tree trunk, Stephanos by name, had stood up and held out his hand for Barra's axe.

He said, "Let me do it. He's my best friend. I want it done right."

"I'll do it fine," she told him.

"His best chance to live is one clean cut," the Argive said with exaggerated patience. "I don't want to stand here and watch you hack his leg like cordwood."

"You don't trust me?" She slid the axe haft back into a scabbard at her belt and folded her arms. "That's fine. Do it yourself."

"I will. Give me the axe."

She showed him her teeth. "Not fucking likely. Nobody touches this axe. Use your sword. Borrow the Hittite's axe, I don't care. You're not using this one."

Now the other Argives were rising to their feet, and gathering behind the trunk-necked one. "I could take it," he said.

A massive presence arose at her side: Leucas was there. He said, "I don't recommend trying."

"This's got nothing to do with you, Athenian."

"Best back off," Barra said. "One dying Argive is enough for today, eh?"

He lifted his chin pugnaciously. "I don't take orders from women."

"I do," said Leucas, his voice chill as the wind. "You can take the order from me, if you like. Back off."

A rustle from her other side was Agaz; even though the discussion was in Greek, the quiet confrontation had been clear enough to stir him from his evil daydreams of war and bring him to his feet with his hand on a spear shaft. Kheperu crouched by the injured man, his hands inside his robes and his eyes glittering, bright as a hawk's. Behind the Argives, Graegduz crouched, watching Barra, waiting for a signal by word or gesture. The rest of the mercenaries, Sherdanu, Philistine, and Hittite alike, watched with a certain detached professional interest.

"This is stupid," the Argive said. "Why can't you just give me the axe? What's the problem?"

"The problem," Barra said through her teeth, "is that nobody touches this axe."

*"Why?"* It was almost a whine of frustration. "Just let me do this. What's worth fighting about?"

"I don't need a reason. Reasons are for peasants." She had no intention of standing here to tell the tale of why she'd cut this axe when she was eighteen, or of the men she'd hunted and slain with it; that tale was one she'd never even told Leucas and Kheperu. "I'll tell you this: the last pair of cockeyed Akhaian sons of whores that tried to take this axe off me now spend their days tripping hand in hand through the forest and braiding daisies into each other's hair. You follow?"

"But—but—this is only—"

"Shut up. You want this done with my axe, it's me that does it. Either find another weapon for it, or sit your fat ass down and let me get to work."

Eventually, when they saw that neither plea nor threat could move her, the Argives stepped aside. They found a fallen tree nearby to use as a chopping block. Its trunk was only a span wide, stunted by the harsh climate, but that was enough for Barra to work with. Leucas twisted tight a tourniquet just below the Argive's knee, and held his leg steady with both hands.

"Careful of my thumbs," he said.

"No fear."

She lifted the axe with both hands over her right shoulder, sighted her target on the Argive's shinbone, and threw her hips into her swing. Not full strength, just smooth and hard and controlled, and the axe crunched sharply through his tibia and fibula, sheared through the thick muscle of his calf, and buried itself in the log. His foot fell away onto the earth in a brief splatter of dark exhausted blood, and she wrenched her axe free.

She met the eyes of the tree-necked Argive across the campfire. "Good enough?"

Stephanos only shrugged.

One of the Hittites had drawn close to watch the operation. He spoke in Hatti, from the side of his mouth, while he watched Leucas bind the Argive's stump to quench the bleeding. "Woulda thought the pain'd wake him up."

Barra responded in the same tongue, "No. When one of the Kheperu's magic powders puts you out, you stay out."

He met her eyes with a gaze flat and blank as fresh-cut stone. "So. Your Egyptian had that powder all this time. He had that powder while my brother died screaming into a rag."

"That's right," she said bluntly.

Blood rose through his neck. "Maybe he just don't understand how much it *hurt*," he said with thick menace.

"Maybe," Barra allowed. "And maybe he doesn't waste his magic on dead men. You got a problem with that, you can argue with my axe. Do we understand each other?"

He held her gaze for a long moment without speaking, then turned and stumped off to sit with his surviving brother.

The rest of the journey had been tense.

The Argive still lived, though he drifted in and out of fever and Leucas didn't expect him to make it more than another couple of days. The Hittites watched Kheperu's every move with predatory loathing, and the Argives seemed to go out of their way to annoy Barra, and the Philistines and Sherdanu seemed to be mostly interested in stoically polishing their armor and sharpening their weapons, all the while eyeing everyone else suspiciously, as though expecting to be attacked at any unguarded moment. Kheperu had lain every night on his trunk of equipment, barely sleeping, one eye open. As he'd put it: "We took this trunk from a dead man. I have no desire to pass it on the same way." The Assyrian whined endlessly about his poor camels and the hardships they faced in the hills until even tolerant Leucas was ready to strangle him. Barra had taken to using her axe for a stone pillow. And through it all, they had still managed to keep Agaz's true identity a secret; they had been calling him Oshea, and pretending that he was a drover from the caravan.

Barra shook her head in wonder as this motley train approached. How in the name of the Loving bloody Mother had she ended up responsible for this ill-matched crew? It defied reason; her only consolation was that they were less than a day's march from Jebusi, when she and her partners could dump them all.

She waited long enough for them to catch up. Most of them looked at the shattered hulk of the city with blank stares, as though it could not be of any possible interest to them.

Leucas smiled wearily. "Not one step too soon. The only way I could walk another mile is to see my camp at the end of it."

Barra nodded in sympathy. "Ay. And we'll get only one night in Jebusi before we haul ass for the Coast Road."

"Don't tell that to my feet."

When Agaz topped the rise, he stared at the scarlet-brushed shadow of the ruins as though it were a sword drawn in naked threat. His face stiffened, and Barra could read his thoughts as clearly as if he'd spoken aloud.

*That could be Jebusi. That could be my home.*

"Come on, *Oshea,* pick it up," she said with a comradely slap on his shoulder. "Sooner there, sooner we eat. Let's go."

He looked at her expressionlessly. "I'm not hungry," he said, and walked on.

Kheperu, though, climbed the hill at the side of the camel that bore his trunk; he was fiddling with one of the clasps, working intently so as not to stop the camel to fix it. When he crested the hill, Barra said, "How's your back?"

"All right." He sighed distractedly. "Very sore, and I feel a bit feverish, but I'm sure it'll pass. I've had worse." He flashed his rotting teeth at her. "Hurts less than my feet—"

His voice choked to silence, and his eyes bulged on both sides of his long, hooked nose, as he stared past her at the ruins of Jericho. All color drained from his face, and he stood for a moment with his mouth hanging open.

"Kheperu? Are you all right?"

"I," he said slowly, "believe so, but I am less than entirely certain." He looked back at her, and his self-possession swiftly returned. "Curious. Very curious indeed. Hmpf. You know, this fever has been giving me some exceedingly odd dreams . . ."

"I take it there's a reason for you to be telling me this," Barra said.

"Mmm. Perhaps there is. Barra," he said in a quizzical, distracted tone, "do you recall that dream I had during the job last autumn in Tyre? About Chrysios?"

She nodded. "Of course."

"I may have had another," he murmured, as though he didn't entirely believe it himself. He stretched a finger toward the hilltop where Jericho lay. "I saw it. Last night, in a dream."

"So?"

He shook his head sharply. "So nothing. I don't know. It wasn't a town, in the dream; it was a hand."

Barra squinted at him and said nothing. She was thinking how it had kind of looked like a hand to her, too.

"Some old man—or old woman, I couldn't tell, for the grey cowl of the cloak he wore concealed him; this . . . individual . . . held up his hand, which was maimed and mutilated, entirely useless, all covered with scar tissue. It was clearly a wound that he'd taken many, many years ago, but as he held it before his face, he wept with a howl like a newborn baby deprived of the tit. But somehow, I'm certain that it was not the pain of the wound that brought these tears."

Kheperu shuddered at the memory. "He was screaming with *grief.*" He hunched into himself within his robe and under his armor. "There is nothing more hideous than the tears of the aged."

"Hey, snap out of it," Barra said. "You're not that young yourself."

His eyes were suddenly raw. "That's true. I am not." For an instant he looked as though this had never occurred to him before, and its implications appalled him. He looked at his own hand as though it belonged to someone else: the hairs on its back were grey as young iron.

"What do you think it meant?" Barra asked, trying to draw his mind back to the dream.

He shrugged. "I haven't the faintest clue."

"And you call yourself a seshperankh?" she said, and punched him on the shoulder hard enough to make him flinch. "Love of the bloody Mother! Don't be asking me to tell you *my* dreams till you understand your own, you old faker."

Some of the gleam returned to his eyes; he drew himself up to his full, unimpressive, height, and puffed out his chest regally. "Faker, am I? Tell me, what does this vaunted *sceon tiof* of yours tell you about your boyfriend *Oshea*?" He waved a lazy hand up the road at Agaz.

She scowled at him. "Nothing. And you know it: he's too close to me already. Shitcake sight won't work that way—it's like trying to read a tablet that's pressed against your eye."

He spread his dirty hands and grinned at her smugly, as though he'd proven something.

"It's not the same thing," she said. "Dreams are dreams, no matter who has them. And I'll be keeping mine to myself, thank you very much."

"Hmpf. The only dreams of yours in which I have the slightest interest are the ones that feature me; and even those are dull unless one of us is naked. Let us go make camp. I think I have a shot at that Greek boy; he's been batting his eyelashes at me all day."

She breathed an inward sigh of relief; a solemn, frightened Kheperu was something too alien for her to handle. Calling Graegduz to her side, she jogged on up the road as night's long shadow fell across it, passing into the lead once again. It was her job to go ahead and make sure the ruins were as empty as they looked, and to pick out a campsite.

Night fell with a whisper like soft spring rain, as she trotted into the deserted streets of Jericho, and the full moon rose at her back, the wind-stirred dust of the desert filling it with blood.

"Barra? Barra?"

An urgent whisper and a hard hand upon her arm shook Barra up from a dream of bloody slaughter. She wasn't alarmed, even rising from sound sleep in full darkness; this hand must belong to one of her partners—otherwise Graegduz would have bitten it off at the elbow before it came close enough to touch her—and the reek that stabbed her sinuses like a needle beside her eye meant that this could only be Kheperu.

Fatigue nailed her into sleep more securely than the horror of her dreams could pry loose. She slapped his hand away, mumbling, "It's not my turn. Go bother Leucas."

"In a moment. Barra, you must wake up. *We are not alone here!*"

She cranked open her eyes by degrees, blinking up at Kheperu's silhouette. With the full moon hanging among the stars behind him, his face was in blackest shadow except for the pinpoint glitter of his eyes.

"You're dreaming," she said thickly. "Another fever dream."

She had scouted Jericho thoroughly before choosing this camp-site. Not only was this shattered ruin of a city deserted, but the ruins were largely untouched; they had built a fire of a luxuriant size out of fallen house timbers and the splintered remains of weather-beaten fur-niture that still lay scattered throughout the broken houses. Much of the tumbled stones and heaps of masonry still showed the blackening of the fire of twenty years ago, but nowhere had Barra found any sign that other folk had used this place since.

This hadn't satisfied Kheperu, though; he'd been rabbity ever since they'd crossed the heaping ridges of giant stones that had once been the city walls. The breeze had kicked up, and he'd jumped at each new whistle or swirl among the ruins, at a scatter of gravel or a creak of settling wall. At intervals he went entirely still, even holding his breath, as though he listened to voices half-buried in the wind.

"I was not dreaming," he hissed. "I was *pissing*—in the bedroom of a little house a hundred paces or so over there."

Barra frowned in sleepy incomprehension. "You were pissing in somebody's bedroom?"

"I hardly think the owner will object," he muttered dryly. "It was interesting, actually—I felt quite thoroughly naughty while I was doing it—but that's beside the point. Even as I was lowering the skirt of my armor, I heard voices, speaking together in low tones. Three, I think. They were moving away from the camp."

"What were they saying?"

"How should I know?" he hissed angrily. "*Wake up,* rot your guts! If I *spoke* this pig-slop tongue, I wouldn't be bothering you!"

Barra shook some of the cobwebs out of her head and rubbed at her eyes. Of course any intruders would be speaking Canaanite. "Sorry. Sorry. All right. Are you sure it wasn't some of our Phili-stines?"

"That was my first thought, but I came straight back here as swiftly as silence would allow. Look about you."

Barra sat up. If Jericho was a hand, their camp would have been in the hollow at the base of the thumb; remnants of what once had been high walls had reflected back the light and heat of their campfire. The fire had been banked to pulsing coals, but the full moon gave plenty of light. The camels rested on their bellies nearby, snuffling through their nose flaps; Pahshannur lay with his head upon a furry flank. The Argives lay scattered in a rough circle around their wounded friend, who moaned softly from time to time in his fitful feverish slumber. The Hittite brothers had made themselves somewhat comfortable on a broad slab of stone a little distance away, and the rest lay randomly here and there, sleeping as deeply as one can, when lying uncovered with the bare earth sucking heat from your limbs. Only Leucas seemed soundly off; he snored with the rasp of an anchor hawser abrading the gunwale of a ship in rolling seas.

"All right," she said heavily. "Wake Leucas and put him to guard. You and I, we'll go see what this's about."

"Wake Leucas? Without shouting and slapping? How do you propose I do this?"

"Easy," she told him with a sleepy smile. "Wet your finger and stick it in his ear. He'll wake up, I promise you."

"Barra, you astonish me," he said, frowning. "I cannot believe I didn't think of this myself."

He immediately put Barra's theory to the test; as soon as the finger went in, Leucas' eyelids popped open as though he'd been stung. His eyes bulged, and he froze for one long second of utter incomprehension, while his sleep-addled brain attempted to make sense of what he felt.

"You know, don't you," he said softly after a moment, once a certain intelligence had chased away the blankness of his stare, "that someday, I am going to kill you?"

"Barra made me do it," Kheperu said, as though he actually expected to be believed.

"I don't care. I'll kill you anyway. I *like* Barra."

"You have to wake up. It's your turn to watch."

He sat up slowly, scratching at his beard. "What's going on?"

They quietly explained. Leucas listened with a growing frown. "You think they could be Habiru scouts?"

"No way to know," Barra said. "Don't worry, I just want to get a look at them. If there's any killing to be done, I'll come back and get you."

"You'd better," he said. "I don't much care for this 'Leucas watch the camp' stuff. I don't want either one of you getting into a fight when I'm not there to look after you."

"No fear of that. I'm not planning to tangle with these guys, and there's not a man in this half of the world that can surprise me when I'm on scout."

Leucas didn't look mollified. He nodded at Kheperu. "What about him?"

Kheperu grinned. Barra shrugged. "That's easy," she said. "We'll just make sure he stays downwind."

Barra lay flat among a tumble of stones that had once been a mighty tower, looking down into a large circular enclosure; it might once have been part of the same building as this ruined tower in which she lay. Thick crumbling walls, stumps of stone pillars here and there within and a scatter of tumbled half-charred beams implied that this huge enclosure had once been roofed. And big it was, big enough for a couple hundred people to throw a party, and have plenty of room to dance.

Even as she settled in, three men wearing dusty burnooses over leather armor stole furtively into the ring. It'd been easy work to track them; she and Kheperu had simply crept in a wide arc downwind of the path Kheperu had seen them take. The scent of soap sweating out of the pores of recently washed skin, and the freshly oiled leather of their armor, had been plenty strong for Barra to trail them until she got close enough to overhear their voices.

The smell alone told her these were no Habiru; scouts don't bathe so regularly. And the way they framed their vowels, when she was close enough to pick up their words, sounded just like the way Agaz did. She was certain of it: these men were Jebusites.

They carried a variety of spears and knives, with round shields slung across their backs, but each man also carried a tool: in evidence were a pair of shovels and a large pickaxe.

They stood close to one another and conversed in low tones, pointing here and there around the enclosure. One of them—a big fellow, wearing a nice-looking kirtle sewn with bronze rings—consulted a scrap of reed paper, squinted up at the moon, then down at the ground.

"Here," he said, pointing to a spot not far from where they stood, his voice thick with excitement. "It's almost midnight, and the shadows we want have to be that one, from that wall, and this one, from the upright timber. At midnight they should be touching . . . right about . . . here!" His face lit with a triumphant grin. "The son of a whore was telling the truth! Curse, my butt. And not a ghost in sight. C'mon, get to work."

Barra carefully slid back down inside the shattered tower to where Kheperu waited for her, squatting comfortably with his back against the night-chilled stone. "Like I said before," she whispered. "Treasure hunters. They've already started to dig."

"It makes a certain amount of sense . . . when the Habiru massed for the attack, folk would have been burying their worldly possessions right and left—and with everyone dead, who knows where to dig? Add a haunting or two to keep people from looking too hard . . ." Kheperu's beady eyes gleamed with avarice. "Let's get Leucas. The three of us should have no trouble chasing them off. Shit—with my trunk, I could do it by myself."

Barra shook her head, grinning. "No, stupid. Let them work. Chase them off now, and *we'd* have to dig."

Kheperu's smile could have been interpreted as paternal pride. "Have I told you lately," he murmured, "that I admire the way your mind works?"

"Hsst—" Barra said, her hand out to stop his lips. "Hear that?"

From somewhere not too far off to their left came more lowered voices, she couldn't tell how many—but once again, they seemed to speak Canaanite with Jebusi accents.

Kheperu met her eyes with a quizzical lift to his brow. "I wonder if our friends within aren't the only folks out with a treasure map this evening . . ."

"Quiet," she whispered. "This ought to be good for a laugh or two. Come on."

She boosted Kheperu up to her previous perch, giving him a little extra help here and there—he was nimble for an aging chubby man, but he was an aging chubby man nonetheless. She handed up his spear to him, then she climbed up beside him as silently as a leopard in a tree.

As she settled in, the men below were quietly gathering their tools and slipping off into the shadows of fallen timbers and jumbled stone; clearly, they'd heard the approaching voices as well. Only a moment later four men, in similar dress to the first three, similarly armed and carrying digging tools, came into the enclosure. One man of the new group had a scrap of reed paper as well, on which the directions must have been nearly identical. He sighted on the moon, decided that the time was approximately midnight, and found the same intersection of shadow. With his partners close behind, he strode to the spot.

Kheperu snickered. "Wouldn't it be funny," he whispered, "if these parties kept on coming? Soon all the hiding places would be full, and men would be jostling each other for the choice shadows—"

Barra shushed him.

"It's here, sure enough," the man with the paper said. Then he crouched for a closer look at the ground within the deep shadow. "Hey! Somebody's been digging here already!"

As his companions crowded around to look where he pointed, the other three men stepped out from shadows at their backs with knives in hand. Without a word, each went to seize one of the newcomers with an arm around their throats and a knife slicing up through the kidney in search of the heart. Blood burst from the mouths of two of them, but the third managed to turn himself and take the knife in his side instead; he twisted away and drew a short broad-bladed hacking sword from a scabbard over his shoulder.

The fight down there was weirdly quiet, three on two as two men jerked in their death throes under their feet; it became an affair of half-breathed grunting and the vivid *sluutch* of bronze entering flesh. No one screamed, no one yelled in anger, fear, or pain, only struggled in grim silence to take each other's lives.

"Run," Barra breathed, barely loud enough to hear it herself. "Why don't you run?"

No one ran.

They couldn't have been veterans, these men below; none of them seemed to have the faintest idea how to defend himself in close combat. Instead they stood toe-to-toe and hacked great chunks out of each other, insensible to pain and fear, until finally they could swing no more.

Only one man still stood, one of the original three, swaying like a drunk in a slaughterhouse. He wouldn't be standing long; his broken left arm hung by a shred of muscle, and his life pumped out of the wound in a wide scarlet spray; his chest hung in tatters and loops of intestine bulged through his sliced-open belly.

Kheperu breathed, "Very well, I was wrong: it wasn't funny."

"Somebody thinks it is," Barra said.

Even as he'd spoken there'd begun an unearthly laugh, a giggling half-hysterical bellow that Barra at first thought came from the standing man; she thought that his mind had snapped in the slaughter. But the laughter grew, louder and louder, and it seemed to come from everywhere at once, first one side of the enclosure, then another, shifting between them faster than a man could run, and it had an eerie resonant echoic sound, like a shout in a canyon.

The hairs on the back of Barra's neck lifted, and her heart tripped between beats.

*Haunted . . .*

"Maybe . . ." she whispered, "maybe we should be going . . ."

"Pish," said Kheperu briskly. "This little joke could hardly have been an accident. I want to see our comedian."

"Are you sure about that? I mean, that laugh—" She shivered.

His eyes glittered and his lips vanished into a thin I'm-so-clever smile. "This was a temple," he said, as though it were an explanation.

"So?"

"So: some of these provincial temples have voice channels cut in the stone blocks when they're constructed. Nothing very complex, just tunnels through the stone about the size of a rabbit run; but there is usually a small room to which they all lead. It impresses the gullible when they hear 'the voice of the god' coming from empty air, or from all around them at once."

The dying man in the enclosure staggered in a small circle, his eyes rolling in terror, making gagging sounds in the back of his throat, and then the laughter was replaced by words every bit as hollow and hair-raising as the laugh had been.

*"The Dead of Jericho call you! I am their Voice! The Dead of Jericho call you!"*

At the end of this simple incantation, the dying man let out one gurgling howl of mortal terror, and collapsed.

Barra translated in a whisper.

"Hmm, nicely done," Kheperu said coolly enough, but his brow was moist, and the hand with which he mopped it trembled ever so slightly. He felt Barra's eyes upon him, and looked down at the sweat on his trembling fingertips. "Fever," he insisted with a deprecating sniff.

Barra chose not to argue with him. She pulled her broadaxe from its scabbard; she needed its reassuring weight in her hand.

Only a few moderately shaky breaths later, a slim shadow detached itself from a larger one on the far side of the enclosure. As it moved close to the scene of the slaughter, the clear moonlight resolved it into the figure of a slightly built man in dark clothing. He carried a smallish strung bow, double-recurved, which he now casually unstrung and set to lean against a timber. He clasped his hands together, the crackle of his popping knuckles clearly audible across the enclosure, and then he began to hum softly to himself as he thoughtfully looted the corpses.

"Here we are at last," Kheperu murmured. "He doesn't appear to be armed, now that he's set down the bow . . ."

"If he wasn't before, he is now," Barra pointed out, as the man picked up the scattered knives and spears.

"Still, there's only one of him, and he can't be expecting an interruption like us. Why should we leave the corpses to him? I could use some new armor, and that big fellow's ring leather looks like it might be salvageable . . ."

She stared down at the dark-clad man, who was chuckling as he removed a ring from a corpse's hand by sawing through the finger joint, and abruptly she said, "All right, why not? I'd like a word or two with this bastard myself."

Without another word she rolled headfirst over the lip of the ruined wall, righted herself in the air, and landed catfooted on the softly crackling earth of the enclosure. The dark-clad man looked up at the noise of her landing, and their eyes briefly met.

His face bore dark lines on his cheeks and around his eyes, like a Nubian's man-scars, and the teeth that showed behind his smile gleamed strong and white. He took in her hair, her sleeveless leather tunic and the breechclout that wrapped her hips, her axe—and then, incredibly, he turned back to his looting as though she wasn't there. He finished disjointing the corpse's hand, and moved on to another.

"Hey," she said in Canaanite. "What do you think you're doing?"

Huffing with exasperated effort, Kheperu managed to scramble down behind her as she paced across the enclosure toward the dark-clad man. "Barra, wait . . ."

She ignored him. "I asked you a question," she said, letting a little edge of threat leak into her voice.

The dark-clad man's head came up again. He gave her a smile tight and competent. "You're not from around here. You should probably go."

"He certainly doesn't seem afraid of us," Kheperu observed in an undertone. "What's that he said?"

"Shut up," Barra told him out of the side of her mouth. "Just get ready to level him if we need to, all right?"

The dark-clad man stepped toward them, placing himself between them and the corpses like a wolf defending its kill, but his hands were empty—he'd even dropped the small knife he'd used to cut off the finger.

"This is my temple. You should leave before you get hurt."

"*Your* temple?" A cold hand stroked Barra's spine. She said in Egyptian, "This guy wouldn't happen to look anything like the one in your dream, would he?"

Kheperu replied, "I'm not sure—and I *am* sure that I don't want to know why you asked me that."

"Of course it's my temple," the dark man said, his voice taking on a thick and brutal edge. "*Everything* here is mine. This temple is mine. This city is mine. These dead men are mine."

*It's all a bluff; he's acting like a madman to bluff us off,* she told herself, trying to ignore how well it was working. "Horseshit," she said strongly. "You're just a man."

"I am," he admitted, a predatory smile spreading wide over his teeth. "I am also the Curse of Jericho. One of these men stole that map from me, when he thought I was drunk. The other won it from me at dice."

"Love of the bloodyfucking Mother . . ." Barra muttered. She frowned, looking at him; he was extravagantly beautiful, despite or perhaps because of the marks—scars? tattoos?—that striped his cheeks and brow. The closer she got, the more beautiful he became, with a brooding power in his stare, a smoldering intensity that seemed half-contained, as though it might explode into brutal violence at any second—but a violence more likely directed at himself than another.

He looked like trouble, standing there waiting to happen to her.

She came closer.

"It's not a treasure map at all," she said.

"Sure it is," the man replied. "Not treasure they'll find here, that's all. It's a map to the treasure they'll *bring with them.* Their armor, their weapons, their horses. Plenty of mercenaries in Jebusi these days are looking for mounts."

"What do you do when it doesn't work—when some are still alive? Is that what the bow's for?" She was mostly trying to keep him talking, while she took deep breaths and let them trickle slowly out through her teeth, staring at him fixedly; in this way, on occasion in the past, she had been able to summon the *sceon tiof.*

"It *always* works," he said savagely. "Always. You stand upon the Dead of Jericho. They scream for blood, and the moon hears them."

He chuckled harshly, and spread his hands like a shopkeeper displaying his wares. "My grandfather always said to plant under the waxing moon, and harvest on the full. You see on the earth before you the sweetest fruit there is—when it's ripe, it falls without a hand to touch it."

The *sceon tiof* blossomed within her, and she saw him.

In one instant, everything that was the dark man entered her, and her breath left her in a sigh that touched on a sob. It was as though his whole being was a suppurating wound, a thin shell of dying skin over raw agony so intense it defied even the expression of a scream—no amount of screaming could ever touch this pain. It left a void in his spirit, a black and windy hole within his heart that could not be filled; into it he poured a furnace of vengeance, white-hot and consuming. Vengeance brought neither light nor heat to him, but still he pursued it as though it could justify his pain.

Though it could not fill his hunger, he had no other food.

Just looking on him felt like she'd plunged her face into a cauldron of boiling fat; she recoiled instinctively, gasping, holding her head, her knees half-buckling.

To look away, to find anything else on which she could fix her eyes, any place safe, any place that wouldn't stab her like daggers through her eye sockets, she bent over and looked at the earth between her feet.

The *sceon tiof* was still upon her, and now she saw the truth of where she stood.

*You stand upon the Dead of Jericho.*

The scream, the ragged throat-ripping howl that she'd thought could not touch his pain, she tried to bring from her own throat, but it wouldn't come. Her chest couldn't summon it, her head was too small to pass the agony, and her legs collapsed; she pitched forward help-lessly, arms and legs flailing in spastic convulsion.

Kheperu cried out and tried to catch her, but the dark man was swifter. His arms went around her and he came to the earth beneath her, trying to shield her, trying instinctively to protect her pain, to muf-fle against his chest her thin, breathless, almost inaudible moan which sounded like an echo of his heart.

Kheperu could only watch in horror as Barra lay convulsing in the dark man's arms, bucking like a maddening horse, her eyes rolled up out of sight in her head and bloody froth trailing from her lips, of her voice remaining only a guttural *uhkgh—uhkgh—uhkgh—uhkgh—uhkgh*.

And the clear pale light gathered strength, bleaching Barra's face corpse white; overhead, the moon seemed to swell, as though it bowed close to watch.

The dark man said something in a calm, sad voice. Kheperu could not understand the words, but his tone sounded as though he'd said *I warned you.*

# 6

# *The Survivor*

**S**he spent more than a thousand years there, convulsing on the lap of the dark man; more than ten thousand years. Immortal gods birthed, aged, and died in senile decay before she opened her eyes and looked up into the dark man's striped face, through the pity underlined by rage that coiled within his eyes, down into the truth of him.

She said, "You're one of them. You're a Jerichite."

His laugh sounded like a snarl. "I'm not one of them," he said. "I *am* them. Didn't I say all this is mine? I wouldn't lie to you, woman. This is mine." His eyes smoked. "I am the sole heir."

"Loving Mother . . ." Barra whispered. "Sweet love of the Mother, *what they did here* . . ."

"Barra, can you understand me?" Kheperu said urgently. He knelt by her side, his face drawn into streaks of concern. "You've had some kind of seizure. Do you remember any of what happened to you?"

She rolled her head slowly to one side so that she could see him; she was afraid to move more than this, for fear her brain might burst from her skull, for fear her whole body might shatter like a faience pot thrown against a wall.

He was so near, so worried, so honestly caring that Barra's eyes suddenly flooded with tears; for a moment, she could have kissed him, just for being Kheperu, for being smarmy and perverse and filthy, for being treacherous and whiny, greedy and brilliant and brave. She could have kissed him just for being alive.

"I remember," she whispered. Her hand shook violently when she reached for Kheperu's, and she squeezed his hand with all her strength.

"He told us that we stood on the Dead of Jericho. It's true . . ." Revulsion beyond control rose up her throat until she nearly choked on it. "This is where they put them. This sand—it blew in from the desert, all these years. Under it, there's only bone and ashes . . ."

"I don't understand," Kheperu said thinly. "Was this some kind of vision?"

"No vision," she said. *"Sceon tiof."*

She tried to sit up, but her body wouldn't yet entirely obey her, and she sank back onto the dark man's lap. He didn't move, except to slide his arms once more protectively around her.

She said, "I called it up to get the truth of this one here, and got . . . I got a bit more than I guess I was ready for. I got the truth of this place."

"Bone and ashes . . ." Kheperu murmured, his eyes distant and cold.

"Ay." Her hold on consciousness still felt fragile, but she forced the words out despite her weakness. "This was the temple . . . they stacked the bodies in here when they were through with them, piled them like cordwood, filled the place wall to wall and nearly to the roof. Soaked them with oil and set them on fire."

It dragged at her, this knowing; it sucked at her spirit and filled her with darkness. The moonlight faded in her eyes, and she smelled the roasting crackle of human flesh.

"They made the temple an oven. They cooked us down to ashes, down to splinters and charred grease. Not all of us were dead, yet—I was a girl, they cut me in the belly, they kicked me in the face, over and over, after they pulled my baby from my arms and smashed his head against the wall so his brains splattered out like seeds of a melon, he was dead but I wasn't, I was only unconscious and I woke up in here in the heat and flames and I heard, I heard, I heard screams that weren't mine, screams of babies, screams of men—"

"Barra, stop it!" Kheperu grabbed her roughly as though he could shake the vision out of her brain, and she returned his clutch, digging her fingers into his arms until he went pale and gasped; she bit her lips until fresh blood flowed into her mouth, using the pain to anchor her, to draw her up from the searing black pool that pulled her down and tried to drown her, and then she clawed herself into his arms and clung to him, gasping, trembling, her eyes streaming unheeded tears.

"Mother . . . oh Mother," she moaned. "How am I gonna live? *How am I gonna live with this in my head?"*

Kheperu was so astonished and disconcerted by her sudden need that all he could do was pat her uncomfortably on the back and murmur helplessly, "Shh, now, Barra, there there, it'll be all right . . ."

She held him tight, just to have a living human being within her arms, and she whispered, "You don't understand. You'll *never* understand. That girl, that's only one . . . her baby is another . . . her husband, her father, her grandparents, her friends, *their* friends . . . I know them all."

Every scrap of their agony and terror howled within her. "All of them. They're all screaming in my head. Every single one. I know them all."

The growing smile that stretched the scars on the Jerichite's face gleamed like the blade of a sword, and his eyes were hot coals of hatred. He had understood every word; in perfectly accented Phoenikian, he said, "Welcome to my home town."

His name was Sheshai. He would give no family name, for his family name no longer had meaning. "My father was a tanner," he said. "If you've got a good arm, you could throw one of those rocks and just about hit what's left of his shop. Everyone who ever met him is dead, so his name isn't even shit. It is nothing at all."

He squatted on the sand that overlay the grave of his family—the grave of his whole people—and told them the short version of the story of his life. He spoke in a dry, precise way with a coldness belied by the fury lurking under his gaze.

"There's no reason not to tell you," he said. He nodded toward the swollen moon. "I'm just like *him*: I see you, you see me, but we'll never touch. It's not important. Nothing matters, except this."

On his back he wore a quiver of long-shafted arrows. He reached over his shoulder and pulled one out that was different from the others. It was fletched in black, as though from the pinions of a crow, and some kind of glyphs were painted in silver along the shaft. Its head was a dull flat grey, a color that Barra knew well: Hittite iron, scoured and oiled to keep the rust off. He didn't have to feel among his arrows to select it—when he reached back, its nock was the first one he'd touched, as though he always knew precisely where this one particular shaft was, as though he had a sense of it the way other people had a sense of their hands and feet.

"I hope it'll fly straight," he said. "I've never used it."

He'd been a trader, back when he was alive—that meant before the sack of Jericho. He was young, and married, and hopeful; he had driven east in the seat of a wagon filled with his father's saddles and belts, to get the premium prices from the Egyptians on the Coast.

"I went alone," he said. "I always went alone. I was the fifth child of seven living; all I ever wanted my whole life was to be alone."

He'd been trading in Gaza when the Egyptian military couriers galloped in with news of Jericho's fall. He was the only Jerichite there. The Jericho Road ran through Jebusi to the Jordan ford; Jerichites didn't travel, they didn't have to. The world came to them.

The Israelites came to them.

They killed his father.

They killed his mother.

They killed both of his grandmothers and his one surviving great-grandfather.

They killed all four of his brothers and both of his sisters.

They killed his wife, a childhood playmate who'd grown into a sensible and strong-willed woman, that he'd married only a year before after a courtship that had begun when he was three, stumbling to her window with a ragged handful of daisies in his grubby little fist, because daisies made her smile.

They killed his infant daughter, and his unborn child, still within his wife's womb.

They killed his boyhood friends, his rivals, his enemies.

They killed the man who once cheated his father in a horse deal.

They killed the woman who used to spit on him when they were both children.

They killed the old man who liked to sit in the sunshine on the roof of his house, drunk as an Egyptian, and pee over the rim.

They killed the twin sisters who'd lived four houses away, of whom he'd had innumerable guilty dreams after once spying through their window while they undressed.

They killed everyone he'd ever known, and everyone who'd ever known him.

They erased his life.

It was three months after his nineteenth birthday.

Five years later, he was a beggar in Gibeon. He'd drifted from city to city, doing day labor and odd jobs until he was too drunk to remember his task. He'd been a prostitute, until the wine he drank to wash away his mind and dull his dreams had so bloated and distorted his features that all he could sell was the occasional half-shekel blow job.

When that trade was slow, he would cut his face with a potsherd and accost travelers, pretending to be the victim of a bandit; later, cutting his face and his arms with bits of broken pottery or glass became something of an end in itself, an amusement of sorts as he came closer and closer to that final state of nothingness in which he could take his own life.

His self-loathing had kept him alive; he hated himself too much to ever want his suffering to end. It would have ended soon enough, though; sleeping in the ditches and eating trash was making sure of that.

But, instead, the Israelites saved his life.

The Hivite elders of Gibeon threw wide the gates when the Israelites approached; in exchange for their lives, they had sold their city and every living thing in it to the Israelites.

Life as a slave had agreed with him. His only worries had been where he'd be able to snitch his next jug of wine, and remembering to always pretend that he'd been a Hivite from birth. One day he woke up too painfully sober because his Asherite master was kicking him in the kidneys, and a beautiful, terrible light had burst into his brain.

He came to the astonishing realization that he didn't have to hate himself.

He could hate *them*.

"That's when I started looking for a way to escape. I served in the camps of Israel for ten years, and I saw—" He could only shake his head grimly. "I saw things you could not possibly believe. They think that what they did here makes them *heroes*."

"It's like Troy," Barra said raggedly. She glanced at Kheperu. "Leucas ever tell you about the end of the war? Once the Greeks took Troy, they slaughtered every Trojan male—all of them, down to the smallest infants. When he tells it, he looks sick—he thinks that the murders and the shipwrecks and all the rest of the horrible things that happened to the captains when they turned for home, were the gods' way of punishing them for this crime."

"Well, the Israelites' god didn't punish *them*, let me tell you," Sheshai said, now some venom entering his voice. "They call him Yahweh; he is a brutal and vindictive god. They say his exact words about Jericho were 'Smite every living thing with the edge of the sword.' Shit. He didn't even let them keep what they looted from us—he took it for himself, so his priests could eat off plates of solid gold."

Sheshai leaned forward, his eyes rolling suspiciously, and lowered his voice into a madman's caricature of a conspiratorial whisper. "*He makes war upon our gods*. He wants to kill them all, because the Israelites fear him so much they'd rather worship anything but him.

Everywhere they go, the Israelites keep trying to find other gods to worship; sometimes, when they can't find any, they'll just invent one of their own. His grip on these people is unbreakable—he kills his own people by the thousand if one of them so much as looks upon a foreign god.

"Mm," Kheperu said softly. "I knew a man like that in Thebes, once—he was a priest, who had a very profitable little sideline in Elephantine ivory and spiced oil. As rich and powerful as he was, he had a terrible fear that his family wouldn't respect him."

Barra watched her friend through bruised eyes. He'd started this tale, she knew, to ease the conversation away from the roots of Sheshai's madness, but as he spoke the story itself seemed to take hold of him, somehow; his eyes went distant and cold as he looked back along the trails of memory.

"A curious fellow," Kheperu murmured faintly. "He subjected his entire household to an endless list of arbitrary rules, down to what they could and could not eat when he wasn't even around, and he beat his wives and children horribly for the slightest infraction; sometimes he beat them for no reason at all. He'd say they were *thinking* about disobedience. He knocked an eye out of the head of one of his sons, for looking disrespectfully at him; he beat his eldest daughter to death for talking with a Nubian in the market. That was the end of him, of course, but the stories his wives told . . ."

He shook his head. "I think of him sometimes, and I wonder if perhaps there was something wrong with his brain, if he had a demon; I'd like to think so. I'd hate to believe that a healthy man could do such things."

Sheshai went on as though he hadn't heard him. He picked up the arrow and held it in both hands, turning its shaft in his fingers. "Their leader is a man named Joshua, son of Nun. I saw him once, at the Beth Horon Valley, when he met the combined armies of the Canaanite League and destroyed them—didn't beat them, you understand, *destroyed* them. I don't think one Canaanite in ten survived that battle."

His fierce gaze drifted out of focus. "Joshua is a big man, bow-legged, and his face is swollen from the blood he soaks himself in. He is decadent and corrupt and raddled with pox. He's an animal—a beast that would open your belly and roll in your guts for play. They say his god protects him, that he can't be killed, that he can't even be hurt."

He lifted the arrow in his fist. "Well, I have a god of my own. Joshua tried to kill him—that's what happened here. But I'm still alive, and while I live to do him honor, so is he. My family has lived in Jericho for three thousand years. Jericho . . . *Tchera'khu—*" The way he pronounced it sounded to Barra like Egyptian: Fortress of Light. "—Tchera'khu hangs above us in the sky tonight, and you saw the sacrifice I brought him. This arrow is tipped with iron, the metal that falls from the moon's house in the sky, and it's painted with silver, and maybe I can't get at their god, but someday *I will see Joshua again.*"

"Perhaps sooner than you think," Kheperu said. "The Habiru seem to be marching on Jebusi."

Sheshai went on as though he hadn't heard. "I know him. He does not know me. Before I die, I will teach him to curse my name."

For one long moment of silence, his words hung in the air beside him like a prophecy; then he looked at the arrow in his fist as though surprised to find it there. He shrugged, and put it away; the fire had gone out of his manner like the sun sliding behind a cloud. He said to Barra, "Are you feeling better?"

She stared at him. She'd never be feeling better. But she said: "Ay, sure."

"Good. Excuse me." He rose and went silently back to looting the corpses.

Kheperu leaned close to murmur in her ear. "He's mad."

"That he is," Barra said. "Wouldn't you be?"

"No: I mean in the sense of *insane.*"

Barra looked at him. "Ay, me too," she said simply. She extended a hand. "Help me up."

Kheperu pulled her to her feet. "You are sure you're ready to stand?"

She sighed. "Can't lie there all night." She went over to where she'd dropped her axe and picked it up, brushing it clean of sand with her fingertips.

Her knees still trembled a little, and she moved with the caution of an old woman, aware of the brittleness of her bones. Her ears buzzed, and her chest ached with the fragile emptiness she remembered from her childhood pregnancy, when she would spend whole days crying herself to exhaustion.

She slid the axe haft back into its scabbard and nodded toward Sheshai, who now filled a large sack with the weapons of the slain men. "I'm gonna ask him to join us."

"Are you as mad as he is?" Kheperu said. *"Why?"*

"I don't know," she said truthfully, and sighed again.

She ignored Kheperu's sputtering and went over to the Jerichite. "Y'know, we've got a camp not too far from here," she began.

"I know," he said, examining one of the knives the Jebusites had used to kill each other. He checked its edge against his thumb, frowned at a bright nick in the blade, shrugged, and dropped it into the sack. "Tchera'khu told me you're not alone. Some more of you are arriving even now, I think."

He waved vaguely over her shoulder, and she turned to see Graegduz scrambling down the scree of the ruined tower. He loped across the enclosure and gravely seated himself at her side, leaning against her legs.

"That's a wolf," Sheshai said, in a blankly matter-of-fact tone like he'd never been this close to one before, but somehow was neither surprised nor particularly distressed. "He's pretty."

"Barra?" Leucas' gentle call came softly from the same place. "I'm sorry, Barra, I couldn't stop him."

He came down into the enclosure, with Agaz close upon his heels. "When Graegduz woke up and found you gone, he just came after you. I couldn't stop him."

"Perhaps not," Kheperu said disgustedly, "but you were hardly forced to follow him, were you?"

Leucas spread his hands. "You were gone so long. I was worried."

"And him?"

Leucas glanced at Agaz. "Graeg's whining woke him up. He was worried, too; I don't speak enough Phoenikian to convince him to stay in camp, and I couldn't let him wander around out here alone."

"It's all right," Barra said tiredly. She buried her fingers in the loose ruff round Graeg's neck. "I'm glad you're here."

"Ba'al in the Muck . . . What happened here?" Agaz said softly, as he took in the scattered jumble of bloody corpses, and Leucas said with a frown, "I thought you were going to come back for me before any killing started."

Barra only shook her head. She was far too tired to attempt an explanation. "Guys, this is Sheshai. Sheshai, these are my partners, Leucas Deodakaides of Athens and Oshea bin Jepno of Jebusi."

"Oshea bin Jepno?" That thick and bloody darkness was back in Sheshai's voice, and his lips twisted back from his teeth. *"Agaz!"*

With no more warning than this, he sprang at the prince, his hands outstretched like the talons of a stooping falcon, going for Agaz's throat. Barra was too exhausted and far too off guard to stop him; she could only gape as Leucas stepped smoothly into Sheshai's path and stiff-armed him with an open palm to the chest. Sheshai went down like he'd run into a wall and lay gasping on the sand.

Leucas said, "Should I kill him?"

"Shit, no!" Barra exclaimed, then added, "But don't let him hurt Agaz."

Now Sheshai found his voice, and he choked out through his bruised chest, "Did you think I wouldn't *know* you, Agaz? Did you think I haven't *seen* you in the streets, seen you at the Citadel? Did you think I haven't dreamed of getting my teeth into your throat?"

Agaz stepped around the shield of Leucas' broad chest, and said coldly, "I have no idea who are you, man. Nor why you would wish to harm me."

Barra came around to stand by Agaz. "He's not the one who hurt you, Sheshai."

"*You* say!" Sheshai snarled. "He's the *prince of fucking Jebusi*, do you understand? Jebusi is a half day's march from here! *Half a day!* Joshua laid siege here for *seven!*"

"Ahhh," Agaz said with a certain chilly satisfaction, as though this explained everything. "You're a Jerichite."

"I'm *the* Jerichite."

"As you say. But what happened here has nothing to do with me."

"We were *allies!*" Sheshai's eyes filled with tears that must have burned like molten lead. "You whoreson shit-eater! You swore you'd protect us—you *swore*! You could have marched out and broken the siege—any day you could have! You sat there behind your walls and *let them slaughter us!*" His voice broke with inexpressible hatred.

"It was the decision of my brother Adonizedek, not mine," Agaz said. If his voice had been cold before, now it was icy enough to freeze beer. "But if I had been the eldest—if I had been king—my decision would have been precisely the same."

Barra now turned to him and stared, stunned beyond comprehension; these words went through her like a white-hot knife. She thought of waking up here, inside the temple with the oil in her hair and in her mouth, with the flames and the screams of her people around her . . .

"And whatever debt my brother may have owed for abandoning you, he has long since paid." His voice seemed to come from some remote mountaintop, miles away from any human remorse or pity, even for himself.

"After Adonizedek my brother led the Canaanite League to the disaster at Beth Horon, he was captured. Joshua paraded him before his army of Habiru, cut off his thumbs, his toes, and gouged out his eyes. He was made to kneel to those savages and suffer each of their captains to place a foot upon his neck before he was finally granted the mercy of death."

"You left out one thing," Sheshai said. He came to his feet with a savage lust in his eyes, a burning itch to inflict pain. "He was *drawn*, Agaz. Along with the other four kings Joshua captured. They slit his belly and pulled out his guts a cubit at a time. I was there. I saw it. I *loved* it, Agaz; the only happy dreams I ever have are when I see it again in my sleep. Look at the men around you here, these corpses on the ground. Recognize them? Any of them?"

He flourished his hands like a conjurer, and took a bow. "They're all Jebusites," he said proudly, "and I laughed as I watched them die."

Agaz stared at him blankly. Then, without the slightest change of expression, he mechanically drew his sword; he raised it to cut down Sheshai where he stood, but Barra caught his arm.

"Haven't you done enough?" she said. "Do you have to kill the last of them, too?"

His eyes widened, then narrowed, and the muscles of his jaw jumped in their sudden clench; her words had somehow stabbed him far more deeply than Sheshai's ever could.

He let his arm fall to his side, and after a moment he resheathed his sword. "Sheshai," he said consideringly, as though memorizing the name. "You are not welcome in Jebusi, Sheshai. If I see you there, I will have you killed."

Sheshai gave him that sword-edged grin. "You won't see me, Agaz."

"Let's go back to camp, and leave this crow to his carrion," Agaz said. "I can no longer stomach the smell."

Barra was silent on the whole long walk back to camp. She paced alongside Agaz, struggling grimly with her feelings; she kept her eyes on the ground before her, pretending that she needed to concentrate so that she wouldn't trip in the moonlit rubble. Agaz made no conversation, either. His gaping silence beside her sounded like an accusation.

She'd hurt him, somehow. He must have expected her to take his side against Sheshai; and she did, intellectually, *rationally* . . . If Adonizedek had come out against the Israelites twenty years ago, Jebusi could very well be today a similarly haunted ruin.

Barra thought of an army twelve times the size of Manasseh's, and shivered.

So she should have been able to apologize. She should have been able to say *I'm sorry, Agaz. I spoke in the heat of the moment, and I didn't mean to say that you—or your brother—had done anything wrong.*

She should have been able to, but she couldn't.

She had too many deaths inside her.

Kheperu spent most of the hike explaining to Leucas what had happened, both on that evening and twenty years ago. The Athenian didn't need it spelled out in detail; he'd fought at Troy, and participated in the sack. His only comment was, "It's not surprising. Let soldiers loose inside an enemy city, things always go bad." His gaze went distant and bitter. "My first campaign was against Thebes, following Diomedes Tydeides and the Epigoni. I saw the gentlest man I ever knew rape a woman twice his age, only a moment after he'd killed her unarmed son in the street outside. He's my cousin, that gentle man is, still lives in Athens. He was born in Thebes—he shares Theban blood, even as I do. It's just war, you know. It does things to people."

After this, he lapsed into a silence so profound that even Kheperu seemed to respect it. Not another word was spoken on the rest of that moonlit hike through the crumbled remnants of Jericho.

The camp looked just as it had when she'd left. The fire was a little higher—Leucas must have built it up some while he sat on watch. The rich coppery stench of blood was still thick in her nostrils as they all slowly lowered themselves back to their chosen spots on the ground, quietly so they wouldn't wake the mercenaries.

Barra sat for a moment with her head in her hands, near the slab where the Hittite brothers snored. The smell of death seemed to cling to her, choking her like smoke from a greenwood campfire. That temple . . .

*I may never eat meat again,* she thought.

Graegduz seemed to want to bother one of the Philistines, until she hissed him back to her side. If anything, the smell seemed stronger, now; would she choke on this reek for the rest of her life?

Wait . . . could memory really be this strong?

She lifted her head and tasted the air, a slow indrawing breath with her mouth half-open. This blood-and-shit smell of death was no memory, no clinging remnant; and it was mixed with the sharp acid sweat of men who have nerved themselves for battle.

"Leucas! Kheperu!" she snapped. "We're in trouble."

But her partners had already laid themselves down; even as they sat up, the Argives leaped shouting to their feet with drawn swords already in their hands.

Barra sprang upright, and a hand locked her ankle from behind and slammed her back to the earth. She tried to roll away from the grab, but a foot planted itself in the middle of her back and pinned her down. She heard Graegduz snarl around a mouthful of something, and heard a Hittite curse.

"Graeg! Run!" she cried in Pictish. "Run away!"

He yelped like he'd been hurt, and she heard his toenails scrape on stone behind her, fading away. "Fucking dog," one of the Hittites growled. "Won't live long."

The shouting woke the camels, and they staggered upright hissing and honking like geese in distress; Pahshannur's wail sounded very much like the camels he loved. "I'm sorry!" he bleated. The camels scattered into the darkness, and he shouted as he chased after them. "They said they'd hurt my babies! I'm sorry!"

Through it all, the Sherdanu and Philistine mercenaries hadn't so much as twitched. None of them would ever twitch again; every one of them had been throat-cut or heart-stabbed in his sleep.

A rough hand removed her broadaxe from its scabbard, then one of the Hittite brothers yanked her to her knees by her hair; she knew him by his smell. Leucas, Kheperu, and Agaz all sat helplessly, blades aimed at their throats, and Barra felt the thin icy line of a bronze edge against her own.

Stephanos, the Argive mercenary with the tree-trunk neck, hefted her axe appreciatively.

"Nice. I can see why you like it," he said in a friendly way. "Bet you didn't know I speak a little Hatti, huh? Not much Phoenikian, but then I didn't need much of the language to know the words *Jebusi*, and *Agaz*. I was curious what you two boys were doing, sneaking off in the middle of the night."

Barra shot a glance toward the murdered Philistines. "What about them?"

The Argive shrugged. "Nobody could talk to them. Didn't know which way they'd jump—and, y'know, we didn't really need them, did we? Just be another five shares out of the reward for nothing." He shook his head. "Why are you so greedy? That's what I can't understand. We travel all this way together, and you goat rapers were gonna cut us out of the money. That's low, Barra. It really is."

*Ay, you'd be an authority on low,* she thought, but held her tongue.

She still had some hope of getting out of this with their lives. "Hey," she said. "Sorry, Stepho. You know how it is."

"Yeah, I do. Sorry I can't leave you alive."

*Shit.* "Not as sorry as I am. Can't we share?"

He shook his head. "Can't trust you. You've proven that already. And I can't let you go, you're too good a scout. The Hittite brothers there, they want the Egyptian dead. You," he said to Leucas, "are a traitor piece of shit—you'd side with a barbarian against your own people."

"Barra *is* my people," Leucas rumbled.

"How do you hope to collect?" Barra asked. "Come on, think about it. You know that Agaz and I have been close . . . You think he's gonna let you go with the money? You're dreaming."

"Got that figured out, too." He tossed the axe up spinning, caught it again with a grin of self-satisfaction. "Not stupid, y'know. People think I'm stupid just because I'm big. Don't have to sell him back to Jebusi at all."

"What, to the Manassites? You'll never get him back there, not without me to lead you. The Benjamites'll kill you and take him themselves."

"Don't have to take him anywhere," he said smugly. "This is a plenty good spot to hold him. Lots of places to hide, and nobody wants to come here in the first place. And I think we can let the Jebusite king and old whatsisname of Manasseh bid against each other."

Leucas' face was grim as iron. He met her eyes fearlessly; he was ready to fight and die.

Kheperu licked sweat from his lips. Both of his hands were in plain sight; no help there.

Agaz had his eyes closed; even without knowing the tongue, he knew what was about to happen.

Stephanos looked at the Hittite who still held her by the hair. "Kill her."

The Hittite yanked her head up and back, so that he'd be able to see her face as he cut her throat. Her hands came up helplessly; the convulsions had left her strengthless, and the numb horror of memory that held her made it almost impossible to resist.

She was going to die on her knees, just as a thousand Jerichites had died twenty years ago, kneeling before their captors. She knew what it would feel like, when the blood began to drain over her chest; she had felt it a thousand times already tonight.

The Hittite smiled down at her, and then with a sound like *crtcch*, an arrowhead grew out of his right eye.

Barra blinked in astonishment. For a moment, nobody moved.

She thought, *Sheshai.*

The Hittite swayed, still smiling, then twisted as he slowly collapsed toward the ground, the fletching on the shaft through his head seeming to glow with the silver of the moon above.

She caught his wrist as he went down, and pulled the knife from his loosening fingers, and all her strength returned in a howling rush. She ignored the other Hittite at her back, throwing herself into a forward roll from her knees that brought her to her feet right in front of Stephanos.

She lunged with the knife in her right, toward his axe side. He cut at her arm with the axe by way of a parry; it might have worked if he'd had a sword in his hand, but the unfamiliar weapon betrayed him. Instead of a sword blade to strike her arm, it was a wooden axe haft, and even as the haft knocked her wrist Barra flipped the knife to her other hand and buried it in his liver.

His eyes went wide and she pressed herself against him like a lover, sawing the blade up along the curve of his rib cage until she could feel the beat of his heart in its hilt.

She looked into his eyes. "Didn't I warn you about touching my axe?"

He freed his arm and swung clumsily; she blocked his swing with a contemptuous forearm and twisted the knife in his heart until his bowels and bladder released and flooded their intertwined legs. She let him fall into his own shit, pulling the axe from his strengthless hand as he went.

Knife in one hand, axe in the other, she looked around. Leucas had taken full advantage of the distraction: the Argive that had held a blade to him now had that blade sticking out of his chest. Another lay pinned beneath the Athenian, who straddled his chest and lifted a chunk of broken wall bigger than his head. As she watched, he brought it down on the Argive's skull with a very final-sounding crunch.

One of the Argives was missing altogether—he must have run off—and Agaz struggled with the last one until Kheperu brained the mercenary with the sword of one of the dead Philistines.

The other Hittite also had arrows in him; one in the guts and another through the knee. He also had a bloody bite wound on his leather-sleeved forearm. He met her eyes, and what he saw there made him try to drag himself away as she approached.

She said in conversational Hatti, "What did you do with my wolf?"

"Fucking thing *bit* me . . . Shit, shit, I'm hurt. It's really *in* me, isn't it? In my guts." He tried to swallow. "I'm gonna die here."

"That's right," Barra said. She stuck the knife behind her belt and put one hand on the white-fletched shaft that stuck out of his belly. "You might imagine that I don't feel too sorry for you right now. Tell me what happened to my wolf and which way he went, or I'll leave you here to die screaming the way your brother did."

"I stabbed it," he said hoarsely. "It ran off that way, over those timbers, and—"

Barra interrupted him with an axe blow to the head that splintered his skull.

"Better than you deserve," she muttered, wiping his brains off her axe with a handful of his shirt.

When she stood up and turned back to the others, Sheshai was there, coming cautiously out of the shadows with an arrow nocked to his string.

"What are *you* doing here?" Agaz demanded roughly, still half-breathless from the fight.

"I followed you," Sheshai told him. "I was going to kill you."

"Why didn't you?"

Sheshai shrugged, with that sword-edged grin. "I suppose I didn't feel like it. Then I was going to let *them* kill you." He took one hand off the bow and turned it palm up; he studied it as though his future could be read there. "I guess I didn't feel like that either."

"You saved my life," Barra said. "You saved all our lives."

He turned his grin on her, and shrugged again. "Maybe it's because you remind me of my mother."

Graeg wouldn't answer her calls, but she could track him by the trail of blood he'd left over timber and stone. She found him in a den made of the corner of a well-built house, where a large piece of the roof had fallen in and was still supported by what was left of the walls. She reached in and gave him her hand; he laid his face against it, and her eyes filled with hot tears at the feel of his breath on her wrist.

"Come on, come out of there," she said. It took a lot of coaxing, but finally she was able to talk him into crawling out to her.

He had a gaping wound in his side; to Barra, it looked as big as his mouth.

"That's it," she said unsteadily, trying to swallow the knot in her throat. "No more for you, you bastard. You live through this, and you're *retired*, you hear me? I'll take your fat spoiled butt back to Tyre and breed you to a bloodhound."

She held him to her, and wet the fur at his neck with her tears. "Oh, Graeg . . . Graeg, I'm so sorry. Never again. Never, ever again."

She could face injury and death. She could lead men into battle: it was their choice, they could run if they wanted, they could refuse to fight. She didn't give one splattering shit for the slain Argives and Hittites; men like them give up any claim on her sympathies with their first murder. The Grey Man—Arawn, Lord of the Grey Lands and the husband to the life-giving Mother by whom Barra swore—required that the lives of murderers be given to him. In the past, Barra had hunted such men for sport.

Graeg didn't have that choice.

He never would; his love for her drove him like a whip. It was her choice that had wounded him. It was nothing more nor less than her own selfishness that had brought him here at all.

He'd been hurt defending her in Tyre, his leg broken by the demon hyaenae of Simi-Ascalon; he'd been threatened with death by her enemies there, and saved only by the foolish valor of a half-senile old man.

She'd taken too many chances with his life already.

One too many.

He weighed as much as she did, and she was cloth-limbed with exhaustion, but somehow she hoisted him across her back. He whined in pain, but didn't struggle; his trust in her was absolute.

She staggered back over the rubble toward the camp. Each time her foot slipped, each time she had to jerk to recover her precarious balance, Graeg would give a tiny whimper that stabbed her in the heart.

Again she was bitterly aware of how expensive this job had become.

*And all just for money?* she thought. *Am I really putting myself through this for silver, nothing else?*

How much silver was Graeg's life worth? How much gold would she need to make her forget how much he'd loved her?

*I hate this fucking work,* she thought. *I hate it.*

This became a litany inside her head, and the subtle moonlight seemed to swell to light her way, as she staggered back to the camp with the wolf she loved across her shoulders.

# 7

# *The Heroes' Welcome*

It was a sadly reduced little band that struggled up the last leg of the Jericho Road toward Jebusi. Leucas walked in the lead, with Kheperu's trunk slung over one rock-hard shoulder; Kheperu came close behind him, leaning hard on an Argive spear as though it were a walking staff, and groaning with every step. In the fight last night he'd somehow taken a kick to the soft muscle just above the inside of his knee. His thigh was swollen and purple, and the rudely stitched spear cut in his back continued to fester, adding fever to his pain.

Agaz walked with his head down and his hands clasped behind him; from the look on his face, there were thoughts going on within him that he could neither endure nor deny. Barra didn't ask him about them. She had problems of her own.

The sweat that trickled down her face got into the cut on her neck, a shallow slice left by the Hittite's knife, and sizzled like pork fat in a campfire. Her legs trembled with exhaustion, and her shoulders and arms were as raw as skin can get, short of actual wounds. Droplets of blood seeped through here and there, staining the leather band that went across her shoulders, behind her neck to the spear shafts under her arms, which trailed behind her on the road to support the travois on which Graeg rode.

The previous occupant of the travois, the Argive whose foot she'd taken off four days ago, had died sometime in the night. He might have gone during the fight, or before, or after—no one knew, and no one cared. His life had slipped away unnoticed and unmourned, and Leucas had tossed his body in among those of his countrymen.

*It's just as well,* Barra had reflected. She would have felt guilty leaving a dying man behind just so Graeg can ride—this guilt probably wouldn't have stopped her from doing it, but she was glad she hadn't faced the choice.

Back at the camp, Kheperu had fed Graeg a piece of sausage dusted with one of his powders to make him sleep, and then bound up his wound; they'd need full sunlight for the internal sewing that must be done. For all his practiced cynicism, Kheperu had the Egyptian love of animals in full force, and it had cut him like knives to watch Graeg suffer.

"We'll need a collar—stiff leather, boiled like armor, in a reversed cone around his face. They're used in Egypt to keep dogs and cats from chewing off their dressings. Perhaps we can improvise something once we get to Jebusi." He reached out and tentatively touched her shoulder. "I wish I could tell you that he'll be all right."

"Ay," Barra said with a weary nod. "Not that I'd believe you if you did."

She had sat with Graeg's head in her lap, stroking his ears as he drifted through his drugged slumber, and watched the others bury the dead.

Sheshai had suggested they be left to the crows and vultures, but Leucas had insisted: "I am not so loved by Zeus that I can risk dishonoring the dead."

"Why not a pyre?" Agaz asked. "Burning is honorable, is it not?"

Barra's heart caught in her throat.

"Yeah," Sheshai said, his eyes alight, "*you* would think so, wouldn't you?"

"No," Leucas had told them with inarguable finality. "Fire is for the funeral of heroes. These men have not earned that honor. Cover their corpses with dirt and leave them for the worms."

"It's a lot of work," Kheperu said. "Perhaps we could bury the Argives and the Hittites, but burn the Philistines and Sherdanu? They were innocent victims, after all—why not make it easy on ourselves?"

"Ask Barra," Sheshai said, his grin sparkling mad. "Ask Barra how she feels about burning the dead in Jericho."

All eyes had turned to her, and the charcoal reek of burning meat had risen up in the back of her throat. "No fires," she'd said thickly, turning her face away from them, so that they would not see the sickness there. "No fires. Bury them."

"Easy for you to say," Kheperu complained. "You're not the one with the bad back."

She shook her head irritably, then closed her eyes and leaned back against the rubble behind her. "Do what you want."

They covered the corpses with stones, and then with a mound of dirt they dug using the shovels of the Jebusites, retrieved from the ruined temple. Barra watched; she could see, through gaps in the stones, the dirt falling into the open mouth of Stephanos, and across his open staring eyes.

They'd hit the road before dawn, to make some time before the heat of the day. Veteran infantry in good condition would take five or six hours on the road from Jericho to Jebusi; none of the four who walked it now was in any condition that would be called good. Barra only hoped to be within the city walls before nightfall.

She watched Agaz from time to time, wondering in an abstract way what he was thinking about. He hadn't said a word all day, barring the occasional curse when he half twisted an ankle or stubbed his foot against a stone that his deep thoughts had clouded from his vision.

She wondered if he was thinking about Sheshai.

She certainly was. She couldn't help it.

She'd watched them both, all through that long, long burial of eleven dead men. Sheshai had stayed close to Agaz, going out of his way to make chatty small talk, wearing a mockingly cheerful grin; he obviously derived a malicious enjoyment from the prince's sullen discomfort. He would have left long before, Barra figured, but for the sport he found in needling Agaz. Staring at the two of them with dull incomprehension, Barra had experienced a strange doubling of vision; she couldn't quite keep them both in focus at the same time. Agaz was a wall between his people and any danger without or within. Sheshai was an avalanche, a flood, existing only for the damage he could do.

She admired the nobility of Agaz's refusal to repudiate the actions of his brother the late king . . . but Sheshai—

Sheshai was a walking wound that humbled her by his very existence. There was a sort of breathless awe, almost religious, that squeezed her chest when she looked at him. This Tchera'khu god that he loved, the moon god for which his city had been named, must have hated him beyond understanding; no loving god would have let him live. A loving god would have struck the light from his eyes on the day his city burned.

In any rational world, she would have come down without hesitation on Agaz's side. Your duty is to your family first, to your friends second, to your people third; everything else is whim.

But the rationality of this world had been blown to tatters by the gale of deaths that had entered her in the temple.

Maybe Sheshai had the right of it: maybe the only answer to a world where such things can happen was hatred and mockery and malice. Through some alchemy of spirit, he had transmuted his unconquerable pain into a reason to keep living. In this, too, there was a sort of peasant nobility, an everyman heroism that sank hooks into her heart that she could neither deny nor dislodge.

She couldn't look at Agaz without hating him a little.

When the long grisly process of burial finally came to an end last night, Agaz's patience had as well. He'd turned to Sheshai and demanded, "What? What is it you want?"

Sheshai's smile seemed a permanently affixed feature of his face. "I suppose I want to go home."

"Go, then. Go! Who's stopping you?"

"My home is in Jebusi, now," he'd said cheerfully. "Since I decided not to kill you, I suppose I'm hoping that you'll do me the same courtesy."

Barra could tell by the vein that writhed in Agaz's neck that his temper had reached a rolling boil, but through some extreme exertion of will he held himself in check. He straightened his back and spoke as though from a great height. "You have the freedom of the city," he'd said. "Come to the Citadel, and my father will add a fourth share unto the reward for my safe return. You have earned it, and more."

"Come to the Citadel? Not fucking likely. How'd you put it? *I can't stomach the smell.* You turn a nice phrase, prince. That's the mark of an educated man. But if you're hot to give me money, my house is seven doors north of the Lady's Temple. Come by and visit. I have some wineskins aging nicely—we can get drunk and talk over old times."

"Don't mock me, Jerichite," Agaz had told him. "You tempt me to add you to this grave, and I have seen too many dead men already this night."

"Too *many*?" Sheshai sneered. "Seventeen? Eighteen? You don't know what 'too many dead men' looks like, *Jebusite!*"

"Neither do you!" Barra snarled, surprising herself with her sudden fury. Graeg whined sleepily from her lap, and Barra slid out from under his head, laying him gently down to rest on the stone.

"Sheshai, get out of here."

"But—"

"Go sell your fucking weapons. Sell your horses. Just shut up and go. I'm sick of both of you."

She turned away, furious with them, furious with herself. She felt a hundred years old and rotting from the inside out.

"The rest of you, lie down and get some rest. We're leaving at dawn. I'll stand watch." She looked up at the moon. "I don't think I could shut my eyes if you hit me with a rock."

"Here?" Leucas asked. "Sleep here? Among the dead?"

"There's nowhere in Jericho that isn't among the dead," she'd said bitterly. "My loving god, how I wish I'd never seen this shitcake town. Kheperu, why didn't you just let me fucking *sleep*?"

She could have used that sleep; the way she felt right now, she thought she might never sleep again. The dead breathed chill within her like ice sliding down the inside of her throat, and a thousand faint and wistful voices had spent the stretching hours till dawn whispering her name.

She could hear those whispers even now, in the scrape of the travois over the rocks of the road behind her, and there was only so much of that she could take; she had to do something to drown them out.

Other travelers sing road songs to pass the time, but Barra had inherited her father's bellowing tone deafness along with his flaming red hair, and so she'd always taken a different tack, to spare her dignity and her companions' ears. She asked questions—often very detailed questions; sometimes downright rude.

She glanced over at Agaz, and allowed herself a melancholy smile. She and he, they weren't so different, down deep. Except his questions were always about things, and hers were always about people. Between the two of them, they could make one pretty damned smart person. Really, y'know, if they put their heads together, they could make an impressive team . . .

She saw in time where these reflections were leading, and she resolutely refused to walk that road, even in her mind.

Instead, she said, "Agaz? Tell me about your brother."

"What about him?"

"I don't know," she said. She would have shrugged, but for the weight of the travois strap across her shoulders. "Anything. What he was like. The games you used to play as kids."

"The games we played as kids?"

"Oh, you know. Like, one of my brothers used to like to wrestle me to the ground; he'd get a hold on me so he could sit on my head and fart on me. That kind of thing."

Agaz gave her a sidelong look. "I find that difficult to imagine."

"Ay, so does he, these days," she said with a forced grin. "He's still got the scars from the last time he tried it. I beat him so bloody that to this day he's hand-shy of me, like a whipped dog."

"Abishai was too much older. We never played that kind of game."

"Abishai?" Barra said. "I thought his name was Adonizedek, like your father's."

He sighed, a soft breath of memory entering his eyes. He answered her absently. "*Adonizedek* is a title, not a name. 'Lord of Righteousness.' Years ago, it was *Melchizedek*—'King of Righteousness'—back when the king was also the High Priest of El, but that name has remained with the priesthood. My uncle, he has that name. It's disrespectful—an insult—to call the king by his given name." His eyebrows lifted. "I never knew my father's name until he abdicated—he'd named my brother after himself, and I'd never known it. A vain and foolish old man. But Abishai . . ."

His eyes began to go distant again, but softly, without the harshness that had lined them these past days. "I was—well, I was only the reserve heir, you know? Abishai was beautiful, and strong, taller than me and broad through the shoulder; he could throw a spear farther than any man in Jebusi. I had two other brothers, and a sister, but they all died before I was born. I never knew my mother; she fell to a fever when I was only a couple of months old. Abishai looked after me. He raised me like I was his son, even though he was only eight when I was born."

"You still miss him."

"Of course I still miss him!" Agaz snapped with sudden anger. He slapped his palm with a knotted fist. "I told him—shit, I *begged* him . . . I knew, you see, I *knew* that marching out to face the Habiru at Gibeon would be a disaster. The one stupid act of a very sensible man. He'd been paying tribute to the Habiru for five years, ever since Jericho—and it *worked*. Caravans had been passing on the road unmolested. Not one single Jebusite was ever harmed."

"Seems reasonable."

"It *was* reasonable. He was the *king*. His responsibility, his *primary duty*, was to protect the people. That's what it means to *be* a king."

She nodded; she'd heard her brother Llem say the same thing a thousand times. She gave him a quizzical look. "It's a long step from paying off the Habiru to forming the League of Five Cities and coming out against them in the field. What happened?"

"He lost his sense," Agaz muttered, with an undertone of sullen fury. "Or rather, his sense was witched away—just as my father's sense has been witched away."

"Witched away?" A chilly tingle pricked up hairs on the back of her neck. "What's that mean?"

He looked at her long and full, his lips compressed into a thin resentful line, then he sighed and pointedly changed the subject.

"Here, that strap looks like it's killing you," he said, putting a hand on the travois pole. "Let me carry him for a while. I'm sorry I didn't offer earlier—I've been"—he waved his other hand in the air—"somewhere else, all day."

Barra shook her head, even though Graeg's weight dragged at her like a yoke of stone across her shoulders.

"No, I've got him. It doesn't hurt," she lied. "It's like what you said about being a king. Graeg's my responsibility."

"Does that mean you can't accept any help?"

"No," she said, "but it does mean I won't."

"All right," he said, and gestured toward the Egyptian milestone beside the road. "It's not much farther now; we should be there in an hour or so."

And though her curiosity nagged at her like an itch she couldn't scratch, she forced herself to leave the subject alone through the rest of that journey. Partly out of respect for Agaz—he clearly wished to speak no more about it—and partly because, as a mystery that she could chew over and over, it occupied the space in her mind that would otherwise have been taken up by the whispers of the Jericho dead.

"Wow," was all Barra could say.

Leucas nodded a thoughtful agreement. "If I had to stand a siege, I guess I'd want to do it there."

From this point on the road, high on the east ridge of the Kidron Valley, they were actually slightly above the city walls, and they could see down into its crowded streets. Jebusi was much smaller than Barra had expected, for such an important fortress city on the only east–west road through the *mâtat Urusalim*; it was only a fraction of the size of Tyre, and you could easily have put the entire city inside Idomeneus' palace at Knossos on Crete.

But in many ways that would be an advantage: it was built on the intersection of the ridges bordering the Kidron and Hinnom Valleys;

three sides of the city were defended by slopes nearly as steep as the high walls that rose from them. The only place troops could come directly against those walls was from the north, and the north wall of Jebusi was barely a bowshot long; a fast runner could sprint it and not breathe hard at the end.

The west corner of the massive megalithic wall was anchored by the Citadel, the royal residence and inner keep of the city, a huge complex of ever-higher inner walls and towers overlooking the Kidron Valley; the east corner was defended by the Gate Tower, an enormous sheer cliff face of a fortress that looked to Barra like it must have been constructed by the same race of giants that had raised up the Sunstone Circles in her native land.

"True enough," Kheperu murmured. "Ten cripples and a blind man could hold that place against the whole Egyptian army—but it's *crowded.*"

It was: from this vantage, the city looked like a kicked-open termite mound, folk pressed nearly shoulder to shoulder in the streets. The city itself sloped far down the eastern side of the ridge, as though it had been thrown by a god and had landed lopsidedly; the long descent from ridgetop to the city's wall was filled with terrace after terrace of close-packed buildings, with streets so narrow only foot traffic could pass, many of the streets so steep that they were constructed as stairs.

Every street, every courtyard, every rooftop was jammed with people. Many of them would have come from the surrounding countryside; every farm they'd passed in the last hour, every vineyard, every house, was as deserted as Jericho. Apparently everyone in and around Jebusi already knew of the coming war.

"More crowded than it ought to be," Agaz said grimly. "You thought Beth Shean was packed with mercenaries? Wait till you see Jebusi."

Apparently the sight of his native city brought thoughts that boiled too hard for him to keep them inside; he had to talk or burst. As they marched wearily through the noonday sun the story dragged out of him, bit by bit.

"I don't think my father ever wanted to be king. I don't think he likes the job now; he certainly didn't, then. When my brother passed his fourth sevenyear and became fully a man, my father abdicated in his favor. He was old even then, over sixty; he said he was tired, and he wanted to spend his age pleasing himself, instead of his people. He was always interested in auguries, bird signs, astronomy, all that sort of thing. He'd always wanted to be a man of learning, instead of a king.

"When my brother was killed at Beth Horon, my father decided it was a punishment sent from El Elyon, for violating the 'natural order'—kingship unto death. As though El would really care whether my father watched birds, or the stars, or kept on polishing the throne with his butt. Instead of allowing the kingship to pass on to me, as my brother's heir, he took it back upon himself. Abishai the elder becomes again Adonizedek.

"I didn't mind. I don't care about being king—I serve my people already, as their prince. But now . . . now . . . ."

He shook his head, wordless for a moment, as his eyes misted over. "My father is very old. He is no longer the man he once was. He wanders in his second childhood, speaking sometimes to my late mother, sometimes calling me by my brother's name and scolding me for the foolishness of getting myself killed. I would take the throne by force, but . . . ."

He shrugged helplessly. "But I cannot. As far as he has fallen, he is still my father. He is still Adonizedek. When you meet him, you will understand. He cannot be pushed. He can only be persuaded. That is what I had hoped to do, with the reconnaissance of Manasseh—to persuade him that what he is doing will lead only to the death of our city, and the slaughter of our people. You see, in his dotage he has fallen under the spell of the witches of the Ba'alath—these priests of the Great Lady, these same witches who stole the reason of my brother and sent him to his death. They have promised him that the Goddess herself will defend the city, if only he does not lose heart."

For a moment, he stopped beside the road, and his face twisted, and in his half whisper was something that stung Barra's eyes like the sweat on her raw shoulders; it sounded like humiliation, like bitter shame.

He said softly, "My father has taken all the wealth that should have gone to the Habiru for tribute, and he has used it to hire mercenaries, to fight them.

"You said it yourself, Barra, back all those days ago in Beth Shean. He's spending all he has to buy nothing but trouble. And I'm afraid I might not be able to stop him. Even now, it's probably too late."

Leucas muttered to Kheperu in Greek, "Did I hear this right? He wants to use mercenaries to fight the Habiru? Who in their right mind

would want to fight the Habiru at all? Has this king never seen what's
left of Jericho?"

Kheperu shook his head, and said flatly, "Those priests of the
Lady must have some magic that I cannot match. What power could
make a man choose suicide for his entire race?"

"We fought for ten years on the plain before Troy," Leucas said
grimly. "What was left of Jericho's walls looked like they used to be
thicker than Troy's—and Joshua took it in a week."

"That's why we're not staying," Barra told them briskly. "We'll get
our money, buy horses and a sturdy wagon to carry Graeg, and then
we'll shake this city's dust off our feet when we're halfway to the coast."

Agaz asked what she'd said, and she reluctantly translated; his
response was a bitter look, and she said, "Sorry, Agaz, but you have to
understand—"

"I do understand," he said, "and I don't blame you. I was only
thinking how much I envy you the luxury of flight."

They were still two bowshots or more from the Gate Tower when
the first shouts went up.

*"Agaz! Prince Agaz! Mercy of El, Agaz is alive!"*

"Y'got somebody up there with bloody good eyes," Barra muttered. "Hope he's an archer; you'll need him."

Jebusites streamed out of the gate to meet them, a shouting parti-
colored river of cheering townsfolk.

"Shit, it's a flood," she said to herself, and soon it was all she
could do to protect Graegduz from the crush. Leucas put down Kheperu's trunk, and he and Kheperu stood close around the travois to keep
the crowd off; no one in the mass of cheering Jebusites even seemed
aware of the unconscious wolf.

In seconds they were at the center of an enormous mob of men and
women who crowded around to touch Agaz, to make sure he was real,
pushing in and jumping up, pressing the shoulders of people in front
of them like pommel horses just to catch a glimpse of him, some
laughing and shouting thanks to Ba'al and El, some of them falling to
their knees and sobbing for joy.

"Your people really love you," Barra shouted close to Agaz's ear.

"What?"

*"Everyone loves you!"*

He pulled away and met her gaze. He mouthed, *Yes, they do.* His
face was bleak as a granite cliff. *Are you surprised?*

She mouthed in reply, *You don't seem too happy about it . . .
Just wait. You'll see.*

He jumped up onto Kheperu's trunk and held up his hands for
silence, ignoring the Egyptian's indignant gasp.

The crowd did not fall silent, but their roar ebbed enough that
Agaz could be heard when he called for horses, to bear him and his
rescuers to the Citadel. Horses were swiftly brought, and a flat-bedded
farm cart with a thick layer of clean straw in it, onto which Leucas
gently laid Graegduz, and then hefted Kheperu's trunk up beside him.
Barra refused a horse for herself; she knelt on the cart and kept one
hand on the neck of the wounded wolf.

Before they even reached the gate, Barra understood the grim
dread she'd seen in Agaz's face a moment ago. A middle-aged woman,
wrapped in ash-stained white for mourning, broke through the press
and clutched at the prince's hand, an expression of wild hope lighting
her red-rimmed eyes.

"Prince! Prince!" she cried, her voice cutting through the crowd's
yells with heart-tearing need. "What of my Yassib? He follows,
doesn't he? Yassib comes behind, with the other boys, with Thimil
and, and, and Ilimu . . ."

Agaz did not reply; he didn't need to. The flat and brutal blankness of his stare, the thin set of his mouth, said everything he could
have put into words. The mourning woman shook her head, blind tears
starting from her eyes; she stood rooted to the spot in the middle of the
road as the parade passed her by.

Distantly, through the roar, Barra heard her begin the keening wail
for the dead.

This crowd differed from the press of other towns in one subtle but
telling way, and it took Barra some few moments to see it: within her
view, there were no middle-aged men. Every man along that sunlit
ridge road was either well past sixty, or younger than thirty—and the
women must have outnumbered them three to one. A tingle grew at the
back of her neck and raced down her arms, as she fully appreciated for
the first time what a disaster the battle at Beth Horon must have been
for these people.

An entire generation of Jebusite men had been wiped from existence in a single day; most of the hundred men that Agaz had led to the
north must have been their sons . . .

Once they passed through the deep shadow beneath the Gate
Tower and entered the city itself, old men pressed around as well, asking about their grandsons; young women with infants in their arms

called questions of their husbands; boys and girls, eight or ten years old, begged Agaz to tell them that their fathers were coming home. With each question, pain chiseled deeper lines around Agaz's mouth and eyes.

But these folk were few, and their grief could not dampen the city's joy at the safe return of its prince. The news spread, and the whole city seemed to brighten and ring with happy talk. People scrambled up their outer stairs and lined their rooftops to wave and lift a winebowl in salute as Agaz passed.

And now, here and there along the streets, in shadowed doorways and narrow alleys, Barra did see men of fighting age, wearing armor, most of them, even in the heat of the afternoon with no enemy in sight, armor of bronze and boiled leather, with spears at their sides and swords at their belts. Their weathered faces carried the map of their homelands, of Mykenai and Tiryns, of Philistia, Iberia, Hattiland; black Nubians released from the Egyptian Army, pale Picts and Kelts—mostly Gaels from Albion by way of Phoenikian longships.

They weren't cheering; the most response the parade received from these lounging mercenaries was a humorless grin and the ironic tilt of a wineskin.

*We did it,* Barra thought, looking about herself and trying to believe the truth of it. *We made it. We're here.*

*Trying to rescue the prince of Jebusi from the Habiru was just about the bloodyfucking stupidest thing I've ever undertaken in a lifetime of foolish undertakings—but we've pulled it off.* But somehow she couldn't summon any joy from this; she couldn't even make herself smile.

Leucas, too, seemed immune to the joy around him. He rode easily, but as he rode he stared this way and that, his broken face solemn and watchful, as though he memorized every home, every shop, every face. As though he knew that no one would ever again look upon Jebusi as a living city, and he wanted to be able to do it justice in a song.

Even Kheperu was unusually grim. He could summon only a pained smile as a pretty girl of twelve or thirteen cast a starburst of spring flowers at him. Not only did he say nothing to the pretty girl, he didn't even leer.

She couldn't find the completion here, missed that welcoming languor she should have felt with the happy end to an arduous task. The pressure to be moving on before the Habiru invested the city robbed her of any real sense of accomplishment. *Sure, we saved him. But what for? A month from now, he'll be just as dead as if we'd left him where he was.*

She felt, in some obscure way, as if this was all her fault.

She feared that the Jerichites who whispered inside her head might have some thousands of new companions soon.

Lowering her naked body into the scalding water turned out to be a long, difficult, and painful process. The potash-and-oil soap found every tiniest cut, scratch, and scrape, and stung like a bastard in each one.

This was her first bath in nearly a month, unless you count getting soaked in the occasional thunderstorm, and the astonishing variety of her minor wounds gave her enough distinct, individual pangs to start tears welling—tears not of pain but of a bone-deep process of unclenching-toward-relaxation that bordered upon the excruciating.

Stone cuts; bramble scratches; skinned knees and bloody knuckles; a broad stripe up one side of her back where she'd skidded down some rocks while dodging a Habiru patrol; the rubbed-raw skin on her shoulders and under her arms; the knife slice on her neck; each announced itself in turn, and then faded behind a general tingle of opening pores and loosening muscles. The last to make itself known came when she slid fully under the water and unbraided her hair, shaking it free and sliding her fingers through it to loosen the sweat and grit and greasy dust that dulled it; this last wound was the knot above her ear, left by that rock during the storm in the mountains above the Manassite camp. Crusted scab and the dried blood that had matted her hair came loose, and she combed it out with her fingers.

The old king had met them at the gate to the Citadel, tears in his aged eyes, pathetically grateful for the safe return of his son. Graegduz had received the attentions of the finest surgeon in Jebusi, and was resting downstairs; Leucas and Kheperu had been given rooms of their own, just as she had, to rest and refresh themselves before the giant feast of welcome that would be held after sundown in the Citadel's East Yard.

Leucas was probably bathing now, even as she was. Kheperu, of course, had made other plans, having at best little interest in bathing—after overseeing the surgeon's treatment of Graegduz, he had wandered off in the company of a burly, hard-faced young man, leading a young goat and a large goose, and Barra had no desire ever to learn what it was he planned to do with them.

She scrubbed at her face under the water, and then surfaced with a splashing gasp, starting to feel human again.

"You have really pretty hair."

The voice was a child's, a girl's, and Barra thought she already knew who this might be. She rubbed soap out of her eyes. A little girl stood near the foot of the washtub, clasping her hands behind her with a show of shyness that Barra guessed was almost entirely pretended.

Barra said, "Thank you."

"My father says you're not a very nice woman," the little girl said with a pretty frown. "But you saved him, and brought him back here, and so I think that makes you nice enough, doesn't it?"

This little girl had been at the side of Adonizedek when the old king had welcomed them all to the Citadel. She had dashed through the king's attendants and thrown herself at Agaz. Barra had watched her with a certain sardonic amusement. Somehow it didn't surprise her that Agaz could spend ten days dodging death in her company and never mention that he had a family. She'd caught herself wondering if there was also a wife that he'd neglected to bring up, and squashed that thought like a roach beneath her bootheel.

It was none of her business. She wouldn't be here long enough to let it matter one way or the other. The king would pay them out tomorrow morning, and they'd be long gone by noon.

Agaz's daughter had braids wrapped tightly about her temples, of black hair that shone like it had been carved of jet. She wore a lovely flounced linen robe dyed with Tyrian purple, its hem embroidered with intricate designs executed in scarlet thread and drawn gold. Her face was a flawless oval, and her eyes were like liquid gemstones; her mother must be exquisite.

*Stop it,* she told herself.

"You're Agaz's little girl," Barra said.

She lifted her chin. "I'm the princess. My husband will be king someday."

*If either of you live that long,* Barra thought, but she said, "Really? I'm a princess, too."

"Oh, you are not."

"I am, really. I swear."

The little princess folded her arms huffily. "Princesses live in big forts and learn to sew and do accounts and get married. They don't run around with dirty legs and great big dogs."

"That's what princesses do where *I* come from," Barra said.

"Really?" Her eyes shone. "Do they *really*?"

"Well, not all of them," Barra allowed. "Some of them—my sisters, for example—are pretty much like princesses down here, except instead of learning to sew and do accounts they learn to herd sheep and have babies."

"I don't think that sounds like much fun."

"Me neither. That's why I run around with dirty legs and a great big dog," Barra explained with a smile. "What's your name?"

"Rachel," the princess replied proudly. "*I* can read."

"Me too."

"You can not."

"I can. Five different languages."

Rachel's underlip stuck out. "No matter what I say, you're going to tell me you do it, too."

"I can't help that," Barra said. "No, wait, I've thought of something you can do that I can't."

"What?"

"Grow up to be queen."

As soon as these words came to her lips she regretted them: they stung her like a splash of wine in her eyes. She saw Rachel sobbing as she clung to Agaz's bloody corpse; she saw Habiru ranging the halls of this Citadel, and one of them coming upon her and sticking a span of bronze through her back, to pin her to her father's corpse for one screaming second before he struck through her neck.

*Loving Mother, I swear, if there was anything I could do to change it . . .*

But these hideous images did not reflect on her face; Rachel only considered her words with the thoughtful concentration of the very young. "But why can't you?"

Barra said simply, "Because we don't have queens. I might live with a king someday and be his woman, but we don't get married, and my sons wouldn't be kings after him; instead, the oldest son of his oldest sister becomes king."

"That's kind of stupid."

"Ay, maybe. Or, y'know, if I want, I might be king someday myself."

"King!" The very idea seemed to make Rachel breathless. "You can be *king*?"

"Oh, ay. My grandma on my da's side, she was king of a good part of Eire. She beat every other contender in single combat. She's old now, though, and she lets my da rule."

Her eyes went wide, dazzled by the thoughts that raced behind them. "I might like to be king . . ."

"Well . . ." Barra said cautiously, "it's a lot of work, and I don't want your father getting mad at me for putting ideas in your head. Who are you going to marry?"

"I already *was* married. When I was a baby. But he died a long time ago. My mother and my brothers died then, too."

This darkened her face for only a fleeting moment; an instant later she was smiling again. "I'll have to marry someone else, only my father hasn't picked him out yet." She clapped her hands with sudden excitement. "*You* could marry my father, and then you *could* be queen!"

"I—" Barra pretended that she'd swallowed a mouthful of bath-water, so that she could cough for a moment instead of answering. "I told you, we don't get married."

"All right," Rachel said with a shrug. "Can I brush your hair?"

"Ay, sure. And braid it, too, if you like. Bring that pitcher and rinse me out."

The water that Rachel poured through her hair was pleasantly chilly, and Rachel helped her towel it down, one long strand at a time, rubbed from root to end so it wouldn't tangle. While she waited for her hair to dry, she climbed out of the tub and got her clothes, to wash them in the grey-brown bathwater.

Rachel's eyes went wide and solemn. "You sure have a lot of scars."

"I do," Barra agreed as she mopped beaded water from her long and muscular limbs. "Nearly every one was a cut that should have killed me."

"Where'd you get that one?" She pointed at the young scar across her right shoulder. "Is that new?"

Barra chuckled. "This one I got from an old boyfriend of mine. He chopped me with a bronze sword—broke my collarbone and nearly killed me outright."

"Did it hurt?"

"No, not really. Didn't feel like much of anything at the time. It hurt later, though. It hurts *now*, if you really want to know—it'll be a year or two before it stops hurting altogether. It might hurt for the rest of my life."

"Why'd he do it? Was he a bad man?"

"No, he was a very good man."

"Then why were you fighting him?"

Barra began to scrub her tunic against itself in the soapy water. "I've been fighting people since before you were born. Maybe it's just a habit."

She chuckled, but then she frowned briefly and shook her head. Somehow she felt that this child deserved better than a flip *you'll understand when you grow up* kind of answer.

"One of the things I've learned in all these years is that just because someone's your enemy, he's not automatically a bad man. Most of the time, the men you end up fighting are the *good* men, and that's the sad truth of it. Bad men won't fight you; they pretend to be your friend until they can stab you in the back. The only time a bad man will let you know he's against you is when he thinks you can't do anything to hurt him."

"What about the Itraelizes?"

Barra gave her a sharp look. "What do you know about the Israelites?"

"Is-rael-ites," she repeated carefully, frowning as she tried to memorize the word, then she shrugged. "I hear my grandfather talk about them, with the High Priest and the Lady's Maid. They're coming here to hurt us. They're bad men."

Barra frowned; she'd seen too much in Jericho to disagree—but she'd also seen into the heart of the Manassite who'd almost killed her in their camp, the one whose throat Agaz had slashed to save her. He'd been as good as men get.

"Some of them are very bad men," she said at length. "Some of them are very good men. Most of them are just men, like the men you know here in Jebusi. You'll hear a lot of stories about how bad they are, and all the horrible things they've done, but I'm going to tell you a secret: in their camp, right now, they're telling each other stories about how bad you Jebusites are, and all the horrible things *you've* done."

"But, but, that's *lying*," Rachel exclaimed, deeply affronted. "We don't do horrible things!"

"Some of the stories you'll hear about the Israelites aren't true, either." *And some of them are.* She wrung her tunic fiercely, clenching her teeth against memory.

Rachel said, "There's a lot of them, though, and they want to hurt us. I heard Grandfather say so. There's way too many for us to fight. How are you going to beat them?"

"I don't think your grandfather wants to fight them," Barra said carefully, hoping she was right. "I think he's going to try to keep them out of the city until they get tired and go home."

"I know what *Grandfather's* going to do," she said with high exasperation. "I'm not a baby. I want to know how *you're* going to beat them."

Barra froze, and her heart lurched in her chest. "What do you mean?"

"Grandfather says you're the Lady's Champion," Rachel explained with innocent solemnity. "I heard him arguing with the High Priest. The High Priest says you're not, but Grandfather says you are, and he's much nicer than the High Priest. The High Priest is mean, and he's really stupid. And my father was there—he kind of started it, because he was telling all about how you rescued him and everything—but then he got mad and he was yelling a lot, and the only one that was standing up for you was the Lady's Maid. I had to go then, because I don't like to listen when my father gets mad and yells. That's why I wanted to come and meet you. I've never met a Lady's Champion before."

Barra could barely hear her own words over the rolling thunder of her pulse. "The Lady's Champion? What's that mean?"

"You're the Hero of the Goddess," Rachel explained, with a scornful *don't-you-know-anything?* look. "You're going to destroy the Israelites. You're going to save us all."

BOOK TWO

# The Lady of Jebusi

# 8

# *The Earth Is of Iron*

The Asherite's face was white-fleshed and blue-shadowed with pain, his eyes rolling up into his skull; blood dribbled from his bitten-through lips in his attempts to hold in his groans of pain as two of his burly clansmen yanked straight his shattered ankle. The finger-sized bone splinter that had torn through his skin submerged into the welling blood, and an Ephraimite tailor swiftly sewed shut the ragged flaps of skin before wrapping the Asherite's ankles with rags and letting his clansmen tie the splints to hold it in place.

Joshua ben Nun watched this operation with thunder upon his brow, then he turned to Phinehas, who was—as always—at his side.

The broad-shouldered priest had, with an enthusiasm more appropriate in a teenager than in a man nearing forty, appointed himself as Joshua's aide in the first days of the march, holding himself ready at Joshua's shoulder to answer the great man's slightest need. He clearly felt that the greatest service he could offer God was to ease every step of His Anointed.

Joshua, for his part, found himself coming to rely upon Phinehas for more than simple errands. The priest's granite solidity of faith became Joshua's talisman against his doubts and night fears; within Phinehas, Joshua saw the crystal depth of conviction that he remembered from his youth, a depth he'd once thought inviolable. But now age and experience had taught him differently; those clear waters had become murky with despair and cynicism, and tainted with blood.

Sometimes only the presence of Phinehas at his side gave him the strength to persevere.

Soon after the murder of the eremite, Joshua had made Phinehas' position official, going to Eleazar for formal release of the minor priestly duties that consumed so much of Phinehas' time and attention. He would still attend his father at sacrifices and rituals—his position as priest was ordained by God and could not be revoked by men—but many of his duties had been of the housekeeping sort, not ordered by Law, and these could be set aside, so that Phinehas could have his heart's desire of remaining ever in Joshua's shadow.

Eleazar had consented with the sour and cynical half smile that now seemed to reside permanently upon his lips.

"Moses the man of God chose you, Joshua, a military man, for his aide," Eleazar had drawled lazily, "to shore up his weakness in matters of battle and siege. Should I take it as instructive that now you, the military man, choose a man of God for yours?"

Joshua had not answered this mockery, but he wished now that he had; every time he remembered Eleazar's words, they carved more deeply the creases of his scowl.

Beside him, Phinehas awaited his orders, his once-glistening black hair and beard streaked brown where their oil had captured windblown sand.

"Make a new camp," Joshua growled. "No more wagons are to be wasted carrying these men. Make camp here, and let the wounded stay, with their women to tend them. And send your father to me."

Phinehas bowed and gave him a respectful "As you will, Uncle," before striding away.

Joshua stumped among the wounded, leaning heavily upon his staff. They lay here and there on the beds of clustered wagons, some leaning in the shadows of their wheels or lying back on tufts of scrub grass that still grew lush from winter rains, some just lying stretched out on the rocky dirt. Here, another man with a broken ankle. There, one with a piece of tree branch through the meat of his arm, broken off when he'd stumbled and fallen against it. And everywhere lay men with feet so bruised and stone-cut that they could no longer walk.

Alongside them were men huddled by pools of thin and stringy vomit; they had drunk the brackish water at the fouled spring the Host had passed yesterday, and now suffered from convulsive cramps. They could keep down neither food nor clean water, nor could they walk.

Many moaned or cried out in pain or delirium; many others stretched out their hands to Joshua as he passed, begging him to intercede with God to bring them relief.

Eleazar appeared, climbing over a small hummock; he stopped

before descending among the men, an expression of mild distaste drawing down the corners of his soft mouth.

Joshua grunted; apparently the High Priest didn't want to get puke on his sandals. He shrugged to himself and picked his way among the injured, climbing slowly up the hummock to stand beside the smaller man.

"I am here at your summons," Eleazar said, with the coldness that had entered his manner on the night of the eremite's death. "What sin here needs atonement?"

"Do not jest with me," Joshua grated. "Look about you."

The sweep of his arm took in wagon after wagon of injured men and women, of lamed horses and donkeys who'd had to be destroyed; the entire depression around the hummock was filled with them.

"We are losing hundreds of men every day. They're breaking bones and slicing their feet faster than we can collect them."

Eleazar sniffed. "Perhaps they lack enthusiasm for throwing themselves against the walls of Jerusalem."

Eleazar's implication was perfectly clear, and it kindled a hot flame at the back of Joshua's throat.

"You think they do this on *purpose?*" His face tightened, and his sun-blackened cheeks darkened further with anger. "I tell you they do not. I tell you: every man who lacks the will to follow the Lord God of Israel shall be turned aside from the path. All who do not wish to fight may stay here, to tend the injured. There is no shame in this."

"There's no *profit* in it, either," Eleazar pointed out. "A man lost to injury on the march still gets a share in the spoils."

"You think this? You believe it? That greed and cowardice drive these men to harm themselves?" Joshua shook his head in disbelief. "You are a small man, Eleazar ben Aaron. I have heard your disrespect for your father, but you are less than he was."

He lifted his gnarled staff and his chest expanded like a wineskin in the sun.

*"Hear me, Israel!"* Heads turned on all sides, for a bowshot in every direction. "Let every man who hears my voice repeat these words to his neighbor, that all may know the truth! Let every man who wishes, stay here to tend the injured. Every man whose mind turns to his wife, instead of to battle; every man who thinks of his child before he thinks of the walls of Jerusalem; every man who fears the sorrow of his aged parents; turn aside! Tend the injured! Go home! Gather food and drink to send ahead to the army. Tend your

fields and grow your crops! You shall receive a *full share* in all the spoils of Jerusalem."

The air buzzed with silence when Joshua finished. He grounded his staff beside his sandals with an audible crunch.

"I have sometimes thought," Eleazar said delicately, examining his slim and dexterous fingers, "that the primary requisite of leadership is a penetrating voice—by that standard, Joshua, you are the world's greatest general."

Joshua ignored him; he listened instead to the swelling murmurs of disbelief, his age-carved face impassive as a granite cliff.

*Full shares?* men asked each other. *Is he serious? How can he give full shares to men who run home to their mother's laps?*

Soon one man approached the hummock, shouting, "Why should they get full shares, when we do the fighting?"

"Because," Joshua rumbled dangerously, "I have said it will be so."

"Why should we share with them? What are they doing to earn it?"

"Earn? *Earn?*" Joshua's face blackened with fury. He leveled a finger at the man as though lightning might fly from his hand. "*Nothing* is earned! All is *given!* Your life, the very breath that enters your mouth and comes out again as these foolish words, is a gift of the Lord! You have done nothing to *earn* your life! You *can* do nothing— the Lord is not some paymaster, bound by law to requite your work! You do not fight to earn a share in the spoils—you fight because it is the Will of God!"

The full force of his righteous anger made him dizzy. For a moment he leaned upon his staff, and when he spoke again, he tried to restrain his voice, but it crept again up into that trumpet blare.

"The spoils of war are as the fruit of your fields. Your crops are not *payment*; you water your fields with the sweat that falls from your brow because the Lord has willed it so. When He wills, your grain grows; at His will, it does not. If the Lord chooses to gift all Israel with the spoils of Jerusalem, *will you argue with Him?*"

The man's indignation had wilted under the blast of Joshua's rebuke like leaves in an oven, and now all he seemed to want to do was slip away as quietly and unobtrusively as possible. "I, I, I'm sorry . . ."

Joshua looked down upon him, and his anger fled; he felt an unaccountable sympathy for this man, and when he spoke again, his voice was low, and warm as a father's.

"Come to the tents of Levi with your best ram, for a sin offering.

Lift up your face and be not afraid. The Lord is merciful, and His love for us is unbounded. If your repentance is true, He will forgive."

The man crept shamefacedly away, and Joshua turned to Eleazar with eyes like chips of stone. "Now," Joshua said, "we shall see if what you say is true. Now the men that throw themselves against the walls of Jerusalem shall do so for the love of God, and not for gain."

"As you say," Eleazar replied with a shrug, unimpressed. "You still have not explained why it is I have been summoned here."

"Walk with me, Eleazar, away from listening ears." Joshua stepped down from the hummock and climbed up out of the declivity, into the hissing wind. He turned his back to the dust and spoke softly. "We lose a hundred men every day, and more. Every slightest misstep brings a broken ankle; every loose sandal strap leaves a festering stone cut. The fruit of the land around us is bitter, when it can be gathered at all, and the springs are foul with rotting animals and their shit. This must end."

"This seems a military matter," Eleazar said, sighing as though bored. "Surely, your scouts can drive off the Canaanites who poison the wells; why bother me?"

"They are not men, that have done this to us," Joshua said. White strings of hair swirled around his face, and his gaze seemed to extend forever into the west. "It is the gods of Canaan. They have turned the land against us."

"Oh, come."

Joshua turned his fathomless gaze upon Eleazar. "It is as the eremite—the man you murdered—had prophesied. The earth is of iron, and our feet break upon it."

He lifted his staff to gesture at the air above them; there was no empyrean blue to be seen, no clouds, only the beige shimmer of wind-borne sand.

"The sky is of brass."

Eleazar swallowed, and coughed into his fist. "Yes, well, even so, Joshua—this is hard country through which we march. Windstorms such as this are not uncommon at this time of year—"

Joshua continued, as though Eleazar had not spoken. "Yahweh has gifted you with power, as His priest. In His name, you must curse these evil gods, and summon an angel to afflict them."

"Summon an *angel?*" Eleazar no longer looked even remotely bored. His voice carried the faintest of tremors. "That's, ah, a little *extreme*, isn't it?"

"You brought the angel of God to stop up the Jordan for our crossing unto Jericho. Are we, today, not equally upon the business of the Lord?"

"That was twenty *years* ago," Eleazar said, licking his lips. "I was younger then, stronger—and vastly more foolish. An Outside Power . . . I don't think you understand the possible *consequences* of such a summoning—"

"Think you so? I have stood in the presence of angels. I have stood in the Presence of God Himself upon Sinai."

"With the skirts of Moses to hide behind," Eleazar muttered.

Joshua stiffened. "Do not defile his name with your mouth, Eleazar. Summon an angel. That is my command."

Eleazar looked away, not daring to meet Joshua's eye as he said, "And if I won't?"

"You have taught Phinehas well. He will perform the summoning, if I ask. He is a true man who loves God more than himself. He understands courage."

At the name of his eldest son, Eleazar startled, then lowered his head. "You are a hard man, Joshua ben Nun."

"If I am, it is the service of God that has made me so."

"I understand courage, Joshua. It's you who does not. You cannot understand courage, because you cannot understand fear," Eleazar said bitterly. "You have none yourself, and so you will never comprehend it in others."

"Shall I call for Phinehas?" Joshua asked, implacable as stone.

Eleazar's voice hushed with something like hatred. "No. You win, Joshua. You always win. The preparations will take only a few hours; you'll have your angel by nightfall, and be damned to you." He turned away and paced toward the Levite Division with his head held low.

"It is the *Lord* that always wins," Joshua called after him, but he could not know if Eleazar heard him.

*I understand fear,* he thought, staring after the priest's departing back, *better than you can imagine. If the spirit of the Host breaks along this march, and the men grumble against God, we will all learn again what real fear is. For instruction in fear, there is no teacher greater than Yahweh.*

And he himself had used a lesson of God's, even here: he had extorted obedience by an implicit threat to the eldest son of a recalcitrant man, a man whose only sin was human fear. The back of his throat burned with bitter gall, and as he walked wearily back toward his place in the vanguard, he felt very, very old.

# 9

# *The Hand of
the Lady*

"**T**hat's it there," Rachel said, letting go of Barra's hand to point. "Where those men are sitting. Those're *guards*," she added confidentially.

"I see that," Barra said. "Is there a back way in?"

"This *is* the back way. If you go the indoors way, all the rooms are full of people waiting to see Grandfather. Or if you want, we could go up over that wall." She shifted the angle of her pointing finger. "There's stairs on the other side, and you can get right next to the vents and hear everything they say."

"I'm not interested in what they say," Barra muttered. "I'll go in here."

Along the curve of an inner wall, the courtyard narrowed toward a point. At that point was one of the few archways Barra had seen here within the Citadel that had a real door. Between her and that door five men sat on a long wooden bench, their backs against the wall, faces upturned to sun themselves for this brief moment of afternoon when the light reached the courtyard floor. They were armed, but they didn't seem too serious about it. Their spears leaned against the wall along with their backs, and two of them were using the plate-sized bronze bosses in the middle of their small wooden shields to reflect the sunlight up under their chins.

"They're still in there, you think?"

Rachel nodded with a concentrated frown. "I think they will be. They were pretty angry. And when my father and my grandfather start shouting, they can go on for a really long time. And then the High Priest—he's my great-uncle—I think sometimes he likes to just make trouble. But the Lady's Maid, she'll be gone by now. She has to be back down in the Ba'alath to sing the sun to bed."

Barra didn't know what that meant, and she didn't ask; she had other things occupying her attention, like the sticky coldness of her still-wet tunic, and a large number of hyperactive butterflies crowding her stomach.

Behind her, the main courtyard through which they walked opened out widely, into a mazy bazaar of workshops and outdoor kitchens, smithies and merchandisers of all descriptions, that in its noisy energy reminded Barra of the Market of Tyre. The Citadel itself seemed to be less of a fortress than a Jebusi in miniature, full not only of the wealthy landowners and their families, but a constantly churning come-and-go of the city's whole population.

Only its maze of successively higher walls and its small archways with heavily reinforced gates advertised its original purpose as the final keep, that can be held even after the city itself has fallen. It looked impregnable, able to hold against any numbers as long as its supplies held out . . .

Until she remembered that Jericho had had a citadel, too.

Barra gravely thanked Rachel for being a trustworthy guide, and told her, "I don't want you listening in on this, all right?"

Rachel's underlip once again showed itself. "Why not?"

"Because I just don't. If I find out you're eavesdropping, I'll tell your father."

"You will not. Anybody can see you're not a tattler, just by looking at you."

*Dammit,* she thought. *Were my boys this smart at her age?* "You're right. I admit it. I don't tattle—but I do spank."

Rachel gasped. "You wouldn't dare! You can't spank a princess!"

*I wish somebody had told my mother that,* she thought. "Yes, I can," Barra said firmly. "If I'm the Lady's Champion, I can do whatever I want. You stay away from that vent, you hear me?"

"All right, Barra," Rachel said. She started to walk toward the door they'd come out of, with a reproachful glance back over her shoulder. Then her brows suddenly pulled toward each other and she stopped. "You're not leaving, are you?"

"Leaving? I—"

"You'll say good-bye before you go, won't you?"

"I—" Barra began, but the little princess's level stare left her no room to wiggle. "Ay, sure," she said, surrendering.

"Promise?"

"Promise."

Mollified, she once again turned away, and Barra muttered, "Good-bye, Rachel," to her departing back.

She strode purposefully along the narrowing curve of the courtyard, pointedly taking no notice of the seated guards, but when she drew nearly even with them, one of those sunning himself with his shield put his foot on the opposite wall to block her path with his leg, and said, "Hold it. Can't go in there."

"I have to see the king," she told him.

"Don't care." His eyes were still closed against the bright reflection. "Can't go in there."

"That's her, Eli," said the other sun-worshiper. "The one I was telling you about. Isn't that her, guys?"

The other guards thoughtfully conferred among themselves, and at length decided that Barra was indeed her. "She's the one as saved the prince. Adonizedek says she's the Lady's Champion."

"Don't give a rat's ass for the Lady, or her witches. I'm El's man, and so are you."

Once again the other guards conferred among themselves, and came to the conclusion that they, too, were El's men.

"It's the Lady as got us into all this trouble, right? Crops are shit, mites in the grain bins all over the city, half the beer's gone bad, and now the Habiru are coming. Wouldn't have happened if Adonizedek wasn't enspelled by the Lady's Maid. If he'd just give all honor to El like we used to, El'd still look after us."

"I just want to see the king," Barra said with forced patience. "I'm no bloody Lady's Champion, all right?"

Eli said without opening his eyes, "Well, you can't go in then, can you?"

Barra spat in disgust on the ground, narrowly missing Eli's foot, then leaned over and snatched the shield out of his hands.

"Hey—" he said, not overly distressed, an attitude that underwent an instant and significant change when Barra slapped him on the head with it, making a hollow-sounding bonk that brought hoots of laughter from his companions.

"I'll *be* the Lady's bloody Champion if it'll get me in there," she growled. "I'll be the man in the fucking moon, if that's what it takes. You let me pass right now, or you and me are gonna go round and round."

Eli got to his feet, rubbing the growing lump over his ear; he was only maybe a hand and a half shorter than Leucas—Barra barely came up to his shoulder. "You want to *fight* me?"

"Sure," Barra said. "You can't win."

He grunted his disbelief from above her. "How do you figure?"

"Simple. You win, and it's no honor to you: slap around a woman half your size? It's *disgraceful*, y'big bully. On the other hand, if *I* win . . ." She gestured significantly at the other men, who watched with broad and happy grins. ". . . it's a tale they'll yarn on you till the day you die—it'll raise a horselaugh ten years past your funeral."

He gave this serious thought, and failed to find a hole in her logic. "I guess I can't stand in the way of the Lady's Champion," he reasoned, and moved aside with exaggerated courtesy.

"Any of you other boys care to step up?" she asked sharply, and they all raised their hands, chuckling and shaking their heads in humorous surrender.

She pushed the shield back at Eli, edge-on to fold him in the middle and sit him back down, then strode past them and banged open the unlocked door. As she went in, she heard one of the men snicker behind her.

"Almost makes you pity the poor Habiru, don't it?"

The back of her neck flamed, and she muttered a curse on every ignorant sorry asshole in this city who was too stupid to understand how much trouble he was in.

Within was a short, narrow corridor lined on both sides with dark spear slits from floor to ceiling. The only light within came from the open door at her back and the thin line of lamplight under the door at the far end. The men's voices that leaked through with the lamplight no longer shouted, but anger grumbled in the very quiet of their control. She tried the door. Finding it locked, she banged it with the hammer of her fist.

"Open up! Open this damned door!"

The voices within had choked off with her first slam of the door, and now she heard Agaz say, "Barra? Is that you? What are you doing there?"

"I'm waiting for you to open this shitcake door."

"You can't come in here."

"Really? That's what the fella outside said," Barra snapped, *"right before I killed him!"*

The bolt slammed back and Agaz swung the door open; experience had made him a firm believer in her temper. "You didn't!"

She stiff-armed him to one side and barged into the room. "Of course I didn't. Don't be an idiot."

The room was small, its close-set walls painted with colorful Assyrian motifs, now faded and stained with lampblack. Only a few faint rays of sunlight leaked in through the horizontal vents that separated the walls from the low ceiling; the rest of the light came from a number of ceramic shell lamps placed here and there on several small tables.

One of the men there she did not recognize; he was well into his seventies and thin as a scavenger-chewed skeleton, his head shaved and beard wire-bound like an Egyptian priest's. He wore a richly embroidered mantle over an ephod of fine linen; his broad pectoral necklace, and every finger on both hands, glittered with gems that were nearly as bright as his penetrating eyes.

"And this must be our champion even now," he murmured, his voice surprisingly deep and rich coming from such a skinny man. She supposed this must be Melchizedek, the priest of El. His sarcasm dripped thicker than cold honey, and Barra disliked him instantly.

"Ay, pleased to meetcha," she said shortly, and turned her back on him to face the king.

Adonizedek sat in a large low-backed wooden chair, his hands upon its curving arms. Age had scoured his face to a shadow of what once must have been formidable beauty. Wisps of cloud-white hair strayed out from under his braided wig of startling black, and his beard was closely trimmed—no doubt to keep it clean of the crumbs and wine that stained the front of his robe. His eyes were clouded with tears as he looked upon her, but even so his jaw jutted like the walls of his city, and his broad and noble brow looked strong enough to break rocks against.

"Barra . . ." he said softly, as though murmuring an incantation. "May I call you Barra? Or is there some title by which you prefer to be addressed?"

"Barra will do," she said. "Listen, about this feast business tonight, I think we're not—"

But he wasn't listening. He slid from the chair to his knees, and reached out to clasp her hands. "Barra, the gift you have given me I can never repay. The life of my son . . ." His voice trembled with barely controlled emotion and tears rolled into the crevices of his face.

A white-flecked gathering of saliva in the corner of his mouth threatened to become drool; once Barra saw it, she had to look away.

"But even this is little compared to the gift you *will* bring," he went on, slurring like a drunk. "The favor of the Lady, and the lives of my people."

Again the back of her neck flamed, and the color touched her cheeks, but where before it had come of anger, now it sprang from embarrassment. *Poor Agaz,* she thought. *How does he stand it?* She didn't dare look at him; it was the only thing she could do to spare his dignity.

She gently pulled her hands free. "I'm not bringing any gifts. Agaz wasn't a gift. He's a *job*. Bought, but not yet paid for. I want my money, and then we'll be leaving. I want to be out of town by night-fall."

Melchizedek snorted loudly. "So. Here is your Lady's Champion, Adonai—she's running off before sundown. I fail to see how one departing barbarian will frighten off the Host of Israel."

"Leaving?" Adonizedek's watery eyes suddenly went shifty and sly. "I think not. You'll be staying. The Lady keeps her promises."

Barra shook her head. "All I want is my money."

"Very admirable," Melchizedek sneered.

From behind her, where she couldn't see him, Agaz said quietly, "You'll not use that tone when speaking of her. She has an honor that would shame you, if only you knew it."

The color on her cheeks deepened.

"Money?" Adonizedek said, still on his knees. "Money is *nothing*. Meaningless. Take what you will. When the city is saved, you will have your pick of my treasury, as much as you want."

"If you care so little for wealth," Melchizedek snapped at the king, real anger now supplanting his mockery, "why didn't you pay the trib-ute? Why didn't you *pay the damned ransom*, instead of throwing away all our *lives*?"

"You think this is about *money*?" Adonizedek rose the way a thun-derhead builds itself in the west, and his eyes flashed as though with lightning. Every scrap of his weakness and age was blown away by the winds of his sudden anger, and Barra found herself taking an involun-tary step backwards.

"Have I not said that money is *nothing*?" he roared. "I would give *every shekel I have* to save the life of a single child! We do not fight for money, but to resist the god of *bloody slaughter*! Death does not frighten me; only surrender. My sole fear is that a failure of courage will let this bloodthirsty slaughtering foreign god rule our land for-ever!"

Melchizedek didn't flinch, didn't even blink; he stepped up and roared right back. "Have you heard *nothing* I have said to you?"

Apparently the king wasn't the only one in his family with a powerful voice and quick temper. Barra felt like she was caught between two boulders that rolled toward each other irresistibly.

"Don't you understand? *Yahweh is not foreign;* He was not always the god of the Israelites. *Yahweh is El!* Yahweh is the name He gave Himself when we turned aside from Him—when this pernicious worship of Ba'al and His Lady supplanted our proper rites! The depredations of the Israelites are El's revenge on us for turning aside from the true way! Of *course* He punishes us. We rejected Him!"

He paused for breath, wiping the back of his hand across his thin and bloodless lips. He glared at Adonizedek, who glared right back, every bit as formidable in his anger as any king Barra had ever seen.

Melchizedek went on in a lowered voice, his words clipped and curt. "They even call Him *El Shaddai* among themselves, telling each other this is only a title. Throughout their conquests, they destroy only the holy places of Ba'al and the Lady; the holy places of El they dedicate to Yahweh. Am I the only one who understands this?"

"What this makes me understand," Adonizedek growled in reply, "is that we cannot rely upon El to save us. Only the Goddess. Only Anat. Does not the Slaughterer conquer even Death for the sake of Ba'al? And in the Song of Ba'al's House, she sings to El:

> I'll push you to the dirt like a lamb
> I'll smash your skull
> make your grey hair stream with blood
> your ashy beard with gore

And when she sings it, even El Himself bows before Her. Who else can save us?"

"I'm not saving anybody," Barra said, slipping out from between the two old men.

Adonizedek's anger seemed to flee as swiftly as it had gathered. He looked at her with a sparkle of deep amusement in his watery eyes. "I was speaking of the Goddess."

"Whatever," Barra said with an irritated shrug. "It doesn't matter. I'm not your bloody Champion. I just want to get paid."

"We shouldn't even *resist* the Israelites." Melchizedek went on as though she hadn't spoken. "The proper course, when faced with superior strength, is to submit. Is this not how the natural world works? With lions, with wolves, with horses, so with men: the strongest rule, the weaker serve. To struggle against this violates the natural order ordained by El, and to violate the natural order brings disaster—as you saw when you made the senile mistake of letting your son rule while you still lived."

Barra braced herself for another explosion, but it didn't come. Adonizedek seemed to wilt, and once again his eyes filled with tears.

"But, but we *must* resist—if the strongest must rule, we'd have a bear for a king instead of a man. Isn't that right?" He appealed to Barra. "Isn't it?"

"Y'know, it's not my business," she said flatly, "and I don't care. I was looking forward to a good night's sleep in that room you gave me. I really was. I was planning to eat too much at the feast, get a little drunk, and sleep till noon. Now I hear that you think I'm some fucking hero of some fucking goddess I've never even heard of, and I realize: this whole city is sliding straight into the shit, and if I don't want to ride along, I'd best collect my money and get out of here."

She turned to Agaz. "And you should come with us. You were right about *him*," she said with a nod toward the king. "No point in dying here with the rest of them."

But that wasn't enough, wasn't the truth of it. She forced herself to add, over the pounding of her heart, "I, ah, *I'd* like you to come along."

He shook his head. "You know better than to ask."

She did, but still his refusal cut her heart cruelly. "At least send your daughter. Give her a chance to live."

"Where? With whom? To what kind of life? Will she be a scullion? A whore? Will *you* raise her?"

Barra couldn't answer. She wanted to promise that she would, but it would be a lie, and she couldn't make the words come from her lips. She'd left her own son in the care of her tribe when she'd left the Isle of the Mighty many years ago; how could she promise to look after a child that she had barely even met? "I guess this is good-bye, then."

She stuck out a hand, trying to act like she didn't care that she'd never see him alive again. "And that thousand shekels? Give me five good horses and a wagon for Graeg, we'll call it even, huh?"

He took her hand gravely. "Whatever I have to give is yours, Barra. It will never be even. As long as there are walls around Jebusi, I will be in your debt, even if the city stands forever."

Her eyes stung, and she turned to the High Priest of El.

"Melchizedek, I wish I could tell you it's been a pleasure to meet you, but that would be a lie. If it's any comfort, I'm on your side."

He sniffed disdainfully and didn't answer.

To the king, she said, "Make that deal with the Habiru, if you can. I won't be the one to save you. Just give us what you owe us, and we'll be gone within a couple of hours."

Adonizedek had already undergone another transformation of attitude; now he sat on his chair and looked upon her like a king from a camp tale, wise and kindly and knowing in a way beyond ordinary mortals.

"You will not save us. The Lady will, through you. As for your payment, you get nothing without the consent of the Lady's Maid."

"*What?*"

"I gave my word that you would not depart Jebusi before meeting with her. Until I hear from her lips that she is satisfied, the reward stays where it is."

While Barra still struggled to grasp this, Agaz came at the king from her side. His face flamed, and veins stood out in his corded neck. The icy prince Barra had come to know was nowhere in evidence; apparently the king brought out a passion in him that she'd never seen.

"What do you think you're *doing*?" Agaz grated, his voice strangled in an attempt to keep it below a shout. "What kind of cheat is this? You dishonor yourself—you dishonor our entire *house!*"

"This is how I *maintain* my honor," Adonizedek replied serenely. "This is how I fight to preserve our people."

"By swindling her with one hand, while with the other you beg for her help?" Agaz snapped.

Fire flared in the king's aged eyes. "Tread carefully, my son. You know not of what you speak."

"Really," Melchizedek said consideringly, "this savage should be grateful to get anything at all."

The blood that had entered Barra's face at the king's word now roared in her ears.

She growled, "Savage?"

She turned toward the High Priest, her lips pulling back in an involuntary snarl. Her right hand hovered trembling a hairbreadth from the cold stone head of her axe, and rage simmered in her voice.

"You want to say that *again*?"

Melchizedek sneered down from his impressive height; he had no idea that only a faintest cobweb of Barra's shredded self-restraint stopped her from killing him where he stood.

"Why should we pay you?" he said. "We have Agaz. What do you have?"

"You really don't want to fuck with me like this," Barra told him between her teeth. "You really don't."

"Threats?" Melchizedek sniffed disdainfully. "Violence is always the first argument of the primitive."

"It's no threat, you sack of shit."

Barra had spent years of her life in practice to speed the draw of her axe; she could pull it and slay before a man could blink. But Agaz knew her temper, and he'd heard the warning in her voice. With a sudden lunge, he barely managed to get a hand upon her arm and keep the axe in its scabbard.

"Barra, don't!" His eyes pleaded with her in a way that his voice couldn't. "Please." He held her a moment, until he felt the killing rage begin to leave her arm, then he spoke with a familiar chill to the High Priest. "Uncle, you shame yourself, and us."

"Pah!" Melchizedek spat. "You would take the side of a savage against your own family."

She shook Agaz off—but met his gaze with a quick flash of shared sympathy. She kept her hand away from the axe.

"All right. You want it civilized? We can do it your way."

She nodded toward the shafts of light that entered through the air vents. "You've got a city full of mercenaries out there. Imagine how they're gonna feel when they hear that you don't pay your fucking *debts*."

Again she showed him her teeth. "Before they're done, you'll be begging the shitcake Habiru to come in and save you."

Adonizedek rose. "Stop."

The habit of command gave his voice a potency that struck even Barra to silence.

He said, "Your reward shall be paid, and in full. I have said so. But it shall not be paid until I hear the satisfaction of the Lady's Maid from her own lips. This, too, I have said. Let any who would make a liar of me, beware. I am Adonizedek, and this land still answers to my word."

Agaz shook his head. "You have made me ashamed," he said bitterly, dropping his gaze to the floor. "I am shamed to be a son of this house."

Adonizedek's expression never altered, but a rasping edge entered his resonant voice. "If it be so," he said, "then so it will be. My word has not changed, and will not."

She looked into his age-ravaged face, at the steady flame that burned within his eyes, and she understood what Agaz had told her earlier.

He could not be pushed.

She shook her head and sighed. "This Lady's Maid, she's the priestess of this Ba'alath of yours?"

The granite determination vanished from the king's face, replaced by an openly boyish enthusiasm. "Oh, yes," he said earnestly. "You'll like her. I know you will."

"Ay," Barra said dubiously. "Ay, sure. Eh, Agaz? Maybe you could show me the way to the temple?"

Before the prince could reply, Adonizedek stiffened like a dog hearing the shuffle of a nearby rabbit.

"Agaz?" he said sharply. "Is Agaz back at last? Just like him, to be haring off when the city's in danger."

Agaz made no attempt to correct his father; he turned away, his eyes raw with pain. "Yes, Barra," he said softly. "I'll take you to the temple."

"You?" the king said. "Absolutely not! Your place is here, Abishai. You are *king*, now, and you must rule, like it or no. I will escort the Lady Barra."

Melchizedek gave Agaz a significant glance that Barra didn't like the looks of at all. "Yes, Adonai," the High Priest said, oozing oil. "Why don't you do that? Your son and I can take care of matters here, in your absence."

"Very well, then!" the king said with obvious relief. "It's been too long since I have walked among my children." He crooked his arm politely for Barra's hand. "My Lady?"

She glared an appeal at Agaz, but he was too lost in his private misery to help her. With a long, slow, reluctant sigh, she took the arm of the king.

"The honor's all mine," she said.

They left Graegduz to sleep in the care of the surgeon, but spent a few minutes collecting Leucas and Kheperu before going to the temple. Between the crushing fatigue of the journey, the pain of her wounds, the dregs of her recent fury still hissing in her veins, and the brittle fragility of her mind with the shades of Jericho lurking in its every shadowed corner, she felt in no condition to deal with the mad king without the support of her partners.

Leucas she found snoring in a bunk, into which he'd fallen while still wet from the now-cold bath alongside it. When she shook him awake, he rose and scratched his hair into place; when he stretched, his joints crackled in sequence like buckeyes in a harvest bonfire. Barra made introductions. Leucas' respectful bow brought his head almost down to the level of the king's.

Adonizedek stared up at him, enraptured in some private glee, and said to Barra with a laugh in his voice, "Why, he's practically the image of Melkarth himself, yes? Thank you so much for bringing him here to my city. I'd never thought to meet him, you see?"

Barra accepted this dizzy sentiment as graciously as she could manage, and led them off after Kheperu.

When they reached Kheperu's room, the goose had been dismembered, as though for an augury, and some of the pieces had been roasted over the hearthshrine; the burly young man with the hard face slept on the floor, his limbs splayed in an attitude of utter exhaustion, a short braided whip still dangling from his wrist by a looped thong; the goat appeared rather decidedly dazed.

Kheperu, on the other hand, was working with his trunk, merrily compounding some new incendiaries and other miscellaneous bits of magic, whistling contentedly through his bad teeth.

After the formal introductions, Adonizedek chuckled gaily and said in accented but fluent Egyptian, "Ah, the self-made man— couldn't you have made yourself into something that doesn't *stink*?"

Kheperu laughed delightedly, and Barra blinked with some astonishment; this was a rather sophisticated pun on the meaning of Kheperu's name.

"You speak my tongue beautifully!" Kheperu said with an obsequious snigger.

"Pish," the king replied. "I so rarely get a chance to practice—but Egyptian is *essential*, you see, all the best texts are in Egyptian. I can muddle through nearly every language of any consequence—except for Greek, of course, you'll apologize to Melkarth here, won't you, dear? No reason to learn Greek; there's never been a Greek writer worth the time to read, and I don't imagine there ever will be. It's an ugly, pragmatic, barking tongue, entirely unsuited to either poetry or science."

Barra left this untranslated; Leucas, like most Akhaians, took an irrational pride in his native language.

She tried to explain to her partners what was going on, as they all strolled down into the lower city toward the temple, but even as the king dictated their leisurely pace, he also dominated Barra's attention with running commentary: the story of the king who built this wall, or that tower, the drunken woman who had waved to him from this rooftop fifty years ago, a moment before plunging headfirst into a dung cart passing below, the poet whose leg had been broken by a runaway horse as it crossed the intersection of these two streets, all interspersed with a laborious disquisition on the mistakes the Egyptian astrologers made in basing their theories on the motion of the sun, when the vastly older Chaldean astrology—predating the Egyptian by two thousand years—was, in its earliest and least corrupted form, based on the motion and phases of the moon, and was enormously more accurate and useful as a predictive tool . . .

He also insisted on introducing the three to what seemed like every bloody godforsaken man, woman, and child that they passed. He had an astonishing memory, summoning instantly the name and family history of even the lowliest beggar by his gates. As they passed on, farther into the lower city, Barra's furious tooth-grinding impatience began to give way to a kind of awe.

Finally, she asked, "How can you possibly remember all these people?" *when you're mad as a drooling badger,* she finished silently.

He favored her with a wise smile. "They are my children. How many children must you have before you can no longer recall their names?"

Barra shook her head wordlessly. She thought of her own father, Ouendail of the Thousand Sons—a name that was no empty boast. The Eirish king at Tara, an immense blustering philanderer of prodigious energy, had scattered his seed throughout the tribes of the Isles and northern Europe—and prided himself that he'd left no child to grow fatherless into manhood. Every one of them knew him; every one could count on his wealth for support and his fist for defense. He traveled endlessly, visiting his bewildering variety of children; he'd attended the birth of every one, or so he claimed—among his many boasts was his claim that he was the best midwife in the Isles.

He was a cheerful braying liar, and a drunkard, and a brawler, and Barra loved him unreservedly; under his dissipated exterior beat a heart as boundless as the sky, and a capacity for outrageous passion that usually pitched him headlong into both love and war. He had offspring by a thousand women, and he loved each child—and their mothers—every bit as much as he did his own wife and queen, and their legitimate children at Tara.

. . . and there was something in Adonizedek, in his passionate conviction that whatever he beheld before him was the single most important thing under the stars, that caught at her heart in the same way her father did. Despite his madness—perhaps because of it—there was joy and pride in his every step, it shone from his face like the sun above each time he introduced another Jebusite.

Name after name, face after face, she met them, shook their hands, blushed at their praise and their thanks for bringing Agaz back safely.

Before long, Barra's heart began to sink, and a taste of bitter ash fouled her mouth. It was as though each of these men, these women, boys, and girls—every one of them—was a face that could be put to a voice of Jericho that still whispered inside her. Meeting them, touching their living flesh, became stunning, overpowering, stinging her eyes and opening a gnawing gap in her belly.

Soon, all too soon, these folk would kneel in their lines, hands bound behind them as they awaited Habiru knives. They would watch each other die. Some of them would carry the corpses of their children to the fires; some would carry their parents.

She looked sidelong at Adonizedek, and muttered darkly from the side of her mouth, "I know what you're doing."

"Doing?" he replied, smiling in senile confusion. "Why, I'm introducing my family—as would any proud father, to an honored guest."

"Horseshit." Senile or not, the old bastard knew exactly what she was talking about. This was a ploy, a trap—not a trick, no, there was nothing dishonest or dishonorable here—but it was a trap nonetheless.

He was taking the abstract concept *Jebusite*, and forcing her to put a face on it, forcing her to admit their voices, their scents, the textures of their skin, the details of their dress and speech, into her mind and heart.

He was making them human to her.

He was using them to bully her into fighting for them.

She laid her hand upon her chest as though she could massage away the pain in her heart—and felt beneath her tunic the carved onyx cylinder seal of Tal Akhu-shabb.

"Where's the Egyptian garrison?" she asked, suddenly, almost gasping in relief at this excuse that had unexpectedly presented itself.

He frowned. "It is only two streets over. Why?"

"I—I have to go there. I, ah, I have a message for the commander. From the Governor," she said, pulling the seal out on its thong to show him, as though she expected him to call her a liar.

"Well, certainly," said the king. "Come along."

As soon as the flag of Egypt could be seen, waving above the garrison, Barra broke into a run, leaving Adonizedek behind with her partners, ran with the Governor's message scorching her heart; she ran to order the might of Egypt to abandon this city, and everyone in it, to the edge of Israel's sword.

Leucas and Kheperu stood together on the street, watching Adonizedek speak with the inevitable crowd of townsfolk that gathered around him.

"I've been thinking . . ." Leucas began slowly.

Kheperu shook his head sadly. "I hate it when you think."

Leucas' mouth twitched toward what might, on a more expressive face, have been a smile. "I've been thinking how much I envy Prince Agaz."

"Envy him what? His senile father? Or the swift approach of his violent death?" Then Kheperu's face broke into a knowing leer. "No, wait, I understand: it's *Barra*, eh?" He chuckled lewdly. "I don't think he's yet had a taste of that particular wine—one which, I must say, I would rather enjoy a sip of myself, someday—she has a certain something, mm?"

The Athenian shook his head. "No, nothing like that. I envy him his people. His home."

"Don't go sentimental, Leucas. Ra's Beard, you're loathsome when you get misty! If the envy becomes overpowering, just remember how this place will look a month from now."

"You ever think about it? Having a home? I mean, how old are you?"

Kheperu sighed. "Forty-eight, to my best reckoning."

"I'm thirty-six. We're neither of us boys anymore, Kheperu. We spend our lives fighting, but what are we fighting for?"

The Egyptian snorted. "Money, you dolt. What else?"

"That's just it. That's all right when you're a boy—it's like a game. And money is how we keep score. It's a boy's game, and we're old enough to know it doesn't mean anything—but we still play it. We're still pretending we're children. That's why I envy Agaz. Even though he'll be dead, and I'll be alive. Because one of these days I'll be dead, too; but I'll be dead because of money. Because of the game. Agaz isn't playing the game. He's fighting for his people. For his home."

Kheperu's face worked as though he wanted to say something snide and cutting, but he couldn't quite find the words; a bleak distance painted itself around his eyes.

Leucas went on. "Even Barra. She invests in her ships, she bargains her people's tin interests at the Knossian Trade Fair. She's trying to build something for her future. What are *we* doing?"

"Living our lives, Leucas. The lives we have chosen. What else is there?"

The Athenian looked far into some grey distance and shook his head. "I don't know. I feel like there ought to be more."

"More? What more? Come on, Leucas, snap out of it. You should get laid; an afternoon's energetic fucking would blow these cobwebs from your head."

"I'm thinking I might take my share and buy myself some land. Have a place, you know? *My* place: somewhere I belong. Something to build on, for the future."

Kheperu looked up into his partner's open face and sighed through the stumps of his teeth. "I will speak to you for one serious moment, my friend, but if you ever repeat this, I'll deny to my death that I said it."

He held up a fist, then opened it as though releasing a moth. He followed this imaginary moth with his eyes as it flew up and away into the sky.

"I don't have a future, Leucas. This is it. This is all of it. I will fight and whore and drink until I'm killed at it. That is the end of my story. Because when you build a home, when you have a family, a tribe—a future—that is nothing but pain. It will be taken from you. It is only something more to lose. If life in this world has taught me anything, it is this: everything that can be lost, *will* be lost. I have nothing to lose except my life. Once that is gone, I will not miss it; I will not be able to miss it."

He waved a magisterial hand at the crowded street around them. "I could watch the slaughter of every man, woman, and child within my view and feel nothing more than the sort of nausea you get from three-day-old meat. But Agaz, on the other hand—when these people are being killed by the Israelites, he will go as mad as the old king before us. He will scream until he has no voice. And that is his sole reward for loving his people and building himself a life among them."

Kheperu straightened the robes over his armor uncomfortably; he frowned as though he closely examined something Leucas could not see. "I had a life once, in Egypt. I had a career, even a family."

"A family?" Leucas squinted down at him. "Somehow I can't imagine you as a married man."

"Oh, but I was. An upright and respectable seshperankh, who worked too hard and drank too much, with a wife who got less of his love than she deserved, children who first adored, then ignored him—

a son," his voice became hushed, "who would now be, oh, perhaps twenty-five . . . I had everything it is you envy in Agaz. A future. It was taken from me—for nothing, on the whim of a mean-spirited woman. All of it. Pht. Nothing left. And for no reason other than that I had offended her vanity." He spread his hands. "Now I pay my women with silver, instead of devotion. It's cheaper in the long run."

"Maybe so," Leucas said, "but at least you had a home, once. And maybe it wouldn't be taken a second time."

"Perhaps," Kheperu said bitterly. "And perhaps you should ask that Sheshai fellow what it's like to have a happy home and a loving family."

When Barra came back out of the garrison, she stopped short at the sight of their brooding expressions. "What's the matter with you two?"

"We were, ah, talking about Agaz," Kheperu murmured, with a whistling sigh through his long nose. "I shall miss him, I think."

"Ay," she said softly. "Me too."

"I get it now," Barra murmured. "I understand . . ."

They stood at the gate to the temple compound. The compound itself was large, a long oval of curving walls now covered with furry climbing creepers, grown lush from the winter rains. The gate, thrown wide with no one attending it, was at the northern tip of the compound; out through it filed townsfolk in ones and twos, some straggling and looking furtively about themselves, others overly erect, their faces set with the kind of humorless determination you see on people who grimly persevere in the face of general mockery.

At the far end of the oval, set well apart from the walls, was a small house-sized structure that must have contained the altar. Wisps of dirty white smoke trailed upward from its chimney gap, and the few remaining worshipers walked dispiritedly out from there. Around the structure stood twelve pillars that overtopped its roof; they stood free, supporting nothing except more climbing vines, rooted in roundish gaps in the flagstones that paved the temple court.

It was the shape of the temple that granted Barra her sudden illumination. All this talk of the "witches of Ba'alath" had troubled her; with her insatiable curiosity, she had learned a bit of the religions of Canaan and the surrounding regions where she had made her living, but she had never heard of any goddess called Ba'alath. Now she understood: Ba'alath was not the name of the goddess, but of the temple: *Ship of the Mistress.*

"My, my, my," Kheperu muttered with a salacious grin. "It's a *vagina* . . ."

Leucas frowned down at him. "What?"

"Don't you see? The oval walls, with creepers for pubic hair? We enter at this end, while up there stands the temple house, the . . . ahem . . . holy of holies, as it were—that's the clitoris, don't you see?"

Kheperu's grin widened. "I'm tempted to make the acquaintance of this goddess myself . . . In fact"—and here he suddenly frowned as though in thought, and turned in a circle to look about himself— "Jebusi is itself a rough oval, isn't it? With its gate to the north, and this temple near—but not at—its southern tip. As though the entire temple is the clit of an even larger—"

He laughed, shaking his head and clapping his hands together in pure delight. "Leucas, I tell you this: if I thought Jebusi had the chance of a fish in the desert of standing another month, I'd make this my new home town. All day long, we've been walking around inside a giant *cunt*! Can you imagine a more congenial abode?"

Leucas only shook his head in bemused wonder, as if he couldn't believe that he'd somehow ended up the friend of such a revolting man.

Barra came to the side of the king. "Where's this Lady's Maid of yours?"

Adonizedek nodded into the compound. "Sarah will be within the altarhouse. She is ill, or she would come out now to tend the vines; I suppose her illness teaches us that even the Handmaid of the Triple Goddess is only human."

Barra felt her jaw go slack. *Handmaid of the WHAT?*

For a long moment she could only stare at him, while a chill like a winter wind raised the hairs along her arms. "The Triple Goddess?" she asked carefully.

Adonizedek nodded indulgently. "Anat, Astarte, and Asherah. The Ba'alathians teach that they are all only faces of a single goddess. Per- haps you think it silly—why should one goddess have three names, after all, but I can assure you—"

"I, ah . . ." Barra interrupted thinly. "Silly? I wouldn't say that . . ."

She looked into the compound, keenly aware of her rapidly beat- ing heart. "Ah, tell me something—Anat, she's the virgin warrior, right, the one they call the Slaughterer? Ba'al's sister and wife? And Astarte, she's Ba'al's Other Self, isn't that what they call her? The one that makes the crops grow after the rains? And then Asherah, she's El's wife, and Ba'al's . . . ah . . ." she forced out the word, ". . . Mother?"

Adonizedek's snowy brows pulled together beneath the oiled ebon curls of his wig. "Yes, that's all true enough. Why does this seem to frighten you so?"

She shook her head. *Shit,* she thought. *Shit, shit, shit.* "No reason," she told him. "I've, ah, heard of this kind of thing before, that's all."

She turned to her partners, her face set into lines as bitter as the edge of a spear blade, and spoke in Greek. "Come on, we're going in to talk to this Lady's Maid. Stick close, huh? This place makes my skin crawl."

As they entered the compound, Adonizedek once again began to prattle his lunar astrology, cheerfully babbling on about how the goddesses correspond to the phases of the moon.

"You'll tell us, of course," Kheperu murmured from behind her shoulder, "if he says anything of any import?"

"Sure," Barra replied from the side of her mouth, "but it's not fucking likely. Right now, he's going on about how this virgin war-goddess of theirs, Anat, is so fierce that if there's no war going on, she brings her furniture to life as toy soldiers and makes her chairs and tables fight each other."

"Virgin war-goddess?" Leucas said with a mild frown. "Like Athene?"

"Well, yes, I suppose . . . but with a really bad temper."

"Athene doesn't have a bad temper?" Leucas said with a sidelong look. "Tell that to the Trojans."

Barra's response was a thoughtful lift of one brow.

"They worship other goddesses here, too?" Leucas went on. "Like Hera and Hecate?"

"Oh, ay."

"Barra?" Leucas said. "Do you think this Anat could be Athene under another name?"

Barra stopped, but didn't look back at the Athenian; her gaze was held by the twelve freestanding pillars that ringed the altarhouse. She was thinking how much they reminded her of the rings of trees that defined the sacred groves of the Mother, back on the Isle of the Mighty.

She said softly, "The druids claim that all gods are only one; that everything, the stones of the earth, the air we breathe, the sun and moon and stars, even our very selves are all portions of the One God. They say that the name of each god or goddess addresses only a small part of the One, even as my name and yours each address only a single small part of humanity."

Kheperu frowned. "The Memphite priesthood says the same—of Ptah."

"Then," Leucas said, "you think it could be true?"

She wanted to say, *I think it's a load of shit,* which is what she had always believed, but here, in the Ba'alath, something stopped her tongue.

Here in the Ba'alath, it suddenly felt all too possible.

So instead she said nothing at all, only shrugged and walked off again toward the altarhouse.

Out from its doorway issued several youngish men and women that Barra took to be acolytes, based on their vine-leafed circlets and robes of spring green. They called informal greetings to the aged king with a much more honest warmth than protocol would require, then turned aside to their tasks. Some carried clay pots, which they used to drizzle water into the flagstone gaps from which the creepers grew; the others had pruning hooks, with which they went to work on the vines that covered the pillars as well as those on the walls.

One nearby acolyte, a boy of perhaps only sixteen, recognized Barra and looked on her with shining eyes. "You're the *Champion,*" he half whispered in awe.

She drew breath to deny it once again, but he went on before she could speak. "I saw you bring Prince Agaz into the city. It's a very great thing you've done, to bring him safely back to us."

"Ay, thanks," she said tiredly. "Where's the Lady's Maid?"

"Please, please follow me," he said, setting down his waterpot. "Everyone? Everyone, look! It's the *Champion*, come with the king to see the Lady's Maid!"

The other acolytes only paused in their work, mercifully restraining themselves from effusions like this boy's, but the smiles of serene joy they turned upon her made her clench her jaw until the grinding of her teeth rose in her hearing like the surf of an incoming tide.

"Get on with it, will you?" she muttered, and the acolyte happily led the four of them into the altarhouse.

Little light entered the altarhouse with them; it took more than a moment for Barra's eyes to adjust.

The interior of the altarhouse was dominated by an enormous rough-hewn statue of the naked goddess, carved of the same native stone as the massive Gate Tower and the walls of the city itself. Leucas would stand less than shoulder-high to this huge statue, and it had a rough and primitive look, noticeably female only in the gross details of anatomy: monstrous breasts, broad hips, and a stylized suggestion of pubic hair at the crotch.

Otherwise, the statue could as well have been male; there was a broad, peasant gracelessness and solidity to it, a suggestion of illimitable strength in the wide shoulders and thick arms. The face was also carved with primitive roughness, a sort of archetypal nonspecificity that should have made it look childish and simple, but somehow gave it an expression of a wisdom both otherworldly and weirdly immediate, a mandrill-look of solemn contemplation.

The statue's lips were oddly dark and smooth, as was the top of its right shoulder, a minor mystery swiftly explained when Adonizedek came close to it and stepped up onto a low pedestal; steadying himself with one hand upon the statue's shoulder, he kissed it respectfully on the lips.

Around the altar were smaller statues of more familiar shape, the axe-armed Anats, gently smiling motherly Astartes with their wide and welcoming arms, the wise and wicked grins of the crone Asherahs.

A hearthshrine not unlike those of Tyre burned before a broad wooden table that seemed to function as the altar; the table was spread with all manner of food and wine, sacramentally bundled.

Leucas favored the small Anats with a long and speculative stare, as though he expected one of the statues to speak to him.

The acolyte had skipped ahead of Barra, and now he leaned through a small archway that seemed to lead into an alcove just off the main room. "She's here!" he said excitedly. "Sarah, it's the Champion! With the king himself to bring her!"

For a moment, the only response he got was a long series of wet-sounding coughs. Once the coughing died, it was followed by a woman's voice, tremulous with emotion, or exhaustion, or both. "Please ask them in, and let them be comfortable. Bring refreshments for the Lady's guests."

The acolyte ducked his head in a perfunctory bow, and then gestured Barra and her partners through the archway with a sweep of his arm. "There's only one stool," he said nervously, "but I'll have more for you in a moment."

"Leave the one for the king, and don't bother with the rest," Barra said. "I don't think we're staying long enough to sit down."

She had smelled the blood and rot when she'd stepped through the door of the altarhouse, but she'd thought it was the remnants of a sacrifice, perhaps, or even of a lamb slaughtered for the acolytes' meal. Only now did she realize from where the smell truly came: the small alcove from where she'd heard the voice of the Lady's Maid.

This woman was dying.

Barra could smell it long before she entered the alcove. The

Lady's Maid lay on a thin and moderately threadbare pallet that rested on a net of ropes suspended from a wooden cot frame.

Adonizedek lowered himself with painful slowness onto the stool next to the pallet. The walk down from the Citadel must have taken more effort for him than he'd shown; perhaps the serene confidence with which he'd introduced Barra to his subjects had been an act as much for their benefit as for hers.

"I have come, Sarah." His words were colored with fatigue as grey as his face. "I have brought the Champion, as I promised."

"Your word, as always, is inviolable. I . . ." Her voice dissolved into coughing.

Barra stopped in the doorway. She really didn't want to have this conversation—but she also didn't want to leave without her money. In the back of her head, the slap of a hundred oars on the open sea sounded fainter than it had in days.

The woman who lay on the pallet waved her in with one hand, while the other held a linen kerchief to her mouth against this series of hacking, convulsive coughs, spasms that jerked her entire long and frail-looking body, lifting her from the pallet and dropping her back again. Only her eyes, large and luminous, seemed unaffected; she watched Barra with an apologetic steadiness that seemed to say *It's only my body—you know how difficult bodies can sometimes be. Please excuse the inconvenience.*

The three mercenaries stood uncomfortably crowded together in the tiny alcove, waiting for the spasm to end; when it finally did, the woman gently mopped a trail of blood from her lips and said, "I am Sarah, the Lady's Maid. You are Barra, Leucas, and Kheperu; I was at the Citadel, and heard Agaz tell of your adventures. Please be comfortable."

For one long-stretching instant, Barra could only stare from the blood on the kerchief to Sarah's face. The Lady's Maid, the unopposable force that had bewitched the king, taken over his city and was leading it down to destruction, was young—and a delicately pretty woman, even now, when exhausted close unto death.

*She's my age,* Barra thought in astonishment. *Not even; twenty-five? Twenty-seven?*

"You're, ah . . ." Barra said, "not quite what I was expecting."

"The Lady wills it so," Sarah replied. "Surprises are her way of teaching us to pay closer attention." She racked into another long spasm of coughing.

Barra looked at her partners with a sort of half-alarmed shrug of

*What do I do now?* Only Kheperu responded; he gave her an encouraging look and the one-handed rub of thumb against forefinger that was the universal symbol of money.

She looked to Adonizedek, but the old king seemed to have sunk into some interior world, as though his last resources had been expended to bring Barra here, and he must mine some deeper will.

When the coughing finally began to subside, Barra said uncomfortably, "Is there anything you need? Is there anything I can do?"

Sarah's smile was vivid with scarlet blood on her lips. "Save my city."

Barra winced inwardly. *Guess I asked for that one.* "No, I meant for you, personally."

"So did I."

Barra rubbed tiredly at her temples; a headache began to pound behind her eyes. "Listen: I have no interest in what happens to this city. All I want here is the money we're owed for bringing Agaz back."

"That's not true," Sarah said in a firm and motherly tone. "You don't have to lie to me, Barra."

"Hey—" she said, a dangerous note creeping into her voice, "sick or not, you really don't want to be calling me a liar."

"Money is not all you seek here," Sarah responded simply. "You want me to say you're not the Champion. You want me to say that it's all right for you to go away and leave us all to the Israelites and their god. I won't, because it isn't, and because you are."

"The money," Barra repeated implacably.

"Your money is ready, and you may take it whenever you wish. In return, I ask only a moment of your time."

"In *return?*" Twin spots of red materialized high on Barra's cheekbones, and anger sang in her veins. How many games were these fucking Jebusites going to play? "That money is *ours*. We've earned it *already*—don't think you can start playing me like—"

Sarah held up her hand. "I'm sorry, Barra, I misspoke. I didn't mean to suggest—well, let me put it this way. Please sit with me for a moment. Give me this gift, of your time and attention."

Barra glowered furiously and lowered her head like a balky mule.

Sarah said, "Why are you so angry?"

"You want to know why I'm angry?" Unaccountable fury burned away any reserve or courtesy. Her words came forth as though she breathed flame from her lips.

"All right. I'm angry because you're *insane*. You're sick with some shitcake idea that is going to kill every human being in this city! This

is all *your fault*, don't you understand? You're the bloodyfucking idiot
who talked that senile old bastard into defying the Israelites in the first
place!"

Adonizedek stirred, but he was still far away within himself; even
Barra's snarled accusation brought only a flicker to his eyes.

"You know what they're going to do to this city?" she snarled. "I
have seen what happened to *Jericho*, you stupid bitch!" Her knotted
fists shook uncontrollably. *"I have seen it!"*

"I have seen, too," Sarah replied, answering Barra's fury with
serenity. "I have seen the whole world forever trapped in the grip of an
angry god. Compared to that fate, anything the Israelites can do to us
is a *blessing*." She would perhaps have continued, but raising her voice
even that tiny amount sent her into a renewed coughing fit.

"You don't know what the Israelites can do," Barra said. "I was
there. I lived every death in Jericho. I *know*."

Sarah forced the words through her spasms of coughing. "And
why would the Lady have given you this knowledge, if there is nothing you can do about it?"

She held up a trembling hand to forestall Barra's answer, and went
on. "The Lady has come to me in dreams, as she did to the Lady's
Maid who preceded me. She has promised that if we resist the god of
slaughter, if our faith is strong and our courage does not fail, she will
send a champion who can save us all."

"I don't give a rat's ass about your dreams! Your goddess hasn't
come to *me* in dreams!" Even as she said it, a leaden weight dropped
into the pit of her stomach; she clenched her teeth against it and
insisted inside her head, *Those were only nightmares. Just nightmares.
Nothing to do with this at all. Nothing at all.*

"She is not my goddess," Sarah said. "She is *the* Goddess, and
even if you do not know her, she knows you well."

"Balls!" Barra snapped, but her voice had more edge than depth.

Leucas, who had been gazing at Sarah's face as though entranced,
now murmured in Greek, "Why are you fighting? What are you arguing about?"

"It's this Lady's Champion thing," Barra said shortly. "I'll explain
later."

"Why argue?" Kheperu said. "Let's just get our money and go."

"Shut up."

Sarah went on, "For a woman who claims to have no interest in
the fate of this city, you certainly become passionate—"

"All right, fine, whatever. So some superpowerful hero is going to come from your Lady and save you. What makes you think it's *me*?"

Sarah wiped the last smear of blood from her lips and gave Barra a raw smile. "Shall we number the portents? You have redeemed the prince already, returned him safe and alive. He is the child of the king; in another sense, we are all the children of the king. The rescue of Agaz is a portent of the rescue of Jebusi."

"That's pretty thin."

"I'm not finished. Your home is far to the west, in the midst of the sea—as is Our Lady's, in her aspect as the moon. Yet you come to us over the eastern mountains—as does the moon. You walk with a wolf—is not the wolf the closet companion of the moon?"

Barra didn't answer. She couldn't answer. She felt like she was drowning.

"Shall I go on? There are three of you, a reflection of the Triple Goddess. Leucas, the Protecting Parent. Kheperu, the Aged Magician. And you, the Virgin Warrior. You even carry the axe, her weapon, with its edge like the crescent moon."

Barra snorted. "I'm hardly a virgin."

"Neither is Anat; she is Ba'al's wife, the bride of the storm. The better word would be Maiden."

"I'm not young, either."

"Anat is as old as the world; she merely looks young. So do you."

"But this is just word games," Barra insisted desperately. "You could make practically the same argument about . . . about Agaz, the king, and Melchizedek!"

Adonizedek lifted his head; the talk of the moon had brought him back from whatever internal mystery he'd contemplated, and now a boyish smile broke over his features. "Why . . . so you could!"

Sarah twitched her wasted shoulders. "And so? Why should they be any less a reflection of the Goddess than you are? Because they are men? Agaz told me that your people believe we should judge each other by our character, not our genitals. Was he wrong?"

"Waiting for me to save this place is going to get a lot of people killed," Barra growled. "Nobody ever *asked* me if I wanted to do this in the first place!"

"No one cares what you want to do: only what you *will* do. I did not want to be the Lady's Maid, but I was the strongest of the acolytes when Ramah died; I did not want this, but if the Lady needs my service, even unto death, I am willing to provide. The Lady has been asking what *you will do* for many days now, and I think you know this."

"You're the High Priestess, and you're dying," Barra said brutally. "How's this Lady of yours gonna save the city when she can't even heal you?"

Adonizedek's eyes sparkled madly. "She isn't going to save the city," he said calmly. "You are."

Barra wheeled on him. "An hour ago you had it the other way around!"

The king shrugged. "It is the same, isn't it?"

Sarah went into another long and agonizing spasm of coughing; her kerchief had become wet with blood and mucus. "I am dying because she is ill. As the Lady's Maid, I am not only her Voice, but also her Shield. I accept the strokes meant for her, and she sustains me as well as she is able. She cannot heal me; it is up to us to heal *her*."

"You have all the fucking answers, don't you?"

"You say that like an accusation. As though it is a crime to understand the truth."

Barra said through her teeth, "Ay, well, maybe it ought to be."

They walked back up toward the Citadel alongside the sedan chair that bore the Lady's Maid. Barra squinted grimly at the sun, in its dip toward the western hills; they'd have little enough light left, by the time arrangements were made. Somehow she didn't feel like she should hope for a bright moon tonight to light their road.

Clouds built up upon themselves in the north, looming half-shadowed by the setting sun, and Barra smelled rain on the wind.

The promised ransom lay in the Citadel's treasury; the companions stayed close to Sarah's chair. The king walked before them, once again filled with joyful strength by the press of his people around him.

They walked as swiftly as they could; soon Leucas had taken the lead, breasting his unstoppable way through the crowds that gathered around them. Through Barra, Sarah had asked him to do this; the hour for the feast of celebration approached, and she feared they might be late—even though no festivities could begin without the king's word. The four broad-chested acolytes that bore her chair—one of them a woman with arms like oaken beams—could make good time through empty streets, but she feared that the crowds might delay them; "and my husband will be waiting."

Kheperu's brows had lifted when Barra translated; Leucas' face had turned a sudden startling shade of crimson. Sarah was married to

Melchizedek, a ritual marriage to symbolize the Lady's joining to El, in her aspect as Asherah.

"It is entirely for the sake of form and propriety," she had explained, "but my husband insists on the show of strict observance of that form, and so I reside in rooms set aside within his apartment."

As they walked, Barra watched an unsettling change come over the crowd. On their way down to the Ba'alath, every Jebusite they'd passed had gladly taken the king's greetings, and had returned them with enthusiasm. Now some men in the crowd turned away, their faces set in lines of hard suspicion, and some women did as well. Adonizedek tried his mumbling best to ignore them, but Barra could see how each rejection stung him, in the brief falter of a wave, or a slow-drawn breath between happy greetings.

The harsh rejections came more rapidly as the tiny procession passed, as though some word had gone out that the king was on the street with the Lady's Maid, and the enemies of both had come out to watch in stares of outright hostility that followed them along the streets; now there came even muttered curses and gestures to ward off magic.

"Not too popular, are you?" Barra said to Sarah quietly.

"No, we are not," Sarah said, and pain flitted across her face like the edge of shadow from her chair's linen sunshade. "I think it is the followers of El—El's Men, they call themselves. They whisper against us."

"I've heard a whisper or two myself," Barra said, thinking of the guards at the Citadel.

"They blame us for everything that goes wrong in the city, from rot in the grain bins to the Habiru."

"I don't know about the grain bins," Barra said, "but the bloody Habiru *are* your fault."

"The Habiru," Sarah said exhaustedly, "are their own fault. They are the fault of the god that chose them for his children—even as our foolishness and weakness is the fault of the gods that chose us."

She turned her head to cough, and then spoke again, more thinly. "The king, he pretends that he does not see how his people turn against him, but more and more seem to do so with each passing day. I would aid him, if I could, but I fear I would only make matters worse. I . . . am the cause of so much of it."

"Can you blame them?" Barra asked with brutal frankness. "You're trying to get them all killed."

"It is not the Lady that threatens them; she is no Yahweh, to turn her sword against her own children."

Sarah's eyes drifted closed for a moment, and Barra thought she had been lulled to sleep by the soft oceanic rocking of her sedan chair, but she was only gathering strength to keep talking.

"Ramah—my predecessor—she would have handled these El's Men the way they deserve: with a bellowed horselaugh and a kick on the rear. She was . . . a great woman, great in body and in spirit. Things would never have gone so badly if she were still alive—the people loved her. Respected her. And they feared her wrath."

"What happened to her?"

Sarah held forth the bloody kerchief to display its contents. "She coughed blood from her lungs until she had no more strength to cough; then she drowned in it. Only a month ago, a little more. She died the day after we heard that the Manassites had captured Prince Agaz."

Sarah stretched her bloody lips in a weak smile. "A month ago, I looked like Peri here, who bears the pole of my chair. Ramah often teased me that I was the very image of the Great Astarte in the altarhouse."

Barra didn't want to buy Sarah's version of this tale; she had seen folk die of consumption before. But as she tried to guess what sort of consumption could reduce a woman built on the heroic scale of the chair-bearer to the loose-knit sack of bone and tendon that was the woman beside her in only a few weeks, imagination failed her. Consumption was a long, slow, wasting process, often taking years to kill.

But, on the other hand, this might not be a sickness.

Sarah had called herself the Shield of the Lady—and this sickness, just as Yahweh's anger had gathered toward her city, seemed too convenient to be mere coincidence . . .

Cloud passed before the sun, and a spit of rain crossed her face. She flicked a finger up toward the sky and said to the chair-bearers, "We'd best hurry up if we don't want to get wet. I don't think it's healthy for the Maid to be out in a storm."

Before them, Leucas stopped in the very act of parting the crowd with a sweep of his arms. He turned his broken face up to taste the rain, and he stared fixedly at the thunderhead above them.

A hollow distance echoed in his voice, as though he called from very far away. "Barra? I think we should get indoors. Now."

She looked up at the tongues of lightning that licked the underside of the cloud, and she remembered Leucas' words from that night in the mountains. "What is it? You have another bad feeling?"

Leucas nodded, the grey of his eyes mirroring the clouds. "This is no natural storm. We are in danger here."

Barra turned to the Lady's Maid and spoke rapidly in Canaanite. "Sarah, we need to find shelter. Leucas—he knows a bit about storms, I guess, and he says this one's about to turn ugly."

Sarah nodded weakly. "Tell the king. With his word, anyone will take us in."

The look on the Maid's face finished the thought. Barra said, "But they won't be too happy about it, eh?"

Sarah's face became even more bleak. "A month ago, they'd have been honored, and cherished the tale to share with their grandchildren. Today?" Her wasted shoulders twitched in an exhausted sketch of a shrug.

Puffs of dust rose from the street around them, struck into the air by the impact of raindrops the size of shekels. Barra jogged up to the king's side, blinking and using a hand to shield her eyes from the pattering droplets.

"Adonizedek—"

He didn't seem to hear her, absorbed as he was in shaking a Jebusite's hand as he kissed the cheek of the fellow's wife; Barra tugged at his arm and he turned his eyes upon her. Faint inky trails began to leak from the dye of his wig, gathering in the creases of his face.

"Adonizedek, we have to get inside," she said with urgency. "You have to ask someone to take us in."

"I think it might rain," he replied absently. "Late in the season, isn't it? Very odd. So much is so odd. My children—"

"Ay, I know." Grey gloom suddenly buried the street as though a god's hand had wiped the sun from the sky. The cropland below the city and the hills above it shone brilliantly in the blaze of afternoon; only the city lay in the shadow of the thunderhead, and that shadow deepened as though cast by a descending heel.

Trepidation sizzled within Barra's veins, adding an edge to her voice and a fresh violence to her yank upon the king's arm as she pulled him back toward the others. "Come on, king, let's go in, huh?"

He frowned down at her, puzzled. "I'm cold. And you're hurting my arm."

The rain strengthened, plastering Barra's tunic to her chest. She let go of the king's arm and turned to the crowd, shouting in Canaanite, "Adonizedek needs shelter from this storm! Whose house will provide?"

No answer came from the crowd.

"Come on, speak up! Who will take in the king and his party?"

All around them, she saw only a wall of hostile faces and warding gestures, a wall that penned them in the street, and struck Barra's heart with a far deeper chill than the icy rain.

She struggled against a superstitious shiver. Not a single supporter of the king, in all this mass of people? How could this be?

But the malice in their eyes could not be denied.

She spat a curse and turned to Leucas with Greek. "Just pick a fucking house," she snarled. "If the owner doesn't like it, sit on him."

The huge boxer nodded grimly, and turned toward the nearest door. But even as he did, the sky opened.

The storm hit Jebusi like a hammer.

With an avalanche roar, a white-foaming wall of water descended upon the city. Like a wave crashing down on the deck of a ship, the water hit with a palpable *weight*, a crushing, dragging mass that nearly drove her to her knees. Barra had weathered heavy seas on shipboard many times in her life; she bent her head forward and shielded her mouth and nose with her hand, because in white foam this thick, a careless breath could fill her lungs with water.

She had never seen a downpour like this on land, never heard of one—Leucas, close enough to hold on to her hand, could be seen only as a featureless blur in the grey-streaked darkness. Faintly around her came choked cries of alarm from the chair-bearers as they stumbled, coughing out the water from their lungs, and the chair was ripped from their hands. It tumbled to the street and the Lady's Maid was jolted off it into the mud, invisible, only her throat-ripping hacks telling Barra where she was.

Leucas' solid grip on Barra's arm kept her upright. "Which way?" he roared, thundering like the cloud above, swinging wide an arm at the impenetrable rain.

"Pick one!" Barra cried in response. "Gotta hit a building eventually! Help me with Sarah!"

She guided him past her to Sarah's side, and he caught up the Lady's Maid like a child in his arms.

Barra turned back, groping for the king. He was nowhere to be found; she shrieked above the storm, "Kheperu! *Find the fucking king!*"

His answer came faintly, barely audible through the water's roar. "I have him! Where are you?"

"Never mind that! Get him off the street! We'll join up after!"

She hooked a hand into Leucas' belt and gave him a go-ahead slap on the flank. He chose a direction at random and strode powerfully against the wind, his head held low to help him breathe. Barra clung one-handed to his belt and stumbled along in his wake. The bearers, Kheperu, the city itself no longer existed around her; they struggled through a universe of rain.

A wall coalesced out of the water before them, and then the black arch of a door. Leucas made for it—but Barra hauled back on his belt.

"Hold it!" she howled above the roar of the rain.

"What—? Barra—?"

That black archway looked suddenly to her like the maw of a great and hungry beast, a beast that waited for them to pass its teeth so that its jaws might close upon them forever.

*Sceon tiof?* she thought. It didn't make any sense—it was probably only a trick of her tired eyes and the strangling downpour, but all this mystical shit had jangled her nerves until more superstition ran in her veins than blood.

"Come on!" Leucas shouted. "We have to get Sarah out of this storm!"

"Not there!"

"There is nowhere else!" He turned toward the door.

The world exploded in a flash of eye-burning brilliance, a searing white that wiped away her vision and hammered her tumbling blindly through the air.

Stunned beyond comprehending what was happening to her, Barra landed facedown in the icy mud.

The mud pressed into her nose and her mouth; her head gradually cleared when she began to cough. She struggled to her knees, and looked before her.

Enough of the rain had cleared that she could see across the street. Leucas lay unmoving in the mud not far away, Sarah beside him, shaking him and stroking his face in an attempt to wake him. In Barra's ears rolled a steady thunderous roar that had nothing to do with the rain around her; she understood that a thunderbolt had nearly killed them all, and had slapped away her hearing.

The house across the street, whose arched doorway they had been about to enter, had been blasted to a smoking ruin, a shattered heap of broken brick and splintered beams.

Lightning flickered in chains across the wreckage, skittered here and there, breaking and recombining, striking flame from the beams, causing the bricks to burst and send splinters sizzling through the air.

Every hair on Barra's body tried to stand away from every other.

The play of lightning over the ruined house did not fade; it was *growing*.

The lightnings came together into a shape, a mass, and bulged upward, extending from its crackling center a shaft of power high overhead; it reared up like a child's drawing of a monstrous cobra, outlined in searing blue-white energy.

Barra could only stare; the *sceon tiof* was upon her in truth now, and what she saw shook her worse than had the thunderbolt.

The rain exploded into steam where it touched the lightningcobra, and the cobra shifted this way and that as though searching out a rabbit that it could smell nearby.

She couldn't make sense of the way it looked—she knew it had a shape but she couldn't comprehend it: all its perspectives wavered in mind-bending ways, as though it grew itself from somewhere, as though it was coming closer without moving, approaching from a direction she could not see or feel, not from the compass points, or from up or down, but from some direction all its own, as indescribable as its shape.

It came from outside the world.

Its outlines wavered, and pulsed and shifted, and spread wings outward to cover half the sky, too many wings, four, six—

And eyes.

Knots of crackling force curled and shifted and sought like eyes, everywhere, on the body, on the wings, eyes like stars, eyes like cartwheels spinning, eyes upon its breast, upon its hands, hands that now became the outstretched talons of a terrible raptor, a falcon, a dragon, reaching, reaching . . .

Reaching for the Lady's Maid, where she lay oblivious in the mud, half-across Leucas, who was only now stirring, opening his eyes, sitting up . . .

Barra's paralysis broke, and she surged to her feet, howling a wordless warning.

The talon swung down, impossibly fast for something so huge.

Barra sprang forward, mud churning beneath her straining, corded legs, too slow, too late—and her feet found one single bit of solid ground beneath the mud, a tiny island of resistance from which she could dive forward.

As though her entire life had been spent in training for this moment, she drew her broadaxe in the air as she sailed across Leucas' body, tangling her legs with his as she came down and again threw herself forward and up, out of the mud—

And intercepted the talon of searing lightning with the blade of her axe.

For a moment, the lightning transfixed the stone, clamping Barra's hand to the axe haft so hard it brought a gasp from her lips.

She hung in the air, interminably suspended from the hook of energy, convulsing, smoke curling out from her hair . . .

Then the basalt head of her broadaxe detonated like a sealed pot left too long upon the fire.

The concussion sent her spinning backward to sprawl in the mud, her face streaked with blood where splinters had cut her. It blew Leucas flat as well, and as Barra struggled to rise, Kheperu came out of nowhere to suddenly appear at her side, trying to help her get up, saying something she couldn't hear over the rolling roar that still stopped her ears.

The creature of lightning filled the sky, and the storm's thunder became its cry of rage—but it was fading, even as it grew, larger and fainter, as though its malice now dissipated like smoke on the wind.

As it faded, that talon swung down again, but this time toward her, and the roar in her ears no longer mattered.

Her head was filled to bursting with its Voice.

BY MY TOUCH WE KNOW THEE, BARRA COLL EIGG RHUM PAGAN WHORE. BEWARE THE WRATH OF THE LORD.

Darkness fell into her head in the wake of the Voice, smothering her vision, her hearing, her touch; she struggled with the darkness, and held it back only for one moment, only long enough to mutter one thought.

". . . not *my* lord, you bastard . . ."

Then the darkness closed over her, and she welcomed the fall into night.

# 10

# *The Voice of
the Storm*

Joshua felt each crash of thunder like a fist that struck his chest. He trudged unsteadily, his head down against the rain, the grip of Phinehas strongly supporting his arm. The thunder's tempo increased as they walked together, coming faster and faster until it rang like the hammerstrokes of some cosmic smith; the rain swirled and spat and lashed them with chill; Joshua's head pounded with wine to the same rhythm as the thunder.

The Host of Israel had pitched their tents in the shelter of low hills when they saw the storm approach from the south. Joshua had reclined upon his couch, with the bulging veins of his brutally swollen, purplish knees raised at last in almost sinful luxury. He'd had a skin of wine to draw the knots from his shoulders, and the gentle surf of rain upon his tent to quiet his mind, and he had been drifting gratefully off to sleep when Phinehas had come with grim face and strong hand to pull him from his rest.

Phinehas had refused to explain his urgent need, saying only that Joshua would understand when he saw. He drew Joshua stumbling into the Levite camps, and now he put his lips close to Joshua's ear, to be heard through the thunder.

"There, Uncle! See there!"

Rain chilled the length of his spine when Joshua raised his head.

The smith hammer of lightning struck, again and again, at the center pole of a tent; the lightning smote it with a deliberate rhythm; a calm man might breathe twice or thrice between each strike.

Joshua recognized this tent through the shroud of rain with a dull shock.

The tent was Eleazar's.

A huge crowd of Israelites gathered around, a crowd that grew with every passing moment, heedless of the rain. They watched the angry strokes at the High Priest's tent, and muttered among themselves. No one approached closer than a stone's throw to the tent, though, not now; Eleazar's tent sat upon a tiny rise, and near its door lay the body of a man in priestly garb, unmoving, smoke rising from its smoldering clothing to mingle with the rain.

"Is that—is that your father?" Joshua spoke loudly, close to Phinehas' ear.

"No," Phinehas replied with a grim shake of his head. "It is Rehabiah ben Eleizer. He tried to go within, and the lightning struck him down."

The name smote Joshua like the blow of a sword, and made him stagger. Eleizer, the father of the dead man, was Eleizer ben *Moses*— Moses' second son. Joshua had held Rehabiah in his arms when he was only hours old; Joshua had blessed his sons, and his sons' sons.

*Ah, Moses,* his inward heart groaned, *do you see how I have failed you?*

For a timeless interval Joshua wandered in the paths of memory, the succor of the very old, sudden tears blending with the rain on his cheeks. He saw again Miriam, and Aaron, and the solemn pride in Moses as he'd consecrated another grandson to the service of God, and for that time, his heart's pain was stilled.

But Phinehas' voice, and his grip upon Joshua's arm, pulled him back to the present. "My father is within, and no one knows if he lives." His voice grated strong and sure, but there was a naked plea in his eyes.

His eyes said, *God shields you from all harm, Uncle. Save my father.*

If it had been another man that lay there, one that Joshua had not known, literally, from moments after his birth, he might have been able to make himself believe that the priest had brought this fate upon himself, by some transgression, or failure of faith . . . but Rehabiah was such an earnest, straightforward, unimaginative man, a true servant of God, who drank in the Law with his mother's milk, until he could no more have sinned than he could have flown through the air.

Joshua lowered his head in the rain, and kept his bitter thoughts to himself.

A hoarsely choking cry came from the crowd not far away; this cry was echoed, answered, increased by other men. They made a ring around something that Joshua could not see, and watched in what he took to be an ominous silence. He pushed through the press.

The disturbance was a man, probably a Naphthalite by his dress, though the mud that streaked his clothing made it difficult to be sure. He writhed upon the earth as though in great pain: boils swelled beneath his skin, pushing outward in great fist-size lumps, on his face, on his exposed arms and legs. The man bucked like a panicked horse, thrashing upon the ground, and the boils split open like overripe pears, spurting corruption into the rain, releasing a stench that made veteran warriors turn away, shaken with nausea. Phinehas gasped and stepped back.

Only Joshua stood unmoved, but within his eyes burned a flame of horror.

The man's belly swelled like a sausage, and his cries of anguish became choked grunts, and finally dissolved into a nerveless *hkk hkkh* deep in his throat, a death rattle to match his last spastic convulsions.

His belly burst from within, and fluid sluiced forth, only roughly contained by his robes, channeled to spill over his knees and out his sleeves, over his neck; where it passed, his flesh shriveled as though roasting, and the earth it fell upon was blackened.

Even as he sagged at last into death, a new hoarse shout came from nearby; Joshua turned to find another man clawing at his arms and face as boils swelled there beneath the skin. Joshua wasted no time in staring—he strode directly to the man, and stabbed at the man's chest with his staff as though it were a lance.

"What have you done?" Joshua barked. "Tell me! Tell me what happened as this came upon you!"

The force of his command struck aside the man's panic for a moment, and the man spread shaking hands, looking into Joshua's flinty eyes with an expression of stark terror barely controlled. Some of his words vanished under the rhythmic crack of the thunder, but the sense was no less clear.

"Nothing . . . nothing, I *swear*! Someone muttered—I don't know who! one of the prophets, I think—that the lightning is a sign from God, that this war comes only to enrich the Levites—that we're fighting for the Levites' gain, instead of—ahh . . . it burns, it burns . . ."

The man dropped to his knees, and his moans became screams, and his eyes rolled up, and he fell convulsing to the ground.

Joshua had no need to watch another man die; he understood now what was happening.

*One of the prophets . . .*

Ever since the death of the eremite, the Host had been attracting madmen, hermits, and wandering preachers as a corpse attracts flies. Joshua's order to leave them unmolested until their falseness could be proven had emboldened all manner of men to step forth, unwashed and dressed in rags, to proclaim themselves prophets. No matter that they spent most of their time arguing with each other; the damage done by their endless mouthings could no longer be denied.

But the prophets were only the outer limbs of the problem; Joshua had to get at the root.

All his former weakness seemed now to him like the foolish maundering of a man's second childhood. He took the thick-muscled arm of Phinehas in a grip like the roots of an oak. "Come. We go now to see your father."

Phinehas would have hung back, even now; even the great power of his faith paled before this eldritch storm. "But—but Uncle—the lightning—!"

Joshua pulled him along with astonishing strength. "Fear nothing, Phinehas. Only trust in the Lord, and know that we do His Will."

He stroked his staff toward the tent of Eleazar. "That is not the work of Yahweh. The hand of God is seen *here*, in these dying men. I have seen this plague before; do you remember Ba'al-pe'or? Zimri, whom you slew? This could be worse. You have learned the tale of Korah—fourteen thousand blameless men fell in that plague, because Korah and his followers contended with Moses. But this tale could end differently—we have no Moses now, to stand between God's wrath and His people. If we do not quell it here and now, thousands will die." His voice dropped bitterly, in a tone that could have been self-accusation. "Tens of thousands."

"Quell—? But how—?"

"For that, we need your father. Come."

Phinehas couldn't have stayed behind if he'd wanted to; Joshua's grip was unbreakable, and he dragged the younger man along as though he were a child.

They broke through the ring of fascinated watchers, and the whip of the rain lessened, as though the lightning that flashed overhead had burned it away. Joshua turned to face the gathered men.

"The plague of Paran is upon us, the plague of Kibroth-hattaavah! Return, each of you, to his tent, and pray to God for mercy! Pray that this plague will come not upon you or yours!"

The crowd stared blankly at him, as though stunned slack-kneed by his words.

"Go!" he roared in a voice to match the thunder above. "Go and pray!"

The men in the crowd began to mill about—and from the crowd came more shouts of revulsion and cries of despair, and some rose from the camp beyond. Joshua could not wait for the men to obey his command; he turned and dragged Phinehas toward the tent of Eleazar.

Phinehas lifted his face in trepidation toward the sky, but Joshua spared the lightning not a glance. Head down, he marched under its crackling flash and pulled aside the door-curtain of Eleazar's tent.

Within, the groundcloth was covered with a heavy thickness of layered linen, scrupulously clean although now greying with age. It had been rolled wide to fill the entire interior of the tent, which was divided into several chambers by hanging curtains. Within the linen groundcloth were woven sigils that to Joshua resembled Egyptian glyphs; these sigils wove in paths both spiral and angular, counter-crossing each other as though one could follow a trail of them, step by step, and read a tale that could change with every choice of direction. The borders of the cloth were woven with gold wire, in sigils vastly older; Joshua could only imagine that this was the script of Ur in the days of Abraham.

When they were fully within, Eleazar appeared, pacing around one of the curtains with a shell lamp in his hand, his head lowered as though in intense concentration.

Each breath Joshua took rasped with thick incense, and some bitter perfume in the lamp's oil.

In his other hand, Eleazar held a short, slim-bladed sword that gleamed dully as though cast in silver. He did not appear to notice his visitors as he paced over the inscriptions on the groundcloth, each stride touching a single glyph; he turned corners at seeming random, and occasionally his foot trembled as he stepped past any number of sigils so that his toe would strike the specific one for which he aimed.

Joshua snapped, "Eleazar!" and the High Priest started so sharply that oil slopped from his lamp onto the cloth.

"What? How did you get in here?"

"I walked," Joshua said heavily.

"Mm, of course—it wouldn't dare strike at *you* . . ."

Then Eleazar's lips pressed into a flat line, and his eyes sparked with desperate danger. He pointed with his sword to Joshua's feet. "Get off that border this instant! And wipe away the mud! Are you insane? Do you want to *let it in*?"

Joshua scowled, but he removed his sandals and set them in the tent's doorway. Phinehas did the same, and then the younger priest stepped onto the groundcloth and knelt to scrub away the mud that had dirtied a portion of the border.

"Are you happy now?" Eleazar spat bitterly. "Are you *satisfied*? I warned you, I *warned* you of the danger!"

Joshua stumped toward the High Priest. "Then it is your angel that causes this. I thought it might be."

"No, Joshua," Eleazar snarled with savage irony, "it's a perfectly *ordinary* storm that has suddenly *decided to kill me!*"

He wiped his lips with the back of a trembling hand. "Of course it's the angel! I charged it to destroy the god that opposes us; it failed, and now it seeks to vent its frustration upon my life. This is the *least* of the Outside Powers—which is probably the only reason that I'm still alive!"

Joshua shrugged. "Get rid of it."

"I am trying! What do you think I was doing when you burst in here?"

"Your angel slew Rehabiah ben Eleizer."

Eleazar stopped in the midst of spitting back a hot retort, and the color drained from his face. "Rehabiah?"

"It's true, Father," Phinehas said. "He tried to come in to you, and was struck down."

Eleazar hung his head, and he set down the sword and the lamp on a low table. He lowered himself slowly to the floor and covered his face with his hands.

"I am sorry, Joshua." His voice was mufffled by his palms, and he slowly lowered them. "But I warned you. Now all that saves my life are my defenses, like this carpet. I pitched my tent upon it when I saw the storm's approach."

He sighed heavily, then raised his head. He was deathly pale, and black streaks shadowed his eyes; Joshua could see the toll that the constant battering of the thunder was already taking upon the High Priest. "The limit of the angel's span to walk the earth was a single day; I made it so, in fear that something like this might happen. I can withstand it for that long, and then it will be gone."

Joshua shook his head. "We do not have a day. Even now, the Lord smites His people with the plague of Paran, because some of them take this—*storm*—as a sign that God is against us. They speak their discontent, even under Yahweh's lash."

"What would you have me do, Joshua?" Eleazar's bitterness grew. "I cannot leave this tent alive, not while the angel seeks its vengeance.

I cannot go into the Tabernacle to make offering for the sin of the people. All I can do from here is *magic*—and magic is *nothing* before the
Outside Powers. So what, then, does your great wisdom say I should
*do?*"

Phinehas drew himself up in righteous outrage. "You should speak
to the Lord's Anointed with respect!"

"Hush," Joshua said to him. "This is your father. Your duty to him
is far greater than his to me."

"Yes, let's speak of *family duty*, shall we?" Eleazar said venomously.
"Do you know how the Lord's Anointed *persuaded* me to this foolish
act?" He glared at Joshua defiantly, as though daring him to command
silence.

The shame that burned within Joshua's breast sealed his lips; all
his strength was required to keep it from his face.

Eleazar jabbed at Joshua with an accusing finger. "This is on you,
Joshua ben Nun. The blood of Rehabiah is on your head! *You* brought
this angel among us by your *threats*—"

"You *dare?*" Phinehas snarled. "You tremble, hiding here within
your tent, and you dare to fault *Joshua* for your cowardice and incom-
petence? I am ashamed to be your son!"

Eleazar flinched as though he'd been struck, and his eyes were
hooded when he turned them upon Joshua.

"My son—for this, too, I blame you, Joshua ben Nun."

"Silence, both of you!" Joshua barked. Bile rose within his throat,
and bitterness gripped the back of his neck. He could not deny
Eleazar's words—he had never in his life spoken against the truth, and
would not do so now. Nor could he affirm them—it was from this that
the bitter gall grew. With all his heart he wished that he had the freedom simply to accept the blame that Eleazar leveled upon him, to say
*Yes, it is my fault, forgive me,* but he could not.

His authority came from God; to take guilt upon himself for these
actions would lay that guilt at the feet of Yahweh Himself.

"This is what shall be done," he said. "Phinehas—on your knees
you will beg the forgiveness of your father for what you have said.
Then you shall make a sin offering to Yahweh, and beg forgiveness of
Him, for breaking His commandment. Never again shall you deny
honor to your father."

Phinehas colored deeply, but he could not bear Joshua's disfavor;
chastened, he lowered his eyes. Joshua turned upon Eleazar.

"The plague upon Israel," he said, "has come of disbelief, and
muttering against the priesthood of Yahweh. This muttering has come

of the bitter march, and the lightning that strikes your tent. Both of these come of the *failure of the angel*; the angel failed because—in your own words—it is the least of the Outside Powers, and it was not equal to the task for which you bound it."

"Oh, no," Eleazar said. "I know what you're trying to do, Joshua. You cannot lay blame for this upon me; the Power that strikes my tent is the greatest that I can command—"

"You do not command!" Joshua thundered, and the lightning outside crashed as though in agreement. *"God* commands; you are His High Priest. You feared to summon a greater power: it is your fear and weakness that have brought this upon you, and upon Israel. You must correct it."

"Oh? And how should I do that?" Eleazar sneered. "Summon another?"

"Yes."

The monosyllable landed like a boulder at the bottom of a well.

Eleazar stared. "You can't mean it!"

"I do." Joshua adjusted his grip upon his staff, and used its support to straighten his back. "I, too, shall do my part. Much of this grumbling will vanish once our warriors sight the walls of Jerusalem. When this storm has passed, we shall strike camp. Jerusalem is now less than a day's march away. We shall march through this night, as we marched from Gibeon to Gilgal. At dawn, the Jebusites will arise to find us camped outside their walls. Their despair will strengthen the heart of every son of Israel."

"A night march through country like this will be a disaster," Eleazar said, and would have gone on, but Joshua silenced him with an imperious lift of his staff.

"Do not presume to instruct me in matters military, *priest*. Tend to your business. We need a greater power. Another like this one will be worse than useless—it has harmed us far more than our enemies. It is crude and valueless in nature; the gods of Canaan laugh at it. You must bring us a Power that can capture the gods of Canaan like flies in pine gum, to hold them fast beneath Yahweh's Fist."

Eleazar said, "I cannot. You can't ask this of me, Joshua. You have no concept of the danger—"

"But I do," Joshua said. "There can be no danger greater than what will happen to Israel if you refuse."

"Don't put this upon me, Joshua. I beg of you."

Joshua set his jaw and turned implacably to Phinehas. "And you? Do you also refuse to serve your people and your God in this way?"

Phinehas straightened, and his eyes flashed fire. "You have only to ask. For Yahweh and Israel, I would summon Shahkhath itself!"

"That," Joshua said, "is precisely what I ask."

The sudden silence was more startling than the outside thunderclaps.

"You speak too rashly!" Eleazar said, horrified. "The Destroyer cannot be called and dismissed like a servant! Shahkhath is a *Throne of God!*"

"Shahkhath is precisely what we need," Joshua said. "We do not contend with men, here, but with their gods. They strike at us subtly, backhandedly, fearing to face Yahweh's wrath directly; we must strike at them the same way. It was not rivers of blood or fiery hail that mastered Pharaoh; it was the silent death of each firstborn. If Shahkhath cannot be summoned, it must be coaxed, bribed, wheedled—promised whatever may be required. But it will not be required. Even Shahkhath will not risk God's wrath. Bind it with the Name of the Lord of Hosts, and it will obey."

"You seem to think," Eleazar said numbly, "that angels are servants of Yahweh, distinct from Him. It is not so."

He rose slowly, and lifted the silver sword, examining it as though help for his words could be found in the glyphs inscribed on the blade.

"Angels are one of the Great Mysteries," he said with slow precision. "I'm not sure that I can make you understand. We treat them as individuals, even call them by name—but that is only . . . ah, a pretense. A convenience. In truth, there is only One Name for all angels: Yahweh Sabaoth, El Shaddai."

Joshua's brow darkened. "Tread carefully around that Name, Eleazar."

"Oh, I do. Believe that I do. Try to understand, Joshua. The Lord is One; He is also Many—a Host of Angels. Have you never noticed how when angels speak of the Lord, they say *We?*—sometimes even *I*, as though it is the Lord Himself who speaks? The names we give to angels—Michael, Uriel, Shahkhath—are ways of addressing parts of the Lord that are . . . not small, but *contained* . . . contained enough for us to understand. Contained enough for us, mortals that we are, to look upon and live. Even Yahweh is, in a sense, only the Name of an angel."

Joshua stiffened and fire crackled in his gaze. "You go too far!"

"No, Joshua. I know the truth. The Lord is unknowable; He is beyond naming. Yahweh is the Name we give to the Aspect of the Lord that sits upon the Mercy Seat, accepts our sacrifices and punishes our transgressions—but that Name is far too small to contain the Lord.

Yahweh is so vast that merely to glimpse His awful majesty would shatter your mind and blast the light from your eyes, yet Yahweh is the merest speck of the Truth of the Lord. The Lord sends a small part of Himself as Yahweh, that He might speak with you without destroying you; and you have told how even hearing the Voice darkens your eyes like a blow to the head. This is why Yahweh does not Speak to me; I have not the strength to endure it. Merely the sound of His Voice would kill me."

"None of this excuses you from the task I have commanded," Joshua told him.

"Do you understand nothing I've *said*? You've seen the anger of the angel that seeks my life; this is the fury of God in miniature. When the angel departs, still angry, its anger *returns to God*. The Lord Himself will feel that anger—in His illimitable vastness, it may be perhaps the merest twinge, but anger nonetheless. A greater power—not even Shahkhath, leave the Destroyer right out of it . . . if something goes wrong, I will not be able to defend myself. Or Israel!"

Phinehas put in nervously, "Uncle—if the Lord truly wishes Shahkhath to afflict our enemies, won't He send the Destroyer without our summoning?"

Stern as granite, Joshua replied, "No. To do so would deprive your father of the opportunity to serve. It is our service that Yahweh requires."

"This could turn God *against* us!" Eleazar said desperately.

"God will never turn against us. He loves us. When he lifts his hand to us, it is as a loving father disciplines a son. That hand is upraised already; if you doubt it—" here Joshua's lips pulled back in a grimace bitter as wormwood "—just look in the plague tents."

He straightened. "I shall send the other priests to you as soon as you have dismissed this storm. I go now to organize the march. When the summoning of Shahkhath is complete, gather your tents and your priests and follow us to Jerusalem. The Lord is not finished with you, Eleazar ben Aaron."

Joshua turned peremptorily and strode toward the door, back out into the lashing storm.

"Get to work."

A sickening dread curdled within Joshua's breast as he numbered the troops for the march. Phinehas at his side, he stumped through the thundering storm.

He took men from each of the tribes—saving only the Levites—

and each of the clans within the tribes, so that no tribe or tribes could claim precedence or right in the spoils over any other. Twenty thousand men would make this march, carrying only skins of water, strips of salt beef, and hard biscuits for provender, slings and spears for weapons. Every third man bore a shovel, and every seventh a pick.

They would march through the night, and erect earthworks to defend the following Host; they would be the initial investing force, who must hold the Jebusites within their city until the vanguard of the Host would arrive in the afternoon or evening. Two days, perhaps even three, would be required for the Host to fully assemble, gathering itself with the tidal flow of a locust swarm creeping through a sinner's field.

Until then, this force he numbered would have to hold the field against Adonizedek's mercenaries, and perhaps the might of Egypt, as well. In former days, when Joshua commanded men in the shadow of Moses, this army would have gone with the Lord before it, and Yahweh's mighty Hand would have swept away the Jebusites. If the Lord chose, he could deliver Jerusalem into Joshua's hand without the loss of a single life.

But the Lord had not so chosen, and Joshua knew it.

The dread within his heart fed on the fear that the Lord had chosen to break the Host of Israel against Jerusalem's walls, to punish them for their sins.

He drained the wineskin he held, and handed it to Phinehas. "Bring another," he said, shortly, so that Phinehas would not hear any drunken slur in his words.

Phinehas looked at the skin in his hand, as though he was reluctant to obey but also unwilling to disobey; as though he silently asked Joshua for permission to defy him.

"Go!" Joshua barked. "This rain chills my bones. The wine warms them, if only for a moment. *Go!*"

Phinehas turned and walked away without comment.

Joshua watched the marchers assemble, seeing them all as corpses rotting in the Hinnom Valley, their eyes and tongues become sweetmeats for ravens and kites.

For a moment, the spin of wine within his head gave him a dizzy vision of simply calling off the war, of throwing up his hands and telling the entire Host to go home.

He steadied himself, his hand reaching unconsciously for the hem of his robe, to gather it and bring the tassel there up into his solemn regard.

There was one blue cord within that tassel, as there was in every tassel on the corners of the garments of every Israelite. This blue cord was there by the Lord's command, that every time one should see it, it would be a reminder to obey God, and His Law, and not go whoring after one's own thoughts and desires.

*Not my will, but Thine, be done,* Joshua prayed as earnestly as he was able. But another prayer, he could give his entire heart to: *I beg you, God of my fathers, to ease my spirit with a promise of victory.*

As though in answer, the day darkened in his eyes, and thunder roared ever louder, beating upon his head until even his bones shook— and he knew, in a single instant's clarity, that the darkness and the thunder came not from the storm above, but from the Voice within.

His staff fell from his hand, and the old man twisted slowly to the earth, pitching forward as a tree falls; he crashed stiffly into the storm-churned mud, and measured his length under the rain like a toppled statue.

He fell with his face to the sky, his eyes staring open to the rain; they showed only an arc of whites like sun-yellowed paper bearing aimless spidery pen scratches of blood.

With shouts of alarm, the men he had been gathering crowded around him, but no one bent to help; they could not tell if he yet lived, and under the Law of God any man who touches a corpse is *tawmay*, polluted, for seven days.

Though the rain still fell when light returned to Joshua's world, a small patch of sky shimmered with God's own blue, a patch of sky that seemed to shine with grace. Between Joshua and that patch of sky was a ring of alarmed faces peering at him as though they'd never seen such a thing before.

As Joshua painfully struggled to pull himself up from the mud to a sitting position, he heard Phinehas growl from not far away; soon his aide had forced aside the men blocking his path. He knelt at Joshua's side, his eyes wide with alarm, the wineskin dangling forgotten from his fist.

"Uncle, what happened? I should never have left your side!"

Joshua pulled the wineskin from his grasp with one hand, while the other took Phinehas' arm in a reassuring grip.

"I am not harmed, Phinehas. Help me up."

As Joshua stood, the weight of years seemed to fall from his shoulders; despite the mud that caked his rain-soaked clothing, he felt as though he need merely turn his face toward the heavens and he might float away into their infinite blue.

"This is a day for rejoicing," he said.

Puzzlement fought with faithful gladness on Phinehas' face. "It is?"

Joshua smiled, his face feeling stiff and weak, as though the muscles to draw his lips into that shape had not been used in a very long time.

Perhaps they had not; Joshua could not remember the last time he had smiled.

He could not tell his aide, or the men around them, that the Lord had answered his prayer, had promised victory; as far as they knew, Yahweh had already done so on the night Eleazar had deceived them.

"There is a new task for you, Phinehas. A way you, yourself, on this day, can bring Israel closer to our victory at Jerusalem."

"Anything, Uncle. Anything. You know I will not fail."

"You must walk among the tribes with questions. Someone, somewhere, will have the knowledge we require."

"What knowledge, Uncle?"

Joshua drew breath with a satisfied, chest-filling confidence that he had not felt in many years. "You must learn everything that is known of a pagan whore named *Barra Coll Eigg Rhum*."

Another forked flash and crash of thunder drew his gaze back toward the tent of Eleazar, and for a moment it seemed that the lightning sparked an answering fire within his eyes. "In fact . . ." he murmured, then turned decisively to Phinehas. "Go, now, and do this thing. Take your best horse, for you will be forced to overtake me at the head of this night's march."

"Uncle, I don't—"

Joshua's smile was kindly, but a fierce flame burned behind it. "I will explain when you return. Go."

Phinehas went.

Joshua looked around himself, and the gloomy, storm-haunted afternoon seemed warmer, friendlier, almost cheery. Humming tunelessly to himself, he walked through the astonished mob of Israelites toward Eleazar's tent.

Eleazar looked up sharply from his dainty glyph-path pacing when Joshua once again ducked into his tent. He snapped, "How am I ever to banish this damned angel if you keep interrupting?"

Joshua stopped at the filigreed edge of the carpet, an unfamiliar gentle smile creasing the folds of his face. "I have an answer to your problem."

"I've already *tried* prayer," Eleazar said snidely. "What other advice do you ever give?"

"Do not banish it," Joshua said. "Only release it."

"Eh?"

"You charged it to attack the gods of Jerusalem. Perhaps its fury comes from a lust to attack its real enemy."

"What do you mean?"

Joshua spread his hands. "Its attack was frustrated by an agent of evil. From whence comes its anger toward you? What does it hope to gain by attacking you? It is *your binding* that frustrates it now. Once you are slain, your binding upon it is broken—and it is free to follow its true desire: to destroy the beast that has defied it."

"You think it is that simple?" Eleazar said with incredulous mockery. "Joshua, if you had the faintest knowledge of what you speak, you would not believe—"

Joshua's smile was serene to the point of smugness. "I do not believe. I know."

"You know? You mean . . ." Eleazar's eyes rolled toward heaven and he made a circular gesture with his hand, as though to indicate all creation.

"Set the angel free. Let it harry this agent of evil out from the walls of Jerusalem; let it slay, if it can. God has promised that when this creature, this Enemy of God, comes out from Jerusalem, the city will fall."

Eleazar swallowed. "That's quite a promise . . ."

"Let it be done. Then, when we reach Jerusalem, we shall see what is left of this . . ." Joshua's face twisted as though the words left a foul taste upon his tongue. "Of this *Barra Coll Eigg Rhum.*"

# 11

# *Axes in the Rain*

**B**arra knelt on the rain-swept flagstones, on the verge of the freshly turned dirt of the garden, and felt the strengthening rain fall across the back of her neck and down within her soaking tunic. She had scooped a hollow in the brown and sandy earth with her own hands, and she laid the fragments of her axe within it, one by one.

Her friends had left the fragments lying in the mud where they had fallen, lying there for horses to kick and dogs to shit on; not even Leucas had thought to pick them up for her. When she'd awakened in the gloom-shrouded front room of some random townsman, she hadn't remembered what had happened. Only the dizziness that she couldn't banish from her head, and the reeking crackle of her fried-crisp hair let her believe them, when they told her she'd been hit by lightning in the street.

They had seen her stand, and charge, howling at nothing. They had seen her draw her axe, and leap—and had seen only the single swift stroke of the thunderbolt from the heavens above.

She didn't mention the creature of lightning. Of them all, she suspected Adonizedek alone would believe her, and the support of a madman would be worse than none at all.

Leucas had remained by the window, his grey and pensive stare directed at the clouds outside. "It's only rain," he murmured. "We can go on to the Citadel, now."

"What do you mean, it's only rain?" Kheperu squawked incredulously. "Every time we go out in a storm, someone nearly gets killed!"

Leucas shrugged. "It was more than a storm, before. Like that one in the mountains was more than a storm. That one was angry; this was . . . cold."

"Oh, please! Winter storms are always chill—"

"No," Barra said from the couch where she reclined. "That's not what he means. Is it?"

"I don't know how to say it," Leucas said. "But it's safe now."

It was when she arose to leave that she felt the empty scabbard at her belt.

Her head spun. She swayed on the brink of memory.

"Where's my *axe*?"

No one answered her. She repeated the question in Canaanite.

The grave and concerned looks everyone exchanged, instead of responding, prickled her neck with creeping horror.

Finally Leucas seemed, by silent and unanimous vote, to be elected spokesman. He said softly, "Don't you remember?"

She remembered a sharp, stunning crack, like the impact of a gull-dropped clamshell upon a seaside rock.

She said distantly, "Oh, no, come on, tell me the truth . . ."

"I'm sorry, Barra. I know what it meant to you . . ."

*You don't know half of it,* she thought. "Where is it? I mean"—her eyes drifted half-closed, and she waved her hand as though she could fan aside the pain gathering in her chest—"where are they? The pieces."

Leucas looked over at Kheperu, silently appealing for aid. Kheperu only shook his head minutely. "There's no helping it," he murmured.

"You left it there," she said numbly. "You left it to lie in the mud."

"It was all in pieces," Kheperu said. "We had to get out of the storm."

She nodded mutely; the pain in her chest spread until it was no longer sharp and stabbing, but instead hung like a diver's stone upon her spirit. She said, "All right." She stiffened her spine and banished all weakness from her face.

"All right. You two take the king and the Lady's Maid up to the Citadel." She lifted a hand to forestall their protest. "No. Somebody has to look after them. Remember the crowd in the street? Take no chances."

"You're going for the pieces of your axe?" Kheperu said skeptically. "Barra, it's just some chunks of rocks, now."

"Shut up."

"You shouldn't even be on your feet—"

"What do you know about it?"

*"Nothing,"* he said, leaning on the word pointedly. "And neither do you. You were *struck by lightning*; who knows what that's done to you?"

"I'm all right."

"How do you know? Barra, I've never even *heard* of someone hit by a thunderbolt who lived; at the very least, you should be resting, not running out into the rain to gather up some useless splinters of—"

"Kheperu, I know you're saying all this because you're my friend—and I really appreciate your concern—but if you don't shut up, I'll break your fucking jaw."

He lifted his muddy hands and turned his face aside in a *don't blame me* gesture of surrender.

She said to Leucas, "You understand, don't you?"

The boxer nodded grimly, reflections of a landslide high among the Manassite mountains in his eyes.

"Good luck."

She went over close to the king, where he sat beside the couch where the Lady's Maid lay. Her knees trembled, their weakness making her stagger; dizzy, she lowered herself into a crouch at the king's side.

Sarah said, "Are you sure you're ready to move? You seem still a little shaky."

"Don't you start," Barra said tiredly. "I've just been through all this with Kheperu—"

"I rejoice that you are well," the king said cheerfully, dye from his wig painting his face like the stripes of a festival fool, "though I expected no less. The Lady would not choose a Champion only to let her fall before the battle."

"Ay, whatever. Listen, Adonizedek, you have gardens within the Citadel, eh?"

"But of course. Do you like gardens? I'll show them to you directly after the feast of celebration."

Barra shook her head. "I don't have anything to celebrate. I'll just need permission to dig in your garden."

The feather-stripes of black that fringed his snowy brows drew together. "Dig? In the garden?"

"I need a place where green things grow." She stood up, and swayed, as colored lights danced madly within her head.

She rubbed her stinging eyes, and said, "I have to bury my oldest friend."

Outside the nameless Jebusite's front door, Sarah's sedan chair lay canted half in the mud, its canopy shredded by the weight of the rain, tatters straggling and streaming, mud caked on the cushions within.

Barra stopped for a moment, and stared; something in its emptiness held her. The chair lay abandoned, and somehow hopeless, and somehow it seemed like her fault.

She shook her head grimly, and tried to keep her trembling knees beneath her as she wove her unsteady path away from her friends.

She walked with her head down. Rain tapped the back of her neck like cold and mocking fingers.

She could not remember ever having been so alone.

By the time she had staggered back to the Citadel, the storm had faded to a drizzling iron grey overcast that darkened toward sunset. The gates stood open and unguarded; torches lit the courtyards like full daylight, hissing and sizzling with the misting rain; tinkling laughter came distantly from the few warm-lit windows high upon the inner walls.

She had slipped aside, once through the gate, avoiding the straggling flow of the important townsfolk who trailed in for the feast. She kept her head down and stayed close to the wall, her muddy hands clenched around three jagged chunks of basalt, clenched so tightly that drops of blood oozed from her palms.

She spared the warm and inviting glow within barely a glance; she was not even tempted to go in, had no interest in the comfort of human contact. The thought of being welcomed and lionized by the celebrating Jebusites appalled her. Even facing her friends, who could come closer to understanding her pain than anyone else in the world, was more than she could bear.

She arranged the three large pieces within the grave, and scattered what few splinters she'd found around them, pressing the stone into the moist and muddy earth, bringing it for one last time back into roughly its original shape.

*Not its original shape,* some forgotten corner of her spirit reminded her, *but the shape into which I cut it.* She remembered the day she'd found that slab of basalt, jutting out from an Anatolian hill; on that day, she had still borne the wounds left her by the three Akhaian deserters who had taken her and used her and left her for dead.

She'd already chosen a hammerstone, and had already practiced her hand by chipping two flint heads to make throwing axes. Flint is brittle, and easy to work—it splits almost effortlessly into edges sharp enough to shave with—and plentiful; she had always made her throwing axes of flint, because they had to be easily and cheaply replaceable. Her throwing axes were tools as much as weapons; she hunted small game with them, and stripped bark from saplings to make traps, and chopped kindling.

But basalt—basalt is another matter entirely.

Basalt is the bone of the earth.

Gently, lovingly, she had brought the shape of a weapon out of the rude stone, day after day, *chip chip chip* until she had heard it in her dreams. She had stroked the edge into the curve of the crescent moon; she had smoothed the cheeks and rubbed them with raw copper until they'd gleamed like oiled bronze; only a practiced eye could have seen that the axe was stone, and not metal.

The eye could be fooled, but not the hand. Any man with knowledge of metalwork or warfare, on lifting that axe, on testing that edge, would have frowned his disbelief. Bronze lacks the solidity, the concentrated heft of a good stone blade, and bronze cannot match its edge. And bronze never quite takes the luster of copper-rubbed basalt; the stone seems to become almost a living thing, a hungering edge that gleams a rich, killing green.

It had been made with the faces of three men floating forever before her eyes. It had been shaped to cut them as cruelly as they had cut her. For a year she had sought them, along the endless curve of the Mediterranean shore.

She had found them, finally, on the far side of Egypt, as they headed into the Libyan Desert. One she had slain; the other two, if they still lived, no longer lived as men.

She'd been eighteen when they'd caught her, a girl, a victim; when she caught them she was nineteen, a woman, a warrior. It was not what they did to her that had changed her.

Her change had begun on the same day she'd begun to carve this axe.

This axe had been the only companion she'd kept from that day to this; her sole friend who could never turn faithless, who would always stand by her side and defend her, no matter what the odds.

Now the faint sounds of the preparations within the Citadel faded behind the rising hush of fresh rain. She bent over the grave she had made, and her tears blended with the rain to fall across the broken stone. She laid her hands upon the pieces, one last time, remembering each stroke that had shaped it, remembering every man who'd fallen before its edge.

This was the only way she could say good-bye.

She wanted to go home. She wanted to be thirteen again, to never have done the things she'd done, seen what she had seen, lived what she had lived.

She wanted to run away, far into the unknown east, away from everything she'd ever known, and bury herself in the infinite green of a nameless jungle.

Slowly, reluctantly, she began to scoop the mounded earth over the remains of her blade.

Distant thunder cracked like the breaking of her heart.

She gradually became aware that she was not alone. She did not bother to wipe the tears from her face; no one could tell them from the rain.

"Barra?" The voice was a woman's, Sarah's, soft and full of gentle concern. "I'm sorry to intrude . . ."

The Lady's Maid stood a few paces away, draped in soft linen now spotting with the rain, the torchlight around her bringing an illusory glow of health to her sunken cheeks. In her arms she carried a bundle, wrapped in some flowing cloth that draped like Indusian silk.

"No intrusion," Barra said hoarsely, from her knees. "I'm finished, here. Should you be out here? Walking—in the rain?"

Sarah shook her head, an expression of ethereal distress making her look very young, and vulnerable. "Coming here has cost you so much . . ."

"What do you know about it?" Barra came to her feet, muscles bunching in her shoulders as though she might throw a punch.

"I had to come out here," Sarah said, her eyes moist with what Barra hoped was only rain—she couldn't stomach this woman's pity. "I have a gift for you—but my husband would deny me, if he knew that I give it."

"Keep it, then," Barra told her with a dismissive wave of the hand. "I don't need anything from you."

As though she did not hear, Sarah began to unwrap the bundle that she carried. Layer after layer of silk unwound, trailing unheeded across the wet flagstones of the courtyard, and the shape of the object within gradually resolved, gleaming and glittering even through the silk that wrapped it.

Barra's heart stuttered madly.

It was an axe.

Sarah held it up. It looked to be forged of a single piece of bronze, double-faced, engraved with curving sigils. The edges seemed to be serrated, with teeth that sparked fire in the torchlight.

"This is the Axe of the Lady—it was used to offer animal sacrifice a thousand years ago, when the Lady still required the life of a bull every spring. It is of bronze, and the edge is inset with cut gemstones."

"I don't mean to be rude," Barra said, "but it looks like a piece of shit." She could see from the way it balanced in Sarah's hands that it would be virtually useless as a weapon, and that ridiculous bronze haft would start to bend with the first stroke—but the harshness in her words came from more than professional disapproval. She grasped for cynicism like a lever, to pry open the bands of panic that squeezed her chest.

"This is less a weapon than it is a *symbol*, Barra. Do you need a clearer sign than this?" Sarah said, holding out the axe to her. "The axe you lost was your old life, shattered here. You must leave it behind you forever."

She took another step closer, and lifted the Lady's Axe up to the level of Barra's eyes. "Now is the time to take up your new life."

Barra scowled at the pretty carving and the lustrous glitter of its serrated edges; the sparkle of gemstones dusted her eyes like sand on the wind. It looked purely decorative—a toy weapon, for little girls playing at being Anat—but also, inexplicably, lethal and terrifying.

"I didn't ask for this," Barra said, her face set and cold while her guts clenched like a fist. "I don't want it."

The wind swirled behind her, and whispered with the voices of the dead.

"I know you don't want it," Sarah said, swaying now with weakness, her face frozen with the effort of holding the axe at arm's length. "Will you take it?"

The rising wind struck her with chill like a knife in her belly; her whole body began to tremble helplessly. "You don't understand," she said, raising her voice so that she could hear herself above the despairing shades howling in her head. Her vision blurred with wind-pricked tears.

"I *can't*." Barra's voice shook as much as her hands; too much had happened to her in too short a time. She felt a yawning darkness open beneath her, and she seemed to be falling into a night crowded with death rattles and the screams of burning children.

Her words seemed to come from outside, as though some distant, barely comprehensible Barra still spoke from somewhere far behind her.

"You can't ask me to take this on myself—I saw, I *lived* every death in Jericho. Don't make Jebusi my fault . . ."

"No one can force you to act, Barra. Not I, nor the Lady herself. We can only ask." The strain of standing, of holding the heavy weapon, pitched Sarah's voice up toward desperation.

Barra swayed; the courtyard spun around her, and she couldn't seem to get her breath. *"Jericho . . ."* she sighed, a whisper of despair; a plea for mercy.

"Would you have saved them, if you could?"

"I, of course I would—I—I . . ."

With the transcendent hush of the earth's indrawing breath, like the sudden surge from a deep dream to perfect wakefulness, the courtyard steadied around her into clarity: she could see the shadows of every grain of sand in the flagstone cracks, cast in red-tinged black by the hissing torches.

It seemed to Barra as though she stood there forever, as though this single instant stretched outward infinitely to compass her entire life. She had always been standing here, on this cusp; she would be standing here forever more.

Hoarse with effort, Sarah said, "The Lady asks you to fight for her children. Will you do it?"

Barra thought of the mist that had risen from the road, to hide them from the Habiru when she'd asked the Mother for help; she thought of the moon that had guided them to safety of the hills. She thought of Sheshai, the moon-worshiper, who had saved her life—all their lives—in Jericho. She thought of Tyre, of Simi-Ascalon's work-shop where the *sceon tiof*, the Mother's gift of sight, had shown her how to save herself and her friends.

*The Lady asks you to fight for her children . . .*

Barra thought of her own children, of Chryl, the son of her body, and Antiphos, the son of her heart, adopted from a Greek slave mar-ket. She thought of Rachel.

She thought of dying here, far from her family in a foreign land.

She thought of facing her sons, carrying the dead of Jericho within her.

She thought of facing each passing day of the rest of her life, won-dering if—with an ounce more courage—she could have saved the children of Jebusi.

The dark and howling pit still yawned within her, but she knew she would not fall; a strong hand upon her arm upheld her.

*Nobody ever promised me I'd live forever.*

The whispers of the Jericho dead hushed, as though waiting.

"All right," Barra said, into the rain-swept silence of the night. She put out her hand and took the Lady's Axe from Sarah. "I'll fight. It's what I'm good at. But it's my *job*, you hear me? You tell your goddess for me—"

She flipped the axe spinning into the air, caught it, and slid its haft behind her boarskin belt; and then she suddenly grinned, a smile as humorlessly savage as a hunting wolf's.

"You tell her I don't work for free."

BOOK THREE

# The Wrath of God

# 12

# *The Feast*

**S**hivering tremors shaking her entire thin frame, Sarah faced Barra, swaying, her brow wrinkled as though she had something more to say, but could not quite put it into words—and then her illness and the rain and the effort of having stood upright holding the heavy axe for so long overcame her. Sarah's eyes rolled up, and she pitched forward senselessly, to collapse against Barra's chest.

Barra caught her easily with one arm—for all her height, the Lady's Maid seemed to weigh nothing at all.

For a moment, she could only stare down into Sarah's face, thinking, *What have I got myself into this time?*

She adjusted the angle of the axe behind her belt—its haft wouldn't fit in the scabbard—hiked the unconscious woman up onto her shoulders, and carried her in out of the rain.

"It took very little time," Phinehas said, his face held deliberately blank and incurious. "She's rather well known in the north."

Phinehas had reined in his short, stocky horse alongside Joshua, who trudged grimly at the head of the column. With stamina that would have been astonishing in a man half his age, Joshua personally led the night march; the promise of God sustained his strength.

But the march under the waning moon had ground away his earlier euphoria. The plague still struck among the men at his back; even as Phinehas rode up, another cry of despair and terror had risen from the ranks, and a man fell into convulsions as the boils swelled and burst within his flesh.

Phinehas looked back over the heads of the men, his face twisting with frightened revulsion. "It hasn't stopped," he said.

"Of course it hasn't stopped," Joshua said heavily. "Ignore these men upon whom God's judgment has fallen. Tell me what you have learned."

Phinehas swung down from the saddle and walked at Joshua's side, one hand upon his horse's bridle. "Many of the Asherites have stories of her. When you cancel out the parts that are obvious fabrications, you are left with this: Barra Coll Eigg Rhum is a mercenary, a woman with hair the color of copper, well connected among the Egyptians of the coast. She's something of a local hero in Tyre, where she was instrumental in one of their petty merchant wars last autumn. The war resulted in a victory for the merchant house that was already the biggest and strongest—little surprise there. Apparently, her major talent seems to be self-promotion."

Joshua scowled. "Merely a mercenary? I think not. She is an Enemy of God; there must be more to her than this. What are these fabrications you spoke of?"

"Uncle, really, they're too fantastic to be credited—"

"In even the most extreme legends there is usually a grain of truth. Speak."

Phinehas sighed. "Well, they say she can turn herself invisible. They say she can vanish in a puff of smoke and reappear atop a building a day's march away. They say she can turn herself into a wolf, and that she fights with a magic axe that cuts bronze like butter. They say that she can summon bears into the midst of a city to tear apart those who offend her. One of her companions is a man made of stone that can break the walls of a city with a blow of his fist; another is a brimstone demon who can roast a whole army with the gouts of fire he casts from his fingertips. The whole crew of them is either supposed to be children of pagan gods, or the pagan gods themselves in disguise—depending upon whom you ask."

"Hmpf," Joshua grunted. "Fantastic enough, I suppose. Well—if these are but stories, we have little to fear. She'll be dead before we reach Jerusalem."


The doorway that she entered, the Lady's Maid over her shoulder, was black with nightshadow; the rain outside had drowned all scents and covered the hushed sounds of slow breathing, and so she nearly jumped out of her skin when Leucas said, "Barra? I've been thinking."

"Bloody *Mother*!" Barra gasped, clutching Sarah to keep from dropping her on her head. "How long have you been there?" Her voice sharpened suspiciously. "You were following me!"

"Hmpf," Kheperu said, for he, too, was close at hand. "We could hardly leave you behind and go to the feast, you being in such a state. This great Athenian half-wit was afraid you'd do yourself some damage."

She looked up at the vague hulking outline that was Leucas. "Ay, well, maybe I have . . ."

"Pish," Kheperu said. "You're strong as a horse. Let's put the Lady's Maid to bed and go to the feast."

Barra sighed. "I'm thinking the same thing." She looked away, back out the doorway, up at the sky.

"What are you looking for?" Kheperu asked.

She shifted the weight of the Lady's Maid, and flicked a hand up at the impenetrable blackness of the clouds overhead.

"I was hoping to catch sight of the moon."

But the only glow against the shroud of night was that of the torches men and women had lit for the celebration.

She turned back at her friends. "So how long are you two lazy bastards going to stand there and let me carry this woman? What am I, your fucking packhorse? Get her up to her apartment and put her to bed—then, if you want, maybe we'll go to the party. Enjoy life while we've got it, hah?"

"This," Kheperu said, a sly smile clear in his voice, "is the sum total of my philosophy."

"Barra," Leucas said slowly, "let me carry her."

He reached out and plucked Sarah from Barra's shoulder as though she were a mannequin of straw. He cradled her in his massive arms, gazing down into her soft oval face with an oddly tender expression, like a father holding his newborn daughter for the first time.

"Come on," Barra said briskly. "We need to get her to her rooms, and then we need to start working on defending her. Follow me."

She strode off, leaving Kheperu and Leucas somewhat bemused behind her.

"She's certainly cheered up," Kheperu said.

Leucas nodded wisely. "She's decided to answer the call."

"Oh, please. The call? You think Barra is buying into this Lady's Champion horseshit?"

"Not only her," Leucas said. He looked again into the face of the Lady's Maid, and for a moment that strange softening seemed to come over him once again. When he spoke, his voice barely rose above a whisper.

"In Tyre, we refused the call until it was almost too late—for the city, and for us. Barra has been hearing the call for weeks. When the gods want you, their voice can become very loud indeed."

They moved upward into the Citadel, weaving around gaily dressed folk on their way to the feast, through knots of slaves bearing spitted pigs and great casks of Egyptian beer. These folk all seemed grimly determined to enjoy themselves tonight; it was as though they all accepted that this might be the last party within these walls, so it had better be a good one.

Many of them looked on Barra's scorched hair and soaking clothes with a certain alarm, but as soon as they saw Leucas approach with Sarah in his arms, their alarm would turn to recognition. Then they'd touch Barra's arm, their expressions blending fear and childlike hope, and speak to her in low, imploring tones.

Neither Leucas nor Kheperu had the tongue, and so they never knew the words, but the meaning of their questions, and of Barra's reply, were overpoweringly clear.

*You're the Lady's Champion? You? Tell us it's true. Tell us that we'll be saved.*

Barra's teeth would flash in the gloom, and an undeniable sparkle would come into her eye.

*Yes. We're the Lady's Champions. We'll fight for you. Hold on to hope.*

"You're going to do it, aren't you?" Kheperu said in Greek as he caught up with her. His face twisted as though he felt more than a little ill. "You're going to stay here and fight the Habiru."

She grinned at him. "Oh, ay."

"You'll die a hideous bloody death here for nothing—for people you never gave a thought to in your life."

"Ah, they're still people," Barra said carelessly. "This 'hideous bloody death' part, that remains to be seen." She ambled along before him, a definite jaunty cheerfulness entering her step.

He flapped his hands in despair. "And how can you be so fucking *happy* about it?"

He'd meant the question rhetorically, no more than a casual gripe, but it caught Barra like a hand upon her shoulder. She stopped and looked back at him. "I don't know," she said seriously, frowning briefly as though she was trying to puzzle it out.

She surrendered with a shrug and grinned even wider.

"But you'll be killed along with everybody else! To save this city, it's impossible!"

"Ay, that's how it looked to me, too—until I decided to do it. Now I'm pretty sure I can pull it off."

"How?" he demanded. "How do you think you're going to do this?"

She leaned close to his ear and whispered, "*Very carefully . . .*"

"You are impossible! Tell me this, then: why? Why risk everything for a bloodyfucking little *caravan stop* in the middle of Buttfuck Nowhere?"

Leucas shifted the slight weight of the Lady's Maid in his arms, and said solidly, "Because it is the will of the gods."

"Screw the gods," Barra said. "I'm doing it for the money."

"Ah—" Kheperu began.

"Barra!" Leucas said with a paternal scolding tone. He shook his head, looking mildly scandalized. "Money shouldn't come into this—"

Barra swung away and began to walk off. "Speak for yourself."

Kheperu began again, louder, "*Ah—*"

Leucas went after her. "*I* wouldn't take silver for serving the gods . . ."

"Swell," Barra said. "Can I have your share?"

Kheperu said again, nearly shouting, "*AH—*"

Barra and Leucas both stopped and looked back at him. Barra said exasperatedly, "Yes? What?"

He frowned prissily at her tone, and said with hesitant, almost reverent delicacy, "—how *much* money?"


"You no longer have a choice!" Melchizedek's sepulchral voice wavered between plea and command.

Agaz rested his elbows on the parapet and turned his face to the wind.

"I do have a choice. And I choose to honor my father."

"He leads us to destruction!"

"Yes," Agaz murmured. "Yes, he does."

Night shrouded this upmost peak of the Citadel's tower, clouds bloody with torchlight drizzling low overhead, a close and airless gloom that mirrored Agaz's heart.

He had come up here to pound his frustration into the stone of the walls with his fists.

Melchizedek's walking staff clacked on stone as the priest came close behind the prince's left shoulder; he spoke in a tone of calm reason.

"I understand your reluctance. I know you love him; as do I. He is my brother. But I cannot be a *brother*, now. I must be the High Priest of El. And you cannot be a son, when you are needed as a king."

Melchizedek had been whispering these treasons in his ear practically from the moment he'd ridden into the Citadel.

Agaz's fingernails scraped at the stone on which he leaned. He stared at them, pretending to examine the grit that painted arcs of mud brown beneath them.

He was running out of counterarguments.

He said, "Only this afternoon, you abused and insulted the king himself, for—what was your phrase?—'violating the natural order' when he abdicated in favor of my brother. Is it less a violation to seize the throne by force?"

"Empty words," Melchizedek snorted. "The people call you to be their king. To *save their lives*. Will you deny them?"

"I have not heard their voices raised to me this way."

"Their *need* cries out to you, Agaz, not their voices. You must put aside your love for Adonizedek. You must think like a *king*, now; love is a luxury, for the king. You must make any sacrifice to protect your people—even if that sacrifice wounds you to the heart. Even if that sacrifice is your father."

Melchizedek placed his hands upon Agaz's shoulders and turned the unresisting prince around so that his moonless stare could strike into Agaz's eyes. "Do you place your love for him above the lives of the people you were born to defend?"

The High Priest's eyes seemed to expand until they filled the world. Within himself, Agaz twisted this way and that, looking for an answer that would satisfy the warring halves of his heart—but he did not find one, and he knew that he would look forever, and never be at peace.

Even that meant nothing; he knew that Melchizedek was right.

The people come first.

Duty over love, always.

Always.

The words burned his throat like acid vomit, but there was no other road.

Before he could bring them forth, the chiming voice of Rachel, his daughter, his sole surviving child, the last princess of Jebusi, came from nearby.

"Father? Great-uncle? Are you fighting?"

He pulled himself away from the High Priest, warm with gratitude for her timely interruption. He crouched down before her, took her hand, and gazed into her limpid eyes, so much like her mother's, and thought that he'd never truly loved her as much as he did at this moment.

"No, no, Rachel. No, we weren't fighting. We were, ah—we were talking about your grandfather."

He shot an emphatic look over his shoulder at Melchizedek, who stood fuming behind him. He tried to say with his eyes, *Do you see? How could I ever explain such treason to her?*

Melchizedek's eyes replied with an icy command to be silent.

"Is he sick?" Rachel said. "You both are upset. I can tell."

"Yes, child," Melchizedek said, striding forward to stand over them and look down from his full spidery height. "The king is *very* ill." A cold triumph lit his face. "Agaz, you should tell the princess about the king's *illness*. Explain how he may not live through the night . . ."

Her fine-drawn brows crumpled together. "He's not *really* sick, is he?" She spoke to her father, trusting him to tell her that the priest was lying. "He seemed fine just now."

"Rachel, I, ah—"

*Does my duty to my people demand this, as well? That I lie to my daughter?*

Then he said, "Just now? Then he's back from the Ba'alath?"

"He's dressing for the feast."

*Then Barra is gone,* Agaz thought. *Gone. Gone and safe. And, I hope, happy.*

"When do the Is-rael-ites get here?"

Agaz lowered his eyes, stung through the heart. Perhaps the only way he could save her life was to betray his father, and himself. "I don't know. Two or three days, probably."

She went on, "Barra told me that they say a lot of bad things about us."

"Mm, *Barra* . . ." Melchizedek made a face like he'd bitten into an unripe peach. "The Lady's Champion . . ."

"You've met her?" Rachel turned back, the Habiru forgotten, her face alive with excitement. "Isn't she *wonderful*? I want to be like *her*, when I grow up!"

*If only you could grow up,* Agaz thought.

If only—he thought of Barra again, of their good-bye this afternoon. Barra Coll Eigg Rhum . . . she was an *If only* potent enough to last a man his entire life.

"Why would you want to be like her?" Melchizedek sniffed. "You're a princess!"

"So is *she!*" Rachel said happily. "She really is! She told me so herself!"

"She," the priest said heavily, "is a savage and a mercenary. Ill-bred, ill-tempered, and unwashed. And also, apparently, a liar."

"She is *not!* Go ask her," Rachel insisted. "Ask her yourself!"

Agaz said softly, "Rachel, honey, all mercenaries tell stories. That doesn't make them liars. It's how they pass the time when they're on the road."

"She *is* a princess!" Rachel said. "Come on, you can ask her right now!"

"She's gone, Rachel. She left this afternoon; she took her money and she's going away."

"She is not!"

"Rachel—"

"She's with the Lady's *Maid,*" Rachel said with that tone of condescension peculiar to children who must explain the obvious to obtuse adults. "She came to get her dog—his name's Graegduz—so she could move him up to the Maid's room, and she asked me to find you for her and tell you she wants to talk to you as soon as you have time."

Agaz's heart leaped. "She's still here!"

Rachel put her little fists upon her hips, in a gesture so exactly like her late mother's that a gentle ache tugged at his chest. "What did I just say?"

His smile pulled him upright like a hook under his chin. "Well then, I suppose I should go see what she wants."

"Now?" Melchizedek said, a storm brewing in his face. "We have unfinished business, you and I."

Agaz allowed his smile to turn far colder than the spring wind. "And it will stay unfinished until I have spoken with an ill-bred, ill-tempered, unwashed savage and liar."

*"What in the name of the Merciful El is going on here?"*

Melchizedek stood in the middle of the sitting room of the cabinet reserved from his apartments for the Lady's Maid, and turned himself in outraged circles so quickly that Agaz feared he'd fall. He swung his long walking staff like a sword at imaginary foes.

Every wall, the floor, and the ceiling were painted with detailed hieroglyphs, in paints scarlet and viridian that gleamed wetly and glittered as though with metallic flakes. The strokes may have been somewhat crude, like a trooper's graffiti, but this was clearly no random vandalism; there was care and a clear intention in every line. The air of the room was still filled with a greenish haze—this had been a thick and choking smoke when Melchizedek had forced his way in here in the company of Agaz and Rachel, but now it dissipated in the cross-breeze past the opened shutters.

Kheperu crouched near one of the windows, a kerchief tied across his nose and mouth, a smoking censer dangling by a chain from his fist. The stubble on his shaven scalp was beaded with feverish sweat; the creased flesh at the corners of his beady squirrel eyes crinkled with either a smile or a grimace of distaste; the kerchief made it impossible to tell. He spoke in Phoenikian, to Agaz, with a nod toward Melchizedek.

"The man of the house?"

"Oh, yes," Agaz said, struggling to withhold a grin of his own. "What is all this?"

"Orders from the *Lady's Champion*," Kheperu said, a distinct edge of mockery in his voice. "You can ask her."

Rachel coughed sharply, from a lungful of the smoke, and Kheperu's eyes glittered like chips of onyx. "Mm . . . I don't believe I've been introduced to *this* lovely young lady . . . ?"

Agaz stepped between them. "She's my daughter, Kheperu."

Kheperu met the open danger on Agaz's face with another ambiguous crinkle of his eyes. "Quite."

"Where's Barra?"

"In the bedroom," Kheperu said. He pointed. "Through there."

Melchizedek stomped over toward Kheperu, lifting his staff threateningly. "*You* did this!" His eyes bulged, and patches of mottled purple spread over his cheeks. *"You did this to my home!"*

"You have a face like a jackal," Kheperu told him in conversational Phoenikian, of which Melchizedek understood no more than Kheperu did the High Priest's Canaanite, "but a jackal has better breath."

Agaz smothered another grin.

"I can have you *killed!*" Melchizedek roared. "I can have you *drawn* on the altar of *El!*"

Kheperu looked at Agaz. "He's threatening me, isn't he?"

At Agaz's nod in reply, he turned back to Melchizedek and pulled the kerchief down from his face.

"No one comes this close to me unless they want a kiss," he said. His broad grin showed what was left of his teeth. "Well, come on then: pucker up, skinny! For a man your age, you have a spectacular ass."

Agaz fled deeper into the apartment while he still had control of his face.

"Who was that man?" Rachel asked, tugging on his arm.

"He's a very bad man," Agaz said, no longer able to choke back his laughter. Oh, how he wished that he'd had the courage to translate for his uncle's benefit . . . "He's a friend of Barra's, but he's . . . well . . ."

He dissolved into laughter once again, an opening, cleansing laughter that seemed to flush a decade of poison from his veins. It wasn't *that* funny, not really, but it had been so long since he'd let himself laugh at anything, it was as though the punch lines to a thousand jokes had all struck him at once.

But then he remembered the glittering gaze which Kheperu had turned upon Rachel.

He sobered quickly, and turned to his daughter seriously. "Even though he's a friend of Barra's, don't ever let yourself be alone with him. In fact, don't ever talk to him or go anywhere with him, unless I'm there, or Barra is. Ever."

"Would he hurt me?"

"Yes, I'm afraid he might."

He grunted softly and shook his head. *I can trust him with my life, but not with my daughter's innocence. It is a strange world, that has such people in it.*

The glyphs and designs spread over every surface of every room. If Kheperu had indeed done all this himself, he must have been hard at work for some little time already. In some of the inner chambers, a haze of the green smoke still hung thickly enough to bring tears to the eye. There were no slaves in evidence in any of these chambers; even in the outer apartments belonging to Melchizedek, the slave quarters were deserted.

Barra met them at the door to the bedchamber. "Thanks for coming," she said.

Agaz reached out to her; only his ingrained aloofness stopped him from gathering her into an embrace. He wanted to stroke the curve of her jaw, but settled instead for a comradely hand upon her shoulder. He became keenly aware of the contrast between the softly smooth skin of her arm and the oak-hard muscle beneath it;

the tight-bound braids of her startling hair gleamed like raw copper, and her eyes spoke to him of slumberous power like the roll of the autumn sea.

He said, "I thought this afternoon was farewell. I thought you'd take your money and go."

"Nah," she said with a wicked grin, "I decided to stick around and save your worthless city instead."

Behind her broad hide belt, she wore a bronze axe that Agaz had not seen before; the lamplight made its edge sparkle like her smile. She moved away into the room. Her walk, the shift of her hips, her every gesture sizzled in his eyes. Some new and potent energy seemed to tingle in her stride, a passionate confidence he hadn't seen in her since the night they first met—the night she'd bet him a thousand shekels she could get him home alive.

And yet she was wet, and bedraggled, and she trailed a reek of burned hair that he could only now register behind Kheperu's incense.

"What happened to you?"

She grinned at him. "I got caught in a storm."

"But—"

"Later," she said. "Adonizedek told me this afternoon that once I save the city, I can have my pick of the treasury. You remember?"

Agaz nodded. "My father's word is law in these lands. But Barra, how—"

"Hah-ah," she said with a quick negative shake of her head. "I know your *father's* word is law, but I want to hear it from you, sunbeam. He's an old man, and not in his best health, and I have a feeling his butt's not exactly nailed to that throne right now, you follow?"

Agaz tried to look shocked and offended, but knew he failed before her oceanic stare. "What do you want me to say?"

"I want to get *your* word: if I go out there and bet my ass that I can make the Habiru go away, there'll be a big pot for me to collect when I get back."

"Of course," he said, spreading his hands in questioning confusion. "But how can you hope to fight the Habiru single-handed?"

She opened her arms in a gesture that included the room, and maybe the whole city—and maybe more than that. "Not single-handed, Agaz. You just have our money ready when we're done."

His gaze had been so captured by Barra that he only gradually came to acknowledge the others in the room. Graegduz lay on a pallet woven of straw in one corner, a boiled-leather cone strapped around his neck so that he could not chew at the bandages that wrapped his belly; he panted his recognition, and Agaz felt a fleeting regret that he had no chunk of cheese or piece of sausage to offer the wounded wolf.

Leucas favored him with a solemn nod, from where he sat on the floor beside the bed. On the bed lay the Lady's Maid; Agaz could only nod to her, and then turn away—he could not bear to look at her.

For all his resentment of her witchery, and that of the late Maid, it pained him to see her so wasted. He remembered the robust, thick-bodied woman she had been before he'd set out on his scouting mission, some fifty-odd days ago; yesterday, when she had been carried into his meeting with the king and the High Priest, he had not recognized her.

"Was that Melchizedek I heard shouting out there?" Barra said.

From the bed, Sarah said faintly, "It sounded like his bellow."

"You might want to hide," Rachel said. "He's really angry. When he's really angry, it's usually best to hide."

"Sarah!" Melchizedek stalked toward the bedchamber along the long hallway, his fury now clamped down into icy control, though rage still burned in his eyes like distant watch fires.

"Rachel," Agaz said, "you should go now."

"*Fa*-ther!"

"Aw, let her stay," Barra said. "C'mon, Agaz, be a sport."

"She's too young for this kind of—"

"You'd be surprised," Barra told him. "She knows more about what goes on around here than you do."

The decision was taken out of his hands when Melchizedek stormed into the room. His walking staff struck the rugs with such force that it clacked against the floor slats beneath them. He spoke with bitter venom as he strode past Agaz, toward the bed where his wife lay.

"You have allowed these savages into our home. You must rid us of them."

Sarah replied, "I will not."

His control was as brittle as porcelain. "You *will*!" The ancient priest lifted his walking staff like a weapon.

Leucas stood up.

The walking staff paused at the top of its arc.

Melchizedek was very tall, and his back was still straight despite his years; it was rare indeed that he ever needed to lift his eyes to look at any man. He looked up into Leucas' wintry gaze with cautious disbelief, as though a mountain had suddenly sprung from the earth to bar his path.

Agaz felt another unexpected smile tugging at his lips—one of his uncle's several unattractive qualities was how he liked to stand too close to shorter men, to tower over them and intimidate them with his height and voice. Now Leucas spoke in Greek with an earthquake-rumble warning tone, and Melchizedek seemed suddenly very old, and frail, like the slim and brittle trunk of a long-dead sapling of birch, tottering beside an oak.

Kheperu, wandering in behind the priest, murmured from beside Agaz's shoulder, "Now, *this* is a party!"

Barra said in Canaanite, "Melchizedek, this is my partner Leucas. You saw him this afternoon, I think. He's been charged to defend your wife." She coughed delicately into her fist, as though she covered a smile. "Even from you."

Melchizedek purpled to the roots of his hair.

"Barra!" Agaz said in astonishment. "You can't believe he would actually *harm* the Lady's Maid!"

She never took that oceanic stare off the High Priest. "I have a feeling you'd be surprised what this bastard is capable of."

"Faugh!" Melchizedek said in disgust, and swung his staff like a petulant child, no longer trying to strike the Lady's Maid, merely daring Leucas to stop him. The end of the stick struck hard against the thick ceiling beam over her bed, and before it could move farther, Leucas' massive hand got in its way and wrapped around it.

He twisted the staff from the High Priest's grasp without effort and shook his head in sad disapproval while he lifted a solemnly admonishing finger. Again he rumbled something in Greek; its tone sounded like *I'll just hold this for you.*

Melchizedek reached out with clawed hands, as though to snatch the staff from Leucas. "Give that back!"

Leucas grounded the staff and leaned heavily upon it, making it very clear that if Melchizedek wanted his staff, he'd have to find a way of shifting all eighteen stone of thoughtful Athenian boxer.

Melchizedek wheeled on Barra. "You're behind all of this! On whose authority do you dismiss my servants and vandalize my home?"

Barra grinned. She pulled the unfamiliar bronze axe from behind her belt and waved it cheerily at the High Priest. "On the authority of the Lady of Jebusi, chuckles."

"I will have all of you thrown *bodily*—"

"That," Barra interrupted him sharply, "is a bad idea. Leucas, here, will kill anyone who tries to enter this room without permission, be they soldiers, or El's Men—or *priests*. How many lives is your pride worth, old man?"

His gaze fixed upon the axe Barra held with peculiar intensity. "Where did you get that?"

"I gave it to her," Sarah said.

"You?" He turned on her furiously, but a simple shift of Leucas' weight stopped him like a straight-arm to the chest. He sputtered, "You had no right!"

"It is the Axe of the Lady," Sarah replied calmly. "She can dispose of it as she sees fit."

"It *was* the Axe of the Lady," Melchizedek snapped. "Now it is a valuable relic. A treasure that is, in fact, mine; it belonged to Ramah, my late *wife*. Even if she gave it to you *herself*, with our marriage, your property—you *yourself*—all became *mine*. Which makes you, both of you, *thieves*."

"Y'know, chuckles," Barra said consideringly, "I disliked you the first time I laid eyes on you, and you've done nothing since to change my mind."

He began to sputter again, but Barra went blithely on. "I wanted to talk to you before the feast tonight anyway. Ever since we hit town I've been hearing a lot of horseshit about the 'witches of the Ba'alath' and all kinds of crap about how everything that goes wrong around here is their fault. Most of it seems to be coming from these pinheads who call themselves El's Men. Why haven't you done something about this?"

Melchizedek snarled, "Who are you to criticize—"

She waved the axe at him. "I'm the Lady's Champion, chuckles. Remember?"

"I want that axe," he said dangerously, "and I will have it."

"You want this axe?"

She stepped forward to where she was nearly chest to chest with him, and she looked up into his outraged face. "If you don't start publicly denouncing these El's Men, and publicly supporting the Lady, you'll *get* it. Right between your fucking eyes, you bastard."

Agaz gasped. "You can't talk to him like that!"

Barra turned her back on the High Priest, dismissing him, and shrugged. "Apparently I can."

Melchizedek gathered all his internal resources and managed to bank the fires of his anger. "Very well," he said icily. "Agaz, come along. We have business to conclude."

"Excuse me," Barra said pointedly, "but *he* was invited here. You weren't." She turned her potent gaze upon Agaz. "You'll want to hear what I have to say."

For a moment, Agaz stood nailed to the floor. Some obscure intuition told him that this choice they asked him to make had any number of unpredictable implications. To stay with his uncle, this man he had known and respected from the very day of his birth, or to take the side—at least implicitly—of a woman who fascinated him, whom he'd come to admire, and more; a woman who could bark at the High Priest of El as though he were a kitchen slave.

*I decided to stick around and save your worthless city instead,* he remembered, and suddenly understood.

With his uncle lay despair, desperate treason and surrender; the shine in Barra's eyes that gripped his heart so powerfully was nothing more nor less than a faint sparkle of hope.

The same hope that had straightened his spine when Rachel had told him Barra was still here; the breath of light that had brought laughter to his lips for the first time in what seemed like years.

He said, "I believe that our business can wait, Uncle."

Melchizedek's fiery stare burned into Agaz's face, but the prince never blinked.

Finally, the High Priest said, "This is a circumstance that brooks no delay. You may waste whatever time you wish with these thugs and your barbarian slut. I will no longer wait. This city must be saved; if you will not act, know that I will."

"Uncle—" Agaz began, apprehension gathering in his stomach, but Melchizedek wheeled and stalked away.

Agaz watched his stiffly departing back, then turned to Barra, shaking his head with a kind of apprehensive sorrow. "You shouldn't bait him like that," he said. "He's a dangerous man."

"I know it," Barra said briskly. "Better than you do, maybe. There's nothing more dangerous than a desperate man with power."

"What, ah, what more business did you have with me?

"It's with both of you." She hid a smile behind her fist and pretended to cough. "I need a couple things for this party tonight. First off, I'm going *nowhere* without something to wear. Rachel . . . ?"

The princess's eyes glowed like candles. "I know just what to do!"

"I knew you would. And, ah, the other thing I'll need"—again she pretended to cough into her fist, now dropping her gaze so she wouldn't have to see how he reacted—"is a date."

Agaz's mouth dropped open. "You chased off the High Priest of El just so you could *ask me out?*"

"He's an asshole, Agaz. What's it gonna be?"

"Well, I, ah, I . . ." His face flamed until he was surprised his hair didn't catch fire. "Well, yes."

"All right, then. I'll meet you as soon as Rachel gets me into some decent clothes."

"Yes, but—but Melchizedek—"

"What about him?"

"He's dangerous, Barra. He truly is. And you have made him your enemy, today."

She shrugged, and the cheer in her eyes faded behind conviction as solid and sharp as flint. "He always *was* my enemy," she said flatly. "I'm just letting him know I know it."

A pair of new bronze scissors, sharp and bright from the forge, had cut away the scorched ends of Barra's hair; what remained piled in coils upon her head like a helm of braided copper.

The dress that Rachel had found for her was a tight-bodiced Cretan design with a broad flounced skirt dyed in vivid autumn colors— it fit rather well, once the lower two flounces had been removed, its original owner having been some few inches taller than Barra. The tasseled shawl she wore over her shoulders partially covered her breasts, which the dress left exposed and rather unnecessarily supported and shaped; the shawl was not for modesty's sake, so much as to conceal her scars and some of her more recent wounds.

Over the dress she wore her familiar boarskin belt, faded and sweat-stained though it was. At the last party to which she'd worn a dress this long, a man had been able to beat the shit out of her because she couldn't get to the daggers she'd strapped to her legs. No such mistake would she ever make again. She hadn't had time to replace her throwing axes, but a pair of keen bronze knives rode in their places, and the Lady's Axe was tucked securely at her side.

Agaz walked beside her. He had not said a word about the belt or the weapons; he had said nothing beyond complimenting the way the dress flattered her. He wore a spiral wrap of a severe black, edged with silver thread, that left one sun-browned shoulder and one thigh exposed, and his hair was bound back by a slender fillet, braided of some silvery metallic thread that seemed to gleam with a moonlight of its own.

They walked alone to the feast; Rachel had gone ahead while Barra dressed, and Barra had asked her partners to stay behind in Sarah's cabinet. Leucas, frowning, had asked her if she thought that Melchizedek would try to strike at the Lady's Maid during the feast.

"Melchizedek?" she'd answered, a little surprised by the suggestion. She tapped her temple, beside her eye, significantly. "No, Agaz was right, he wouldn't hurt her—not on purpose, anyway. He actually cares for her, believe it or not, and he's not a bad man: he's just a desperate one."

"Then who are we protecting her from?"

"I can't really say."

"Then why miss the feast?" Kheperu asked.

"Because she's *important*. She's what this whole thing is about."

"I don't understand."

Barra had shrugged, frowning. "I'm not sure I can really explain. She says she's the Shield of the Lady, that she bears the strokes meant for the Goddess. I think she's hooked into the land, into the Goddess, somehow; I think as long as she's alive, we still have a chance. And I think that's why something's trying to kill her."

"Oh, come now, Barra," Kheperu had scoffed in his most withering superior tone. "You cannot truly believe this—this tale for simple children!"

"Can't I?" Barra said. That monstrous cobra of living lightning reared again, within her mind. She said, "Just protect her, that's all."

"You know I will," Leucas said, his face warming as he gazed down at Sarah, where she lay watching their conversation with uncomprehending eyes. "While I draw breath, she will come to no harm."

Kheperu, whose beady eyes missed little, no matter how fever-raw they might be, had squinted at the blush on Leucas' face and cocked an ear to his oddly gentle tone, and had declared that he, too, must stay behind. "There's nothing worse than a smitten Akhaian. I'd best stay here, to keep an eye on this Athenian oaf and remind him that she's another man's wife."

Then he turned his feverish gaze upon Barra, with mocking speculation. "But if the defense of the Lady's Maid is so allimportant, why are you going out on a *date*? Our Agaz truly makes you runny, eh?"

She ignored his mockery and answered him bleakly. "It's Melchizedek," she said. "He's about to blow his cork, and the Mother alone knows what he'll do then. I think I've pissed him off enough that when he explodes, he'll go after me, instead of Agaz or the king. So I *have* to be at that feast; I have to give him a target."

"Hmpf," Kheperu had said sourly. "Very convincing; but I still think this is mostly about getting in a slow dance or two with Agaz."

Barra decided not to belt him while she was wearing a borrowed dress, and left them there with a promise that she'd send servants up with enough cartloads of food to burst their bellies.

The feast was well along when Barra and Agaz arrived; it filled the

Hall of Assembly with shouts and laughter, and spilled out into the Citadel's various courtyards now that the rain had ended.

Kitchen slaves brandished knives long enough to fight with, around tables covered with quartered roasted cows, with whole pigs, disjointed lambs, young goats stewed in milk; there were enormous platters with every imaginable variety of cheese, with figs and dried apricots, huge jugs of ripe olives, tray after tray of pastries and sweets ranging from crystal honey to fried locusts baked into sweet yogurt shells, Tyrian wine, and Egyptian beer.

Each plate on the low tables surrounding the sprawling couches still held food, but much of the serious eating was already past; now most of the feasters reclined at their ease, sipping wine, listening to the festive music and watching a dozen or so young girls and boys, professional entertainers who danced with great skill and erotic enthusiasm as they sang songs of ritual seduction.

Some of the feasters appeared already to be drunkenly snoring, others spoke among themselves, many sang along with the dancers, but when Barra and Agaz arrived, a shout began that streaked outward through the feast as though carried on the east wind, a roar of applause and good wishes so intense that it became fierce; everyone leaped to their feet, cheering and clapping as though all Jebusi believed that happiness alone could hold off the Habiru.

And over it all, in great braying voices like happy trumpeter swans, came "Barra! Barra Coll Eigg Rhum! I *knew* it! I told you it was her! I told you!"

Barra looked around for a convenient way to slip out.

Those shouts had come in Pictish.

A sickening hole sucked at the bottom of her stomach as she watched a pair of nearly Leucas-sized men shoulder their way through the party toward her. But there was no escape; they had seen her clearly, and it was no use pretending she hadn't heard their shouts— they'd just bray louder and louder until their voices shook the Citadel down upon their heads.

She turned to excuse herself from Agaz; he didn't even seem to hear her, surrounded as he was by a sudden press of well-wishers who shoved and pulled him in all directions, gradually forcing him away toward the couches where the king reclined beside Rachel, with the High Priest at his side.

Barra was left alone to face the men approaching.

One of them was tall and dark, with a spray of unexpected freckles across his nose, and eyes of startling blue; he wore a vest and kilt of rawhide and had muscles like knotted ropes beneath skin translucent as marble. The other was a span shorter, with hair as red as Barra's and a twinkle of lunacy in eyes that were green as summer leaves; he wore a sleeveless tunic of greyish wool, belted tightly over a belly every bit as impressive as his chest and shoulders, hugging thighs like the trunks of hairy red trees.

She didn't recognize either of them. This neither surprised nor discomfited her: on her trips home she'd done quite a bit of traveling in the company of her brother the High King, as he toured the islands settling disputes and defusing minor wars. She had met thousands of people, and remembered only a few—they, on the other hand, never forgot meeting the High King's half-Gael sister with her boy's figure and her temper so quick and lethal that it had become a byword.

She could only stand helplessly, her stomach twisted and sour, as they approached. What could she say to them? How was she supposed to act?

She told herself these feelings were childish, they were stupid, she had nothing to be shy about or ashamed of, but that only made it worse. She felt as though everyone at the feast was staring at her, and judging her to be unworthy.

The ill-matched pair shouldered cheering Jebusites aside, heedlessly shoving them to stumble against each other in their wake, and she tried to say something, but that familiar obscure shame rose up in her throat and choked her.

Then they stood before her, and before a word could come from her lips she found herself gathered into a pair of bear hugs that took her breath away. She couldn't tell exactly who was hugging whom, whether the Pict held her and the Gael held him, or the other way around, but it didn't matter.

"I *knew* it was you," the Pict crowed. "What other redheaded girl in the whole buggering world has the balls to bring back the buggering *prince*, eh?"

"Sure you knew; you knew what I told you and not one whit more, you great bloody dolt," said the Gael happily.

Their arms were warm around her as they lifted her from her feet and spun her around, and their breath smelled of wine, and their skin of flesh fed on Eirish deer and mountain sheep, of heather and haggis and peat fires, and she found that it didn't matter what she could or couldn't say.

This sharp sting in her eyes could only be joy.

"Loving Mother," she gasped breathlessly in her native tongue, "if

I could only tell you how good it is to see some *real* men for a change!"

"Oh, ay," the Pict said, holding her off her feet in one cabled arm and looking around with a derisive grin. "They're a pack of punypants in these parts, aren't they? Little skinny pale little fucks—some of them are smaller than *Gaels*, can you believe it? I'm always watchin' where I walk, for fear of crushing a dozen-odd with every step. That's what happened to Ross, here—as a lad he was stepped on by a Pict."

"Keep it up, y'great Pictish ass-pirate," the Gael responded with a cheerful growl. "We can have it on outside like gentlemen, or right here like bloody Pictish savages, whichever you like."

"Here," she said breathlessly, "put me down before you start fighting. This is a borrowed dress."

"Ay, and you want the prince to see you in it before he sees you out of it, eh there, Barra?" the Gael said with a broad wink.

Without warning, the Pict slammed him on the side of the head with a knotted fist hard enough to send him sprawling.

"That's the *princess* you're talking to, y'drunken pukepuddle!" he roared at the top of his considerable lungs.

The Gael sat up with his hands behind him and shook his head, grinning like an idiot. A trickle of blood trailed down beside his eye, and some seconds passed while his wits gathered themselves together enough to allow him to speak.

"Oh, sure," he said dizzily. "Just like a bloody Pict to take the cheap shot—"

He started to get up, and the Pict's eyes lit up with joy as he raised his fists, but Barra stepped between them.

"Cut it out, both of you. Everybody's staring."

The Pict looked around. "So they are. P'raps they're curious how *full*-size men fight."

Now the Gael was on his feet, and the look in his eyes matched the Pict's perfectly. "I'll show 'em how men fight. You can show 'em how they fall."

Barra squinted at the shorter man. The build and coloring was right, as was the attitude . . .

She let out a happy sigh, and stepped between them.

"You wouldn't happen to be one of my brothers, would you?"

The Gael's grin broadened and he offered her a sweeping bow. "Ross mak Ouendail, if it please the princess—and if it'll earn a hard-workin' man a kiss from his little sister."

Barra grinned; he had a touch of her father's Eirish charm, too.

"Where are you from, Ross? Not from around Tara, eh? I'd remember."

"I'm a northern lad, from the Sperrin Heights, and would you kindly inform this Pictish lout behind you that I can speak about my own sisters any way I please?"

"I don't give a squirt from a goat's butt what you say about those whores," the Pict proclaimed loudly, "but when you talk to the princess, you'll keep a civil tongue or you'll keep no tongue at all."

"You're a brother too, are you?" Barra asked, wincing.

"Oh, no, no, Barra, not at all," he said cheerfully. "I'm your nephew."

She looked him up and down. He had to be at least five years her elder.

"It's true," he insisted. "The great shame of my life is that my da was another of Ouendail's red bastards. I'm also your third-or-some-such cousin." He extended an arm. "Bertram Dhui Maud Rhum."

Instead of shaking his hand, Barra covered her eyes and massaged her temples. She had a headache coming on, the same headache her family always gave her.

It felt wonderful.

"How many of the brothers are here, do you know?"

Ross shrugged. "I think only two or three besides me. There's about four hundred Gaels, and maybe a few more of these ass–pirates from the big island—p'raps a thousand, to end the tale. I don't know them all, y'know. We're not all of us so famous as you, Barra."

His smile stretched a little thinner, and his voice went a bit quiet. "We did lose one on the caravan down from Beth Shean. We got hit by some Habiru raiders, and Brandon was killed when we fought our way clear."

Barra only squinted at this news. This brother she'd lost was one she'd never known; he might have died only steps away from her, there on the watershed road. He could have been the one she'd turned her face from, only a moment before the attack.

This didn't hurt as much as it could have; as it would have, if she learned it from foreigners. She looked from the Pict to the Gael, and back again, marveling at the strength she drew from simply being near them.

She was silent for one long moment, as were they, a respect for the passing of blood kin, but then she broke a smile and sighed out her silence into speech.

"C'mon," she said. "I'll introduce you to the prince."

"That the fella you came in with?" Bertram asked. "He's pretty enough, I guess, but I don't understand what you see in these little dinky-dick runts."

Barra shrugged. "He's got a nice butt."

Ross slapped her on the back. "Oh, you're a sister of mine, all right!"

"That's right, Ross, it is," Bertram said. "The butt's the first thing you look at on a man, isn't it?"

Ross squared off and spat on his palms, then rubbed them together and spread his hands into a wrestler's arc. "Come on, then. It's a fight you're after, and I'm your man. Knock me out, and y'can have your way with me."

"Hey," Barra said, just sharply enough to get their attention.

They both stopped and looked at her.

"You two play nice," she said mildly, "or I'm gonna get angry."

Their eyes widened just a hint.

"Is that what you want? You want me to get angry?"

Ross frowned.

Bertram bit his lip.

Ross said, "*He* started it—"

Apparently her reputation hadn't suffered in the years since her last visit home. For Pict and Gael alike, a bare-knuckle brawl was a sport, a recreation, as much a part of a celebration as dancing. For Barra, though, fighting was purely business, and they knew it. Somebody who got playful that way with her ran a sharp risk of having the brawl settled with her axe.

She'd done it more than once, and tales grow in the telling.

"I don't care who starts it," she said. "I'll finish it, and it'll be a finish you'll never forget."

They exchanged glances. "I don't think that'll be necessary," Bertram said, a little thinly.

"Good. You boys behave yourselves, and come meet Prince Agaz."

One long coil of ash-colored smoke spiraled up from the censer.

The white-fleeced, spotless ram bent backward over the block, its horned head hanging by scraps of flesh. Three golden bowls beneath it had caught the blood from its slashed throat; the first two lay empty and discarded nearby.

Sweat poured across Eleazar's naked body, and his hand shook with an old man's palsy as he reached for the third bowl.

*Blood. It's always blood.*

His hand froze at the errant thought; it had been years since his concentration during a rite had been scattered enough to permit thoughts outside his ritual intention.

He steadied himself again, and lifted the golden bowl to his mouth as though to drink the crusted scabbing that rimmed it, but he only kissed its golden lip. The eating of blood was forbidden to the sons of Israel. *Only God drinks blood.*

He dipped his fingers into the bowl, then flicked them above the censer, scattering the crusting blood onto the coals.

A ruddy thickness swelled into the coil of smoke, growing red, and the smoke began to pulse like the beating of a heart.

The invocations were complete; all the dances had been danced, and the chants had been chanted. His sweat-damp ritual robes lay wadded upon the floor, half-covering his silver sword, outside the binding ring near which he knelt.

Shivering with exhaustion, Eleazar scattered yet more blood upon the coals.

The smoke coiled, and pulsed, and now began to slowly rotate within the borders of the binding ring woven into the carpet that floored Eleazar's tent.

Eleazar glared at the smoke through stinging eyes. It filled the cylinder of air above the binding ring, yet never strayed beyond it.

Shahkhath was coming.

Eleazar seized all that was left of his courage with both hands and stepped into the ring with the angel.

He kept his eyes firmly closed—the merest glimpse of Shahkhath's face could strike him dead—as the angel's power seized him within the binding ring, buffeted him as though with fists, as though with stones, battering him and bruising him and lifting him into the air to dash him again to the ground.

And all the while, the angel howled its fury into his mind, scattering his wits in a shrieking maelstrom of burning, a lake of fire poured out upon his brain. He was forced down screaming into flaming sulphur, and felt the sizzling roast of his flesh, felt the molten brimstone close over his head, felt his lips burn from his face and his eyelids char while his eyeballs boiled and split and burst . . .

Through it all his will never faltered, never flinched.

He pressed out from himself with his mind, as though breathing out forever.

A veil draped across the fury of the angel; it seemed to be happening to someone else.

Then, he *inhaled*.

In through his nose came the choking brimstone, the scents of charring flesh and seared eyes, in came the pain of stone blows and fist blows and slaps and pinches and the sweet savor of burning blood, in came the refined essence of hatred, and with them all flowed Shahkhath the Destroyer.

And to the angel now entering his body, he showed his intention.

He brought Shahkhath into his intention, and made the two one.

Barra kept Ross and Bertram beside her through the whole long feast. During the interminable speeches, and hymns of rejoicing to the gods, and the dancing and singing and thunder of tymbals and shrill of pipes and flutes, she kept shoveling food into her mouth and washing it down with watered wine and questioning her kinsmen for news from home.

She ignored the formal parts of the feast as completely as she did the acid glares that Melchizedek directed at her from the couch beside the king. She didn't even bother to provoke the High Priest; she'd stoked him up enough already, and she figured she owed herself this brief interval of peace. Here, with her kinsmen to either side, soaking in the blessed luxury of speaking her native tongue, nothing could touch her.

It was like coming home.

She learned from Bertram that her brother Llem the High King had gone entirely gray; that one of her sisters was widely rumored to have murdered a rival by magic and was enjoying the notoriety; that her son Chryl Barra Coll Eigg—now fifteen—was making a certain name for himself as a ladies' man; that her adopted son Antiphos had taken his first Eirish deer, and done it fair like a Pict: no arrows, no spear, using only a sword Barra had sent him the year before.

From Ross she learned that her Eirish grandmother Maeve was ailing, and that the old sorceress had cast a gloom across Tara that kept the whole stronghold abed for days at a time; that her father's wife, Brigid, was suspected of being the agent behind her grandmother's illness, with poison being mentioned; that her father was once again voicing his displeasure with his household and threatening to abdicate, move to the big island and marry Coll, Barra's mother.

"As if she'd have him," Barra snorted.

"Oh, sure, like she could resist," Ross laughed. "No woman born can turn aside from Ouendail of the Thousand Sons. How else does he get that name?"

"Eirish women, maybe," Bertram said, bristling. "There's not an Eirish woman alive who can keep her ankles crossed with a pig in the house . . ."

"Hey, now," Barra said, as sternly as she could manage. "What did I tell you boys about playing nice?"

These two had been invited to the feast along with the other mercenary captains. The Picts and the Gaels, finding so many of their kinsmen scattered among the various mercenary companies, had decided to band together—mostly to protect themselves from each other. These newborn companies, enormous by the standards of the Canaan District, had elected their captains in the usual Isles way, voting to the seven or eight top candidates, then letting the candidates settle affairs with a last-man-standing brawl.

Barra approved of this method; to win, one must be not only popular and extremely tough but smart as well—and lucky. All four characteristics are equally important in a successful captain.

When the speeches and the hymns and the toasts were all done, the floor was opened for dancing. Ross and Bertram each—almost in unison—asked her to dance beside him. A smiling general refusal was the only way to prevent a fistfight; she managed to indicate, without actually saying so, that she was obligated to remain at Agaz's side.

Without hesitation or any discernible regret they excused themselves, rather unsteadily gained their feet and lurched onto the dance floor, breaking into the rings of dancers by main force; they linked their arms to those of the men to either side and immediately shouted at the musicians in pidgin Phoenikian to pick up the tempo.

Agaz leaned close beside Barra's ear, his face flushed with wine, but his eyes showed the weariness that comes of being forced to pretend that the babble of formal speech means something of significance. He nodded tiredly toward Barra's kinsmen, where they danced with drunken abandon.

"They're certainly, ah, enthusiastic," he said.

"They're three sheets to the wind," Barra told him, smiling fondly at them.

"Are all your people so . . ." His shoulders twitched expressively. ". . . happy?"

"Ah, nah. My brother Llem, say: he's a grim bastard, he barely breaks one smile a season. But even he'd be dancing and drinking tonight."

There was a cold distance in his stare; he looked far beyond the dancers in this room. "Oh?"

"It's the war, Agaz. They know they're going into battle—they could die soon."

"So could we all. Is this cause for celebration?"

"It's not the death we celebrate," she said. She reached up and put a hand upon his shoulder, pulling his face just a touch closer to hers. "It's life. This is how we thank the Mother for the life she gave us, and how we thank Arawn Deathgod, her mate, for reminding us how precious that life is. A party like this on the Isle of the Mighty might go on for a couple days. It's bad luck to go into battle without a hangover—who wants to be killed on a clear head? So we spend a couple days drinking, dancing, and fucking."

Agaz blinked. "Fucking?"

"Sure. It's almost a prayer, y'know."

His brows drew together in puzzlement.

Barra chuckled broadly. "What, you Jebusites don't scream *'oh God'* when you come?"

Much of the weariness in his eyes seemed to have been replaced by speculative interest. "Barra," he said slowly, "would you—"

"Yes?"

One of his cold smiles crept up his face, but something he saw in her eyes melted it into a warm and wistful half grin. "—would you like to dance?"

For long minutes the only sound in the cabinet of the Lady's Maid had been that of the clink and scrape of flatware, teeth tearing roasted meat, and the occasional slurp of wine.

Sarah sat up on her bed with a tray across her lap, pushing her food this way and that in its bowl, occasionally taking tiny bird-like bites and glancing curiously at the two mercenaries that guarded her.

Kheperu had glumly chopped his food small, and mashed all he could, to make it possible for his rotting teeth to chew. He sat hunched on a small stool beside the pallet on which Graegduz lay, and he occasionally fed bites of meat to the drowsy wolf.

Rather furtively, Leucas watched Sarah; he had no desire to be caught staring by Kheperu, and so be forced to endure another round of what passed for the Egyptian's wit. Sometimes he sighed as he looked at her, wishing idly that they had some common tongue.

When he'd held her in his arms, she'd felt so frail, like a woman of straw and sugar crystals, yet when he looked into the fine-drawn bones of her face and the fierce determination in her eyes, he saw a strength that reminded him forcefully of Barra's.

She could hardly be content in marriage to that desert-dried skeleton of a priest, he was sure. He caught himself imagining how she must have appeared before her illness, a powerful, heavy-bodied woman . . . with the face of a goddess . . .

He smiled to himself. *Idle dreams,* he thought, and gave his full attention to his meal. He bit great fist-size chunks of blood-rare lamb from the steaming leg that he held in one hand, and washed them down with long draughts of wine from the large pelike that he held in the other.

Sarah glanced up toward the ceiling, a pretty frown drawing her eyebrows together. Someone had been pacing in the room above for some time, now, his tread growing heavier and heavier as though growing anger caused him to stamp. She said something in Canaanite, and pointed upward with her knife.

Kheperu made some weary smacking sounds with his lips, wearing an expression of distaste as though his fever had killed his appetite. He set down his utensils in defeat and sighed.

"What do you think she's saying?"

Leucas shrugged. "I think she's saying, 'Cheer up, Kheperu,' " he said happily, around an immense mouthful of meat. He brandished the leg like a weapon. "She's saying, 'You're not the only man who didn't go to the feast. Listen to that fellow upstairs.' "

He sniffed. "I *have* been, thank you very much. And he doesn't seem very pleased about it, either."

Now he frowned, and mopped at this forehead with his sleeve. "Damned fever—I can't remember. I seem to recall that above this room there is only rooftop, not another room."

Leucas shrugged. "So he's a sentry. So what?"

"No—no, he *isn't.*" Kheperu shook his head and waved a damp hand at the joining of wall and ceiling. "If he was, he'd be patrolling the edges. You see? He's been pacing that entire floor, a straight line from one wall to the other, then taking a step sideways and starting again as though he wants to cover every span of it—very methodical, that fellow, whoever he is."

The stomping got louder; now plaster dust sprinkled down. Leucas squinted upward. "Funny, too, the sound. Not so much like he's stamping, anymore. It's like he's getting *heavier* . . ."

"And," Kheperu said nervously, "if that's the roof, it's stone. *Stone,* Leucas. How could we hear him through stone?"

"Well, then, it's not the roof," Leucas said reasonably.

Kheperu replied tightly, "I'd be more comfortable with your logic if we could ask Sarah and find out for sure."

A thunderous crash shook the whole room, rattling the crockery and making Kheperu clutch at the seat of his stool. Fist-size chunks of plaster broke away and thudded to the floor. "Now the idiot's jumping up and down! Is he trying to . . ."

His voice trailed off as he stared up over Leucas' head, looking at the spot above which the crash had come, and he was suddenly very pale.

Leucas followed his gaze.

There, on the massive beam of cedar that supported the ceiling over Sarah's bed, where the High Priest's staff had struck it, one of the protective glyphs Kheperu had painted was scuffed and smeared, nearly obliterated.

Kheperu said, "Ah, Leucas—?"

But Leucas was already in motion as another crash thundered overhead; the beam snapped like tinder, and two tons of ceiling fell in.

When Barra and Agaz returned to the royal family's couches after the dance, Agaz frowned into his winebowl. It was full enough that wine slopped over its rim when he picked it up.

"I could have sworn I drained this."

"I took the liberty," Melchizedek said darkly, raising his bowl in what would have been, from another man, a polite toast.

"Well, *mine's* empty," Barra said.

"As is mine," the king added.

Melchizedek said with great precision, "Apologies. I suppose I thought the Lady's Champion could throw a pinch of dust and conjure wine from thin air."

He lifted a single finger, with a significant glance toward the row of wine stewards that stood against a wall. One of them nodded expressionlessly, and approached them bearing a large twin-handled stamnos.

"Perhaps I'm unclear on the way such things work, having never before met a Champion of the Lady," Melchizedek went on, a keen edge in his formerly rich voice, as though some unknown tension stretched it thin. "Tell me, what powers does the Lady grant her Champion? Will the stones fight like men for Jebusi? Will you raise the seas until the Habiru drown? Will you summon a wind to blow them back over the mountains?"

"You're windy enough for that by yourself, y'old fart," Barra muttered, softly enough that only Agaz could hear. "One blast from your butt, and they'd never come down."

Agaz nudged her reprovingly, but she could see he was smothering a smile.

"I beg your pardon?" Melchizedek said sharply.

She let the steward fill her winebowl before answering; he poured carefully from his brimming stamnos.

"You've got this whole Champion thing backwards, Melchizedek. The Lady doesn't grant me any special powers at all. Just the opposite. She's asked me to use the power *I already have* in her defense—and the defense of her city, which includes, unfortunately, you."

Melchizedek tried to summon his superior sneer as he waved the steward irritably away, but he looked more like a cornered badger showing its teeth. Something was happening, Barra was sure; something had the High Priest almost shaking with dread. He was holding onto his self-possession with both hands.

All she could do was watch, and try to be ready.

The king laughed openly, gesturing for the steward to hurry and fill his bowl as well.

Barra went on, "And you seem to think I'm the Lady's only Champion. It's not so."

"There are more savages and tarts among us?"

"Great-uncle, that's mean," Rachel said. "You shouldn't say things like that."

"It was said, and it was meant, Rachel. It is more important to speak the truth than to be nice. The Champions of the Lady are tarts and savages, nothing more."

"Is that how you speak of your king?" Barra asked with an aggressive smile.

"Me?" Adonizedek sat up suddenly, slopping a little wine. "Me? A Champion of the Lady?"

"Aren't you doing everything you can to save your city from Yahweh and his Habiru? She asked for your help the same as she asked for mine—and she's getting it, from you and me, and my partners. She asked for *your* help, too, Melchizedek; and if you don't mind my saying so, it's a coward of a man who won't come to the aid of a lady in distress."

Melchizedek purpled to the silvered roots of his hair, and Barra hid her smirk behind the rim of her winebowl. The wine had a pleasant fruity fragrance, of apricots and a hint of almond.

"I'll drink to that!" the king said unsteadily. "I'll drink to being a Champion of the Lady."

"Oh, by all means," Melchizedek said with a certain breathless overenthusiasm. "Let's drink to the Champions, all of them." He lifted his winebowl in salute, and brought it to his lips.

Barra lifted her own, and her extraordinarily acute sense of smell caught a shade of bitterness beneath the almond fragrance in the wine, and she suddenly remembered Kheperu once giving her a lecture on what happens when one combines almond oil with water.

She had drunk a great deal of wine this night, but she'd have to be a great deal more drunk before she would forget the scent of hydrocyanic acid.

In a single flash it all came clear.

Melchizedek had waved away the steward.

Melchizedek had refilled Agaz's winebowl earlier, from a different jug.

And now the king lifted his bowl to his lips.

Barra dashed her wine to the floor. *"Poison!"*

The king had already tipped his bowl back as he took a mouthful; from lying on the couch she could never get up in time and she had no options at all.

She threw her cup at him.

The cup spun past the amazed Agaz and the stunned Melchizedek and clipped the king over his left eye. The bowl shattered and cut him and blood sprayed—but so did his mouthful of wine, bursting from his lips along with his astonished exhalation.

Suddenly it seemed like everyone was shouting at once.

"What? What?" the king said, holding his bloody brow and looking around in confusion. "What happened?"

Barra sprang to her feet, pointing at the steward and yelling, *"Get that jug!"*

The steward met her gaze for one timeless instant of blank, insensate hostility, just like the eyes of the crowd on the street before the storm; then he deliberately opened his fingers and let the stamnos slip from his hand to shatter on the floor.

The wine soaked through the rug and ran away through cracks in the stone.

Rough hands seized her from both sides.

"What the fuck do you think you're doing?" she shouted, struggling in the grip of strong men. "The wine was poisoned—that man, *stop that man!"*

But the steward vanished out through an archway, and was gone.

"Will you let me *go?"* she snapped. "Agaz, tell these monkeys to get off me!"

Agaz only looked at her with wide and helpless eyes.

Melchizedek stepped before her and said with acid triumph, "Lady's Champion or mercenary whore, the price for striking the king is the same." His grin showed teeth as yellow as sun-bleached sand.

"Kill her."

As the ceiling crumbled with a roar and a choking cloud of dust, Kheperu scrambled backward into the relative safety of the doorway.

Leucas sprang *forward*.

He got beneath the mighty timber, a hand to each side of the crack, and he caught it like Herakles taking the sky from Atlas' shoulders.

Even Kheperu, well acquainted with the power in Leucas' arms, was struck momentarily speechless.

"Sarah!" Leucas rasped, choking on stone dust that filled his nose and blinded his eyes with tears. Cords bulged up his neck and every muscle of his shoulders and legs sprang out in high relief. He held the beam above his head, his arms nearly at full extension. "Kheperu, get her out!"

Kheperu skipped around him, through the cloud of billowing plaster and the rain of stone splinters, and slapped the tray off Sarah's lap. He grabbed her roughly by the shoulders, dragged her out of bed; she helped as much as she could, driving her nearly useless legs to take some of her weight as together they struggled toward the shelter of the doorway.

Another crash came from above, striking the break in the timber like a boulder falling from a cliff. Leucas grunted, his knees buckled, and the stone above the plaster began to crack and break up into smaller chunks with sounds like the dull popping of Leucas' joints.

Then, with strain that rang in his ears like a scream and threatened to snap his spine, Leucas straightened his legs.

"That's nothing human," he said in a strangled voice. "It's coming in, and *I can't stop it!*"

"Come *on*, then," Kheperu shouted from the doorway. "Get out of there!"

"Graeg . . ." he said thickly, strangled with effort. "Or Barra . . . kill us both . . ."

Snarling a continuous string of curses, Kheperu darted back into the room.

Leucas could *feel* it now, feel the malice and bloodlust from above; it raised the hairs along his arms and seemed to strike sparks within his head.

It struck from above again, making the room buck like the deck of a storm-tossed ship; Leucas' vision filled with bloody haze and an agonized groan escaped his lips. Muscle overload sank red-hot barbs into his shoulders to drag down his arms.

"Shit!" Kheperu wheezed behind him. "Fucking dog is heavier than the Lady's Maid!"

"Get clear," Leucas panted through clenched teeth. "Get clear *I can't hold it . . .*"

"One second more!" Kheperu said. "One second! Hold it one second!"

"I can't do it! Kheperu, *get out!*"

"Sure you can." Now his voice came from close behind Leucas— the shit-eating fool had come back *in* again!

"Just one second—where is that fucking thing . . . ?"

Darkness descended upon Leucas' eyes like a chillingly swift nightfall. "Kheperu . . . this is no joke . . ."

"One second!"

"You don't *have* a second!"

"All right . . . all right . . . all right—*go!*"

With a single convulsive thrust, Leucas threw himself backward; he fell to the ground and scrambled through the doorway even as the force above struck.

The ceiling fell in with a roar, two tons of stone smashing the entire room to splinters, crashing through the floor, and from the sound of it, through the next floor as well. Leucas could see firelit clouds through the hole above, but he had little eye for them.

Something was in that room.

He could see only a swirl of plaster and stone dust, but he knew it was there, he could feel it—he could feel it in that cloud of dust itself, and he knew what it was.

He had felt this before.

Even as he had felt the sullen fury of the storm in the mountains, he had felt the passionless malignity of the storm this afternoon—and now, again here in the cabinet of the Lady's Maid, he felt a cold hatred, so utterly alien that he didn't know if there were any words to adequately describe it.

All he knew was that the connection, the pulse of relationship that he could always find humming deep within himself—whether he looked on a man in battle, or a stone, a horse, the sea, a cloud, the stars themselves, he could always feel a tug of joining, an inarguable sense of being part of a whole that included all he saw, a single creation—that pulse had not been there, and in its place he'd felt a revulsion and contempt so profound that he could only think of it as *otherness*.

Turning it over in his mind, in his slow and thoughtful way, he discovered a flutter in his stomach and a metallic, coppery taste on his tongue, and he thought, *I believe I'm afraid . . .*

It seemed that he stood apart from himself, and he turned these sensations over in his thoughts the way a jeweler examines a precious stone.

*I am frightened,* he thought with a dawning wonder.

*Interesting . . .*

"We have to go," he panted. He felt like a man made of string as he tried to stand. "It's in there. It'll come after us."

"No, I should think not," Kheperu said judiciously. He gave a wicked grin and lifted the remnants of Leucas' leg of lamb. "The advantages of a classical education."

Leucas eyed that alien threatening swirl of dust warily, but it did not seem to be attacking. "How do you mean?"

"Well," Kheperu said, "many years ago, the Habiru in Egypt called down a plague spirit upon us. It killed the firstborn of every house in Egypt—including my brother Tet."

"I'm sorry," Leucas said reflexively.

Kheperu waved the sentiment away. "I never knew him. It was ten years before I was born. Every firstborn died—even cattle, cats, dogs, hawks . . . The Habiru, on the other hand, lost no one. After they ran off into the desert, the priests of the area—being men of science—naturally investigated, searching for whatever it was that had protected them. It is still taught in every House of Life in Egypt; it's so elementary that I had completely forgotten it."

He lifted the leg of lamb. "Every one of the Habiru houses had lamb's blood on the lintel and doorposts, and the spirit of slaughter did not pass within."

Leucas nodded thoughtfully, still watching the swirl of dust. It showed no signs of settling, but instead coiled out, rotating slowly, giving an impression of the limitless patience of a snake watching a rabbit hole. "You have a good memory."

Kheperu shrugged. "I am Egyptian."

Barra's mistake was in letting her instincts take over: she went for her axe. The unfamiliar decorative knob, on the end of its bronze haft, hung up in her belt when she tried to draw, and the men to either side of her had time to yank her arms straight and hold them fast.

Melchizedek pulled the axe from her belt, and triumph lit his eyes. "I told you I would have this back," he purred.

One of the men drew a shortsword—it was Eli, the lazy guard from this morning, still in his gear. But as he stepped toward her, Rachel grabbed his arm from behind.

"Don't!" she cried. "She didn't mean it! You can't hurt her!"

He pulled his arm free with a sharp tug and gave her a shove that sent her staggering back into Agaz's arms.

"Father, don't let them hurt her!"

Agaz was beyond worrying about Barra for one hot instant. He stared frozenly at Eli, his face suddenly white with rage. "You dare?"

"Don't do it here, you fool," Melchizedek snapped. "Take her outside."

"Agaz!" Barra said desperately. "The wine—he *poisoned the wine!*"

"Easy to say that now," Melchizedek sneered, the brittle edge easing from his voice. "Where is this poisoned wine?"

But Barra's cry had brought the prince back to himself. He stepped forward, moving between them with regal authority.

"Stop." His voice rang with command. Only his bloodlessly pale face showed the level of fury that he now forced into icy control.

"Do nothing hasty, here. Let her go."

Instead of complying, the men who held her looked to Melchizedek.

His face was as pale as his nephew's, and there was no hope of mercy in the thin slice of his mouth. "You are El's Men, and I have told you: take her outside and kill her."

Agaz could only watch, dumbfounded, as these men yanked Barra backward off her feet and dragged her toward the door. She fought and thrashed, but they were too strong for her; she couldn't even pull one near enough to get her teeth into him.

"Adonizedek!" she shouted. "I saved your life!"

The old king still sat upon his couch, examining the blood on his hand with puzzled concentration. "Here, now," he murmured. "Here, now, what's this . . . ?"

*All right, that tears it,* she thought. She wouldn't be the only one who died here this night.

"Ross! Bertram!" she cried in Pictish. *"Get these motherbuggers off me!"*

From somewhere back in the room came a pair of leviathan roars, and men suddenly seemed to fly outward in all directions.

Ross and Bertram descended upon the men who held her like twin avalanches.

One of the El's Men made the heroic choice, obeying his master, keeping both hands clamped to Barra's arm. Bertram's fist struck his face with a solid *chunk* like an axe entering oak, and the El's Man dropped bonelessly to the floor.

The other let go and got his hands up to guard his face before Ross could swing, so the Gael cheerfully kicked his legs out from under him. The El's Man hit the floor with a thud and a whoosh of driven-out breath; Ross chuckled in a friendly fashion while he kicked him in the head.

Eli snarled and lunged at Barra with his shortsword extended for her belly, but her arms were free and she had her feet under her and he never had a chance.

She swayed around his lunge while she whipped one of the knives from her belt. As he tried to recover his balance she drove the knife between the bones of his forearm.

He gasped, staring at the span of bronze sticking out the inside of his wrist. Barra gave the knife hilt a sharp twist, so that its double-edged blade grated on bone to both sides.

Eli gave a high falsetto screech of pain; his hand sprang nervelessly open, and his sword clattered to the floor. His knees buckled, and she yanked the knife free as he fell to the floor clutching at the spray of blood.

Barra faced the assembled Jebusites, her knife dripping gore and the twin mountains of her kinsmen flanking her. Experienced tavern brawlers, they put their backs to her, to cover each other and her as well from the men around them, and in the room beyond the doorway arch.

She muttered in Pictish, "What the fuck were you two apes waiting for?"

Bertram spread his hands. "For you to ask, princess Auntie."

Ross added, "It'd be an insult to just *assume* you need help."

Barra sighed and shook her head. "Next time, you have my permission to jump right in."

"Ay, thanks," Ross said. "Don't mind if we do."

Now she spoke loudly in Canaanite. "Nobody's dead, yet," she told the room in general. "Let's try to keep it that way while we settle this, can we?"

"There's nothing to settle," Melchizedek said from a safe distance away, "except your execution."

She squinted at him, judging the distance, calculating her chances of taking him in the throat with the knife in her hand, but Agaz stepped into her line of throw.

"There will be no executions," he said. "Not tonight."

For one moment, everyone seemed to think that things would calm down, now, and this would be resolved in some reasonable fashion; everyone except Barra. She was watching the High Priest.

Melchizedek had been nervous, even frightened, only moments before, terrified as he did the unthinkable; but now he knew he'd turned an irrevocable corner, and with that same cold courage that she had admired so much in Agaz, his self-possession had returned. He'd committed himself to this path, and he would walk it boldly to the end.

He fixed his imperious gaze upon his nephew, the prince.

"If you defy the Law of God," he said with delicate, quietly enunciated malice, "even you, Agaz, may be branded an enemy of El."

"What?" His voice hushed with disbelief, Agaz turned slowly toward the High Priest, his eyes wide. "Are you threatening me? *Me?*"

"Of course not, Agaz," Melchizedek said calmly. "I am only *reminding* you."

He lifted the Lady's Axe over his head and swung it in a small circle, to include the entire room in what he now said.

"Take them. Kill the men, too, if they resist."

Agaz shouted, "No! Stop, all of you stop!" but no one paid him any attention at all.

Every man in the place had that hostile glare she'd seen on the steward. Many of them produced knives from within their festival clothing, and the few guardsmen in full gear drew their swords.

Barra said, "Shit."

But even as the armed feasters closed in around them, the entire Citadel bucked like a spurred horse, with a rolling, thundering boom like God's own tymbal and distant rending crashes of shattering pottery and splintering wood.

It sounded, impossibly, as though part of the Citadel was collapsing. Men and women staggered, clutching at each other and flailing their arms for balance.

And over this confusion, Agaz yelled, "See how El rebukes you! Fear his anger—*put down your weapons!*"

Barra flicked him a nod of professional admiration. He certainly was quick with that shit, no doubt about it.

The armed feasters and the guards exchanged dubious glances, and looked to Melchizedek for guidance. The High Priest was silent; even he couldn't argue with an earthquake.

"Listen, you two," Barra murmured in Pictish. "If they come for me again, I'm gonna break for it. Get back to your companies; once everybody calms down they won't bother you—they can't risk turning the mercenaries against them."

"But Barra—" Bertram began.

"Are you gonna *argue* with me?" she said dangerously.

Before he could respond, the festival rooms filled with flame.

Every fire in the rooms around burst and flared, showering sparks from censer and hearth; torches exploded like Kheperu's bombs and even the candle flames leaped to the height of a tall man and spat fire.

Barra dropped flat, her kinsmen beside her. Screams of men and startled shouts were all that could be heard; panicked feasters threw themselves to the ground, batting at their smoldering clothes. The fine oils that had brought a pretty gleam to the braided beards and hair of feasters now caught furious flame that sent howling men in all directions.

Barra lifted her head, and she knew.

The *sceon tiof* was not upon her, but she had no need of it.

As she looked into the heart of the flame, the fire that burned from every torch and hearth without consuming them, the Voice in her head scoured her flesh with acid hate.

WE HAVE COME FOR YOU, BARRA COLL EIGG RHUM PAGAN WHORE. THE WRATH OF GOD IS UPON YOU.

*And me with no axe,* she thought. *I guess I'll be leaving, then.*

She was already in motion as she finished the thought, rolling onto her back and popping to her feet with a bulldancer's kip. A gout of flame from behind her scorched her heels as she sprang away, and charred the stone on which she had lain.

She sprinted out through the Citadel.

Her first thought had been to make for Sarah's cabinet and the protection of Kheperu's glyphs—but she didn't have all that much faith in the Egyptian's magic, and it would have meant leading this angry spirit through any number of rooms packed with feasters; hundreds could die.

Each torch exploded and lashed flame at her as she passed it; she ran a weaving course to stay away from them, dive-rolling under the fires she couldn't dodge, screaming at astonished slaves and feasters to *Get the fuck out of my way!* as she raced through them.

Some were not quick enough, and roasted screaming in the flames meant for her.

Finally she broke out through the Citadel gates, into the street. No torches burned here, no fires through which the spirit could strike at her, and she paused for a breath to collect her wits.

But a ravening wind howled out from the Citadel and buffeted her, whirling upward to loosen stones from the rooftops and fling them down at her.

"Shit shit *shit*," she snarled as a slingstone-sized chunk drew blood from the spot on her head still sore from the rockslide in the mountains.

*Holy ground,* she thought. *If I have a chance, it's on holy ground.*

She sprinted away into the darkness, with fury at her heels.

Melchizedek, of course, had an appropriate explanation ready by the time the confusion died down. Agaz cradled his terrified daughter in his lap and listened in blank-faced astonishment.

"It was the Goddess," he told his followers. "We were attacked by the Lady, to protect her Champion—yet her Champion *ran from us.* Even the Lady, herself, cannot stand before the humblest servant of El. The destruction you see around you is only a foreshadowing breath of what is to come, if we do not resist the witches of Ba'alath."

This reasoning pleased El's Men a great deal.

All the small fires here and there had been extinguished, and the injured had been moved away to rooms to be cared for. Adonizedek still sat with bloodied brow upon his couch, blinking in senile puzzlement as though he could not recall where he was.

Agaz set Rachel on her feet and made her meet his eyes. "You have to be strong, now, Rachel. You have to help your grandfather get to his apartment. Can you do that?"

She wiped frightened tears off her cheeks with the back of her hand, and nodded bravely, sniffling. "Yes, Father."

She pulled reluctantly free of his grasp and went over to the king. She held out her hand. "Come on, Grandfather. It's time for bed. Come on."

The old king tentatively gave her his hand and rose unsteadily to his feet.

Melchizedek indicated three of El's Men with a gesture. "Go with them. Make certain the king reaches his chambers *safely.*"

"That won't be necessary," Agaz said coldly.

"I think it is." The High Priest waved them on. "Go."

And the three El's Men followed the king and princess from the room without so much as a glance at their prince.

Agaz took several long, slow deep breaths, to make certain he had his temper fully under control, before he moved close to his uncle and spoke in a low and chill voice.

"By what right do you encourage your men to defy my authority? I am the crown prince of Jebusi!"

"No, you are not," Melchizedek said with a skeletal smile. "Now, you are the king."

Agaz's heart stuttered. "You wouldn't dare!"

"Kill him? Hardly. I don't have to."

"Barra said you'd poisoned the wine."

The High Priest snorted. "She also says she's a princess, and the Lady's Champion. No, Agaz. The old king—Abishai—was *badly injured* here tonight. He lies in his rooms . . . shall we say, dying? In this emergency, *you* are Adonizedek."

Agaz looked around the room—and found that there was not a single man here that he could call his friend. He, himself, was the only one in the room who was not a Man of El.

"I won't do it."

"You will do what neither Abishai nor your mercenary savage could. Negotiate with the Habiru. Save the city."

"And if I don't?"

Melchizedek's stare was flat as slate. "Then *I* will."

Agaz took his meaning perfectly.

The story could just as easily be given out that the prince was mortally wounded, along with the king. Melchizedek could eliminate his brother's entire bloodline. The king, Agaz, and—

"Rachel," Agaz said softly.

Melchizedek shrugged. "Tragic, isn't it? How much more tragic if we all die for nothing, and the city is still destroyed. While you played at being the returning hero and wasted time with your mercenary slut, I have acted to save the city. Now, you must do the same . . . *Adonizedek.*"

*I have always prided myself,* Agaz thought, *on being a practical man.*

He said, "All right."

Battered, bruised, her breath coming in ragged exhausted gasps, Barra staggered into the open mouth of the Ba'alath.

The howl of the wind's fury cut off as though sliced with a knife.

A few steps more, on legs of cloth, she forced herself in away from the gate, clutching handfuls of ivy along the wall for support; near one of the trees that grew from the flagstone gaps, she fell to her knees.

Here, within the Ba'alath, no stones battered her, no flames burned her, no lightning struck.

In the blessed peace, darkness gathered within her eyes. She rolled onto her back and saw briefly the waning moon, showing through a gap in the clouds.

She slept; she could not say for how long.

It felt like only seconds later that she was wakened by a shadow falling across her face, and she opened her eyes.

Haloed by the moon behind his head, only the feral gleam of his white teeth could be seen.

"Fancy meeting you here."

"Sheshai—!" Barra gasped. "How—?"

His voice sounded openly mocking. "I followed an angry wind."

She struggled up to a sitting position, some of her strength having returned with her breath. She squinted up at him; the moon-shadow covering his face was black as the night sky.

"Y'know," she said, "I've been kind of expecting to bump into you again."

# 13

# *Parley*

**W**hen the sun first breasted the mountains and spilled across Jebusi, the city had already become a tiny island in a sea of Habiru.

A few clouds like wisps of threadbare linen floated high in a sky clear and snapping blue, and in the bright splash of the morning sun, the Host of Israel looked decidedly festive. Scattered among the tents of black, brown, and red goat hair, were many that were dyed and woven in carnival colors, vivid stripes and patterns to catch and hold the eye.

The camps ranged from far below the city to the south, deep in the Hinnom Valley, to the high ridge that looked down above the city walls to the north. Men poured from these camps like foam down the sides of a boiling pot. The dazzling array of their colorful wraps, their galabiyehs, and their robes covered the earth like a patchwork blanket.

Laughter and snatches of song came clearly on the wind; many of the men ranged just barely out of bowshot, in gangs of twenty or more, working with picks and wooden shovels, throwing up long lines of earthworks.

The high walls of Jebusi were crowded this morning; armed men stood nearly shoulder to shoulder along their tops, staring in bleak silence.

Kheperu watched from the sole open window in Sarah's cabinet.

Sarah sat up on a couch beside him, peering around the window's lower corner. He didn't think she'd gotten much more sleep last night than he had; her child-weak hand upon his arm had wakened him this dawn from a feverish, half-aware doze, and had pointed him to the window; she must have heard the activity outside, and somehow from the events of the night before had intuited the danger. Kheperu had moistened some of the dried lamb's blood with leftover wine and smeared it onto the stonework around the shutters.

So far, so good.

"Leucas?" he said, only loud enough to get the drowsing Athenian's attention. "You might want to come look at this."

Instead of his usual dead-to-the-world slumber, Leucas had spent the night lightly napping, sitting up with his back against the barricade they had hastily built to hold the door that connected Sarah's cabinet to the rest of the apartment: a wardrobe, a dresser, and several couches wedged in to fix them in place.

Not long after the demon's attack last night, men had come to force the door; Kheperu had heard the sneering voice of the High Priest outside, egging them on. Leucas had held the door against them for some time before they'd heard Agaz march up, snapping harsh-voiced orders, quarreling with Melchizedek—and the attempts had broken off.

After some moments of silence, Agaz had returned.

"I think they won't bother you again tonight," he'd said through the door in Phoenikian. "Barra's not in there with you, is she?"

"I thought she was with you," Kheperu had told him, puzzled. "What's going on?"

"I can't explain right now. The two of you had better stay in there until you hear from me."

"No fear of that," Kheperu had said feelingly.

"And let no one in unless you hear me say so."

Kheperu shivered. "No fear of that, either."

Now, in the morning light, Leucas scratched his head, looking around with sleepy uncertainty.

Kheperu understood precisely what he was looking for. "Use the doorway."

"The doorway?"

"You have a better idea?"

Kheperu gestured toward the arch that opened onto the gaping ruin that had been Sarah's bedchamber. The chamber pot with which it had been supplied now lay buried in the rubble two floors below, a rubble of stone and wood and plaster above which dust motes danced all the way up through the yawning sunlit hole in the roof above.

With only a single shrugging glance at Sarah, Leucas went to the doorway and bunched his kilt in front so that he could relieve himself. His back and shoulders were striated and blotched with angry red, the blood vessels having burst under last night's strain, and he moved stiffly, awkwardly, occasionally scowling as though in considerable pain.

He smoothed his kilt back into place as he came to the window. He narrowed his eyes at the besieging army, and then he looked beyond them, out into the northern hill country, and said nothing.

Kheperu mopped sweat from his brow. The day was not yet warm, but the fever from the inflamed spear cut on his back had given him a restless, sleepless night. His bruised thigh ached fiercely, despite the willow-bark tea he had drunk several times since retiring. He'd been tempted to use a more potent narcotic—but he feared the dreams that might come with it.

He glared out at the gathered *shasu*. There were thousands of the filthy beggars, tens of thousands. He imagined that they gave off a peculiarly rancid odor that choked his nose like dust.

Deep in his heart, last night, he had still fancied the notion that this morning would see him and his partners on the road to Ascalon. That dream now curdled like the milk of a sick cow.

*Perhaps,* he thought, *that law of theirs about being nice to Egyptians will still be in force.*

Leucas gazed with dour professional admiration at their earthworks. "They're good at this."

Kheperu winced; somehow he'd been obscurely hoping that Leucas, in his experience with sieges and soldiery, would tell him that the *shasu* were really nothing more than a mass of smelly rabble, a conglomeration of bandits with no skill or discipline.

He said painfully, "Oh?"

Leucas nodded. "At Troy, it took us weeks to raise and fortify the wall that defended our ships. Their earthworks will be near to done by noon. And well done: whoever their master engineer is, he knows what he's doing. There won't be a single straight stretch the length of a good spear throw to get up speed for a chariot charge."

"And—ha ha—" Kheperu laughed nervously, "there's a *lot* of them, too, isn't there? Nearly, ah, *nearly* as many as you had at Troy . . . ?"

*Please,* he thought, *say to me Oh, no, Kheperu. Don't be silly. These are barely a fraction of the Greek army . . .*

"Oh, no, Kheperu," Leucas said distantly. "Don't be silly. This is only the advance guard. The rest of them are still coming through the hills."

Kheperu followed his gesture with his gaze, but his aging eyes saw nothing except rolling green-and-brown hills, shading to pulsing grey down their sides.

He blinked. *Grey?*

"What?" he said, his voice hushed with awe. "That's them? All *that?*"

Leucas nodded. "In ten years of war at Troy, we brought maybe a quarter of a million men—that includes all the reinforcements that joined us through the decade. I'd guess there are about twice that many Habiru coming through those hills right now, maybe more like four or five times."

Kheperu coughed into his hand, and massaged his burning forehead.

"And the Trojans," Leucas went on meditatively, "they had allies from all over Asia; maybe eighty or a hundred thousand of their own—"

"That's enough," Kheperu told him. "Don't try to cheer me up any more."

A hot desert wind came from the east and stirred the grey hairs on Leucas' head into the black. His gaze ranged now not upon the besiegers, but through memories of distant years.

"It is a long and tangled road I've walked, to die behind these walls."

His hands crossed upon his lean, battle-scarred chest, exposed by the shirtless Cretan kilt he wore, and he scratched at his head, and Kheperu supposed that in his mind he stroked the armor and helm he'd worn at Troy, the armor lost in the mountains a tenday and more ago.

Kheperu stared blankly out at the approaching Host of Israel, appalled. Last night's attack of the demon had been frightening, but they had weathered it, and Kheperu had been able to pigeonhole supernatural assaults, in general, as a manageable threat.

This, though—this unimaginably vast army . . .

"We have one advantage," Leucas rumbled.

"Oh?" Kheperu said encouragingly, desperate for some good news.

"Their army's too big."

"That's an advantage?"

He nodded. "They'll never be able to keep it supplied. It means this'll be a short siege. They'll have to storm the walls and take it before their food runs out. Probably won't even have time to build a siege ramp."

"You call this good news?"

Leucas shrugged. "At least we won't starve."

Now on the ridge to the east, an old man stepped out through the rising earthworks, leaning heavily on a knotted staff. At his side walked a broad-shouldered man of about Leucas' age, richly dressed—but he stayed a pace behind the old man's left shoulder, like a servant.

The old man stood as tall as the biggest warrior he passed, and his short, bowed legs and barrel chest gave his rocking stride an inexorable, elephantine look, as though he were a granite boulder come to life. For a moment, one of the drifting clouds must have crossed the sun, for it seemed that the earth darkened, save for a single blazing lightfall around the old man that turned his white and drifting hair to a corona of gold, and it seemed that while he spoke, his face outshone the sun.

"HEAR ME, MEN OF JERUSALEM! THE DAY OF YOUR DESTRUCTION IS AT HAND!"

Kheperu blinked. "That is an exceptional voice . . ."

The old man spoke an archaic, overformal Egyptian, the language of this land's titular conquerors. The broad-shouldered servant shouted what Kheperu presumed to be a translation into Canaanite.

"They're within bowshot, with no flag of truce or herald's staff," Leucas murmured. "Why don't they shoot?"

With each phrase, the old man paused for his servant's translation.

"I AM JOSHUA BEN NUN, JUDGE OF THE NATION OF ISRAEL. I SPEAK FOR YAHWEH SABAOTH, EL SHADDAI, GOD OF ABRAHAM AND ISAAC. THE UTTERMOST SPAN OF YOUR DAYS UPON THE EARTH IS SEVEN. COME OUT; SURRENDER YOUR SINFUL CITY TO THE JUSTICE OF GOD."

"What's he saying?" Leucas asked.

Kheperu looked down at Sarah, more than half-expecting to see on her face some of the dismay he felt in his heart, but her expression was only intent, as though she listened carefully.

He said, "He's going to destroy the city within seven days."

"Huh," Leucas grunted. "Probably only brought food for a tenday. He's cutting it close."

Now the mercenaries that crowded the walls did shoot: first only one, then several, then a flood, a high-arching flight of arrows soaring over the Kidron Valley.

Joshua lifted his chin as though to greet them, and raised his staff like a flag, but he made no other movement; the arrows fell around him like spring rain, but left him untouched. His richly dressed aide looked decidedly nervous, shifting his weight and obviously restraining himself from flinching, but he, too, was unharmed.

It seemed some wind caught the arrows and swirled them away, some even falling beyond their range, over the earthworks; from the men beyond came some cries of pain and dismay, but Joshua never budged.

Kheperu murmured, "He has a great deal of faith in this god of his . . ."

"Kheperu," Leucas said softly, "mind if I borrow your spear?"

The spear Kheperu had been using for a staff ever since the caravan raid leaned in a corner by the barricade; Leucas went over and got it without waiting for an answer.

"Why?" Kheperu asked.

Leucas hefted the spear, measuring its weight and balance thoughtfully. He took three deliberate strides back from the window.

"Because there seems to be a crosswind in the valley, today."

He bounded forward those three strides for momentum, and his breath exploded in a mighty shout as he hurled the spear high into the sky over the Kidron. Cries of amazement and wonder rose both from the walls and from the earthworks outside as the spear sailed on and on as though it would never come down.

Leucas stood watching at the window. "Just don't move," he muttered, as though he could conjure Joshua with his words.

Joshua didn't move. He didn't even watch. He closed his eyes and spread his arms wide as though receiving grace from above.

The spear seemed to turn in the air, first this way, then that, as though opposing winds struggled over it, then it slashed down from the sky—

And struck the head of the staff in Joshua's left hand.

The impact stripped the staff from Joshua's grip, sent the spear skittering one way and the staff another, with a bright new scar in its age-darkened wood.

A cheer went up from the walls, as though the defenders had won a great victory—a cheer answered an instant later by the Habiru, who seemed to think the victory was theirs.

The aide swiftly retrieved the staff and returned it to Joshua, who had not moved.

"Damn," Leucas said. "Thought I had him." He looked down at Kheperu. "Sorry about your spear."

"That's *two*," Kheperu said, flaring his considerable nostrils. "You still owe me for the one you broke on the bear last year."

Joshua took a breath so deep that Kheperu could see his chest expand from across the valley.

"THERE IS A WOMAN AMONG YOU WHOSE WORD GOD WOULD HEAR."

Kheperu frowned. A new note had come into the old man's bellow, an overprecision of speech, as though Joshua chose his words with great care: the sound of an honest man skirting a lie.

"WHEN THE SUN STANDS STRAIGHT ABOVE THIS VALLEY, LET BARRA COLL EIGG RHUM COME OUT FOR PARLEY."

Leucas blinked. "Was that *Barra's* name? How would he know Barra's name?"

"Yes it was, and I don't know. Be quiet."

Something fierce sparked within Sarah's eyes.

"BARRA COLL EIGG RHUM, COME OUT! GOD CALLS YOUR NAME. COME OUT, BARRA COLL EIGG RHUM!"

Joshua lifted his arms as though in benediction.

"TRUST IN THE MERCY OF GOD. OUR TRUCE SHALL STAND UNTIL NOON. WHEN NOON COMES AND BARRA COLL EIGG RHUM HAS NOT COME OUT, THE ATTACK WILL BEGIN. SO SHALL IT BE."

The old man dropped his hands and turned away. With his aide at his heels like a faithful puppy, he strode back among the earthworks, out of sight.

Kheperu and Leucas looked at each other for a long silent moment, then both turned again to stare back out over the Habiru.

"Well," Kheperu murmured under his breath. "Well, well, well."

And between them, Sarah wore an expression of grave satisfaction.

Barra knelt at one of the large gaps in the Ba'alath's flagstone courtyard, beside the bare earth from which sprang the vines that covered its curving walls. Sunrise haloed the eastern mountains, and the waning moon still hung above, giving her enough light to see what she was doing.

Soon the acolytes would arrive to begin their morning devotions. She wanted to be gone before then.

This was going to be a busy day.

Her hair was piled high above her head, packed with blue-dyed clay, the color of a thunderstorm; spikes of hair, stiff with clay, descended behind her neck like streaks of rain. Jagged streaks of the same clay painted her face like thunderbolts, striped her arms, swirled out in spirals from her bared breasts, and formed sigils of power upon her naked legs.

She wore only her weapon belt of boarskin, and a breechclout of twisted cloth to swaddle her hips. In her hands she held a small wooden board, of the sort that the Jebusites used to pull flatbread from their stone ovens. On that board was the last remaining wad of leftover clay, moistened with her spit and nine drops of her blood, dyed with the powdered pigment she carried in a pouch on her boarskin belt.

Sheshai had stood behind her on the flagstones, watching silently with his fixed manic stare, as she had mixed this clay and painted it across her body. Now he watched her scrape a small hollow in the earth by the rooted vines, lay the board with its clay within, and reverently cover them over again.

She'd asked him to teach her everything he knew about the Habiru. He never asked her why she wanted to know; he'd simply crouched beside her and begun. His personal madness served her well, here: he never tired of speaking of the Habiru and their ways, and his obsession had made him rehearse everything he knew about them over and over again in his mind. He had forgotten nothing.

He'd been a slave among them for ten years. He knew a lot.

They had spent the night here, upon these flagstones, talking in low voices. He knew enough of their customs, laws, and history to fill a book—shit, to fill *five* books.

Toward the end of the night, crouching on his heels, he had begun again.

"First, most important, no blood, understand?"

Barra shook her head; she was so exhausted she could almost hear the scrape of her eyelids when she blinked.

"There's no point in this. I'll never remember them all. Forget the dietary laws, screw the cleanliness and all the shit about mildew and pox and everything else. How about this god of theirs? What's he look like?" She glanced toward the altarhouse, thinking of the enormous Astarte inside. "How big is he?"

"Nobody knows."

Barra frowned. "What do you mean?"

"I mean nobody knows. They carry him around in this box, a big box, they call it Arawn."

"What?" Sudden panic had thundered in Barra's chest. "Arawn? They call the box *Arawn*?" That was the name of the Grey Man, the Lord of the Twilit Lands, the Judge of the Dead and the mate of the Mother by whom Barra swore. *Who the fuck am I fighting here?*

"No, you're pronouncing it wrong. It's *awrown*—it's a Habiru word, it means *coffin*."

Chills skittered along Barra's spine. That mishearing, mistaken though it was, had been creepy enough to make her hands shake. "Go on."

"The only time they uncrate him is when they set up their temple—that big tent of the Tabernacle, remember? Only the High Priest or Joshua himself ever goes inside the inner chamber; for anyone else, it's death. No exceptions."

"What about their other gods?"

"They don't have any."

Barra blinked, momentarily speechless.

"It's true," Sheshai insisted. "This Yahweh of theirs told them he created the world and everything in it, and they're not allowed to have any gods but him."

"But—" Barra frowned incredulously, "doesn't he even have a *wife*?"

"I told you: no other god but him."

She felt a half-hysterical laugh rising up her throat. "No wonder he's irritable!"

"Sure," Sheshai had said with a shrug. "If you hadn't gotten laid since the creation of the world, you'd be cranky, too."

Now, in the strengthening dawn, Barra rose and dusted dirt from her hands. The Triple Joining of the Rite of War was complete, and as it had in Tyre the previous year, it brought the *sceon tiof* as a living presence to inhabit her eyes.

She saw the rot and decay that ate at the walls of the Ba'alath; she saw the desolate shadow that darkened the altarhouse. She looked at the raw wound that was Sheshai.

He shook his head, grinning like a hungry dog. "It'll never work, y'know."

"What?"

"What you're thinking. It'll never work. You don't have the experience. They'll catch you in less than a day. There are a thousand things you'll never learn in time, a million. The first time someone asks you a question you can't answer, you're cooked."

She shrugged. "I'll burst into tears. That usually works."

"Does it?" Sheshai's scars twisted. "Did it work for my wife? For my daughter?"

No answer could be made.

"That's why you're going to help me."

"Eh?"

She needed him. The city needed him, and the Lady as well.

And he had no reason to value any of the three more than a fart in the wind.

She faced him squarely, and within her mind she summoned an image of the Lady, of the Mother, of Hera and Artemis and Hecate, of Isis and Inanna; she imagined every one of them standing at her shoulder, a host of goddesses looking out through her eyes, fixing Sheshai with a stare that pinned him to the floor.

The imaginary goddesses at her shoulder whispered, *Command him.*

She said, "Follow me and help me," and somewhere within her voice was a power that made him cringe.

"I . . ."

"I am the Lady's Champion. Serve truly, and the Lady shall grant your fondest desire."

"Will she?"

"I have said so."

His grin sharpened like steel on stone. "I want Joshua's blood."

"You shall have it." The conviction in her voice was absolute; no man alive could have heard the lie.

*And maybe I wasn't even lying,* Barra thought. *Shit, this Lady's Champion stuff could have its advantages.*

He came close to her. His breath smelled of blood and old meat.

"What do you want me to do?"

She turned away from him, toward the gate of the Ba'alath.

Without giving herself time to change her mind, she walked out into the street.

For one long, breathless moment, she waited. She waited for the thunderbolt, for the hail of stones, the snarling winds and gouts of fire.

A crow cackled, somewhere far off. A few houses away, a townsman scratched at the dirt in front of his door with a bronze rake. He looked up at her curiously, then shook his head and went back inside.

The glare of the rising sun chased shadows eastward down the street.

She let her breath trickle slowly out through her lips.

*Well, all right, then. It's working.*

She turned back to Sheshai, who leaned against the gate of the Ba'alath, watching her fixedly.

"First," she said, "there's an errand I want you to run."

*"Adonizedek stands here, ready to answer for his people. Let Joshua come forth! Here is our herald's staff! Adonizedek would speak with Joshua ben Nun!"*

Agaz—he might play at being king, but he would never call himself so in his heart—wiped spittle from his lips. He glared red-faced at the mercenaries that stood watch upon the parapet. Some of them returned his glare expressionlessly; most ignored him altogether.

As did the Habiru beyond the walls.

This is what burned in his face, and made his stomach boil with humiliation. No matter how he shouted, what he said, the Habiru did not respond. They didn't even condescend to jeer at him, as if they could instinctively sense that he was only playacting the part of king.

His uncle's followers watched him from a short distance away. His first lesson in kingship he had learned last night: he was every bit as much a prisoner as was his father.

Melchizedek scowled, only a step away. "Call them again. Perhaps they do not hear you."

"They hear," Agaz said. "And I will not call again."

He turned his back upon his uncle and walked toward the door at the end of the wall's arc. The El's Men that accompanied him shifted their weight as though to bar his path, but he never slowed, his eyes inviting them to put their hands upon him, if they dared.

At the last moment, they parted to let him pass. Melchizedek came after him.

"You must keep trying," he insisted stridently. "It is the only way!"

Melchizedek had explained his plan through the long sleepless night. He felt that the Habiru might accept a doubled tribute—which could be extorted by the mercenaries from the Jebusites who crowded the city—if the offer included Agaz's life.

"The king can redeem his people by sacrificing himself," Melchizedek had insisted. "It is their way."

He'd certainly made his plan sound reasonable, and Agaz was willing enough. If the city could be saved at the cost of only his life, he was happy to do it.

The sole flaw seemed to be that the Habiru weren't interested.

Melchizedek was clearly puzzled by this, and flatly refused to accept it. He snapped at Agaz's departing back, "Tell them you'll come out. Tell them they can do what they will with you."

Agaz never slowed. "Uncle, they will do what they will with me anyway, when they take the city."

"You must try again. I did not make you king for nothing!" Melchizedek's voice rose. "You know whose lives depend upon your cooperation!"

Agaz stopped in the doorway, and cast a cynical glance back at the

High Priest. "I may be your puppet king," he said flatly, "but I find it less than comfortable to have your hand up my ass."

While Melchizedek was still sputtering, Agaz stalked away.

The Men of El followed him, as they had ever since last night. A handful of sullen, stupid men enjoying their sudden new authority, they kept him on as tight a leash as had his Manassite captors.

He did not speak to these men; he had wasted words enough on them last night. He knew most of them by name—they were young, under twenty-five, some of them the younger brothers and sons of the men he'd led on his ill-fated northern expedition. He knew them, and would have sworn by their loyalty, but somehow Melchizedek had managed to corrupt them. They steadfastly insisted that their duty was to El first, and the king second, and nothing Agaz could do or say would sway them.

Melchizedek's control was not complete, however. None of these peasant El's Men were truly comfortable defying their prince and their king, no matter what El might say. He'd seen a hint of it last night, when he'd managed to stop Melchizedek from breaking into the cabinets of the Lady's Maid. He had no idea how he could possibly protect Leucas and Kheperu from the vengeful High Priest for any length of time, but at least they were safe enough for the moment.

He wished he could get some clue what might be happening up there. Practically half the wing had collapsed last night, and men he could ill afford to spare from the walls were occupied trying to clear the rubble and discover what had caused the collapse.

He wished with all his heart that Barra were here. He was sure that if she were here, she could give him an idea what to do.

He had found within himself an unexpected faith that she could do the impossible.

And he wished she were here so that he could tell her that he believed in her, that he'd never doubted her, not even last night. He knew she'd saved his father's life, and had nearly been killed for it, and he'd simply stood there—like an idiot; like a *coward*—and let it happen.

That humiliation burned more deeply than the rest. The enormity of the situation had frozen him; he'd been unable to think straight enough to do anything, and he despised himself for it.

She must despise him for it, as well.

*If I ever get another chance,* he swore to himself for the thousandth time since the feast last night, *I will not hesitate.*

*I will not fail.*

But Barra had vanished into the night like smoke from a campfire. No one had seen her go, no one knew where she might be; riding the wind, perhaps, far beyond the city walls . . .

There was no way to know if she'd heard Joshua's summons.

*Perhaps our last hope,* he thought, *hiding like a hare from my uncle's hounds.*

Another part of him knew that even this was vain and foolish optimism; he'd seen the Habiru Host flowing through the hills like honey from a broken jug spreading over a table.

Barra was not Jebusi's last hope: there was no hope.

He strode through the public rooms of the Citadel, the Men of El close behind. Everywhere he went he was stopped by slave or townsman, gravely concerned for his father's health. Perhaps by worrying about the king, they could relieve their minds of the weight of what awaited them when the Habiru Host stormed the walls. For some, though, for many, perhaps even all, the concern was genuine as well. As it always did, it struck his heart how loved his father was by the people he ruled.

To each of them he gave the answer that Melchizedek had prescribed, "My father sleeps, and cannot be wakened. He may never waken again. Until he returns to lead us, I am Adonizedek."

And *Adonizedek* was what the Men of El called him, although in their mouths the word had an edge of contempt.

A number of the mercenary captains awaited him in a private room, ostensibly to hear his directions for organizing the defense. More likely, they had decided what they would do, and now would give orders, rather than take them.

He dourly half expected them to tell him they were marching out the gate to join the Habiru.

In the small entryway to that private room, he found his daughter sitting on a couch, her hands between her knees and tear streaks on her face.

"Rachel, what's wrong?" he said, crouching beside her.

"Everybody says Grandfather's going to die," she said solemnly.

Agaz's heart twisted. "Yes. That is what they say."

"They won't let me in to see him! They won't let me talk to him or even *sit* with him!"

The *they* she spoke of, would be the pair of El's Men who stood guard at the king's hall door. Agaz nodded. "He's very sick, Rachel." He put his arm around her tiny shoulders and drew her close. "I'm sorry."

And when her little face nestled into his shoulder, he was astonished to hear her bare breath of a whisper: *"I know he's not really sick, Father. You need to make them let me go in to him."*

He pulled back and stared at her. She caught her underlip in her teeth and looked at him with enormous liquid eyes that begged him to believe her, to trust her, to let her do whatever it was she was planning to do.

He remembered Barra saying: *She knows more about what goes on around here than you do,* and abruptly his mind was made up.

He stood. "By whose authority is the princess forbidden to visit the bedside of her grandfather?" he said, loudly enough that the mercenaries in the room beyond would be able to hear him clearly.

One of the Men of El muttered, "You know by whose authority, *Adonizedek.*"

He stepped close to the man who'd spoken, and said softly, "Why not just put her up there with him? Then you filthy bastards will have both your hostages in the same place."

The man blinked and exchanged looks with his companions, and none of them could find fault with this idea.

One of them held Rachel's hand as she led him away. She flashed a quick and grateful look over her shoulder, and Agaz wished he had some idea what she was up to.

Even as he turned to go in, a Jebusite in guardsman's armor jogged up. "Prince Ag—ah, Adonizedek, I mean. There's a townsman here that wants to see you."

Agaz shook his head. "I'm too busy."

"He said you'd see him, though, if you knew he was here. Him and his friends, they're right behind me."

Agaz waved him off. "I have no time."

But even as he did so, around a distant corner came a pair of pale, heavily built European mercenaries, who bore a suspicious resemblance to the kinsmen of Barra's he'd met at the feast.

And between them was a small man in dark clothing, with black hair, swarthy skin, a jackal's grin, and curving black scars across his cheeks.

"So, it's Adonizedek now, eh?" Sheshai said. "Suits you."

Agaz's mouth was suddenly dry. "You!"

"Sharp as ever. I have a message from our mutual friend."

Agaz coughed into his fist and turned to the Men of El. "Tell the captains I'll be with them in a few minutes."

Sheshai's grin spread like flames on a pool of oil.

\*  \*  \*

The commander of the Egyptian garrison oversaw the organization of his troops with a sharp pain in his heart. He'd been posted in Jebusi for ten years now, and he'd come to love the city as though he'd been born here, and the Jebusites as though they were his own blood. He understood the necessity of abandoning them, to preserve the fiction of Egypt's control over the *mâtat Urusalim*, but to actually do it, in the face of the enemy, burned him like he'd swallowed a hot coal.

His troops stood in ranks, sweating under their armor in the hot spring sun, while he went back into the garrison building to inspect it one last time.

As he passed, he shuttered each room into darkness, and fixed each door with a massive bronze lock.

This garrison would be left as spotless as human hands could make it, even though the Habiru would undoubtedly destroy it in the sack of the city. When they were done, when they occupied the city as they had so many others, he and his men would march back in and rebuild, and life would go on as before . . .

Except that every Jebusite he'd ever met would be dead.

He half wished that he had some excuse to defy the Governor's order; he half wished that he could stay and fight.

He was sure his feelings had shown upon his face when that northern axe-woman had come with the letter and the seal of Tal Akhu-shabb. His display of weak emotion had shamed him, but he could not help it, any more than he could now stop his eyes from stinging or swallow the knot in his chest as he locked each door for the last time.

He came at last to the room that had served him for an office for a decade, and found that he'd left the shutters of one window open. He shook his head in mild self-mockery. He, who insisted on meticulous perfection from his men, was the one who'd gone lax.

He rounded his desk to close that shutter and darken this room for the last time.

"I'll thank you to leave that open," came a hushed voice from the shadows. "I'll be using it again in a moment."

He froze, steeling himself against an imagined blow, and when it did not come, he said, "Who are you? I can't see."

"There's a letter on your desk. It's for the Governor. He'll want to get it today."

"But—but—who—?" But this was an empty question; now he had recognized her voice. His heart stuttered to a sudden gallop.

"He'll be in Gezer by now. A good horse can take you there before nightfall. You have a good horse?"

"I, yes, I, but . . ."

"Beside the letter you'll find the Governor's seal. That'll get you straight in to see him."

"But—what's this all about?"

"It's about saving the bloody city."

"This city will fall, no matter what—"

"The city will stand. Jebusi will stand if I have to hold it up with my bare fucking hands. If you get that letter to Gezer before dark, I *guarantee* it. Can you do it?"

"Well, I, ah . . . ah—*yes*," said the garrison commander, coming to a sudden decision. From some unknown corner of his spirit, a fresh breeze seemed to blow. He felt light inside, as though laughter bubbled within his chest. "Yes, I'll do it!"

The opened window darkened for just an instant, as someone bounded through to the sunlit street. The garrison commander got only a fleeting impression of bare flesh, and stripes, blue stripes . . .

When he went to the window to shutter it for the final time, the street beyond was empty.

He latched the shutters tight and put his hands on the letter and the seal that lay upon his desk. He stood motionless for one long breath, marveling how *good* he suddenly felt . . .

Then he snatched up the letter and the seal and ran for the street, shouting for his aide to ready his horse.

The entire procession arrived at the door to Melchizedek's apartment: Agaz, Sheshai, the two Pictish mercenaries, and the trailing knot of El's Men. Their conversation was conducted entirely in Phoenikian, to keep it private from the suspicious Men of El.

When they arrived, Melchizedek's slaves were busily chipping off the green glyphs Kheperu had painted on the door and walls the day before. Agaz shooed them away with a few short words and a stern look, then he turned back to the knot of El's Men.

"You can wait for me here in the hallway," he said coldly.

"Uh-uh, Adonizedek," their informal leader said. "We understand our duty. Where you go, we go."

"Not today."

A word with the pair of towering Pictish mercenaries, and they took up positions to either side of the door. Agaz and Sheshai went in without a backward glance. When the Men of El moved to follow, they found the closing doorway suddenly filled with smiling Picts.

The Picts stood half a head taller than any of the Jebusites, and they seemed every bit as friendly and relaxed and unthreatening as sleepy bears.

The Men of El decided to wait in the hallway.

The knock sounded dull and distant through the barricade, as did Agaz's soft request for entry.

"Before we open this door," Kheperu told him, "I must be certain that the outer door to the hall, the one with the green glyphs upon it, is closed and will remain so. If both doors are open at the same time, I cannot answer for the consequences."

"The hall door won't open until I say so," Agaz replied. "There's about forty stone of mercenary standing out there to make sure of that."

"Mercenaries guarding the door?" Kheperu said with a frown. "You think they're reliable? Will they stand against Melchizedek and his apes if they come back?"

"They're men of Barra's tribe."

Kheperu blinked. "Oh, well, come in, then."

He and Leucas cleared aside the barricade in only a moment, and when they opened the door Agaz came in, with Sheshai at his side.

Kheperu and Leucas exchanged glances, momentarily at a loss; it was like seeing a lion and a hyaena strolling casually arm in arm.

"And a good day to you, sir," Kheperu said in Phoenikian. "I, ah, rather expected to see a certain black-fletched arrow shot at Joshua this morning . . ."

Sheshai snorted broadly. "Shoot at Joshua when the *sun* is in the sky? What am I, crazy?"

Kheperu forbore to answer.

Sheshai brushed past him and knelt at the side of the couch where Sarah lay. They seemed to know each other; soft words passed between them.

"We heard you shouting from the wall," Kheperu said to Agaz. "I take it some things have changed around here?"

Agaz nodded distractedly; he passed by Graeg's pallet with a pat for the wounded wolf and stared through the archway into what had once been Sarah's bedchamber. Two floors below, men were at work among the broken stone and splintered timber.

"Yes, things have changed," he murmured. "Melchizedek tried to murder my father last night. The Men of El have taken the Citadel; they call me Adonizedek, but my uncle rules here now."

Kheperu coughed dryly as though the words had choked him. "I've heard better news."

"Melchizedek wants me to pay off the Habiru, and offer my life as part of the price."

"Pay them off? With what? I thought all your tribute money had gone to hire the mercenaries."

Agaz's response was the silent compression of his lips.

"Oh . . ." Kheperu said. "Oh, this is a very bad idea . . . Does your uncle have any idea what ten thousand mercenaries can do to a city when they discover they're not going to get paid?"

Agaz shrugged. "Better than the Habiru."

"Hmpf. Well, speaking as a mercenary myself, I should point out that my loyalties are to the man who counts out my silver," Kheperu said significantly. "Melchizedek may rule here now, but I'd wager the mercenaries don't know that yet."

For a moment, a light kindled in Agaz's eyes, but it was swiftly snuffed by cold despair. "But my uncle holds my father and my daughter in his hand."

"What about Barra?"

"She saved my father's life last night; now, when Melchizedek catches her, he'll kill her for it."

"More easily said than done, that. Do you know where she is now?"

"I do," Sheshai said from across the room. He stood. "At least, I know where she'll be at noon."

"Oh, not really—!" Kheperu made a pained face. "She's not going to go *out* there!"

"Yes, she is," Sheshai said with that jackal grin. "And so are we."

The tunnel was a long, step-cut stretch of dank stuffy hole in the rock; it ran at a steep angle from the foundation of the Citadel to the level of the spring in the Kidron Valley, a spear throw below Jebusi's east wall. It had been laboriously chipped from the stone centuries ago; used only in time of siege, it had nonetheless seen enough traffic that the steps were worn smooth and bowed in the middle by numberless passing sandals.

Once reaching roughly the spring's level, the tunnel ran horizontally until it came upon the short final slope down to the spring itself.

A wall of close-fitted stone blocked its end, a wall that was easily knocked through in time of need.

The tunnel probably would not be used during this siege; here at the end of winter, the catch basins all over the city were brimming with rainwater, and it was sadly unlikely that the city would hold out long enough to run short.

It was at the rock wall that a small group of Pictish mercenaries worked, while Kheperu and Sheshai watched from a short distance up the tunnel. Beyond the wall lay the spring itself, well below ground level; stairs beside the spring would lead them up to the small well-house—up on the floor of the Kidron Valley, outside the wall.

The Picts pried at the wall, only occasionally striking with leather-wrapped hammers to seat their levers between the rocks; the sharp clank of bronze on stone might carry up the shaft to the besieging army.

Kheperu licked sweat from his upper lip and glared at Sheshai. This Jerichite bastard's mad grin hadn't altered a whit in three hours, and Kheperu didn't trust him at all.

"Are you sure you have it?" Kheperu hissed. "Say it again."

He shifted the weight of a small satchel he carried over one shoulder, and arranged his Hivite-style galabiyeh. "First the cook pot. Then the water. Then the fires, one two three four. Easy. Relax."

Kheperu chewed at a thumbnail. "Why are you doing this? What do you get out of this?"

"Mm?"

"You knew they were coming; you could have left yesterday."

"And miss the party? I don't think so."

"You're not interested in saving this city—you went for Agaz's throat on sight. You hate these people."

"Sure," Sheshai said. He nodded toward the spring end of the tunnel. "But I hate them *more*."

Kheperu shrugged irritably, and fingered his new staff, which lay across his folded legs—a nice piece of work, a gift from Leucas. "All right. I suppose that makes sense. I only wish that someone could explain why *I* am doing this."

But this was only reflexive grousing; he knew the answer all too well.

Back in Sarah's cabinet, hours before, when Sheshai had finished explaining Barra's incredible, foolhardy plan, Kheperu had stared at him and exclaimed, "You can't believe this will work!"

"Sure I can," Sheshai had responded cheerfully.

"Of course," Kheperu muttered. "I forgot: you're completely mad."

"What's your point?"

Leucas might have been carved of mountain rock; he looked as grey and solid as the wall that defended the city. He leaned on the windowsill and gripped the edge; his knuckles whitened and the stone creaked beneath his hands.

"I used to wonder how the Trojans felt, when they saw us sailing up. It's kind of interesting." Then a gentle smile cracked the broken planes of his face as he looked at Kheperu. "Remember? Only yesterday, I was looking for something to fight for, that meant more than money."

"You were talking about a home, a *family*," Kheperu said; in his voice was a whiny edge of desperation that he loathed, but could not control.

Leucas lifted his shoulders and let them fall again. "You and Barra *are* my family—maybe as much family as I'll ever have. And wherever I'm with my family, that's home."

He gestured at Sarah, and nodded toward Sheshai and Agaz. "Tell them that I'll do my part. Tell them that while I live, no harm will befall this woman."

"Well, I'm *sorry*," Kheperu said, "but I just don't see how being slaughtered here in Jebusi is so much better than dying peacefully in the bed of a Coast Road whore. The Egyptian garrison will be marching out in an hour or two. Why can't we *all* leave? Together?"

"Because Barra isn't leaving," Leucas replied with inarguable finality. "And I follow Barra."

Kheperu whined in frustration. "What is *wrong* with you? Perhaps I should go alone!"

"Yes," said Leucas. His grey eyes gleamed like ice in the winter sun, and he spoke with heavy-handed significance. "You should go. You have to think about your *future*."

The inflamed spear cut on his back throbbed in the rhythm of his pulse, and sizzled fever into his face. He thought about being old, and sick. And *poor*. He ran his tongue thoughtfully over the roughened ridges of his decaying teeth, probing them for sore spots, and thought about mashing his food with a spoon so that he could swallow it without chewing.

He thought about going up the Coast Road alone.

"That was cheap, Leucas. Cheap."

The Athenian only shrugged.

Kheperu thrust his hands past each other, into the opposite sleeves of his heavy robe, and clutched the hard muscles of his forearms as he glared once again out at the assembled thousands of Habiru.

"This is as good a place to die as any, I suppose."

As the group broke up to go their separate ways, Leucas held out Melchizedek's walking staff to Kheperu. "Here."

Kheperu took it and tested its heft appreciatively. "For me?"

Leucas shrugged. "Don't think I'll be giving it back to Melchizedek. And you look naked without one."

Kheperu summoned a semblance of his usual leer; it was forced, but it made him feel a bit better anyway. "Really? You don't like to look at me naked?"

Leucas had replied solemnly, "Like the glory of the sun, I'm sure that it would leave me stone blind."

Now with his back against the stone, Kheperu tightened his grip on the staff, and tried not to think about how much he would miss Leucas, and tried not to wonder if Leucas will miss him.

One of the Picts came back from the crew working on the tunnel wall and told the pair in halting, thickly accented Phoenikian that the wall was loosened enough that a sharp shove would break through. Then he summoned his men, and they trudged heavily back up the tunnel.

Their footsteps, and the light from their lamps, faded into irrevocable night.

Deep within the stone below the Kidron Valley, Kheperu crouched beside the mad Jerichite and waited for the first explosion.

Agaz leaned on the Citadel's parapet, his elbows grinding against the age-smoothed stone, and watched the troops of the Egyptian garrison march away from the city.

They were a couple of hours up the road, far in the eastern distance, a tiny cloud of dust raised by marching feet heading for the coast. The Habiru had parted politely to let them pass; as soon as they were beyond the Habiru perimeter, one of their officers—at that distance, Agaz couldn't tell which—had galloped away on horseback.

Many, many more Habiru had arrived in the hours between dawn and noon, perhaps three times as many as the initial force. They came walking in loose, disorganized tribal bands, not only fighting men, but women and slaves and livestock and numberless wagons.

They had pitched tents out beyond the earthworks, and now, as the sun crept toward noon, these newcomers began the meticulous, painstaking construction of an enormous enclosure high upon the central ridge, to the northwest above the city, walled with fine twined linen of blue and purple and scarlet, hung with silver hooks from silver-filleted poles set in sockets of brass.

"I know what you've been up to," Melchizedek said from behind him, among the knot of El's Men that had followed Agaz up to this vantage.

Agaz didn't move. "Uncle," he said distantly.

"You've been in my apartment, with my wife and those mercenary thugs."

Agaz shrugged.

Out in the Habiru camp, a wagon approached, drawn by men in harness rather than oxen.

"I know that you've been to my brother's dressing room. You stole one of my brother's wigs, and some of the dye that colors them. I know what you're up to."

"I am up to nothing," Agaz said. "I am the king. I am the most helpless man in Jebusi."

Now the High Priest came to the wall beside him, and followed his gaze. "What's that?"

"They call it the Tabernacle," Agaz murmured. "It's the tent where their god lives. That wagon, there, with all the silver and brass—the one the men are pulling over the ridge? That'll be him coming, even now; their god, riding in his box in that wagon."

Melchizedek frowned at him suspiciously. "They carry their god in a box? How do you know all this?"

Agaz only smiled.

"Well, then," Melchizedek said, "this must be why they refused to negotiate. They can't make a deal with us until their god has arrived to witness it—many of these primitive bandit tribes are stubbornly superstitious. You must approach them again."

But Agaz was clearly not listening; he lifted his face to the sky and squinted at the sun, then looked down as though to judge the angle of his own shadow.

He leaned over the parapet and called in Phoenikian, "Open the gate!"

On another parapet, below and some distance away, a pale and sun-freckled mercenary with blazing red hair waved in acknowledgment, then turned and bellowed the message toward another.

From voice to voice the message leaped; seconds later the mighty timbers that barred the gate began to creak as hands pulled them from their resting places.

Fury rose up Melchizedek's neck and spread into his face. "What are you *doing*?"

"I, Uncle? I am being king, for so you have made me."

"If you dare to cross me, Agaz—"

"*Adonizedek*," Agaz said coldly. "You hung me with that name; I'll thank you to use it."

Melchizedek went purple, and Agaz turned away to look back down over the parapet.

Below the walls there lay a flat and open area, filled only with scrub grass and scattered spring wildflowers. It surrounded the city, wide to the precise distance of a bowshot from the wall, a ring of land within the range of both arrows from the city and slingstones from the hulking Habiru earthworks.

This would be the killing ground of the coming battle, the slaughterhouse floor over which the Habiru clan chiefs would lead their men against the walls. It had an eerie blasted look, yellowed and sickly in the noon light, as though the blood that it would soon soak up had poisoned it already.

The wind stilled. The sun hung like a brass medallion nailed to a cloudless sky.

A solitary figure moved out from the shadow of the Gate Tower.

Carrying a large satchel over one shoulder, clad only in a breechcloth and sandals and a broad belt of boarskin, she looked outlandish, utterly alien, her flesh striped with patterns of vivid blue, eldritch spirals curling out from her bared breasts, streaks like lightning from her eyes, hair spiked with blue mud into a fantastical sunburst helmet.

She walked parallel to the walls, along the middle of the killing ground, slowly, thumbs hooked in her belt, almost sauntering.

A hundred thousand eyes followed her every step.

Melchizedek said, "What in the Name of Merciful El is *that*?"

As if in answer a shout went up, first from tribal mercenaries of the Isle of the Mighty, dour Picts, then joined by the laughing bellows of the Gaels, and soon picked up by Hittite and Greek and Phrygian and Philistine.

*Barra! Barra Coll Eigg Rhum!*

The name became a cheer.

As she passed beneath the Citadel walls, she looked up and her painted face split into a fierce grin.

Agaz shook his head, marveling. More than anything else, she looked like she was enjoying the attention.

"All right," Melchizedek hissed petulantly. "All right. She has gone out. But I can make certain she never comes back in." He swung a hand at the Men of El. "Go and see that the gate is closed and barred. See to it personally."

As the man ran off to comply, Agaz said mildly, "No need for that."

"I think there is," Melchizedek sneered. "That woman is under sentence of death. Let the Habiru fulfill it."

"What I meant," Agaz went on, "is that the gate is *already* closed and barred."

Barra's heart hammered under the hot noon sun.

Her jaunty walk was entirely an act; under her breath she muttered prayers that the Habiru wouldn't start shooting at her until she got within spitting distance of the wellhouse in the Kidron.

It was the only cover she had.

The creak of the gate as it closed behind her had made everything suddenly real. Now she was out here to bet her life—everyone's life— on her wits and on the intelligence she'd gotten from Sheshai.

*He was their slave for ten years,* she told herself for the thousandth time. *Slaves know things about their masters that the masters themselves never learn.*

Out here beyond the walls, with the stares of tens of thousands of Habiru beating down on her like the sun, she couldn't find a lot of comfort in that.

Worse, between her nerves and the noonday heat, she was starting to sweat. What might happen if the blue-dyed mud that painted her body started to rinse off, she didn't want to think about.

She reached the wellhouse, passed it casually, trying not to look like it had been her destination.

She faced the Habiru and slung the satchel she wore behind her back so that she could put both fists upon her hips. "Well?" she shouted. "I'm here!"

In the Rite of War she had performed this dawn in the Ba'alath, she had ritually joined herself with the Earth, the Sky, and the Sea; she wore their symbols painted on her body with clay from the tree roots in the Ba'alath, colored with the powdered extract of the bark of a small shrub from the Isle of the Mighty, and moistened with her spit and nine drops of her blood. The knife which had drawn that blood, she carried naked in her right hand; the Rite required that she carry it naked until it had been used in battle.

It was potent magic, was the Rite of War. She performed it only at great need, for its single side effect was appalling.

As she walked between the city wall and the massed Habiru, the *sceon tiof* lived behind her eyes and cradled her with its power. Every man she looked upon, she knew as a brother; she knew better than she knew her sons.

She was looking forward to learning what the *sceon tiof* might show her about this Joshua ben Nun.

She had seen a great deal with it already this morning.

Lurking in Jebusi, hiding from the Men of El who sought her life, she had seen the city itself. She had seen that this siege was only the beginning.

No matter what the outcome, battles would be fought here for centuries. For thousands of years, men would shed each other's blood at the intersection of the Kidron and Hinnom Valleys. Not only in these hills but in the plains below, these lands would bathe in blood from now until the end of time; a day would come when men would *invent* reasons to fight here, make them up out of smoke and daydreams, because the land itself called out for battle.

The fundamental nature of the *mâtat Urusalim*, the Land of the House of Peace, was war.

She was sure it hadn't always been this way, and she couldn't see what had caused the change, but she didn't give a rat's ass about the land. This was for the people that lived there, and for the Goddess that loved them.

*And for the money,* she told herself; a *lot* of money.

When she had looked upon the Habiru Host, these tens of thousands of men drawn up in ranks with their weapons and siege ladders ready, more arriving behind them every minute, all poised, waiting only for a single command to attack, in their rows from the Gate along her stroll over the blasted ring below the walls, what she had seen had surprised her.

Looking on the besieging army, this titanic massing of force that slowly gathered itself to crush Jebusi and slaughter every living thing within its walls, she had expected to see its fury, its greed for loot, its *hunger*; she'd expected the Host to appear to her *sceon tiof* as a ravening beast, drooling with mad, foaming bloodlust, crouched to spring.

And she had seen those things, scattered here and there among the Host, tiny pockets of madness and greed, but far less of them than she had seen, for example, among the mercenaries that lined Jebusi's walls.

What she saw most, when she looked on them, was fear.

The songs they sang while they built up their earthworks, the laughter and the chatter among the camps, all these were precisely equivalent to her swagger as she walked toward the wellhouse.

Sheshai had told her they had a saying, a proverb: "The fear of God is the beginning of wisdom."

She could have thought of them as dogs: whipped, cringing, begging for a chance to obey their master—but the *sceon tiof* showed her also a fierce, stubborn pride, enormous courage, and the kind of passionate devotion to each other that one sees in resistance fighters among a conquered people.

These weren't dogs. They were strong, proud, and warlike men that someone was trying to *turn into* dogs, using beatings, starvation, terror, all the cruelly efficient weapons of a dog trainer; the weapons of a slave master.

The Israelites were fighting back every step of the way—Sheshai had told her how they'd turned countless times to other gods to rescue them, and how each time their god had come among them as a master retrieves escaped slaves, slaughtering at random until their spirit broke and the survivors came crawling back.

They had not chosen Yahweh; they had never had a choice. He had chosen them.

Perhaps the better word would be *captured*.

Now through the Host strode toward her a man who could only be Joshua ben Nun.

She hadn't seen him this morning—she'd been still in the Ba'alath when he'd addressed the city—but she could not be mistaken.

His back was straight, as a temple pillar is straight. Like a pillar, it did not bend under the titanic burden it bore, but was compressed ever straighter, its flaws crushed away until only its essential core remained. Strings of hair trailed down from his sun-blackened scalp, and his unbound beard flowed across a chest as massive as a bull's.

The *sceon tiof* saw him clearly.

Here was a man who was pure warrior, forged as a weapon is forged, a sword annealed and tempered and crafted by a master smith to fit precisely in the hand of his creator. Perfectly made, of a single piece through and through, every part integral to every other, no more capable of weakness or falsehood than is a sword itself.

And yet his features bore the scars of drink and doubt, of countless wineskins drained to ease some unbearable pain, half-concealed even from himself.

*He was taken,* she thought, *as I took the stone for my axe. Neither I nor Yahweh ever thought to ask the materials we carved for their permission.*

She understood him, in her head; but in her heart the Jericho dead screamed for vengeance.

Behind his shoulder marched a broad-shouldered man wearing the vestments of a priest, his hair shining and curly as the fleece of a black ram. *Loving Mother,* Barra thought at random, *they sure grow 'em pretty around these parts.*

The *sceon tiof* saw this man clearly, too. Here was the dog, indeed, that she hadn't seen among the Host of Israel; but he was no whipped cur. He was a guard dog, a fighting dog, walking with stiff-legged pride and fierce strength: he lived to obey. His master's word was his only law, and any that defied his master would fall with this man's teeth buried in their throat.

*No wonder I like him,* she thought. *He's a human Graegduz.*

The breeze in the Kidron swirled for just an instant, bringing to Barra the scents of the perfumed oils that glittered in his hair and beard, as well as the acidic sour-grape smell that she assumed came from Joshua himself—the smell of an old man, sweating wine.

Joshua waved his follower to a halt and came forward a few paces alone, until he was close enough that Barra could see the red tracery that discolored his nose and the whites of his eyes. He leaned on the knotted staff he bore, a staff worn and darkened with use, but bearing a fresh white scar on its head.

"That," he said heavily, with a pointed look at the knife in Barra's hand, "is no herald's staff."

"True enough," she said. "And this is no parley."

Joshua's only response was a pensive compression of his lips, but the big man at his back stepped forward, affronted. "What do you mean by that?" the follower barked. "Are you *threatening*—?"

"You tell him, old man," Barra said. The voices within her snarled and spat, and she fought against a trembling that started in her guts and wanted to seize her limbs. "We both know you called me out here to kill me."

"You *dare*?" the follower snapped. "You dare to question—"

Joshua silenced him with a glance. He turned back to Barra, and sighed tiredly; his shoulders seemed to settle themselves, as though he were a wrestler, preparing for a match.

"It is better this way, perhaps."

"Sure it is," she said. "Saves us both a lot of breath we'd be using to bullshit each other."

The man at Joshua's shoulder gaped at them openly. "Joshua—Uncle—what . . . ?"

"My aide," Joshua said, with a nod of introduction. "Phinehas ben Eleazar. I am Joshua ben Nun."

"Ay, I know. Barra Coll Eigg Rhum. Pleased to meetcha." *Phinehas ben Eleazar,* she thought, filing the man's face away in her memory. That would probably make him the son of this High Priest of Yahweh that Sheshai had told her about.

"I am curious," Joshua said, "why you have come out, knowing that you are to die."

The knife in her right hand twitched, as though it were a living thing. She bared her teeth. "Why did you?"

"Uncle—" Phinehas sputtered. "This treachery—you *admit to it?* I don't understand—I *can't* understand!"

Joshua never took his eyes off Barra. "*You* understand," he said to her, his face as hard as slate.

"Sure," she said. She glanced at Phinehas, and she could almost feel sorry for the hurt and confusion painted on his open face.

"It's a god thing, Phinehas. Honor, integrity, honesty—these are *human* things, between men, and women. As soon as gods like Yahweh start mixing in our business, or us in theirs, all that shit goes right out the window. Yahweh doesn't give a rat's ass about honesty. He wants *results.*"

The aide's handsome face suffused with blood, as though she'd delivered a deadly insult, but Barra had lost interest in the aide's delicate sensibilities, and Joshua had never seemed concerned with them in the first place.

"You're shorter than I expected," he said.

She looked him up and down: he was nearly the size of Leucas. "So are you."

"I suppose," Joshua said slowly, "I wanted to see what you are, Barra Coll Eigg Rhum. I wanted to see a woman who can be an Enemy of God—who can stand against an angel of the Lord without fear."

"*Without fear* might be a little bit of an exaggeration," she said. "What's that you call your demon? An *angel?*—a messenger, huh? Well, I met your messenger, and I got your fucking message."

"And yet you stand here before us all, even now."

"That's the easy part. When pursued by angry spirits, you run like shit from a sick cow for holy ground. All I did," she said, gesturing to the blue mud designs that painted her body, "is take my holy ground with me."

"Pagan magic," Joshua said, nodding judiciously. "You still haven't answered my question."

The knife's hilt grew warm against her palm, and the dead hissed inside her skull, but she stood up straight and mastered her trembling and thought, *I know you, Joshua ben Nun. I have seen you.* She knew his heart of hearts, and she put as much of that supremely compassionate knowing into her words as her fatigue-roughened voice would allow.

"I came out here to ask you to call off this war."

Phinehas gasped at her audacity, but Joshua only frowned, and squinted at her sadly.

"It is not up to me," he said.

"I know that," Barra said. "I know that if the decision was yours, none of us would be here now. I know the struggle within your heart."

Joshua stiffened and his face went pale, then reddened like the rising sun. "What do you know?" he snapped harshly. "What can you possibly know? Nothing! You know *nothing!*"

A vein pulsed in his forehead, matching the furious knots that rose around his eyes and up the sides of his neck. "Look at you! A painted savage—a pagan whore with her breasts bare! *What can you know?*"

Barra matched his fury with a level, passionless stare. Again, as she had with Sheshai in the Ba'alath, she summoned the goddesses to stand at her shoulder, to see through her eyes, and add their power to her voice.

"I know that the land on which you tread is sacred to the Lady," she said evenly. "I know that I am Her chosen Champion. I know that most of the blood that will spill into this earth will not be Jebusite. I offer you this chance to give over this war, Joshua ben Nun. Pack your tents. Go home."

With her eyes upon him, even Joshua ben Nun, the Lord's Anointed, could not summon the words to answer her. He stared past her, through her, inexpressible pain in his eyes, and she knew he was looking at a future in which every man he'd brought with him on this march returned to his own home, to his wife, his children, his own lands, his parents.

Phinehas strode forward now, blood suffusing his face; his voice was barely more than a strangled croak. "The God of Jacob calls for this city's destruction. *Yahweh*—the True God, not your lumpish whore carved of wood! How dare you presume to command the Lord's Anointed?"

"The Lady does not command," Barra said softly. "This is not a command. It is an *offer*."

Finally, Joshua found his voice. "It cannot be. Yahweh has decided that Jerusalem will be destroyed as though it had never stood. The only man who might have persuaded Him differently has been dead for twenty years."

Phinehas stared at Joshua, aghast. "Uncle, you speak as though you wish this could be done! To defy God is a sin that can only be expiated in death—and the sins of the fathers are to be visited upon the children unto the third and fourth generation! The destruction of Jerusalem was decreed on the very day that Adonizedek stole his son out of the hand of Manasseh; when he set his will against the Will of God."

"Is *that* what this is all about?" Barra said with a dawning incredulous smile. She had seen all that she needed; there was nothing to be done now except to move on to the next phase of her plan. She was reluctant to begin; one of the sad effects of her *sceon tiof* insight into Joshua was that she really kind of liked the old man, and pitied him.

But what was to be done, had to be done. "This is about Agaz?" she asked. "This Yahweh of yours is kind of a pinhead, isn't he?"

They turned to her, and the dumbstruck astonishment on their faces drew from her an irrepressible horselaugh.

"That wasn't Adonizedek," she said. "That was *me*."

"You?" Joshua said, his powerful voice gone small with awe. "You stole Prince Agaz from Manasseh? *You?*"

"That's right. And I haven't been paid for it yet, either."

"Then . . ." A new light seemed to enter Joshua's eyes, a sudden clearing of some cloud that had hung within his spirit. "Then *you're* why God has ordained this war. This is all *your* fault—"

He seemed so happy about it, so *relieved*, in some fundamental way, that he'd forgotten everything else. *Can't have that,* Barra thought.

"My fault?" She snorted, and pitched her voice so that she could be heard clearly both by the mercenaries on the wall and the Habiru that stood upon their earthworks.

"Are you trying to tell me that this Almighty God of yours lets himself be pushed around by a little half-naked Pict girl? What kind of a sissy god are you following here, anyway?"

Phinehas spluttered, and hoots from the mercenaries brought a dangerous flush to Joshua's cheeks; from the Habiru Host came only a frozen, deathly silence.

"Hey, *Israel!*" she called. "Your crops getting a little dry? No problem! Tell this Yahweh whiner of yours that if he doesn't send rain, I'm gonna kick his ass!"

The hoots from the walls at her back swelled into jeering laughter, as Jebusites among the mercenaries translated for their benefit. Phinehas was livid; he started for her, and Barra lifted her knife invitingly, but Joshua restrained him with a backward sweep of one thick arm.

"Have a care, Barra Coll Eigg Rhum—" he began, but before he could summon the full thunder of his voice, she cut him off with a scornful laugh.

"Or what? You're gonna *kill* me? *Fuck* you," she said, dismissing him with a snap of her fingers. She spread her arms wide to include the entire Habiru Host. "Fuck you all! And *fuck your scabrous old blood-drunk sack of shit god Yahweh!*"

"Just so," Joshua said coldly. Staring at her fixedly, he raised one arm as though reaching for a cloud, then with decisive emphasis, he let it fall to his side.

At this signal, ten thousand Habiru warriors boiled up over the earthworks, and more joined them every second; the rush began at Joshua's back and spread outward in a wave in both directions to encircle the city and meet on the far side. The cry went up from ten, twenty, thirty thousand throats:

*Attack! Attack! For the God of Jacob! Attack!*

And Barra, standing alone in the Kidron Valley with numberless Habiru warriors howling down upon her like a cresting wave, thought, *Now, that's more like it.*

# The First Day

**L**eucas had been gnawing on the inside of his lower lip as he watched Barra and the two Habiru speak, far away outside the walls; this was as close to fidgety as he ever got. When the younger one started toward her, he gave a relaxed smile. He looked at Sarah, who sat beside him, supporting herself by leaning on the windowsill, and he offered her a silent wink as he lifted one of the five large tar-covered globes at the base of the window.

A fuse of twisted cloth protruded from one side, smelling strongly of naphtha. Leucas lit this fuse at the lamp beside the window, stood, and even as the massed Habiru Host broke into a run to charge the walls, he cocked his arm, reared back and threw this globe so high and far it seemed to vanish into the limitless blue of the noonday sky.

As soon as he released it, he bent to pick up and light another; he threw them so hard and far that two more were in the air by the time the first one struck, only five paces from where Barra stood, by the wellhouse in the Kidron Valley.

The first globe hit the ground and exploded with a blinding flash and a deafening boom; the several hundred charging Habiru nearest to the wellhouse screamed in sudden terror at this inexplicable thunderbolt and threw themselves flat to the ground.

Whistling down from the clear blue sky came another globe, and another, then two more; all of these burst with very little report, spewing forth instead a thick and choking white cloud that spread like oil down the slope of the valley, filled it, and began to climb again, obscuring all vision within its scope.

Confused shouting took the place of battle cries, there in the Kidron, as the frightened Habiru blundered about within the dense smoke.

"FIND THAT PAGAN WHORE!" came the roar of Joshua. "FIND HER AND KILL HER!"

But as the smoke spread farther and farther and began to thin away, exposing the Habiru beneath it, arrows rained down upon them from the wall above, finding flesh among the stones. Joshua's cries began to drown within a sea of shouted pain and dismay, and the Israelites turned; some, wounded, staggered back up the slope toward their defensive earthworks.

The rest, every man of them, stormed the walls.

Barra had withheld her hand from striking Joshua before the smoke had filled the Valley because she needed him alive and nearby to discourage the Habiru slingers. Once the smoke closed over them both, she had no need for him at all.

She lunged for him, her knife seeking his heart.

A loose stone shifted under her sandal, and she stumbled, dropping her knife as she caught herself with her hands and rolled to her feet. She picked up her knife once more, but by that time Joshua could not be seen within the dense and drifting smoke, nor could Phinehas.

*Shit,* she thought. *Should have done him while I could, and just taken my fucking chances with the slingers.*

She shifted the satchel's strap higher onto her shoulder and moved downslope, following the thickest of the smoke. She had a lot of ground to cover before this shit started to clear away, and plenty to do once she got there.

She heard Joshua's bellow from not far away, though, and for one indecisive moment she paused, weighing her chances of finding him within this cloud; she felt a sharp twinge at her passing wish that she had her axe with her. She missed its cold solidity beneath her hand as she tried to decide.

Then, for one miraculous moment, a rift appeared within the cloud, a channel that opened precisely between them.

He saw her at the same instant that she saw him, and despite the screams and shouts and sounds of battle that rang out upon all sides, for that one timeless moment they were the only two people in the world.

He was a bare stone's throw away, too far for her to charge before the rift would close and he'd be lost again within the smoke.

She lifted her knife above her shoulder.

His eyes crinkled, and he spread his arms wide, as though offering his embrace.

She snapped her arm forward, and her knife streaked toward his belly.

It tumbled slowly in the air, spinning through a single revolution until it hit him square, an inch above his navel, and bounced from his robes and fell to the ground.

It had hit him pommel first.

Barra stood frozen, openmouthed, too shocked even to feel the anger of frustration. She hadn't missed a throw that easy since she was ten years old.

She remembered Sheshai's words, back in the ruined temple of the moon-god in the ruined city of Jericho: *They say his god protects him, that he can't be killed, that he can't even be hurt.*

Despite the heat of the sun and stifling closeness of the cloud that enveloped them, she felt a chill of gooseflesh up her legs and along her arms.

He leveled his arm at her as though his gesture could strike her dead. "SHE'S RIGHT THERE, YOU FOOLS! TAKE HER!"

She clutched her satchel to her side and dodged away into the smoke.

She had too much still to do, and only one knife left.

At the dull thump of the explosion overhead, Sheshai kicked through the wall, and the stones crumbled away from his foot. Faint light filtered down the well from the wellhouse above. He turned back to Kheperu for one flashed grin and a muttered, "May Tchera'khu bring luck to us both," and then he vanished up the winding stair above the wellspring.

Kheperu looked up the shaft at Sheshai's legs vanishing into the milky light above. "All right," he said to himself. "I can do this. I can. These are nothing but ignorant *shasu*. Like taking sweets from a baby."

Like taking sweets from an enormous, ill-tempered, really *vicious* baby—one that will tear your fucking arms off if it catches you so much as sniffing around its cradle . . .

With a deep and reluctant sigh, Kheperu climbed the stair, wincing at every twinge from his back.

He came out of the wellhouse, blinking dazedly through the pall that still hung over the valley, the smoke that blazed a brilliant white in the bright sun.

Shouts and screams and battle cries sounded from all sides, though all he could see were indistinct shapes moving through the smoke; he peered around himself, but Sheshai was nowhere to be seen, and no more was Barra. An instant later, an arrow hit the stone of the wellhouse beside him with a sharp crack, and bounced up to rap his elbow.

This was more than enough to remind him to get moving.

He stumbled downslope toward the pool below the city, angling outward closer to the earthworks. As the smoke thinned around him, he saw that the Israelites threw themselves recklessly at the city from all sides, scrambling up the steep, nearly clifflike slopes through the rain of arrows and stones from above. With alarming dexterity, they seated their siege ladders and swung on up them, while their companions raked defenders from the walls with volley after volley of slingstones.

He shook his head in private derision—following this primitive tactic could easily cost the Israelites twenty men to each defender. His derision faded as he realized that if Leucas' estimate of their eventual numbers was correct, they could do this until every single defender was gone and still have more than half their men left to take the city.

And the ratio would drop as defenders fell and as arrows ran short. The defenders upon the walls would not be able to replenish their supply from the return fire; few of the Habiru had bows at all, preferring their traditional cheap and deadly slings.

And years would pass before an army that holds these valleys would run short of stones . . .

Even as Kheperu watched, he began to wonder just how primitive this tactic truly was. By attacking from all sides simultaneously, they spread the defense; the mercenaries on the walls could not concentrate in any one place to repel them.

Even now, only minutes since the attack began, Kheperu could see scattered knots of hand-to-hand fighting atop Jebusi's walls.

Kheperu tried to swallow through his dry throat. For all he could see, the city might fall before Barra's plan had a chance to work.

He hustled toward the earthworks as fast as his stubby legs could carry him.

He scrambled up over the nearest berm and slid down its leeward face. Already some casualties were limping and staggering back from the walls, but still the attack swelled as more and more Habiru streamed into the camps surrounding the city.

No one seemed to be paying attention to him so far . . .

He began doing his Confused Old Man walk, a sort of bewildered wandering that shortly caught the attention of a solicitous youth. This young man, a bloodied rag tied around his arm where an arrow had punctured him, very respectfully guided him back into the safety of the nearest camp, before returning to the fight.

Kheperu spent a moment turning in dazed circles, staring at the sky, and then began to wail in a high and piercing nasal screech.

"The Word of God comes to pass before your eyes! Yahweh speaks, and you do not listen! You are a stubborn, stiffnecked people, bent upon your own destruction! *Hear the Word of God!*"

Apparently Sheshai had given him the proper formula; he certainly had their attention now. Wounded and whole alike, every man within the considerable range of his voice turned to stare at him, the elders among them muttering to the younger men, translating his Egyptian into their tribal slang.

Kheperu spun faster, dancing into a dizzying whirl.

"Israel goes down to destruction before Jerusalem! Again Israel has turned her back upon Yahweh, and His Wrath descends upon you all! I gave you this prophecy at dawn: that Yahweh's thunder would strike, to teach you that Joshua leads you astray from the will of the Lord! The Lord spoke, but you would not hear! *Now you go to your deaths upon the wall, because you defy the will of the Lord!*"

Now men began to gather around him.

"I *told* you! I speak the Word of God! You have seen the First Sign of which I warned you, but *you still do not believe!*"

"Easy to say that now," one man snorted nearby, his Egyptian clear, though thickly accented. "I didn't hear you prophesying *shit*. Hey, this morning I told everybody some stinking Egyptian would walk into camp claiming to be a prophet—I guess I'm a prophet, too, eh?"

Kheperu stopped his whirl and fixed the man with an imperious glare. "I spoke, and it has come to pass. I am a true prophet of the Lord."

The fellow snorted again, and several other men laughed derisively.

So it went for some few minutes; Kheperu continued to insist that he'd predicted the entire thing, while the crowd turned more and more against him. Really, for superstitious primitives, these Habiru had nasty suspicious natures . . . He began to sweat profusely beneath his robes and his armor; where in staggering fuck was Sheshai?

*I knew this would happen,* Kheperu told himself. *I knew it.*

The mutters of the crowd began to be talk of false prophets, and stoning, and still there was no sign of Sheshai. More and more men joined the crowd, more interested in this than in rejoining the attack which still raged on not far away; after all, stoning a man was more fun than storming a city wall, and infinitely safer.

The crowd now numbered several hundred, and their battle nerves had them in a jumpy, aggressive mood. Men edged closer to him, gathering their courage to place their hands upon him and drag him from the camp.

But then an unfamiliar voice came from the fringes of the mob. "It's *true*! I heard him! He spoke in the western camps this morning, and he said that a thunderbolt would strike between Joshua and the woman of Jebusi!"

"There, you see?" Kheperu crowed triumphantly.

The disbelievers turned to each other, and then looked around themselves. "Who said that?"

Another voice came from a different part of the crowd. "I was there, too! I *saw*! He is a true prophet of the Lord!"

The crowd parted, showing a man in the striped galabiyeh of a Hivite slave; his face bore curving black scars and an expression of pious awe.

Sheshai said, "I stood as close to him as I am standing now. Everything he says is true."

That was the agreed-upon signal; Kheperu smiled upon him benevolently.

The disbeliever sneered, "But this is only a slave! Should we take his word?"

"No!" Kheperu barked rapidly. "Yahweh speaks to me. A new sign shall come before you all, that my words are His very Voice. There is a man among us who does not believe—there is a man that doubts me in his heart of hearts, and sneers at the word of the Lord."

"Only one?" the disbeliever said with broad sarcasm.

Kheperu sailed on, pretending he had not heard. "Even now, Yahweh draws back His Arm—but in His Mercy, he shall let the disbeliever live. *Strike instead his fire, Yahweh!* Strike the food he had thought to eat! *Let your thunder show my truth!*"

And only a few paces away, the cookfire nearest to the mob exploded with a *boom* that shook the earth on which they stood.

Kheperu raked the crowd with a stare as bright and glittering as an eagle's, while cinders of reeking brimstone rained around them.

They stood in silence, and the disbeliever looked decidedly pale.

*We're off to a running start,* Kheperu thought.

He lifted his arm and intoned, "This is the Word of the Lord. Let it be heard throughout the camps of Israel. Yahweh commands that you cease this blasphemous violation. The thunderbolt at Joshua's feet was only the first of the Signs and the Wonders that the Lord shall do before you . . ."

Joshua stood by the spring-fed pool, his thick arms crossed over his chest. He occasionally glanced up at the city above, where his people still threw themselves against the walls, but for the most part, he watched Phinehas—and the small group of men he'd dragooned—examine the slaves.

Before allowing any of the slaves to depart with their water jugs and filled skins from the pool, the hoods of their burnooses, and their veils, and anything else that they wore to cover their heads, were removed or pulled aside by one of Phinehas' men.

Phinehas had had some trouble rounding up men for this hunt; all the Israelites in the area believed that this Barra Coll Eigg Rhum was some sort of desert demon who had vanished in the flash and the smoke, and gone back to the land of the spirits from which she'd sprung.

Joshua knew better, knew that she was flesh and blood. Furthermore, he had a bloody good idea where she'd gone.

It was the satchel that she had carried: that was his clue. That satchel could have held clothes. It would take only a moment to scrub the paint from her face; then a loose robe thrown on and a burnoose to cover the mud-spiked hair, and she could walk among the Children of Israel with no one the wiser.

She was loose in the camps. Joshua was sure of it.

When he explained this to his aide, Phinehas had instantly volunteered to lead the search. They started down here at the pool because it was straight downslope of the cloud; she could have easily made it here under cover of the smoke and then blended in with the water carriers.

One of the slaves seemed to hang back reluctantly from the searchers. Joshua suddenly strode forward and snatched her wrist roughly. She let out a little squeal, but she didn't struggle.

"You avoid these men," Joshua snapped. "Why? What are you afraid of?"

She seemed too small to be this fearsome mercenary warrior, but Joshua recalled that the whore's apparent size was deceptive; though she'd seemed large and impressively powerful when he'd first seen her from some distance away, when he'd come close he'd discovered that she was so tiny that the top of her head had not even reached his chin.

This slave kept her eyes properly downcast, and she spoke in a frightened, doelike voice. "I, I, I don't know, master . . . the fighting . . . all the blood . . ."

"Look at me when I speak to you, child." He took her chin and forced her face up.

She had eyes of brilliant, luminous blue-green, the color of nearby seas on a cloudless day. Joshua couldn't recall ever having seen eyes of quite that color—and there was something striking about the way she looked at him, too, as though she saw within him, and through him, as though she *knew* him . . .

He had been looked at that way only minutes ago.

"I'm sorry . . ." she whispered. "My master, he does not wish that I look upon him . . . I'm sorry . . ."

And her throat, the soft flesh beneath her chin, was *damp*—it could have been sweat; the day was warm.

It could have been water used to wash away blue paint.

A face could be washed in seconds; mud-caked hair, on the other hand . . .

Without warning, he snatched off the hood of her burnoose.

She gave another little squeal, but the hair beneath was dry, and shining, and black as a spear shaft of ebony.

"Master . . ." she whimpered, "Master, you're frightening me . . ."

"Uncle!" Phinehas called from below. "We've found something! Come and look!"

He retained his grip upon her chin a moment longer—dry hair or no, those eyes . . .

Perhaps he should kill her anyway. She was only a slave. He could give her master an ox, or one of his own slaves . . .

*"Uncle!"*

She said, "Please, you're hurting me . . ."

He released her. "You can go, child. Return to your master with his water."

"Thank you," she said humbly. "Thank you." Pulling her hood back up to cover her head, she moved off toward the camps.

Joshua stumped down over the broken ground to where Phinehas stood. His aide pointed to something that was lodged in a shadowed crack between two sizable rocks. Joshua peered at it, moving closer for a better view.

It looked like a dead animal of some kind.

"What is it?"

Phinehas bent down grimly and pulled it out into the sunlight.

It was a handful of long and tangled hair, spiked hard and trailing clods of dried blue-grey mud.

Phinehas said, "It's a wig."

"A *wig*!" Joshua roared. He spun furiously. That slave with the sea-green eyes!

But all he could see was the crowded camps below, the gently swaying slaves vanishing among the tents with their burdens of water. From here, there was no way to tell them apart.

"I had her," he snarled. "Phinehas, I had her in my hand."

"Uncle . . ." Phinehas began helplessly.

"It does not matter," Joshua said through clenched teeth. "Because we know that she is out here. And we know that she is in the guise of a Hivite slave."

He turned back to his aide and allowed himself a humorless smile.

"Better still: she does not know that we know."


The shouts and screams, wails of the dying, smells of blood and shit and the clash of weapons drove Agaz to a sudden decision. With a snarl he pushed away from the parapet and shoved through the knot of El's Men behind him.

"Where do you think you're going?" Melchizedek snapped.

"To my chambers," Agaz said, walking away.

"Why? Is your heart so weak? Can you not bear to watch this battle, which you could have prevented? Can you not bear to watch lives lost that you could have saved—that you could *still* save!"

Agaz stopped, and turned back to face his uncle. "In my chambers," he said evenly, "is my armor. My shield and my spear. Whether I am indeed Adonizedek, or in fact still merely Agaz, my place is upon the wall."

"You cannot," Melchizedek said firmly. "Your life is too valuable as a negotiating point. If we are to save the city, we must be able to offer your life to the Habiru as atonement. You cannot risk it in mere battle."

"If we are to save this city," Agaz replied with perfect calm, "we must *fight*. And if these useless cowards you call Men of El wish to keep their watch over me, they'll have to put on their armor and bloody-fucking well fight at my side."

He strode through the knot of El's Men, and none of them dared put out a hand to stop him.

Leucas watched the battle from the window, every beat of his heart aching to join the mercenaries upon the wall. He winced at every cut, cheered every toppling siege ladder, groaned each time a defender fell.

Once the battle had begun, Sarah had become pale and faint once more; Leucas had helped her return to the couch, where she lay now with a wet cloth folded across her feverish forehead.

The smell of blood and clash of weapons had roused Graegduz as well. He whined sleepily from his pallet, stirring as though he wanted to rise.

"Yes, I know," Leucas told him from the window seat. "I'd like to get my teeth into a few of them myself."

When he watched the fighting he could not help but think of his armor, lost in the mountains. He kept a wistful hand upon the hilt of his iron scimitar, but it was just as well that he was stuck on guard duty up here, he decided. Without armor, he'd be useless on the wall. In that kind of close-quarter confusion they'd carve him like a roast.

"Still, though . . ." he muttered, and: "Even so . . ."

Footsteps in the room behind him made him whirl, his scimitar scraping free from its homemade scabbard—but it was the two hulking Pict mercenaries, looking rather sheepish but also eager.

"All right?" one of them said in thick Phoenikian, gesturing toward the window. "Watch fight?"

Leucas shrugged. "Mmm, door?" he asked, nodding out toward the outer apartment.

"Mnn, locked. Chair, table," the Pict said, miming blocking the door with the items he mentioned. "Break, and we hear. All right? Watch?"

Leucas nodded, allowing himself a broken smile. He slid his precious iron blade back into its place at his belt. "Watch."

The Pict grinned in response, and said carefully, "Thank you."

As they came to the window, he yelped something that was probably a Pictish curse, and hopped on one foot, holding his other in both hands.

Chuckling loudly, his partner lifted his sandal to crush an enormous scorpion, a big scuttling bastard nearly the size of Leucas' fist and the color of desert sand. His foot came down hard and the scorpion splattered across the thick woven rug, crackling and squirting like a nutshell with rotted meat inside.

Leucas frowned at the mess on the rug. He hadn't seen a scorpion since they'd left Jericho. How had one that big gotten all the way in here?

Now the wounded Pict gingerly put his foot down and began to limp painfully to the window seat, much to the amusement of his partner; then his face went red and he began to make choking noises in the back of his throat, which made his partner laugh even louder.

One step later he stiffened, clawed at his throat, and pitched forward onto his face, his limbs jerking in spastic convulsion. Leucas was at his side in an instant; he rolled him onto his back while the other Pict stared in confusion, suspended on the cusp of laughter and fear.

The Pict's face went from red to blue, and his lips turned black, and his tongue swelled into a blue-grey stalk sticking out from his mouth; he clawed at his throat until blood came under his fingers, and Leucas restrained his arms, but only for a moment; soon the strength went out of them as the light fled from the Pict's staring eyes.

Crawling up over the dead Pict's chest came another scorpion as large as the first, its pedipalps lifted threateningly and its powerful tail poised to sting.

With a cry, Leucas flicked at it backhanded, sweeping it off the dead man's chest, and the other Pict stomped it, his teeth bared in a naked snarl—and an instant later the Pict cried out, his eyes wide and terrified, leaping away. He fell to the floor with a crash and clutched at his ankle; from where he had been standing, three more scorpions scuttled toward him.

The rug over which they skittered began to ripple and pulse as things ran beneath it like rats under a blanket. Leucas whipped the rug aside.

There were hundreds of them.

Up from the cracks between the floor slats they came, a cascade like sand pouring uphill, out of splits and crevices and innumerable tiny cracks that were far too small to admit these creatures . . .

They weren't coming in from outside at all.

It was as though, Leucas realized with a knot of revulsion rising into his throat, every grain of sand that had ever lodged in the tiny imperfections of this floor was ballooning to the size of a rat, growing pincers and a sting.

They rustled as they came, like dry leaves blowing over a rocky hillside. They filled the center of this room and the room beyond; some had already made it to the walls and climbed upward; some already surrounded the archway that opened upon the shattered floorless bed-chamber beyond.

The room sizzled with their odor. Though the scar tissue that blocked his sinuses prevented Leucas from smelling them, he could *taste* their reek, a rank and musky back-of-the-throat foulness like the spoor of the cockroaches that infest Tyrian inns.

The other Pict struggled on the floor, thrashing in convulsions, smashing scorpions by futile hundreds; he was already covered with them, on his chest, his arms, his face, their tails striking again and again into his neck, his hands, pinning his eyelids to his corneas . . .

And they converged upon the couch where Sarah lay.

Leucas' horrified paralysis broke and he leaped to her side. He swept her up into his arms and jumped onto the couch, holding her high as though that would somehow protect her.

Something large landed on the back of his neck, tiny clawed feet digging for purchase into his hair.

He looked up in time to see another one drop toward him from the ceiling.

Sarah, in his arms, hissed something in Canaanite and slapped one away; the one tangled in his hair she caught by its barbed tail and yanked it free.

"Leucas! *Seshet—seshet!*" she cried.

He had no idea what that meant. Kheperu had told him: *Under no circumstances are you to leave this room. Outside, you have no pro-tection at all.*

Leucas grunted. Some protection.

He looked down into the face of the woman in his arms, and he winked.

She gasped and clutched him tightly as he sprang from the couch to the windowsill in a single bound, caught himself there with one hand while the other supported the Lady's Maid, and peered down over the dizzying drop.

Six stories to the stone-flagged courtyard below: a killing fall. A pair of broken legs was the best he could hope for; more likely he'd kill them both.

He saw no sense in that sort of surrender: why do the demon's work for it?

He threw himself back from the window, Sarah once again gasp-ing in his arms; he leaped to the couch—flailing his free arm for bal-ance as his momentum caused the couch to skid a couple of spans, nearly dumping him on his back onto the carpet of scorpions, which now scuttled hissing up the legs of the couch. He recovered his precarious balance and judged his distance.

His best jump would take him only two-thirds of the way to the bedchamber door. There had been men working below much of the morning to clear the debris, he knew—he also knew that they weren't finished when the attack began, and nothing had been done down there since then.

It had been a jumbled ruin of shattered stone and splintered timber—but it was only a two-story drop.

Without giving himself time for second thoughts he leaped from the couch. He came down with both feet flat, crushing and crackling and squirting scorpion guts across the floor. Letting his legs bend to take the impact, he leaped again, blindly, his feet slipping in the crunchy paste he'd made of the scorpions he'd landed on, nearly falling, barely clearing the bedchamber door.

The fall took longer than he expected; at each fractional passing second he thought he'd feel the rubble strike his feet, but it seemed he'd never land. And yet, despite the stretching eternity of the fall, he wasn't nearly ready for the spine-crushing impact when he did finally hit.

His knees buckled instantly, and he slammed onto his back on broken stone with Sarah's full weight across his chest. Something broke inside him, and the ragged circle of blue sky through the shattered ceiling far above turned grey, then black.

He snarled the light back into his eyes: unconsciousness was a luxury he could not afford. He rolled to one side, shoving Sarah off. She lay where he pushed her, her mouth working feebly and her limbs twitching, stunned by the fall.

He put fingers to his lips as he'd seen Barra do many times, and he let out a shrill and piercing whistle.

"Graeg!" he called. Barra had taught her partners only a few phrases in Pictish, but this was one of them. "Graegduz! *Oiman nu,* boy! *Oiman!*"

His fingers came away bloody from his lips, and he barely managed to struggle to his feet as the grey wolf hurtled from above. He put up his arms and got under him; the wolf's weight flattened him again, but Graeg managed to stagger to his feet.

Leucas lay on his back for a moment, curled around the jagged pain in his chest.

From the doorway above, scorpions flooded toward them down

the walls. Some of them fell free, from too high up; they landed squirming and broken on the rubble, but it was clear that some would soon be low enough to survive the drop.

He had to keep moving.

He spat blood and sat up.

Graegduz stood panting and whimpering faintly with pain, looking fiercely out from the inverted cone of his postsurgical collar. Fresh blood spread through the bandages on his side, but his bright yellow glare said he could walk—could run, if Leucas asked him to.

Leucas pushed himself to his feet and went to Sarah, crouching beside where she lay gasping across a litter of beam splinters and shattered roof stones.

She met his gaze through eyes filmed with pain and exhaustion. "Leucas," she said softly. "Ba'alath."

Leucas nodded. He'd had that part figured out already.

He gathered her once again into his arms. The hall door stood closed upon this enrubbled room; Leucas splintered it with a kick rather than waste a second to learn if it was locked.

Scorpions rained around them like a desert cloudburst as Leucas and Sarah, with Graegduz just behind, slammed through the corridors of the Citadel, heading for the gates, for the open air, the lower city.

Heading for holy ground.

The long afternoon stretched behind Agaz like a road littered with corpses. With day fading from the sky, he still ran along the wall with armored men at his heels. All day long, wherever men on the walls had come against one another with bronze and furious courage, he had been there. He had shot arrows from the bows of fallen men; he had tipped cauldrons of boiling water; he had stripped the frenzied valor from the breasts of Habiru warriors with the edge of his spear.

Ever in motion, running along the wall, running down into the streets to cut across the city, he had halted the breaking floods sometimes with his presence and voice alone. When arrows ran short, he and his men had knocked down homes near the wall and had run the bricks up by hand to the defenders; a brick hurled down from the height of the wall could kill as surely as any arrow.

Twice during that endless afternoon the Habiru had forced a breach in the defenders and poured down into the streets of Jebusi to burn and loot and slaughter, only to meet there the city's grim prince and men behind him; they fought from house to house, driving the invaders back with implacable ferocity to pin them against the wall's megalithic base and slaughter them.

Night slowly gathered in the sky. Agaz leaned, gasping, upon his spear, and looked with some surprise at the men he'd led this day.

Only three of the self-styled Men of El were left standing, all of them bleeding from minor wounds, as was Agaz himself—but his followers had grown from a handful to a company. As Jebusites fell from his side, fractured by slingstones or hacked by swords or the sharpened shovels the Habiru used for axes, their places had been taken by Philistines and Hittites, by Picts and Kelts and Nubian spearmen.

He had heard the voices of other mercenaries on that long day, muttering among themselves in the broken Phoenikian that passed for a common tongue. He had heard them speak of surrender, of slipping over the walls in the dark of night, of buying their lives by opening the city's gate to the Host of Israel, and he had despised them in his heart, though he had said little and done less.

And yet here beside him now were men just like those, men whose only stake in this city was the silver it paid, and they had fought and bled and died for it. These men had watched Agaz rush to the fight, had watched the men fall at his side, and something in that spectacle had drawn them from their resting places to silently fall in beside him as he ran to his next melee.

Now he spoke to the three remaining Men of El.

"The attack will end with sundown," he said. "You have fought at my side, with honor, all through this bloody day, and now as we take our rest and food this evening, you must choose. Are you Men of El, ready to give up this city and our lives as my uncle demands? Or are you men of Jebusi?"

The three looked at each other, as though each was uncertain what the others would say; they looked mildly surprised at the answers they found in each other's eyes.

One of them stepped forward. "We're *your* men, Prince Agaz. We're with you. As long as you'll have us, we'll be there."

Agaz accepted this with a silent nod, and turned to the assembled mercenaries that made up the balance of his men. "You men can return to your companies this night, with my gratitude for your valiant service. Only stay with me as far as the Citadel, and my own wealth will express my gratitude more keenly."

One of the mercenaries, a gruff Hittite who spoke better Phoenikian than most, gave him an approving nod. "You're a good captain,

Agaz," he grunted. "You ever wanna give up this princing shit, I'd follow you on the road."

"Very well, then," Agaz said, not quite knowing how else to respond to this compliment. "Let's go and see what my uncle has gotten up to since we left."

"*No,* Grandfather!" Rachel's voice came thinly through the heavy barred door, shrill with panic. "No, you *can't*! You'll *fall*!"

The two Men of El posted outside the king's apartment—there, they were quick to inform any who asked, to deter any well-meaning citizen from disturbing the *seriously ill* king—exchanged glances. What was the old fool up to now?

The muted drumming of a tiny fist now came against the inside of the door. "Help me!" she screamed. "You have to help! He'll die! He'll fall and he'll die!"

The smaller El's Man sighed. The old fool had probably climbed up on his bedside table to swat at a fly, or somesuch. He lifted the heavy bar and set it beside the door. He opened the door only a crack to speak with the hysterical princess.

He set his face into what he imagined was paternal concern. "What's the matter?"

"You have to help!" she wailed, pressing herself frantically against the door, pointing back into the room behind her. "He'll *die*!"

"I'm sure he's not in much . . ." His voice trailed off as his gaze followed her pointing finger.

She pointed at an open window.

"Shit!"

"He's climbing down to the fight!" Rachel wailed. "He's *climbing*!"

Both El's Men realized simultaneously that, even supposing the old fool didn't fall to his death, having half the fucking city see the supposedly bedridden king climbing along the Citadel wall would not please Melchizedek one little bit.

The Men of El threw open the door and charged into the room. They ran to the window and leaned out to scan the ledge.

Adonizedek was nowhere to be seen.

From behind them came the crash of the door slamming shut, and the dry wood-on-metal rasp of the bar sliding into place.

They turned around and discovered that they were now entirely alone.

The larger of the two dashed back across the room to yank futilely upon the barred door, which rattled but did not budge.

The smaller one only leaned back upon the windowsill, and said, "This is a problem."

A ring of bonfires blazed upon the eastern ridge of the Kidron Valley, and thousands upon thousands of men converged upon it. Some came bearing bandages from the camps of the wounded; some came with the fierce swagger of men who have faced death and come away unscratched; some came footsore and weary, having only arrived off the march at dusk. Some of them brought their entire households along to watch and listen.

For a new prophet had arisen in Israel, so it was said, and they would hear the Word of God.

The stories had become already extreme, of this man of Egypt who spoke the word of Yahweh. Far from being one of the ragged doom-criers to whom all upon the march had become accustomed, he spoke not in riddle and parable, but in plain language, and God's own thunder had become a sign of his truth.

It was the chance of a Sign that brought them, more surely than any desire for the Word, no matter what they might have claimed. How many times in a man's life does he have the chance to see a real prophet do real signs and wonders?

So by the thousands they came, and listened, and watched.

Kheperu stood in the midst of several thousand curious and anxious Habiru. He tucked his stolen staff in the crook of his arm, and rubbed his hands together to dry them of sweat. It wasn't only his fever that dampened his palms; the Habiru crowded around him, pressing close to beg his blessing or touch his hand, some only to stroke the filthy hem of his ragged robe. Even in the chill of the clear spring night, so many bodies and so much breath warmed him like high summer in the Delta.

He had to struggle to keep a leer from his face. Being the center of so much attention had a rather thrilling effect on him, one that had only increased as the day wore on; he'd developed an erection by midafternoon, one that still showed no sign of abating. It had become positively painful, and for the thousandth time today he cursed the rigid Law of Israel. If he'd pulled this act in a *civilized* country, his hosts would have fallen all over themselves to provide for this particular need.

This was yet another grudge he held against these *shasu* bastards.

He raised his arms once again, ignoring the aches this brought from his shoulders and back—how many times had he done this

already today?—and the thousands around him fell silent to hear his
words.

"The Second Sign comes tomorrow!" he called. "The Flame of
Yahweh shall descend upon the Tabernacle in rebuke to Israel! But
*even then*, you stubborn and stiffnecked people, you will not repent!
You will see the truth in the Tabernacle's flame, but you shall seek to
deny! Not until Egypt Herself mounts upon Gilgal will you admit the
truth! This is the Third Sign, and you shall see it on the Third Day! The
Hammer of Egypt shall crush Israel against the Jebusite Anvil! *Flee
the Wrath of the Lord!*"

He went on, improvising in this vein. Really, this prophecy business was all too easy; it was nothing more than a variation on his well-
practiced Wandering Seer act, and these superstitious savages *wanted*
to believe in him; probably every man of them had been dreaming that
Yahweh would tell them to pack up and go home.

But out farther away from the circle of firelight, at the far fringes
of the considerable carrying power of Kheperu's voice, the crowd
began to grow restless. Cynical murmuring began to bury the words of
this new prophet. Most of the men here had little interest in being
preached at by the prophet, and even less interest in waiting until
tomorrow for a Sign.

They were here *now*, they reasoned in sullen grumbles. If he's a
real prophet, he can just as easily do a sign tonight as tomorrow, can't
he?

Not everyone in this crowd had come to hear him. Many men and
women, here this night, moved through the crowds hawking sweets
and snacks of smoked lamb and the like. One enterprising fellow had
apparently been planning ahead; he'd had a pair of his slaves bring a
whole wagonload of water casks and wine barrels, selling their stock
by the ladleful to the immense and thirsty crowd, a gerah of silver for
water, three gerahs for wine.

They moved through the fringes of the crowd, their wagon hauled by
four patient asses, until word of their presence had spread through the
mob. Soon after that, they could no longer move for the press of thirsty
men around them.

As they collected silver and doled out their water and their wine,
one of the slaves turned to the other and muttered softly, "I think this
is going to work . . ."

"Work?" his female companion replied in the same tone. "Shit,
Sheshai, this'll do more than work; we'll turn a bloody profit!"

Barra had found Sheshai without any difficulty, simply by following rumors of the Egyptian Prophet. Then a little adroit bargaining, using silver provided by Agaz, had purchased the wagon and team of asses, ostensibly for their supposed master, a mythical Asherite by name of Jerubal—a safe enough lie, the camp of Asher being on the opposite side of the embattled city. The same story and a similar amount of silver had procured the water barrels and the wine.

The potent alkaloid dissolved in that water and in that wine, however, had come by way of Sheshai's satchel from Kheperu's voluminous trunk.

Now, as the levels of fluid in their barrels dipped toward zero, Sheshai stood up on the drover's bench and waved his arms, shouting, "No more! Sorry! All gone! We'll be back tomorrow! Sorry! No more!"

Far across the darkness and the grumbling crowd, up within the ring of bonfires, Kheperu couldn't hear him clearly, but he didn't have to; the actual signal was the waving of his arms.

"My friends! My children!" he cried, his hand raised for silence. "Tomorrow, we shall come to the very walls of the Tabernacle, to see God's Second Sign with our own eyes. *Who will come with me?*"

The crowd roared as though with one voice.

"Ah, my friends, my friends," he said chidingly, squinting to hide the twinkle in his eye, "this was not asked of you, but of God! Many are called, but few are chosen. Only the *Elect*, the greatest and purest among you, those that God loves above all the rest—only they can walk beside me to the Tabernacle! Only they can witness, when I am taken up alive into the heavens, to sit at the *Right Hand of God Himself*!"

His voice rang out triumphantly. "Look above! Look up into God's heavens! Look!"

All around him, necks craned as men turned their faces skyward.

Kheperu smiled to himself. "Know ye now, that you look not up, but *down*! The stars are below you, and you might fall from the face of the earth!"

Cries rang out from the crowd around, and men clutched each other, some stooping to grip the earth beneath their feet—the alkaloid was in full effect—while others, who had drunk no poisoned wine, snorted and looked at their cowering brethren with puzzlement verging on disgust.

"It is God's mighty Love that holds you here! You, who are the Elect, the Beloved of Yahweh, look up and see that the stars are caught in the golden net that Yahweh has spread across the heavens, the golden net that binds you to the earth, that will never let you fall. See the strands that bind the stars together? He gathers you to Him, as a fisherman draws in his catch. *See the Net of Yahweh!"*

*I see it,* someone cried, and then another, then twenty, a hundred. *There! The Golden Net of Yahweh!*

All through the huge crowd, men dropped to their knees in worship, tears of joy streaming down their cheeks.

Kheperu beamed. Now these silly drugged bastards would believe anything he told them. No matter that many in the crowd saw nothing; the very disbelief of their sober brethren would reinforce his command, as these chemical visionaries insisted on the reality of what they'd seen. He'd have a thousand men behind him when he went up to the Tabernacle in the morning, a thousand fanatical followers who knew beyond the possibility of doubt or argument that they were the Elect of God, and that he was Yahweh's True Voice.

*Heh. Almost too easy.*

Well into the night outside the circle of ecstatic believers, Sheshai turned to Barra and said, "What now?"

Barra swung down to the ground and stretched her aching muscles. "Nothing now. Sleep now."

"Sleep?" Sheshai's eyes glittered with reflections of the distant bonfires. "You expect me to sleep?"

"I don't give a shit what you do," Barra told him. "I'm sleeping under the wagon. If you wake me up before dawn, I'll kill you."

She crawled under the wagon to be well out of the dew, lay down on the hard, stony ground, and fought the urge to scratch. The dried mud and pigment that still painted her body beneath her spiral wrap itched fiercely, but it was probably the only thing hiding her from that vengeful demon of Joshua's—and it'd take more than a little itch to keep her awake tonight. The way she felt, she'd sleep through a colony of fire ants crawling up her butt.

Sheshai crouched beside her, his scars black in the fading moonlight.

"On bare ground," he said. "In the middle of half a million men who'll kill you the instant they know who you are. Chased by demons, and planning to face down a god in the morning, you're going to *sleep?"*

"Are you kidding?" Barra murmured exhaustedly. "This'll be my best night's rest all month."

She rolled over, cradled her head on her folded arm, and was instantly asleep.

Sheshai crouched there beside her for a long time.

If she had seen the expression his face wore, she might have had some trouble sleeping after all.

# 15

# *The Siege (Inside)*

Leucas leaned on the vine-covered wall of the Ba'alath's gate, and watched the heavens fill with dawn.

The body of one of the acolytes who had greeted them the day before lay now a few feet away, facedown in the street, his flesh already torn and ragged and rat-chewed. Leucas didn't waste much attention on him; his was not the only rat-chewed corpse on the streets around the Ba'alath this morning. Rats and mice swarmed over the body, and streamed out among the streets as well, as did ants and scorpions and spiders and cockroaches, until the dawnlit streets seemed themselves alive.

But they moved *away* from the Ba'alath.

Leucas frowned thoughtfully and shook his head in grim silence. He could not comprehend what the demon was up to now, and he was rapidly losing confidence that he'd be able to handle it.

He wiped blood from his lips as he looked up into the brightening purple sky. He could no longer taste the blood that had run into his mouth all through the hours of this night; he was so tired he could barely see it.

Something was broken inside him. He could feel it, a swollen looseness in his belly, beneath the tightly tied bandages he'd wrapped around his chest and stomach to try and keep his guts in place.

*If I could get some rest,* he thought, *this might not kill me.*

He was not the only one within the Lady's temple with blood upon his lips. Behind him, within the altarhouse, he could still hear Sarah's occasional thin cough. Her coughing had become quieter during the night, less frequent; if Leucas had a more optimistic nature, he might have let himself believe that she was getting stronger. But he knew the truth: blood and phlegm filled her lungs until she was too weak to expel it.

She didn't have long to live.

And Graegduz, too, lay within the altarhouse, his teeth stained red as though he'd been eating a fresh-killed deer. The wolf's leap had torn stitches inside him, and he'd been intermittently vomiting blood ever since the three of them had arrived at the Ba'alath at dusk.

Leucas had carried Sarah in his arms as he dashed through the streets of the city, like a mother bearing her child from a burning building. He had sensed the malignancy of their pursuer building at his back, had felt its hand in the deepening pain and weakness that spread out from his guts, in the way his heart hammered as though it might burst at any step.

Entering the gate of the Ba'alath had been like closing a door upon a noisy street; the malignancy was still there, could still be felt, but it was muted, distant, definitely outside.

Three acolytes had been there to take the ailing woman from his arms. Sarah had, Leucas presumed, explained the situation to them in detail, and they had agreed to stay through the night. In moments, Sarah was once again on her pallet in the alcove beside the Great Astarte, and the acolytes had improvised beds for Graegduz and Leucas by gathering piles of fleeces that had been left there as offerings to the Lady.

Only moments after he'd tumbled into his pile of fleeces, one of the acolytes had shaken him awake and tugged him out into the open yard. Without any sense of smell, Leucas at first couldn't understand what was happening out there; it seemed as though the moonlit night dropped occasional dirt clods upon the flagstones of the yard. Then one of the "dirt clods" *splattered* when it hit, and through his exhaustion Leucas felt an alien malice that grew like the clamor of an approaching mob.

Someone was throwing shit into the Ba'alath.

No one needed to explain to Leucas where this led; the ultimate end of this desecration, he could feel in the strengthening lust of the demon. He had driven himself stumbling toward the gate, and had his hand upon its bar to pull it open, when he saw the body of one of the acolytes only a few feet away, half-concealed in a deep moonshadow just outside the gate.

Apparently the acolytes hadn't bothered to awaken him until they'd decided they couldn't handle this themselves.

It took only a moment for him to devise a simple plan to meet the threat without leaving the temple's protection. With the two remaining acolytes to give him a boost, he easily gained the top of the wall around the courtyard, a stone's throw away from the source of the shit: a man standing by a large-wheeled dungbarrow, mechanically hurling one clod after another over the wall.

Standing atop the narrow wall, Leucas caught the fist-size chunk of flagstone the acolyte tossed up to him. He said no word of warning; why give the shit-thrower a chance to dodge? He fired his chunk of flagstone overhand. It struck the shit-thrower solidly on the hip and knocked him spinning to the ground.

"Now get out of here!" Leucas had shouted, waving his arms. "And don't come back!" The fellow could have no understanding of his words, but the rock should have made his meaning clear enough.

Slowly and painfully, the man had pulled himself to his feet, supporting his weight with the side of the barrow—the rock might have broken his hip. Balancing carefully on one leg, he had once again dug his fists into its load of dung and hurled handfuls of it over the wall. Leucas shouted at him again, but the man spared him not even a glance.

The second rock that Leucas threw crushed the man's skull and dropped him flopping spastically to die on the street, shit leaking from his bowels to mix with the dung he had sought to throw.

And so the night passed: between the sporadic attempts at defilement, Leucas and the acolytes had done their best to clean the courtyard, and turn the flung shit to a positive use by spreading it gently as fertilizer for the trees, and for the vines that climbed the walls.

Each desecration ended the same way: a man dead or incapacitated on the street. Leucas was forced to handle every one, for neither of the two remaining acolytes had the strength to kill a man with a thrown rock. None of the defilers ever spoke, and nothing could stop them while they had strength to continue.

They never even tried to take cover.

Leucas occasionally allowed himself the idle speculation that they might not even know what they were doing, that they might be unconscious dupes, innocent victims, themselves.

It didn't stop him from killing them.

An hour before dawn, the attacks had ceased. Now Leucas could only watch the outflowing vermin and wonder what might be next.

The answer was not long in coming.

A woman came into view, far up the street, peering at the river of vermin that streamed past her, her eyes swiftly tracing this river back to its source. From far away, she pointed, and began to shout.

Other folk appeared on the street, and on other streets, their eyes wide with revulsion and horror, and the woman's shouts were answered first by a few of them, then by a chorus like the baying of hunting hounds, old men, children, women—they all came streaming back against the current of rats and spiders and cockroaches. Leucas could understand only their tones of furious anger, and one word among their Canaanite: *Ba'alath.*

He watched them gather, feeling a dull ache gather more tightly around the broken swelling in his chest. Without the support of the wall, he wasn't sure that he could stand.

These were the Jebusites themselves, this oncoming mob, the same aged parents and children and widows that he and Kheperu and Barra were fighting to defend, and they came toward the Ba'alath with violence in their eyes.

He had sworn to protect the Lady's Maid with the last breath of his body.

Dread and despair hung weights of stone upon his arms.

This would be a bloodbath.

Another man might have slipped away then, from fear of an angry mob; another man might have faded aside from compassion, and let them through the gate rather than fight and harm children and old folk; another man, from prudence, might have realized that one man alone could never hold the gate against so many, and would have bowed to the inevitable.

Leucas only shook his head. This was not the first time in his life he'd wished he was somebody else.

He drew a deep, sad sigh, pulled the iron scimitar from his belt, and waited for them to arrive.


"Where is my father?"

Melchizedek turned to face him as Agaz plowed into the room with a double handful of mercenaries at his back. The High Priest stood among a crowd of his El's Men sycophants, but the smug consciousness of power that had ridden his face through the past day was conspicuously absent.

"Agaz," he said, ignoring the prince's question, "we must arrange the surrender *today.* We are utterly out of time. During the night—"

"I will have an answer," Agaz grated, his stride never slowing until he stood nose to nose with the skeletal priest. "Where is my father? Where is my child?"

Melchizedek snapped, "Precisely where they were when you

asked that question last night! Yes, they are safe, and no, you cannot see them. The stores your mad father laid up for this siege are ruined—*ruined*! There isn't a grain bin in the city that hasn't more rats than wheat in it right now!"

"Then we'll eat rats," Agaz said.

"We will not. We will give up this city and save the lives of our people. We've lost a thousand men to death and wounds already! And another *hundred thousand* Habiru marched into their camps overnight! You must call for parley with Joshua ben Nun, and offer your life in atonement for this city's sin."

Agaz's squint became openly calculating. "If I don't?"

Melchizedek drew himself up to his full height, towering over the prince. "If you refuse to pay for this city's rejection of the true El, you know who will. They await their fate in your father's bedchamber."

"Thank you," Agaz said coldly, and turned to the mercenaries that followed him. "We can go now."

"What?" Melchizedek sputtered. "What? What?"

"I have just come from my father's chamber," Agaz told him with a humorless smile. "Here, I merely sought to make certain that you had not moved them. But if you had any idea where they are, you would not have attempted this pathetic bluff."

"I, but, I—"

"I'll find them myself. Good day, uncle."

"You cannot leave!"

Agaz barked a cold laugh as he strode away through his men and they fell in behind him. "I have a dozen mercenaries that say I can. What do *you* have?"

And he was gone before Melchizedek could summon an answer.

The rivers of vermin that streamed outward from the Ba'alath entered not only the grain bins and cisterns of the city, but also the kitchens, pantries, vegetable cellars, stables, every smallest cranny that could possibly hide food. Soon there was not a loaf of bread or length of sausage in the city that didn't show rat-gnawed corners and the black specks of cockroach eggs; there was not a house where no infant squalled from spider bites, where no man was sick from scorpion stings or woman bandaged a rat bite; soon the streets flowed with men and women beating against the current like spawning salmon, seeking the source of this flood of vermin.

This flow of humanity created a current of its own, its eddies being knots of men who stopped to gather picks and hoes and shovels as makeshift weapons, and backflows of bustling officials carrying the news of this invasion back to the Citadel.

This current drew along many who were not directly concerned; some merely curious, having awakened to the sounds of angry voices in the street, some drifting vagrants and beggars, who had no stores to ruin and who took no more notice of spiders than they did of fleas, some idle mercenaries, and one very young, exhausted and hungry girl, who stumbled along holding the hand of a half-mad old king.

Rachel had understood that her grandfather was being held hostage against her father's behavior. She had approached that situation in the fashion that she'd imagined Barra would—she'd *rescued* him, exactly as a hero should.

A scullion's dress for her, a cowled robe and a face with no makeup or wig for Adonizedek had been enough of a disguise to get them out of the Citadel, but that had been the extent of her tactical planning. She had somehow expected everything to get better as soon as she and her grandfather escaped from her great-uncle's men. If anyone had asked her, she would have stoutly exclaimed, "I'm not even ten years old. I've done *my* part," and trustingly waited for someone else to take over from there.

But no one had asked, and no one had taken over.

Adonizedek's day of captivity had made the old man insanely suspicious. He would trust no one, not even her; they had wandered the streets all night, Adonizedek holding on to her hand with the grip of an eagle carrying a rabbit in its talons. He refused to seek shelter in any townsman's home, though Rachel wept with exhaustion—he wouldn't even let her go for food. He spent the night stalking the narrow alleyways of his beloved city like a specter, peering warily at shadows and muttering obscenities under his breath.

She guessed that it must have come as a terrible shock, when his brother turned against him, and when he discovered that men he'd regarded as his sons would treasonously lay hands upon him—but she wished all the same that he'd calm down and let them at least get something to eat. She'd had a couple of sausages and some hard cheese stuck in the apron of her scullion's dress, but the last of those had been finished hours ago. Now as he practically dragged her along the street, she no longer cared where they might be going, as long as it would be somewhere she could sit down for a while.

There was a big crowd at the end of the street, and everybody seemed to be angry. Over their heads, she could see the ivycovered walls of the Ba'alath. When they reached the back of the crowd,

Adonizedek began to push his way through, elbowing people sharply to both sides and dragging her along behind him.

At the front of the crowd, standing in the gate of the Ba'alath, was that big Greek friend of Barra's, Leucas. He stood angling one shoulder toward the nearest people, and in his rear hand he held a big curving sword low along his thigh.

A lot of people in the crowd were shouting at him, but he didn't say a word in response, only stared at them like he was worried, and trying not to be angry. She noticed that the people closest to him weren't shouting much, though, and they looked like they didn't really want to get any closer; they pushed back a little against the people that pushed them from behind.

So many people were shouting at once that it took Rachel a while to figure out what everyone was angry about. A lot of people were talking about rats and food and stuff, but she couldn't begin to guess why that would make them all angry at Leucas.

When Adonizedek reached the front of the crowd, he let go of her hand so that he could throw back his cowl and face the crowd to speak. There was a crepidoma at the base of the wall a couple of spans high, and he climbed up precariously onto it to address the crowd. He'd torn the bandage from his forehead sometime during the night, and the gash on his forehead was ragged and black with crusted blood.

Rachel left his side and came over to Leucas, looking up into his cavernous face from barely the height of his belt.

"Hello, Leucas. Where's Barra?"

He frowned down at her, and then his face cleared as he recognized her through the dirt on her face and despite her servant's dress. He said something that she couldn't understand, and put out his hand as though to shoo her on her way.

Rachel had no intention of being shooed, and she understood how to get her way around adults. Instead of letting him push her, she took his hand with hers as though he were her father, and clung to it as she turned back to watch what the crowd was doing. She'd been a little scared before, with so many people making so much noise, but with Leucas' enormous hand in hers she felt as safe as she ever had in her own bed.

He said something else in his big rumbly voice, but he let her hold on to his hand.

Now she began to gather what was going on. Rats and bugs and stuff had gotten into everyone's food, and somehow they'd decided that it was the fault of the Lady's Maid. Some of them wanted to just go in and talk with her, but some of them wanted to knock down the Ba'alath—some of them even said they should kill Sarah herself. Then somebody shouted something about a dead man lying in the street— and then everyone was shouting and screaming, and *everyone* wanted to hurt Sarah, because of some men who had died by the temple wall. They wanted to drag her out into the street and stone her.

Rachel was really, really glad she'd rescued the king, because now he was here and he was going to make everything turn out all right. Even though he didn't look much like a king today, in his dirty robe, with no wig and no face-paint, no one really wanted to argue with him.

He knew every person there by name, and when he scolded them for behaving like children, they blushed and hung their heads and sulked exactly as though they *were* children, little kids younger than Rachel herself.

"Now go home," Adonizedek said. "None of this is the Lady's doing, and well you know it. Go home and give an offering to the Lady. Ask her to forgive your wrath, and ask her to protect you. She brought my son back alive and well; she will preserve us, if we only have faith."

The people milled restlessly; they'd start to break up any minute, and drift back to their homes.

"They said you were sick, Adonizedek," someone called. "They said that barbarian girl poisoned you, and you were dying!"

"I—" the king began, suddenly a little confused, and weaker. "I have . . . been sick, I suppose. A little."

"You don't look a *little*," came a reply. "Maybe the Lady's Maid witched your mind away. Maybe you won't get better while this witch house stands!"

"A *little*," Adonizedek repeated. "Only a little. But now I am well. I am Adonizedek, and I tell you all: go home!"

"But you are not Adonizedek," came a new voice, deep and oily like a barrel of pitch.

Melchizedek came forward within the crowd, wearing the full flowing robes of his office and leaning upon a stout new walking staff. Around him stood ranks of hard-faced young men in armor. Rachel recognized most of them: they were all El's Men.

"Come home, Abishai. Come home and rest. You have been ill."

"No," the king said. "No . . . only a little . . ."

"You passed on the kingship, Abishai. Do you not remember? Now your son is Adonizedek."

"My son . . ." the old king murmured, his eyes beginning to fill with tears. "My son—"

"It's you who must come home, Abishai," Melchizedek said reasonably. "These good people will handle what needs to be handled down here."

There came a low and frightening rumble of agreement from the crowd.

"I'm not the king?" Adonizedek asked, his hands trembling and his head shaking from side to side. "Really not?"

"Really not, Abishai. Come home. Rest."

Suddenly Rachel could stand it no longer. She had no doubt whose side *she* was on: anything her great-uncle wanted had to be bad. She released Leucas' hand and clenched her little fists at her sides, shrieking in that ear-piercing squeal that only young girls seem to be able to summon.

"You are a *bad man!*" she shrilled. "You're a nasty awful old man! You liar! You *cheater!* You—you—" She struggled to remember the worst thing she'd ever heard. *"You suck the shit out of goats' butts!"*

Instead of being angry, Melchizedek smiled; many in the crowd laughed rudely.

"Hush now, Rachel," he said serenely. "You're too young to be mixing in this. Come along home with your grandfather."

She turned back to Leucas. "Do something! Don't you see what's going to happen?"

He only met her eyes, and shrugged, and said something in his own tongue.

"Grandfather," she said desperately, "you *are* the king! Don't believe him! You don't have to go!"

"Perhaps . . ." Adonizedek said, his voice breaking with an old man's uncertain whistle. "Perhaps it's best . . ."

Rachel thought back to the party, to the last moments before everything had gone so terribly wrong. "Well—even if you're not the king, you're still the Lady's Champion, aren't you?"

"The Lady's Champion . . ." Adonizedek's brows drew together, and he cocked his head as though he could not quite remember where he'd heard that phrase before.

"You're a *Champion!*" Rachel insisted. "You don't have to go home!"

"Yes, he does," Melchizedek said. "He's very ill."

He gestured toward the armored men he'd brought with him, and a pair of them came forward as though to help Adonizedek step down safely from the crepidoma.

As he looked down on their reaching hands, his eyes seemed to finally come into focus, and fury gathered upon his brow. "You dare?" A drop of blood trailed down his forehead from the gash. "You would lay hands on me without my leave?"

The men hesitated in the face of his sudden anger, and Melchizedek said, "Don't stand against us, Abishai."

All the smooth reasonableness had fled the High Priest's manner and voice; in its place was dark threat. "The Lady is the enemy of Jebusi. She has brought us to the very brink of destruction, by gathering the Habiru against us. Now she has sent her creatures out to befoul our food and water, to destroy our ability to withstand this siege. Look at the men who lie broken around this place of filth—the men who lie dead in the street, with no one to do them honor. True men, each of them, men of El, husbands, fathers. Heroes, slain by this Lady you claim will save us. She will not. She hates us. She wants to kill us all. If you would defend her, you, too, are our enemy, king or no: the enemy of every living being in this city. We cannot afford the luxury of mercy. All who serve the vile goddess must die, if the true sons of Jebusi are to survive. Even my wife. Even you, Abishai. To fight this ravening monster is our only hope."

There came a general mutter of agreement, a low and dangerous sound like the hunger rumble of a giant's stomach.

Once again the El's Men reached up for Adonizedek's arms, but over Rachel's shoulder came a hand the size of a lion's paw that seized a reaching wrist. The Man of El let out a thin gasp of pain, and Rachel clearly heard a wet crackle, like the sound of one of her father's hounds splintering a chicken bone in its jaws.

Leucas said something again, in that voice that made Rachel's chest hum in sympathetic vibration, and let the man go.

The Man of El fell to his knees, clutching his wrist as tears leaked from his eyes and he tried to gather enough breath to moan. The other El's Man backed away warily, trying to watch Leucas and Melchizedek at the same time.

The High Priest lifted his staff and pointed it at Leucas. "He who stands against a servant of El stands against God Himself! You see before you the very monster who treacherously slaughtered your husbands, your friends. Do you need further proof? Our only hope is to destroy this Lady and all who would defend her! All your lives, the lives of your *children*, depend on this!"

Leucas smiled brokenly and moved a step closer to Adonizedek. Without leaving the gate, he pushed Rachel behind him, then took Adonizedek's arm, and did the same with the old king.

He stood, with his chest a shield between the king and the hostile mob, and raised his sword.

Blades scraped free of scabbards throughout the crowd.

The children and women in the crowd began to move back, and the Men of El pressed forward with many sideways glances, none wanting to be the first within reach of Leucas' sword. There was some jostling and one of them was shouldered forward by the others, stumbling, lifting his blade to the level of his determined, terrified eyes.

Even then, Rachel thought that somehow everything would turn out all right. Wasn't her grandfather here? Wasn't Barra's friend Leucas here? And the man who stumbled forward, he was only barely a man—she knew him: his name was Jaalah, he was seventeen, the big brother of one of her playmates, he'd caught her once pulling flowers from the Citadel's gardens and he'd never told on her. It was obvious that he didn't really want to fight Leucas; after all, who would?

She was so certain that somehow something would stop them that she didn't really see what was happening when Leucas' big curved sword slashed down through Jaalah's shoulder and neck, crunching through bone and causing a huge crimson spray of blood to burst from his mouth. It didn't make sense to her; Jaalah had always been around, for his sister to pester and his mother to complain about. How could he be this same boy whose head flopped sideways, who fell to the ground with his heels kicking, whose blood sprayed like a fountain of rubies sparkling in the sunlight high over her head?

It didn't make sense. It was wrong, it was completely wrong, everything was wrong; and when everything was wrong, Rachel had only one solution.

She closed her eyes and screamed.

Her scream rose with transcendent power, dulling the clash of weapons and the grunts of fighting men, striking through all other noise like a nail driven into the eardrum.

She would scream, and scream, and scream, and never stop until things made sense to her again.

Agaz and his company of mercenaries were already approaching the Ba'alath when the fighting began.

He'd realized that the Ba'alath was the most likely destination for Leucas and Sarah, after their dash from the Citadel—he'd gotten that story from three different people, each of whom had been knocked down by the Greek's headlong sprint. He'd meant to check on them last night, but the exhaustion of the day's fighting had overtaken him as soon as he'd gulped down his evening meal. Now, in search of his father, the Ba'alath seemed a likely place to look.

Then, once on their way, he'd heard the rumor of the gathering mob, and a sick dread in the pit of his stomach had warned him that his father was probably somehow in the middle of it.

He heard the rumble of the crowd, and then its sudden silence, followed by shouts of mixed fury and dismay—and over the top of it, cutting through its roar, the high keening wail of a young girl.

He knew that scream; he'd last heard it at the death of his wife.

His heart froze within his breast, and he broke into a run. His men followed crisply, with no need for an order.

They hit the rear of the crowd like a charge of heavy chariots, battering people aside and trampling the ones that could not move in time. Agaz tore through the crowd, tossing men to the ground like broken scarecrows.

There came a whirling confusion of shouts and flashes of blades, and Agaz found himself standing in the gate of the Ba'alath behind a screen of mercenaries who faced off against a deep arc of El's Men, with his father at his side and his sobbing daughter in his arms.

For a moment all he could see was the blood that caked Rachel's hair; it struck his chest like a knife and made his frozen heart thump painfully.

"Rachel!" he rasped, his terror making his voice harsh and angry. "Are you hurt? What have they done? Have they hurt you?"

Her body trembled against his, and words began to spill from her lips between the sobs. Gradually Agaz gathered what was happening, and as he understood that the blood on her hair was not hers, he found he could breathe again.

Leucas towered beside him, his scimitar dripping gore in slow splats to the flagstones. Three men lay dead or dying just outside the gate, and the huge Greek's whole right flank ran with blood that steamed faintly in the sunlight.

He gave the prince a nod. "Agaz. Good to see you," he said in thick Phoenikian. He nodded out toward where Melchizedek stood back in the midst of the crowd. "Sarah's husband. Big, big asshole."

*For a man with a limited grasp of the tongue, he's unquestionably eloquent,* Agaz thought. *Big asshole, indeed.*

He turned to his father, who stood glowering furiously at the Men of El. "Adonizedek," he said formally. "I am glad to find you well."

"Do you know that they put their *hands* on me?" Adonizedek

seemed as astonished as he was angry. "Do you know they had me locked in my bedchamber all day, and hunted me through the streets all night?"

"That is over, now," Agaz told him firmly. He gently disengaged himself from Rachel, who looked up at him with enormous, luminous eyes. "He has gone too far for forgiveness, or even tolerance."

Agaz stepped to the fore of his men and leveled his sword at Melchizedek. "Your treason is exposed, uncle; now you must pay its forfeit. I know you believe that what you've done was right. For that reason, I will let you live. Surrender and return to the Citadel."

"I think not," Melchizedek said crisply, as though he'd come to a sudden decision.

Agaz's men lifted their swords and shifted their balance as though to start for him. Their looks were grim and confident; seasoned mercenaries, they knew the young and nervous El's Men could never match them.

Agaz held them back with a gesture. "Surrender. Spare the lives of your men. Everyone here has seen your treason; there is no denial, no defense."

Melchizedek smiled thinly. "What everyone here has seen, Agaz, is that you, along with your father—your entire *house*—have declared yourselves enemies of El today. Enemies of Jebusi. You would defend my whoring wife, and her decadent slut of a goddess, who is bent on the destruction of every righteous man. You have thrown aside each chance I gave you to save this city. What did the Habiru promise to pay you, while you relaxed as their guest this past month? How did they convince you to betray your own people?"

Agaz stared, gaping speechlessly. This was so outrageous that for a moment he couldn't understand how Melchizedek even spoke the words.

"Is that why only you, alone, returned?" the High Priest continued. "Because the *loyal* sons of Jebusi who rode with you would have exposed your betrayal? Did you merely laugh while the Habiru murdered them, or did your masters let you kill them yourself?"

Agaz felt something give way within him, some barrier that snapped and flooded him with warmth and ease and savage joy. For at that instant, he thought that he could lift the burdens of the entire world with one short stroke of his sword.

He started for his uncle with bloody intent.

The Men of El drew together to deny him. He moved to cut through them, but before he could even lift his blade, a stone sailed from the depths of the crowd and struck him on the forehead. A new sun blazed briefly within his brain, and blood rained swiftly down over one eye, and before his vision could clear, more stones flew, and the Men of El advanced.

And behind them, a crowd of old men, and widows, with the children of Jebusi surging at their backs to support them.

In a single instant of terrible clarity, he saw in each pair of eyes that faced him a blank, unreasoning hostility. Their terror of the Habiru had been transformed as though by magic into savage hatred of him, and his father, and the Goddess and all who would defend her.

If he did not retreat, his sole course would be to order these outland mercenaries at his back, these ruthless foreign bloodletters, against his own people.

If he had been the man his uncle had described, he could have done it. If he had been the man Melchizedek told these people he was, his uncle would lie dead in the street right now.

Even for a man whose taste in humor ran naturally to irony, this was too bitter to raise even the coldest smile.

In a voice as bleak and bereft of hope as a night wind in winter, he ordered his men to fall back into the Ba'alath; they would hold the gate against attackers, but no more.

They backed in, shields up against the stones of the crowd, and the gate clanged shut like the door of a dungeon cell. He stood once again between his father and his daughter, and looked out at the hungry, hostile crowd.

Melchizedek, satisfied that he had all those he'd styled as Enemies of Jebusi safely imprisoned, left in the company of three of his men. The rest stayed, occasionally encouraging the crowd by chucking rocks of their own.

Leucas laid a hand upon his shoulder, and Agaz looked up into his lucid, wise eyes. The Athenian said gravely and with difficulty, "This is the siege."

Some hours were to pass before Agaz would realize that Leucas' limited Phoenikian had not caused him to misspeak, that he had meant precisely those words and no others.

*This is the siege.*

# 16

# *The Siege (Outside)*

"**F**ather? Father, you must wake!"

A hard hand upon his arm brought Eleazar ben Aaron up from a horrific dream: ten thousand children screaming in lakes of molten sulphur, flames licking from their wailing mouths.

The summoning of Shahkhath had left him exhausted, beaten in body and spirit, but still restless and largely sleepless, snatching only scattered moments of slumber between nightmares. He rolled uneasily upon his pallet, each bruise on his battered body announcing itself afresh. His every joint was packed with sand, and his eyes felt scalded as he forced them open.

Phinehas knelt at his side, and there was a fierce light upon his son's beloved face. For one instant, Eleazar's heart lifted and opened like a flower.

"Please, Father. Joshua asks for your help."

"Joshua?" Eleazar said thickly, smacking his lips against the vile taste of sleep. He should have known: even one instant's pleasure of seeing his son happy would be taken from him by Joshua. Phinehas was a man now; that light upon his face could never be kindled by his mere father . . .

"There is a new prophet in the camp, an Egyptian who proclaims disaster for us, here at Jerusalem. The Egyptian shows great signs and wonders, and has a huge following among the Host already."

"Huh." Eleazar grunted sourly as he sat up and rubbed at his face. Phinehas handed him the pitcher and cup from the water stand by the door, and Eleazar drank. "And so?" he asked, wiping his lips. "What does the great man require of me?"

Phinehas stiffened slightly at Eleazar's tone. "Joshua would have you examine this prophet and test his truth."

Eleazar made a face as though he would spit bile. "Convey my apologies to the great man, and remind him that he himself forbade me making such tests. He proclaimed himself the Judge of Israel. Let him judge."

"It was God that proclaimed him—" Phinehas began severely.

"Spare me. Preach to me of God's proclaimings after my bruises heal."

"Father—" Phinehas gritted his teeth. He stopped whatever angry words were about to come from his mouth, and said with forced softness, "Even as we now speak, the Egyptian who styles himself a Man of God marches upon the Tabernacle with thousands at his back— thousands! He has said that the Tent of God shall *burn*, Father. That it shall burn as a sign from God that He has forsaken Joshua, and this siege."

"Joshua's relationship with God is not my concern—"

"The pagan whore, Barra Coll Eigg Rhum, has a servitor who is reputed to be an Egyptian sorcerer. Joshua suspects that this Egyptian is a fraud, that he is the very man who serves the pagan whore. A false prophet. That the signs and wonders he has shown are conjuror's tricks. Thus, he sent me to you."

"Because I am the expert on false prophecy and conjuror's tricks," Eleazar said bitterly.

"Father—"

"No!" Eleazar spat. "Enough! I have done Joshua's bidding enough to last my lifetime."

"He is the Lord's Anointed! There is no higher honor than to serve—"

"Phinehas—" Eleazar rubbed his eyes; his anger slipped away like water through his fingers, and he sighed tiredly. "Yes. Joshua is the Lord's Anointed—but he is not the Lord. He is only a man; sometimes I think he is not even a very good man. To treat a man as though he stands alongside Yahweh—that is a dangerous thing, Phinehas. You should take care that this honor you cherish does not cost your life."

"I stood beside him when the Jebusite arrows fell around us like rain. In his service, the power of God protects me, too. Father," he said, leaning forward to clasp one of Eleazar's hands in both of his, "you must not let your petty rivalries with Joshua turn you aside from the service of God, and Israel; this is too important."

"Petty *rivalries*?" Eleazar began, but Phinehas cut him off.

"If you will not answer Joshua's call, come then for the sake of Israel. Please, Father. It is not only Joshua who asks for you. I ask you now, too," he said humbly. "Please."

Eleazar had to turn his head and blink away the hot sting in his eyes. When was the last time his son had come to him, to ask him for his help, as other sons ask their fathers? Had it been twenty years? Twenty-five?

How could he possibly refuse now?

He sighed, and shook his head, and began to stiffly rise. A groan escaped his lips at the pangs from his bruised body and grit-scraping joints, and Phinehas scrambled upright to assist him gently.

His son's strong arms beneath his shoulders gave Eleazar unexpected warmth, and his pangs subsided.

"All right," he said. "Because you ask, I will come. But not for Joshua. Only for you, Phinehas."

*Only for my son.*


Barra lay on her back, enjoying her sleepy languor despite the rocky ground that was her mattress. She stared, unseeing, at the splintery age-greyed bottom of the wagon's bed, now underlit with glaring sunlight reflected from the pale earth around it.

Now, in the morning sun, the ground grew hot; last night, it had been cold as a stone in winter. Sand fleas had made a meal of her tender flesh; their bites itched only slightly more than the flaking blue-dyed mud inside her slave dress. The Habiru camp had been abuzz with activity all night long, as more and more tribesmen marched in, pitching new tents and cooking late meals, shouting greetings to friends and relatives.

None of this had even remotely disturbed her rest.

She had told Sheshai the truth, last night—this had been her best sleep in weeks.

For that long moment, she actually felt pretty good, until she stretched. The motion awakened all her bruises and minor wounds, and she sighed disappointedly.

*Ahhh, shit,* she thought. *I suppose waking up healthy would have been too much to ask for.*

She reminded herself that waking up at all meant she was still ahead of the game.

The wagon shifted above her, and a pair of sandal-clad feet descended to the ground at her side. "Barra?" Sheshai said, leaning his grinning face down to peer at her. "He's started the march on the Tabernacle. It's time to go."

She answered his grin with one of her own; she found something about his manic confidence infectious. "You look cheerful this morning."

His grin spread wider, becoming even more crazed. "Sure. Why not? It's good to be alive. Come on."

"Oh, ay."

She rolled out from under the wagon, and stood, patting the dirt off her spiral-wrapped dress. As she did so, she felt small dusty slitherings down her skin, and she frowned downward.

Across the tops of her feet, and on the earth around them, was spread a small quantity of blue-dyed dust.

She shrugged. It could not be helped.

She bent over and wiped the dust off her feet so that it could not give her away, then shouldered a small satchel and followed Sheshai, abandoning the wagon.

It was time to get this shit over with.

The messenger spoke breathlessly. "We found the blue dust, just as you said we would. It was beside and beneath a wagon, over in the eastern camp—the camp of the warriors of Gad, where the Egyptian prophet showed the crowd the miracle, the Vision of Yahweh's Net—"

The messenger went on at length, but Joshua lost the thread of his tale; his attention was taken by the dispute going on between the Kohathite perimeter sentries and an enormous mixed-clan assemblage on the slope below the Tabernacle.

Eleazar and Phinehas stood beside him, also staring downslope to the argument. "I cannot see him," Phinehas said.

"He is there," Eleazar replied. He turned to Joshua. "They all are there, Joshua."

That assemblage below was undoubtedly this Egyptian prophet and his followers, demanding to be allowed to approach the Tabernacle. The Kohathites resisted, and shouting growled on both sides. More Kohathites approached now, in support of their sentries, and even some Merarites and Gershonites strode downhill from their respective perimeters behind the wedge of Kohath.

Joshua shook his head grimly, a sickly dread gathering weight in his stomach. This could turn ugly any second.

This could turn into a riot.

He was aware of the frost in Eleazar's manner, but he had no leisure to consider it now. If the argument below turned into a fight, the

Tabernacle itself could be in danger; at the very least, sons of Israel would spill each other's blood.

Eleazar said, "Without examining the man personally, I cannot say for sure, but I can tell you this: every sign and wonder that has been accomplished at the behest of this prophet, I could do myself, with no aid from Yahweh."

He ticked them off on his fingers. "The thunderbolt, and the smoke that hid the pagan whore from you—a firebomb, and the smoke pots that Egyptian magicians use to impress the gullible, thrown by a good slinger, or shot from a mechanical catapult. The exploding fire in the camp, the same sort of thing, placed in a cookpot by a confederate."

"And this vision?" Joshua rumbled. "This Net of Yahweh, filling the sky, that thousands saw last evening?"

Eleazar gave him a crooked, cynical smile. "There are poisons, well known in the laboratories of Egypt, that will give a man visions— he will see precisely what he expects to see, or what someone tells him he is seeing. This is how the Egyptian priests dupe their people into following gods that do not exist."

He turned to the messenger. "That wagon, where you found the blue dust, what was in it? Empty wineskins? Water casks, also empty?"

"Why, yes," the messenger said, startled. "How did you know this?"

"There you have it," Eleazar said lightly. "This man's confederates offered poisoned drink to a thirsty crowd."

Joshua muttered, "But this suspicion is useless. For the crowd at his back, *they* believe." He came to a sudden decision, and said abruptly, "Phinehas, descend to the Kohathites, and tell them to let this man and his followers pass. Otherwise, it will come to violence, and that we cannot allow."

"Let him *through?*" Phinehas asked, dumbfounded. "Let this false prophet and his rabble approach the Sanctuary?"

"I have said so," Joshua told him. "Eleazar, you and I will meet him there, and we shall test this prophet, and learn his truth."

He met the High Priest's eye, and found Eleazar staring at him speculatively, as though trying to discern just how far he was willing to allow this test to go; in Eleazar's gaze was a mocking reminder of Joshua's fury on the night of the eremite's murder.

Joshua did not answer this unspoken question. He could not answer it; the answer he wanted to give, he feared to even think.

"—but how did you know?" the messenger was asking. "What is the meaning of this blue dust, and how did you know that we would find it there? Is this a word from Yahweh?"

"Take your men," Joshua said brusquely, "and go into the crowd that gathers below. There will be women among them, women in the dress of Hivite slaves. From every Hivite woman that your men find, they are to remove the dress. One among them will have blue paint on her skin. It is the pagan whore who mocked God yesterday. You are to bring her to me."

"Alive, Joshua?"

He shrugged. "It does not matter."

*"Beware Egypt! The Hammer of Egypt falls from Gilgal upon the Host of Israel! The Sanctuary burns, it burns, it burns!"*

Kheperu paused, his throat rasping dry from his ceaseless screeching. Instantly, one of his followers passed a bulging wineskin forward to his hand. Another sliced away the cork, and Kheperu tipped the skin high, directing an amethyst stream in an arc to his lips.

The wine eased his throat, but did nothing to quell the leaping of his heart or untie the knots in his stomach.

Yesterday, it had been positively intoxicating, having a thousand men compete to do his bidding; today, it filled him with a dread that approached mortal fear.

He had vastly more than a thousand at his back this morning; not only all those who had seen the drug-induced vision of the night before, but in addition another thousand or two who claimed they had. Whether or not they believed it themselves, he couldn't say. It seemed vital to them to be considered among God's Elect, and so they insisted they'd seen the vision as well, and who was he to argue? And many brought their households, their friends, and their slaves, and following them all came a vast throng of the merely curious.

And they all gathered around him, and pressed close to touch his robe, and whispered among themselves, repeating every syllable that came from his mouth, and shouting translations at each other; already this morning he had been called upon to settle three lawsuits, and to judge a man accused of stealing another man's donkey, all on the presumption that Yahweh Himself spoke infal-libly from Kheperu's lips.

This swindle had taken on a terrifying life, spinning out of his control. His fanatic followers were never satisfied with a repetition of his previous prophecies—everyone wanted one of his own. And so he gave them prophecies in an endless babbling stream, as swiftly as his lips could move, he told them how their crops would grow next year, and that their firstborn sons would be mighty Men of God, that a dream of croaking ravens was a portent of new wealth, and on and on until sometimes he himself was astonished to hear the nonsense that came out of his mouth.

But they lapped it up like stray dogs at a puddle of beer; no matter how ridiculous his words became, they believed him. He tried to maintain a properly Egyptian contempt for their gullibility, but he could not. Their fierce attention, their instant and savage fury against any who would breathe the faintest doubt, their unhesitating willingness to follow him—even against their own *kinsmen*—awed him, and left him breathless with dread.

The men at the front of his crowd were even now prepared to kill the Tabernacle guards, if these guards had the temerity to deny him an open path to the Tent of God.

They had a lust to believe, a desperate need to feel that their God was speaking to them—or perhaps it was fear; perhaps they did not so much believe as they feared to disbelieve. So they struggled to outdo each other in their shows of conviction, as though by their actions they proclaimed, *Behold! I have more faith than he, I have more faith than she, I will do anything for Yahweh! Anything!*

More disturbing still had been the outcome of the donkey-stealer's case. To dispose of the matter, Kheperu had mentally shrugged and arbitrarily decided the fellow was guilty, simply because he reminded Kheperu of one of his childhood acquaintances, an apprentice that had tormented him mercilessly many years ago.

As the unfortunate fellow was being dragged away, he had *confessed*.

This was a coincidence that Kheperu did not allow himself to think about too closely.

Now, that big man with the curly black hair—the one that had stood, shouting in Canaanite, at Joshua's side yesterday morning—came scuffling down the slope to talk with the captain of the guarding clansmen that were barring Kheperu's progress to the Tabernacle. Kheperu was sure that the big fellow was even now ordering the sentries to let Kheperu and his followers pass.

"*Beware!* Woe to Israel, if the Bride of Yahweh is bent across the Jebusite Anvil for the fall of the Egyptian Hammer! Thus saith the Lord God, *I will number you to the sword, and ye shall all bow down to the slaughter: because when I called, ye did not answer; when I*

*spake, ye did not hear, but did evil before mine eyes, and did choose
that wherein I delighted not!"*

Kheperu found that once begun, there was a certain rhythm, a kind
of swing to this prophecy business, a comfortable meter that he fell
into quite naturally. It didn't require much of his attention, really;
though he often found his mind drifting off, the words continued to
flow.

The clan captain grudgingly ordered his men to give way, and
Kheperu started up the long slope with thousands of chanting fanatics
at his back.

*"And ye shall leave your name for a curse unto my chosen: for the
Lord God shall slay thee, and call his servants by another name!"*

There, that was a particularly apt phrase, a sonorous, memorable
line, something that his followers could repeat among themselves.
Inwardly, he began to relax and allowed himself a sigh of happy contemplation, and let the words continue to tumble out in time with his
rolling gait, climbing up the rocky slope to the scarlet-dyed wall of the
Sanctuary.

He resisted the urge to wink at the big curly-haired fellow as he
passed; instead he shouted out, "Behold, thus saith the Lord: *I will
bring evil among you, which you will not be able to escape; and
though you shall cry unto me, I will not hearken to you."*

At his back, ten men and more shouted out the meaning of his
words in Canaanite to the benefit of those farther back among the
crowd, and Kheperu lifted his brow in a superior fashion at the big
scowling bastard as though to say, *Joshua had only you, you tiresome
ill-tempered nincompoop, as a translator. I have* ten *tiresome ill-tempered nincompoops, because I am ten times the prophet that Joshua is.*

Kheperu couldn't tell if he'd gotten his message across or not, but
the fellow's scowl deepened perceptibly.

"And before your eyes, you will see me taken up alive, to sit at the
Right Hand of God!"

The fabric walls of the Sanctuary were spectacular, rising high
above him as he approached, as blue as a summer sky, as purple as
young wine, as scarlet as arterial blood. They were scrupulously clean,
even here in the dusty wind, and the sun struck eyedazzling splinters
of light from the silver hooks and the brass sockets of the poles, and
nowhere was there to be seen even the faintest speck of tarnish.

*Hmpf,* he thought. *Not surprising, from a nation of rug beaters.*
Sheshai had told him that three entire Habiru clans made caring for the
Tabernacle their life's work—they even made their camps around it,

and served as its perimeter guards. There must have been more than ten thousand of them here, perhaps twenty thousand, or even more; they made the band of his followers look small indeed.

Their openly suspicious and hostile eyes followed his every step.

And this was it: the big show.

In a moment, his skill at deception would save Jebusi.

He reached the Sanctuary wall, and reached out despite himself to stroke the fabric. It was beautifully made, of linen so fine-twined it slid over his fingers like soft butter. *Mmm, nice work,* he thought reflexively; material of this quality was a treasure in itself; it would fetch a high price in the Market of Tyre—not to mention the hooks of silver, and the silver fillets and capitals of the poles . . .

*Almost a shame to burn it,* he thought, *but sacrifices must be made. Let me stall a moment or two for Barra and Sheshai to set the firebombs, and we shall see who is the real prophet, here.*

And, with this phrase ringing in his head, he turned back away from the Sanctuary wall and found himself face-to-face with the towering bull-necked presence of Joshua ben Nun.

Barra said, "We're in trouble."

Even as she spoke, she watched another knot of hard-eyed men purposefully surround a woman in the dress of a slave; not far away, the same thing happened to another female slave.

She kept herself screened by the taller men around her, all walking half on tiptoe and craning their necks to catch a glimpse of Kheperu, high up the slope above them. The crowd of his followers had spread out now, spilling between the tents of Merarites and Kohathites that surrounded the Sanctuary. As she looked back down the slope, she saw more and more small groups of men moving purposefully through the crush, to lay hands upon every slave girl within their path.

They were stripping away the girls' shifts and spiral wraps.

This was bad.

They were on to her.

For half a second Barra even considered pouring water down her dress and smearing the mud, wiping it off before it could be found on her.

Of course, there was still one big reason why she couldn't do that.

She swung her gaze through the visible arc of the sky. Ever since she rose this morning, her *sceon tiof* had been intermittent, fading in and out like the sun's light on a cloudy day; this meant that the ritual designs on her body were flaking away.

She couldn't see the demon out there, but she could feel its approach. It was as though it came a step closer to her with each flake that fell from her skin.

Soon the sigils would not protect her at all; only enough of the pigment would remain to betray her to the searching Habiru.

"Come on, Sheshai. We have to get moving."

The Jerichite made no response. He stared off into the west, unheeding.

Up above, near the gate of the Sanctuary, she saw Joshua towering over Kheperu, and she cursed harshly under her breath. Where in bloody fuck had *he* come from? And who was this natty-looking little man beside him, some kind of priest? He'd be this Eleazar ben Aaron that Sheshai had told her of, she decided.

She could all-too-clearly imagine Kheperu sweating, and licking his lips, and stammering under Joshua's smoldering gaze.

She told herself that if anyone could bullshit Joshua ben Nun, it was Kheperu. And she tried very hard to believe it.

"Sheshai, come *on!*"

But instead of answering, he only made a guttural snarling noise in the back of his throat, a low, unconscious growl like a cat tearing at the body of a dead bird.

"Sheshai—"

He said, *"Rahab."*

She followed his gaze with her eyes. He was staring at a bent-backed old woman—prematurely aged, to judge by the vivid black of her hair—who stood a good bowshot away.

Barra frowned; she seemed familiar, somehow, in a way that the other Israelites did not.

Then the *sceon tiof* brushed her gaze, and what she saw wrinkled her brow in puzzlement and sudden pain. This woman carried a brutal burden, nearly as deep and as harshly painful as Sheshai's, some septic wound on her life that she denied with all her strength.

This denial, this refusal to accept, this was what had bent her back and aged her before her time; she spent every waking minute of every day of her long life telling herself that she wasn't hurt, that she wasn't damaged, that whatever had happened hadn't really happened, that it wasn't her fault. Barra saw her too clearly to doubt it, and she saw that in this broken woman's dreams, she saw herself with clarity that sucked the conviction out of her like a dog sucks the marrow from a well-chewed bone.

"You know her?" Barra asked, frowning.

"Yeah," Sheshai said thickly, as though his throat were filled with clotting blood. "I know her. And she knows me."

Then this woman's odd familiarity clicked into place like the tumblers of a well-oiled lock.

She looked like Sheshai. She looked enough like him to be his cousin, his aunt.

Barra said softly, "She's a Jerichite."

Sheshai didn't respond. He stared at her across the crowd like a hungry lion that crouched in the rocks above a well-fed goat.

"I thought you said you were the only one left."

"I *am* the only one," he said in a low snarl. "Rahab is Israelite now. She is a hero of Israel."

"I don't understand."

"She used to be a temple prostitute. She was a friend of my mother's—not a good friend, she was too bitter to have any good friends. When her looks began to fail, she opened an inn, up on the city wall. That much I knew; the rest I heard after I was slaved at Gibeon. Every man in Israel knows the story."

The words came from his mouth absently, and hollow, as though someone else spoke through his lips. "Joshua sent two spies to check the town—to make sure we were weak and helpless enough for him to slaughter. They stayed at Rahab's inn. She fed them, and protected them, and helped them slip out of town after dark one night."

His voice thickened, and he began walking mechanically through the crowd, muttering his tale as Barra kept pace. "Do you see? She *knew who they were*. In exchange for her wretched life, she gave them Jericho. Even after they were gone, she said nothing, only waited, stewing in her poison, waiting for Joshua to come. She killed my family—my people—as surely as if she put the knives in with her own hand. I've dreamed of her for twenty years—and there she is, right in front of me, in broad daylight."

"Hey," Barra said, catching his arm and murmuring in Phoenikian so that no man in the press through which they moved could overhear, "we have business that's more urgent right now, remember? Come on, we've only got a couple minutes before those fires need to go up."

"Go on without me."

"*Listen*, you ratfuck!" Barra whispered fiercely. "Kheperu's hanging his balls in the wind up there! It's his *life*, you understand? She's not going anywhere—she's here for the show, like everybody else. First things first, Sheshai, all right? Come on."

She looked around. One of those little groups of purposeful-looking men had left behind a red-faced, half-naked slave girl, and was coming right toward her.

"Shit! We're out of time," she said. "We've got to go *right now.*"

"Too late," Sheshai said, nodding toward the west, where Rahab stood. "She's seen me."

Even as Barra looked, Rahab's distant lips pulled back in a silent *Sheshai*—the word became a grimace of stunned dismay, then a twisted snarl of fear and hatred. The old woman turned and began to scrabble up the slope as fast as her tired legs and bent back would let her.

"She's going for Joshua," Sheshai breathed with triumphant malice. His eyes glittered. "She'll tell him there's a Jerichite here—they'll stop everything till they find me and kill me. We'll never make it to the Sanctuary in time to set the firebombs."

He turned to Barra with a beautiful, glorious smile. "We have to stop her."

"You *let* her see you!" Barra snarled furiously, gathering a handful of the front of Sheshai's galabiyeh. "You did it on *purpose!*"

He met her fury with indifferent madness. "So?"

"So *this*, you son of a whore," she said as she drove her right fist through the short arc of a shovel hook to sink deep into his solar plexus.

He folded around her fist, gasping, clutching his belly. Surprised murmurs and laughter came from men in the crowd around them.

"Anyone who thinks that was funny," she said in Canaanite, "can step right fucking up and get one of his own. Now *piss off!*"

They backed up, chuckling, lifting their hands in mock surrender. She tangled her fingers in Sheshai's hair and hauled his reddened face up to meet hers.

"Come on, you shitcake bastard," she said. "Like you said: we have to stop her."

"You are a fraud, Egyptian."

Kheperu barely heard the High Priest's words. His gaze ranged desperately over the crowd near the Sanctuary wall. Sheshai was nowhere to be seen; no more was Barra.

How in bloody fuck was he supposed to time his prophecy if he missed their signal?

"What is it you search for?" The High Priest studied his fingernails, deliberately avoiding Kheperu's eyes. "Some sign from your confederates?"

*Oh, please,* Kheperu thought with more of an edge of contempt than he really felt. *Am I a child, to be caught out with such a tactic?* He clasped his damp palms together over the heel of his stolen staff and said with impenetrable smugness, "I am in league only with Yahweh Sabaoth, El Shaddai. It is His Word you mock, when you accuse me."

"Piffle," replied Eleazar. "I could eat an omer of pickled cabbage and *fart* better prophecy, you faker. Firebombs and smoke pots and rye-mold poison, that's what you have. Nothing more."

Kheperu drew himself up to his full height and glowered at the High Priest of Yahweh, and he raised his voice to be heard clearly by his crowd of followers.

"When fire comes from the Lord God to destroy the Sanctuary that *you have profaned with your unbelief*, fall then to the earth to repent and beg the forgiveness of Yahweh the Merciful!"

He turned to address the crowds upon the slopes below, not only his devoted followers but all the rest who now gathered there, tens upon tens of thousands spread out like a forest on the slopes of the valley.

He pitched his voice to its most nasal and penetrating; if he couldn't see Barra and Sheshai, he'd have to hope that they would hear him and play along. They'd had plenty of time to set the incendiaries, hadn't they? He was sure they had; it seemed to him that he'd stood here in the presence of Eleazar and Joshua and Joshua's hulking aide for a very long time indeed.

"See now how the Lord God has turned against these, His false priests! See how Joshua has forsaken the Lord, and the Lord lifts His Hand against him! *See the anger of Yahweh strike flame into the Sanctuary!*"

He breathed deeply, for a dramatic pause.

A faint breath of breeze rippled the Sanctuary walls.

No shouts, no cries, no lick of flame, not even the barest whiff of smoke came with that breeze.

This was bad.

"You shall see," Kheperu went on as smoothly as he was capable, "God's Wrath against Joshua and those who follow his blasphemous path! You shall see the sign of my truth, as a fiery chariot descends to carry me alive up to the heights of the holy mountain, at the Right Hand of God!"

As he drew breath to continue, Joshua himself spoke for the first time, quietly for Kheperu's ears alone.

"It wouldn't be Barra Coll Eigg Rhum for whom you wait, would it?" he said darkly. "It wouldn't be the pagan whore, that you expect to set fire to this holy place?"

Kheperu licked sweat from his lips. "Who?"

"I am not so swift to doubt as is my friend Eleazar. But I must learn the truth of you, Egyptian. My duty to my people, and to God, demands it. I am told of your signs and wonders. I have heard that the Sanctuary will burn, but I would prefer that you show another sign. A *new* sign."

"God is not to be tested," Kheperu began.

"If God is truly with you," Joshua suddenly said in a voice that blared like a trumpet, turning out toward the gathered crowd and spreading his arms wide, "if I have strayed from His True Path, let him strike me dead where I stand. Let Him destroy me, for if my service is not pure, I have no life worth living. *Let it be so!*"

*If wishing could stop your heart, you* shasu *bastard*, Kheperu thought, *you'd get an answer to that prayer fast enough.* "Yahweh does not demand your life," Kheperu said, very nearly as loudly as Joshua, "but your *obedience.* You must *live*, that you may turn Israel back onto His True Path. As an ignorant shepherd, you have led them astray; with the instruction of Yahweh for wisdom, you may yet shepherd them to safety."

"Do you know the penalty for false prophecy?" Joshua asked quietly, and then did not wait for an answer. "It is to be dragged outside the camp and pelted with heavy stones until you die."

He swung back to face out over the valley and roared, *"If this man truly speaks with the voice of Yahweh, let there be a sign unto us, and let it come now."*

"Now?" Kheperu said weakly. *How much does he know? Does he really know I'm with Barra, or was he only fishing?*

Another thought struck his belly like a falling brick: *What if they caught her?*

Barra stepped out from behind a tent not far from the frightened, bent-backed old woman's path. "Rahab!" she hissed urgently. "In here! Quickly!"

Rahab looked at her with uncertain panic. "What? I—you—there's a *man*, a man is following . . ."

"I know," Barra said. "Quickly! Inside, before he sees you!"

Barra held the door-curtain aside for her, and the old woman scuttled breathlessly into the empty tent. Barra followed her in and closed the curtain behind her.

"That man—that man, he's from *Jericho*!" Rahab's eyes rolled in terror, and she could barely speak for panting. "He should be dead!

He's supposed to be dead—they're all dead. He's dead, *he's dead but he's come back for me!"*

Something dark began to howl in a deep and shadowed corner of Barra's mind.

The bloated, pocked face of this old, harmless-looking woman before her seemed to transform into a monstrous leering creature, and the sun-bright walls of the tent, its scent of the sweaty robes of the man who slept here, even the feel of the earth beneath her sandals began to fade, and swirl away into a distant darkness.

Whispers hissed inside her skull, hushed with hatred and muttering a hunger for this old woman's life.

"How do you know me?" Rahab asked, squinting now at Barra, slowly realizing that something was wrong.

Barra could only stand in the tent and sway like a poplar in a cold north wind; the struggle against the memory of the Jericho dead consumed her.

She'd had a plan, when she'd circled wide to intercept the Jerichite woman, a plan to persuade Rahab to hide here while Barra pretended to carry the message to Joshua. It would have been simple and effective— she only needed to buy five minutes, at most—and it would have worked.

But she could no longer speak, nor move. Even a gesture would collapse her resistance, and she would leap upon this woman and sink savage teeth into her throat.

"Who are you?" Rahab asked, her face now turning to suspicion and crafty malice. "What's wrong with you? Are you sick?"

Barra knew that in another breath, the old woman would brush past her and scurry out of the tent, and that she could not allow. As Rahab shifted her weight to move, Barra's fist lashed out of its own accord, striking the old woman hard enough across the cheekbone to knock her flat.

Rahab writhed on the floor of the tent, squalling like a child with pain and fear. Barra stood over her, rigid, shaking, trembling with her need to kill this woman, and shivering with her absolute resistance to this need.

The *sceon tiof* had shown her this woman's life.

It showed her the unconquerable fear that had driven Rahab to betray her people; she'd done it because she had seen no other chance to save the lives of her children, and her father. It showed her the acid self-loathing which had burned away any joy Rahab could ever take from any day. It showed her the terrible judgment of her children, who despised her.

It showed her the fierce courage she'd once had, the courage to renounce herself and everything she'd ever been or believed in for the sake of her children's lives, and it showed her how that courage had shriveled into a cackling hatred òf herself and every other human being.

Barra swayed, balancing on the edge of a knife; to one side lay murder, and to the other, a burst of sympathetic tears.

The same hand that had struck Rahab to the floor now extended to help her back up. The old woman looked at it fearfully, as she would at some alien insect crawling up her dress.

In that short moment of suspension, the door-curtain swished aside, and Sheshai came in.

Rahab saw the murder in his eyes, and she squawked like a frightened goose. She tried to get her hands up to hold him off, but he brushed past Barra and kicked her with brutal accuracy in the side of the head. Her eyes glazed and her arms relaxed, and he forced her onto her back. He dropped one knee into the pit of her stomach, got both hands around her throat, and squeezed.

Rahab's face went red, then purple shading toward black, and her blackened tongue stuck out from her swelling lips as her eyes rolled in mad panic, and she clawed desperately at Sheshai's arms.

Sheshai never said a word. His manic grin never slipped, only sharpened like a knife being whetted against the stone of her death. He moaned, deep in the back of his throat, like a man reaching a sexual peak.

Rahab's heels kicked the tent floor, and her eyes bulged as though they would leap from their sockets—and, at the end, they fixed on Barra as the last of their light faded.

In the grip of the *sceon tiof*, Barra knew Rahab's death as she had those thousands of others—as though it was her own.

And like those thousands of others, she could only watch.

Rahab's sphincters relaxed with her death, spreading a thick fecal reek throughout the tent, but Sheshai's grip never faltered. He held on to the corpse's throat, shaking it, and squeezing until the cervical vertebrae snapped under his hands.

Barra found she could move again. She put her hand on Sheshai's shoulder. "It's over, Sheshai. She's dead. Come on, we have to get out of here."

No hint of reason showed in Sheshai's face. "If only she had another neck I could twist," he muttered, his hands flexing and clenching as though they hurt him. "And another . . . and *another*—"

"Come on," she said. "We have to move. Kheperu's probably feeling real fucking lonely out there by now."

A grinding roar sounded, low, below the voices of the crowd. It came from outside, but also from *inside*, from here within the tent—below the tent; it vibrated through the soles of Barra's sandals—and she staggered as the earth beneath her pitched as though the land had become a stormy sea.

*"Let flame rain upon the Tabernacle, if this man speaks truth!"* Joshua had thundered from the very gate of the Sanctuary. "But: if *I* am the true prophet, let the *very earth shake with God's Wrath at this fraud beside me!"*

Then Joshua had stamped his foot, and fifty thousand men staggered, for with a great subterranean roar, the valley itself had trembled beneath them.

Kheperu lost his footing, and found himself clutching Eleazar for balance. Eleazar took in the expression on Kheperu's face with a thin smile, and spoke softly while only barely moving his lips.

"Let's see you match *that* trick, eh?"

Joshua wheeled on Kheperu, his raddled face blazing with triumph and righteous fury.

With neck-bulging effort, he choked his voice back to a flat and level tone. "Stone this stinking pile of dung."

Barra had been through earthquakes before—Tyre, where she made her home, was known for them—but this had a different feel, somehow, a shorter, sharper bounce, as though the earth were a table struck by the fist of a strong man, and it alarmed her.

She had a feeling this was a bad omen.

She grabbed Sheshai by the back of his collar and yanked him to his feet. She took both of their shoulder satchels in her other hand and dragged them all out of the tent. For a moment, the brilliant sunlight on the valley slope blinded her, and into the stinging whiteness that seemed to consume her brain came thunderous shouts from the crowd all around, a chanted roar of triumph that seemed to shake the earth again.

*Joshua! Joshua! Joshua!*

"Shit," she growled, "shit shit shit," knuckling fiercely at her eyes. Finally, her vision began to clear.

Her words were prophetic: in the short interval she'd been within the tent, everything had gone to shit.

Up at the gate of the Sanctuary, high above her, a ring of hard-faced men closed grimly in upon Kheperu, who backed away, holding his staff in a futile guard stance.

Beside them stood Joshua, his arms upraised as he addressed the crowd, his voice like the crash of mighty waves, invoking the followers of the false prophet to repent and pray to Yahweh for forgiveness.

And here, close by, two of those little groups of determined men converged on her, one above her on the slope and one below; both had their eyes on her, and were moving toward her with all deliberate speed.

She had no time to waste on subtlety.

She drew Sheshai close. His face was still blank with sexual afterglow; she slapped him hard, then again, until intelligence returned to his eyes.

"I'll give you a five-second head start," she hissed. "Find out where that High Priest of theirs keeps his tent. If I live through this, I'll meet you back near where we left the wagon. Understand?"

He nodded dumbly, and she gave him a shove that sent him stumbling downslope.

Then she slung the two satchels crosswise over her shoulders, put the back of her hand to her mouth and let out a shrill scream of raw terror.

All around her, heads turned at this horrible sound.

*"Murder!"* she screamed in thick and panicked Canaanite. "Oh God, she's *dead*, dead, she's *murdered*, right *here*, here in this tent! Help! Murder! *Help!*"

Men and women rushed toward her, converging from all directions. The two groups of searching men found themselves suddenly swept along in a river of humanity that buffeted them first in one direction, then another. Barra, on the other hand, ducked low and scuttled upstream, dodging whoever she could and letting her sharp elbows and judicious use of her knees clear a path when she couldn't find one open.

There came more screams and shouts as the tent was swept open and Rahab's body was found within, and by that time Barra was well away—even if her pursuers saw which way she went, which she doubted, it would take them some time to spot her again in this sea of Habiru.

Up above her, in the Sanctuary Gate, strong men held Kheperu's arms and legs, and they carried the struggling Egyptian like a calf to be branded.

Muttering an Egyptian prayer that Kheperu had taught her, Barra strode into a gap in the crowd, and drew from one of her satchels a pair of spheres slightly smaller than one of her fists, each covered with some sticky black tarlike substance. With the prayer still upon her lips, she peeled back a layer of the tar with her thumbnail, and the balls began to smoke.

"Kheperu! *Run like bloody fuck for the god-box!*" she cried in Greek. There was no way to know if he could hear her, and she immediately hurled one of the smoking balls high up the valley slope, over the crowd.

Barra rarely missed a throw of any kind, and she did not miss this one. The black ball struck one of Kheperu's captors and clung to the back of his burnoose. The fellow stopped, and looked around himself at the ground, not hurt but puzzled, wondering what had hit him.

A man near Barra strode toward her. He pulled a knife from his belt and demanded, "Here! What did you just throw? I saw that!"

"You want one?" Barra said. "Here, catch!"

She lobbed the other sphere to him underhand, and he caught it instinctively. He lifted the ball up to his eyes to examine it in the sunlight, and it exploded with a *whoosh* into an expanding burst of white fire. He fell back, screaming, inhaling the flames and charring his lungs, already dead as he thrashed on the ground, spasmodically trying to roll away from the flames that still fed upon his flesh.

On the slope above, the man Barra had hit also screamed, spinning in panicked circles as he tried to rip away the clothes that burned in swirling flames around him.

Shouting people surrounded both burning men, and Barra sprinted through the crowd. She scrambled up the slope while she again muttered the short Egyptian prayer and primed two more fire balls. These she flipped at random into the crowd, not aiming at anyone in particular. They detonated behind her, and she kept moving.

Now many of the Habiru around her had realized that she was the killer in their midst; most pressed back away from her, frantically fighting to get clear before she could burn them as well; the rest fought, cursing and battering about themselves with knotted fists, to push through the fleeing mob so that they could come at her and cut her down.

Barra still sprinted up the slope, her breath shortening into choppy gasps. She couldn't see what had happened with Kheperu, but huge blazing fountains of flame spat toward the sky from somewhere near the Sanctuary Gate—that would be the enormous incendiary he'd been waiting to use as his "flaming chariot." She wasted no time gawking; he'd either make it, or he wouldn't, and she had problems of her own.

Armed men closed in upon her from all sides.

Barra's next two fire balls arced above the valley's crest, and clung to the fabric walls of the Sanctuary. She managed to get two more off before the first ones exploded, and in a single moment a stretch of the Sanctuary wall nearly a bowshot long suddenly bloomed with flame.

Thousands upon thousands of Habiru below, who had seen the other fires and heard the shouting and knew something was wrong, although they could not have said what, now saw Kheperu's prediction come true with a vengeance; some few may have glimpsed the balls that Barra had thrown, but all saw the sudden blossom of flame. A mighty roar arose within that valley, louder by far than the earlier chants of Joshua's name.

When one of the men holding him was suddenly consumed by fire, Kheperu knew exactly what to do. There was one place of refuge to which he could flee, and only one.

It had been, after all, his goal all along. He hadn't planned on getting there precisely in this way, but no plan is perfect.

Sometimes, one must improvise.

The burning man twisted and howled, and the other Israelites released Kheperu to try to smother the flames that roared up from the clothing of their unfortunate comrade. Kheperu reached within his robe and pulled open the knotted belt that held his false belly in place; this false belly was a pouch of *sh'asbiu* bigger than his head, along with one small, black, tar-covered ball.

Joshua roared something incomprehensible and furious, and lunged at Kheperu with his staff upraised; Kheperu skipped nimbly aside from the old man's rush, and broke the fire ball into two parts that instantly began to smoke and hiss. He ripped the false belly in half with a twist of his arms, threw the powder into the air and ignited it with the halves of the fire ball, closing his eyes and throwing himself to the ground against the thundering eruption of blinding white fire.

When he opened his eyes again, men on all sides of him reeled, their clothes afire, their arms thrown across their scorched faces. Piles of *sh'asbiu* still flared here and there on the ground, sending cascades of fire fountaining toward the sky.

Kheperu sprang to his feet. He needed a weapon; a quick glance around didn't show that staff that the Habiru had taken, and he had only a shaved moment before they'd be all over him again.

A couple of steps away, Joshua blundered about sightlessly, rubbing at his eyes with the back of one wrist, smoke wisping from his hair—and a thick, knotted staff in his other hand.

"Give me *that*," Kheperu snapped, snatching the staff from Joshua's hand. Joshua clutched blindly at the air, and Kheperu lifted the staff. *Cracking the old general's skull should do wonders for* shasu *morale,* he thought with grim satisfaction, but before he could swing, a hard shoulder slammed into his back and drove him, breathless and stunned, to the ground.

He barely managed to turn faceup. Joshua's burly aide straddled his chest, his face swollen with unreasoning fury. His hands found Kheperu's throat, and his grip filled Kheperu's eyes with darkening clouds.

The black-bearded aide was large and powerful, younger and much stronger than Kheperu—but he was, after all, a priest, not a fighter, and Kheperu's trade for many years had included fighting for his life.

The broad-shouldered aide never had a chance.

Kheperu hooked his thumb into the aide's throat at the notch in his collarbone, and jabbed sharply. The aide reared back, gagging, and for an instant his grip loosened upon Kheperu's throat, which was all the time the Egyptian needed. He got ahold of one of the aide's thumbs and bent it backward until it gave way with a wet *pop*, and the aide howled with the sudden pain, yanking his hand free and half-standing to get away. While the aide clutched his broken thumb, Kheperu sat up and punched him solidly in the testicles.

The aide's eyes nearly bulged from his head, and he froze, motionless except for convulsive gasping, in that long stretching second between the first searing pain of impact and the following hammerblow of nausea.

Kheperu scrambled out from between his legs and stood. All around him was shouting confusion. Half the men nearby were blind from the *sh'asbiu*; many of them still beat at their smoldering clothing or rolled on the ground to snuff the flames that climbed their robes; the Sanctuary had caught fire, and the priests and nearby men all fell over each other in their haste to yank down the walls and put it out.

Eleazar, of all people, the aging High Priest, was the only man who turned to attack him, his eyes staring in fury and his staff raised to strike.

*Shit*, Kheperu thought, *if I have this much trouble with their priests, I'm glad I don't have to deal with the bloodyfucking warriors!*

He swept up Joshua's staff in time to block Eleazar's swing—the High Priest was even less of a warrior than was the aide. Kheperu struck Eleazar's staff aside and doubled the priest over with a sharp jab to the solar plexus—which brought another enraged roar from the aide, who staggered toward him yelling *Abba! Abba!*

Kheperu cursed him for being tougher than expected, and struck him a powerful blow across the face that shattered his cheekbone and turned his limbs to cloth. Blood burst from his broken eye socket, and Kheperu felled him with an overhand strike that brought the end of Joshua's staff down squarely on the top of the aide's head.

The aide pitched forward with the boneless flop of a dead man.

Eleazar howled like a woman in labor; inexplicably, he fell to his knees beside the downed aide and gathered the broad-shouldered man into his arms.

Kheperu took advantage of this opportunity by bolting like a startled cat.

He scuttled between shouting blind men and around others who were raising great clouds of dust and smoke as they pulled down the burning cloth walls of the Sanctuary and stamped out the fire in the dirt. Before anyone had any idea where he was headed, Kheperu stood at the door-curtain of the Tabernacle, and he pulled it to one side.

Within stood a large golden lampstand with six arms, worked in a fancy flowering-almond motif, a large table of some dark wood, its top covered with beaten gold, with about a dozen loaves of bread on golden plates on it, and in the middle, a large altar, also covered with beaten gold, its four corners decorated with large curving horns that were stained with what looked in the lamplight like dried blood. Kheperu slipped past them, thoughtfully snagging one of the loaves of bread and tucking it inside his robe, and he went to the inner curtain.

This curtain would lead into the Holy of Holies.

He stared at the curtain for one long moment, taking a deep breath to steady his nerves.

Within would lie the box in which the Israelites carried their god. To enter here was death, for any man or woman on earth saving only the High Priest and the Lord's Anointed—which meant that no one could follow him in here except Eleazar and Joshua. An effeminate priest and a man nearing ninety, Kheperu was fairly certain he could handle.

With one last glance over his shoulder, he flipped the curtain aside and went in.

\* \* \*

The armed men that pursued Barra were not impressed with the playing-out of Kheperu's prophecy of the burning Sanctuary. They surrounded her just below the crest of the valley, and approached her with drawn swords and leveled spears.

She stood in the middle of the tightening ring of sharp and hungry bronze, panting harshly, with her hands upon her knees. She couldn't get through them; the longer they took to close in around her, the more of her breath she'd recover.

"Take me to Joshua," she panted. "He'll want a word with me."

"We'll take you nowhere but *Sheol*, you vile cunt," one of the men snarled. "You have attacked God Himself, and I will personally shove this spear up your ass until it comes out your throat."

"Oh, it's like that, is it?" she said. As they approached with another cautious step, then another, her hand dipped into a satchel and came out with a fire ball. She muttered the prayer, peeled back the strip of tar with her thumbnail, and displayed it to the men who closed upon her.

"We don't fear your fire, cunt," the man said.

"No?" Barra said. She dropped the smoking ball back inside the bulging satchel. "Glad to hear it."

The man's eyes widened, and now the other men that surrounded her were no longer quite so eager to close in.

"Hey—" he said, "hey, don't—"

She swung the satchel through a short arc and tossed it at the Israelite's feet. "You don't fear my fire? Really?"

The man's nerve broke and he lunged to one side. The men near him parted, scattering like pigeons away from a cat, and Barra dashed straight at the satchel.

One shaved second after she leaped over it, the satchel detonated with a shuddering boom that sent flames shooting past her, ignited the back hem of her dress and slapped her tumbling along the slope, skidding downhill with rocks slicing her dress and shredding her skin beneath it.

She rolled up to her feet, frantically disentangled her legs from the long strap of the other satchel and sprinted away, trailing smoke and clutching the satchel to her chest.

Too many people had cleared away here, though, and the men behind her began to cast spears; she ducked and dodged, thanking her gods that the Habiru were less expert with spears than they were with slings, and ran in the random jags of an antelope with a lion on its tail, working her way toward the Sanctuary Gate.

Toward Joshua.

There he was, she could pick him out now, barely a stone's throw away. He stood near the Sanctuary Gate, where men now had the cloth walls down and were stamping them out. Eleazar knelt nearby, cradling the head of Phinehas in his lap. Joshua pointed down at her and thundered something in his powerful voice, and men left off stamping out the burning cloth and started down the slope toward her, producing knives and short Greek-style swords.

Kheperu was nowhere to be seen.

Barra gritted her teeth and took a deep breath. She still had a chance to make this work.

She dug into the satchel and brought out one last fire ball. She held it high with her thumbnail set against its skin and the mouth of the satchel held open below.

"Back off!" she snapped. "This bag has *triple* the incendiaries of the other. If I set this off, you'll all burn with me."

This bag, in fact, held sausages and cheese and a skin of wine, a couple of loaves of hard bread and a double handful of dried fruit; nearly all of the incendiaries had been in the one she'd already used, but the threat alone was enough to slow them.

"I want to talk with Joshua," she said. "That's all. Just a few words with Joshua ben Nun."

The men exchanged wary glances, wanting neither to give in nor to call her bluff.

Blood trailed a ticklish line down from the fresh scrapes on Barra's back.

After what seemed like a very long time, Joshua's gravel voice rumbled from above, "Let her approach. I would have words with her, as well."

Joshua turned away from the pagan whore's approach and came to Eleazar's side. Phinehas lay in his father's lap, breathing shallowly in random, hitching gasps; occasionally one of his fingers or a foot would twitch like those of an uneasy sleeper; his eyes were slitted, partially open. Eleazar rocked him as though he were an exhausted child.

"Eleazar," Joshua began, "you should—"

"He'll live," Eleazar said. "He'll live, don't you think, Joshua? He's strong, still young. He can live through this."

"As God wills," Joshua said.

"And as *you* will," Eleazar said. "God loves you, Joshua; if you ask for it, He will keep the life within my son."

"God does not grant my every wish," Joshua said sternly. *If He did, we would not be here, at war, right now.*

But as he looked down at Phinehas' broken, bloody face, his heart hurt him, and he wished that he had the gift of gentle speech, that he could give comfort as others do. Instead he could only set his mouth into a grim line and shake his head. "I am sorry, Eleazar. You know I care for him."

"And you'll pray for him, won't you?" Eleazar's voice sharpened, honing the plea into a command. "You'll ask God for his life?"

"I will." *Even as I pray for every son of Israel.* Joshua caught the eyes of several nearby men and beckoned them to Eleazar's side. "Help the High Priest carry his son to his tents," he told them, and then he said to Eleazar, "You can better care for him there."

Eleazar glanced downslope to the pagan whore, now nearly upon them, and his gaze became a lance of hatred. "Leave you? Leave you now, when *she* is here?"

Joshua put a restraining hand upon the High Priest's shoulder. "Go with your son and tend his wounds. He needs you more than I do. Leave her to me."

"Don't let her get away," Eleazar said thickly. "No matter what happens, don't let her escape again."

"Fear not," Joshua rasped. He tried to put the force of conviction into his voice, but it came out, against his will, sounding vaguely sad. "She is now in the Hand of God. She cannot escape."

*Any more than I can,* he thought. *Or any of us.*

He turned away from the men who now gently lifted the still form of Phinehas, and went to face the whore.

Her wrap was torn and stained with blood, and a line of glowing embers still climbed a short section of the hem. Sweat drew black-edged trails down from the dye that darkened her hair, and intermittent flashes of blue-painted skin showed through the rents in her dress.

Her face wore an expression of animal ferocity, the lethal determination of a lion that holds the throat of a bull in its jaws; he fancied that he saw there as well a sort of sullen adolescent rebelliousness, the look he'd see on teenage children of his neighbors when they'd been caught stealing, or fondling each other, or looking upon foreign idols: a look of guilt and shame mixed with stubborn defiance.

*But perhaps,* he told himself, *that is only wishful imagination. Perhaps that is only what I hope she is feeling, or what I think I would feel, in her place . . . perhaps it is only a vain hope that she might have human feelings at all.*

The armed men moved with her as she approached, keeping as close as they dared. She still held the black ball in her hand, and she came up the slope at a slow walk; her gaze darted this way and that, taking in everything, especially the men who carried away the limp form of Phinehas, and the charred remnants of the Sanctuary wall.

"What was it," he demanded, "that you hoped to accomplish by this? What have you achieved here that will be worth your life?"

She didn't seem to hear his question; for some reason, she seemed more interested in Phinehas. "What happened to him?"

"Your false Egyptian prophet stole my staff and cracked his skull. What words did you want with me?"

"About the Egyptian prophet. I'm glad I got here in time to stop you."

Joshua's eyes narrowed. "To stop me from what?"

"From killing him. You wouldn't want to hurt a true prophet, would you?"

Joshua seemed to hear a thin edge of mockery under those words, but he could not be sure—it should have been there, but she seemed sincere. "He is no prophet."

"No?" she said. Now her wind seemed to be coming back, and she stood straighter, with a certain arrogance that brought Joshua's blood up to a slow boil.

"Every prediction he's made so far has come true, hasn't it? Even to the fire that struck the Sanctuary."

"Fakery," Joshua spat. "Fire sands and poisons and treacherous pagan whores, nothing more."

She grinned at him. "Who are you to dictate to God what tools He will use to work His Will?"

Her unknowing quote of Eleazar's mocking question stirred sudden fury; for an instant, Joshua wavered on the brink of a command to cut her down where she stood, but before he could speak, she said, "And I can do a bit of prophecy, once in a while, myself. Like, for example, I can tell you where the Egyptian prophet is, right now."

Joshua glanced around with a sharp frown. He couldn't remember seeing the Egyptian after the foul little man had felled Phinehas. Where had he gotten to? He could not have escaped, could he?

He put on a sarcastic face. "What, you mean to tell me he isn't sitting at the Right Hand of God, as he proclaimed?"

"No," Barra told him. "I mean to tell you that he *is*."

She showed her teeth, their edges stained with blood from her lips. "He's in the Tabernacle."

Joshua felt like he was choking, like his breath had turned to molasses in his lungs, and he was drowning. He clutched vainly at the air, seeking the support of his stolen staff. In the *Tabernacle*? In the Holy of Holies, face-to-face with the Mercy Seat and *God Himself*? It could not be. It was unthinkable!

All the men who had ringed her stared at him, their faces blank; they waited for him to laugh aside this futile lie, waited to be told that no man could enter beyond the vestibule of the Tabernacle and live, saving only Eleazar, and Joshua himself.

"This is a lie," he rasped. "This lie gains you nothing; it is only a weak and silly tale."

"Sure it is," Barra said, and now her mockery was unmistakable. "Go see for yourself, old man."

The impossibility of what was happening unstrung him; nothing in his life had ever prepared him for such a moment. For what seemed an eternity, he could only stand and dither, looking from her to the Tabernacle, and back again to her. The useless words rang senselessly inside his head. *In the Tabernacle? Impossible! Unthinkable! In the Tabernacle?*

Because something in her voice, in her manner, told him this was truth.

And if he had dared to doubt: a young Levite, his priestly raiment loose upon him, pelted toward him across the Sanctuary ground, and squeaked in a high and breaking voice, "Joshua! Joshua! The Egyptian—he's inside the Tabernacle! He shouts through the wall that if any approach, he will *burn the Ark*! Joshua, he will burn the Ark of the Covenant! What do we do?"

Joshua felt as though his chest was collapsing under the weight of massive stones. The impossible, the unthinkable had come to pass.

This vulgar little whore and her reeking flunky had taken God hostage.

Slowly, painfully, Joshua turned back to the pagan whore. "All right," he said hoarsely. "What do you want?"

Barra grinned at him. "I told you once before: I want you and your playmates to pack up and go home."

"Impossible," Joshua rasped. "God has commanded the destruction of Jebusi."

"Fair enough," she said, mockingly cheerful. "Let *him* handle it, then, why don't you?"

"Do not mock."

"I'll take my chances with Yahweh. It's you and the army that I want out of here. You have until noon tomorrow. By that time, the only Habiru I want to be able to see from the walls of Jebusi are the minimum necessary to cart away this tent of yours."

"This order I cannot give."

She shrugged. "Then we'll all be getting a whiff of what roasted Yahweh smells like, I guess."

"You cannot threaten God," Joshua said. "I am no savage, to believe that the Ark holds God Himself. It is only a vessel, that Yahweh fills with His Spirit—"

"Ay, whatever. So what? When your Host sees it go up in smoke, what are *they* gonna think? Shit, you can't even tell them Kheperu's *in* there! They'll panic, and you know it. Look at these guys here," she said, waving the black ball in a gesture to include the men that ringed them.

Their weapons drooped, and on their faces was blank disbelief, mixed with anger—and growing fear. Joshua could read their minds as though their thoughts were printed upon their faces.

*Why does Yahweh allow this? Has He deserted us? Why does He not destroy these blasphemers?*

*What have we done to offend Him?*

*How will His Vengeance fall upon us this time?*

Joshua knew their thoughts so well because he heard their echoes within his own heart.

"We *can* tell the people," Joshua said slowly, realizing the truth of this even as he spoke. He felt obscurely pleased, to have summoned an answer as swift and clever as any of Eleazar's. "You have made of him a prophet. They will believe he communes with God, and be comforted."

"And when he sets fire to this god-box of yours?"

Joshua's heart thumped painfully within his chest. He said, "I cannot say what will happen, if your false prophet succeeds in burning the Ark, and the Tabernacle. I do know what will happen if I surrender to your extortion. I have seen God's Hand among us already, slaying any that speak against this war—slaying even those that innocently hear the words of others. If I turn my people aside, God will not spare them."

"That's not my problem," Barra said. "And it's not just Yahweh that you need to be worrying about, right now. It's the Egyptian army."

A sour, sickening taste grew in the back of Joshua's throat. "What Egyptian army?" he rasped, dreading the answer. "Your tiny garrison marched out yesterday."

Barra shook her head. "Joshua, Joshua, Joshua," she said with mock sadness. "You haven't been *listening*. Don't you remember the Third Sign of the Egyptian Prophet?"

*Egypt mounts upon Gilgal . . . Woe to Israel, if the Bride of Yahweh is bent across the Jebusite Anvil for the fall of the Egyptian Hammer . . .* These words whispered in Joshua's ears, and he shook his head sharply to drive them away.

"I don't believe it."

"Fine. Don't believe it. You've got, what, half a million Habiru here, something like that? I've seen them fight—they're very brave. Brave, at least, as long as they're sure that Yahweh is with them. If, on the other hand, something were to happen where they thought Yahweh *might not be on their side* . . . I seem to remember a story about the First Battle of Ai . . . ?"

She let her voice trail off significantly, and Joshua's habitual scowl deepened sharply.

She went on in a friendly, admiring tone. "Ay, you've got a great huge Host here, don't you? Hundred fifty, two hundred thousand fighters, maybe more, with their wives and their daughters and their slaves and all. How many of them have armor? How many of them have swords, or axes, or real spears?"

Her voice sharpened into spiteful derision. "How many are fighting with shitcake *farm* tools, with scythes and shovels and fucking *pruning hooks*?"

Joshua glowered at her, but made no answer.

"Were you listening to the prophet? He hasn't missed one yet— and if he's right again, every fucking Egyptian soldier in the Canaan District and every district adjoining are marching up Gilgal right now!" she spat harshly. "You served in the Egyptian army, Joshua. You know what a *hundred thousand Egyptian regulars* are going to do to your hoe-swinging farm boys?"

She stepped closer, slowly, deliberately, as though she was stalking him. "Just imagine them, Joshua. Imagine them marching down in their ranks, with spearmen in front, axe companies behind to protect the archers. How many chariots do you have? A hundred? Two? The Canaan Division alone has *five thousand*."

He could see it in his mind as vividly as though it happened before his eyes. He saw the undisciplined bravado of the Israelites as they threw themselves against the ranks of bronze and were cut down like winter wheat; he smelled the blood and shit, and heard the agonized cries of the dying.

"They are going to pound you to paste against these walls," Barra said. "And you know it."

He could not speak. Within his heart, he clung desperately to the promise of the Lord, to the victory to which Yahweh had given His Word.

"It is a lie," he forced out. "Egypt is a tottering oak, rotten at its core. She will not interfere."

"You could be right," Barra allowed calmly. "But think what'll happen if you're wrong."

She took another step closer to him, and pitched her voice low, so that the men around them could not hear. "I know your secret," she said.

He scowled down at her. "I have no secrets."

"Joshua, I *know*. I know that in your heart, you do not want this war. I know that you have searched for an excuse to end it. And I know that you can see now that you will not win. You cannot win. Save your people, Joshua. Take them home."

For one long wavering moment, her soft words, her tone of understanding and fellow feeling, weakened his resolve, but then he straightened and put aside his sinful doubt. "Cannot win? *Cannot?* The Lord created the heavens and the earth, and if He chooses to level this city, it will be as though these walls had never been built."

She shook her head sadly, reaching out to him as though to put her hand upon his arm in comfort. "Don't do this, Joshua. It's over. Go home."

He flinched away from her touch, and she turned her palm up, in a sad sketch of a shrug. "Go, Joshua. You won't get another chance."

He stepped back from her as he would from some venomous beast. "And while I live to serve the Lord, we will never submit to extortion. Your, your attempt to . . . to *terrorize* Israel will fail. The Lord is at our backs, and we cannot be pushed."

Barra sighed, and dropped the ball of black tar on the ground. She held open the satchel with one hand, while with the other she pulled out a bulging wineskin.

"I guess that means you're going to try to kill me again, huh? Mind if I have a drink, first?"

He snorted. "Very well." He lifted his head and raised his voice for the armed men around her. "Let her drink. Then cut her down."

"But Joshua," one man protested, "to spill blood within the camp, it is forbidden!"

"I will personally petition Yahweh for exception," Joshua growled darkly. "I believe He will grant it; He has done so before." He turned once again to Barra. "Drink, then. Delay serves nothing. You cannot escape."

"You could be right," she said with a cheery grin that belied her words. "It'd take a bloody spectacular diversion to get me out of the middle of this camp, wouldn't it?"

Again, Joshua snorted. "More than that: it would take an act of God."

While they spoke, the pagan whore had sliced the pine-pitch seal from the wineskin with her thumbnail, and now she tilted the skin high above her head. But instead of into her mouth, she directed the gushing ruby stream down into the neckline of her slave's dress, over her breasts and belly. The wine stained her dress, made it almost transparent, showing the curve of her taut ribs and the blunt hardness of her nipples.

Joshua stared. "What are you doing?"

Barra shrugged, smearing the dress back and forth across her body with both hands, as though wiping something away. She said, "You'll find out."

A breeze sprang up between them, freshening with astonishing rapidity toward a howling gale, picking up sand in dusty swirls, then gravel.

"Why make your boys spill blood?" she called, shouting to be heard above the rising roar of the wind. "If Yahweh wants my ass, let him come and take it himself!"

Flying sand scoured his eyes, and gravel stung his flesh, and now even larger rocks sprang upward on the back of the wind.

He understood now.

He understood the risk she took, in hopes it would cover her escape.

*When pursued by a demon,* she'd told him, *run for holy ground.* Then she had gestured at the blue mud that had painted her body. *I brought my holy ground with me.*

He lifted his hands to shield his face and cried, "Kill her! Kill her now, before she gets away!"

But the wind slashed the words from his lips, and he could not know if his men had heard. The cries of alarm from his people nearby became shouts and screams of pain as the uncaring wind sliced their flesh with the stones that rode it.

He could see her no longer; he could not open his eyes in the swirling grey-brown soup of dust and sand and stone; wind and flying rock buffeted him, and he thought, *If even I am struck so, how much worse must it be for the rest of my people?*

And he saw, within his mind, her fleet-footed dash back down the valley's slope, blind in the wind but knowing her way from the incline of the ground beneath her feet. He heard again his word to Eleazar, his promise that she would be taken . . .

Fury boiled within his breast, and a thundering roar rose to his lips.

*"In the Name of God, I command you to be still! In the Name of Yahweh, cease! Be gone!"*

And he staggered in the sudden silence.

Cautiously, he opened his eyes.

All around on the sunlit slopes, men and women and slaves picked themselves up gingerly from the ground, cringing fearfully with timid glances toward a sky of tranquil, indifferent blue.

"Find her!" he snarled to the men nearby, who even now feared to rise. "Find her and kill her. Kill her before she gets back inside the city!"

But even as he spoke, he knew his words were futile.

Far, far below, an astonishing distance into the Kidron Valley, he spied the figure of a slim woman running in a torn dress, only for one moment, until she vanished behind a fold of earth, and was gone.

For a long moment, he stood staring after her, stricken, wounded to the heart that this tiny pagan whore had once again mocked Yahweh to His very Face, and Yahweh had not seen fit to crush her.

Why did He forbear?

Was it that he *couldn't*?

But an instant later, he realized that these thoughts were only the treacherous weakness of an old man, maundering and senile. The failure was not God's, but his own.

He knew what must now be done, without question or hint of doubt. He could not risk that Barra Coll Eigg Rhum might have told him the truth; if Egypt did indeed come against the Nation of Israel, his best hope to save his people lay in being inside the city when the Egyptians arrived.

Within the city, those same walls that he now strove to break would defend his people.

Twice on the first day, the vanguard of the Host had broken onto the streets of Jerusalem; since that first day, the balance of the Host had assembled, and his army had more than doubled in size.

But still he hesitated, as he had hesitated and stalled all morning long. He had not forgotten that God's promise of victory was conditional. He had not forgotten that lives spent now may well be wasted—bloodshed in the service of futility.

There were three words that he must say, and each one would cut him like the stroke of a knife.

He said, "Cry the attack."

# 17

# Night in the House of Peace

**A**ll through that long spring afternoon, the Nation of Israel threw its strength against the walls of Jebusi.

Most of the defenders' arrows had been exhausted on the first day, and rocks and bricks were not enough to keep the Habiru back from the walls, nor could water be boiled fast enough to scald them; the fighting raged along the tops of Jebusi's walls all day long.

Again and again, the Habiru seized and held portions of the wall. Instead of ranging down into the city, as they had on the previous day, they defended their portions of the wall, holding them while further masses gathered below. The mercenaries and the pitifully small Jebusite city guard retook every section, but at terrible cost to them both.

Once the Habiru even took the wall on both sides of the Gate Tower and broke its doors; for a time, the fighting was room-to-room within it. When the mercenaries finally took it back, they cast the corpses of the Habiru down from its windows, and the bodies made a pile at its base taller than a man.

And the Habiru kept coming and coming, in wave after wave of fresh troops; they had more eager attackers than could be thrown at the walls at one time.

Each time a mercenary fell, he left a hole in the defense that could not be filled.

By midafternoon, the mercenaries no longer attempted to hold the entire wall; they formed themselves into flying patrols, concentrating their force at each Habiru breakthrough in turn. In close combat, their superior weaponry and experience gave them a decisive advantage— but the Habiru never stopped coming. A man might fell five attackers, only to take a wound from the sixth, and be killed by the ninth, and be borne under the rolling tide of Habiru to vanish and be forgotten as though he'd never fought at all.

But late in the day, with the sun dipping into the west like a swollen and festering wound in the sky, the Habiru finally fell back, dragging such of their wounded and their dead as they could.

A ragged cheer went up from the walls, a cheer that died away as quickly as it arose, for the cheer was so thin, from so few voices, that it was more frightening than the attack itself.

The mercenaries looked at each other, and themselves. More than half of the surviving defenders were seriously wounded; the men without some bleeding cut were few indeed.

They had held the wall for two days.

They all knew they wouldn't hold it for three.

The more experienced among them shrugged grimly. They knew the next attack—the final attack—wouldn't last an hour.

Joshua did not watch the attack. He spent the day among the camps of the wounded, watching the rivers of bleeding, broken men limp back from the walls of Jerusalem. Most of the wounded went back to their own tribes to be cared for; those who could not make it that far were brought here, to this sprawling city of tents, with its still air thick and foul with the bowel stench of gut-pierced men. He walked among them, listening to their choked-back whimpers of pain, to their fevered ravings and the rare, pitifully rare, screams of agony.

These men summoned every minah of their courage, expended every ounce of their will for no other reason than to die in honorable silence.

Most of them wanted nothing more from Joshua than a squeeze of his hand and a nod of approval. They wanted only that someone would acknowledge their courage, that someone would say to them, *You're very brave*, as they slipped into the darkness.

He had sent scouts out this afternoon, riding for Gilgal on several of the Host's few horses; they still had not returned. As he walked among his dying kindred, Joshua did not know whether he had sent these men against the walls, to fight and bleed and die, for no reason other than a pagan whore's easy lie.

As the afternoon had slipped toward night, Joshua's nerve failed him, and he could not stand it anymore.

Men had come to him with word of the pagan whore: she had gained the wellhouse in the Kidron Valley and vanished inside it. The men who pursued her there had found a tunnel cut through the rock, a tunnel guarded by enormous howling savages that had driven them back—of the ten men who had followed her into the wellhouse, only three returned. By the time more men could be organized to go in, the tunnel had been blocked with a barricade of stone and timber, and they could not force it, down in those cramped quarters.

She had escaped.

Joshua had ordered the men who brought this news to guard that wellhouse themselves, to kill any that might emerge. Perhaps they could not use this tunnel to gain entrance to the city—but they could, at least, deny its use to the Jebusites and their pagan whore.

But none of this changed the fundamental truth of the situation.

Barra Coll Eigg Rhum was back within the walls of Jerusalem.

He could not throw away the lives of these men uselessly. He could not allow another ten thousand to stagger back from the wall, to die here with no family at their side.

Through runners, he gave the order to retreat.

It might take an hour for the command to filter through the Host, an hour during which more young brave men would throw their lives away.

He could not watch.

He had paced up to the high ridge, near where a ring of archers encircled the Tabernacle in hopes that the Egyptian blasphemer would show himself. He had listened to the archer captain's shouted conversation with the false prophet inside, and heard the Egyptian's screeched replies, dire threats on both sides, and had merely shook his head and paced on without comment, walking unsteadily, wishing for his staff with every step.

All day long, it had chewed at his belly, the image of this foul Egyptian within the Tabernacle. He'd struggled to push aside these thoughts, but they had always lurked at the fringes of his mind, eating his confidence.

There had been no way to keep this from the Host; rumor ran wild through the camps. In some, the Egyptian held the Lord Himself hostage within the Tabernacle, and the Host was doomed. In others, Yahweh had descended to gather the Egyptian to His Breast in a whirlwind of fire, crying in a great voice that all had heard, that here was his True Prophet, defiled and abused by Israel, saved by the Hand of God.

Dozens of men had volunteered to go inside and slay the Egyptian, but Joshua could not accept their offers. The Lord's own law demanded death for any man who enters the Holy of Holies, save only the High Priest and Joshua himself; he could not allow them to throw away their lives, when it was likely that the Egyptian could carry out his threats despite them.

He had seen how quickly those fire bombs could burn.

There was nothing he could do; with half a million men at his command, he was helpless.

He moved on, walking deliberately away. The only answer to his futility was to concentrate on a problem he could do something about.

From the highest point upon the ridge, he scanned the surrounding countryside until he found what he sought. There, along the road, perhaps an hour's march away or a little less, that broken ground would serve.

If he brought his army there, to do battle where the Egyptians would be constricted, where they could be surrounded, and their column chopped into segments like a venomous snake, he could face them. Not to destroy them—that was a vain dream—but to bloody their noses so badly that they'd retreat and regroup; it would buy him at least another day or two to take the city before he'd have to hold it against them.

He knew, too, that he was not the only man who could lead night marches. If the Egyptians were already on Gilgal, they could easily be here by dawn tomorrow. They would press through from the west and push the Host of Israel toward the sea, to crush them against the fortified garrison cities of the Coast. Israel would be trapped, with nowhere to turn for shelter, and Pharaoh would finally satisfy his lust, after this half century and more since Israel had escaped his grasp at the Sea of Reeds: Ramses would finally drive the Nation of Israel into extinction.

What the Egyptian blasphemer had said was true in this part: *Woe unto Israel, if the Bride of Yahweh is bent across the Jebusite anvil for the fall of the Egyptian Hammer.*

Woe, indeed.

It was decided, then. Again, he had no choice. If the scouts returned with word that the army of Egypt was indeed camped upon Gilgal, he would have to march out to meet them, to choose his own ground for the battle.

He stumped back down into the camps and watched the retreat.

As the attack ebbed like an outgoing tide, Joshua wove through the camps back to his own tent, and ate a solitary meal in silence, the slaves making a ring around him to keep petitioners at bay. After his meal, he rose and moved heavily toward the tents of Eleazar.

It seemed to take hours to get there, for with every step, another man would call out to him, or grasp his arm with anxious questions.

*Is it true that Ramses' army marches upon us? Is it true that the Egyptian prophet lies with God in the Tabernacle, and none dare approach? Is it true that the same evil desert spirit which defied you before the walls yesterday noon was the one to burn the Sanctuary, or was that a fire from God, as the prophet's followers insisted?*

Joshua answered these questions, and many others, as best he could, without telling so much as to cause undue distress. He reserved that distress to himself; each question bit him like a sand fly.

Each question was only surface, like clouds reflected in the ripples of a pond; all these questions, every one that he faced on that walk, were but faint distorted images of the one true fear in every man's heart.

*Is it true that God intends to punish us? Is it true that you have led us here to be destroyed?*

The sun sank below the horizon an hour or more before he finally reached the High Priest's tent. Eleazar sat outside, on the ground with no cloth beneath him. He sifted sand and ash back and forth through his fingers, as though he considered pouring them upon his head in mourning, while his slaves prepared a meal around his small fire. He stared blindly into the rising sparks, and when Joshua first inquired about Phinehas, he did not answer.

When Joshua asked again, Eleazar said faintly, "He lives."

"That is well, then," Joshua said. "He is strong. With the help of God, he will survive to succeed you as High Priest."

"He should have succeeded me long ago," Eleazar muttered tonelessly. "He'd have been a better High Priest than I ever was."

"Eleazar—"

"You called the retreat with an hour of daylight left," he said. "Why? Why did you do that? And I was told that she got away—they say an angel came and raised a storm to cover her escape. And Phinehas—Phinehas lies with one eye pierced and bloody, and his skull broken, he cannot speak, he cannot move—why? Why, Joshua? Why would Yahweh punish him? God had no more faithful servant than my son."

Eleazar sifted the ash from hand to hand. "Why do I find that now, this late in my life, nothing seems to make sense to me anymore?"

"I called the retreat," Joshua said slowly, "to spare the lives of our men."

"But *why?*" Eleazar insisted. "If they must die, they can die as well tonight as tomorrow. Look! The moon is only waning, and there are no clouds above—you could attack again! There is light enough for fighting—send them back against the wall, Joshua. Send them now!"

Joshua scowled at him. "This bloodthirst—is this because of the injury to your son?"

Eleazar rose, and his eyes shone red with reflected firelight as though embers had been set within his skull. "Phinehas gives his life to your war. It cannot be *wasted* . . . I fear—I have heard—there is talk of retreat." He looked away, and his voice was hushed. "I am afraid I have given my son for nothing . . ."

Words rose to Joshua's lips, oaths that there would be no retreat, that he would spend every life in Israel to bring Jerusalem down, but before he could speak, he was interrupted by a clatter of hooves on stone and shouts of excited men.

A scout had returned.

Someone had directed him to Eleazar's tent, and when he galloped close enough to see Joshua there, he reined in and slipped off the horse's back. He threw the reins to one of Eleazar's slaves and dashed to Joshua's side.

"I *saw* them!" he gasped breathlessly. "I saw them—campfires upon Gilgal like the stars in a clear sky!"

Joshua passed a hand before his eyes, and massaged his temples against a growing pain. "How many?"

"They could not be counted!" the scout said, his eyes rolling like those of a spooked horse. "Fires enough for a hundred thousand men, or more!"

People heard him all around, and suddenly the chill night was filled with whispers.

*The prophet . . . !*

*The Third Sign . . . !*

Joshua ground his teeth together and bunched his hands into enormous knotted fists. "Eleazar," he said, "Phinehas will be in my prayers tonight. I must leave you now. I must whip our exhausted men through another night march."

"March—?" Eleazar's face twisted with sudden fury. "You can't! You can't abandon the siege!"

"I do not abandon this siege. But if Egypt comes against us here in our camps, she will destroy us. We must march out to meet this threat."

"Joshua—" Eleazar stopped his voice, his face working through unnameable emotions.

"What?"

For one instant, the High Priest's eyes blazed with some fey, fatal light, of fanatical extremity and danger, but then this faded and he lowered his head.

"Nothing, Joshua. Make your march."

Joshua stood and watched him for another moment, then he nodded shortly, and left.

Barra woke with tears in her eyes, from a dream in which she'd stood at the mast of a Phoenikian longship. In the dream it had been *her* ship, hers alone, a hundred-sweep battleship with a ramming-prow of bronze; in the dream its sails had crackled in a fresh sea breeze that bellied them out and sent the huge ship skipping over the waves as lightly as a gull.

Her chest ached with sharp sorrow as she woke; she wanted that ship to be real, and this city to be the dream.

For a while, she couldn't quite remember where she was, or how she had come here. It was dark, here, and smelled of goats and poultry and men, of leather and oiled bronze and wool shirts soaked with sweat; there was a fire outside, somewhere nearby, built of dried horseshit by the smell, and over it boiled a pot of rich barley and chicken, spiced with cinnamon and nutmeg.

She sat up, and found that her chest and arms were tightly tied with neatly torn bandages, some of them already stained and crusting with dried blood. One thigh was bound up as well, and another strip wound around her head.

Many of the bandaged wounds didn't hurt at all, but that small comfort was erased by all the places she hurt that *weren't* bandaged, knotted bruises hard as nutshells over what seemed like half her body. She was in a small room, a couple of paces square; three steps up from the floor was an open door at street level.

This was a Jebusite house.

She remembered now, vaguely, some of it, racing away from Joshua in the hail of rocks and blast of sand, remembered tumbling down the ladder to the spring below the wellhouse and landing hard on the stone, remembered being grabbed by strong supporting hands that smelled of home.

She remembered nothing else.

No sign of the angel; since she was still alive, she figured it must have found somebody else to pick on.

Her leg seemed able to bear her weight, and she limped up the stairs to the door.

Maybe a dozen Picts squatted around a fire they'd built in the middle of the street. One of them looked up, his face red-lit by the flames below, and grinned at her.

"Hey, princess! Glad you're about. Come have a squat and a bowl of barley chicken, eh? I'll go tell Bertram you're up."

Barra's mouth watered, and she discovered a yawning hole where her stomach used to be. Carefully, she detached herself from the doorway and joined the circle around the fire.

"Thanks, fellas. Don't mind if I do."

She accepted a clay trencher filled to its brim, and used her fingers to scoop the steaming stew into her mouth, barely tasting it in her hurry to ease the nagging gripe of her belly. She felt one guilty twinge, when she thought of Kheperu, cornered, alone in the dark, up there in the Tabernacle, cold and no doubt desperately hungry as he held off the entire Habiru Host, but that didn't slow her down.

She thought, *Fuck it. My going hungry won't help him any.*

At least, she hoped he was still there; if he wasn't, he was already dead. He'd better be still alive; she was going to need him. And Sheshai.

She'd been *so close* with Joshua, so fucking close she could *taste* it. He'd almost gone for it, almost caved right then and there and called the whole thing off.

He was rattled, though; she had him reeling, she just hadn't quite managed to knock him down. The old bastard was tougher than he looked—and he looked plenty damned tough.

*So much for that plan,* she thought. *Now, we have to do it the hard way.*

At least Leucas was all right, and Graeg, back in the Citadel, safe as anyone in this doomed city, warm and snug in the cabinet of the Lady's Maid; that much was a comfort to her.

Soon Bertram approached, threading his way through his men, offering whatever words of encouragement he could summon. His right shoulder bore a bloody bandage, but his arm still seemed to work as he clasped hands with nearly every man he passed. He came to the fire at which Barra squatted, and lowered himself to her side.

His smile was exhausted, but none the less bright. "How y'doing, Barra?"

She shrugged. "Well enough, I guess. You?"

He copied her shrug exactly. "Better than I'll be come this time tomorrow."

They exchanged a slow, silent nod—a shared appreciation for his grim joke.

"How'd the fight go, today?"

"It was a good fight." He compressed his lips and shook his head. "We'll not stand another, y'know."

Barra stared into the fire. "Ay. Listen, where's Ross? I'll need him here for this, too."

"Ross?" Bertram's face went entirely bleak. "He's dead, Barra."

She stared at him.

He looked away. "The Habiru took the Gate Tower for a while this afternoon. If they'd held it, they could have opened the main gate and the city'd be theirs right now. Ross—he led the men in that took it back. First man in like the Gaelic fool he was."

Bertram looked back at her again, and his eyes glistened. "For a fat Eirish sheepfucker, y'know, he could fight like a Pict."

Barra turned her gaze back to the fire, and for a long time neither of them spoke.

"But, hey, y'know," Bertram said at length, "there's a rumor old Joshua's packing up and moving out. Nobody knows why—shit, right now he could have this city for a strong fart—but he's doing something for good and sure. Y'can see the signs of it from the wall."

"Ah, he is," Barra said. "He'll be marching out to meet the hundred thousand Egyptian regulars that his scouts say are sweeping down from Gilgal."

"Egyptian *regulars*?" Bertram's jaw dropped. For a moment, a wild hope lit his face so brightly that it stung Barra's heart. "Are you fooling? Are there really a hundred thousand Egyptian troops coming?"

"Joshua thinks so," Barra told him with a sigh. "His scouts will have come back a couple of hours ago to tell him they saw campfires for a hundred thousand on the mountain."

Bertram's face fell. "How many are there, really?"

"Five thousand, I guess. Maybe a few less. Just enough to chop the wood and set the fires."

"And they're going nowhere, I take it?" he said heavily.

"Ay. And it won't be long after dawn that Joshua figures it out."

"Well, what good'll that do us, then?"

Barra met his eyes. "It'll move fucking near all his men an hour's march away, that's what it'll do. Listen, who's Ross's lieutenant among the Kelts? Is he a Gael, too?"

"Sure enough. You know Ross wouldn't trust anyone but his own kin to second him."

"Good. You get this Gael and bring him around. My father's his king; he'll do what I tell him. And so will you."

"Barra—"

"Shut up. Don't even think about arguing with me. I want every fucking Pict and Kelt—and every other mercenary you can round up—armored and ready for action. Empty the walls. We don't have enough men left to hold them anyway. Get the men assembled at the Gate Tower an hour before dawn."

"And just what do you think we're gonna do with them, eh?"

She tossed what was left of her stew into the fire and stood up.

"We're going to *attack*."

He stared at her for a long astonished second, then he rose and stood beside her, and his eyes sparked like greenwood in a fire. "Why not?" he said. "We can't defend, and it's no use to surrender. Let's fuck 'em up."

"Ay. And in the meantime, I need a couple dozen of your men to go up to the Citadel with me." She started peeling the bandages off her arms and swinging her fists to loosen up.

"I have to see a man about an axe."


Eleazar ben Aaron stood before the tent where his eldest son lay dying, and looked down upon Jerusalem.

In the hours since Phinehas was struck down, Eleazar had passed through shock and outrage, through fury, to grief, and now beyond even that.

As he gazed down upon fires that burned on the walls and in the streets of the city below, he believed that he was entirely calm, he thought that he saw with perfect clarity; that everything around him, everything that was, everything that happened—the waning moon, the breeze, the fading coughs of wounded men nearby, the smells of blood and shit on the southeast wind, and the coming death of his son—passed into him and through him without leaving any trace of its passage.

He felt as though his flesh had become as cold and transparent as Egyptian glass.

He had had *enough*.

The time had come to end this war.

And Eleazar, he could do it. He knew exactly how.

He could bring the Finger of God Himself down from the sky, to erase Jerusalem like a scribe preparing a palimpsest; and he could do even more than this.

He could call upon a final Power; a Power whose summoning would certainly destroy him, but he cared little for that.

He could call upon the Name of God, and make of the *mâtat Urusalim* what the Lord had made of Sodom and Gomorrah, in the days of Abraham and Lot.

*When Phinehas dies, so dies Israel,* he thought.

He couldn't make himself care.

He turned away from the city, and away from his life, with a single gesture of contempt for them both. He went into his tent to begin the first summoning.

By midafternoon, the shit and other offal that the crowd outside continued to throw over the walls made the Ba'alath smell like a freshly manured field.

By sundown, it smelled like a dung heap that had been piled with rotting meat.

By midnight, the mercenaries began to go crazy.

Leucas watched it happen through a head-size window in the wall of the altarhouse. Behind him, Sarah tossed fitfully on her pallet in the small alcove where he'd first seen her, and whimpered vague childish moans out of her fever dreams.

At first, he didn't understand what was happening. The early signs were unremarkable: the men began to draw away from each other, seeking their own little spaces of the courtyard, tiny plots of flagstone circumscribed by the small rings of light cast by each man's lamp.

The high walls around the Ba'alath cut so much of the wind that no fires needed to be lit; tiny shell lamps of baked clay, their wicks of twisted lamb's wool, shone as steadily as the stars. But each man wanted his own, as the night wore on, and they guarded their lamps as though the flames that burned in them measured out their heartbeats.

They'd snarl at each other over the slightest gesture, and twice brief scuffles had broken out when one tried to take a skin of olive oil away from another. When a man would move away from his own little plot—to get another scrap of bread or piece of hard sausage from the offering table within the altarhouse, or to relieve himself against its rear wall—he would weave among the tiny pools of light cast by others' lamps, sticking to the darkness as though he feared to cast a shadow.

Graegduz, who had spent the day curled into a knot of silent pain behind the altar, began to growl softly, his labored breathing making it sound sometimes like a whimper.

Leucas didn't see what started the first real fight. He heard a snarl of angry words and saw the dirty gold flash of blades in the uncertain light, then Agaz was between the two men, barking in Phoenikian, his own blade in his hand.

The two turned away from each other, and one of them was bleeding.

For the first time in all that long day and night, the crowd outside the walls had fallen utterly silent.

Leucas scowled, and started looking around the altarhouse for something he could use to bar the door.

Outside, he recognized the voice of one of the two acolytes who had tended his wounds and cared for the Lady's Maid all last night and through this day. Both of them had been out in the courtyard, bringing sacramental food and wine to the mercenaries. Leucas couldn't understand what the acolyte said, but his tone of frightened pleading was unmistakable, as was the moist gurgle of breath bubbling out of a cut throat that replaced it.

Then, all was quiet.

Agaz panted harshly in the eerie silence, his sword still in his hand, his gaze flicking rapidly around the courtyard as though he might be attacked from any side.

Leucas frowned out through the tiny window at him, thinking. Lack of a useful common tongue had prevented him from getting to know Agaz very well, though he had fought at the prince's side more than once. He might or might not owe Agaz a debt for intervening with the mob that afternoon, but he knew that Barra cared for him, and that settled it.

He hauled himself painfully to his feet, his guts shifting loosely inside the wrappings that strapped his chest, and went to the door of the altarhouse. Mindful of his recent experiences in the Citadel and down here, that was where he stopped.

No breath of wind stirred the silence outside. The waning moon peered down from just above the eastern mountains. All around, the mercenaries glared at him suspiciously from where they crouched, each within his own steady ring of lamplight.

"Agaz, come inside," Leucas said in his halting Phoenikian.

"Stay back—stay *back!*" Agaz panted, leveling his blade at the Athenian. "I don't know what you are, but if bronze can cut you, you will not take me while I have my sword in my hand."

Leucas leaned on the doorjamb, and in his slow and thoughtful way he turned over these words in his mind, looking at them from every side. No matter how he turned them, they could mean nothing good.

Behind Agaz, a mercenary let out a shrilling scream of high terror and a desperate invocation to Ba'al; he whipped his spear around his head, striking at something only he could see. The flame of the lamp on the flagstones by his feet snapped back and forth, making the shadows seem to leap wildly for his throat.

Grimly, with no real hope that he could succeed, Leucas tried one more time. He took a moment to organize the unfamiliar Phoenikian in his mind, to make his meaning as clear as he could. "Agaz, it is me, Leucas. Come into the house with me, while you still can."

"In *there*?" Agaz said, his eyes wide and staring. "I can't go in there! She'll cut off my balls—she'll chop my cock at its *root*, that's what *she* does. That's what she wants us all to do—it's the only kind of man *she* doesn't hate!"

He took a step forward, and rasped a hoarse, conspiratorial whisper. "She wants to eat the city—she wants to eat the *whole world*!"

Leucas stared at him for one long, hopeless moment, then he nodded to himself. There was nothing he could do for Agaz now, except try to keep his family from harm.

Adonizedek sat on the ground near the door, his aged head nodding back against the wall; he'd seemingly watched this exchange through half-slitted eyes, but Leucas couldn't tell if the old man was awake or asleep. Rachel lay on the ground beside him, her head in his lap; she'd been asleep until the shouting had begun, and now, awake, she lay staring with a rabbit's panicked stillness.

"Adonizedek," Leucas said slowly. "Rachel."

They both turned their heads to look at him, and he beckoned for them to come inside. Rachel said something in Canaanite, and her grandfather answered her; the conversation went back and forth for a moment, and Leucas sharply wished he knew what they were saying.

Agaz also listened, and he crept closer with his head cocked as though he could not believe his ears, and even in the shifting lamplight, Leucas could see his knuckles whiten around the hilt of his sword.

"Adonizedek," Leucas said more forcefully, and when the old man looked again to him, Leucas' gesture was emphatic: *get in here!*

The old man pulled himself up the wall to his feet, Rachel rising beside him, and suddenly Agaz shouted and sprang toward them with his sword upraised.

Leucas murmured, "Athene . . ." half in prayer, half as a curse, and leaped from the doorway into Agaz's path.

He got there before Agaz even knew he was in motion; the prince had barely begun to swing when Leucas' huge hand locked his wrist.

Leucas squeezed—not too hard—and the sword rang when it hit the flagstones.

"Agaz," he said softly, though he knew the prince could not understand his Greek, "Barra would never forgive me if I hurt you. If you hurt your family, you'll never forgive yourself. You're coming inside."

He dragged Agaz unceremoniously across the threshold of the altarhouse. He hoped that bringing the prince within the sacred space would protect him; he half expected Agaz to recover himself as soon as he was inside. Instead, Agaz fought wildly, scratched and bit and struggled in Leucas' grip, howling in incomprehensible Canaanite.

Leucas' next thought was to tie the prince up, and keep him in the altarhouse, to protect him from the mercenaries outside, but as he tried to shift his grip Agaz got his feet firmly planted on the floor and drove a short and powerful punch against Leucas' broken ribs.

Nausea spread from his chest like ripples on a pond, making his vision swim and his grip dissolve, and Agaz darted back out into the courtyard before Leucas could summon the strength to stop him.

Adonizedek slammed the door after him, saying something in a harshly rasping voice. Rachel stared up solemnly at Leucas, tears shimmering in her eyes.

Leucas looked from her to her grandfather, and back again, then he shook his head sadly and set about barricading the altarhouse door. He worked one-handed, hugging the other arm to his injured chest against the nausea and growing pain.

The door itself was small, and sturdily built of oaken planks; he shifted its heavy bar into place. He pulled apart the offering table— also oak—and used these boards to brace the door, footing them with the heavy stone figures of Anat and Asherah that surrounded the Great Astarte.

He thought this should hold well enough; the bracing would resist the rush of any one man, and the door was too small for two to work together. And the mercenaries outside were armed with sword and spear, of little use in chopping through a door. For that, they'd need an axe.

He stood for a moment, regarding his handiwork, a thoughtful frown on his face. He hadn't been affected by whatever was happening to the men outside, even when he went out there to stop Agaz; neither, apparently, were Adonizedek and Rachel, who'd been out there all along.

"If it's not the altarhouse," he murmured to himself, "what makes the difference?"

In his deliberate, methodical way, he began to consider possibilities, but his answer came from an unexpected voice.

"It is because they call upon their man-gods to protect them, upon Ba'al and El, Dagon and Marduk."

For one spine-chilling instant, Leucas thought the voice had come from the statue of the Great Astarte at his back, but when he turned, he saw Sarah standing in the archway to her small alcove.

She did not now lean on the wall beside her; she stood tall and straight as a young poplar, and the lines of her illness had faded from her face. Her hair spilled around her shoulders, and Leucas thought he had never seen a woman so beautiful.

Then he thought, *Wait—Sarah doesn't speak Greek . . .*

She swayed as though a wind from the west stirred her branches. "But you, Leucas, in your rare moments of need," she said, "like Adonizedek, you call upon *me*."


The two Men of El who guarded the door to Melchizedek's apartment scrambled to their feet as Barra approached with two dozen heavily armed Picts at her back.

They made a halfhearted show of lifting their spears, apprehension clear on their young faces.

"Stop," one said, his voice cracking boyishly. "Stop right there."

Barra didn't even slow down. "Put down your spears. Lie facedown on the floor with your hands behind your heads."

"I'll shout an alarm," the El's Man said, "and a hundred men will answer it . . ."

His voice trailed off as Barra stopped with the points of their spears an inch from her breasts. "Maybe so," she allowed, "but none of them will get here in time to save your lives. Put them down, boys. Live another day."

They looked past her shoulders, their eyes round and filled with massive, axe-armed savages. They looked again at her and saw no hope of mercy.

They put down their spears and lay beside them on the cold floor of the Citadel hallway.

"You and you," she said in Pictish, "tie these kids up, and don't hurt them more than you have to."

"Hmp," one of the Picts snorted grumpily as he complied. "Why don't any of these little buttrags want to fight?"

Barra showed her teeth. "It could have something to do with the ten-to-one odds."

"Pisswater," the Pict pronounced decisively as he yanked tight a knot around the boy's wrists. "Are we gonna get to fight at all?"

"Oh, ay," Barra told him. "Come dawn, you'll get all you want, I promise." She measured the door before them with her eyes, its heavy construction, the scars in the wood where Kheperu's glyphs had been scraped away.

"Fuck knocking. Bust it in."

Without hesitation, the Pict nearest the door kicked the door hard with the flat of his sandal; it gave way with a splintery screech and Barra strode in, the Picts piling through behind her.

"Toss the place," she said. "The axe I'm looking for is made of solid bronze with lots of fancy carving, and its edges are inset with splinters of gemstone."

The Picts swarmed through the High Priest's apartment like a sacking army, ripping down wall hangings, shattering furniture, overturning chests, and shaking out their contents onto the floor.

Melchizedek appeared in a doorway, his eyes filmed with sleepy horror, bedclothes in disarray.

"What in the name of Merciful El is going on here?" he barked with as much authority as a rudely awakened man can muster.

Barra stepped over the jumble of broken furniture and looked up at him with a humorless grin. "I was hoping I might find you at home," she said, and roughly grabbed his long wire-bound beard. "Come with me."

He squalled in outraged pain as she yanked him along. He yelped, calling for his slaves, but none of them were willing to risk the wrath of the marauding Picts; the slaves stayed huddled in odd corners, watching with wide and frightened eyes.

She got to the inner door that led to the cabinet of the Lady's Maid, and she pounded on it with the heel of her hand. "Leucas? It's me, open up!"

"He's not there!" Melchizedek squawked, tears of pain filling his eyes. "What—why are you here? What are you doing?"

"I came for my axe," she said shortly, then called down the hallway to a couple of Picts to come and break this door for her. They trotted along, set their lamps on the floor and went to work with shoulder and blade.

"Please," Melchizedek said, "please, you're hurting me . . ."

"Am I?" She yanked his face down close to hers. "Can't have that, can we? The Loving bloody Mother knows I wouldn't want a murdering shitcake traitor like you to get *hurt.*"

The door gave way with a splintering screech, and the Picts shoved the rest of the barricade clear. Looking in, one of them gasped, "Duncan—aw, Dunny, what'd they do to you?"

Through another arch, Barra could see the swollen, blackened corpse sprawled on the floor, and could smell the thick corruption of its flesh. She snarled under her breath and yanked Melchizedek into the chamber after her.

The rising moon dropped a shaft of light through the broken roof, just enough that Barra could see the shattered hole that was once Sarah's bedchamber; the Picts set lamps on the floor behind her, and their glow underlit the room, throwing huge and menacing shadows upon the walls of stone, outlining the corpses of the two dead Picts in gold.

She could see herself reflected in the High Priest's eyes, distorted and demonic, shadows rising up her face.

"All right," she said, "where are they? Leucas, Sarah, where'd they go?"

Melchizedek gave his best impression of a sneer through the pain that misted his eyes. "I'll tell you nothing until you unhand me."

"Wrong answer, shithead."

With her free hand, Barra pulled the dagger from her belt.

Now fear joined the pain in Melchizedek's eyes. "You wouldn't *dare!*"

"Haven't we gone over what I'll dare already?" she said, deceptively calm. "Where are they?"

"They—they ran to seek shelter from their foul goddess," he said, surrendering. "They are under guard in the Ba'alath."

Barra nodded to herself. *Good move, Leucas,* she thought. The Ba'alath would protect them, she hoped, as it had protected her. She leaned around the High Priest's skinny chest and shouted down the hallway in Pictish, "How're you coming with that axe?"

"Is this it?" A Pict stepped into view, holding the Lady's Axe up for her regard.

"Ay. Hang on to it for a minute, till I finish up in here."

She let go of Melchizedek's beard, and he straightened, panting and smoothing his bedshirt, trying to recover his self-possession. "This insult shall not be forgotten—"

"Shut up," she said, lifting the knife. "I'm already under your sentence of death, you shit-sack bastard. There's not a lot more trouble I could be in, is there?"

"You think not? You forget that I am High Priest of the Most High God. El's vengeance is not bound by the endurance of your earthly form. He can wreak punishment on you and yours for all eternity—"

"Ay, really? If he's so powerful, let's see if he can save your life."

Melchizedek stiffened, and he took a cautious step backward.

"I don't know how the customs run in these parts," she went on. "You may have noticed I'm not from around here. Back home, the druids teach that the Grey Man, Arawn, demands that the lives of murderers be given to him, so that their sickness can be eased in the Cauldron of Rebirth. You poisoned the king. You tried to poison me. You seized this city by high treason. You're a murderer and a traitor, and back home, you'd die for it."

Melchizedek said boldly, "Everything I have done, I did in the service of El and the folk of this city—"

"I believe you," Barra said seriously. "That's why I haven't jammed this knife in your belly already. I can't decide whether that excuses you or not. But I can see, now, that it doesn't have to be up to me. We can both let the gods decide."

She waved the knife toward the yawning blackness of the archway to the shattered bedchamber. "Jump."

"Jump?" The wavering light of the lamps picked up a glint of panic in his eyes.

"Ay. A leap into the dark. Have faith in your god. If you're right, El will see that you land safely. It's only a couple of floors deep. Go on, jump."

"But—but, it's full of broken *stone*, and *timbers*, and in the dark—"

"You'll just have to take your chances with that, won't you?"

"This is madness!"

She took a step toward him and prodded the skin over his heart with the point of her knife. "That's the only way out of this room for you, Melchizedek."

He stepped back, closer to the archway. She moved with him.

"Jump."

He lifted his eyes to the ceiling, and intoned, "Merciful El, if the savor of my sacrifices has ever pleased you, come to me now, to give me the strength—"

"That's enough," Barra said. "I don't have all fucking night." Now he teetered with his heels at the broken threshold. She raised the knife to his throat. "Jump or die."

He summoned the last shreds of his tattered dignity and turned to face the darkness.

"El! Give me strength for your work!" he cried. "I give myself to you! Revenge me!"

Just as Barra was about to give him a shove, he stepped off into space.

There came no heavy thud of a falling body, only a vivid *sluutch* of ripping flesh, and a thin, despairing *hukh . . . hukh . . .* of breath leaking from stilled lungs.

Barra retrieved a lamp, and went to the archway, holding the light out into the shaft.

At the bottom, Melchizedek stood bent over like a scarecrow with a broken back; he'd landed on a huge splinter of beam that had pierced his groin and angled upward to spear out from his back above his kidney. His hands and feet still twitched with their last nervous convulsions.

"Well," Barra said to the air, "I guess that settles that."

Kheperu's every breath trembled with fever.

He crouched in the blackness of the Holy of Holies, hugging his knees to his chest and shivering, with his eyes squeezed shut.

He'd had a lamp, earlier, years before at some previous point of this eternal night, but he'd doused it; he couldn't bear the flickers of motion at the corners of his eyes, the growing, stifling sense of *presence . . .*

He could not bear the misty unsolidity that hung in the air between the upraised wings of the golden kherubim that faced each other from opposite sides of the Mercy Seat.

Even now, in darkness so deep that he could not tell if his eyes were open or closed, he could see that shapeless pulse of night, he could feel it on his face like heat from a black fire.

He could hear the whisper of its voice, a hissing chewing sound like some burrowing animal that dug a path within his skull.

*You are alone, Kheperu. The gods you worship are only pieces of wood and stone. Your companions desert you unto death. Your strength fails, and night closes your eyes. All things come down to death, for so I made them. Wise and foolish, rich and poor, strong and weak, their end is the same.*

*In the end, there is only Me.*

In silence so complete that he could *hear* the gangrene consuming his flesh around the festering wound near his spine, Kheperu fought back the only way he could.

He dreamed of the smells of the sea, and the cry of gulls echoing from their soaring spirals, of green fields in springtime, of the happy smoky dark taste of sex, and the scent of roasting lamb basted with beer; he recalled the solid warmth of Leucas' handshake, and the sharp sting of Barra's comradely slap on his arm. He thought of anything and everything that would take his mind far from this whispering darkness.

But as the night wore on, these memories and dreams fell away. He could no longer see the face of his long-abandoned wife, or recall the color of the sunset above the Nile flood, or remember the flavor of Tyrian wine. It was as though every memory to which he turned was stripped from him in his very act of summoning it, leaving him alone and defenseless against the whispering night.

He was alone here. He had always been alone here; his life before this night in the Holy of Holies had been only a dream, a passing fancy, gone in an hour.

This fear-stinking blackness was the only truth.

This was forever.

Earlier in the night, when he'd still had some hope of living through this, he had managed to blackmail some food out of the men who surrounded this tent.

"If I don't smell some food in here by the time I count ten," he'd screeched, "the next thing you'll smell is the smoke of a burning Yahweh!"

After much delay and discussion, he'd heard the bass rumble of Joshua ben Nun join the argument outside. Shortly thereafter, a large wooden trencher heaped high with steaming meat and a loaf of flatbread had been borne into the Holy of Holies by Joshua himself.

Joshua had pulled aside the Inner Veil and boldly entered. "Your food, false one."

Kheperu had gaped soundlessly up at the imposing Israelite general, then scrambled to his feet and leveled the staff at him like a weapon. "Keep your distance."

The skin around Joshua's eyes bent into leathery creases. "You would threaten me with my own staff?"

"I'll crack your bloody skull with it, if I have to."

"I think not," Joshua sighed. "My fighting days are behind me, false one, but God Himself defends me, while I am about His business."

"But He doesn't defend Himself, does he?" Kheperu said snidely. He showed Joshua the powerful incendiary—his last. "Just in case you thought I was only bluffing."

"Nothing you do can harm God," Joshua said heavily. "I wish only to protect these sacred relics of Moses, the Ark and its tables of stone. What can you possibly hope to gain? Destroy the Ark, and it will only be rebuilt. It is a symbol, nothing more."

"Oh?" Kheperu sneered. "Then why has no one come in after me? And what do you tell your people that I am doing in here?"

"I have told them that you are communing with God."

Kheperu snorted.

Joshua went on. "We will not retreat, even if you burn the Ark itself, and there is no escape. I ask you again: what do you hope to gain by this?"

"A few more hours of life," Kheperu said. "That's worth something, isn't it?"

"Is it?"

Joshua stared at him steadily, as though expecting a serious answer, then he shrugged. "Here, eat."

He skirted the gold-covered Ark, set the trencher on the tent floor between them, and lowered himself to sit beside it. He unslung a bulging wineskin from its thong across his shoulder and offered it to Kheperu. "Drink?"

Kheperu sneered at him. "You first."

Joshua shrugged and tilted the wineskin above his lips, directing its ruby arc into his mouth, then he passed it to Kheperu's hand.

"You see? No poisons, to slay or even sedate you. Only wine. Good wine, as this is good meat and good bread, a gift from the Lord." He lifted a strip of meat, and broke off a piece of bread to wrap it in. He stuffed the whole bundle into his mouth, indicating by gesture for Kheperu to do the same.

"Tonight," Joshua said thickly while he chewed, "I go to fight Tal Akhu-shabb, and his Canaan Division, which is hugely overstrength. He must be reinforced by every contingent of every district between Egypt and Hattiland."

*So that much, at least, is working,* Kheperu thought.

As long as he held out, the Ark would go nowhere; Joshua would send his army marching to battle without the Ark at its head for the first time in history. He only prayed that the rest of Barra's plans would go as well.

"Tal Akhu-shabb," Joshua murmured meditatively. "Do you know,

I knew his father? He was an officer in my division, when I was a foot-man in the service of Ramses."

"Really?" Kheperu said distractedly, while he frowned with suspi-cion at the wineskin. He was terribly thirsty, after all, but he still could not trust the Habiru . . .

"He wasn't my officer, but he had a good reputation. A good man, fair and stern but never harsh. Solid and competent—his companies always won the division games. Ah, those days—I could never have imagined being as old as I am now. But that's not so strange, I sup-pose. Now that I am old, I cannot imagine myself much younger." He shook his head and chuckled into his beard, then asked abruptly, "What's your name?"

"I call myself Kheperu," he answered automatically, now sniffing cautiously at the steaming meat, weighing the demands of his belly against the possibility of falling asleep and being taken in the night.

"Kheperu?" Joshua said. "Morning Star? What a peaceful name. How can anyone who names himself Lightbringer be an Enemy of God?"

Kheperu lowered the meat from his lips and squinted at the old general. *Why, he's drunk,* he thought in amazement. *The old bastard's positively boiled! No wonder he's gone all misty.*

"I can't really say," he replied slowly. "It simply seemed to hap-pen this way. Almost by accident. You understand."

Joshua nodded gravely. "I suppose I do. It's a pity that you have to die."

"Yes, isn't it?"

"If you hadn't come in here, if you hadn't violated the sanctity of the Holy of Holies, perhaps we could have reached some compromise. After all, you don't have to be a false prophet. That pagan whore you follow, she had a good point. All your prophecies have come true . . ."

"Why are you so concerned for me?"

Joshua hiked up his massive shoulders as though with great effort, then let them fall again.

"It has been so long," he murmured. "More than twenty years, since I last sat with a man who could remember how the fields smell in the spring at the Nile's first flood, who has seen the dawn light spark from the white face of Khufu's tomb, who knows the crocodile's cough, and that bellowing the hippos make, sometimes, at twilight, when they're in rut and dangerous . . ."

Something in the old man's voice struck Kheperu with a pang of homesickness so intense it unstrung his knees. He sat on the tent floor, a pain in his heart that no medicine could ease.

"Yes," he said. "I understand. It's been ten years—more—since I left home."

"Home," Joshua murmured. "Yes. I live in Timnath Serah, but that is only a house. I was born in Egypt, Kheperu. I grew from boy to man there, and I shall never see it again. Of all the Israelites who marched out from there at Moses' word, only Caleb and I still live—and Caleb wanders his halls without wits, waiting for God to take him to his ancestors. Between you and me and God, here"—he waved a hand unsteadily at the Ark—"I never wanted to leave."

Joshua blinked a few times, and sighed heavily. "If only Israel had not become a slave to Egypt—"

"Oh, pish," Kheperu said. "You were never slaves. We don't keep captive populations to do our work, we never did—"

Joshua forestalled him with a lifted hand. "It was Moses' phrase," he said tiredly. "The chains that bound us in Egypt were not those of bronze, but were fetters of ease and comfort and plenty. None of us ever knew want—the fertile Nile ensured that; after Seti took the throne, we never saw civil war. We were safe in our snug houses. Every year that passed in Egypt, we became more and more Egyptian, less and less Israelite. You would have swallowed us altogether. That was the slavery out of which Moses led my people."

Kheperu lifted the wineskin in sardonic salute. "Here's to killing men with kindness."

Joshua smiled. "I'll drink to that. If only there were no other kind of killing at all . . ."

And for a time, then, in that lamplit tent, the old general and the exiled seshperankh sat together on the floor, and spoke in low tones of what they had both loved best.

Some time thereafter, Joshua pushed himself to his feet. "I must go now, to fight the Egyptian army. I don't suppose I'll see you alive again."

"Don't be so sure," Kheperu said.

Joshua shook his head. "You have condemned yourself by your own actions, and there is little help I can give you, even if I would. You cannot hope to escape, after this—thirty thousand men of the Tribe of Levi surround this tent. There is no one who can rescue you. If you come out now, with me, perhaps you can be given a quick death, with little pain. I would not care to watch you suffer."

"You won't," Kheperu said. He rose as well, and the fever made his head swim and clenched his guts into a nauseous knot. "You won't see me suffer, Joshua. But we will meet again."

"You think so? Why?"

Kheperu swallowed nausea and tried to focus his eyes. "You should go now, Joshua. You should take your troops and march away—otherwise, there will be destruction such as you cannot imagine. The Tabernacle will be destroyed, and the Ark lost, you yourself will fall in battle, and Israel will be the mockery of Canaan unto the seventh generation . . ."

"Without your confederates to make things come to pass," Joshua said stiffly, "you are not much of a prophet." With that, he had turned and strode out of the tent.

*Ah, well,* Kheperu had thought at the time. *It was worth a try.*

But as the night filled his spirit with darkness, he saw that it hadn't been worth a try; nothing was worth a try. All his hopes, all his pleasures, every single thing that had ever brought him joy in his life, seemed to him futile and worthless, nothing more than useless attempts at self-deception.

Attempts to forget death.

That voice no longer chewed the inside of his head, and he knew, now, that it never had; there had never been any voice there except his own thoughts, his own knowledge of the final truth.

There was no Habiru god, seeking to drive him to despair. The bleak stillness within himself came purely from the inescapable horror that death waited for him, just like everyone else, that he would die alone; in the face of that extinction of self, all the sunlit joys of life are nothing more than the capering of a madman on the brink of a cliff.

And the life that he would ache for, that he would scream for as he died—if that life were somehow given to him, it would be every bit as futile as the wasted years that had led him into this tent.

He turned to the gods of his youth, to Ptah and Hathor and Horus, and found he could not think of them without contempt. Useless, empty pretense, to kneel before Anubis—another deception, to pretend that death is not the end.

He remembered, fuzzily as though through a veil, praying to such gods and feeling the breath of their regard upon his spirit, the warmth of love that his creator felt for him; but even that, now, was clearly vanity and deception.

No prayer could help him, for there was no one to pray to.

The gods are only pieces of wood and stone.

He was alone, trapped inside his skull, waiting for the final extinction.

He weighed the incendiary in his hand. Why bother to wait? He could place the bomb against his own chest, in his own mouth.

Even better, he could open his wrists with the small knife he wore inside his robe.

That final extinction seemed far more attractive, for all its horror, than the wasted futile minutes he would spend in waiting for it.

He fought back as best he could, turning his mind this way and that like a rat in a trap, trying to remember what he loved about life, trying to call upon his gods, but his memories faded, and his gods were only figments of his imagination.

In the darkness, he laid the edge of his knife against the veins of his forearm.

But his hand did not move.

Barra needed him.

She was counting on him to deny the Ark to the Habiru.

And she would come for him. She wouldn't leave him here to die.

Alone in the endless dark, without the faintest breath of hope, without a shred of belief in any god, he still had faith in Barra.

In the darkness, unseen by human eyes, the twitches of Melchizedek's corpse did not fade away. Instead they strengthened, and the dead hands curled into fists, and slowly, with the graceless spastic lolling of a badly made puppet, his back straightened, and his head came up, and the light that came from his eyes cast red-tinged shadows on the rubble at his feet.

He had offered himself; something had taken him up on it.

Those dead hands wrapped around the impaling beam, and crushed it as though the thick cedar was fragile as the paper husk of an abandoned wasps' nest. The rest of the beam tore from the corpse's belly with a wet sucking sound and was cast aside.

It staggered across the rubble to the broken door and into the lightless hall beyond. Its head lifted, and quested this way and that as though it sniffed the air, then it limped along the same path Leucas had taken on his dash from the Citadel on the previous day.

It, too, had business at the Ba'alath.

"Come to me, Leucas."

Within the lamplit altarhouse, Sarah lifted her arm in a gesture that was half-beckoning, half an offer to take his hand.

Leucas frowned at her.

Beside him Adonizedek had slid down against the wall, and Rachel had laid her head once again in her grandfather's lap. Her eyes were closed, and the old king snored faintly.

Leucas said, "I am not entirely sure what's going on, here."

The shifting light of the lamp flames cast huge moving shadows behind the Great Astarte, and made the small Asherahs and the axe-armed Anats seem to lean forward with attentive expressions.

"I will not compel you, Leucas. I only ask. Come in to me."

The invitation in her voice, the soft curve of her cheek, the spark of reflected flame in her eye, caught at Leucas' chest and he stepped forward, closer, closer, until he stood next to her, not above her, for she nearly matched his height. She lifted her lips for his kiss.

"You are another man's wife," he said.

"El has not been a husband to me here."

"You mean, Melchizedek." He cleared his throat. "Don't you?"

"He has not been my man. You have defended me as he would not, but I need you for more than that, Leucas. I must share your strength. I want you to be the man for me, Leucas."

She reached up and touched his beard. Her fingers were impossibly soft, and gentle, and her touch woke a passion in him that made him tremble.

"I . . . Sarah, I . . ."

Her hand trailed down his chest to his kilt, and slid within it, her fingers exploring with the confident and unashamed familiarity of an old lover's.

"Come into me, Leucas. I cannot ask you a fourth time."

She turned away from him then, and went back to her pallet within the alcove. She paused there, her back to him, and her robe parted and fell in folds around her slim and delicate ankles.

Her body seemed to be made of sunlight shining through cream. The curve of her back could have been the arc of a wave's crest.

She turned to face him, and opened her arms.

He went in to her.

Barra squatted in the tunnel that led to the spring, rocking back and forth on her heels. The last lamp had been doused some minutes ago; now she only waited for the word from above. The Axe of the Lady dug into her ribs behind her belt, but she didn't mind. Around her in the utter darkness squatted a dozen Pict warriors, stripped down to breechclouts and wearing the battle paint of their respective clans.

They were nervous, these men; though they made no noise, not even shifting their weight, Barra could smell their acid sweat. At her word, these men around her would break down the barricade in the tunnel and fight their way up out of the wellhouse.

A few of them bore eastern swords and shields, and one had a spear. Most of them carried axes of granite and basalt, the axes they'd brought with them from the stoneworks of Great Langdale, freshly burnished with hunks of raw copper.

She could smell the metal on the stone, and it made her heart ache.

Her nephew Bertram would lead the sortie at dawn, every able-bodied mercenary in a mass charge straight out the main gate and straight up along the ridge. She'd gone over the plan with him as he stood among his men near the Gate Tower, waiting for dawn.

"No reserves, no nothing," she'd told him. "Come howling out the gate and make for that big fucking tent of theirs on top of the north ridge."

Bertram had nodded gravely. "Oh, we can do that, sure enough, what with Joshua marching the main body out and all. How many d'you think we'll be facing, Auntie?"

Barra scowled at him. He'd taken to calling her "Auntie" in the past few hours, and the couple of good whacks she'd given him for it didn't seem to discourage him at all. "Thirty or forty thousand," she said.

"Ay, sure, but most are women and slaves, eh? How many of them are fighters?"

"Those *are* the fighters."

Bertram seemed to settle into himself, his rangy form becoming more compact: a smaller target.

"Well then," he said slowly, "guess I'll tell the boys to keep close together, so they can't come against us all at once. So, when we cut through the fifty or sixty thousand Habiru and make it to their big friggin' tent, what then?"

Barra met his eye, straight and level. "You won't make it that far."

"*You* say," he disagreed grimly.

"Fair enough. Look, I don't want you to waste men pushing through; we're better off if the fighting centers about halfway between the city and the tent. You shouldn't be out there more than about half an hour, and most likely the Habiru won't waste men surrounding you to cut you off; they'll be too worried about protecting that big tent out there. When you hear trumpets sound from the city, that'll mean the plan's worked and we're going to win. Get everyone turned around and get them back into the city as fast as you can—you might have to hold the wall for a few minutes, right at the end."

"And if there are no trumpets?"

"There will be."

"Ay, but if?"

Barra let out a slow, grim breath. "If you look down, and your shadow's shorter than your wingspan, go for the tent. You might make it. If you do, there might be a box in the middle of the tent, covered with gold, and a couple of big four-faced bird-looking things with their wings spread on top of it. Grab it, and run like shit for the city."

"And what then?"

"Nothing then. If that box is still there when you get there, it means everything's gone to shit, and I'm already dead. You'll never make it back into the city with that box, not unless you cut the Habiru down to the last man."

"What are we goin' out there for, then?"

She grinned at him. "You're the diversion."

"Diversion? What, you're gonna sneak off and kill Joshua or something, in the middle of the fight?"

"Joshua's not the enemy," she told him seriously. "Neither are those poor mopes who follow him."

"How do you figure?"

She touched her forefinger to her temple, beside her eye. "You've heard of my ma Coll?"

He nodded. "Ay—they say she has the *sceon tiof.*"

"She does. I have a touch of it myself."

His eyes widened.

"I've been as close to Joshua as I am to you, and I know him better than I do my own da. The real enemy is that god of theirs, that Yahweh bastard."

Bertram frowned at her. "You're going to fight their god?"

"Fight him? Shit, no!" Barra had said with a dark laugh. "I'm gonna *steal* him."

Before going down into the tunnel, she'd rounded up a couple of detachments of Picts, one to locate Agaz, to make sure the prince understood what was going on and wouldn't interfere, the other to get down to the Ba'alath and help out Leucas however they could. She found a Pict who could get along in Greek pretty well and gave him directions to the temple.

"How'll I know this Leucas, princess?"

"Ah, that's easy," she said. "He's a good hand taller than the High King, and his face—imagine Llem with a face like he's spent a few years playing Eirish Stand Down with my da."

The Pict flinched at the thought. "Shit, my great-uncle played Eirish Stand Down with your da once, and to this day he's cockeyed and deaf in one ear. This fella must be a sight."

"You won't mistake him," Barra said. "Get on, now."

Now, rocking on her heels in the tunnel's utter night, feeling her battle nerves sing in her veins like lyre strings, with the scents of her people all around her in this alien place, she allowed herself one indulgence, one last moment of reflection.

"Y'know," she said softly to no one in particular, "this reminds me of a story. There was a city up north once, a place called Troy, and all these Akhaian bastards came to sack it, a thousand ships' full."

From the darkness around her came the sounds of her tribesmen settling themselves into more comfortable positions to listen; Picts love a good story nearly as much as Greeks do.

"Sounds like a short fight," someone muttered.

"Ay, you'd think so," Barra agreed softly, "but it seems that bloody near everyone on both sides was the son or grandson of some god or other—all those Akhaian gods are randy bastards; some of them have near as many by-blows as my da. Anyway, there were these two Akhaian kings—one an Argive, by name of Diomedes, and the other from Ithaka, Odysseus. They got a prophecy that Troy would never fall so long as a statue of one of their gods—Athene—was still inside the city."

"Tough problem," the someone said, and there came a general rumble of agreement.

"Ay. Most anybody else would have given up and gone home—can't get the statue out without taking the city, can't take the city while the statue's still there. But these two, Odysseus and Diomedes, they never gave up. They dressed themselves up like Trojans and snuck over the wall. Into the enemy city. And into the temple to Athene—the most heavily guarded place inside. They stole the Palladion—the statue—and snuck it back out. By themselves."

She shook her head and grinned into the darkness. "I always thought that was about the stupidest bloodyfucking thing I ever heard of. What kind of puddle-brained foolishness would lead a man to do that? How could they possibly have ever thought they'd get away with it?"

There was general silence around her, as the Picts considered the question.

"Well," one offered slowly, "all Greeks are crazy. Everybody knows that."

"True enough," Barra said. "But I tell you one thing: one of those two guys is still alive. If I live through this, someday I am going to go to Tiryns, I'll find Diomedes, and I am going to shake his fucking hand."

She crouched there for one moment longer, listening within herself to the ghostly murmurings of the Jericho dead; she felt there might be some comfort to be taken, even from them.

But they did not cry for revenge. They only whispered of death's long, cold stillness.

She rose to her feet in the darkness, and shook the knots out of her shoulders.

"Knock over that barricade," she said. "Let's go do this."

Eleazar ben Aaron breathed out malice within his tent.

Power poured upward with his breath, its current tugging his guts along in its wake. A dreadful shuddering racked his fame, spread from his heart outward to shake him until he thought he must fly to pieces like a shattered pot. The howl of winds roared within his skull, rising in concert with the lightning that boiled his eyes.

The angel within him yanked at his life as it left.

With grim, hopeless tenacity, he held on.

Hatred gave him the power to live, until the howling brilliance crested and began to fall away.

He collapsed bonelessly on the gold-worked carpet inside his tent. No longer was he the vessel of power; now he was only a naked aging man, whose flesh sagged in folds across his prominent bones.

Soon, though, he dragged himself to his feet. This had been only the summoning of the Finger of God; his intention was not yet completed. The acid fury still ate his belly, and the clawing darkness of his son's descent into death had not been appeased.

These must be answered, before he would allow himself to die.

The Finger of God would not requite him; for that, he required His Fist.

Slowly, with great care, as though his body were fragile as Egyptian glass, he began to dress in his ceremonial vestments.

He had settled Jebusi already. Now he would settle all Canaan.

He would make a desert of the land of milk and honey. He would make all this land as dead as his son, to be his everlasting monument.

He dressed because this final power could not be summoned; he must go to it.

For this, he must go to the Tabernacle.

*   *   *

The first shouts brought Sheshai up instantly out of his light, dreamless nap on the fresh straw in the wagon's bed. His hand fell upon his quiver, safely hidden beneath him, and his fingers traced the shape of his black arrow. Not even Barra knew he'd brought these along; he hadn't been able to bring his bow, but he assumed that Tchera'khu would provide one at need.

He sat up. On the far side of the Kidron Valley, a knot of shouting men hacked at each other with spear and axe all around the tiny wellhouse on the slope. A couple of Israelites raced away from the fight toward the camp, crying, "Get up! Awake! Arm yourselves! The savages attack!"

Ram's-horn trumpets sounded mournfully within the camp, and men poked their heads sleepily out from their tents, or sat resentfully up from their bedrolls under the stars. No one looked too excited about this; it obviously wasn't that much of a fight, and all of the sleepers had been looking forward to a full night's rest after having been excused from the march. A few of the armed sentries ran to the aid of the men who had guarded the wellhouse, and soon the attacking mercenaries had been beaten back; they retreated inside, and the fight was over.

One of the Israelites who had cried the alarm approached the wagon where Sheshai sat. This Israelite wore a flowing burnoose that mostly concealed a large axe stuck behind a leather belt, an axe with an edge that glittered like Sheshai's eyes.

He grinned. He was no fool—and Tchera'khu had told him who this was.

"I'm glad you're alive, Barra. I wasn't sure I'd see you again."

"You and me both, Sheshai," she said as she swung up into the wagon's seat. "I was afraid you wouldn't show up."

"You still owe me the blood of Joshua ben Nun. I intend to collect."

"Ay, whatever. Did you find the High Priest?"

"Better." Sheshai showed her his teeth. "I found his only son."

"All right, then. Get the fucking donkeys hitched up. Dawn's coming soon. We don't have much time."

"Dawn?" Sheshai said. He pointed at the sky. "We have less time than that."

Barra's eyes followed his gesture toward the western horizon, where a line of advancing thunderheads threatened to swallow the moon. "Shit," she said. "That's all we need. Think you can find him in the dark?"

"You don't understand," he said, still pointing toward the sky.

In the south, another line of storms blew in so swiftly its leading edges billowed like sea spray.

From the north came more thunderheads, lightning flickering within them like a wick guttering inside a paper lamp.

From the east, clouds devoured the stars.

Sheshai watched comprehension slowly enter Barra's eyes, as she gradually came to understand what was happening. From all sides, storms converged upon Jebusi.

Her face went slack and bloodless in the moonlight.

"That's not *possible*," she breathed.

"Of course it isn't," Sheshai said. "Are you ready to go?"

"Ay," she said slowly. "I suppose I am."

Afterward, Leucas held Sarah tenderly in his arms as they lay together, skin against skin on her small pallet. She had gathered strength throughout their lovemaking, a growing tidal power that had increased until her climax had rocked him like a swimmer cast ashore by heavy surf.

At first, he had feared that through some magic she drew this strength from him; he did not grudge sharing it with her, he only feared that what little he had to spare might not be enough. But he found, as they moved together and sought their ancient harmony, that his pains eased and his strength began to return, as though the act of love was some unexplainable wellspring, from which they both could drink and come away refreshed.

As dawn neared, she whispered, "I have always loved you."

Leucas' response was a silent caress; he never forgot, even in passion, that forces were at work here that he did not understand.

The glow that seemed to come from Sarah's beautiful face filled his eyes, and breathless awe held him motionless; but then the glow faded, and a cough brought blood to her lips, and she said, "It is too late."

The altarhouse shook as men threw themselves against its door in a sudden fury of shouting and chopping blades. Leucas came to his feet, his hand instinctively finding the hilt of his iron scimitar at the wall, where his sword belt hung on a peg. From the main room came the keening wail of a young girl awakening to terror.

Leucas looked out the tiny window; the mob from the street had streamed through the gates, and some of them had brought axes, and now the crazed mercenaries applied themselves to the altarhouse door with a will. It would take only a moment to chop through the barricade.

He'd have to hold that doorway himself.

He came into the main room, wearing only the bandages that tied his wounded guts in place, his scimitar naked in his hand. Adonizedek looked up at him with uncomprehending eyes, cradling his howling granddaughter, and Leucas gestured sharply for them to get inside the alcove at his back. The old king rose unsteadily, and carried the little girl through the arch.

The door trembled under the mercenaries' assault. Leucas stood alone in the middle of the main room, the Great Astarte at his back. He tried to think of some way he could stop these men without killing them; Barra would never forgive him if he hurt Agaz. But if it came to a choice between the prince's life and Sarah's . . .

He hefted the scimitar, and swung his arms to loosen his shoulders.

He'd apologize to Barra, later.

Then, over the noise of the mob outside, came a great shout in heavily accented Greek, and the accent was one he recognized— it sounded like the lilt that took over Barra's Greek when she got angry.

"Leucas! Hey, Leucas! Where are you, man? Barra sends us to help!"

Leucas' face split into a smile so broad it hurt his cheeks. He sprang back into the alcove and went to the tiny window. Outside, a dozen huge barrel-chested Picts shouldered their way through the mob, shoving the smaller Jebusites this way and that with abandon.

"I'm in here!" Leucas called. "Inside the altarhouse! Don't let anyone get at that door—but try not to hurt them, they don't know what they're doing!"

The teeth of the Greek-speaking Pict gleamed in the moonlight. "I should think we can manage that."

As the Picts shoved their way toward the mercenaries at the door, Leucas turned away from the window. "It's Barra's tribesmen," he said with a grin. "She sent them to rescue us. Everything's going to be all right."

But on her pallet, Sarah had turned weakly on her side, and now she vomited black blood across the floor. Rachel howled again, and Adonizedek looked down in puzzlement as the blood lapped up over his bare feet. Leucas was at her side in an instant, cradling her head tenderly.

"No," she said. "It is too late. You must go. Run, while you still can."

Outside, the mob had fallen into deathly silence.

Leucas looked up. *I hate it when that happens,* he thought.

Gently laying Sarah back down upon her pillow, he rose and went once again to the window.

Through the gate of the Ba'alath stalked the tall and skeletal figure of a man with shaven head and tightly bound beard.

He wore only a tattered bedshirt, with a gaping hole opening at the groin; from this hole to its hem it was awash in blood, more blood than a man should be able to lose and still walk with the kind of ethereal, floating stride that carried this man through the mob. The people parted around him like the sea, and through the hole in the bedshirt, Leucas glimpsed a pale tangle of intestine spilling from a wound, and he knew that this man should not be walking at all.

He felt a high, thin tightness in his throat, and realized that it came from an irrational, almost overwhelming urge to giggle.

He said, "It's your husband."

Sarah forced words out through blood that bubbled freely from her lips. "Run. There is no help for me, now. Save yourself."

Leucas turned back to the window.

The mob had cleared to the sides of the courtyard, pressing themselves in a solid, silent mass against the Ba'alath's walls. The mercenaries, Agaz among them, began to tremble, then to shake, their limbs jerking faster and faster in uncontrollable spasms until they each fell convulsing to the flagstones. They writhed across the courtyard floor like blind worms scorching on sunlit stones, twisting and scraping toward Melchizedek as though he were the sheltering darkness.

He passed among them with a mincing stride, lifting his feet high as though they would be soiled by a mercenary's touch. He never looked at the men who squirmed at his feet, nor did he glance toward the mob to either side, even though they now began to voice a low and guttural sound that seemed to come from the backs of their throats, midway between a moan and a gagging retch. The sound resolved gradually into an animal rhythm, an urgent, lustful thumping like the beat of a rapist's heart.

As Melchizedek strode inexorably toward the altarhouse, his eyes began to shine red like the night-eyes of the forest creatures that gather just outside the circle of a campfire's light.

The Greek-speaker outside said hoarsely, "I'm guessing you don't want that fella getting inside, either."

"If you can stop him," Leucas replied, "I'd be much obliged."

"You want us to be gentle?"

"I don't recommend it."

The Pict spoke in his own tongue, and three of his men moved toward the advancing High Priest. All three of them suddenly darted at the old man together; two of them grabbed Melchizedek's arms to hold him steady, while the third stepped forward, a short sword in his hand, and jammed a double span of bronze into the old man's belly, sawing upward toward his heart.

The priest blinked, regarding the man who had stabbed him with a sort of disinterested puzzlement, then with a negligent shrug of his shoulders sent the Picts that held his arms flying backward to either side. They fell, skidding across the flagstones with the force of his throw.

He ignored the blade in his belly, grabbing instead the arm of the Pict that held it. With one hand on the Pict's wrist and the other on his bicep, he broke the Pict's arm at the elbow with a sharp twist.

The Pict gasped, his knees buckling and his face going slack as the High Priest twisted his arm again, back the other way, working it this way and that like a dog worrying a bone off a joint, until the splinters of the man's elbow ripped through the skin and he was able to tear the forearm completely free, holding it by the wrist like a club.

The Pict dropped to his knees, and Melchizedek dispassionately slammed him on the side of the head with his own arm, slapping him to the flagstones, unconscious, swiftly bleeding to death. Melchizedek tossed the arm aside and withdrew the blade from his belly. He flipped it away as well, then began once again to walk with solemn deliberation toward the door of the altarhouse.

Leucas murmured, "Ah, shit."

Another Pict charged him, screaming in battle rage, and swung a stone axe at the High Priest's head. Melchizedek didn't even try to dodge, made no move to defend himself.

The axe sliced open the skin of his forehead, and shattered to splinters against his skull.

The impact knocked Melchizedek down, but instantly he rose again, brushing the hanging flap of torn skin back up over his forehead like an errant lock of hair.

The other eight Picts, who had watched all this with motionless horror, now howled their war cries and threw themselves upon the High Priest all at once, burying him beneath their combined weight. The whole pile went down upon the courtyard floor, and within that snarling mass of flesh, daggers worked busily.

But the snarls began to turn to gasps and yelps of pain, and then trailed into the liquid rip of tearing flesh and the wet crush of splintering bone.

In only a moment, Melchizedek arose from the mass, lifting the Greek-speaking Pict in his hands like a sack of meal. He raised the Pict high over his head and cast him like a stone at the door of the altarhouse. The door, its barricade of timber and stone, the wall itself, none could stand against this; with an earthshaking crash of rending wood and crumbling stone, the middle of the altarhouse's front wall collapsed.

The Pict lay broken and dying amidst the rubble. He looked up, and met Leucas' eye, and spoke. But in his final extremity, he had fallen back into his native tongue, and Leucas had no idea what he'd said.

Melchizedek stalked into the altarhouse over the corpse.

Leucas moved out from the arch of the alcove, naked save for his bandaged chest, scimitar in hand.

Melchizedek said, "I have come for my wife."

The sense of his words was perfectly clear.

Leucas didn't blink, gave no sign that he understood.

The High Priest took the collar of his bedshirt in both hands and tore it from his body. Beneath, he was naked; the sword wound in his belly grinned with bloodless lips, and his guts hung in coils below a long pale penis that now began to twitch and pulse with life.

"My quarrel is not with you, Child of Melkarth. Stand aside, and live."

Leucas said, "No."

"You cannot stand against me. Stronger men than you have fallen before powers that are only a shred of what I am."

Leucas shrugged.

He was exhausted, and wounded, without armor or even the strength to wear it. This creature, that once had been the High Priest, could rip whole limbs from living bodies, could throw a man bigger than Leucas through a stone wall.

It didn't matter.

He'd given his word.

From the alcove behind him, Sarah's voice came with the dry spastic rattle of death beneath it.

"Go, Leucas. Save yourself, beloved. There is no helping me, now. Go. I command it."

"How can you command me," Leucas asked reasonably, "when we both know that you don't even speak Greek?"

"You must save the king, Leucas. And the princess . . . save—"

Her voice failed her.

He compressed his lips, and sighed. Saving the king and the princess wasn't his job.

They'd have to take care of themselves.

He measured Melchizedek with his eyes, taking in the flap of loose skin that hung below the red-streaked bone of his forehead, bone that had shattered a granite axe, then looked down at his precious iron scimitar.

Nodding grimly to himself, he set the sword aside.

Melchizedek said, "I will not offer again. Run, and live."

Leucas lifted his right fist to his cheekbone, to where he could just see it at the bottom of his vision. He extended his left forward, with his open palm toward the High Priest of El.

Over the web of skin between his left thumb and forefinger, Leucas' eyes of winter grey met the inhuman scarlet glitter of Melchizedek's.

Leucas said, "Come on, then."

Melchizedek came on.

In the first grey-tinged hint of the coming dawn, the Host of Israel lay in ambush.

Joshua stood just far enough below the summit of a hillock that he would not be skylined by the growing light, and gazed unseeing at the sky. The clouds that gathered above had been met by others coming in from the sea, and had covered the moon; Joshua saw this, but its significance did not register. His mind was miles away: his thoughts with a dying priest who lay in his tent near the Tabernacle.

He was astonished at how *bereft* Phinehas' absence made him feel. He felt dismembered, as though that vile Egyptian had taken his hand, instead of striking down his aide. In the sobering dawn, a sharp sting grew behind Joshua's eyes; had he really been so drunk that he'd sat beside that murdering blasphemer and waxed maudlin about his childhood home?

In his heart, he knew that Phinehas' death was his fault; Joshua had led him to it. It had become so easy for Joshua to depend on Phinehas, so necessary. Not so much for his willingness to serve, and his constant helpfulness and efficiency, as for the simple presence of his unshakable faith, forever at Joshua's side, a rock on which he could lean when he needed to rest from his burdens.

Dismembered . . .

And Joshua had betrayed him, had broken bread with his killer, before the breath had even left his body.

Joshua was certain that Phinehas would not live until his return from this battle.

*Oh, Phinehas,* he thought. *I am weak, and old. You deserved a better master.*

And in the vivid waking dream of the very old, he heard Phinehas' imagined reply.

*Yahweh is my master, Uncle, not you. My life is given in His service, even as is your own.*

The imagined voice brought a melancholy smile to Joshua's lips in the growing grey light, as he looked down upon his massed troops, crouched to spring upon the Egyptians when they passed along this road. This sight, too, brought Phinehas' voice to him; Joshua knew exactly what he would be saying if he were here, where he belonged.

He would shake his head in disapproval, is what he would do, and he would turn to Joshua and say, *Uncle, this makes me afraid. We should have never come out to battle without the Ark going before us; Israel without the Ark is like a body without its head.*

Dismembered . . .

Joshua nodded to himself. It was too true, what this dream-Phinehas whispered in his ear. He should never have come here without the Ark—he never would have, if he'd had a clear choice. Separate the head from the body, and even a nation will die.

Then, with a flash that drove the breath from his lungs and buckled his knees, he understood.

Separate the head from the body, and even a nation will die.

"Oh, my God." His muttered words sounded far away, harsh and strange to his ear.

"Oh, my *God!*"

His voice cracked like thunder, and men near him jumped in sudden panic to their feet.

"Up!" he cried. "Up! Up and run for Jerusalem! Run for the sake of God Himself!"

The army leaped from their ambush as one man; suddenly the hills were filled with warriors. "But, Joshua!" someone shouted. "What about the Egyptian army?"

*"There is no Egyptian army!"* he roared. *"There never was!* Bring a chariot for me, and let the cavalry go first at a gallop!"

He raised a fist at the clouds, and lightning flashed beneath them as though called by his fury.

*"They're after the Ark!"*

# 18

# *Dawn*

**B**arra slid like a ghost between the tents of the Levites.

The other tribal camps had been nearly deserted, as she and She-shai had driven slowly past, the creak of their wagon wheels sounding like screams in the predawn silence. Mostly, these camps only had a few women or slaves rising in the grey, uncertain light, yawning, adjusting their clothing with one hand while the other held back a door-curtain, before venturing out into the mist. Many of those they passed looked askance at the wagon as it rolled by, pulled by its team of four patient asses.

They left the wagon at the far fringe of the Levite camps, for the Levites had not followed Joshua on his night march to meet the nonexistent Egyptian army; all thirty thousand Levite tribesmen had stayed behind in their camp, around the Tabernacle of Yahweh.

Barra and Sheshai had slipped into the Levite camp on foot; someone might wonder what a pair of slaves might be doing out on a wagon before the dawn.

Overhead, the clouds swung around each other, in a wheel the size of the world, with Jebusi as its axis. They looked swollen, and weirdly solid, a maelstrom of boulders the color of iron.

The air beneath them, as Barra slipped from tent to tent, the Lady's Axe jabbing her ribs with every step, was still and grey and damp, warmer than dawn mist should be, thick in her lungs as though she tried to breathe with someone's hand over her mouth.

Sheshai was back in the tent where Phinehas lay, crouching like a jackal over the dying man, a knife in his hand, ready to spring on any that would try to enter.

And beside him, there in that tent that stank of sweat and death, there would lie another pair of corpses.

Those two deaths sat uneasily in Barra's stomach, even now. One was an old woman, old enough to have been Phinehas' mother; the other had been a thin, pallid woman of perhaps Barra's own age. It hadn't required even a flicker from the *sceon tiof* to make their corpses inhabit a sickly, heavy place in Barra's heart.

They had been there to tend to the needs of the wounded man; there was only one way to ensure that they wouldn't escape to raise an alarm.

Sheshai hadn't understood her reluctance to kill these two women, whose only defense against bronze blades had been their utter, pleading helplessness. He'd murmured in his toneless voice, "They're not *innocents*, Barra—they didn't come to Jebusi to throw you a fucking birthday party. Go along and get Eleazar. I'll take care of this."

He was right. She knew he was right. These were enemies; they'd chosen to come here, and they deserved no more mercy than did the fiercest Habiru warrior.

But she'd seen something in their eyes that she still felt inside her, in the squirming whispers of the Jericho dead.

She'd heard Sheshai's knife entering their bellies, even from outside the tent, the vivid smacking sound of wet meat parting before a keen edge, and it had burned the back of her throat with bile.

She thought, *That's it. I've had enough of this shit; I don't have the stomach for it anymore. I need a new line of work.*

Now the sharp tingling smell of nearby lightning brought her head up, though she'd heard no thunder.

She stopped, her lips stretched thin in a silent snarl.

She stood before a wide, ornate tent, its walls woven into a colorful brocade, its roof rimmed with golden tassels. A thin trail of smoke issued from within, rising straight up in the still air.

All around her, the camp of Levi stirred as men roused themselves in the strengthening dawn. Soon, the usual morning buzz of activity would be replaced by the cries of battle and the screams of dying men.

The door-curtain was still tied shut; she drew her knife to cut the ties, then frowned and put it back.

Some things, she decided, simply demand to be done a certain way; sometimes style is indistinguishable from substance.

From her belt she drew the Axe of the Lady, and in a single smooth arc, she cut through the door-curtain of the High Priest to Yahweh.

Thick grey smoke, reeking of burnt blood and incense, billowed out through the cut. Axe in hand, she stepped inside.

Within the enormous tent was only a single, small man, dressed in ceremonial robes, his back to her. A brazier smoked upon a horned altar before which he knelt, and cast a bloody pulse of light on the ceiling. He did not look around as she entered.

She threw back her hood. "Eleazar ben Aaron," she said. "I have your son."

He rose, touching his forelock toward the altar, and spoke without turning.

"God has my son, Barra Coll Eigg Rhum. Not you."

His voice had an eerie, inhuman hollowness that kicked her heart into a flutter and sucked the moisture from her mouth. Her tongue scraped her lips as though both were covered with sand, and she tightened her grip upon the axe, trying to draw strength from the bronze as she once had from stone.

She said, "That's as may be. But it's not God's knife at his throat right now. That knife belongs to the last survivor of Jericho. If you want your son to live out the day, you're coming with me."

Eleazar shook his head distantly, as if he were only barely paying attention. "I cannot. I have somewhere else I need to be."

Barra took a step forward, and lifted the Lady's Axe to remind him that she was armed. "You're coming to the Tabernacle, Eleazar. Or I'll cut you down right here, and your son won't live to see the dawn."

"The Tabernacle?" Eleazar's clouded eyes shifted and sought and finally found hers, as though he peered through a deep and roiling fog. "Of course. I should have expected this. Come along, then."

He brushed past her, moving awkwardly as though none of his joints worked quite right, and climbed through the cut in his door-curtain without a backward glance.

Barra's heart thumped harder. She didn't understand what was going on with him, and right now, anything she didn't understand might kill her.

"This is a great day, Barra Coll Eigg Rhum," Eleazar murmured as she came out beside him. "Today you will see the Finger of God erase Jerusalem as a scribe scrapes clean a papyrus sheet. Today you will see His Fist strike Canaan as it has not been struck since Abraham's day."

Dread clutched Barra's heart like a cold hand inside her chest. She wished that she'd made some better plan, she wished that she had more time to think, more room to improvise, that somehow she'd managed to arrange things so that she didn't have to go through with this right now, in the face of the High Priest's eldritch, dissociated stare. She wished that he'd been surprised, had been angry, resistant—she'd rather he shouted an alarm than spoke one more word in that flat and awful voice.

She spat her fear out onto the ground, and tucked the Lady's Axe behind her belt.

She'd built this boat, and now she had to sail it.

"Come on," she said. "Let's go collect your son."

Leucas could barely see past the red haze that lowered over his eyes; he could taste only blood and black bile. Random, spiky tingling was all he could feel from his right leg, and the flesh over the knuckles of both his hands had split into bloody shreds over the rock-hard bone.

He pushed himself up against the pier of the alcove's archway, sliding erect on the slickening blood that poured down his back from some forgotten scalp wound. His lungs felt like he had inhaled shards of broken pottery, and he struggled to lift his hands once again.

Melchizedek moved toward him, as unstoppable as a landslide.

Leucas' fists had fallen like rain upon Melchizedek, had delivered a beating that would have killed ten men. He had moved with the grace and skill of the professional boxer that he was, darting in to strike, cracking the old man's head to the side with hooks and pounding uppercuts to his bare chest that lifted Melchizedek off his feet and sent him hurtling through the air, landing whistling crosses to the chin that had slapped the old man to the ground like a blow from a hammer.

No matter how strong Melchizedek might be, he had only the weight of a skinny old man, and Leucas could knock him down at will.

But though his fists fell like rain, like rain they were ignored. Melchizedek rose from each pounding as though he had not felt it.

Leucas couldn't win this fight. He'd known from the start he couldn't win it.

He also knew he wouldn't give up.

*I didn't expect, though, that it would be quite this short,* he thought dazedly, as Melchizedek closed with him.

Perhaps it had been his broken ribs and lacerated guts that had betrayed him; perhaps it had been the weeks on the road, the accumulated fatigue of more than a month without a real night's rest; perhaps the demon had been only playing with him, and had now tired of the game. Melchizedek's fist had seemed to flash from nowhere, impossibly fast; it had struck him like a thunderbolt, unstringing his knees and wrapping a black veil across his eyes.

After that, he could only stagger and try to duck, and hold his guard up, try to roll with the crushing blows that blasted him from one wall to another, tossing him tumbling through the air like a doll cast aside by a petulant child, splattering the walls of the altarhouse with his blood.

Melchizedek had stalked after him expressionlessly, methodically, one blow at a time, with the mechanical deliberation of a smith hammering flat a shield, each a stroke that could shatter a tree or pulverize stone, each a stroke that could kill an angry bull.

Now Leucas barely had the strength to cover his head with his bloody hands as Melchizedek strode toward him for the last time.

The High Priest's eyes glowed with fire as lifeless as embers of charcoal; muscle, laid bare by the mercenaries' daggers, flexed within his shredded chest, and his long mottled penis pulsed upward as though with lust.

*Damn,* Leucas thought, his own voice inside his skull oddly calm and detached. *Damn, he's going to kill me.*

Melchizedek seized his arm above the elbow, and a sudden sadness as sharp as nausea overtook Leucas. *He's going to tear my arm off,* he thought. *I hate that,* as though he didn't mind dying, really, but he'd much prefer to be killed in some other, less awful way.

For what seemed like a very long moment, he experienced it in anticipation, so vividly that he felt only vague relief when Melchizedek seized his thigh with his other hand, his grip so powerful that his fingers tore bloody gashes into Leucas' flesh like knives, then lifted him high and threw him through the wall.

The earlier damage to the wall saved his life; the mortared stones gave way under his impact and he landed hard across them in a choking cloud of stone dust. He lay stunned, his back arched over a pile of rubble, staring at the wheeling clouds above.

*The sun's come up,* he thought.

He lifted his head in time to see Melchizedek turn away from the ragged gap in the wall and stride toward the alcove where Sarah lay.

With an effort that sent a spray of blood bursting past his lips, Leucas sat up.

A few of the Picts had apparently run away, and Leucas didn't blame them; those that hadn't lay torn and dead upon the flagstones. The mob still stood silently pressed against the inside of the Ba'alath's walls. The mercenaries stared at them, and each other, awakening into obvious puzzlement.

"Leucas!" Agaz snapped, confusion harshening his voice until it sounded like rage. "What's going on?"

Leucas didn't have time to answer.

Melchizedek had reached the arch to the alcove.

With a heavy sigh for the sunlight, for the world he was leaving behind, Leucas climbed brokenly to his feet, and limped after him.

The sun splintered a pass in the eastern mountains, bloodying the circling storm above, and Bertram Dhui Maud Rhum looked out over his men.

He stood on the slope of a Gate Tower buttress, leaning on a spear that was twice his own height, and thought about the strange fortunes of war.

A sea of faces returned his regard, pale Picts, ruddy Kelts in all their variety from Gael to Briton to Scot, grim Akhaians, Philistines with their long golden braids, sweating Hittites and Nubians the color of charcoal; in every face Bertram read the sure knowledge that to leave these gates was death.

*On the other hand,* he reflected for the thousandth time, *stay here and we're dead just as sure.*

There were many Jebusite faces in this crowd as well, boys who held a blade with uncertain grip, their hands unused to weapons, old men who refused armor, knowing that their strength would not support bronze in a charge. And some of those boys, to Bertram's eye, looked a bit too old and and world-wise to be quite so beardless: wives and mothers of the Jebusites had chosen to put on the dress of their husbands, of their sons, to fight and die alongside their men.

Bertram shrugged. He would not tell them no. It was not the way of his people to deny anyone the right to choose their own fate.

He had gone to every mercenary company, to each campfire and Jebusite guardhouse. Few had refused him, and those that had he could cajole or bully; with six-hundred-odd Picts and assorted Kelts at his back, no one dared to argue.

Not even the remaining Jebusites turned him down. Melchizedek was reported to be dead; Adonizedek had vanished during the first day's attack. Agaz was nowhere to be found. Bertram Dhui Maud Rhum captained nearly all the surviving mercenaries. For the few short hours between midnight and dawn, he had been, effectively, the king of Jebusi.

And now he was where a Pictish king should be, when his people face danger: at their head, leading them into battle.

The clouds like a wheel of stone overhead had brought wind now, a rising gale that whipped Bertram's hair in stinging lashes across his face.

*I've really come up in the world,* Bertram thought.

The wind would slap any words from his mouth and bury them in its rising rush, but words were not required; he raised his spear over his head, and five thousand fighters answered his gesture with their gold-flashing spears, swords of bronze and iron, axes of bronze and granite and basalt.

*Ma would be proud. Pity I'll die before I get the chance to really enjoy it.*

The men who worked to dismantle the timbered bracing that had held shut the gate now rolled the last of the logs to one side and picked up weapons of their own.

The gates swung open.

On the ridgetop above, the bright colors of the Tabernacle were bleached by the grey light into something pale and malignant, like a poisonous fungus that fed on the rot of the land around it.

In the vast forest of tents that surrounded the Tabernacle, thousands of Habiru looked toward the open gates, their mouths wide with shouted alarms that vanished behind the wind.

Bertram swung his spear above his head, and sprang down from the buttress into the forefront of the mass. With a single shout from five thousand throats, a shout that for one instant overwhelmed the whistling roar of the wind, the Army of Jebusi made its first and final charge.

Guiding Eleazar through the Levite camp from a careful two paces behind his left shoulder, Barra watched her plan begin to bear fruit.

She walked with the cloak of her burnoose folded over her axe, directing Eleazar with muttered commands; he shambled before her like one of Simi-Ascalon's soulless chryseids, mindlessly following her orders, his face blank as a river-smoothed stone.

All around them, the camp twitched in confused amazement as the gates swung open and the mercenaries howled their charge; like a herd of sleepy hippos in the Nile that sees a lone crocodile stalking toward it through the muddy waters, its first overwhelming reaction had been *Is this some kind of joke?*

But as the shrieking mercenaries took advantage of the Levites' disbelief to hurl themselves over the earthworks that separated the camp from the city, to trample tents and carve through unarmed Levites who stumbled unprepared before them, the amazement faded behind alarm, and then bloodthirsty fury. Battle horns blared, ringing echoes from the walls below and the clouds above, and Levites threw on their armor and swept up their spears and slings, their sickles and sharpened shovels.

The Kohathites took the brunt of the first charge, their clan's camp being closest to the city. Half-armed, panicked, furious, they threw themselves at the mercenaries and were slaughtered by the dozen, then by the hundred, but even in death they began to absorb the mercenaries' charge: the advance slowed as men stepped more carefully around corpses and fallen wounded, and over earth treacherously slick and muddy with pooling blood.

Instead of spreading into a broader front to engage the Kohathites, the mercenaries kept themselves tightly packed, like antelopes harried by lions, and ground relentlessly toward the Tabernacle. A shock bigger than the first rumbled through the camps when the Levites understood the mercenaries' objective; suddenly the clans of Gershon and Merari realized that the Tabernacle itself was threatened, and the men of both clans flew to its defense.

For a time, Barra and Eleazar threaded through a stampede of running men, getting shoved and jostled this way and that, as the Levites pounded downslope toward the mercenary army, to place their bodies between it and the Tent of Yahweh.

This was what she had been counting on: the Levites were priestly clans, not warriors, charged with the care of the Ark, the Tabernacle and its fittings, not with battle. They didn't have even the elementary discipline to hold their position.

She guided the High Priest to where she'd left the wagon, and ordered him onto the drover's seat while she untied the hobbles around the ankles of the lead asses. She swung up beside him and drove in an arc around the rear of the Tabernacle, below the crest of the ridge and out of sight of the battle, through a maze of tents that seemed every bit as deserted as the camps through which she'd driven before the dawn.

*This might actually work,* she thought, her heart clenched with agonizing hope. She had Eleazar to get her past whatever Tabernacle guards remained—she had his story planned in detail: he would tell any guards that the Ark itself was in danger, and he must go in first to cover it so that these servants in the wagon could bear it away without committing the crime of looking upon it; if any asked where were the Merarites who customarily transported the Ark, Eleazar need only gesture toward the battle. Kheperu was inside, ensuring that the Ark was still there, and would be able to help her load the Ark onto the wagon . . . and she had a clear path through the empty camps, to swing around toward the wellhouse, where her tribesmen waited within.

Then, if Sheshai was right, the Habiru would take the loss of the Ark as irrefutable evidence that their god had deserted them. They wouldn't just retreat, they'd run like their own fucking angels were after them.

If Sheshai was wrong . . . well, dead is dead; she wouldn't be any more dead than she would have been if she hadn't tried.

As the wagon neared the tent of Phinehas, she tried not to think about what could happen if the mercenary attack collapsed before she was safely back inside Jebusi. *It won't,* she told herself. *It's my nephew and my kinsmen leading them. They'll fight as long as a human being can, and longer.*

She prayed it would be long enough.

She reined in the asses alongside the tent of Phinehas. "Sheshai!" she barked, raising her voice to be heard above the rising wind. "Come on, move it!"

The stony clouds overhead wheeled faster now, their undersides churning like stew at a rolling boil; lightning clawed the sky, reaching toward the earth like talons. At the axis of the wheeling clouds, something dark and powerful was massing, bulging downward, but Barra had no attention to spare for it right now: she'd caught sight of something far more alarming.

Along the Jericho Road, perhaps a mile away or a little more, an enormous cloud of dust rose as though the earth echoed the thunderheads above. She sprang up to stand on the drover's bench, and squinted down the road, trying to swallow past the cold hand that squeezed the inside of her throat.

At the head of the dust cloud raced chariots.

He was on to her.

*Joshua, you bastard!* Her thoughts snarled like angry wolves inside her skull. *How'd you know?*

How did that bastard *know*?

Beside her, Eleazar gave a thin, high moan, the unconscious whine of an old man in pain. She looked down to find that Sheshai had brought Phinehas out from the tent, slung over his shoulder, and now tossed him carelessly into the wagon's bed.

Phinehas looked bad, his beautiful hair matted with mudcolored clots of blood, one side of his face swollen purple and black over his shattered cheekbone. The eye on that side had swelled shut, but through his lashes leaked some transparent fluid only faintly tinged with blood. The eyeball had been punctured by splinters of bone, and he'd be half-blind, if he lived, but Barra didn't expect him to regain consciousness.

His irregular breathing came in ragged, shallow gasps, and his arms and legs twitched in random spasms.

For one moment, as Eleazar looked upon his son, Barra caught a glimpse of human emotion cracking through his mask of detachment.

His lips formed words: *Phinehas. Phinehas, my son.*

But then his face sealed itself like a riven breastplate being brazed together over a furnace, and when he looked up at her, his eyes were empty.

"We're wasting time," he said calmly. Barra could barely hear him; the winds had risen to a howl like the screams of the Jericho dead.

He said, "Let's go. I want to get to the Tabernacle before Joshua arrives."

"Ay," Barra said. "Me too."

"Joshua?" Sheshai showed his teeth as he swung up into the wagon's bed and began to bury Phinehas in the straw; when he looked at Barra his eyes sparked with reflections of the lightning above. "He's coming back, isn't he? He's really coming!"

*And we're going,* Barra thought, dropping back onto the drover's bench and taking up the reins. She did not speak, for the winds now rattled the wagon as though it would blow onto its side, and from the sky grew a roar like thunder, a thunder that did not crack and fade away but gathered, louder and louder, until it filled her head with a rolling blast that threatened to burst her skull.

She had never heard anything like this; and she had never seen anything like this, either.

From the wheel of clouds above Jebusi descended a whirling mass of darkness, a maelstrom of air like a swirl of water draining through a bunghole the size of the city itself. It reached downward, a funnel-shaped cone of incredible, monstrous proportions, a mountain that stood on its head.

Barra screamed into the wind, "What in every name of the bloody Mother is that?"

From Eleazar's lips, she read her answer.

*That,* he mouthed, *is the Finger of God.*

As it lowered upon the city, it seemed that the earth itself swirled up to meet it, a column of sand and broken stone, of wood and living things that shot upward like the spume of a volcano.

The Finger of God touched the massive, Kyklopean rock of the Gate Tower, and the Gate Tower exploded.

It blew apart into fragments consumed by a spinning shroud of black dust, boulders bigger than horses whirling upward into the air like bits of straw; Barra glimpsed among them tumbling men, men who had thought to stay behind in the safety of the strongest fort in Canaan, carried upward to the clouds, vanishing high beyond her vision.

And the Finger did not recede; after shattering the wall as though it were a child's fort made of sand, it swung out through the Israelite camp, scouring the earth in a broad arc, leaving nothing in its wake save shattered stone, heading straight for the ridge slope where the Levites struggled with the mercenaries.

"You did this?" she screamed. "You?"

Eleazar answered her gaze with eyes that burned like Sheshai's, and mouthed his reply.

*This is only the beginning.*

The screaming wind covered the sound of his footsteps.

Melchizedek had paused for one instant, in the archway, and in that instant Leucas seized him from behind. One hand on the back of his neck, the other taking his naked, grey-haired thigh, Leucas lifted the High Priest over his head.

*Let's see how you like it,* he thought, and threw him through the wall.

The wall shattered into individual bricks and the roof above it collapsed with a long, sustained groan like the sigh of a toppling tree. Leucas hurled himself after Melchizedek, diving awkwardly under the falling roof, skidding across the bloody flagstones, and barely managing to grasp the High Priest's ankle before Melchizedek could rise.

He yanked Melchizedek to the ground again and scrambled to his feet, coughing blood, holding on to the ankle, and praying that his numbly tingling right leg would support his weight. He whirled as though he were throwing the hammer at the Olympian Games, spinning Melchizedek out at arm's length. He slammed him again and again into the flagstones as he spun, scraping away huge chunks of the High Priest's flesh to expose the twitching muscle beneath.

His breath chopped into short gasps, and his head began to spin faster than he did, and Melchizedek reached down and hooked an unbreakable grip around the edge of a flagstone the size of a Pictish tower shield.

The sudden jerk broke Leucas' grip and sent him staggering dizzily across the courtyard. Melchizedek rose, lifting the flagstone as though it were a child's ball, and threw it at Leucas. The Athenian weaved to one side, and the stone ripped into the silent mob against the wall, tearing through the shoulder joint of one man before striking edge-on into another's sternum, crushing his rib cage into splinters that pierced his heart.

*That would have killed me, if it hit,* Leucas thought with that same odd detachment. *But it missed, and I'm alive.*

His battered face split into a grin. This wasn't over yet.

And he was starting to have fun.

He lifted a flagstone of his own, smaller than Melchizedek's; he needed both hands to do it, and had to shift unsteadily to balance its weight. Taking a few running strides for momentum, he faked his throw like a boy in an apple fight; when Melchizedek instinctively ducked, Leucas fired the stone and pegged the old man squarely on the top of his head. The impact broke the stone into pieces and flipped Melchizedek into the air, sending him rolling and skidding backward across the courtyard.

When he rolled over to get up, Leucas pounced on his back.

He slid his arms beneath Melchizedek's armpits, bringing his hands together behind the priest's neck; he wrapped his thighs around Melchizedek's naked hips and locked his ankles together in front. In this leverage position, he could deny Melchizedek the use of those slaughtering arms for as long as he could hold on.

*That's the trick,* he told himself. *I just have to hold on.*

Barra fought the reins, her head down against the wind-whipped gravel that stung her face. The wind kept shifting unpredictably, and whenever it came at the wagon broadside the whole thing would rock sideways and threaten to tip over; only Sheshai's weight, thrown in reckless leaps from one side of the wagon to the other, kept the wheels on the ground. The asses brayed in panic, writhed under their yokes, tried to rear and kick. Flying sand and gravel darkened the air like a heavy rain.

Eleazar sat like a wooden statue on the bench beside her, eyes open and uncaring, as though nothing that happened to his body could touch him.

Some of the Levites who guarded the Tabernacle had stayed at their posts, clinging with astonishing courage to their duty even as the battle raged ever nearer up the slope of the ridge and the Finger of God towered above them, but they waved the wagon through when they saw Eleazar on the drover's bench.

The elaborate story she'd planned for Eleazar was never used; no one could have heard it over the roar. No matter. With the descent of the Finger of God, her plans had exploded like the Gate Tower.

Below, the mercenaries and the Levites were joined in a line of slaughter, pressed together to make a border of bloody blades and dying men. The Finger of God swung across the lines once, obliterating Levite and mercenary alike, but the rest threw themselves at each other with increased frenzy, as though the storm fed rage into their hearts.

The Finger of God seemed to pause, as though waiting, feeding on the stone and earth of the valley, pulsing and twisting with its gargantuan power, until the wagon reached the Sanctuary Gate itself. Then, once again, it began to move.

Slowly, with obscene deliberation, it advanced on the Sanctuary.

She turned the asses and cracked the reins around their ears, sending them bolting through the gate toward the Tabernacle. The door-curtain of the Tabernacle whipped wide in the wind, and Barra drove the wagon straight through it, the asses knocking aside an enormous golden candelabra, toppling a large table and kicking over a big horned altar covered with beaten gold. They twisted and stamped, trampling golden plates under their hooves, braying in confusion and distress.

*We're in,* she thought numbly, for an instant unable to believe it. *We made it. We're in.* Then she leaped down from the wagon, her heels skidding on trampled bread loaves and spilled oils.

"Kheperu!" she cried. "Kheperu, come on! Let's go!"

"Barra?" came a weakly hopeful voice from beyond an inner curtain; an instant later the curtain whipped aside and Kheperu stumbled through, his face shining with sweat, his eyes raw and streaming tears. He threw himself upon her as an exhausted swimmer throws himself on a beach that has barely saved him from drowning. She staggered under his sudden weight, but managed to hold him upright.

"Barra, oh, Barra," he sobbed. "Oh, you came, you're really *here!*"

"Of course I am, you pinhead. What did you expect?" she snapped, but her arms tightened around his chest, and she felt a heat in her eyes that threatened tears of her own. "Come on, help me load the fucking wagon. We don't have much time."

"It doesn't matter," Kheperu said. He lifted his flushed, tear-stained face. "At least I don't have to die alone."

The tent muffled the roar of the Finger of God, but she could hear it coming like an avalanche.

"Die, nothing," she said, pushing him away. "We get that god-box into the city, and we win it all."

"But it's futile," he said hopelessly. "Don't you see? It all ends in death—now, later, it's doesn't matter. Why struggle?"

Barra squinted at him, measuring his despair. She understood him perfectly, but she didn't have time for sympathy, or a debate. Her fist flashed faster than the eye could follow; before Kheperu knew she had swung, he found himself on the ground, blood streaming from his freshly broken nose.

He gaped up at her, gasping through the pain and the blood. "What was that for?"

"To remind you that you're still alive. Get the fuck up."

"Indeed," he said, his face clearing. He blinked once, then again, then scrambled to his feet with startling energy. "Indeed!"

She turned to Sheshai. "Pull Phinehas out and leave him here, then help us with the god-box."

From the back of the wagon, Sheshai glared at her with inexplicable fury. "What about *Joshua*?"

"He's going to be here any second," she said. "That's why we have to hurry!"

"You're going to take the Ark into the city," he snarled. "That's all! You're just going to take it and run."

"Sheshai," she snarled right back, "don't pull any shit with me. I don't have time."

"All you *care* about is the *city*!" The bitter accusation of a betrayed child filled his voice. "*What about Joshua?* What about his *blood*? You promised!*"

Barra wanted to scream with frustration: everywhere she turned, another bloodyfucking thing got in her way. Instead, she pulled the Lady's Axe out from her belt and cocked it back over her shoulder, pointing at Sheshai with her other hand.

"Either get to work or make peace with your fucking Tchera'khu, because I'm about to send you to see him."

His face twisted with lunatic hatred and his scars burned red. He brought something up from beneath the wagon's sideboard; Barra almost killed him, thinking it was a weapon, before she saw it was his quiver of arrows.

"Remember this?" he cried, shaking it at her. He whipped the silver-tipped black arrow out from its place. "Do you *remember*?"

"Sheshai, we don't have—"

"Joshua doesn't!" His cry carried the bleak, bottomless despair of an old woman burying her sons. *"Joshua doesn't even know who I am!"*

Before she could answer, he leaped down from the wagon and streaked out the door of the Tabernacle, vanishing into the screaming dusk of sand and flying stones.

Kheperu was at her side, pinching shut his bleeding nose. "Go after him?"

"No time," she said. "And he'll be dead before we find him, anyway." She turned to grab Phinehas' ankle, and began to drag him out of the wagon. "Guess it's just you and me, partner."

He replied with a pained smile, and Barra thought, *Just you and me? Oh, bleeding shit!*

She'd lost track of him—between Kheperu and Sheshai and everything else she had to worry about, he'd slipped away unnoticed.

She said aloud, "Where's Eleazar? What happened to fucking *Eleazar?*"

From within the Holy of Holies came a laugh like a shout of power, that made the earth beneath her feet tremble like a drumhead. The Tabernacle filled with a brilliant white light, more blinding than the noonday sun; Barra squeezed her eyes shut and clapped a hand over them, but the light struck through her flesh; even through her closed eyes she could see the faint outlines of her finger bones.

The power of the silent voice within her skull drove her to her knees.

The silent voice said:

I AM.

# 19

# *The Fist of God*

Sheshai stumbled into the path of the oncoming chariots, his head down, staggering against the blast of the wind. The gale ripped tears from his eyes and scoured his flesh with gravel until his face and hands streamed with blood.

He let the blood run into his mouth, and smacked his lips over it, pretending it was Joshua's.

Behind him, the maelstrom hovered over the Tabernacle, poised like an unimaginable mouth to devour it. The hooves of the galloping chariot horses shook the earth, and their eyes rolled white, and behind the chariots ran the entire Host of Israel.

The chariots thundered around and past him; the shoulder of a charging horse grazed him and battered him spinning to the earth, breathless, clutching his quiver to his breast as though it could save his life. As he struggled to his feet, both horses of a chariot team reared up rather than trample him, pawing the air with their hooves. The driver cursed him in a high, piercing screech as he fought for control, and Sheshai saw here a gift from Tchera'khu: the chariot's passenger bore a long, recurved bow of laminated horn.

His God had provided.

He whipped an arrow from his quiver and leaped at the team, holding the arrow like a dagger. He stabbed it into the neck of the nearest horse; the horse reared again, screaming. Its scream panicked the other horse as well, and they both bolted uncontrollably. As the chariot plunged past him, he leaped up and caught the arm of the startled passenger, yanking him out of the chariot onto the ground.

Sheshai pressed himself against the stunned Habiru like a lover,

gazing passionately down into the man's dazed eyes. He lowered his
face and kissed the man on the lips even as his knife slid into the
Habiru's belly and sawed upward. The man bucked beneath him,
screaming his death into Sheshai's mouth.

Sheshai leaned over and nuzzled the corpse's ear. "Thank you," he
whispered, then he picked up the man's bow and rose.

Now past him, a bare stone's throw away, charged Joshua himself,
the old general had no driver but stood wide-legged on the bucking
chariot, handling the reins himself. Other chariots and their drivers
passed between, denying Sheshai his shot, and the following warriors
had seen him kill the man at his feet: they raced toward him, weapons
poised to bite.

Sheshai ran from them, fleet as a hare, pursuing the chariots.

Tchera'khu had given him this bow; surely he would give him a
shot, as well.


Twilight filled Leucas' eyes with grey fog. He clung grimly, desperately, to Melchizedek's back; he could no longer remember if it was
day or night, where he was, why he was fighting this old man; he no
longer knew his own name.

He only knew he must hold on.

Melchizedek's hands, locked behind his head by Leucas' hold,
scrabbled at Leucas' wrists, at his hair, his eyes; Leucas clung grimly,
twisting his head and shifting his arms to keep them out of
Melchizedek's killing grip.

The old priest hurled himself across the courtyard for the tenth
time, or the hundredth, or the thousandth. The preternatural power in his
skinny legs hurtled them both at a terrific speed. As they approached
the altarhouse wall, or the outer wall of the Ba'alath, or one of the tall
stone pillars that made the ring in the courtyard, Melchizedek spun
once again and Leucas' back crashed against the stone with crushing
force.

Again, stone crumbled; all twelve of the stone pillars now lay in
pieces across the courtyard, broken by Leucas' back. The wall around
the Ba'alath gaped with three Leucas-sized holes. The altarhouse was
nothing more than a pile of rubble, the hulking Great Astarte rising out
of it like Aphrodite from the surf. Only the tiny alcove of the Lady's
Maid still stood, covered by the remnants of the roof; each time
Melchizedek had charged toward that, Leucas had managed to summon enough strength to throw his weight to one side, to shift the High

Priest's balance enough to make him stumble and blunt the force of his attack.

And now the High Priest began a new tactic. He lumbered over to the towering megalith of the Great Astarte, turned his back to pin Leucas against it, braced his feet against the floor, and pushed.

The Great Astarte weighed tens of tons; even so, it rocked backward on its pedestal, its balance shifting, and every time it rocked forward again it crushed the breath out from Leucas' chest.

The darkness before his eyes thickened until he could no longer see, and his ribs began to give way before the strain. He could feel them break individually: *crack* went one, wet and sharp inside him, then another, then two more. Blind now, gasping for air that would not come, he couldn't feel his hands anymore, he couldn't tell if he still held his grip or not.

But he did feel Melchizedek's hand take his wrist, and he did feel his bones grind together within that grip, and he did feel his arm being forced inexorably away.

And he felt Melchizedek's hand touch him on the hollow of the thigh, and he felt his leg break with a sickening *pop* like a cork bursting from a jug of spoiled wine.

And, finally, he felt Melchizedek's hand tangle in his hair, yank him from his back, and slam him to the floor like a side of meat.

Stars fountained across his vision, and then he felt no more.

Barra knelt at the door of the Holy of Holies, blind and deaf in the screaming whiteness, and the light peeled her like an apple.

It tore away her hair in smoldering hanks, and stripped the flesh from her skull. It chewed her fingers from her hands and sliced her breasts down to her bare and bloody ribs. It chipped away her bones, gnawed into her belly, and cracked her skull like an eggshell.

In that merciless brilliance, she knew the truth.

She was nothing, and He was All.

Shame overpowered her, shame more potent than the sizzling agony of her dismemberment. She was only dirt, after all, clay and shit with breath inside; the light that dissolved her was all purity and majestic strength.

That light was the countenance of He Who Commands the Morning, Who Opens the Gates of Death; it was the face of He Who Laid the Foundation of the World, the Master of Behemoth, the Strangler of Leviathan; faced with the Creator of Heaven and Earth, what was she?

She was low and vile, a clod of earth polluted with menstrual blood, pathetic and contemptible. She was weak, worthless, a vessel of base desires and revolting lusts; she took into her all the fine things of Yahweh's Creation, every apple and pear and olive, cool clean spring-water and savory herbs and roasted meat, and her sinful, loathsome body transformed them into foul shit and stinking piss.

The flames of dissolution that burned away her flesh were more than justice; they were her only chance to escape the disgust that choked her. Free of the defiling flesh, she could be as pure as this sear-ing light.

How could she have ever struggled against Him? Everything she had ever done, everything she'd ever believed was so horribly, humil-iatingly wrong; she was a child, an infant, squalling in befouled swad-dling; like a child, she should never have been trusted with her own life. If only someone could have looked after her, directed her, shown her the way, led her in the path of Light, protected her from herself . . .

Boiling tears ran from eyes that cooked beneath His Gaze, scald-ing her cheeks, etching them like acid.

She reached instinctively for the axe at her side, but instead of cool basalt, her fingers found only unfamiliar bronze. This crushed her more finally than the rest; there was nothing left.

Death was her only hope.

*Father, I'm sorry.*


Sheshai sprinted behind the chariots, the front ranks of the Host of Israel at his heels. The Finger of God roared above the Tabernacle, and from the Tabernacle rose a shaft of searing light that bleached all color from the earth around; it entered the howling mouth of the Finger, kin-dling light within like a faience lamp. Shadows lay sharp as knife-edges on the ground, and the clouds above blazed as though they burned with white flame above the battlefield.

The shaft of light thickened, and strengthened, filling the throat of the Finger until it was impossible to look upon; Sheshai turned his eyes away, but even the reflection on the lowered heads of the follow-ing Habiru burned his eyes like a splash of wine.

He put his head down, and kept running.

A rising note entered the Finger's roar, a whistling shriek that grew into the scream of an angry god. Light the red of a sunset in a dust storm flared and painted the shadows with blood, and the ground vanished from beneath his feet; his legs kept working, still trying to run, scrambling for purchase on the empty air. He went tumbling down to meet the earth as it rose again and struck him like a hammer.

Stunned, he lay on his back and gasped for air, staring dazedly up at the boiling clouds overhead. Somewhere to his left, a fountain of smoke and dust and molten rock sprayed toward the sky.

A new angry whistling shriek grew, joined by another, and another, a deafening chorus of fury that opened rippling mouths within the clouds, mouths which spat lines of flame toward the earth, impossibly straight, impossibly bright, scratching his eyes and battering his ears.

In a single flashing instant, they struck the earth, making it leap and buck like the deck of a racing chariot; from each impact gouts of smoke and flaming earth splashed overhead like water around a rock thrown into a pond.

And Sheshai, lying on his back with his stolen bow across his chest, looking up with detached, unsurprised calm, realized that this was exactly what was happening.

*It's Yahweh,* he thought. *He's throwing rocks at us.*

He sat up. All around him, men were staggering to their feet, wandering dazed and aimless over their brethren, most of whom still cowered on the ground. The battle between the mercenaries and the Levites on the slope below was utter shambles, blood-soaked men clutching in mortal terror whoever happened to be beside them, desperate for the touch of another's hand but tearing and stabbing at each other nonetheless.

The Habiru cavalry cursed and fought their panicked horses closer to the Tabernacle, and there, skylined above Sheshai, against the blinding brilliance of the shaft that rose from the Tabernacle, stood the silhouette of a balding old man with heavy arms and a bull neck, alone in a chariot.

Sheshai rose.

The black outline of Joshua ben Nun lifted its arms to the sky.

Sheshai reached into his quiver without looking, his fingers finding a certain arrow with absolute surety.

Above the Tabernacle, the Finger of God ended its hesitation, dipping downward with majestic deliberation.

In a single smooth gesture, as though he had trained for this moment his whole life, Sheshai nocked his arrow of iron and silver, drew the shaft back to his ear, and let it fly.

He stood motionless, his eye following his arrow's beautiful arc.

His lust for vengeance, the bottomless hunger that had eaten his life, paused and stood poised for its final fulfillment.

As the Finger of God dipped closer, his arrow turned in the air, caught by its winds.

Sheshai's mouth formed a silent *No*.

The arrow twisted, and lurched, and turned its barbed head upward as it began to tumble in the air; the winds grasped it and swirled it away to vanish up among the clouds.

"No! *Noooo!*"

Sheshai's howl vanished unheard behind the wind.

He fumbled with his quiver, trying to find another arrow, stumbling into a run to get closer for a flatter shot. Another shrieking sky-stone hurtled down and blasted the earth nearby, slapping him to the ground, and this time he fell on his bow, and it snapped in his hands. One curved section of laminated horn whipped across his face, tearing open his cheek so deeply that he felt the wind on his back teeth.

He still knelt on the ground, staring dumbly at the bow that had betrayed him, when a Habiru warrior finally reached him and hacked into his shoulder with a sharpened shovel.

Sheshai looked expressionlessly at the bronze blade that separated bone from muscle in his chest as the warrior behind him wrenched it free. Another warrior reached him, this one bearing a dull and ragged-edged bronze sword that struck off the forearm he lifted to guard his head. He stared at the spurting mess of bone and muscle and fat that was the stump of his arm, and thought, *My hand. That was my hand.*

The third warrior to arrive kicked him unresisting flat upon the earth, and drove a spear down into his guts, sawing upward through his spilling intestines, severing his liver, his stomach, slicing toward his heart.

Sheshai said, blood bursting from his mouth, *"Do you know me? Do you know who I am? I am—"*

He fought to get his name out, to tell them, to tell somebody, but instead of words all that came from his mouth was bloody vomit, and death crushed his heart.

Joshua ben Nun looked in openmouthed awe at the whirling tower of the white-flaming Finger of God that loomed over his head, and now swung down toward him.

All around him, the sky blazed with the light of the rising shaft and the searing streaks of sky-stones; Joshua stepped down from his chariot and his horses bolted, tearing their reins from his grasp and running in panic down toward the valley floor.

The ground on which he stood tossed like the open sea.

*Eleazar,* he thought. *Eleazar, what have you done?*

The rest of his cavalry gathered around the Tabernacle; Joshua could see the panic in their faces, but he could not hear their shouted pleas over the constant roar.

Eleazar's words snarled within his skull: *This could turn God against us . . .*

All around, as far as the eye could see, the land burned under the sky-stones' fall.

Joshua gathered breath to the depths of his massive chest, and roared in a voice to match the winds above, "Begone! In the Name of God, I command you to be still! *In the Name of Yahweh Sabaoth, El Shaddai, CEASE!"*

As though by way of answer, the Finger of God swung down upon his head.


The bronze of the Lady's Axe felt smooth and warm as skin beneath her fingers, and Barra thought, *Hey, wait.*

This light that had burned her to ash, this purifying flame that had dissolved her flesh and charred her bones in an instant, had left the axe at her side untouched? Not even *hot*?

How could she feel it, with her hands burned away? How could she feel anything at all?

How could she still live?

She pulled the axe from her belt and clutched it with both hands. She felt the strength of her own grip, the clean health of her muscles; she felt new breath surge into her lungs, and she felt the grace of her balance as she came inexorably to her feet.

She thought, with unwilling admiration, *Why, you lying son of a bitch!*

She lifted the axe up before her face and felt its cool shade upon her cheeks.

In the shadow of the axe, she could open her eyes.

The power of the Light, within the Holy of Holies, struck through even the warm solidity of the bronze, transforming it into a filmy golden translucency; she looked through the axe, into the room beyond.

There on a pedestal lay the god-box, showering the Tabernacle with brilliant reflections from its covering of beaten gold. At each of its corners, a golden figure crouched in hideous detail, each with four wings spread wide, arms and legs beneath them beweaponed with hooked talons, and eyes, far too many eyes . . .

With the Lady's Axe held before her like a shield, Barra stepped over the threshold.

Eleazar stood between her and the god-box, his head thrown back and his arms thrown wide. Even through the sheltering axe, he was impossible to look upon: it was from Eleazar himself that the screaming brilliance came.

The vague smoky outlines of a cloud hung between the upraised wings of the angels on the god-box, swirling and boiling, a long, doubled tendril extending from it to pour into Eleazar's nostrils, as though the High Priest inhaled a never-ending breath. The smoke itself was barely existent, the merest shadowy hint on this side of nothingness; only by passing into and through the priest's body did it find expression as this unimaginable gout of power.

Barra took another step.

Now Eleazar turned to face her, his body swinging around with mechanical precision as though he stood on a potter's wheel, the tendrils of smoke parting around his head, still flowing into his nostrils, the twin streams embracing him from behind like insubstantial hands. The light from his face stabbed her eyes like knives through the axe, and she stood transfixed by the full force of the alien malice that poured from him.

What she had felt before, in the outer room, had been only a shadow of the terrible power that beat against her now. All that fear, all that loathing of her body and her self, all of that brutal self-surrender now roared tenfold within her, growing every second, now a hundredfold, a thousand . . .

But now she knew better, she knew that this came from outside, not from within; she knew that this was what He wanted her to believe.

She said, growling like her wolf in anger, *"Liar."*

And she took another step.

The light sharpened even more. Who was she to judge Him? Could she thunder like Him? Could she lighten? Could she order the days into seasons and set the sun in its path? Could she rain destruction upon the land?

Lips full of blood and life pulled back from her teeth; she had learned better lessons than this one long ago.

*I'm not buying,* she thought. *Being strong doesn't make you right.*

Faintly through the screaming brilliance she heard explosions, and the awful roar of the Finger of God. Now the earth shook beneath her like a horse that bucked and tried to throw her, but some answering power rooted her feet like an ancient oak, and she rode the earthquake forward.

Now there were no longer words, only meaning, only power that beat at Her and tried to strike Her down, only Her implacable step-by-step advance into the teeth of the white hurricane.

The god She faced roared at Her of decay and disease, of misery and death; She answered Him with sunlight and birdsong, with wine and sweaty sex.

He howled Corruption.

She sang Love.

He thundered Violence, and She replied: *All right.*

The Axe of the Lady was never intended to be a weapon; its balance was all wrong, its head far too large for the meager counter-weight of the pommel, its haft of bronze too slender to withstand the shock of combat. It had been designed, forged, and balanced as a sac-rificial tool, to cut the throat of sacred bulls a millennium ago, when the Lady still demanded blood and life each spring, and it was as a sacred tool, not as a weapon, that it was now used.

She stepped close, and swung, and the serrated edge of broken gemstones chopped rudely into His side, hacking through liver and kidney to notch his spine.

The power that fountained through Eleazar held him upright, and shot through the bronze haft of the axe, locking tight hands that Barra now discovered were once again all too mortal. Bound together by the power that rushed through them both, they could only stand and shake; but where the power in Eleazar shot upward, that which entered Barra was grounded into the earth.

Her hair burst into flame, and her clothing cindered to ash in a bare second, and she smelled the pork-scented smoke of her own roasting flesh, and the Tabernacle exploded into fire around them, a sudden blaze that ate through its hangings of linen and goat hair, its skins of rams and manatees, that blew them to pieces which swirled up the limitless throat of the Finger of God.

There came a shattering crack and final flash that seemed to scorch the eyes from her head.

She knelt on the bare and smoking earth, blind and deaf and naked, and her salt tears streamed, stinging like fire, into the charred ruin of her hands.

                                    \*   \*   \*

Leucas opened his eyes to see Melchizedek standing over him, holding high in his spindly arms a chunk of stone wall larger than he was. Leucas knew that he had only this one brief second of light before that stone would descend and crush the life from his skull; in that second he thought, *Barra, I'm sorry, I did my best,* and even as he did so, a vision flashed across his eyes, of what his life could have been if he hadn't lost, a vision of a home, of a family, of Barra playing with his sons and teaching them to use the axe and bow, of an ancient Kheperu telling them lies around a warm hearth on a winter night, and always, over it all, of Sarah. Of Sarah whole and well, hearty and filling their home with laughter and love.

Hot tears rushed his eyes, the first he had felt in nearly twenty years.

*If only I could have lived,* he thought. *If only . . .*

From the corner of his eye, he spied a stealthy movement; his gaze flicked to follow it . . .

Behind the High Priest, unsteadily, staggering under the weight of the upraised iron scimitar, came Adonizedek.

It was a futile gesture, too late and too far away; the old king could never reach Melchizedek before that stone came crashing down. But the stone stayed up, still raised over the High Priest's head, and Melchizedek's head now cocked to one side as though he listened to a distant sound.

In that suspended moment, Adonizedek struck.

The scimitar flashed down into Melchizedek's shoulder joint, slicing through muscle. It grated against the invulnerable bone, and stuck there, wedged into the joint as Melchizedek's arm gave way and let the huge stone fall to his side. Melchizedek wheeled sharply on the old king, and the trapped scimitar snapped like a twig.

Leucas raised an arm, caught a projection at the foot of the Great Astarte, and pulled himself up to a sitting position. He looked around himself for something he could swing, something he could throw, anything to regain Melchizedek's attention and save the king, but he found nothing.

Melchizedek's fist rose, and fell once. He buried it in his brother's skull as deep as his wrist, and when his fist rose again it dripped with the brains of the king.

A scream of raw unbelieving anguish came from a voice that Leucas knew: across the courtyard Agaz charged toward them with leveled spear.

Leucas got his good leg under him and steadied himself on the Great Astarte so that he could rise.

The Great Astarte rocked on its base. Leucas clung to it; he needed its support; if it fell, so would he. Melchizedek's use of it to crush the breath from Leucas had shifted its many tons to a precarious balance.

Leucas felt that balance, and nodded to himself.

The charge of Agaz drove his spear deep into Melchizedek's belly; the High Priest snapped the spear shaft with a contemptuous backhand, and reached for the prince's arm.

"Graegduz," he gasped hoarsely, and another Pictish word: "Enchlao!"

From somewhere out of sight, behind the piles of rubble, Graegduz lurched like a broken puppet; he pushed himself into a limping scramble, and somehow he knew whose ankle Leucas meant.

Agaz had drawn a sword, and hacked toward the High Priest's head, his face a mask of unreasoning grief. Even as Melchizedek caught the blade and wrenched it from the prince's grasp, Graegduz's teeth locked around his ankle, and the High Priest fell.

Leucas had only one second before the High Priest would kill Graeg with a single blow, only one second before he would rise and strip the life from the prince of Jebusi—but he had learned, just a moment ago, how a man can live a whole lifetime in that brief span.

The Great Astarte balanced precariously, but still it was far too massive for any ordinary man to move. Leucas put his broken wrist against it alongside his good one, splinters of bone ripping through his skin, and he shifted weight onto his broken leg, and he used every scrap of agony in his battered body to shove against that hulking figure of stone.

The broken ends of his thighbone ground together, darkening his eyes, but with the slow majesty of a mountain crumbling into the sea, the Great Astarte toppled outward.

From somewhere above the world came a flash as though the sun had exploded, wiping away vision.

When Leucas could see again, he found himself sprawled across the back of the Great Astarte. From beneath it projected one clawed hand of the High Priest; from the other side, his ankles. Agaz stood nearby, rubbing dazedly at his eyes.

*I won,* Leucas thought. *We won.*

Leucas lifted his head now, to seek the alcove where Sarah lay.

There was no alcove, not anymore; where it had stood was only a pile of bloodstained rubble.

The last of his strength drained away.

Too late; he'd awakened too late.

Despair closed over his heart, and brought darkness to his eyes, and he knew no more.

The charred husk of Eleazar's body lay at her knees. The Axe of the Lady had melted across it like a puddle of candle drippings, the white-hot bronze slowly going red and solidifying as it cooled.

She was more tired than she thought it possible to be, and as her vision began to clear, she saw bone and tendon through the cracked flesh of her palms. The overpowering nausea of the onset of shock stripped breath from her lungs. She wanted nothing except to lie down now, to rest, even if it meant being pinned to the ground with an Israelite spear, but a hard hand took her shoulder, and Kheperu's voice shrilled in her ear, high-pitched and panicky over the roar of the winds.

"Barra, get up! You have to move! Move! Come one! *We still have a chance!*"

She looked around them. On all sides, there were Israelites. Many were lying on the ground, dead or stunned, but many, many more were now rising. Above, the Finger of God dipped toward them, swelling as though it would swallow the world; with all her hair burned away, she could not judge the full force of the wind, but she felt it press against her naked flesh like an invisible hand.

There was nowhere to go.

She couldn't fight—her hands might never hold a weapon again. She couldn't run, she could barely walk, and the whole Host of Israel spread across the ridgetops and through the valleys.

Striding toward them through the storm, his unbound beard whipped like a pennon by the wind, came Joshua ben Nun; at his back marched warriors who flicked frightened looks at the descending funnel-shaped cloud above, yet kept marching as though they feared Joshua more. They walked forward with shielded eyes and averted faces, to avoid the mortal sin of looking upon the naked Ark; only his shouted commands gave them direction.

"A chance for what?" she said dully.

"Barra, you must *trust* me," he said, leaning close to stare into her eyes. Blood still streamed from his nose, and his gaze glittered like broken glass. "Go to the Ark, Barra. You must stand before the Ark!"

She returned his gaze blankly, uncomprehending. He didn't seem to understand that to do that, she'd have to get up.

*"Get up!"* He grabbed her blistering shoulders roughly, as though

he could shake life back into her eyes. "Do you want to die on your knees?"

"On my knees . . ."

Like the Jericho dead.

Convulsively, with a groan of agony that made her head swim and her stomach twist toward vomiting, she lurched to her feet.

"Go to the Ark!" Kheperu insisted, his voice cracking into a screech.

"Why?"

"*Because we can still win!*" He shoved her sharply away; the wind's blast made her stagger. "You must *trust* me! You must believe me! If you stand before the Ark, we can still win!"

She raised her eyes; above her gaped the roaring mouth, with teeth of lightning that shot back and forth within it, seeming so close and solid she could reach up and touch it. All around her, swirling walls of dust and sand sprang up from the ground like mountains raised by a god, reaching toward the descending maw. Far, far away, up this unimaginable throat, she saw a ring of sky, clear and impossibly blue.

In the center of that ring of sky hung the pale shadow of the waning moon.

*All right,* she thought. *All right, but this is the last time.*

She leaned into the wind, stumbling forward blindly through the stinging sand and the larger stones that now lifted up to batter and cut her.

The Ark still stood upon its pedestal, scorched and blackened by the fire that had burst from the body of Eleazar. The four winged demon-figures at its corners seemed to turn and watch her come.

Finally she reached it, and stood swaying there, blood streaming down from the stone slices all over her body. Where was Kheperu? Why wasn't he beside her? She turned around, looking for him, but he was nowhere to be found within the howling darkness. Faintly, far away through the blasting murk, she saw the wagon move. Was that where he was? Making a run for it?

The betrayal struck her to the core. How could he do this? After all she'd done for him, how could he leave her to die alone?

Out of the darkness came Joshua, and the men at his back, their faces still averted. Joshua stopped and stared at her as though he could not believe his eyes. His mouth moved, but if he spoke, Barra could not hear him above the shriek of the wind.

That was all right; the time for words between them was long past.

She straightened her back, forcing herself to stand with defiance and a semblance of pride. She stood before the Seat of Yahweh, bald as a newborn child, armed only with charred and useless hands, clothed only in her blistered skin.

He mouthed, *Surrender.*

She replied, *Fuck you.*

His mouth sealed itself into a grim-set line and he strode toward her, and down from the shrieking mouth above her whirled something that struck her hard in the back, stabbing through her chest and sending her stumbling to meet him.

She tried to clutch at it, uncomprehending, but her left arm no longer worked. She looked down, and saw a barbed and bloody arrowhead protruding a full span from her chest; it had ripped out through the flesh of her left breast.

The barbed head was the silvery grey of Hittite iron, and the black shaft was worked with runes of silver.

She thought, *Sheshai . . .*

She lifted her head to look at the distant moon above. This was a betrayal more final than she could fully comprehend: it was as though the Lady herself had shot her in the back.

Had this all been a hideous mistake? Had she been on the wrong side from the beginning? Was that why she stood here now, abandoned by her friends, betrayed by her gods?

Now Joshua stood over her, and she looked up into his creased face, a face lined with pain and hard-won wisdom. This face held no joy, no triumph, only a kind of resignation, as though *he* was the one who had lost, after all.

He opened his arms to her once again, as he had in the Kidron Valley, with half a flicker of hope in his eyes, and she understood. Unlike the Anointed of Yahweh, she'd had a choice. She had not been abandoned. She had not been betrayed.

To stand here, now, naked and burned and wounded, was a *gift.*

The favor of the gods is always bought with pain.

She threw herself forward, and leaped against his chest.

Joshua's eyes went wide, and breath escaped him in a long gasp as the barbed arrowhead of Hittite iron pierced his breast. She hung in his grasp, her arm wrapped around his shoulders, hugging him as their blood mingled along the black rune-worked shaft.

She put her lips against his ear, and said, "Hurts, doesn't it?"

The Finger of God descended around them, and the men at Joshua's side were swept away, and all there was left in the universe of dark and shrieking chaos was Barra and Joshua, pinned together at the chest, and the scorched Ark of the Covenant behind them.

"How—?" he gasped against her ear. "How—?"

"*Sheshai,*" she told him. "Remember that name. Sheshai of Jericho. Remember."

"Jeri—" he began, but the winds ripped them apart.

For a single tearing second, they hung from the shaft that joined them as though it were a meat hook; one merciful instant later it snapped. Joshua tumbled away, the barbed head deep within his lung, and Barra staggered back with the arrow's fletching still sticking out beside her shoulder blade.

She reached out blindly, clutching for anything that might steady her; her hand brushed the wingtip of a golden kherub, and lightning blasted away the world.

# 20

# A Practical Man

**B**arra spent a long time waking up, a gradual surfacing of consciousness in a warm, gentle sea of sleep. When she finally opened her eyes, she turned her head to the side; a shaft of light fell across her face, and she flinched helplessly away from it.

"Shh, it's the sun," came a voice that seemed to whisper through distant layers of wool. "It's only the sun."

This light leaked in through a small crack in closed shutters; it was golden, not brilliant white, and a slow swirl of dust motes wheeled through it, and some fist that had been clenched inside her slowly relaxed.

She lay on a deep featherbed that had molded itself around her. Her body seemed very far away—ominously distant, as though her connection to it was as tenuous as the touch of the sun on her cheeks. She knew she was hurt, and badly, but the pain was even farther away than her body.

She thought, *My hair . . .*

She lifted a hand that felt heavier than her axe ever had, and tried to touch her scalp, but she could feel nothing; her hand was wrapped in thick bandages that were heavily oiled with some kind of salve. She could hear, though, a soft scrape as she passed the bandages over her head, the sort of rasp she could make by rubbing Kheperu's scalp stubble.

The effort exhausted her, and she let her hand fall back to her side.

"It's quiet . . ." she whispered, and a slow, steady warmth grew within her breast, a blossoming of serenity that was almost joy.

Someone leaned close—she could not tell who. "What? What did you say?"

"It's quiet inside my head," she whispered, and fell back into blissfully dreamless sleep.

Discomfort woke her, sometime later: a gnawing, burning itch in her left shoulder, and an icy sizzle in her hands. When she opened her eyes this time, she recognized Kheperu, who sat on a low stool beside her bed, his back against a wall, his eyes closed, and spit-bubbles bursting across his half-open lips with each light snore.

"Khe . . ." she tried to say, and had to cough something thick up from her lungs, that she spat on the floor. "Kheperu . . ."

Her voice was barely above a whisper, but his eyes sprang open and he jerked himself straight as though he'd been pinched. He shook his head sharply to drive the sleep away, and showed her his bad teeth in a warm grin.

"Why, good morning!" he said brightly. "How are you feeling?"

"Am I . . ." Each word was an individual struggle against exhaustion. "Am I gonna live?"

"Oh, I should think so. You've made it this far; you've been a bit dicey for a few days, but I think you've turned for the better."

She wanted to ask about her hands, but she didn't dare; she remembered their charred ruin all too well. "How . . . Leucas? Where's Leucas?"

A shadow crossed Kheperu's face. "He's wounded, Barra."

"Worse . . . than me?"

Kheperu nodded. "But he'll live, that's the important thing. We're all alive."

"Graeg?"

"I believe so. Now that you're awake, I think we can let him in here; his confounded howling for you has kept half the Citadel sleepless for days."

Her last question, most important, she forced out through the gathering twilight of exhaustion. "When . . ." she said faintly.

Kheperu leaned close. "What? When what, Barra?"

"When do we get paid?" she asked, and fell back into sleep before she heard his answer.

When next she woke, Agaz was beside her, on the little stool by the bed, feeding strips of smoked fish to Graeg.

"Good morning to both of you," she said. She reached out to stroke Graeg's shoulder behind the cone collar of boiled leather, and found her hands still muffled in oiled dressing. She didn't want to think about that; she quickly tucked her hand back under the sheet that covered her. Graeg heaved himself onto his feet and put his front paws on the bed, craning his neck to lick her face. He was thin, and weak, and his breath reeked of fish, and Barra finally began to believe that everything was all right.

Agaz looked on her with eyes that shone as though they were filled with tears. He tried for a smile, but could only stretch his lips into a wider, grim line.

"Hey, cheer up, Agaz," she said. "Nobody's told me the news, but it seems like everything's turned out for the best."

He looked away. "Thanks to you and Leucas and Kheperu, everything has turned out better than I had any right to hope," he said, "but you must now call me Adonizedek."

"Adonizedek," she repeated slowly, getting the feel of the name in her mouth as she matched it to his face. "Your father . . ."

"My father fell at the Ba'alath, defending the Lady's Maid—defending the Lady—with the last breath of his body."

The half-mad, half-wise old king, who knew the name of every one of his subjects . . .

"Agaz, I'm sorry. —Adonizedek," she amended.

He accepted this with a slow nod. "He was a better king—a better man—than I ever knew. He was better than he knew himself. It is . . . humbling, and painful, that I cannot now clasp his hand and tell him he was right, and I was wrong."

Barra looked away; she couldn't help thinking of her own father, back at Tara, in Eire. *I have to go home,* she thought. *I have to see him, and Coll, and Llem . . .*

"The funeral?" she asked.

"Three days past," he said, offering Graeg another strip of fish.

"Hey," she said, "you could give *me* some of that, y'know. I'm starving. And you could tell me how you finally beat the Habiru."

Now he did smile, just faintly, as he held the strip of fish to her lips. She devoured it greedily; it was salty and bitter and utterly delicious.

"I didn't beat them," he said. "You did. I . . . had nothing to do with it."

While he fed her fish and cheese and sips of water from the pitcher by the bed, he told her the story. After the explosion of the Tabernacle, the storm had run wild, the cloud striking at random in the city and the camps beyond, like a wounded scorpion stinging itself to death. The sky-stones had ravaged the countryside, setting fires everywhere, destroying much of the Habiru Host's provisions and livestock. With random death raining from the sky, battle had been impossible.

By the time the storm and the rain of sky-stones had abated, the Ark was securely in Jebusite hands within the city. The first blow to the Habiru had been the discovery that Joshua himself had been wounded; to find that Yahweh wouldn't—or couldn't—protect him had shaken their faith as little else could.

Then, when the Ark had been prominently displayed upon the parapet of the Citadel, the Habiru had apparently decided that their god had abandoned them, and they began to abandon him. The camps bled warriors back into the countryside; they had scattered like straw before a wind. There had even been some intertribal warfare in the camps, as some of them seemed to blame the Levites for the loss of the Ark.

"Did you see Joshua?" Barra asked around a mouthful of bread. "Did I kill him?"

"He lived, at the last time I saw him. He was bandaged, on his chest, and he coughed as though afflicted by consumption. He hardly seemed like the same man; he stammered, and coughed, and there was a trembling of weakness in his voice and his hand. He seemed as though he had grown old, overnight."

Barra nodded. It must have been a terrible shock to him, to be wounded after all these years, and to lose the seat of his supposedly omnipotent god.

And, somehow, she was obscurely pleased that she had not killed him. She felt a certain kinship with him, a feeling she was sure wasn't mutual, but was real for her nonetheless. She had been used hard by a god, even as he had; as difficult as it had been for her, over these past days, she could not imagine what burdens Joshua must have borne through all his years as Yahweh's Anointed.

"And Phinehas?" she asked, reaching out to ruffle Graeg's fur with her bandaged hand. "Joshua's aide? Did you see him?"

"Yes; he stood as witness to the treaty of peace," Agaz said. "He is Joshua's aide no longer, though. He has been anointed as the High Priest of Yahweh, though he is half-blind and drags a foot, and has lost the use of his right arm."

Graeg nuzzled her hand, and for a while she stroked him, and considered the dangers of standing close beside a tool of the gods.

"And where is this Ark of theirs now?" Barra asked at length. "Can I see it?"

Agaz's—Adonizedek's—eyes went flat and cold. "No, you cannot."

"I can't?" Blood pounded in Barra's temples. "You mean, I can get myself wounded, and roasted, and nearly bloodyfucking *killed* to get that fucking thing into the city, and I can't even *see* it?"

"I gave it back."

She gaped at him, speechless.

He looked down at his hands. "Barra, you must understand. The Gate Tower is destroyed. The wall is broken in many places, and there is no one left to defend it. We could not withstand a single attack by a single tribe, by half a tribe, let alone the entire Host; if they chose to come and take the Ark by force, we could not have stopped them. When Joshua sent his offer of peace, I took it. It was the only practical thing to do."

"And what did you get?" she asked bitterly. "What did you get for it?"

"I got Joshua's word that Jebusi would stand, unmolested by any tribe of Israel, unto the seventh generation. That's more than *two hundred years*, Barra."

"And you think he'll keep that word?"

"Don't you?"

He was right; she knew he would. Joshua's word was as unbreakable as the old man himself, but still it burned her like she'd swallowed acid.

"What about after he dies? He's an old man, and he's sick now, sick in his lungs, you said."

Adonizedek nodded. "I considered that. As a condition of returning the Ark, Joshua has pronounced a curse upon any tribe that attacks us before that time, that a 'hundred generations shall not be enough to encompass the misery' visited upon the tribe that violates this peace. You know how superstitious the Habiru are, Barra—even now, Joshua's curse from more than twenty years ago keeps them out of Jericho. I should think that the prospect of three thousand years of misery should cause any of them to think twice about attacking us."

"So you bought two hundred years of peace for your people. What then?"

"That's more than enough. These tribal confederations always fall apart; two hundred years from now, no one will have ever heard of the Nation of Israel. This Yahweh of theirs will be swallowed by history, and forgotten forever."

She wished she shared his confidence, but she had seen how durable some gods could be. She wished he had destroyed the Ark, had hacked it to pieces and melted down the remains—but that wouldn't have been *practical*.

She rolled painfully onto her side, facing away from him, and wished she could just tell him to leave.

He read the gesture perfectly; she heard him rise, and his voice sounded heavy, and sad. "As part of the bargain, there was also silver, and gold. A great deal of both, and it's all yours."

She stared at the shaft of sunlight that leaked in through the shuttered window, and growled, "It had fucking well better be."

Many people spent time with her, as she recovered some strength. Rachel came in, wan and hollow-eyed, gone silent and shy, but some animation returned to her lovely face as she described how she had rescued the king from his captivity in the Citadel; she would not yet speak of anything that had happened after she and the old king had reached the Ba'alath. She insisted that she did not remember, and perhaps it was true.

Barra did not press her on it; she had memories of her own that she wished she could forget.

Tal Akhu-shabb, the Governor of the Canaan District, had also stopped by to pay his respects, on his way back from Gilgal to Gezer. He'd arrived the day after the Habiru Host pulled out, while she was still unconscious, and had put his five or six thousand troops to work in the city, clearing rubble and erecting temporary stockades in the breaches of the walls. When he was finally able to see her, his age-creased face had paled slightly, at her blistered skin and uneven brush of regrowing hair, but decades of diplomacy in the service of the Pharaoh had kept his voice smooth and hearty.

"You have a gift," he'd told her wonderingly, "for finding your way into the center of the most extraordinary events—and, perhaps more important, for finding your way out again."

"I wouldn't have made it without you, Tal," she'd said.

"Pish," he said. "It was nothing. The men needed the exercise, anyway."

"I'm serious. I owe you one."

"You do not," he said quietly. "And you know it."

She let it go. She was too tired and too injured to waste breath arguing, and besides, if the old man wanted to insist he was still in her debt, let him. She might need another favor, someday.

It was from Sarah that Barra learned of Leucas' epic battle with the demon-ridden Melchizedek. She had seen the whole thing from her pallet in the alcove, except for the death of the king and Leucas' final victory; once Agaz had recovered his senses in the courtyard, he had swiftly and accurately assessed the situation, and had carried her to safety in his own arms.

Barra had grunted sourly at this news; from the visits of Bertram and other Pictish mercenaries, she had already heard of Agaz's heroism when the Habiru had first stormed the wall. Bertram himself insisted that it was only because of Agaz that the city had stood through the first day.

*This,* Barra thought, *is what Agaz calls "having nothing to do with it."*

And Bertram's visits had started a little mystery niggling at the back of her head. She had assumed that his charge had carried the mercenaries through the Levites, and that he and his men had brought the Ark and her and Kheperu back into the city, but when she thanked him for it, be looked honestly puzzled.

"Nah, it wasn't like that, Auntie," he'd said. "When everything blew up and all, we broke ranks and ran like bunnies for the city. You and your Egyptian pal were already inside."

"Then how'd we get there?"

He shrugged. "Don't you remember?"

"No."

"Then how should *I* know?"

She braced Kheperu on the subject when next he came to look in on her. He checked on her every couple of hours, to examine the dressing that bound her arrow-holed shoulder, and to force her fingers straight and then curl them again, in hopes that her hands might recover some of their use as they healed. This was incredibly, excruciatingly painful, and she was glad to have something else to think about while he manipulated her hands.

Forcing her words around the grunts of fiery agony that shot up her arms, she said, "I've been meaning to—*hgh*—meaning to ask you. *Ghowh*—how did we get back into the, *hgh,* the city?"

His eyes glittered. "You mean you don't remember?"

"No, shithead. I'm asking because I love the sound of your fucking voice."

A tiny, tight smile played over his mobile lips, while he pretended to be absorbed in bending her fingers. "It was the cloud, you know; it sucked us up like an elephant's snout, Ark and all, and spat us out as light as a feather on the Citadel's roof."

"Horseshit," she said, blinking back tears of pain.

"If you like," he said with a shrug. Now he no longer worked her hand, but held it gently in both of his. "In fact, it was a great pale hand that came down from the sky, to scoop us up as though we were living dice . . ."

"Don't make me hit you. I swear, I'll make it hurt you more than it does me—and you don't even want to know how much I hurt."

"Perhaps the earth opened and swallowed us, but we gave it such indigestion that it puked us all the way into the city."

"Kheperu, I'm warning you—" she began.

"Pick a tale, or make up one of your own," Kheperu said, an oddly calm and serious look in his eyes. "They are each as true as any other."

"All right," she said, surrendering. "Forget it. I'll ask someone else."

"As you wish."

"One thing, though, that I can't figure out. What made you push me over to the Ark? How'd you know I had to stand just there?"

His eyes went completely opaque, like beads of glass. "I can't really say. I just knew."

She shook her head, chuckling. "Almost like you're a real prophet, huh? How do you get to be a prophet, when you're such a fucking liar?"

"Prophet? Liar?" He shrugged carelessly. "Perhaps they are the same, mm? Now, enough talking. Let's get started on your left hand."

The first place she went, once Kheperu pronounced her fit to walk, was to visit Leucas. Sarah was there with him, when Barra came into the room. A certain flush warmed her cheeks as she rose and excused herself; Barra watched her go with some bemusement. Sarah seemed to have recovered fully, her face filling out and her hair taking on an astonishing glossy sheen. She was still painfully thin, but her gracefully swaying walk showed already the return of her strength. Barra sighed, and lowered herself onto the seat that the Lady's Maid had just vacated.

The Athenian sat up in bed, in a room almost identical to hers. His wounds had done nothing to dull his enormous appetite; he'd waved her in with a mutton shank the size of his forearm. Enormous splints were bound to his left leg and right forearm, and his entire chest was strapped so tightly that it barely moved with his breath. His body, what she could see of it, was covered with bruises shading from red-black to a pale greenish yellow; his face looked like it had been painted by a madman. But, durable as always, he was clearly healing swiftly: his swelling had already receded, and his eyes sparkled like ice in a bright winter sun.

Leucas gave her good morning, and asked her how she was feeling, and she answered him before she realized that he'd spoken in Canaanite.

She gave him a sharp look. "You've been studying."

His bruised face twisted toward a slightly pained smile. "I have a good teacher."

Barra glanced speculatively toward the empty doorway through which Sarah had passed, and asked, "Just what's between you two, anyway?"

Leucas frowned, and drew breath to speak, let it out again in a sigh; he did this again, and yet one more time, as though the words he needed were simply not to be found.

"Now, don't be upset . . ." he said, at length.

"Upset?" Barra squinted at him, puzzled. "Why should I get upset?"

"I think . . ." he said slowly, then drew a deep breath, and said solemnly, "I think I'm going to ask her to marry me."

Barra's mouth dropped open.

While she continued to gape in astonishment, he told her the whole tale.

". . . and that was when I knew that I love her. I really do, Barra," he finished, "and so I'm going to ask her to marry me."

"But . . ." Barra said helplessly. "But . . ."

"I knew you'd be upset."

"I'm not upset!" She heard the lie in her own voice. This *did* upset her, more than she could have imagined; it struck her like a blow to the chest. It wasn't jealousy—her feelings for Leucas had never been romantic—but rather it felt like the earth had shifted under her feet, and a rock that she had thought was solid had turned to sand.

"You're going to retire," she said softly. "You're going to retire here, in Jebusi?"

He shrugged, and turned his face away. "We have the money. I'll never have to work. I've been thinking I might buy some land, maybe have a vineyard . . ."

"You're a long way from home."

"Home is wherever my family is," he said, and she could hear the pain in his voice, and began to understand how much this decision was costing him.

"But," she insisted, hating the edge of desperation in her voice, "it's not even *her* you love—it's not her you made love to! Don't you understand? That was the *Goddess*. Sarah was only a vessel—"

"We are all only vessels," Leucas said seriously. "Yes, I fell in love with the Goddess in her—but maybe that's what we always love in the women that touch us; we fall in love with the echo of the Goddess."

"I, ah . . ." She sighed in surrender. "I don't know what to say. Congratulations, I guess."

"Thank you."

She rose; she could no longer bear to be in this tiny, stuffy room. "Well, I'll see you."

"Barra?"

She paused in the doorway, and looked back.

"You could stay here, too," Leucas said hopefully.

She shook her head. "This isn't my home."

"Do you know that Leucas is going to *retire* here?" Barra demanded angrily, stomping into the room and batting clouds of reeking gas away from her face with her bandaged hands. "That he's planning to marry the bloody Lady's Maid, settle down, and *breed*?"

Kheperu looked up from his worktable, where he was compounding a number of noxiously smoking chemicals over a small brazier, and nodded solemnly.

"Yes, he told me. And from the looks that Sarah gives him when she thinks no one is watching, I imagine she'll accept."

"What are we gonna do about it?"

"Do?" Kheperu said, giving her a cautious, sidelong look. "Why should we do anything?"

"Don't tell me," she said, squeezing her eyes shut. "You think you're going to retire, too."

"It's not such a bad idea," Kheperu said defensively. "Do you have any idea how *wealthy* we are now? The ransom paid by the Habiru for their god-box was beyond comprehension, and it's all *ours*. It seems a little silly to risk one's life for money, when one is already rich."

He turned back to his chemicals, so that she could not see his face. "We have cut a little too close to the bone," he said, "both at Tyre, and now here. Heh, I barely survived bringing Agaz out from the camp—that clumsy hamfist they laughingly call a surgeon here, had to chop a hole in my back nearly the size of my head to get the infection out. I'm not a young man, anymore. I don't heal as fast as I once did."

"What will you do, though?"

He shrugged, and stroked the long hook of his nose with one stubby finger. "I've been thinking about the priesthood."

Barra snorted.

"Don't scoff. That night I spent in the Holy of Holies . . . was as bad a night as I've ever had, and you might believe that I've had a few rough ones, in my day. There is a hole in my life, Barra; thrown back upon my own resources, I discovered that I had none. My lack nearly killed me. The only thing that kept me alive that night was . . . well, never mind. It's not important. I have been, in my humble way, something of an . . . mm, adherent of Astarte for many years now, have I not? Perhaps I will see if I can take the orders at the Ba'alath."

"You'll never stand it. You'll be bored out of your skull."

He shrugged. "Perhaps. If so, I'll do something else. I should think I'd be able to find something to keep me busy—something in my particular field of expertise . . ."

"What, open a brothel?"

"Of course. Who knows more of whoring than I? Perhaps in Ascalon, where I'd get the Coast Road traffic, or perhaps here in Jebusi—more money in Ascalon, but also more competition. And here, I'm, ah, well connected, you might say. And I could have a profitable sideline in aphrodisiacs and abortifacients, as well as suitable narcotics and hallucinogens. You know," he said consideringly, "I could always use a partner with sharp trading sense— especially one who can double as a bouncer . . ."

"No."

"Don't answer right now. Give it some thought."

"I don't have to. The answer's no."

He spread his hands. "This is an offer that cannot be revoked. Should you ever change your mind, you have only to speak—"

"Ay, thanks." The bitter sting in her eyes came from the smoke, she was sure of that. "Listen, I have to go—I have to find someplace where I can breathe."


Agaz came silently up beside Barra, where she leaned on the uppermost parapet of the Citadel and looked out over the blasted fields of the *mâtat Urusalim*. He leaned his elbows on the wall at her side, without saying a word, and stared out just as she did.

From the base of the wall to the farthest horizon, the earth was pocked with impact craters, scorched black in wildfire streaks. Broad arcs and scattered splotches of bare stone glared among the craters, places where the Finger of God had touched down and consumed the land down to its uttermost bedrock; from here they made an almost-comprehensible pattern, like an illiterate child's scrawled imitation of writing.

Distant figures moved through the battered land, farmers and herdsmen returning to their holdings, picking their way across the broken stone and around the craters, some of which still leaked smoke up into the cloudless sky. Barra wondered what might be going through Agaz's mind right now—*Adonizedek*'s mind, she reminded herself. She didn't want to ask; she had a feeling that all he was thinking about was how lucky it was that the Habiru had come and gone while there was still time for another spring planting.

*And that's what he* should *be thinking about,* she told herself. *He's the king. He has to worry about feeding his people, now that all their grain stores were ruined during the siege.*

It still stung a little, though; more than a little.

Without quite realizing how she got there, she found herself leaning comfortably against his arm, which slowly slid around her shoulders.

They stood this way a while longer, in warm and pregnant silence.

Finally, Adonizedek murmured, "What are you thinking about?"

She breathed half a chuckle through her nose. "I was wondering what you're thinking about."

"All right." He stared out over his people's lands, the creases around his eyes deepening. The salting of grey at his temples seemed to have increased over the past few days, but it suited him well. "I was wondering," he said slowly, "if there is any way I can convince you to stay."

She turned her face away, looking into the wind. Her bandaged hands ached bitterly; if her hands were whole, she could stroke his face . . .

"I don't think so," she told him.

"Rachel worships you," he said, "and everyone in this city knows what you have done for us; they adore you."

"And you?" Barra hated herself for asking, but she couldn't help it. She needed to hear this, needed it more than she had guessed. "How do *you* feel?"

Adonizedek was silent for a long, empty moment, in which cold winds blew through her heart. "I don't know," he said. "I could say I love you. We've been through so much . . . You remember what you told me, up on those rocks overlooking the watershed road?"

She nodded.

He said, "I do know, though, that this city, my people, I myself, owe you more than money can ever repay. I know that the only way we can begin to answer that debt is to do you honor every day of your life." His voice dropped to barely above a whisper. "I know that you would make the finest queen . . ."

Barra stepped away, out from the warmth of his encircling arm. "Are you asking me to marry you?"

He shook his head. "Not yet. I know you better than to back you into that kind of corner. What I'm asking is that you stay. Stay with me, at least until we know if what we feel for each other is real."

"It's real enough," she said. "I know that already. I've been through plenty of close fights, with plenty of men, and none of them has ever made me feel . . ." She couldn't finish. She shook her head. "But I can't stay."

"I don't understand."

"You'll be a fine king," she said, "but you're just a bit too much the practical man."

"Barra—"

"No. There's nothing you can say. See, the thing is, I know that if it ever came down to it, if shit ever broke in such a way that things came right down to the nub, and you had to choose between me and your people, I already know which you'd choose."

"But that would never happen," he protested. "How could that ever happen?"

"Doesn't matter. The same qualities that'll make you a good king, make you the wrong man for me. I need . . . I need somebody who's with me *first*, and everything else isn't even second; it's fifth, or tenth. If you weren't king, maybe you could do that. With your people to look after, I know you never will."

He could not answer. He only stared at her, inexpressible pain shadowing his eyes. She couldn't bear to see it; once again, she turned and leaned on the parapet, staring off to the north and east, toward Tyre.

Toward the sea.

"That's why I'm leaving," she said. "After all this, after everything I've gone through, I just learned that my two best friends in the world have found something that means more to them than I do."

"Did you put *them* first?" he asked.

"Maybe not, I guess, but that's not the point, is it?" She shrugged. "I didn't say it was rational. It still hurts. And I'm *jealous*."

She sighed and looked down at the oiled wrappings around her ruined hands. "I always thought I was the ambitious one. I always thought I was the one who knew what I wanted. Now Leucas is going to get married, and start a family. Kheperu's entering the priesthood. You have your city and your people to tend. Everyone has decided what's really important to them. Everyone knows what their lives are going to be about from here on. Except me. What do I have? What was I doing all this for?"

"I don't know, Barra," Adonizedek said sadly. "I wish I did. If I knew what you wanted, I would give it to you."

"Oh, ay?" She gave him a sidelong look, and a hint of a gleam came into her eye. "I can tell you one thing I want. The sky-stones."

"What?"

"I want the sky-stones," she said. As she thought about it, her black mood began to lift, and she felt the beginnings of a smile. "When your farmers and whatever start clearing them from their fields, have them bring 'em in here. I want them."

The king frowned. "What for?"

"Iron," she said. "Sky-stones are loaded with iron. It's the wave of the future, Agaz; it's the rising tide. Nobody thinks about iron much, because no one can work it into weapons except the royal craftsmen of Hatti." Her smile spread. "With the Hittite Empire falling apart, I have a feeling that, before too long, some enterprising ironsmiths are going to be looking for work. I want those sky-stones."

Adonizedek's eyes creased toward a ghost of a smile of his own. "They are yours."

"Your word on it?"

"I have said so."

Hours became days, and days turned into weeks. The bandages came off Barra's hands forever, revealing knotted scar tissue across her palms. Kheperu visited her every day, during his breaks from taking instruction at the Ba'alath, and badgered her into doing painful and repetitive flexing exercises, meanwhile keeping a variety of his healing salves rubbed into the scars to keep them supple.

Barra stood at Leucas' side when he married Sarah; the bride was already showing, by that time, the beginning curve of belly from the child which grew within her. The Athenian's leg healed a little crooked; he walked with a heavy limp, and used a cane from time to time, for his leg became painful whenever he was tired.

Graegduz recovered as fully as could be expected; he was gaunt, and tired swiftly, but his spirit returned and he became once again the happy companion that Barra needed so much; they spent long hours together, ranging the *mâtat Urusalim*, looking for sky-stones the farmers had missed. Many of the small landholders had brought the stones into their houses, as talismans against bad luck. Barra never objected. One entire grain bin in Jebusi now brimmed with tons of nearly pure iron.

Whenever Adonizedek could steal away from the consuming task of rebuilding his city, he spent the hours with Barra; knowing that they had no future together made those hours seem even more sweet. She showed him the Egyptian trick of the tied-off sheepgut; he showed her the Canaanite technique of the lemon-peel cup. Love is love, and rare enough even in its briefest forms; for those weeks, they both were happy.

She thought, sometimes, of Jericho, and of Sheshai. He had vanished into the battle, and no one knew what had become of him, but he still lived inside her, in her bruised memory: he was the last echo of the Jericho dead, and she did not begrudge them this small piece of her heart.

For this time, at least, she was at peace.

But the seasons were turning, and soon Barra decided it was time to go. She had places to go and things to do, and shortly after the equinox, one morning found her arranging her belongings on a wagon, in the caravan that had assembled outside the growing shell of the new Gate Tower. Many of the men who would walk with this caravan were her tribesmen; her nephew Bertram, as the captain of the remaining mercenaries, would himself be serving as the caravan master.

"Let's go, Auntie," he called to her. "Say your farewells; we're burning daylight."

All Jebusi had turned out to see her off, and her friends stood at the front of the crowd. Kheperu hugged her close, smelling only of clean sweat and incense; for the first time, her keen nose took in his own, natural scent, and it brought tears to her eyes.

"I'll miss you," she said.

His eyes gleamed with moisture of their own. "If missing me becomes intolerable, you will always know where I can be found."

"You never did tell me how we got back into the city with the Ark."

"Eagles," Kheperu said seriously.

"Eh?"

"Eagles, great huge ones, the size of elephants, swooped out of the clouds—"

Barra waved him to silence, and sighed her surrender. "Oh, never mind."

Sarah and Leucas stood together, as they always did, arms about each other's waists. She released him long enough that he could step forward and gather Barra to his enormous scarred chest.

"You have to come back," he told her softly. "Remember your promise. You have to help me dig for my armor."

"I will," she said. "I swear it."

She pulled away and went to Sarah, taking her hands and standing close to look up into her face, nearly as far above her as Leucas' had been. "You take good care of him," Barra said. "You're not so big that I can't kick your ass."

"You know I will," Sarah responded. "And know, too, in your travels, that you are loved, here. Never forget that, no matter what happens. Not only by your friends, but by the Lady. She will always be with you."

"Just like a bloody priestess," Barra said. "Always bringing the gods into it."

Sarah smiled. "They bring themselves, as I think you have learned."

"Don't remind me."

The king stood a little apart from the others. She went to him and put her arms around his shoulders and kissed his lips. She held him close, and whispered, "You'll always be Agaz to me, you know."

"I would be whatever you like," he replied, "if it would keep you here."

"I'll be back," she told him. "It may take a long time, but you'll see me again."

"Will I?"

"You know you will," she said with a cynical grin. "You've got all my iron."

"Barra, I—"

She put two fingers against his lips, and shook her head. "Don't. This is hard enough as it is."

She turned away quickly, and went back to the wagon, so that he would not see her tears. She made a show of checking her gear, then looked around.

Where was Graegduz?

"Hey, Graeg!" she called. "Come on, it's time to go!"

She looked back at her friends, and at the people of the city that spread out from the Gate Tower and lined the walls above. "Has anybody seen Graegduz?"

"I saw him this morning," said the king. "He was digging in the Citadel gardens."

"Dammit, Agaz—Adonizedek—you should have stopped him. He gets these bad habits—"

"Stop him?" the king said. He shook his head in disbelief. "I don't think so. It's like trying to stop *you*."

She flashed him a grin, then put two fingers to her lips and let out a piercing whistle. "Graeg! Graeg, get your hairy butt out here!"

There came a disturbance in the crowd, and people parted to let someone pass; Graegduz appeared through this rift, trotting toward her unconcernedly, with something large and green in his mouth.

Barra's heart stuttered madly.

It was an axe.

He came to her and laid it at her feet, and she stared down at it, afraid to move for fear that she was dreaming, and a sudden motion might wake her.

It was a stone blade of basalt, with no haft. She knelt slowly beside it, and ran her scarred hands over it. The workmanship was impeccable; this had to be the product of Langdale stonework. She lifted it, breathless, hoping against hope, but the two small chips, on the axe's blunt side, where her hammerstone had struck at the wrong angle, were not there.

She looked up, from her knees, and met the warm, knowing eyes of the Lady's Maid. "It's not mine," she said.

Sarah said, "Yes, it is."

"I thought . . ." Barra's heart seemed to rise up her throat to choke her, and she lowered her head. "I thought, at first, that it was my old one, somehow . . . I thought it would be the same . . . but it isn't. It's not the same at all."

Sarah spread her hands, and gave Barra a wise, loving smile.

She said, "Neither are you."

# Epilogue

The sweating scribe picked his way nervously through the busy mess of haulers and carpenters and shipwrights. He didn't like this one little bit; he was new in Tyre, had only arrived here a month before, and he had made it a rule never to leave his tiny stall in the bustling Market, but the generous terms of this summons had netted him like a fish. Now, with his precious pencase and a bundle of papyrus under his arm, he had to endure the japes and glares of the common laborers, the beach sand that rasped his feet despite his sandals, and the blazing sun of Tyrian summer.

Simply being in the busy shipyard itself made him nervous, with its constant traffic of men bearing heavy curving beams across their shoulders, and towering masts being erected on all sides; he expected that one would fall and crush him at any moment. And he was well aware of the jealous resentment an educated man receives from his inferiors—he was quite sure that the hulking porter whom he had asked for directions was, even now, snickering behind his back.

When he finally reached the destination to which the porter had directed him, he decided that what he should really do is turn about, find that porter again, and have him flogged. There was no office here, not even a tent or so much as a coach or sedan chair. The wealthy Tyrian woman he sought would never be caught out here, in full sunlight, in the midst of these arching ribs of half-built ships.

"You! You there!" he snapped at the nearest person he saw, a barbarian girl with short, ragged red hair, wearing, of all things, *animal skins* that exposed flesh burned red-brown by the sun. "Do you speak Phoenikian? I'm looking for the ships of Barra."

"You've found them," the girl said, without a trace of an accent. "I'm Barra."

"No, I don't think you understand. I'm looking for *Barra*. The shipowner," he explained.

"You're the one that doesn't understand, pally. Come with me."

She turned her back on him and clambered up a short ladder to a bench on the half-completed deck above. "Come on," she said encouragingly.

The scribe carefully followed her, his distaste for this entire process plain upon his face.

"Sit down," she told him, and he was about to tell her that he most certainly would not, but then his eyes fell upon a large green battle-axe that rode her hip, its haft in a smallsword scabbard.

He sat down.

"You know what you're sitting on, right now?"

He frowned at her. "A ship," he said blankly.

"*My* ship, you pinhead. This is my ship. A hundred-sweep battleship, with extra draft for cargo. So is that one, right there." She pointed to the neighboring skeleton. "And that one, over there, that's a merchantman, and she's mine, too. I'm Barra, all right? Now get your shit in order, I want you to take a letter."

He sniffed disdainfully, and began to untie his rolls of papyrus.

She went on, "You know Egyptian, right? Demotic will do."

"Of course."

"Don't shit me, pally. The last bastard scribe I had up here lied to me, and I sent him home still looking for his teeth, you follow? I can read this stuff as well as you can."

"Hmpf. If you can read and write, what do you need a scribe for?"

She shoved both her hands at his face, and he flinched back from the knotted mass of scar tissue that was her palms. "Now you want to get started, or do you have another stupid fucking question?"

"I, ah, I, ah, well, all right, I think we can—"

"Good. Shut up and write."

She took a deep breath, looking out over the sunlit shipyard, and for a moment some soul-deep satisfaction brought a beauty to her face that stole the scribe's breath. She caught him looking, and he flushed and lowered his head to his work.

She began, "Dear Antiphos and Chryl . . ."

*It looks like I won't be home for Midsummer's . . . but that's only because my ships won't be done in time.*

*That's right. Ships.*

*I'm a big-time Tyrian shipmaster now. By the time you read this, I'll have three ships under my command, and still have the quarter shares in the* Skye Swift *and* Langdale's Pride, *too. That little job with the prince of Jebusi turned out to be kind of a big deal, and I made a lot of money off it, and that's as much of the story I'll tell you right now.*

*You'll hear the rest from my own lips.*

*That's what this letter is about. This is the last one you'll get from me, because I should make landfall in Great Langdale not much more than six weeks after you read this.*

*I'm a little battered, but unbeaten, and I'm bloody rich. I've decided to quit while I'm ahead.*

*I'm retired.*

*And I'm coming home.*

> *I love you both very much.*
> *Mother*

*P.S. Tell your Uncle Llem that I think we'll be able to cut the Phoenikians out of the tin trade after all. All it'll take is a little luck, and I feel like we'll have plenty.*

*Luck, after all, is the Mother's favor, and she owes me.*

*See you soon.*